THE BRIGHT SWORD

Also by Lev Grossman

Warp

Codex

The Magicians

The Magician King

The Magician's Land

The Silver Arrow

The Golden Swift

THE
BRIGHT
SWORD

A Novel of King Arthur

LEV GROSSMAN

VIKING

VIKING
An imprint of Penguin Random House LLC
penguinrandomhouse.com

Interior illustrations on pages 1,167, 373, 529 by Wesley Allsbrook

LIBRARY OF CONGRESS CATALOGING-IN-PUBLICATION DATA
Names: Grossman, Lev, author.
Title: The bright sword : a novel of King Arthur / Lev Grossman.
Description: [New York] : Viking, 2024.
Identifiers: LCCN 2023030353 (print) | LCCN 2023030354 (ebook) |
ISBN 9780735224049 (hardcover) | ISBN 9780735224056 (ebook) |
ISBN 9780593833568 (international edition)
Subjects: LCSH: Arthur, King—Fiction. | Knights and knighthood—
Great Britain—Fiction. | Great Britain—History—To 1066—Fiction. |
LCGFT: Historical fiction. | Novels.
Classification: LCC PS3557.R6725 B75 2024 (print) |
LCC PS3557.R6725 (ebook) | DDC 813/.54—dc23/eng/20231016
LC record available at https://lccn.loc.gov/2023030353
LC ebook record available at https://lccn.loc.gov/2023030354

Printed in the United States of America
1st Printing

Designed by Nerylsa Dijol

For my family:
Sophie, Ross, Hally, and Baz

anoeth bid bet y Arthur
a hidden thing is the grave of Arthur

—"The Stanzas of the Graves,"
from *The Black Book of Carmarthen*

BOOK I

A WAR OF WONDERS

Strange women lying in ponds distributing
swords is no basis for a system of government.

—*Monty Python and the Holy Grail*

One

AZURE, THREE SCEPTERS, A CHEVRON OR

Collum punched the other knight in the face with the pommel of his sword gripped in his gauntleted fist, so hard the dark inlaid metal dimpled under his knuckles, but his opponent showed absolutely no sign of falling over or surrendering to him. He swore under his breath and followed it up with a kick to the ankle but missed and almost fell down, and the other knight spun gracefully and clouted him smartly in the head so his ears rang. He would've given a thousand pounds to be able to wipe the sweat out of his eyes, not that he had a thousand pounds. He had exactly three shillings and two silver pennies to his name.

The two men backed off and circled each other, big swords held up at stiff angles, shifting from guard to guard, heavy shards of bright sunlight glancing and glaring off the blades. They'd dropped their shields after the tilt to have both hands free. No mistakes now, Collum thought. *Circles not lines*, Marshal Aucassin whispered in his mind. *Watch the body not the blade.* He threw a diagonal cut that glanced harmlessly off the other knight's shoulder. The inside of his helmet was a furnace, sharp smells of hay and sweat and raw leather. He'd come here to test himself against the flower of British chivalry, the greatest knights in the world, and by God he was getting what he came for. He was getting the stuffing beaten out of him.

They stepped lightly, testing, offering, up on the balls of their feet. Every tiny movement made their armor squeak and clank and jingle in the quiet of the meadow; even the tips of their swords made tiny *whips* in the stifling air. Why—why had he thought this was a good idea? Why hadn't he stayed back on Mull? Heatstroke prickled at the back of Collum's neck. They weren't fighting to the death, but if he lost he'd lose his horse, and his armor, which he hadn't gone through all the trouble of stealing it from Lord Alasdair just so he could hand it over to some nameless knight who probably had half a dozen spares waiting for him back at his cozy castle.

And without his horse and armor Collum was nobody and nothing. An orphan and a bastard, poor as a church mouse and very far from home. And he could never go back. He'd made damn sure of that, hadn't he?

He didn't even know who he was fighting; he'd stumbled on this man purely by chance, or possibly by God's will—thanks a bunch, as always—sitting under a crooked ash in a meadow, head in his hands, as if the weight of the sunlight itself were too much for him. He'd looked up and shouted a challenge at Collum, and who did that anymore? It was like something out of the stories. Whoever this was, he was a knight of the old school.

His armor was old-fashioned, too, the breastplate black steel damascened with a pattern of fine silver whorls and a rose at the center. A rich man's armor. A nobleman's. His helmet had a pointy snout like a beak, and like Collum he bore the *vergescu*, the plain white shield of an unfledged knight. Collum bore it because he was not technically—as he'd tried to explain—a knight at all, not yet, he hadn't sworn the vows, but there were other reasons to bear the vergescu, like to hide your identity if you were in disgrace. Or Sir Lancelot bore it sometimes because otherwise no one would fight him.

This man was no Lancelot, but he was pretty damn good. Thoroughly fledged. Collum was taller but the mystery knight was faster—he barely saw him move when *bang!* his wrist went numb and *ping!* a tiny fastening pin sprang off his gauntlet and disappeared forever into the grass. He stepped neatly inside Collum's reach and grabbed for his wrist with his off hand, and Collum skipped back, panting like a bellows, but he stumbled and the man jammed his blade in the gap where his gardbrace didn't fit right, shaving off a sharp curl of bright steel.

He pressed his advantage, whipping a backhand strike at Collum's head that just missed—

There it was. The knight let his follow-through pull him round just a little too far. He was tired, or he'd overcommitted, either way he couldn't quite stop the stroke and it left him off-balance. Collum's blood broke out in a martial chorus and with the last of his strength he barged ahead behind his gauntleted fist *MANG!* to the side of the knight's helm, and twice more, *MANG! MANG!* Just like that he was through and into that other place, the one where he felt like a solid shining steel godling and nothing could stand against him, certainly not this soft, staggering wretch he saw before him! Collum regripped and delivered a clean, high, two-handed horizontal cut and the knight's head snapped round and he sat down backward on the grass.

Sir Vergescu tried to raise his blade but only dropped it again, as though fairies had cursed it so it weighed a thousand pounds. Collum let himself bend over panting, hands on hips. Sweat stung his eyes and gathered and dripped under his chin. Had he won? Really won? The man just sat there. He'd won.

He dropped to one knee and pressed the top of his helm against the cross of his sword. Thanks be to almighty God in Heaven! Thank you God for giving me—your unworthy servant—this magnificent fucking victory! He'd fought a British knight in a British hayfield and he had won. He could keep his precious armor, for now at least. In the darkness of his helmet un-knightly tears prickled in his eyes. Somewhere inside him there was strength, the strength he'd always longed for but never quite believed in. Not really. Not truly.

Or was there? Was there not something about this victory that was just a little bit too easy? Collum pushed that unappealing idea away, sniffed, and hauled himself to his feet again.

"Well fought, sir," he said. "Do you yield?" Collum thought in Gaelic, the language of the north, but for the occasion he used the courtliest, most correct, most Roman Latin he could muster.

The man didn't answer. That beaky bird-helmet just gazed up at him, expressionless. It looked quizzical and a bit funny.

In fact, now that Collum had a second to take it in, the man's appearance was stranger than he'd realized. Armor hid his face but in other ways it spoke volumes. That pretty silver rose on his chest had been scratched and scribbled over; somebody had taken a nail or a sharp rock to it. On top of the knight's helm, where a lady's favor might have been, a knotted hank of dry grass was tied instead.

There were streaks of rust on his mail undercoat where the armor plates overlapped and trapped the wet. Sir Vergescu's cozy castle was far away, if he even had one. He must've been out on the road a long time. Maybe not so different from Collum after all.

He shook off his gauntlets and fumbled with his bare fingers at the buckles and catches at the back of his head and tore his helmet off and dropped it on the grass. The bright world blasted in on him from all sides, loud and acid-green. He rubbed his face vigorously with both hands. The hot summer air felt marvelously cool. The rush of victory was fading now, and the heat and hunger and thirst were coming back. His knees felt weak. He hadn't eaten in two days.

He hoped the man wasn't hurt. He'd actually been looking forward to having a chat with him. Breaking down the combat, talking some shop. Maybe he knew how things stood at Camelot. Maybe he even knew Sir Bleoberys of the Round Table.

"Well fought, sir," Collum said. "Do you yield to me now?"

"Fuck your mother."

The man's voice was hoarse and weary. Somewhere a woodlark sang: *loo-loo-loo-loo-loo tlooeet tlooeet tlooeet.*

"Beg pardon?"

"Your mother." His Latin was surprisingly refined. A lot better than Collum's. "Fuck. Her."

Maybe they weren't going to be having that chat after all.

"That is ill said of you, sir." Collum cleared his throat. "I ask again: Do you yield to me now?"

"Well, that all depends," the man replied, "on whether or not you've fucked your mother yet."

He was angry, obviously. It was embarrassing, losing to an un-fledged knightling. God knows he, Collum, wouldn't have wanted to lose to himself. But it wasn't his idea to fight, was it?

Maybe he was hurt after all. Maybe he was in pain. Collum put out his hand to help him up, and the mystery knight held out his own—but then quick as a lizard he grabbed Collum's wrist in-stead, and with his other hand he whipped something thin and dark out of a sheath at his waist—a misericord, a long, thin knife made for slipping between armor plates—and thrust it up at Collum's groin.

Purely on instinct Collum twisted his hips and took the blow smartly on his steel skirt. He caught the man's knife hand and for a heartbeat they strained against each other, trembling. The knight kicked Collum's ankles out and rolled on top of him with all his weight, and Collum lost the knife hand—God's blood!—and panicked and scrabbled and caught it again just in time to keep his throat from getting laid open.

He threw his other arm around the man's shoulders, heaved with his hips, and rolled them back over.

"God's nails, stop!" His voice cracked hysterically. "Just yield!"

Collum fumbled for his own knife and forced it through the slit in the knight's helm. The knight trembled like a rabbit in a snare and clawed at Collum's face and thrust wildly with his pelvis. Then he coughed once and went still.

The sound of insects was loud, like dry seeds rattling in a dry pod. Silent pillars of golden country sunlight were slowly burning the green timothy grass into hay.

The knight lay flat on the ground as if he'd fallen there from a great height.

Jesus. Collum scrambled to his feet, breathing hard. *Shitting Jesus. Thou recreant knight.* He'd never killed a man before. *God have mercy on us both.*

The man kicked once and then stopped moving forever. The only part of him that was exposed was that one fish-pale hand, the one he'd bared to go for his misericord. There were brown speckles on the back of it, some ropy blue veins. Sir Misericord had not been in his first youth.

And now he was dead. And for what? Nothing. A game, played for no one, in an empty field.

And to think that they were barely a day's ride from Camelot, the sun that bathed all of Britain in the golden light of chivalry.

"God have mercy," Collum whispered. An hour ago he'd been no one, then he was a hero, and now he was a murderer. He stood there for a long time, he didn't know how long. A cloud passed in front of the sun. The two horses, his and the dead knight's, watched him with long-lashed disinterest.

Then Collum knelt and with a shudder drew his knife out of the man's eye socket. He walked over to where the fallen knight's shield lay face down on the matted grass and turned it over with his toe. You could still make out the arms under a hasty coat of white paint: Azure, Three Scepters, a Chevron Or.

Two

ROMAN ROADS

It was late afternoon. Collum rode on through a cool June rain, sitting bolt upright in the saddle, staring straight ahead into the misty distance. The drops stepped down from leaf to leaf through the trees overhead and strained ticklingly through his armor. Why didn't he just yield? Collum was a problem solver by nature, but his mind could get no traction on this one. Or on this: What was a knight that skilled, that well armored, doing fighting and dying in the middle of nowhere? Against a nobody like him? Just a big boy with a sword, from a nowhere island at the edge of the world, green as grass and fresh as dew.

The low sky was like a tent the pale creamy gray of unwashed linen. The water was cool on his face, which burned where the dying knight had scratched it.

Death itself didn't shock Collum. People were guttering candles, always on the brink of going out, from measles or pox or childbirth or a cough. They starved or shat themselves to death or were eaten by bears or wolves. But nobody should die the way that man had. The doorway from life into death was a perilous one, fraught with misadventure, and he'd stumbled through it naked and unprotected, with no friends or family around him, no priest to absolve and anoint him. Only his murderer for company.

Before Collum rode on he had buried him—he could do that much, though the dirt was packed with roots and stones and he had to use the dead man's own sword to dig with, a fine, slim blade with a pommel shaped like a wheel, thereby ruining its edge. Then he laid the knight to rest under his crooked ash tree and hung his white shield over him on a crooked branch. Unlucky tree, ash. Any crops its shadow fell on would wither. Collum couldn't bring himself to take the man's fancy armor, he wasn't going to strip his corpse like a scavenger, but he did have a silver medal on a thong round his neck with a curious device on it: a twisted rod of knotty wood like a crooked walking stick. The metal had an old look about it. Collum added it to his St. Christopher and St. Lawrence. You could never have too many medals.

And he took a brown apple and some dried beef from the knight's saddlebags. Sorry, friend. Should've yielded. He spent an eternity on his hands and knees combing through the grass for that damned fastening pin and not finding it.

Then he rode on toward Camelot.

He wasn't sure what would happen when he got there. At seventeen Collum was tall, ungodly strong, virtually ambidextrous, and terrifyingly quick on his feet, with the shoulders of a stevedore and the delicate hands of a goldsmith. He was the best fighter on the island of Mull, not just now but in living memory.

But Mull wasn't exactly a hotbed of world-class knightly talent. It was a cold, humpy place of treeless green hills, their flanks streaked with silvery streams, their peaks dragging low white clouds like tufts of wool caught on brambles. If it had a distinction it was probably that it was, in the face of stiff competition, the rainiest of the Out Isles. Wind scoured it. Chilly lochs penetrated deep into its interior. Huge shaggy red cows and tiny brown kittenish sheep wandered its coarse meadows.

Not many knights wandered the meadows of Mull. It had been years since Collum had faced anyone in his own league or anything like it, not since he was thirteen and beat the house knight at Dubh Hall who said he'd fought with Arthur at Bedegraine, in the War of the Eleven Kings. He was good, but was he good enough? The knights of the Round Table were fantastically, legendarily elite. The Table was a golden hoop that bound this shattered world together, and it drew to itself the greatest fighters in Britain and beyond: Sir Tristram from Cornwall, Sir Marhaus from Hibernia, Percival from Northgalis, Lancelot from Gascony, and Palomides from even farther away, the far East, Sarras, or wherever the hell he came from.

But if there was a place for Palomides, maybe there could be a place for Collum. He couldn't be more of an oddity than a Saracen. And he did have one single gossamer-thin connection to the world of the Table, namely Sir Bleoberys, who supposedly was his brother's wife's godfather's second cousin.

It was a long way from Mull to Camelot. Adventures were quick and exciting when you heard about them, but when you were inside one they happened very, very slowly. There were no maps of Britain, and Collum followed the sun and the coast and the drovers' roads and directions from strangers, some of whom spoke unfamiliar tongues and seemed never to have seen a man in armor before. They stared at him as if he were a gleaming metal angel who'd fallen to earth.

Collum passed through a dog's breakfast of northern realms: the

Royaume Sauvage, whose fractious kings and queens claimed descent via Brutus Greenshield from the first of the Britons, Brutus of Troy; mountainous Rheghed, domain of the boy king Carmac; the Duchy of Cambenic, ruled by Duke Escant, whose people had been driven off their land by Picts and forced to lay claim to a sere and bitter peninsula. These rulers had their own kingdoms but all of them were kings under King Arthur, High King of Britain. Arthur's law governed them, and it was at his pleasure that they sat in their thrones.

For long stretches, days sometimes, Collum saw nobody at all. The world was vast, and people were few. He bedded down in fields, wrapped in his cloak, with the Milky Way howling across the black sky above him. He clopped along sunken holloways and past isolated farmsteads, their little square fields scratched lengthways and crossways like a chessboard. He circumnavigated more lochs than he could imagine a rational Creator creating. Innumerable dogs barked at him. The further south he went the more verdant and lush the land became.

But the most amazing thing about Britain was Rome.

Collum knew that Rome had ruled Britain for three hundred and fifty years, in theory, but the Romans had never reached the Out Isles in person. He knew Rome only in the form of little things, bits and bobs, glass beads, coins with the heads of emperors on them. Errant particles of a distant empire.

But here in the southlands Rome had thrived and built, and its ruins were everywhere, the bleached bones of an empire. Having crossed Hadrian's world-girdling wall at Luguvalium, Collum found himself on a magnificent Roman road, level and cambered and paved and astonishingly straight, bashed uncompromisingly through woods and swamps and over rivers and chasms. He peered into collapsed villas with rain-worn mosaic floors and terra-cotta tiles scattered all around them in the tall grass. He passed crumbling aqueducts, roofless granaries, dry baths, entire empty towns slowly being picked apart by scavengers.

It all seemed desperately sad, like the broken architecture of Heaven. The Romans had brought civilization to Britain. They'd brought apples and pears and glass and plumbing and fine pottery. They'd brought God and the written word. They gave Britain trade routes to the Continent and beyond, as far as India and China. The Romans brought peace too. Before they came, every man's hand was at his neighbor's throat.

And then they were called back over the sea by their distant emperor, and the light went out. The secrets of civilization were lost and forgotten in the lengthening shadows. People scurried back to the old hill forts, which they barely remembered how to live in. Abandoned legions became tribes, and masterless legates became warlords. Britain went back to being a dark, fractious, divided place. A crackwork kingdom.

And through that kingdom rode King Arthur, and wherever he rode, order and peace returned. He was the last light in the darkness.

Collum chopped the heads off cow parsley with his sword. He chewed clover and sorrel to stop his stomach rumbling and picked at the peeling calluses on the palm of his sword hand. He stopped and prayed by the roadside. He snapped a thin branch off a tree and shoved it down the back of his armor in a desperate attempt to scratch his back. Gradually his horror at the events of the day began to give way to the boredom of the road. He told himself the man was just a villain, that was all. The world was full of villains, they were the darkness that King Arthur was driving out, which

Collum was—possibly, hopefully—going to help him do. For an hour or two his whole world had wobbled on its axis, the incident in the meadow bespoke some deep chaos, deeper even than evil, from which his soul instinctively recoiled—but now the world was regaining its balance. He'd met an uncouth knight on the road, they fought, and Collum slew him, as any knight of the Round Table would have done. As God had willed it. And God would forgive him.

It was a good story. It made him feel better. Stories were useful that way, they smoothed over the gaps and sharp edges of the world. There was no great mystery here, or if there was then there was no need for him to solve it. And if it wasn't quite the whole story, well, it wasn't the only lie he was going to tell when he got to Camelot.

COLLUM COULD TELL he was coming to a town because there were no more fallen branches under the trees. The locals gathered them all up for firewood. He found the town itself around sunset, a jumble of sprouting gardens and wattle-and-daub houses standing at odd angles to one another, as if a giant had thrown them as dice. It had an inn, too, a sturdy, respectable-looking building with an arched doorway and a sign painted with two crescent moons.

A drunk was passed out on the grass outside, an absolute giant of a man, his greasy tunic riding up over his white belly. A couple of kids were throwing clods of mud at him.

"Oi! Leave off!"

Collum scowled at them. The children looked at one another and collectively made a calculation, correct as it turned out, that he wouldn't actually chase them, and went back to clodding the drunk.

He doubted he could afford a bed for the night, but he left his horse in the courtyard anyway and ducked into the hall. The inn-keeper, a middle-aged man with a torch of red hair and the iron face of a jailer, sniffed at Collum's northern accent but informed him that the village he had attained was called Ditchley, in the kingdom of Logres, and that Camelot was only ten miles to the south and east. Follow the river Brass and the trail of countless other naive, hopeful young men.

Ten miles. After all this time, tomorrow would be the day. In a grand gesture Collum handed over a quarter of his life savings for a bed and a meal. He'd never stayed at an inn in his life before but he'd need a good rest, and after all, if things went right, if he did win himself a place, he would never have to worry about money again. The innkeeper lifted his chin toward a woman in a green smock who was scrubbing the floor.

"Watch out for her, she's a live one."

The woman winked at him.

Upstairs, Collum took the opportunity to get out of his armor for the first time in a week. Like a lobster carefully molting its steel shell he removed all thirty-seven pieces, one by one, each with its own hinges and pins and buckles and fastenings, and piled them on a bed. There were a couple of replacement parts that didn't quite match—right cuisse, left gardbrace, now scratched—but only a couple. (And now that missing fastening pin, too, dammit.) Collum traveled with a little hammer and a metal file to hammer out dents and smooth out nicks and dings. Etched on the inner face of each piece were the maker's mark and the lioness of Brescia. There were few decent armorers in Britain.

He dried each piece and rubbed it with mineral oil. If you left them too long, like the late Sir Chevron Or had, they got rusty and you had to roll them in a barrel of sand to scrape them clean.

He cleaned and oiled his blade too—for a killing weapon swords were surprisingly sensitive. Even touching one bare-handed would leave fingerprints that could turn into rust spots. When he was done he let his hair down—like most knights he grew it shoulder length and then pinned it up under his helmet for extra padding. He washed his grubby hands and feet and face in a basin. Then, feeling almost human again, he went downstairs.

The woman in the green smock placed a cup of ale and a plate of lamb stewed with onions and red wine in front him, and after that he couldn't think about anything else for a long time. He ate till his stomach hurt. His damp clothes steamed in the warmth. He was full, he was safe, he was almost there.

The sun was down, and the innkeeper prodded the fire to life. He argued with two customers and the woman over whether or not the big drunk in the gutter outside should be removed, and if so who should do it, and how, given how very big and drunk he was. Collum couldn't help noticing the woman watching him, bold and unembarrassed. People were always interested in a man in armor. She said something and the others laughed. Her hair was cut very short, shorter than he'd ever seen a woman's hair. Lice maybe. Or they shaved your head for adultery. Shave a cross on your head, cure for madness.

He'd turned away and decided he'd be better off ignoring her for the rest of the night when she abruptly sat down across from him.

"You a knight?"

Her age was hard to guess. Her eyes were a curiously pale gray.

"Not yet."

"I told them a real knight wouldn't stay in a shithole like this. Where from?"

"The Out Isles." He had to clear his throat. Collum was out of practice at making conversation, not that he'd ever had much practice in the first place. "And yourself?"

"Local girl." She had a winsome, lopsided smile and a funny accent that didn't sound local at all. "What happened to your face?"

"Lost a fight with a hawthorn bush."

She snorted.

"They won't let you lie like that when you're a knight. What's this?"

She reached across the table, so suddenly he flinched, and took the dead knight's silver medal in her hand.

"Medal."

"Obviously it's a medal." She weighed it in her palm. "Where'd you get it?"

He'd already resolved never to tell anybody what happened with the knight in the meadow; in fact, he'd firmly resolved to drink some water, go upstairs, and get the best night of sleep he'd ever had. But now he found himself spilling everything: the challenge, the fight, the ugly words, the ugly end. It just came tumbling out, as if she were his best and oldest friend.

He supposed he was lonely. He'd talked to two people in the last week, one of whom he'd killed. Her eyes were wonderfully large, and she had a way of looking at him as if he were the most interesting person she'd ever met.

"Dark times," she said. "I hope you buried him."

"Yes."

"Can't leave a body out like that. Spirits'll take it. Owls, even."

"Mm-hm."

"Can't have an owl running around in a knight's body."

Collum agreed that one absolutely could not have owls running around in knights' bodies.

"His arms were three gold scepters and a chevron," he said. "Do you know them?"

She shrugged.

"I can never keep track of that stuff."

"But here's what really bothers me." Collum stared into the fire. He'd called for ale because it felt like the kind of thing a knight would do, but he wasn't used to it and now he felt woozy. "I don't think that knight was trying to kill me. I think he was trying to make me kill him. I think he wanted to die."

The woman tapped her lips with a finger, thinking, her large eyes gleaming.

"Of all the animals," she said, "only man can feel a despair that is beyond his power to endure."

"God wouldn't've sent him more than he could endure."

"I find your God is a great optimist when it comes to the question of how much people can endure. Can you read?"

Your God. A pagan then. Collum felt like he'd begun this conversation with one person and now was having it with someone completely different, who was several times more intelligent than he was.

"I can read."

"Just Latin? Or do you know your Beith-luis-nin?"

"Just Latin."

Beith-luis-nin meant Ogham, the old writing of the druids. More pagan stuff. Each letter was supposed to be a tree: *beith* was a birch, *luis* was a rowan, *nin* was an ash, or something like that. Back on Mull the elders made you feel guilty if you didn't learn it. Collum hadn't. He was a good Christian, like King Arthur.

Still he couldn't help wanting this woman to like him. There was something terribly exciting about her—her quickness, her smile, that wonderfully attentive gaze . . .

"Stay with me, Collum." She snapped her fingers under his nose. "You're off to Camelot tomorrow, yes?"

An enormous iridescent beetle lit on her shoulder then flitted away again, so quick he wasn't even quite sure he'd seen it. There was a cold smell, like winter woods.

"I cherish the hope that—"

"Yes, of course you do. Well, I can't stop you. At least you can use a blade. Or stab somebody in the eye with it anyway." She stood up as suddenly as she'd sat down. Whatever game they were playing, she'd gotten tired of it. "Just don't waste any more time, you're late as it is. The sword's in the sea, and the last ship has sailed."

"I don't know what that means," he said, feeling stupid.

"I know you don't. I'm telling you now so that when you find out, you'll know that I knew."

She took off her smock and dropped it on the table.

"I quit," she called to the innkeeper.

Then she walked right out into the night. Collum stared at the open door.

He supposed it was traditional for a knight errant like himself to be accosted by mysterious maidens. Though usually in the stories they had longer hair. And what did she say about the sword in the sea? And there was something else, something important that he'd forgotten the moment she'd said it. He took a swig of his sour ale. She was one of those vibrant people who seemed to be part of a more interesting story than he was, and when she left she took it with her and left him behind in the dreary margins. She, the damsel, was the hero, and he the foil, soon discarded and forgotten. He fingered the rough fabric of her abandoned smock. *Stay with me, Collum.*

But that was it. He sat up straight. That was it. He'd never told her his name.

The bench clattered over behind him as he got up and ran out into the courtyard, three-quarters drunk. The noise and light and heat of the inn shrank away to nothing. The woman was nowhere in sight. He jogged out into the wet road.

He dithered frantically then picked a direction at random and set off at a brisk walk, past a looming barn, a well, a market square with a carpet of mashed onions and cabbage trampled flat. The cozy inn dwindled away behind him. He'd forgotten all about Camelot, now it seemed like the only thing that mattered was that he find the short-haired woman and receive whatever message she had for him. Adventure had come looking for him and like a fool he'd let it slip away!

The rain started again. Somehow the road had left the houses behind, thinning down to two wheel ruts with a tall ruff of green grass sticking up between them. A loose-limbed hare lolloped lazily across the road. Bugs burred and trilled in the night around him. Maybe he'd made a mistake. Maybe she was an enchantress who'd lured him out here to do him mischief. The nape of his neck prickled. The world was coming undone again, like it had with the knight, just when he'd almost got it back together again. Why couldn't it behave?

Maybe she was a fairy. He stopped walking. This felt like fairy business. Collum swore under his breath and patted his thigh softly, but he'd left his sword back at the inn. Stupid. Stupid. He touched his medals—but she'd touched them, too, so were they cursed now? Fairies liked a bit of fun, but they played rough and didn't care if their toys got broken. They'd been gods once, who'd shrunk and faded with the coming of Christ, and now they lurked in hollow hills and at the borders and edges of things, places even God seemed to forget about or else why wouldn't He just get rid of them? They had their own world, too, the Otherworld, and if you put a foot wrong, on a thin place, you could fall right through into it and be trapped for a hundred years . . .

He bounced nervously on the balls of his feet. Did the ground feel thin? God's neck, he was an idiot. Just when he was almost there. "Grant unto us, we beseech Thee, O almighty God," he whispered, "we, who seek the shelter of Thy protection . . ." He should've just gone to bed. He swore a solemn vow that if he survived this he would always, for the rest of his life, if given the choice, go to bed.

He squatted down in the grass, his head spinning, and prayed to God some more. Maybe they'd get bored and leave him alone. How precarious this world was, he thought, how easily one left the straight path, even with the best of intentions. Or at any rate with pretty good ones. He thought about tomorrow. If he didn't win a place at Camelot he'd just have to keep going. To Astolat maybe; he'd heard the duke there wanted men. If not there then Londinium. If not Londinium then Rhydychen, Norholt, Caer Loyw, Aquae Sulis, cities he'd never seen, where he would swear service to a lord he'd never met, and fight for him, and kill for him, and die for him. It was nothing out of the ordinary, thousands of people did it, landless, masterless knights like him. But how strange that that would be his life.

But first Camelot. He didn't have to be a knight, he'd be a squire, a servant, he would do anything if they would just let him stay, anything! He would work in the kitchens like Gareth Beaumaynes had . . .

A footstep crunched behind him in the road. For a moment of total horror he thought it was the recreant knight, restless and owl-possessed, back to take his vengeance—

But it wasn't. It was just the big drunk. The one who'd been lying on the grass outside the inn.

"Evening, friend."

He was tall, even taller than Collum, and he had a missing hand, the sleeve tied off short with a piece of twine. An old wound. How did he get all the way out here? But Collum wasn't all the way out anywhere. He was sitting in the wet road right in front of the inn, right where he started. The whole thing had been some kind of trick.

"Evening," Collum managed.

"You're from the north."

"Mull." His accent didn't seem to be fooling anyone.

"That's an island."

"It is an island." He picked himself up. His bum was wet with cold mud. Suddenly he was very, very tired.

"And what brings you all the way down here?"

"I'm on my way to Camelot."

"Camelot? Ha!" The man seemed to find that hilarious. Like Collum was the filthy broken-down drunk.

"Yes, Camelot," Collum said, with a heroic effort at manly casualness. "I'm looking for a knight, his name's Sir Bleoberys."

"Oh, you're too late for that." The big drunk chuckled some more and shook his head. "Old Blueberries is gone. Long gone!"

He turned and walked away, still laughing, looking for a better party than this one.

"Camelot," he muttered. "Good Christ. Too late for that. Go home."

Something about the way he said it made Collum's mind go still, the way small animals do before an earthquake. The rain was gone now, the clouds swept clear, and bright stars swarmed overhead. In the moonlight the fields and gardens, having drunk in the rain, were breathing out a white fog.

The moonlight showed him something else too: he was standing in a perfectly round fairy ring of bone-white toadstools.

Three

A Yong Knight

The next morning Collum rode to Camelot.

He hadn't slept well. All the way here he'd had actual fantasies about spending a night at an inn, in a real bed, but when he was finally in one—alongside an itinerant ropemaker from Garlot—the mattress felt like it was stuffed with needles, and he couldn't seem to force his thoughts down into sleep. First there was the disaster of the uncouth knight. Then there was the clever fairy-woman at the inn, and then the giant drunk who said Bleoberys was gone. None of it meant anything, or it shouldn't have meant anything, but in the Otherworld of the night things had a way of meaning things they shouldn't. And what they meant to Collum in the darkness of the inn was that something was wrong where nothing could be wrong, where he needed nothing to be wrong. At Camelot, the heart of the heart of the world, something was wrong.

By the time the sun rose his mood had cooled and stiffened into grim determination. He roused the innkeeper's daughter—who remembered nothing about any woman in a green smock with short auburn hair, none, never seen or heard of her—grabbed a heel of barley bread, and set off just as the sun pulled stickily free of the rim of the world and began heating the steaming meadows.

He kept saying it under his breath rhythmically as he rode: "going to Camelot—going to Camelot—going, going, going to Camelot." This was it, the greatest day of his life. He pushed his horse for no reason, his jaw set like cement. It felt like if he didn't hurry he would miss it. It would all be over, Camelot would've collapsed into a heap of rubble before he got there. *You're late as it is*, said the woman with the short hair. *Too late*, echoed the drunken giant. *Go home.* But that was nonsense. Camelot was eternal. He pasted a smile on his puffy sleepless face. It was time. Today his future would be decided one way or the other.

Though probably, if he were being brutally honest, it would be the other. He'd been strenuously trying to avoid thinking about it, but it was entirely possible that he was about to be publicly humiliated in front of the greatest men in the kingdom.

The problem was not that he wasn't a knight yet. That was easy enough to explain. If anybody asked, you just said that they'd wanted to knight you—they'd begged for the august privilege of knighting you!—but you'd refused to be knighted by any lesser hand than King Arthur's. The problem was that although in theory membership in the Round Table was awarded on the basis of virtue and chivalry and skill-at-arms, in actual fact every knight at the Table was of noble birth, and most of them were royalty of one stripe or another. Even when they did let someone of humbler origins in, it would inevitably come out after the fact, surprise surprise, that he'd had noble blood in him all along, only nobody knew about it. Like Sir Gingalin, Le Bel Inconnu, who turned out to be Gawain's son. Or Percival, who was raised in such total isolation that he didn't even know what a knight was, let alone who his father was. (His father was King Pellinore.)

But Collum wasn't bluffing. His father was a tradesman, a wool broker, and while it was true that he was a candidate for knighthood, it was only in the most technical possible sense. Furthermore his father wasn't even really his father at all. His mother had had him out of wedlock with a fisherman who was lost at sea before he was born, which meant that Collum wasn't just a commoner, he was a common bastard who had no business showing up at Camelot looking for a place at the Round Table. He knew this and he'd come anyway. He couldn't stop himself, it was like he craved humiliation, like he had a perverse compulsion to see the greatest in the land and to prove to himself and them and the whole world once and for all how definitively unworthy he really was.

The whole disaster had begun with Alasdair, Lord of Mull; he'd been the laird of Mull once, but after King Arthur took his conquering armies north of the wall the local clan leadership had been made over in the image of the southern aristocracy. An idle, feckless man, Alasdair had run up significant debts with various moneylenders, goldsmiths, wine merchants, mountebanks, and gambling buddies, adding up to the stupendous sum of forty-five pounds.

Collum's stepfather, Peadar, wasn't noble but he wasn't poor either, nor was he stupid. He needed some way to dispose of his illegitimate stepson, who wouldn't inherit his livelihood, so he sent Collum to Lord Alasdair's household, Dubh Hall, where Alasdair promised to educate him as a knight. In return Peadar would pay Alasdair, in regular monthly installments, enough money for him to service his massive debt. So far as he was concerned he was giving Collum the greatest gift a boy could have.

Dubh Hall was deep in the countryside, miles from the muddy

streets of Mull's only proper town, but it wasn't a terrible place to be a little boy. It was drafty and leaky and constantly at war with creeping damp, but at its heart was a massive, double-sided, ever-warm stone chimney stack that supposedly went back to before Roman times—they'd found it standing alone in a field and built the manor around it. One of its stones had a crude image carved on it of a naked woman with her legs apart, and the other boys of the house made jokes about it, but when the older servants passed they always touched it for luck.

Collum touched it too. But it didn't bring him luck.

He quickly discovered that Lord Alasdair had no intention of training or educating him. He had no interest in Collum at all except as a scapegoat on whom he could vent his anger at the many humiliations of his life, which included being conquered by King Arthur (through base southron trickery) and having to beg a tradesman to get his title out of hock for him. Nobody was permitted to speak to Collum. He was dressed in discarded clothes. A motherless boy—she'd died when he was three—he'd always loved cozy, warm places, but now he slept with the servants on a thin pallet on the floor of the drafty cruck-roofed great hall, with a log for a pillow, listening to strangers all around him, grown-ups, sniffling and shifting and muttering and farting and sometimes—though he couldn't admit it to himself—having sex.

Alasdair beat and whipped Collum for the tiniest infraction. He sent him crawling up the chimney to sweep out the soot, where he nearly suffocated. There were other adults at Dubh Hall with a taste for cruelty, and Alasdair encouraged them to indulge themselves. There was a baker who held Collum's hand over a candle after he dropped a loaf of bread in the ashes, and a chaplain who forced his head underwater in a bucket for no good reason at all that Collum could see. He was locked out of the house at night and kicked down flights of stairs; on one such occasion he broke his leg, and it was badly set, leaving it forever slightly shorter than the other. Once somebody sprinkled lye on his blanket.

And that wasn't the worst thing in his bed. There were men at Dubh Hall who wouldn't scruple to make use of a well-made boy with no powerful protectors, who couldn't afford to make trouble or throw around wild accusations.

All he could think was that it was his fault somehow. There was something wrong with him, and this was just what he deserved. He never once resisted, though when he slept outside he sometimes prayed he wouldn't wake. He didn't even dream of freedom, or rebellion, or revenge. He despised himself as much as they despised him. Collum worked and ate and slept at the bottom of a dark ocean of misery, head down, lost in the depths where no light reached him. He felt like the weight of it all would crush him. Father Conall called this listless despair *acedia* and he told Collum it was a sin. If it was, then Collum sinned and sinned and couldn't stop sinning.

His one refuge was the smithy, a snug bolt-hole where he would retreat sometimes when it was cold or rainy or snowy out. The smith kept it dark even in the daytime; he explained that it was so he could see the heat in the metal. Sitting in a corner, hugging his knees and rocking, Collum imagined the forge as a demon—the fire was its demon brain, tormenting it with red-hot thoughts. He watched sparks scatter across the stone floor and followed their individual fates as they shone defiantly and then winked out one by one. As his father's spark had, and his mother's. As his own spark one day would.

The blacksmith had come to Dubh Hall from a post at Caerleon, which he had left for reasons he firmly declined to elaborate on, and he brought with him a deep fund of stories about the knights of the Round Table, which he liked to tell as he worked. Most people on Mull dismissed such tales as propaganda for the despicable southrons, but the smith found a rapt audience in Collum.

Like him, the knights of the Round Table were despised and forsworn, but unlike him they weren't fazed by it. They were too far away and too strong. They lived in a warm, safe world wrought of old gold, rich with strength and love and fellowship, where evil was great but good was greater, where God was always watching, and even sadness was noble and beautiful. That was the world Collum wanted to live in. Those were his people. It was only after he heard those stories that for the first time he actually wanted to be a knight.

That meant being a Christian, too, though Jesus was if anything even less popular on Mull than Collum was. Good Gaelic folk mistrusted Jesus as a newcomer who stank of the south. But King Arthur loved Jesus, and God, so Collum resolved to love Them, too, and worship Them, though he had to row across a narrow, icy strait to do it, to a tiny island off Mull that had a monastery on it. Services there were presided over by chipper, bent-backed Father Conall. The few other churchgoers were mostly there to catch up on gossip—which they did during the service, over the persistent objections of Father Conall—and to collect the bits of magic bread he gave out, which were well known to bring good luck.

And unlike the chimney stone, the magic bread did bring Collum good luck, or something did. On one unseasonably warm morning in April, two years after he'd come to Dubh Hall, it happened that, miraculously, there was nothing for Collum to do. He'd cleaned the other boys' boots. He'd been shooed out of the kitchen and the stables. Nobody anywhere needed him. So he wandered out to the practice yard.

Collum had seen the other boys there, training with swords. There were three of them, Alasdair's son, Marcas, and two fosterlings from other islands. At first he just watched. Nobody looked at him. The boys weren't fighting one another, they were just cutting and thrusting at the empty air in response to the barked commands of the marshal, a slender, dark-skinned Frank who looked like he had more than a dash of North African blood in him.

This was what Collum had been promised. This was why they'd sent him here. He'd almost forgotten. The boys were red-faced and sweating in their lumpy padded clothes. They complained about the heat. When they stopped for a rest Collum cleared his throat and spoke. It was like a voice spoke through him, he didn't know how or whose it was. It was like a wonder from the stories—a sword offered up from dark water.

"May I start my training now?"

The boys burst out laughing. The marshal looked at Collum with heavy-lidded eyes: a ragged child, desperately thin and ill-kempt, with a sore on his dirty cheek.

"Not today, boy."

"But when may I?"

"The hell would I know? Take it up with Lord Alasdair."

"He won't say." Collum's face was on fire, but he couldn't let it go. "He promised my father!"

He found he couldn't say "stepfather."

"A lord always keeps his promises, but till he does it's none of my business."

Every instinct told Collum to slink back off to the smithy. But somewhere inside him, somewhere even he couldn't see, he had come to the end. He'd waited and suffered as much as he could. It was like a plough hitting a buried boulder in a field, and the blade striking a secret unseen spark underground and stopping dead.

He stepped up to the nearest boy, a wide-eyed, jug-eared child whose name he didn't even know, and yanked the sword out of his hand. The boy was so surprised he didn't even resist.

The others grinned and hooted. This was going to be good.

Collum didn't hear them. He was looking at the sword in his hand. He flipped it round and grasped it by the hilt. He'd never held one before. Branches, broomsticks, any number of pretend swords, but never a real one.

Even this one wasn't real, it was just a wooden training sword— wasters, they called them. It was surprisingly heavy; later he would learn that they were weighted with lead to be heavier than the real thing. But to Collum it felt like he'd grasped a lightning bolt directly from the hand of Jupiter himself. He had a dizzying, rising feeling, as if he were shooting up from the very bottom of his ocean of acedia, from the black depths all the way to the sunlit surface in one glorious go. The crushing weight was gone, all the colors were bright again, and he could breathe sweet air. It was like waking from a terrible dream.

The jug-eared boy tried to grab his sword back but Collum wasn't ready to let go. He scurried back out of reach. Jug Ears then made the mistake most boys do in a fistfight, and a lot of men, which is that he reared back to throw a great big punch, which meant that Collum saw it coming a mile away. Before he could throw it Collum whacked the boy on the side of the head then quickly jabbed him in the eye with his free hand. The boy put his hands over his face; Collum punched his face through his hands three more times and then kicked him in the balls.

He wasn't weak or a coward. He'd just had the bad luck to be in the way when Collum discovered the one single thing in life he was good at.

Now Marcas and the other fosterling closed in, swords held in both hands in front of them. They had him two to one, but Collum understood instinctively that he had several advantages in this situation. They had the numbers, but that made them overconfident. It also meant they had to avoid each other, and that each of them was waiting for the other one to go first. Collum noted that he was the only left-hander in the yard, which made him an unfamiliar challenge, and even though the other boys had always seemed like giants to him, he saw now that he was actually spotting them both a couple of inches. Also unlike them, Collum was untroubled by any inconvenient notions about the correct way to use a sword.

Circling to the left, so his adversaries were lined up in front of him, he batted Marcas's blade aside with his own, then bashed him on his hands so that he dropped his sword, and rushed in and kicked him hard in both shins, one-two, and kneed him in the nose when he doubled over.

The third boy's fighting spirit was rapidly deflating. Collum screamed at him and charged, and he turned white and ran for the safety of the house.

To this point the marshal hadn't interfered, just observed it all silently, arms folded. He was a small, elegant man. His name was Aucassin. Now he sighed and slowly, unhurriedly, bent and picked up Marcas's fallen waster from the worn grass.

Collum had moved beyond fear into a state of total focus that bordered on the mystical. He was no longer Collum, he was a god among mortals, Jupiter Triumphans. He was Sir Lancelot du

Lac himself, the lightning-struck sword Arondight bright in his hand!

He woke up an hour later with bruised knuckles, a splitting headache, and a broken nose.

MARSHAL AUCASSIN DIDN'T EXACTLY take an interest in Collum after that, but he made room for him in the yard. The marshal seemed to be above the rules that required the other masters of Dubh Hall to ignore or abuse Collum; maybe it was the fact that he could've beaten any of them with a sword, or maybe it was his air of Continental sophistication. For the marshal of an utterly obscure household in the Out Isles, he was a pretty well-traveled fellow. He could speak any number of languages, though he spoke them all with a thick Frankish accent. He'd fought under King Bors of Gannes and later King Claudas of the Land Laid Waste and studied with several interesting Continental swordmasters. He'd sought out the Saxon adepts Octa and Baldulph, and even an Egyptian master who'd somehow fetched up in Paris.

He had a pronounced mystical bent, and his training often took the form of obscure aphorisms—*A straight arm is the essence of man-hood; a moving leg is the manhood of essence*—and cryptic verses:

> *Only circles, never lines*
> *Only movement, never still*
> *Nimbly wind and counter-wind*
> *Long the journey to the kill*

But over time Collum began to discern in all the flowery talk and puzzling metaphors an orderly system that reduced the chaos of combat to something almost comprehensible. In the art of the longsword there were fourteen guards, five major and nine minor. No more, no fewer. There were eight cuts, all linked by flowing motions and arcs that chained them together. There were four thrusts and four parries. All else arose from combinations of these fundamental elements.

Collum's world was now sharply divided between the humiliating abuses of his life as a servant and his steady progress in the promised land of the training yard. It occurred to him early on to steal a real sword and kill Lord Alasdair with it, but that seemed unnecessary now. He wasn't worth it, it would just be a distraction. As prodigies will, Collum outstripped first his peers and then the motley gang of household knights who lodged at Dubh Hall, who learned quickly that they wanted nothing to do with Alasdair's terrifying feral fosterling. He spent a lot of time alone fighting the pell, a thick, stripped-pine post six feet tall that was a staple of knightly training. Aucassin taught him an antique poem about it, called, naturally enough, "The Poem of the Pell," which began:

> *Of fight the discipline and exercise*
> *Was this: to have a pale or pile upright*
> *Of mannys hight, thus writeth olde wyse;*
> *Therwith a bacheler or a yong knight*
> *Shal first be taught to stand & lerne fight*

The pell had a red demon face painted on it by hands unknown, a cousin to the forge-demon, with a wide fangy mouth that gleefully ate up the blows he rained on it.

Collum bashed the pell to the point of exhaustion, day after day, year in and year out, the courtyard echoing with the dull, arhythmic clonking sound of wood on wood. High cuts and low cuts and cross-cuts, diagonal and vertical, upward and downward, weak edge and strong edge. The Squinting Cut, the Scalp Cut, the Battle Cut. The Father Strike, the Crooked Strike, the Crosswise Strike. A hundred of one, then on to the next, then start the cycle over. All he could think was that if he kept training and fighting he would one day refine the taint out of himself, burn it away, the one that made it impossible for anyone anywhere to love him. He would fight his way off this island, over the sea and all the way to Camelot.

As he got bigger Collum was no less resented and despised by the folk of Dubh Hall, not just for his connection to Lord Alasdair's debt but also increasingly for his vocal Christianity and allegiance to the southern swine at Camelot. The beatings he received were no less harsh, though he found himself better able to tolerate them. His body accumulated scars, from burns and whippings, but that did not stop it growing strong. He was biding his time now. This wouldn't go on forever. Once he was eighteen they would have to give him his knighthood and let him go. If nothing else they had to give him that.

Since they couldn't face him one-on-one, the other boys would track Collum down when he was alone and attack him in a gang, any way they could: sand in the face, stone in the fist, thumb in the eye, knee in the groin. Practice yard rules did not apply.

Collum complained to Marshal Aucassin.

"Let those boys be your masters," the marshal said, "as I have been." He was whittling a votive figurine, which was his hobby, though he was in no other obvious way devout.

"What, fight like them?" Collum said irritably. "Like a dirty coward?"

"Is that what I've taught you? To fight the way your opponent does?" Aucassin closed his heavy lids and shook his head at the tragedy of Collum's stupidity.

"No, master."

"No. Not like them. You must fight worse."

So when they went low, he went lower. He went for the nose, the Adam's apple, the corners of the mouth. The knees, the instep, the balls. He shouted "For Camelot!" while he did it.

Collum was right that it couldn't last forever, but wrong about everything else. An incurable optimist, Lord Alasdair invested in another one of his friends' speculative enterprises, a scheme to send ships full of otter and seal skins to the Frankish kingdoms and bring them back full of wine. Contrary to all historical precedent, the business was a spectacular success, and Lord Alasdair was able to scratch his way back to a state of solvency and then modest wealth. That meant he didn't need Collum's stepfather's money anymore. One cold spring afternoon he told Collum to collect his things and get out by sunset.

Collum took this news as stoically as any beating. It would be the end of beatings, at least there was that. They would never whip and burn and drown him again, though he would always have the scars. He would always have a limp. But where would he go now? He'd been at Dubh Hall for so long he could barely remember the time before it.

Of course he could go back to his stepfather's house and beg his younger half brother for a place. But he knew he wouldn't. Collum gathered up his things. He felt around inside his thin straw mattress for the four much-clipped silver shillings he kept there. From under a loose flagstone he retrieved a stolen hatchet and silver spoon, both engraved with the arms of Dubh Hall, a hedgehog, that were worth two more shillings. They would be worth a spell in the stocks, too, or worse, if he was caught with them.

He went to the practice yard and gripped by a rage he didn't even recognize he hacked at the pell with his hatchet till he'd chopped it off at the root and it flopped over, finally defeated, its red demon face face down in the dust at last. Then he strode back to the house.

Lord Alasdair himself was a knight, of course, and he owned a marvelous armor. Every piece was edged in brass, and its breast-plate was set with lines of fancy decorative rivets and covered in rich red velvet. It stood on a stand in a place of honor in the hall. Collum had never seen him wear it.

Slowly, piece by piece, barely knowing what he was doing, he put on Lord Alasdair's glorious armor. It was awkward, and he quickly discovered that you couldn't really do it by yourself, not correctly, but halfway through Marshal Aucassin appeared and wordlessly, with no expression on his narrow face, buckled and strapped and bolted and tied the fine old steel into place. When he was done he knocked his brown knuckles on Collum's armored back.

"Go on, boy," he said.

On Collum went. He walked clanking out into the afternoon sunlight. Lord Alasdair's armor was worth a small fortune, fifteen pounds easily, but in that moment Collum didn't care. He was Collum of Mull, the wool-broker's stepson, and he would sooner be hung for a sheep as for a lamb. Alasdair hadn't expelled him, he'd released him.

He went to the stables, knocking down a house knight along the way (*for Camelot!*), took a horse, and rode the eight miles into town, stopping only for a last look at his father's house. How he'd longed to go back there, night after dark cold night, and how small and ordinary it looked now. It held nothing for him. By the time he got to the docks the sun was almost down but the wind was fair, and he traded the hatchet for a ride on a fishing boat across the Firth of Lorn to the mainland.

As soon as they left the shallow bay the wind kicked up, speeding them out past low-lying sandbanks and into open water. Land sounds gave way to soft sea sounds: creaking, sloshing, slapping, the crying of seabirds. The temperature plummeted shockingly fast. Collum had never been to the mainland. You could see it on a clear day, green hills with halos of cloud over the tallest ones, not obviously that much different from the hills of Mull.

Crouching in the stern, he watched the umbilical of wake that connected him to his island home disperse and fade away. The sky above Mull was wild and windblown, here dropping curtains of gray rain, there lighting up a headland with a clear shaft of sunlight that made it look like a lost paradise. The island's bumpy silhouette got thinner and thinner till he could cover it with two fingers, and it became the small, insignificant thing he always knew it was.

Proper ocean swells arrived, and the wind kept rising. He shivered in his stolen armor. Suddenly all his bravado blew away and he longed for his familiar berth on the floor of the Great Hall. Where would he sleep tonight? What was he doing? He knew no one on the mainland. His whole soul burned with regret. He'd given in to a childish impulse to prove that he was something more than what he really was, which was nobody at all. He was the motherless, fatherless stepson of a tradesman. He was a bastard and a thief and a fool, and that's all he ever would be.

He could still go back. Grovel and pay a fine, do his time in the stocks. He could go to work for his half brother. Let his hard-won muscles go slack, his belly fill out, his calluses soften, live out his days as an oversize clerk who had once, years ago, shown some promise with a sword.

But he needed to know who he was. They had told him he was nothing and nobody, and before he died he needed to know if that was true.

Night fell, the wind dropped, and the fishermen made him row. By the time they reached land he'd been sick three times. He spent what little was left of the night in a haystack. But he was on his way, seventeen years old, strong and healthy, with a rich man's armor and little money and no prospects whatsoever, and somewhere far to the south was Camelot. He felt so broken that nowhere and nothing else could fix him. Camelot was the one crucible hot enough to burn away all his weakness and shame and confusion, leaving him whole and pure and bright. *Therwith a bacheler or a yong knight.*

Four

CAMELOT

He started getting coy glimpses of it, peeking over hills and between trees, but superstitiously Collum avoided looking straight at it till he topped a rise and it was right there square in front of him.

As a castle there was nothing fancy about it, none of your new-fangled circles or star shapes. Camelot was a massive stone box, not quite square—irregularities in the terrain and the whims of generations of kings had pulled it from a true rectangle into a lumpy, nameless five-sided shape. It stood on a gently sloping bluff, guarded on four of its sides by a lazy loop of the river Brass, and on the fifth by a moat that had been diverted from the river.

A low, wandering outer curtain wall separated the castle grounds from the town that clung to its skirts. Inside it Collum could make out a high inner curtain with massive muscular towers topped by crenelated battlements. From within that rose roofs and more towers and finally the upraised fist of the inner keep, the oldest part, a huge blunt mass of stormy gray rock.

The sight washed away Collum's sleepless night and soothed his

41

bleary red eyes. There was nothing wrong here. Knights could curse at you, fairies could trick you, it didn't matter. Camelot would go on forever and ever, world without end.

As he rode closer, through fields of flowering blue flax seething with brown butterflies, he picked out things he recognized from the stories. The triple-arched Gate of Three Queens. Camelot's notorious Rain Gate. That green strip of cleared ground must be the tiltyard. The tower with the curious domed top was Merlin's Tower, which was sometimes there and sometimes not.

There was the outlying Tower of Stars, linked to the keep by a single delicate footbridge. That fat one was the Bakehouse Tower, and there, tallest of all, was the Godsfall, so named because King Uther was accustomed to hurl the idols of the pagan peoples he'd conquered and converted from the top of it.

Camelot town was quiet, the streets all but empty. A distant hammering came from somewhere, and he smelled baking bread, but otherwise the whole place could've been in an enchanted sleep. A tabby cat lounged slit-eyed in the morning sun. He crossed the drawbridge. He thought he'd have to beg or bribe or bluster his way inside but the crook-backed old man on duty just took his sword and his horse and waved him through, under the heavy ironshod double portcullis.

Strolling up through the gently sloping grounds, Collum startled a couple of tame deer. Camelot was a fortress but it was also a royal palace, with some concessions to civilian luxury: a hornbeam maze, an orchard, fountains, a pond. The famous Rose Garden, planted with seeds from as far away as Crete. He'd never been anywhere so grand and clean and orderly. Everywhere the Pendragon dragon was worked in stone and wood and paths and topiary. Back at Dubh Hall there had been a small cabinet that held the household treasures: amber beads all the way from Egypt; a little clasp knife with an ivory handle in the shape of a leopard; a cup made out of a hairy exotic thing called a coco-nut; a dried pressed olive sprig that was said to have come from Gethsemane. But this was a whole world made from treasures, a world of emerald leaves and white stone shot through with threads of golden sunlight.

Camelot wasn't always a seat of British royalty. The curtain walls were speckled with stones and ornaments scavenged from Roman buildings, and some of the exposed foundations belonged to the imperial fort that had stood here once, identical to all the other forts the Romans had stamped all over Britain. And it went back further than that. Broad banks and waves of earth rippled out from around the castle, the kind you saw around the oldest hill forts, made in ancient times by the Old Ones, who worked the landscape like a blacksmith works hot metal. Camelot had always been a place of power.

Collum proceeded on foot through the Rain Gate, so named for the rain of boiling water and hot sand it offered invaders, courtesy of its many murder holes and machicolations. A couple of ancient guards watched him from above—too old, he would've thought, for active service, but Camelot was turning out to be something of a rest home for elderly soldiers.

But that's it. Of course. He was too late. Arthur's court must've moved on to Caerleon for the summer. He'd thought they'd wait till after Whitsunday. Dammit, now he'd have to go all the way to Glamorgan. His journey wasn't over after all.

Well, he could at least have a look around first.

Collum marched unopposed across the outer bailey, which had a great green curtain of ivy spilling down one wall, and through an archway into a huge grassy interior courtyard. The mountainous keep peered down at him through narrowed arrow-slit eyes, a few of Arthur's azure-and-gold banners dripping down its sides. A couple of bored white geese were investigating a neat garden in one corner, and an anvil and some smith's tools lay temporarily abandoned in a circle of bare ground. It was all real. The promise of the stories in the flame-lit darkness of the smithy had been kept. White linens had been left to soak in a wooden tub, and he wanted to run over and touch them. The linens of Camelot! What heroes had slept and dreamed in these sheets!

A high slate-roofed hall formed one side of the courtyard. The Great Hall.

There was the door, right there. Did he really dare? Collum's head was spinning. He blinked his eyes hard. He sniffed and tweaked his nose with his fingers. Yes, he dared. He'd waited for this for nine long years, and that was long enough. He whispered a prayer, straightened his spine, and opened the door.

The Great Hall of Camelot was vast and shadowy, more like a forest at dusk than a hall. A massive chandelier hung from the roof beams, a grand celestial double wheel of candles, though only a few were lit. Narrow sunbeams speared down at steep angles through rows of high slit windows. Drifting motes glowed in the light and vanished into shadow again. Sparks on the smithy floor.

He'd arrived at the center of the turning world.

The Round Table was even bigger than Collum had pictured it, a hoop of thick varnished oak a hundred feet across, worn and scarred, darkly gleaming. You noticed the chairs as much as the table, a hundred of them set around it in two perfect fans, one on the inside of the O, one on the outside. Each chair was tall and straight-backed and varnished black, with the name of a knight written across the back in gold; supposedly Merlin himself had done it by magic. Collum had always imagined the Great Hall loud and full of people, but on this particular morning it was still and silent.

It wasn't quite empty, though. As his eyes adjusted, Collum picked out a man sitting at the table with his head down on his folded arms, apparently asleep. Another one, wide and frog-mouthed, sat with a cup of wine in front of him, even though the bells were only just ringing for terce. A ridiculously tall fellow with long, loose blond hair stood contemplating one of those green slit windows with his hands clasped behind his back, apparently lost in thought. A fourth man lay full length on his back on top of the Table, his eyes closed, as if he'd been laid out there for burial.

No one spoke. A banked fire slumbered in an old-fashioned open hearth in the center of the circle, a thin spire of gray smoke spooling up from it toward the ceiling, where a complicated-looking system of wooden louvers waited to vent it out into the summer morning air. The broad man took out a steel and began sharpening a long-bladed knife with slow rasping strokes.

He wore armor from the waist down and a thick quilted gambeson with bits of mail sewn into the elbows and armpits. The air smelled of smoke and sweet herbs and spilled beer.

"Boy." His head and jaw were frosted with silver stubble. "What do you want?"

"Boy?" The knight on the table lifted his head. "Magic boy, or regular?"

He let his head drop again with a clunk and closed his eyes.

"Regular boy."

Collum felt like he was melting into pure radiance. With his curious accent and rich brown skin like tanned leather, the man on the table could only be Sir Palomides, the famous Saracen knight.

The Knight of the Questing Beast. Collum had scaled the cliffs of Olympus and was staring at the gods themselves as they took their ease.

He went to one knee. Gray cathedral light fell around him like sleet. I will not lie, Collum thought. They will look at me and see a nobleman and I will simply do nothing to disabuse them of that notion. Then they will anoint me and gift me with lands and—in a way that will cause almost no actual blame to accrue to me—the lie will thereby become the truth.

"An it please you, my lords." It came out a note higher than he'd meant it to. "My name is Collum of the Out Isles. I have come to Camelot to present myself to the Round Table."

He'd said it too fast. He should've waited. It would've been better if Sir Bleoberys had done it, wherever he was. *Old Blueberries is gone.*

"The what now? The Round Table?" The grizzled knight kept on sharpening. "Never heard of it."

"You're in luck." The man with his head on his arms didn't raise it. "At the present time we find ourselves with several vacancies."

He said it like it was a joke, but nobody laughed. Collum walked a few paces farther into the hall, trying to hide his limp, then went back to one knee.

"God's bones," someone said quietly.

"Gentlemen." Collum cleared his throat. Years at Dubh Hall had trained him to drop his gaze when dealing with his elders, but now he forced himself to keep his eyes up. "It is the greatest honor of my life to be in your presence! An it please you, I beg you to judge of my worthiness!"

There was a deep echoing belch.

"Who's your f-father, Sir Collum?" the tall blond knight said, not unkindly.

"Lord Alasdair." The lie was so repellent that he nearly choked on it, but it wrenched itself out of him. "Also of the Out Isles," he added miserably.

"I see." The tall man had a slight stutter and an aristocratic drawl. "My boy, I'm afraid that through no f-fault of your own your arrival is ill-timed."

"What my companion means," the knight with the knife said, "is that circumstances bein' what they are, we would much prefer it if at this time you fucked off"—he made his fingers do a little run along the table—"back to those isles you spoke of earlier. An it please you."

"That will I not," Collum said.

"Eh?" The knight did an actual double take. "No, actually, that will you fucking will!"

But no. He wouldn't.

It had happened again, just like it had that first day in the training yard. The plough had hit the boulder, struck a spark, and stopped cold. He would not go. Maybe it was pride, fatal pride, but he wasn't leaving before he'd given them a good look at him.

"With the utmost respect, Sir Villiars, I am your servant in all things but this." Collum could tell the flowery talk was annoying them but he couldn't seem to stop. "I will not go until you and your comrades have judged of my worthiness."

"How do you know my name?"

"Begging your pardon, my lord, but everyone knows your name." It wasn't as obvious as Palomides, but by the man's size, shaven head, pugnacious manner, and thick Northgalis accent, he could only be Sir Villiars the Valiant. "You fought with Arthur against the Eleven Kings."

"Yeah, I know who I am. And who I fought."

"Whom," the tall knight said. "You want the direct object. Accusative case."

"I have come many miles to swear fealty to the—!"

"To the what? What? The fuckin' table? Do you see any fuckin' table?" Sir Villiars dropped the sharpening steel and tossed the knife over his shoulder; he did it casually but the knife spun in a precise arc and stuck upright in the tabletop with a soft *tok*. He flowed to his feet in one terrifyingly lithe movement.

"Of course he can see a fucking table." Bored, the knight with his head down rolled a bit of spilled green candle wax into a ball between his fingers. "It's right in front of him."

"I'm going to teach him some table manners."

Chairs scraped in the silence as people turned to watch.

"Don't listen to him, my boy," the blond knight said. "Villiars's table manners are revolting."

Sir Palomides sat up, blinking.

"In Sarras," he rumbled, "we would settle this at the chessboard. But I do not judge."

"I meant no disrespect—!"

"None taken, lad," Villiars said heartily. "My fist here is just going to judge of the worthiness of your face!"

Sir Villiars shuffled toward Collum, massive hands raised. And now for my next trick, Collum thought giddily, I shall fistfight a knight of the Round Table. How was this all going so wrong so fast?! Had he really come all this way just to get yet another beating? Villiars had a heavy jaw and pouchy eyes—he must've been a quarter-century older than Collum. One eyebrow was warped by a knot of silvery scar. Boulders rolled around in his upper arms.

Every instinct in Collum's body told him to backpedal, or better yet just cut and run as fast as he could, back to those isles he spoke of earlier, but he didn't. He would give no more ground. Instead he dropped into a boxing stance: hands up, elbows down, chin down, knees bent, feet unsquare. At least they would see him fight. Villiars would be expecting him to back up, but in a fight you always did the unexpected thing, so he shuffled forward, too, setting up for a couple of nice neat jabs to the face—

A whirlwind hook practically knocked him over. It was like being run over by a bull. Collum only escaped with a full-body duck and cover.

"Shit!" He didn't mean to say it.

"Come on, kid!" somebody called, but cracked up at the end of it.

Collum reset himself, breathing fast and shallow. His pulse was a runaway cart clattering downhill. This was his chance, this was the test. Whatever he did next he would remember for the rest of his life. He took a poke at Villiars's side, which was as indifferent to his knuckles as a tree trunk, and followed it with a cross that Villiars dismissed politely with a tiny movement of his bicep.

Villiars jabbed at his face, one, twice, jab-hook. Collum fended off the blows with his forearms, which hurt tremendously. He uncovered, and Villiars's fist glanced off his cheekbone, but it gave him a hard shot at the man's kidney. *Boom* and the joy of the fight flared inside Collum once again! Gentlemen, feast your—!

Time skipped. He was on the floor.

His ears rang, his nose buzzed, and one whole half of his head felt hot and twice as big as it should be. It was as though his mind had wandered off in the middle of doing something—but what?—and he'd just decided to lie down for a restorative nap on this pleasantly cool floor.

There were sweet herbs scattered on it: fennel, lavender, pennyroyal, hyssop. His body felt much, much heavier than usual. A pair of large booted feet stood in front of Collum. He couldn't remember who they belonged to, but they made him strangely uneasy.

One of the feet reared back to stamp on his head.

"Enough." The voice was deep and infinitely weary of bullshit.

"Oh, go to hell," said the owner of the feet.

The feet rose clear off the ground. Now they were being propelled backward through the air away from him. Was this a miracle—was this that merciful God Collum had heard so much about, finally making Himself useful? At last! *All glory to Jesus Christ!*

"Apologize to the boy."

Whoever he was, man or god, he'd picked up Sir Villiars with one hand by the front of his tunic and sat him down on the Round Table like a naughty baby.

"Fuck off!"

The man pushed Sir Villiars backward and onto the floor with a clatter.

Collum struggled up onto his hands and knees and a big callused hand hauled him the rest of the way to his feet. His savior was an older man, fiftyish, very big, sharp eyes in a blunt, unsmiling face. He almost looked familiar.

He did look familiar. It was the drunk from last night. But he was transmogrified. He'd washed and dressed and shaved. If he recognized Collum he didn't show it. He was sober now, but along with the drink the light had gone out of his blue eyes. The party was over.

"We are ill prepared for visitors, but I hope you will accept what hospitality we can offer."

Of course. A man that size, missing one hand. How could he not have seen it?

"Thank you, Sir Bedivere," Collum croaked. "That's very kind of you."

"By our custom I cannot offer you a seat at the Round Table itself, but please, take one nearby."

He indicated an extra, non-sacred chair with the stump of his left wrist.

"I thank you."

"And don't do the thing with people's names," he said, with infinite patience. "Wait till you're introduced."

"Yes. Of course. I thank you."

"You're welcome."

"My name is Collum of the Out Isles."

"Sir Bedivere."

Collum sat obediently, like a schoolboy who'd just escaped a whipping, dabbing at his bloody nose with the back of his hand. It throbbed, and so did his head, and his arms, and his ribs, but the pain was nothing. Sir Bedivere was Arthur's oldest companion, his body man and best friend, there from the very beginning, through all the wars and the quests and adventures.

By now Villiars had climbed back over the table, but his appetite for violence was temporarily sated. He reached for his cup of wine but it was empty. He threw it into the fire and put his head in his hands.

Two servants in livery brought in more wine and bread and pickled carrots and radishes on a tray. The other knights drifted over and the unsmiling Bedivere introduced them one by one. Sir Villiars, you've already had the pleasure. Sir Palomides. The round-faced man was Sir Dinadan, a minor knight with a reputation as a wit. There was a heaviness to Bedivere—like Atlas he seemed to be bearing more of the world's sorrows on his broad shoulders than other people did. He wasn't going to complain about it, but you could see that he'd appreciate it if everybody else could just do as they were told and not add to his burden.

The tall man with the long blond hair, as shining and pretty as a woman's, turned out to be Sir Constantine. Collum knew the name: he was a prince, his father was Cador, king of Cornwall. Of them all he was the only one actually dressed like a nobleman, in a magnificent form-fitting blue doublet embroidered with white lilies and featuring a new fashion that Collum had heard about but never seen: buttons.

"What on earth happened to your face?" Sir Constantine asked. "I mean, besides the o-obvious."

"Lost a fight with a hawthorn bush," Collum said.

"Ah, yes. They can be vicious when cornered."

Sir Palomides raised a cup.

"Muhammad teaches us that wine is the sweat of the denizens of Hell."

"That would explain the smell." Constantine sniffed at his cup of wine and set it aside. Palomides drank.

With that the knights of the Round Table appeared to lose interest in Collum, which gave him the opportunity to observe them as a group. They were a curious assortment, tall and short, thick and thin, with accents from all over. Dinadan looked so ordinary Collum could've mistaken him for a greengrocer. But there was something in the way they all moved—every gesture had a smooth deliberate precision to it, a sense of speed and strength held lightly in check. Never for an instant was any one of them off balance. There was a secret they shared, which was that they were all members of the most elite military order in all of Christendom.

Collum just wondered where the rest of them were. Gawain. Gareth. Bors. Lancelot. The heroes. Maybe they were off at Caerleon. Maybe being a hero meant you could sleep in of a morning.

Dinadan drained his wine and strode off to the far side of the room to practice forms, his blade flickering in the half-light. It was an extraordinary weapon, with a broad chunky blade made of blued steel so matte it didn't even look like metal. His left hand, his off-hand, was bandaged. Constantine had a black eye too. They must've seen action recently.

Collum wasn't in such great shape either. Many parts of his body were reporting damage. But he was still here. You couldn't call it a strong start, but they hadn't thrown him out yet. He didn't have to go to Astolat. Not quite yet.

Maybe some wine would help. He took a sip and set it down.

"Is King Arthur at Camelot presently?" he said, in an effort at making conversation.

"The king is dead." Sir Bedivere's face and voice were empty of all emotion. His gaze was fixed on the far distance. "He died at the Battle of Camlann along with most of the Round Table. We are all that's left."

Five

THE TALE OF SIR BEDIVERE

ong ago on a sharp crisp morning in early autumn King Arthur and Sir Bedivere chased a deer deep into the Tamwood, a glittering green forest north of Caerleon.

The campaigns for Pictland and Scandinavia had ended in triumph that spring, after three years of hard fighting, and Camelot was enjoying a rare and welcome interval of peace. Arthur and his court had spent the long lazy summer in Glamorgan, and nobody wanted to make the long trudge home yet along the old Roman Southway to Caer Loyw and then Camelot. So they lingered, trying to stretch out the season a few days longer. Now it was the eve of the autumn Feast of the Holy Cross, the damp gnawed stub of the season, and the weather had finally and undeniably begun to turn, but the king had wanted one last day out.

Arthur slowed his horse in a sunlit mat of white yarrow.

"If I weren't the king of Britain," Arthur said, "I might admit that I'm wondering where the hell we are."

He shaded his eyes and squinted into the half-light of the forest.

"But as you are—"

"Unlike his subjects, the king does not enjoy the freedom to be uncertain."

"Well, if we find that damned deer we can ask it," Bedivere said. They'd long ago dropped any formality between them when they were alone.

Yellow leaves slipped ceaselessly down through the branches. Arthur was a tall, handsome, black-haired, pale-gray-eyed man, not yet thirty, clean-shaven in the Roman manner—beards were for barbarians. He still had the sharp cheekbones of the half-starved foundling he once was, but otherwise he was radiant with health and goodness and genius and the certainty that there was no problem in this world that he could not solve, whether with laws or with charm or with faith or with an army.

It took some doing for the king to get lost on a hunt. He hunted in the grand manner, *par force*, accompanied by Master Huntsman Edward, five assistant huntsmen, three horn blowers, four archers, ten beaters, and a small army of dog handlers handling relays of lymers, bloodhounds, brachets, greyhounds, and so on, shouting at them *So how! So how! So how! Sa say cy avaunt!*

"I suppose," Arthur said, "that from the deer's point of view this is a great victory. It must think of itself as a mighty hero."

"You don't really think God bothered to give deer a point of view?"

"Of course He did, He's a fiend for details."

"Well, maybe it deserved to get away. Maybe it's a virtuous deer. If animals can be virtuous."

"I had a cat once," Arthur mused, "who has almost certainly gone to hell."

Bedivere wasn't much practical use hunting deer—one-handed, he was clumsy with a bow—so lately he'd been practicing hunting calls with a little brass horn shaped like a bull's horn that he wore slung around his neck. It wasn't polished bright but instead waxed a dull green for camouflage, one of many details of woodcraft about which Arthur was obsessive.

He blew it now. There was no echo. The dense fabric of the deep forest absorbed the sound completely.

"That's the wrong call," Arthur said. "You don't want a recheat, you want 'straking from covert to covert.' You know—" With his fist to his mouth the king did a fair imitation of a hunting horn sounding "straking from covert to covert"—but broke off halfway through.

"Shh!"

He pointed.

Bedivere didn't see anything. The silence was so thick it seemed to roar around them. He stifled a sneeze.

"Shh!" Arthur took his arm and pointed again.

Bedivere was sure they'd long since lost the deer—and anyway they weren't going to bay it without the dogs—but suddenly there it was, maybe fifty yards away, alone in the leafy dusk, staring off at something else even as they stared at it. Without taking his eyes off it Arthur slithered down from his horse and nocked a barbed hunting arrow. He gave Bedivere a look that meant, *Stay here you one-handed lumbering lummox.*

Arthur was only middling competent with a sword but the ritual complexity and deep seasonal lore of the chase appealed to his hungry intellect, and he was a past master at it. Bedivere watched him step carefully through the woods, toe-heel, mimicking the gait of his quarry. Most nobles went in for flashy colors on a hunt but Arthur wore the greens and browns that peasants wore, the better to blend in with the forest. To complete the look he twisted a small leafy branch off a tree and gripped it between his teeth, to hide his face.

If Bedivere were honest with himself he didn't really care whether Arthur got the deer or not, except that it would make Arthur happy, and Bedivere wanted Arthur to be happy because he loved him. Not just as a king but as a man: Sir Bedivere was in love with King Arthur.

He'd never done anything to betray his feelings. The risks would've been grave; sex between men was a serious sin, as was adultery. But he thought about it. A lot.

Did Arthur love him back? Almost certainly not. Not that way anyway, though it was hard to be sure. No one knew exactly what Arthur and Guinevere got up to in the royal bedchamber, but whatever it was, it hadn't produced an heir. And Arthur definitely spent a lot of his time in the company of a lot of big, strong, sweaty men.

Suddenly the deer raised its head and looked directly at Arthur, curious but still unalarmed, a solemn verger in a chapel of ash and oak. It shivered its hindquarters primly. Arthur paused, his bow drawn. He frowned, vexed, maybe, by some merciful impulse. The hart took the barest beginning of a step toward him.

Then it threw itself violently down headfirst, as if it were trying to burrow into the ground. A long arrow was stuck square through his skull.

A huge knight in bloodred armor came trotting out of the woods on horseback. He dropped smoothly out of the saddle and with monstrous strength hoisted the dead deer on his shoulder like a sack of flour, then remounted and was off again, its head bouncing limply against his back.

Arthur spat out his leafy twig.

"Look at that," he said. "This isn't a hunt. It's an adventure."

Sir Bedivere was part of Arthur's story from the very beginning, and he was there at the bitter end, but he was never the hero. He led no armies and worked no miracles. He was only ever the companion. The story was never about him.

People liked to speculate about Bedivere's missing hand, but that didn't make much of a story either. He didn't lose it in battle. He didn't trade it for passage home from the Otherworld, or sacrifice it to a demon to save an innocent maiden. He was born without it. His left forearm ended in a rounded pink stump and always had.

His father, King Reitheoir of Dyfed, told Bedivere that God kept his hand because Bedivere was too precious and He couldn't bear to let all of him go. A priest told him that the left hand was the one that did evil, and God had withheld it from Bedivere's body as a sign that Bedivere would do only good. Privately Bedivere thought that if God thought he was so precious He had a pretty funny way of showing it, and furthermore he was confident that he could get up to any amount of evil with his right hand if he put his mind to it. But he didn't brood about it. Until such time as God saw fit to clarify His intentions, he would get on with his life.

After all, he had plenty to live for. He was tall and strong, with fine, tousled dishwater hair and a long, blunt-chiseled face, and as the scion of one of Dyfed's great families he stood to inherit the throne of a small but prosperous kingdom. His good arm was disproportionately strong, and his master-at-arms helped him develop a fighting style that took advantage of it. Not many men had the strength to wield a war hammer, not properly, but Bedivere was made for it, and he carried one worthy of Thunar, the Saxon thunder god.

Likewise in the age of plate a lot of knights dispensed with a shield, but Bedivere doubled down on shield work. When he was seventeen and had come into his grown-up frame he had one specially made for him, iron-bound and spike-edged, with the great eclipsed sun of Dyfed on it, and it was a thing to be feared.

He would need it, because he was coming of age in uncertain times. The high king, fierce white-haired Uther Pendragon, had brought order to the chaos of Britain in the turbulent wake of Rome's departure. He'd bound together Britain's muddled warring kingdoms and secured its borders and harassed its pagans. Uther's ancestors had been Roman generals, or so legend had it. He fancied himself the second coming of Julius Caesar.

But Uther's Britain wasn't as solid as it looked. It was under constant threat of invasion from the Saxons and the Franks and riven with internal grudges and rivalries. Bedivere's own father was a loyal Camelot man, but some of his neighbors balked at the taxes the high king levied to pay for his endless wars. Matters were not improved when the old king died suddenly, leaving no obvious heir.

The news spread quickly, like flames through a house, and wherever it went Britain began to burn. Long-smoldering private wars between great houses sprang back to life. Cornwall and Orkney and Pictland buzzed with talk of secession, and half a dozen of the realm's big landholders began jockeying for the throne. Bedivere's family stockpiled grain and arrows and dredged the moat.

But before Britain could descend into civil war, a miracle occurred. A great irregular gray stone appeared in St. Paul's churchyard in Londinium. On top of the stone rested an anvil of rough black iron, and thrust down through the anvil and into the stone was a shining steel sword, its hilt wrapped in crimson silk thread.

Chiseled into the stone, in plain Roman letters, was an inscription:

**WHOSO PULLETH OUT THIS SWORD OF THIS
STONE AND ANVIL IS RIGHTWISE
KING BORN OF ALL BRITAIN**

It was certainly a novel and highly dramatic way to conduct a royal succession. A great tournament was announced, and candidates descended on Londinium in a royal mob: red-faced, crooked-legged King Erec of Destregales; beanpole King Cador of Cornwall; enormous, laughing King Rience of Rheged, who was rumored to be part giant. Hibernia sent three kings: Marhalt, Anguish, and Yon. They came down from Pictland and Orkney and the Out Isles and up from Lyonesse and from across the Channel. There was no shortage of kings in Britain—it was a kingdom made out of kingdoms—and the news sent them into a frenzy.

Some came to try their luck with the sword, while others were there for the lucrative aftermarket in lands and properties. Whoever won the crown would promptly neutralize his rivals by stripping them of their holdings, which he would then hand out to his friends and allies as rewards for their loyalty. There were dynastic fortunes to be won in that churchyard.

Bedivere's father, King Reitheoir, had no illusions about pulling the sword out himself, or even about making a fortune. He was there to personally make sure that somebody pulled it out, anybody, because any succession, however farcical or contrived, would mean peace, and civil war would mean poverty and suffering. He didn't want other people's armies tramping across his farmland, maiming and press-ganging his peasants.

Bedivere went with him intending to win the tournament. Also he wanted to see Londinium for the first time and, if possible, have sex.

WHEN THE ROMANS left Britain, most of the cities and towns they built were abandoned, but somehow Londinium had stubbornly held on to the greater part of its population, which was said to number almost ten thousand people, if such a thing were actually possible.

To a country princeling like Bedivere it looked like they simply couldn't get out: Londinium was ringed by a great ragstone wall ten feet thick and thirty feet high. Its wide streets were crammed with magicians and jesters, mercenaries and priests, gamblers and pimps and prostitutes in their striped hoods, Moors and Jews, pigs and dogs and rats. The river was crowded with swans and flat-bottomed fishing boats and cogs and hulks and Saxon longships. Bedivere peered down whole alleys devoted to a single trade each: tanners, pelterers, poulterers, bakers, fullers, spice mongers, wine sellers, apothecaries, gold- and silversmiths, merchants of silk and velvet and samite and damask. The air was full of the sound of bells from a dozen churches and so heavy with coal smoke you had to wash your face after a day out in it. And the smell! The gutters overflowed with sewage and rotting fish and vegetables and the discarded entrails of animals. And the Londoners bragged about how much they'd cleaned up for the occasion.

A hundred and fifty knights were expected to compete at the tournament, with many more coming to watch and trade gossip and talk shop. Children scrambled up walls and scaled rooftops to get a look at the arriving champions, who indulged them by rearing their horses and flourishing their swords in the air. Long, thin gonfalons curled and flapped and snapped from poles and spires and steeples. Banners—some professionally sewn, some enthusiastically homemade—were hung out of windows in support of this or that favorite, bearing an impossible gallimaufry of heraldic devices: fish, towers, lamps, bees, birds, fists, wings, horns, trees, slashed and quartered and counterquartered, shields within shields within shields.

North of the city, outside the massive wall, a marvelous tilting ground of surpassing greenness and smoothness was rolled out and then surrounded by ranks of seats on earthwork embankments, which were in turn surrounded by a whole improvised city of stalls and canvas tents and stripy silk pavilions. The crowds feasted on pasties and pies, strawberries and hot sheep's feet and flampets—a flampet was pork and figs that had been boiled in ale and then baked in cheese and *then* encased in pastry, and it was the first food item Bedivere had ever encountered that he couldn't actually finish. A troupe of lady jousters competed in a special exhibition, and the crowd cheered them lustily in the hopes that somebody would be unhorsed and expose herself immodestly.

As for that sword and that stone, a swollen river of humanity shuffled past St. Paul's churchyard to gawk at them. You heard a lot about miracles but it wasn't every day you got to see one right plain in front of you, just sitting there, a visible, tangible incursion of the divine into the everyday. God had reached down personally with His great hand to seize the helm of this listing nation and set it right again.

But that wasn't the only miracle afoot. By this age Bedivere had discovered in himself a longing for the love of men, and while he was fuzzy on the details and hadn't really thought through all the practical steps, what exactly went where and how it got there, he sensed that Londinium might have answers. Back in Dyfed the love he longed for was forbidden to him, it was kept under seal, but here in Londinium, he suspected, that seal might weaken. Something might leak through.

Just in case, he was dressed in his absolute finest, scarlet stockings and a mi-parti cotehardie, half black and half orange, short as he dared and tight fitted to show off his barrel chest and flat stomach. In and among and through the crowds of Londinium ran flashes of connection, glances and relays of eyes meeting, like veins of a wild, precious metal. Some of these glances were between man and man, and they were full of meaning. After a couple of hours of this Bedivere felt like a piece of amber that had been chafed and rubbed till it was crackling with energy. His cock felt like it was radiant with St. Elmo's fire.

There was a man, older than Bedivere, late twenties maybe, with a large, round, friendly face and shiny cheeks—Bedivere met his eyes and glanced away, then met them again, and then a third time. Almost immediately the man turned and walked away down a side street.

Bedivere followed. It was like a secret silver thread connected them. He let it tug him forward, away from his father and his brother Lucan and their retinue, who didn't even notice he was gone. He forgot all about the tournament and the succession. Bedivere followed the man down the skinny doglegged streets of Westcheap, stepping across trickling streams of equal parts water and shit. Brown-and-pink pigs bulled roughly past his knees. It was like he was penetrating deeper and deeper into the city's forbidden, intimate passages. This was the hidden world, the world of love and passion. The seal was about to give way.

The crowds thinned out around them, and the day went quiet.

Old women and cats watched from doorways. Where would the man lead him? What would they do there? I mean, actually do? The man's form was fascinating. He was shorter than Bedivere but with wide shoulders, a deep chest, an oddly narrow waist, and that great globe of a head. Just to be alone with him for a minute, to kiss, hard stubble against his face, the taste of another man's tongue—the thought froze Bedivere's breath in his chest. With no warning his quarry ducked into an open doorway.

It was a small dirt courtyard. It smelled like a barn, dung and straw, and the walls around it were four stories high. Even in late morning the yard was half in shadow.

The man waited for him in the shadow half, leaning back against a wall, arms folded, hips thrust forward lewdly. He was as relaxed as a cat, with a heavy-lidded half smile. Their eyes locked. Lust forced a shuddering breath out of Bedivere's chest. He hoped the man knew what to do.

He knew. Bedivere was lucky, not once but twice.

Once because the first stone didn't knock him out. He didn't even really feel the impact, just noticed that the back of his skull had abruptly gone numb. More rocks stung his shoulders and his back. He heard the laughter of children overhead.

Blinking, his erection not even faded yet, Bedivere put his hand to the back of his head and looked up. They were children, a whole gallery of them laughing delightedly and throwing rocks down at him from the roof far above.

Then he was lucky a second time because he spotted the knife. A blade can be hard to see in a fight, and often you don't find out about it till it's already in you. The man with the large head held it low, by his thigh, but it caught the light. He moved in briskly and without ceremony, looking for the quick kill. All business.

The last thing Bedivere thought was that they must have done this before.

AFTERWARD, WHEN HE FINALLY got to the churchyard, no one asked Bedivere where'd been, or what happened to his head, or why his tunic was like that, because by the time he found his way back to the inn something else had happened. The whole tournament, which started out as such a magnificent pageant, had abruptly ended as a farce. There was barely half a morning of competition before some obscure country knight's squire snuck into the churchyard and pulled the sword out before anybody else had a chance.

What a fiasco! The boy claimed he hadn't even known what he was doing, he was just looking for a replacement sword for his master who'd left his back at the inn. The inn was shut, so he grabbed the first sword he saw, which turned out to be the one stuck in the stone. He didn't even notice the inscription. Probably he couldn't even read.

Bedivere would've been happy to vent his anger and confusion and disappointment on the boy, but he couldn't even do that because he looked so hopeless, a pathetically skinny yokel, miserable and terrified as he demonstrated his party trick over and over again for skeptical bishops and kings and whoever else demanded to see it. He could only have been a couple of years younger than Bedivere but he looked like a child. He kept pushing his black hair out of his eyes and wiping his nose on his sleeve—he had a summer cold.

They kept him at it all afternoon till it started to look kind of obscene: in, out, in, out, in, out. Every time he put the sword in, with a satisfying *chunk* like a door closing, you could see he was praying it would stay there for good so that somebody else, the real king, whoever he was, could have a go and leave him out of it.

And they all tried, pushing and shoving to get at it. The sword looked like a toy in Rience's giant hands, and he yanked on it till his face turned red and the skin on his fingers tore, but it stayed where it was. Gawky Cador put his back into it, elbows and knees sticking everywhere, his supporters hoarsely cheering him on. People said that King Marhalt of Hibernia offered the boy a dukedom if he'd help him fake it.

A chill rain began to close in, and the mob of royals and nobles and their consiglieri and hangers-on and knights-of-the-body was getting surly. The miracle was supposed to avert a bloody civil war, but something had gone wrong. This boy had made a mockery of God's intention. They didn't even get a proper tourney! Factions were forming and dissolving, nobles were spreading gossip and accusations and swapping sides. Bedivere's father was shouting and clapping hands on people's shoulders, trying to play the voice of reason, but nobody was listening. No one was in charge.

A rumor went round that what they were witnessing was a coup, staged by Uther's ratty old enchanter, Merlin, using gramarye and stagecraft to install a weak-willed nobody whom the wizard could then manipulate from behind the scenes. It made as much sense as anything else.

By sundown the crowd's mood was black. The wheel of fate was spinning like a top, and where would it stop? You could argue till you were blue in the face, but when it came right down to it nobody really seemed to know exactly what it was that made a man a king. How did you work the alchemy that turned human dross into royal gold? God, blood, armies, faith, luck? Miracles were all well and good, but at the end of the day it was all in the interpretation, wasn't it?. They could damn well lynch this little hayseed, hand the sword to whoever they wanted, and work out the explanation later.

Bedivere barely noticed what was happening. He was in a fugue state, from the blow to the head and everything else. That man must have seen his stump and thought he was simple, a harmless cripple, dressed up in fine clothes, with a fat purse on his hip.

But Bedivere was far from harmless. Even out of armor, even unarmed and half crazed with lust and longing, he was still a knight of Britain. When Bedivere saw the knife, he made a blade of his own out of the stiff fingers of his right hand and stabbed it hard into the hollow of the thief's throat, collapsing his trachea. The man dropped the knife and reached for his neck with both hands, groping vainly for some way to undo the damage. Bedivere scooped up the knife with his good hand. The dying man wobbled and made tiny squeaking noises as he suffocated. Bedivere swept him into an embrace, locking that great round head in the crook of his enormous muscular elbow.

The kids had stopped throwing stones now and were just staring, a row of dark little heads silhouetted against the sky. A sadness came into Bedivere then, a disappointment that felt bigger than he was, that spread its dark wings over the courtyard and over the whole of Londinium. Here's my miracle, he thought. Gazing up at the children, holding their eyes with his, he cut the man's throat and let the blood jet out like a slaughtered pig's.

Bedivere dropped him and he pulsed the rest of it out into the black dirt, shivering as he died. Every man believes that killing will come easily to them, and in Bedivere's case it turned out to be true. How can I be so strong, he thought, and at the same so weak that I followed a stranger down a dirty alley in search of love?

Hours later in the churchyard, Bedivere's head still hurt. He felt the lump under his rain-wet hair. The bells of all those churches felt like they were clanging in his brain—how many fucking churches did one city and one God need? It seemed like there was no place on earth for one such as himself. He was deformed and perverted in both body and soul. It was no mystery: God had denied him a hand as an outward sign of his inner corruption, so that everyone could see it and shun him.

Someone was singing.

A hale, hollow-cheeked old man had come to stand next to the miserable boy—Arthur, they said his name was—and placed a fatherly hand on his shoulder. Arthur was nobody but everybody knew who the old man was. He was the archbishop of Canterbury. In a thin high voice he chanted:

> *Te Deum laudamus: te Dominum confitemur.*
> *Te æternum Patrem omnis terra veneratur*

The sound quieted the crowd. It brought them back to themselves.

> *Tibi omnes Angeli; tibi Caeli et universae Potestates;*
> *Tibi Cherubim et Seraphim incessabili voce proclamant:*

To Bedivere it was like cool water in the desert pouring over his hot throbbing head. He opened his eyes and looked into Arthur's for the first time. They were so helpless and lost, both of them.

The world had gotten them both so wrong, it couldn't see the least thing about who they really were. For a moment Bedivere saw Arthur as God must see him, with total understanding and compassion. Arthur hadn't sought this burden, but God had given it to him, and he would have to carry it all his days.

But not alone. This Arthur had in him a spark, a guttering flame, and Bedivere would feed it and protect it till it lit up the whole world. His life meant little to him, but he could make of it a gift for a king, and that was something. God might have withheld Bedivere's hand, but at least He had given him this moment.

Without thinking he slipped forward through the crowd. The archbishop of Canterbury nodded to him kindly, familiarly, still singing, the way a street musician would when you put a coin in his hat:

> *Fiat misericordia tua, Domine, super nos,*
> *quemadmodum speravimus in te.*

With all eyes on him Bedivere knelt at Arthur's feet and placed his one hand gently on the teenage boy's filthy boots.

He was the first.

> *In te, Domine, speravi: non confundar in aeternum.*

Six

The Tale of Sir Bedivere, Part II

t was only then that Merlin finally came forward.

Bedivere had already noticed him: a smiling, heavyset man who didn't dress like a nobleman but seemed to mingle with them on an even footing. He had long, lank gray hair and wore a robe and an array of rattling fetishes around his neck. His arms were covered in blue tattoos. He projected an air of inscrutable calm, indefatigable omnicompetence, and unlimited energy.

It wasn't till after the archbishop sang and the crowd settled down that Merlin sprang his big reveal: Arthur was no yokel, he really was royalty, the only son of King Uther Pendragon and Queen Igraine. He'd spent his childhood hidden deep in the countryside, in the care of some rural nonentity named Sir Ector. No one else, not Ector, not even Arthur, knew who he really was till the miracle showed them.

It was only later that Bedivere thought to wonder why Merlin hadn't just explained all that first, rather than risk an ugly scene, but Merlin was a dark horse if ever there was one. He might've been testing Arthur—Bedivere would learn that Merlin enjoyed putting people under pressure and then studying their reactions.

Merlin himself looked like he could withstand any amount of pressure. He was a court institution: he'd served Uther as counselor and sorcerer and all-purpose royal fixer, and Uther's father before him, and his father before that. Nobody knew how old he was. Some people said he was the last of the druids, or even one of the Old Ones who'd built the stone circles. Some said he was a devil's son. But what would a druid, or an Old One, or a devil's son for that matter, be doing in the service of a Christian king like Uther? Bedivere mistrusted him on sight, and nothing that followed would change that.

Whatever Merlin's true intentions were, Arthur was part of them, because without his help Arthur would've lost his throne as soon as he gained it. A coalition of Eleven Kings immediately rose up to challenge Arthur's claim; apparently for some people even a miracle was not enough to make a man a king. Merlin, armed with the gifts of prophecy and far sight and a surprising amount of practical military know-how, ran Arthur's campaign against the rebels. When the sword Arthur drew from the stone broke in a duel with King Pellinore, it was Merlin who led Arthur deep into the swampy labyrinth of the Fenlands, to a hidden pool where the Lady in the Lake presented him with Excalibur. It shone like a burning brand when he drew it.

And what did that mean? Bedivere wondered privately. It wasn't the Lady in the Lake who anointed the monarchs of Britain, it was God. But the sword was ancient magic, and men surrendered at the sight of it.

In those early days Arthur was silent and practically catatonic with shock. He'd come to Londinium for a break, hoping to see some tilting and a few pretty girls before he got back to his rural drudgery, and instead he'd been scrubbed and groomed and crowned, dressed up in armor and sat on a horse, and not long after that he was being chased through forests and fields by people who wanted to kill him while a thousand-year-old wizard barked orders at him.

Bedivere rode with Arthur all through the War of the Eleven Kings. He wasn't Arthur's counselor—that was Merlin—and he would never be his champion-at-arms—that was Lancelot. But he was Arthur's best friend and bodyguard, good-humored and level-headed and utterly trustworthy. He devoted himself entirely to the young king—he formally ceded his own claim to the throne of Dyfed to his younger brother Lucan. He made it his business to be the only person in Britain who asked nothing from Arthur other than that he stay alive and on the throne.

Which took some doing, because as soon as the Eleven Kings were put down, Arthur had to fend off the Saxons, a tribe of enterprising pagans who spoke a barbarian tongue and worshipped grim barbarian gods: one-eyed Woden, Thunar the thunderer, and the war god Tiw. They'd stayed on the Continent until one of Britain's Roman governors had the bright idea of bringing over a bunch of Saxon mercenaries to help fight off the Picts. The cure turned out to be worse than the disease. The Saxons discovered that they liked Britain better than Saxony, and they invited their friends and relations to come join them. Every British king since then had been trying to kick them out, and every spring and summer more Saxon fleets came howling across the North Sea bent on conquest.

With Uther gone, and his untried, unpopular, so-called son on the throne, the Saxons saw their chance. A week after the Eleven

Kings surrendered, twenty open boats full of Saxon warriors rammed ashore on the soft beach at Brancaster under Woden's single watchful eye.

Everybody panicked. Even Bedivere panicked. The army was exhausted, and the political situation was still critically fragile. The only one who didn't panic was Arthur. To the amazement of all, he picked up the reins of power as easy as you please, using a voice they'd never heard before, calm and confident and firm. He issued a stream of precise orders with the clear expectation that they would be obeyed. The nobles, somewhat to their consternation, did as they were told.

If his royal blood was Arthur's first revelation, this was his second: he was no figurehead, he was a warlord, a *dux bellorum*. He had only the most perfunctory training with a sword, but Arthur was a natural with a much more fearsome weapon, an army. He'd spent two years watching Merlin beat the stuffing out of the Eleven Kings, and not a second of it had been lost on him. He had the general's knack for reading a landscape, creating mismatches and natural killing grounds. He had an instinctive feel for when to show his forces to the enemy and how far to stretch a supply line. He could chill his soul down to the temperature necessary for the sacrifice of loyal men.

It was enough to make the Saxons nostalgic for the reign of good old King Uther. When they sued for peace, Arthur laughed. When they tried to retreat, he burned their boats. Merlin could only watch and stare. The Saxons called him *Blaec Artair*, Black Arthur, and he had an armor made to match, black as charcoal.

Having scrubbed Britain's eastern shore clean of Saxons, Black Arthur proceeded to do what the Romans never did, what even his father never did, which was to march north and conquer Pictland, the Orkneys, and the Out Isles. He crossed the Clear Sea and took Hibernia. In all their history the British Isles had never before been one nation. Arthur was the very first to reign over it all from Camelot as high king. By the time he got back from the north, six years had passed since the sword left the stone, and the skinny country boy had sprouted up and straightened up and filled out. Power had transformed him.

Arthur was so ruthless a general that Bedivere worried about what would happen when he finally came marching home. At Camelot there would be nobody to turn all that raw aggression on but his own people. But now the world met a third Arthur, Arthur the king, and as surprising as his skill at war was Arthur's genius for peace.

Uther had had little interest in dusty laws and regulations, and as long as his nobles turned up for battles, he let them administer justice more or less however they saw fit. But there was much cruelty in their justice—King Lot's idea of due process was seeing how far the accused could walk on red-hot irons, or whether they could retrieve a stone from the bottom of a cauldron of boiling oil bare-handed. Arthur disliked cruelty and made war on it as coldly and efficiently as he had on the Saxons. He decreed that there would be only one law in Britain, and it would be the king's law, which was derived in turn from the laws of Rome in the golden days of the Pax Romana.

All this was annoying to Arthur's fellow aristocrats. The king's law usurped their power in their own realms and curbed their ability to extract money and amusement from their serfs. They muttered about Arthur's obscure upbringing—practically a commoner himself. Too much of the lowly Briton in him, not enough sturdy Roman! They called him weak and sentimental and spoke of his father's legacy. Arthur replied that he would be more than happy to talk it over with them the minute his fellow aristocrats pulled a sword from a stone. In the meantime they could go ask the Saxons if Black Arthur was weak and sentimental.

He was naive at first—he started on most topics from a position of unlettered ignorance, but Arthur always finished streets ahead of everyone else in the room, and he never had to be told a thing twice. He was so clever, his brain ran so hot, that paradoxically it made him a little cool to the touch. Arthur was hardly ever wholly present—even the trials and tribulations of an entire empire were not enough to occupy his capacious mind completely. His thoughts were always racing eagerly ahead to the next, and the next, leaving his most loyal knight panting far behind. Where Uther had clamped the disparate parts of Britain together crudely, with fear, Arthur welded them together with—there was no other word for it—love. People loved him. People who agreed on nothing else agreed on Arthur. The British had never in their long history been one people before; no matter where the borders were drawn, they were always at best a collection of feuding and irritable neighbors. But Arthur made the British for the first time actually want to be British.

It didn't hurt that he was lucky in his looks. Bedivere wasn't the only one; everybody fell for Arthur, men and women alike. He was tall like his father but not barrel-chested or big-shouldered; people compared him to a gazehound, a greyhound or a whippet, lean and rangy, with that same intense seeking expression. He dressed in midnight blues and grays and deep blacks, velvet and silk spangled in silver. He rarely smiled, but when he did you knew he meant it. His deep-set eyes were such a pale gray that they made you think of cataracts, but they saw everything.

And the people looked back at him and thought, *Lo, there is greatness alive in this land after all, for there stands a true king.* When they saw Arthur they knew who they were, and where they belonged, and that they were home at last.

THAT DAY IN THE COURTYARD Bedivere thought he would spend his life nursing a guttering flame, cupping his hands to shield it from the wind, but the flame had become a roaring bonfire. Most people were content to be dazzled by it, but Bedivere looked deep into the flames, and he saw things there that other people didn't. Some of those things troubled him.

Arthur didn't quite make sense. He didn't add up. How could a man who was born with so little power wield power so effectively? How could a man who grew up unloved command the love of so many? How could the boy from nowhere and the High King of Britain be one and the same person? Bedivere made it his business to inquire discreetly into Arthur's origins. Not with any sinister intent, or even with any particularly good one either, but with the inexhaustible curiosity of a lover, for whom every last detail of his beloved's life is precious and charged with meaning. If he couldn't have Arthur's body, Bedivere could at least have his secrets.

From the outside Arthur's life looked like a fantasy, the one that all children dream of: he was an orphan, raised in obscurity, who discovered that his parents had actually been a king and a queen. He was really a golden princeling and his real home was a castle. But what Bedivere came to suspect was that the fantasy came at a cost, because it meant Arthur's whole childhood up until then, everything he thought he knew about himself, had become a lie. It was stripped from him like a hat in a high wind and whirled off into the darkness. And it had seemed so real! And what was real looked so much like a dream! The confusion must have been profound.

In a way, that was the birth of his genius, because after that Arthur doubted everything. He never once mistook the surface of a thing for its real nature. It was like he'd found an enchanted ring, like in the stories, that allowed him to see through all illusions. Appearances were merely reflections on the surface of a still pool, and he saw into the depths.

But in the stories a gift was always a curse, too, and this one was no different, because once you donned the ring you could never take it off, and sometimes it made Arthur mistake real things for illusions. Sometimes it made him doubt himself, and his own goodness. He'd been sure he was a yokel, and he was wrong, so what made him so sure now that he was a king? Where was the catch? Who was paying the price? Maybe if Uther had been alive to love him and look him in the eye and say, *Yes, you are mine, this is who you truly are, and always were.* But Uther had sent him away and then died, and all that Arthur had to tell him who he was was the testimony of a gray stone and a sword that broke. Could you ever really know you were a king if you'd never been a prince? *You've no idea how silly the game of lords and ladies looks,* he once told Bedivere, *when you've won it just by pulling a knife out of a rock.*

Bedivere traveled to the scene of Arthur's childhood, Sir Ector's country seat of Little Dunoak Hall. This took some doing because Little Dunoak wasn't just nowhere, it wasn't even on the way to anywhere. It was a ragged village with some patchy fields, lodged deep in the guts of the Weald like Jonah in the whale, and well on its way to being digested. An oasis of rural dreariness. It was a perfect place to hide a king, but it was no place to make a king.

Nobody in Little Dunoak remembered anything much about Arthur, or if they did they wouldn't cop to it. He was "a good boy," apparently, and "quiet." He'd passed his seventeen years there as a complete nonentity, making no impressions, leaving no footprints. His genius had not yet chosen to show itself.

But what really surprised Bedivere about Little Dunoak was how old it was. He hadn't known there were still places like this in Britain, that had been so comprehensively left behind by the march of history. Over the course of three and a half centuries of occupation, Bedivere's family, like most families of any social standing whatsoever, had become thoroughly Roman. They'd learned Latin and built villas and taken up the Roman gods, and when the Romans changed their minds and became Christian, Bedivere's people had too. On state occasions Bedivere's father still wore an old, much-mended *paludamentum*, the crimson cloak of a Roman general, fastened at one shoulder with a gold clasp in the shape of an eagle.

But Rome had missed Little Dunoak entirely. It was a left-behind scrap of the Old World, where life went on much as it had a thousand years earlier. Its houses were roundhouses, and the castle was little more than a hill fort, a sad relic of a primitive age. There were pagan shrines, to an exotic god from the east called Serapis and to Durelas, a deity of doorways and dreams. People still lit bonfires on hilltops on the quarter days—Imbolc, Beltaine, Lughnasadh, Samhain. Sir Ector put on the necessary courtly airs when the quality stopped by to hunt his woods, but at heart he was still a tribal chieftain of the mighty Cantii. At Christmastime he would dance through the village under a white sheet carrying a horse's skull, trailed by a man wearing women's clothes and a bull's tail. He duly acknowledged the birth of Jesus, but the real hero of the midwinter season was Sol Invictus, the Unconquered Sun, who banqueted with the mystery god Mithras on the hide of a stag.

This was the place that shaped Arthur, this backwater, where the deep British past persisted the way scraps of winter snow last late into the spring in the shadows of trees and gullies. This would've been the world of Arthur's mother, too, Bedivere knew. Queen Igraine was a daughter of Cornwall, with an iron-rich bloodline that ran unbroken all the way back to the kings and queens of the proud Dumnoniae.

Ancestral voices must have whispered to Arthur here. Old stories, old secrets. And Arthur never had to be told a thing twice.

But this wasn't the solution to Arthur, it was yet another mystery, because when Bedivere looked at the king now he saw no trace of the Old Britain. To all appearances Arthur was the quintessence of a Christian king, like his father, speaking Latin like a tribune and attending Mass daily. He never once went back to Little Dunoak. He even gave lip service to the idea, which only the deeply fanatical or sentimental took seriously, that one day the Romans would return from across the sea and fold Britain back into the embrace of their resurrected empire.

Arthur showed no discernible interest in witchwork or quarter days, standing stones or harvest festivals. Probably to him they reeked of his unhappy childhood. Probably it felt like if he so much as acknowledged them then the royal dream would vanish and he would have to go back there. So he'd buried the Old World along with the child he'd been and built King Arthur on the gravesite.

But what is buried is not gone.

. . .

OF COURSE A GREAT CHRISTIAN king needs must have a queen. Loyal courtiers put it about that Arthur's marriage to Guinevere was a love match—as the story went, they'd begged him to make a more politically advantageous marriage, but the king's passion for Guinevere carried all before it, just as his father's passion for Igraine had. It was a romance for the ages, and people sang a lot of songs and sobbed a lot of poetry about it.

That was the story. Bedivere thought it was bullshit. Arthur married Guinevere for one reason only, which was that she was an Eastbrook. The Eastbrooks weren't royalty, they were of at best middling rank, but they were a vast and wealthy family with rich holdings all across the north and east—between them they held as much land as any kingdom in Britain. They'd been slow to accept Arthur as king—a few had even joined the revolt against him—but a marriage to Guinevere bound the Eastbrooks to the throne, pulling in landholders from all over the map and giving them a solid stake in Arthur's reign. In Bedivere's eyes it was the quintessence of Arthur's kingliness that he sacrificed whatever unnamed yearnings lay in his heart on the altar of his royal duty.

She was not unbeautiful, though she was hardly what Bedivere would've called womanly. Just sixteen on her wedding day, Guinevere was almost as tall as Arthur. She stood straight as a mast, thin and curveless, with a pale round face and wavy dishwater hair; she looked, Bedivere thought in his less kind moments, like a mop dressed up as a queen. But she made a professional job of it all, smiling and waving and dancing and laughing whenever Arthur whispered to her at a banquet. He'd give her that.

The Round Table came to Camelot from Guinevere's father, King Leodegrance, as part of her dowry, and in all honesty it was a bit of a white elephant. It was so big they had to take it apart just to get it inside. They couldn't throw it away, but what the hell to do with it? But Arthur quickly realized that the Round Table was the kind of problem that could solve several others.

One of them was that Britain had a surplus of knights. Arthur had needed them for his military campaigns, and he'd egged them on and made sure they were properly trained and kitted out, but now the campaigns were largely over and the knights were still here, knocking around Britain in great numbers with nothing to do. They were getting bored and starting to push people around. He was catching glimpses of that old Utherian cruelty again. They needed to be put to work.

So Arthur started an exclusive club, answerable directly to him, with a lot of prestige and badges and silly rituals and fancy perquisites attached to it, and of course everybody wanted to be in it. But there was a catch: membership in the Round Table required adherence to a strict code of honor. Arthur would take all that military muscle he'd used to expand Britain's frontier and steer it inward, to keep order and do good at home. Britain was a big place with a lot of dark corners. The knights would roam at will, exploring, investigating, seeing that justice was done according to God and king. Then they would return to Camelot and tell Arthur all about it over good food and excellent wine.

But as the Table evolved and the knights pushed deeper into the wilds of Britain, they reported curious things. Wonderful things. They began to catch coy glimpses of the marvelous, the divine weft threaded through the mundane warp of this earthly fabric.

They began to have adventures. They were discovering a new frontier within Britain, invisible and passing strange. A new war was starting, and it was a war of wonders.

A mysterious maiden would turn up at Camelot lugging a magic shield, or a broken sword, or the severed head of her husband or brother or occasionally even herself. A little dog would come yapping into the hall and lead the knights off into the forest where its master lay dying of a cursed wound given him by a floating sword. Giants thundered and ravaged. Sulfurous fumes issued from marble tombs.

Bedivere watched these developments with a mixture of awe and unease. To be sure there was greatness afoot, undying glory to be won, and he himself was not immune to its siren song. But the stakes were rising too. These adventures were testing the knights, urging them on toward a transcendence that hovered always just out of their reach. God had personally put Arthur on the throne, and now He seemed to have come back to scrutinize his investment. Bedivere loved God, but he loved Arthur more, and he felt nostalgic for the days when the great game of knighthood was just a game. He would have given his life to protect Arthur, but he couldn't protect him from God.

Arthur didn't seem to want him to. The Round Table became his obsession. The knights of the Table were a great force for good, but it went beyond that for Arthur. It was personal. His bottomless intellect had finally met an inexhaustible mystery, a puzzle to consume his entire attention, his whole mind, and his soul along with it. And at the end, at the center of the labyrinth, waited his father.

Not his earthly father, not Uther, the bad cruel father who'd sent him away. These adventures came from God. A king is the father of his nation, but even a king needs a father of his own. Arthur longed for God's attention and approval the way any son would, and every time an adventure arose, Arthur felt his father's eyes on him. Here was the certainty he longed for, that even the sword in the stone couldn't give him. If he could prove himself to God, he would know who he truly was.

And there was no end of adventures. It seemed like they would go on forever.

THEY CERTAINLY WENT ON for a long time. Twenty years, twenty glorious years, as the young King Arthur gradually became the great King Arthur. His reign was so joyful and peaceful and prosperous that people forgot all about the Arthur that was, the terrified country squire who one morning blundered into the wrong churchyard and inadvertently detonated a miracle.

But Bedivere didn't forget, and one night he glimpsed that boy again.

It was late, very late, and Sir Bedivere and King Arthur sat surrounded by the spectacular wreckage of yet another Round Table feast. Servants were mopping the floor and dragging away tablecloths heavy with spilled wine and gravy. They ferried trays piled with bowls and goblets and pitchers and sodden trenchers back to the kitchens, where the almoner would collect the leftovers to give to the poor.

Lancelot had retired early, along with other holy joes, and by now even most of the serious drinkers like Villiars and Gawain and his brothers had ceded the field. But tonight for some reason the king was drinking deep. Bedivere had already been sick once, but he wasn't going to let the king drink alone.

They'd been silent for a good while, their drunken thoughts

staggering in their own separate circles. The cellarer had left them a jug of sticky-sweet hippocras and a board piled with bread and melting wedges of cheese. A servant with a harelip was with great concentration putting out every second candle in the chandelier with a long-handled candlesnuffer to save precious beeswax. Another, thin and somber, was carefully arranging the tall black chairs one by one back into their perfect fans.

"You know I'm illegitimate," Arthur said, apropos of nothing. "Mother and father weren't married when they conceived me. Couldn't wait. Child of lust."

"Everybody knows that, Arthur," Bedivere said. "Nobody cares."

"I care."

"Jesus was a bastard, too, you know. Mary and God weren't married. At least yours got married after."

"That's right." Arthur snorted. "Me and Jesus. And I've got one too now. Bastard I mean. Just like my father. And God."

He meant Mordred, of course, who'd shown up at court a few weeks earlier with no advance notice. Wound tight as a crossbow, that one. He was Arthur's son with Morgause, his own half sister, and therefore the illegitimate half brother of Gawain and the Orkney gang. But of course Arthur made a place for him. Unconsciously he was turning over an old silver coin in his fingers, a keepsake, worn almost smooth, that he took out when he was thinking.

"You know he raped her."

Bedivere felt cold at that. These were things not spoken of.

"My father killed my mother's husband and then he raped her. And Merlin helped, and God watched and did nothing. That's how I was born. She must've hated him like poison." He poured himself some more wine but didn't drink it. His face was flushed. "Must've hated me too."

"Arthur. Stop. Your parents would be so proud if they could see you."

Bedivere was embarrassed to find himself choking up. He cried easily when he was drunk.

"If my father were still around to see me, I would hang him."

Arthur's black hair looked flat and lank. He took another sip and blotted his lips with a napkin. He was lost in thought, and he stayed there for a long time. Finally he closed his eyes.

"Little bear," he whispered. "I was a little bear once."

He said it in the language of his childhood. Bedivere had never heard him speak British before. Arthur began to snore softly.

For once Bedivere felt free to study his beloved as much as he liked. Asleep, the king looked childlike and at the same time older than his years, all stubble and clogged pores and broken veins. Gazing at him Bedivere felt for a moment every bit the prophet that Merlin was. He could see it all, past, present, and future, and what he saw made him afraid.

Arthur wasn't wrong. There was a terrible truth at the heart of his life that colored everything he did and everything he was. Maybe all men had such secrets; certainly he, Bedivere, had one. Arthur's secret was that when he was hardly more than a child they had handed him the whole world, and that world had a flaw in it, and the flaw was him. He was conceived in sin and deception and murder, and no matter how great a king he became, how passionately he pursued perfection and devoted himself to God, he could never change that. That was the catch, that was the cost, and he could never make it right. It was like one of those cursed wounds from the stories, that would never heal.

Typically a son like Arthur would destroy his father. If he couldn't, if his father was beyond his reach, then he would destroy his father's legacy, the world his father had made, and himself along with it. Bedivere would back King Arthur against any general who ever lived, against Alexander the Great and Julius Caesar put together, but God help Arthur if he ever went to war with himself, because no man could stand against Blaec Artair. Not even Bedivere could save him then.

And when Arthur fell so would Camelot. And Camelot was the pillar of the world.

Bedivere woke from his trance to find the hall empty except for a few servants still waiting to clear away and see the weary king safely to bed. The air was full of birdsong. Earlier there had been a pie with live swallows inside that came fluttering out when it was cut open. Now the birds had flown up into the rafters, where they were chirping and twittering away as if it were morning, foolishly, even though dawn was still hours away.

Seven

THE LAST BATTLE

W hat do you mean, he's dead?" Collum said.

"What the fuck do you think he means?" Sir Villiars said.

Bedivere shot him a look, but Villiars ignored him. Collum looked around helplessly, but it was true. He could see it in their faces. He'd been seeing it all along, he just hadn't known it for what it was. He felt like a sailor swept overboard by a cold, silent wave. He was far from land, lost at sea, watching the warm lights of his cozy caravel disappearing among the towering swells.

Nobody had seen. Nobody was coming.

"He can't be—"

"He's definitely dead," Sir Dinadan said.

Collum was breathing hard the way he had after he'd killed the knight. Cold sweat squeezed out of his pores, and for a heartbeat he thought he was going to throw up. It was unimaginable, but he didn't have to imagine it because there it was, right in front of him. The world in all its unlimited horribleness had imagined it for him. Arthur was dead. And now—he thought miserably, selfishly—who's going to fix me? Of all the horrible things he'd imagined happening when he got to Camelot, this was so much worse than the worst of them.

"What happened?" he whispered.

"Mordred killed him." Villiars said it like he was reporting the weather. He sliced the head off his ale with two fingers and sucked them noisily, an operation that made Constantine blanch. "His own son. Arthur ran 'im through with a spear first, but Mordred pushed himself right up it and then—"

He mimed an overhand sword stroke and made a clicking sound. Another silence descended, deeper this time.

The truly strange part was that everything looked the same. The light, the chairs, the tiny dust motes, the smoke going up through the wooden louvers. The world had died unexpectedly, with no prior symptoms, but its appearance hadn't changed. All the color should've run out of it, all the light should have vanished, endless night should have fallen. Instead it kept on going. The only difference was that now it all meant nothing.

"It started when Lancelot—" Dinadan began.

"Oh, don't." Constantine cut him off.

"You're not going to defend him?"

"Can you not stop talking about it?!" Bedivere snapped incredulously.

"One night while Arthur was away hunting, Lancelot slept with the queen," explained Dinadan, who apparently couldn't stop, "which is treason. So Arthur had to sentence her to death, but he knew Lancelot would rescue her. What Arthur did not know was that while rescuing her, Lancelot would kill Gawain's brothers

Gareth and Gaheris. Gawain swore bloody vengeance, and he and Arthur chased Lancelot back across the Channel.

"Except some of us weren't so sure Lancelot was guilty, because we were accursed fools, and we went with him. Which is why we're still alive and our betters are all dead. Except for Bedivere. He stayed with Arthur."

"Lancelot was wr-wrongfully accused," Constantine said wearily.

"Cease your arguing," said Palomides.

"Stop," Bedivere said. "Leave it alone."

Collum said nothing. But he knew in his bones, in his soul, that what Constantine said had to be true. Sir Lancelot du Lac would never have betrayed his liege lord.

When Collum was three his mother died in a blizzard. His step-father was stuck on the mainland at the time, leaving his mother home with him and his little stepbrother, Eoin, who was only six months old. They were hungry, and they'd eaten everything in the house, so their mother threw a thin blanket round her shoulders and went out for more food. But it was a complete whiteout, and she must've gotten turned around somehow. She walked the wrong way, lost her bearings, and ended up in the woods. It was a month before a dog found her face down on a frozen pond, a mile and a half from home. They had to saw her out of the ice.

Collum knew he must have loved her, that his tiny heart must have been wild with uncomprehending grief, but he couldn't re-member it. He'd lost both his mother and his grief for his mother too. He sometimes wondered if it was gone completely, or if it was still there inside him somewhere, locked away in an unmarked chest with his memory of her voice, and her face, the silver key lost forever.

But now he knew what it must have felt like.

"In what might charitably be called a lapse of judgment," Dinadan went on briskly, "Arthur left his incestuous bastard son Mordred in charge of Britain while he besieged Lancelot. Did you really not know about this? As soon as he was gone Mordred told everyone Arthur was dead and seized the throne for himself. He rallied half the country to his side. Arthur came straight back across the Channel and there was a battle at Camlann.

"Arthur died. So did Mordred and practically everybody else."

"Why was Arthur fighting with a spear?" Villiars said, as if it had just occurred to him. "When he had Excalibur on his hip?!"

He said it as though if he poked enough holes in the story it would cease to be true and Arthur would be alive again.

"Lancelot and the queen are innocent. Both of them." Constantine wouldn't let it go. He really was incredibly tall, easily the tallest man Collum had ever seen. "Don't drag them down, too, it just makes it w-worse. I know it and so does Palomides."

"Do not speak for me," said the Saracen.

"For God's sake!" Dinadan said sharply. "They were in the queen's chamber!"

"Because she sent for him!"

"What the hell does that prove?!" Villiars said. "She sent for him to sleep with him!"

"According to who?" Constantine said, his face pink with exasperation. "Mordred? He's your witness? Lancelot was set up! It was all an Orkney plot! It couldn't p-possibly be any clearer!"

"It doesn't matter," Bedivere said grimly. "There's no point in talking about it. So don't."

It was clear that they'd had this argument many times already and that they were going to go on having it. They were stuck in it, whirling in circles in an eddy of grief.

But obviously Lancelot was innocent. He was the greatest knight in the world. Not that it mattered anymore. Collum walked a few steps away and sank down on the floor with his back to a pillar and his head in his hands. Suddenly he was exhausted. He closed his eyes.

"They sent a dozen knights to take him," Constantine said, "and Lancelot beat them all single-handedly. And he was unarmed. And out of armor."

"He's a beast," Villiars said, with grudging respect. "Whatever else he is."

"My point is that God protected Lancelot. He cannot be a f-fornicator because he demonstrated his righteousness upon their bodies. Surely that proves something."

"Do you really think that is how it works?" Palomides gave him a hard look. "You think that God still cares who wins a sword fight? If He really cared, then why did He not save Arthur?"

A deep quiet invaded the room. The dream was over and Collum had only just now realized it was a dream.

Though some part of him noticed that they were using the present tense about Lancelot. Arthur might be dead, but somewhere out there Sir Lancelot was still alive.

"I always thought it'd be the Saxons who got him," Villiars said.

"We didn't need them," Bedivere said quietly. "We did it ourselves."

"Britain is a waste land now, and this is not a Round Table anymore." Palomides knocked his fingers on the tabletop. "It is a zero."

"What the fuck is a zero?" Villiars said.

"You see what we are, don't you?" Constantine was addressing Collum directly, his long limbs draped limply over his chair like a puppet with its strings cut. "We're the d-dregs of Camelot. The last battle's been fought, all the best died, and we're what's left."

The fire had burned low, and Dinadan got up to add another log. It was cool here in the Great Hall, even in June. Collum's eyes lit on an enormous steel gauntlet hung from a rafter, that must have belonged to a giant. What happens now? he wondered. He didn't even know who was king.

"I might keep bees," Dinadan said. "Put my armor to good use."

"I had a bee in my armor once," Palomides said. "Tournament in Surluse. I could not think about anything else. Galahalt nearly killed me."

"Sir Galahalt." Villiars smiled. "The Hault Prince."

"He did kill my horse," the Saracen said. "Very poor form."

"As if you never killed anybody's horse."

"He killed Lancelot's!" Dinadan hooted. "Remember?"

It was true, Palomides admitted. Once at a tournament he'd chopped Lancelot's horse's head half off in a fit of rage. Now he couldn't even remember why; it was Tristram he'd been angry at, not Lancelot. He must've been mad.

And then when the tournament was over Lancelot had insisted that Palomides be awarded first prize anyway. But that was Lancelot for you. They spoke as if it were already a lost age.

"All right. Somebody has to say it."

Bedivere got heavily to his feet, as if he were carrying a tree trunk across his shoulders.

"My friends, it's over. Camelot was the center of the world, but the center's gone somewhere else now, Constantinople maybe, Jerusalem. I don't know. Maybe there isn't one anymore."

He looked out over their heads, as if he could see all the way to Jerusalem.

"But I can't pretend. Grails and spirits, marvels and quests—time to let it all go. Time to go back to whatever we were before this. Ordinary men."

The age of enchantment was gone, it had slipped away mere moments before Collum arrived, as the day steals away across the land, silently and without ceremony, to distant parts unknown. Without Arthur they were all ordinary men, their names written in sand, playing with sandcastles, and soon time would roll over them like a wave and smooth it all away to nothing.

On to Astolat then. At least he could tell his children he saw it.

"Or," said a woman's voice, "you could all stop whining like a lot of giant babies."

THE KNIGHTS GAVE a collective groan.

"We should really put a lock on that door," Dinadan observed thoughtfully. "People just come walking right in here."

The woman did walk right in, and not slowly and obsequiously the way Collum had, though she couldn't have been much older than he was. She was pale, with freckles, a sharp nose, and a bright steady gaze. Her clothes were plain but not cheap. (Linen from Flanders, thought the wool broker's stepson.) Unlike the knights she didn't seem sapped and beaten down by grief; in fact she radiated energy and determination.

Collum stood up out of respect, hastily scrubbing away his tears. Arthur might be dead, but you still stood for a lady. The woman ignored him. The rest of the knights stayed seated. Collum sat down again.

"What do you want, Nimue?" Bedivere said.

"I was worried you might be sitting around wallowing in shambolic misery, but thank merciful God I was wrong."

She took a seat at the Round Table. Any magical prohibitions or issues of protocol evidently didn't apply to her.

"The Knights of the Round Table are in conference."

"Excellent. What are we conferring about?"

"You fail to take my point. You have no standing—"

"My standing with respect to the Table is unimpeachable." She didn't say it defensively but as a statement of simple fact—she had a rapid, precise way of speaking that was obviously very difficult to interrupt. "The king is head of the Table. I am the king's adviser in all matters magical and supernatural."

"The king is dead," Sir Villiars said.

"Well, that leaves us all in something of a pickle, standing-wise, does it not? Just for example, who is that?"

Her gaze fell on Collum for the first time.

"I am Collum of the—"

"None of your business who he is." Bedivere folded his arms. "He's a guest of the Table."

Collum wondered what exactly you had to do to become adviser to the High King of Britain in matters magical and supernatural at the age of twenty-something. And anyway wasn't that Merlin's job? And Collum was no connoisseur of courtly Latin, but by her accent Nimue hadn't been raised in a castle any more than he had.

"All right then," she said. "Tell me the news."

"There is no news," Dinadan said. "What news could there possibly be?"

"I've got some: King Rience is rallying the Old North."

"Yeah?" Villiars said. "So what?"

"So what? So we'd better do some rallying ourselves or we'll be kissing King Rience's shit-caked boots. And we'll be lucky if that's all we're kissing."

Dinadan picked at the bandage on his left hand. Palomides examined the backs of his knuckles.

"He can't possibly be coming," Constantine said. "Not really."

"Well, he's not going to sit around Din Guarie plaiting his beard and mourning the glory that was Camelot." Nimue's long hair was braided and wound into two tight fierce ram's horns. "Rience is the last of the Eleven Kings. When he heard Arthur was dead he probably pissed himself he was so excited."

"He's got no claim," Bedivere muttered.

"Of course he doesn't have a claim. What were you expecting?"

"A God damned sword," Villiars said, "in a God damned stone."

"I wouldn't count on any miracles this time, Villiars. It's a free-for-all and Rience is an old dog, he knows how the game used to be played. While you sit here contemplating the impermanence of all men's hopes and dreams, Rience is putting riders on the roads. He's getting the word out, getting the barons in line. Next thing you know he'll take Londinium, seize the privy seal and the treasury, and mint a bunch of coins with his face on them. Then he deeds the Isle of Wight to the church, the archbishop slaps a crown on his head, done, bang, he's king!" She slapped the table. "That's a claim. No miracles. Just politics."

"Whose army is he going to use?" Dinadan said reasonably. "Mordred's is gone."

"Yes, and so is ours, and everybody knows it," Nimue said. "I hear Rience has enough gold to buy himself a new one."

"Who in hell would give that ingrate coin?" Villiars said.

"The Franks, I expect. Who knows? Doesn't matter. The point is that we have to fight back."

Dinadan started to say something clever back but Bedivere held up a hand.

"She's right."

Everybody stared at him.

"What?" Villiars said. "No, she's not!"

"She's right. Arthur wouldn't have given up, nor will we."

He looked around, daring anybody to disagree with him. He obviously didn't relish being on the same side as Nimue, but it didn't stop him. Collum said nothing. He wanted it to be true. He recognized Nimue as a fellow problem solver, and he wanted her to be right. He wanted to fight. But there wasn't much left to fight for.

"There is no 'we!'" Dinadan said, exasperated. "Arthur emptied the treasury fighting Lancelot, Mordred licked it clean, and the Table's down to these sorry bastards."

"Find some more sorry bastards!" Nimue said. "You could take him!"

She pointed at Collum again. The knights looked like they hoped it wouldn't come to that.

"Listen: the longer we wait the worse it's going to get. Rience is just the beginning, everything Arthur built is coming apart. The Saxons've already got half of Essex, and you can bet the Hibernians have heard by now. I know for a fact the lairds of Orkney are sitting in council this very moment at Kirkwall. Then there's the Franks and the Picts and John Strongarm and the Free Companies and the fairies. Cantium's got a witch king. In Londinium they're forming a commune, they're going to pick their own king!"

"Disgusting," Villiars growled.

"And Mordred left a son," Palomides said.

"Right." Dinadan snapped his fingers. "What is it—Melga—? Meliant—?"

"Melehan. He is Arthur's grandson. He has a claim."

"Over my d-desiccated corpse he does!" Constantine said.

"I was never a leader," Bedivere said. "I was only ever Arthur's shadow, but Nimue is right, we will defend Arthur in death as we did in life until God grants us a new king."

"He gave us one king, and we killed him," Dinadan said. "Do you really think He's going to give us another?"

"If God won't give us a king then we'll make our own," Bedivere said grimly.

"How? How do we make a king without God?"

"I imagine something could be arranged," Palomides mused. "A hollow stone with a slot cut in it. A chamber underneath concealing a man. We secure the sword in place, then at a signal the man releases it—you see?"

This idea was so depressing that nobody could even summon the energy to object to it.

Servants arrived ferrying in platters of food: roast chicken, boiled venison, brawn with mustard. It was lunchtime. The knights stirred like heavy beasts, grateful for the animal comforts of food. There was the scrape and rattle of cutlery.

"I have an idea."

Collum blurted it out before he had a chance to second-guess himself. Everybody turned and looked at him. He had the impression most of them had forgotten he was here.

"I thought—" His voice dried up. Say it, he thought. Or die wishing you had. "I was just thinking, when Arthur wanted a miracle, didn't he used to swear an oath not to touch his food till he'd seen one?"

People's eyes flicked from him to their food.

"Yes?" Bedivere said. "And?"

Dinadan was holding a chicken leg an inch from his mouth.

"Maybe we should ask for one. Like Arthur did. Maybe then God would show us who's supposed to be king."

It sounded even stupider when he said it out loud. Collum glanced at Nimue for support, but she looked miles away, lost in thought.

"Ah—Collum, is it?" Dinadan said. "Arthur did do that, but—"

"But we're not Arthur," Villiars finished.

"And that was the old days," Bedivere said. "There hasn't been anything like that since the Grail."

"Even then it was just little things," Dinadan said. "A talking stag, a floating candle. You wouldn't get a sword in a stone."

"But we did," Palomides said. "Remember? That was how the Grail Quest started. A big block of marble with a sword in it, floating on the river."

A few of the knights pushed their food around on their plates and snuck looks at Bedivere.

"Why don't we just try it?" Collum was sounding increasingly strident and hopeless even to himself. He was hungry too—that crust of bread from the inn had been a long time ago, and the wine he'd drunk on top of it wasn't helping. "What's the worst that could happen?"

"Who are you again?" Nimue asked.

"My name is Collum."

"Of the Out Isles," Dinadan added.

"You're right," she said. "He's right, we should find out."

"You fast," Villiars said. "I'm eating my damn lunch."

"Take one bite," Bedivere said, "and Nimue will summon a demon who will turn you inside out through your asshole." Villiars opened his mouth and then closed it. "We are in a changed world. If we are to bring back the Old World, we must first discover the nature of this new one."

Then he pronounced the formula that Arthur used to use: *We shall not go this day to our meat until we have heard or seen of a great marvel.*

There was a general sigh of resignation. Some of the knights grudgingly knelt and prayed. Collum did, too, but his mind was already roaming ahead to Astolat, where the market for freelance men-at-arms ought to be freshening up nicely with the imminent collapse of the rule of law. What had been a flash of brilliance a minute ago already seemed like another disastrous blunder. It wouldn't work, his tenuous perch on Olympus would fail, and he would tumble back down to earth again, back out through the Rain Gate into this cursed and empty new world.

Constantine leaned his chair back and practiced spinning a dagger across his knuckles until he dropped it with a clatter and Nimue glared at him.

The bells rang for sext.

Collum kept his face neutral and his spine stiff and avoided any eye contact. At least he'd tried. At least he'd said something. His shorter leg ached at the site of the old fracture, as though to remind him where he came from, that he didn't belong here, as if he could have forgotten. He looked around the Great Hall hungrily, trying to memorize it in case he never came back. The whitewashed walls were hung with captured banners, retired shields, ceremonial swords and lances and outlandish pole arms, the stuffed heads of griffins and boars and wolves and wyverns and something that might have been a giant house cat. In a place of honor hung a pole twice the height of a man, decorated with battered silver bosses and crescents and a tattered red flag embroidered in gold, all surmounted by a silver eagle on top. A Roman battle standard, presumably belonging to whatever legion was stationed at Camelot before it was Camelot.

"It should not take this long," Palomides said.

"It was always more of a Christmas thing," Dinadan said.

"Well, I ain't waiting till Christmas to eat my lunch," Villiars said.

"It only took about ten m-minutes with Arthur." Constantine fussed with his buttons.

"That's probably because Arthur didn't whine like a little bitch," Bedivere said.

"There's your problem." Villiars jerked his head at Collum. "Look at him. He's a Jonah if I ever saw one."

"Oh, leave him alone," Dinadan said, but without much conviction.

Villiars put his head down on the table and began to snore. Bedivere closed his eyes too. He must've had a hard night.

Collum was determined to stay awake, but he was coming off a sleepless night himself. He thought about Christmas at Camelot. Thin snow in the courtyard, swept into piles in the corners. The voices of ragged carolers, and masked mummers at the gates, and inside the Great Hall a roaring fire, hot mulled wine, damp woolens steaming. Rafters crowded with masses of holly. The castlefolk playing King of the Bean and Queen of the Pea.

And in the air, hope. Hope for forgiveness. In the teeth of midwinter, hope for renewal.

Something soft hit him in the forehead and he twitched awake.

It was a bread roll. Nimue was chucking them at each of the knights in turn to wake them up. She put a finger to her lips and pointed, and for a heartbeat Collum thought he was still dreaming because the back wall of the Great Hall had vanished.

Eight

THE TALE OF SIR BEDIVERE, PART III

All that afternoon, King Arthur and Sir Bedivere followed the Red Knight.

The chase took them through the forest and out into a strange barren land they'd never seen before, a desert of dead grass and powdery gray sand like ash. They rode through groves of blasted white trees that looked like they'd been murdered by lightning and then had their bleached white skeletons twisted a half turn by some great cruel hand.

It wasn't hard to track the knight: his horse left pristine hoofprints in the fine dust, accented with occasional drops of blood from the deer carcass. After a few hours the trail ended at a modest castle built on what was clearly the site of an old hill fort, with a moat and an unusual design: it had four drawbridges and four gates placed at the four compass points.

In front of each gate a knight with a long-handled ax stood at attention.

"Decorative," Arthur remarked. "But tactically unsound."

It was already late afternoon, they'd ridden away most of the day, but when Arthur was on an adventure time meant nothing to him. He would've ridden all night if that's what it took. They were in dream time now, the timeless time of adventures, which had a different texture from ordinary time.

The water in the moat was still and blank, reflecting the blank white sky. A few reeds grew in clumps around the edge, the only living plants they'd seen for miles. The thirsty horses snorted dust out of their nostrils. They didn't like it here.

"You know there's plenty of venison back at Caerleon."

"Not the point." Arthur squinted at the nearest of the ax-knights and frowned. "This is a legal matter. Red deer are royal property."

"Well, we'll fine him stiffly." Bedivere knew his objections would be ignored, it was part of their game.

"What shall we call this? The adventure I mean? 'Of the Red Knight'?"

"'Of the Four-Gated Castle'?"

"'Of the Stolen Hind'? I suppose we'll have to fight one of those axmen. Maybe all four."

"I hope it's just the one," Bedivere said.

They left their horses by a dead tree and trudged across the sand toward the castle. As they got closer Bedivere saw that there was something odd about the men guarding the four gates. Their armor was lit from within with a blue light.

It was blue fire: the knights seemed to be made of it. Tufts of flame poked through the slits in their visors and wherever there was a gap in the plate. The edges of the metal glowed orange where the fire licked it. The dry grass around their feet was burned black in a circle, and the air above their heads rippled.

"Look at them," Arthur breathed. "What a wonder. Pure British magic."

He was like a bird-watcher who'd spotted a rare warbler.

"Never trust an axman," Bedivere said. "Give me an honest war hammer any day. We should go back to Camelot for armor." They were still in their hunting greens.

"We'd never find this place again. You know how these things work."

The king trotted in the direction of the nearest flame knight, drawing Excalibur as he went, which shone with its own pale radiance. Arthur had a tendency—touching in a man who was otherwise so keenly perceptive—to vastly overestimate his own abilities as a swordsman. Bedivere had saved his life more than once on the battlefield, hauling him out of the press, swords and axes drumming like hail on his great sunburst shield.

Of course Excalibur helped, though it was a funny thing about that sword. Like all the great blades it was made by fairies, not by God. But why not? Was God, for all His power, not much of a swordsmith? Or did He fear to arm His mortal creations? The flame knight showed no sign that he'd even seen them. He stood with the wooden haft of his ax planted on the ground in front of him. It was a heavy weapon, its single flared blade backed by a spike.

"Sire, let me face this challenge," Bedivere said.

"No."

"I beg it as a boon."

"Denied."

"Then we'll fight it together."

"What, two on one?" the king said. "Not very knightly."

"That's not a knight! It's made of fire!"

In the end Arthur advanced on the flame knight alone while Bedivere hovered nervously, ready to jump in if things went pear-shaped. The knight stood stock-still till Arthur crossed an invisible line about ten yards away, when he suddenly came frighteningly alert, brought up his weapon, and gripped it two-handed.

Arthur was completely unafraid, as if the flame knight were a legal loophole or a trade agreement he could solve just by thinking about it. The flame knight started weaving and spinning his weapon in circles and figure eights, a continuous flowing pattern. Arthur hesitated, then backed up again. An ax could be a perplexing proposition if you hadn't faced one before. It was a crude weapon, unbalanced and single-edged. You couldn't thrust with it and you could barely feint or parry. But it was heavy, and all that weight was in its head, so when it hit it cut deep and broke bones.

The king poked at the weaving ax-head, testing the range. The knight slapped Excalibur aside. Arthur retreated some more. The knight chopped and the king lurched sideways and lost his balance but rolled to his feet again.

"Stop his weapon!" Bedivere called. "Break up his rhythm!"

"How?!"

"With your damn sword! Your Highness!"

Arthur aimed a hard cut at the ax's handle—maybe he thought he could hack through the wood, or get at the knight's fingers. He didn't do either, but he did interrupt the weaving pattern, and he had the sense to press his advantage with a string of wild hammering blows. Excalibur rang at different musical pitches in the stillness, a chiming anvil chorus. Now it was the flame knight who gave ground, backing up toward the drawbridge.

"Ha!" Arthur shouted.

Bedivere stole a glance at the other axmen, but they were still at their posts, indifferent to their comrade's fate.

The king and the flame knight circled, Arthur sweating visibly in the dry air. Bedivere winced as the knight tried to hook the sword out of Arthur's hand with his ax-head. He didn't get it, but he did yank Arthur close enough to catch him in a bear hug. The king grunted with pain and wriggled and tore himself loose. One side of his face was red where it had touched the hot metal.

"God's bottom!" It was about the worst profanity Arthur would utter.

He bulled inside the knight's reach and shoved him off balance—a knight made of flame couldn't have weighed very much—and forced him back a couple of steps into the shallow moat. When the knight touched the water steam exploded around his ankles with a high whistling noise. He dropped his ax and fell to his hands and knees as if stricken with agony or regret. More steam burst out. He tried to crawl out of the water.

But he got no mercy from Blaec Artair. With a look of studied concentration, the king kicked the knight onto his side and the water sizzled and hissed around him. A shroud of steam hid them both for a moment, but Bedivere heard Arthur banging on the knight's armor with Excalibur like a bell as the knight wallowed helplessly in the moat. The king struck his helmet once, twice, and on the third try it came off completely and a blast of heat exploded from where the knight's neck would have been, a jet of flame so blue it was almost clear, boiling the water and sending up still more white clouds.

Arthur skipped back. Even from where he was standing Bedivere could feel the heat on his face.

"Well fought, my king," he said. "Magnificently fought."

Arthur was breathing hard but already calming down.

"Poor beggar," he said. "I wonder what he feels."

"I doubt he had a wife and children, if that's what you mean. I would imagine he feels a great contentment. He spent his life here waiting for a fight, and he was granted a magnificent duel with the king of Britain himself. His fellows must envy him."

The moat was a burnt umber now from the sunset, and the steam was a towering white pillar, alone in the emptiness, taller than the castle.

"You think that's his head?" Arthur said. "That—form of fire? Or is it his blood, and he's bleeding to death?"

"I suspect the latter. He does look like he's dying."

"Probably phlogiston comes into this somehow. Merlin would know."

The flame was dwindling. In a minute they would cross the drawbridge and the true nature of the adventure would reveal itself. The holy secret of the four-gated castle. Arthur took off one glove and dabbed at his burned face with a fingertip.

"How bad's my ear?" he asked.

Bedivere took this as an excuse to lean in close. The king smelled of sour sweat and sweet cloves. What exactly did Arthur know? Bedivere wondered that every day. After all, did the king not see everything for what it was? Was that not his gift of gifts? If Arthur had closed his eyes then, angled his chin just a little, Bedivere could have kissed him. Would his touch scorch the king, the way the embrace of the flaming knight had?

But Bedivere did nothing. Sometimes he didn't know if he was a brave man or a coward.

"Your ear looks fine," he said.

INSIDE, IN THE GREAT HALL, they found a young woman seated at a long oak table. She was slender and straight-backed, with dark braids and two spots of high color in her pale cheeks. A fire roared in the hearth.

It took a moment for Bedivere to recall what the place reminded him of: it was like Little Dunoak Hall, Arthur's childhood home. Bronze shields and crossed spears adorned the walls, and the beams were carved and painted with curling, twisting, spiraling designs. There were no Roman trappings here, and no crosses either. This was the old Britain, from before the invasion. The cooking smells were different, too, plain and simple, no Roman spices, no olive oil.

But unlike Little Dunoak this hall was rich and beautifully appointed. Most Old Britons were farmers and peasants; Bedivere hadn't known there were Britons who lived like this, like lords. There must be a whole kingdom here, a shadow kingdom within Arthur's kingdom. Or was it Arthur's kingdom that was the shadow?

If Arthur noticed—and how could he not have?—he said nothing, and his face gave nothing away. He never talked about his childhood. Bedivere scanned the room for avenues of attack or escape. There were still places in Britain where kings didn't go without a significant escort.

The woman wore an intricately braided golden torc around her neck that must have weighed at least a pound. A big man with an ostentatiously barbarian mustache and forked beard stood at a table carving slices from a haunch of roasted venison, pointedly ignoring them. The Red Knight, presumably, now out of his red armor.

The woman rose, with a smile.

"You must have beaten one of the Burning Brothers."

She spoke Latin but with a strong British accent. They were siblings, Bedivere hazarded, not a married couple. He had the sense that he and Arthur were interrupting a long silence.

"My lady," Bedivere said, "the man you address so familiarly is King Arthur Pendragon, son of Uther, Lord of Camelot, King of Logres, Pictland, Glamorgan, Cornwall, the Out Isles, Orkney, and many lands beyond."

"My name is Elidir," the man said bluntly. "And this is my sister, Ystradel. We recognize no king but our father, King Bran."

That was treason, pure and simple, and Bedivere would've laid hands on him but Arthur raised two fingers slightly: let it go.

"We would be grateful for whatever hospitality you could offer us," the king said.

If Ystradel was awed by the company she was in, she hid it well.

"Of course. We don't have many visitors."

"That's probably because of the Burning Brothers," Bedivere said.

The venison was in fact excellent, tender and rich, though to go with it they were served mead, which Bedivere found unpleasantly sweet, and he knew it would give him a ferocious hangover. He drank it anyway. There was no hurry now. Once the divine machinery of an adventure was in motion Arthur liked to draw it out, study it and savor its every last wrinkle. After a suitable interval Ystradel rose and began what sounded like a well-rehearsed speech, like a docent at some minor, rarely visited historical landmark.

"You will have seen that there is a curse on this land."

"Hard to miss," her brother muttered.

"Our father the king brought it on us by misadventure. Years ago on his travels he came across a strange ship steered by an elderly man. The ship carried a spear on a velvet cushion. It dripped blood from its tip continuously. The man told my father that it was the Holy Lance, the same that had pierced the side of Jesus, and it could be wielded only by a perfect king.

"My father was a good pagan, and he sacrificed faithfully to many gods, including Jesus. He was as loath as any man to refuse a challenge. And why would the spear have come to him if he wasn't supposed to use it? So he took it up.

"This proved to be a mistake. The moment he grasped it the

spear turned on him and stabbed him through both his thighs. At that very same moment the sky turned white, and the soil was bleached, and the trees died. His kingdom became a Waste Land.

"Our father survived and was carried home in a litter, but his wounds have never healed. Ever since then he has lain in his chamber, in the dark, in pain, with this blasted country all around him. He lives—indeed he cannot seem to die—but until he is healed, our land will not heal."

Logs shifted in the grate. The place had the dry chill of the desert at night. Those curious curling designs tugged at Bedivere's vision, always on the verge of becoming tendrils or snakes or waves but never quite doing so.

"My brother and I are waiting for a knight of purity and goodness to come and anoint his wounds. If the prophesy is true then when he whom we await touches them, the wounds will heal. When the king is whole again, the land will be whole too."

Her speech finished, Ystradel stood up. She seemed eager to wrap up the formalities.

"I understand." Arthur stood too. "We will try this adventure, and may God have mercy on us all. But a word with my companion first, if you please."

He took Bedivere aside.

"You think I can do this?" he said in a low voice.

"No."

"Be frank. On no account spare my feelings."

"My liege, I think it extremely unlikely that you will accomplish this adventure."

Arthur was a brave knight, and a zealous Christian, and the best of all kings, but he was not without stain, at least as God judged these things. He'd had a child out of wedlock with his own half sister, which seemed like the kind of detail God was unlikely to overlook. For some of the more rigorous adventures you had to be an actual virgin.

"If it were a question of bravery alone," Bedivere said, "or goodness, or perspicacity—"

"Then the question becomes, why would God give us an adventure we can't perform?"

"Why would He give their father a spear he couldn't pick up? You are a good man and a great king, Arthur. The rest is up to Him."

"So it is. Keep an eye on the brother, he could be a fiend in disguise."

King Bran's bedroom was up a flight of stairs, directly above the great hall. Bedivere wondered if he could hear what was said down there, and if so, how many times he'd had to listen to his children rehearse the story of his disgrace. It was fully night now, and Elidir led the way with a torch. They stopped at a wooden door into which small, neat black letters had been burned, as if written with a red-hot iron:

THE KNIGHT WHO FULFILLS THIS QUEST WILL NOT FULFILL THIS QUEST

"What do you make of that, Bedivere?"

"A riddle, my king. Or a paradox."

"It's always been there," Ystradel said. "Or at least as long as we can remember." There was a low groan from behind the door. "Please. He's in pain."

Bedivere wondered how long they'd been here, hostages to their father's error. Arthur squared his shoulders and pushed open the door.

Nauseous sickroom air breathed out at them: warm and damp, hints of vomit and rot. Arthur showed no fear or disgust. It was a feat Bedivere had watched him perform a thousand times: striding into a room as if he were entering a feast in his honor, filling it with calm and goodwill, no matter what it contained before he arrived. Bedivere could make out the white shape of a bed and a pale attenuated body lying on it uncovered, wearing only a loincloth.

Dark spreading stains bloomed around it. The sight brought to mind the deposed Christ. The old king coughed. He was emaciated, with long, lank, white hair. Arthur bent over him without the slightest squeamishness.

"Ah, my friend," he said gently, "this will never do. Let us see if we can help you."

He dabbled his fingers in a dish of oil and laid them on the old man's wounds. His tenderness made Bedivere's heart ache: pettily he envied the old king for receiving Arthur's attentions. The spear must have gone through his thighs front to back, though by luck or divine mercy it had missed the femoral artery. Bedivere scanned the room continuously for sudden movements, but Elidir did not appear in any danger of throwing off his mortal seeming and becoming a fiend. They were only an old man in pain and his children.

Next Arthur washed the wounds, which made the man gasp in agony. Ystradel and Elidir kept their faces studiously neutral, betraying neither hope nor disappointment.

"Arthur—"

"I know. I know!" Arthur threw down the towel in frustration. "God's bones!"

He kicked the wall.

"By my faith, I have failed!"

"Now him," Elidir said.

"Yes, all right, all right." Arthur recovered his equanimity immediately. He picked up the towel. "Come on, Bedivere. Do your worst."

112

Bedivere dutifully took the cloth and rinsed it in the bowl. He at least had never touched a woman with lust in his soul; in that narrow sense he was as chaste as any hermit or anchorite. But he'd touched his share of men, other knights even—how could he not have, with all the time they spent out questing, bedding down together in empty fields and lonely pavilions and the drafty spare rooms of far-flung castles? He'd dallied with Sir Aglovale, a tender and passionate lover, and Sir Colgrevance, and even the doughty Sir Lamorak, brother to Sir Percival. Though the next day Lamorak blamed it on Bedivere's seductive wiles and threatened to kill him. How much easier, how much simpler his life would've been if he could've given his heart to one of them—or to Sir Tully, who trailed after him like a puppy for months after. But Tully wasn't clever like Arthur, he didn't instantly grasp Bedivere's meaning the way Arthur did, and finish his thoughts for him even as he had them. His eyes weren't gray like Arthur's, his nose wasn't just a little off center. He didn't rub a coin with his thumb when he thought.

But he regretted none of it. Bedivere was as God made him, and he did not think he could have done otherwise.

The old king's legs were ghastly pale and hairy and slick with sweat. Bedivere was as gentle as he could manage, but after a short while the pain was too much and King Bran begged him in a hoarse voice to stop.

It was finished. There would be no miracle today. The adventure was a failure.

Old King Bran fell back on the bed panting. Now he would suffer on, moaning and turning in the darkness, while the corpse of the land he killed moldered around him. How long, O Lord? How long had he lain here already? He must dream endlessly of that long-ago day, of taking it back and leaving the spear alone.

But you could never take anything back. Words and deeds, once said and done, flew away and never returned to you, like Noah's dove after the Flood. Bedivere made their apologies to the prince and princess and they all filed out together in discontented silence.

Halfway down the stairs Arthur stopped.

"That's your father calling to me," he said. "Sounds like he wants a quick word."

Surely the adventure was over? Reluctantly Bedivere descended the stairs with the prince and princess. The great hall was empty now, soundless servants had cleared away the venison, and the candles were guttering in pools of wax, like martyrs wallowing in their own blood. No one sat. In the afterglow of failure there wasn't much to say. It was hard not to feel a little ashamed. Lancelot probably could've healed him before breakfast.

But for his hand Bedivere might have been like that, one of the great ones. But for his hand and but for his heart. As it was he would only ever be the companion—faithful Bedivere, always there to back up the leading man, ready with a bit of wry wisdom maybe, but not too much. Never enough to steal the scene.

It was one of his functions, making small talk with people who were waiting for King Arthur. Have you had a lot of people try? What's the point of your Red Knight routine? Terribly dry weather here, is it not? And so on. He promised them that once he got back to court he would try to send Lancelot over, or if he was busy then one of the lesser lights. Sir Gareth maybe. He's young but very promising, I assure you.

"What happened to the spear afterward?" Bedivere asked.

"After what happened to my father, no one wanted to touch it," Ystradel said. "So the old man put it back on its cushion and they sailed away again. To the far north, he said."

"We had no trouble here till you Christians came." Elidir had apparently decided to speak his mind. "Then your Jesus maimed my father with his spear, and broke our land, and now we must wait for an eternity for some other Jesus-lover to come heal him! How long will it go on? The Romans killed our druids, and without them we barely remember who we are." He gave Bedivere a hard look. "But at least we know we are not Roman."

At last Arthur appeared, trotting briskly down the stairs.

"What is it?" Ystradel's face was all hope and confusion. "What did he want?"

Arthur had the weary air of a doctor just out of a long surgery. A telltale arterial spray crossed his front.

"The king is dead." He held out the old king's crown to his son. "Long live the king."

Arthur tried to place it on Elidir's head, but the young man shied back as if it were red-hot.

"You killed him." His face was white. "Didn't you? You killed my father."

"I am sorry." Arthur looked almost as shaken as Elidir did. "I truly am. He asked me to release him from his suffering and I did. Sometimes the king must die so that his land may live. I will pray for your father and for you."

"Save your prayers, Christian scum!" Ystradel spat a white fleck onto Arthur's chest. "Murderer!"

Elidir lunged at Arthur but Bedivere stiff-armed him so hard he slammed down on his back on the stone floor and the wind went out of him.

"Understand this." Arthur's voice deepened and hardened. It wasn't Arthur the knight errant who spoke now; this was Arthur Pendragon, King of Britain. King of Kings. "Your father died the day he picked up a spear that wasn't meant for him. The curse he brought down has held you and this whole kingdom hostage ever since. It's time you were free.

"And he was suffering. You wouldn't let a dog live like that."

"Are you going to tell me he's in Heaven now?" Ystradel sneered. "My father was wounded, but you *are* a wound. I can see it! You are killing this land, and the worst part is you know it! If your mother were alive to see you now she would die of shame."

Ystradel tried to spit again but her mouth was dry. Arthur placed the crown on the table. Elidir groaned and rolled onto his side, trying to get his breath back.

"You are king now, under me," Arthur said, looking down at him, "and life will return to this dead land and it will flourish again, if our holy savior Jesus Christ wills it."

He walked out of the hall without looking back.

THE BURNING BROTHERS were no longer at their posts. Their duty done, they'd vanished or departed, gone back to wherever such beings came from, leaving behind only four black charred spots in front of the four gates. Bedivere imagined them in retirement, engaged in peaceful civilian pursuits. A vegetable garden. Amateur woodworking. Recorder duets.

Two men rode away from the oddly shaped castle together into the night, back across the sand and the dead beaten grass. It was late, and no stars showed in the gray sky, but neither of them felt like making camp for the night. It was too chilly, and too dusty, and they hadn't packed for a night in the open. They would push on till dawn.

From a distance we might be anyone, Bedivere thought. Tramps, tradesmen, brothers, lovers. Knight and king, the endgame of a chess match.

For a long time they didn't speak. The mead hangover was coming on.

"'Of the Maimed King,'" Bedivere said finally.

Arthur nodded. Another long while passed before he spoke.

"I would've preferred a nice clean fight," he said. "Or resisting the temptations of a beautiful enchantress. Or succumbing to them, either one really. This is the first adventure I ever had where I don't know if I've succeeded or failed."

"You fulfilled the terms of the paradox. You both accomplished the quest and you didn't. You clove the Gordian knot, like Alexander the Great."

"You know he was only thirty-two when he died? That would give me five years." Absently the king gave his horse's withers a scratch. "Do you think it was right, what God did? Punishing a man like that, and his family, and his whole country, just for attempting a task that was too hard for him."

"Whatever God does is right, by definition. Ipso facto."

It was a glib remark, and its glibness annoyed Arthur. Bedivere didn't even know if he meant it or not. He lied so much, with every waking moment, that sometimes even he wasn't sure when he was telling the truth.

"If I hadn't lain with Morgause I could have saved that man. I would've been good enough then."

"You don't know that."

"Those children were prisoners. If they were my children, I would've killed myself to free them. And did you see—did you see how much they loved him?"

Even now, when Arthur saw a family like that, where the parents and children obviously loved one another, he was still amazed. It was a sight as strange to him as the Burning Brothers.

They were heading home, back to Camelot, which always put Bedivere in a bad mood. At Camelot Arthur was always on display, always watched. He couldn't chat with Bedivere the way he did when they were alone together. They couldn't be close like they were now, everything was stiff and formal and distant. At Camelot Guinevere was Arthur's lady love, and Lancelot his champion, and Bedivere was furniture. He was like everybody else who wanted a scrap of Arthur's attention.

He wondered whether Arthur hid his affection for Bedivere at Camelot behind a false indifference, or whether it was their closeness now that was false. Was this the illusion, and Camelot the reality, or the other way round? Bedivere let his thoughts wander back the way they came, to poor old King Bran. If God truly wouldn't let him die, then even a blow from Excalibur might not have killed him. He might be living on as a severed head. Like— who was it? Odysseus? Orpheus?

Orpheus. Torn to pieces by the Maenads, because he would take only men to his bed.

His head carried by wind and wave, still singing, to the isle of Lesbos.

They entered the dead forest of white trunks.

"He warned me God would punish me if I did what he asked." Arthur said it so quietly that Bedivere almost didn't catch it. "King Bran did. He told me that one day I would be as he was, trapped between life and death. But I did it anyway.

"What does it mean, Bedivere? I wanted to be good, and I wanted to serve God, and I found I could not do both. How can that be? When a king quarrels with God, nothing good can come of it."

He might have said more, but just then an extraordinary thing happened. A faint soft creaking sound came from all around them. Tiny green buds were appearing on the bare flayed branches of the trees. Living bark spread over the bleached, tortured wood. The air filled with the smell of sweet sap forcing itself through dry veins, filling parched channels.

The curse was lifting. Frozen branches flexed stiffly, and they heard the tiny, tender noises of flowers opening and grass pushing up through dead soil in the moonlight. The Waste Land was coming back to life.

"Look at that," the king said in wonder and confusion. Stars were coming out overhead, in the black dome of the sky. "It worked. The king is whole, and the land is whole. God is terrible, and God is merciful. Bedivere, how could I ever forget that God is merciful?"

Seeing the king's face in the starlight, so glad and so troubled at the same time, Bedivere fell in love with him all over again. According to the priests, sex between men was a sin because it was not in the interest of reproduction, because it wasted the man's seed. But what about the waste of love? Was that not a sin too?

As the desert bloomed around them Bedivere's love for Arthur hurled itself against the walls of his heart, battered at them, trying to get out, again and again, until finally it fell back exhausted and bloody. It would die inside him, alone and starving. He would never bloom. Bedivere looked down at the steel cap where his left hand would have been.

"I've never been whole," he said. "I wonder what it's like."

Arthur nodded.

"So do I."

Nine

THE GREEN KNIGHT

I don't believe it," Dinadan breathed.

"It's been a long time." Bedivere's face didn't change, but his voice was hoarse with emotion.

"My word," said Constantine. "That is as great a marvel as ever I saw. Even in the old days."

Villiars said nothing, just stuffed a bread roll into his mouth in unselfconscious awe.

It was as if the wall, though it appeared solid, had been a painted curtain that was now thrown back to reveal behind it an eldritch forest, dark and still. Sunlight lanced in through the windows of the great hall of Camelot, but in the forest it was night and the moon was up, and the two lights, sun and moon, met and mingled together in an impossible pool on the floor.

Nimue screwed a ring off her finger and squinted at the forest through it, as through a peephole, studying the apparition with a professional eye.

Summer and winter met, too: snow was mixed in with the dead leaves on the forest floor. A few trees had boldly poked the tips of their branches out of the forest and into the hall, like a painting escaping from its frame. The corners were getting a bit mossy, and a couple of ferns had pushed up between the flagstones in front of it.

"Look, Vil," Palomides said, with a trace of a smile. "Maybe he was a magic boy after all."

No one was more surprised than the boy himself. Collum had already abandoned any hope whatsoever that his idea would work, but look: they'd called for a marvel and it had come. They'd pounded this dead world on the back till it coughed one up. Arthur was gone, and the world was a dry husk, but deep underground a taproot of life still persisted. Something had survived.

Cold, woody air rolled through the room in a wave. The apparition gave Collum a vertiginous feeling—it was deep where it should've been flat, like looking at a mirror or a painting and suddenly realizing it was an open window. Something was stirring in the depths of the winter forest, a dark figure on horseback winding its way toward them between the trees, passing in and out of the moonlight.

The horse moved stiffly, awkwardly, not like a living creature moved. Maybe he should've kept his mouth shut after all. We called, but who answered? What if the world was dead, and here was its terrible ghost come to haunt them? Only when it finally stepped out into the hall did they see it clearly. The horse's body was formed of tree limbs and roots and bracken and woody vines roughly twisted into the shape of a horse, with a few rocks and dirt clumps caught in them as if they'd just been ripped out of the ground. It had two staring flint cores for eyes. Its hooves were flint, too, and struck sparks from the flagstones.

On it rode a knight. His armor was in a style long out of

fashion—not even true plate, just a coat of mail with steel plates riveted on at the vulnerable spots, covered in places with moss and lichen as if it had been left out in the forest for years before being picked up and pressed back into service again.

It was hard to tell who or what was inside. A couple of thorny green twigs poked out at the joints, and a spray of them stuck out through the eye-slit in the helm.

"The hell is that?" Villiars said softly.

"Well, it's not a sword," Dinadan said. "Nor is it, unless I'm very much mistaken, a stone."

"Did God send it?" Palomides said.

"Does that look like an angel to you?."

"It's a Green Knight," Bedivere said.

"Nonsense," Constantine said. "The Green Knight w-wasn't twiggy l-like that. He was just a normal-looking person with green skin."

"Well, this one's twiggy."

"Where God does not tend His garden," Palomides said, "weeds will grow."

The Green Knight, if that's what he was, swung his leg over his tree-horse and dropped lightly to the stone floor. His ancient armor squeaked and rattled. He placed his gauntleted hands boldly on his hips, one resting on the pommel of his sword. Unlike everybody else in the room he seemed perfectly at ease.

"Who speaks for this company?"

His voice was disconcertingly high, like a harsh birdcall.

"I do," Bedivere said.

"Speak then. Why have you summoned me?"

"We sought a marvel, as in days of old."

"You have found one. But not as of old."

"Well, you are welcome here in our hall. Please. Sit and join our feast."

"One such as I does not eat," the Green Knight said. "But I have a secret, and if anyone among you can defeat me, I will tell it."

Oho. So that was the game.

Collum was raising his hand to volunteer but he never even got near it because every single knight in the room was already on his feet. They crowded around Bedivere loudly explaining why this adventure belonged rightfully to them and no other.

Sir Villiars emerged the victor, though on what grounds Collum couldn't tell. Maybe Bedivere wanted to make up after their spat. He exited the scrum looking fiercely triumphant and dispatched a couple of servants for his sword and the rest of his armor, then he threw a foot up onto the table and bent over till he touched his nose to his knee. Dinadan patted him on the rump and said something in a low tone, and they both laughed.

Having said his piece, the Green Knight waited, unmoving, impassive, and aloof. Servants swept away the herbs on the floor in a wide circle. More candles were lit, and the knights dragged their chairs around for a better view. Now that the surprise was sprung they didn't seem at all disconcerted by this magical incursion, but why would they be? They did this sort of thing all the time.

Sir Villiars inspected his sword, a big two-hander. He placed the blade across his knee and carefully flexed it. Having seen him in a fistfight, Collum was looking forward to watching what Villiars could do with it, especially since he wouldn't personally be on the other end this time. Villiars stepped out into the middle of the hall and executed a fancy flourish, tossing the blade up in a flat spin over his head and then catching it behind his back.

Then he kissed it where the hilt made a cross and donned his helmet, which was made like the head of a bear, and with his broad shoulders Villiars did look like a bear cast in steel. He held his sword out lightly in front of him, angled up in the starting guard that Aucassin called the Plow. The easiest and most common guard, but for good reason—you could start any number of cuts and parries from the Plow. The other knights clapped and yelled his name, though the noise got a little lost in the big hall. It must've sounded empty if you were used to the full roar of the Table.

"Hah!" Villiars feinted once, twice.

The Green Knight—who also led with the Plow—stood motionless, with the stillness of a boulder half buried in the ground. Collum leaned forward. Suddenly he was glad he hadn't won the bidding for this particular adventure.

"Hah!" Villiars barked again, but faced with that ancient silence the shouting and posturing looked a little silly.

At exactly the same moment, as if they'd rehearsed it, both knights began circling widdershins. Villiars shifted stances, snapping the sword up by his ear (the Ox), then high over his right shoulder (the Roof), and then back down into the Plow again, his movements quick but unhurried. Aucassin used to talk about this, the measuring phase of the fight, the mutual sizing-up. It could go on absurdly long, ten minutes or more, before the first stroke was struck.

But apparently Villiars was satisfied that he'd taken his opponent's measure because with no warning he stepped in behind a hard cut that knocked the Green Knight's sword off-center. There was a blur of movement and a racket of blades colliding, and for a heartbeat the two knights were locked together, grappling hard, then they broke apart again and a cloud of rust-dust flew as Villiars got in a hard clout to the knight's collarbone going away. A sword couldn't cut through plate, but it could traumatize the delicate flesh underneath, and a shot like that would've bruised him to the bone, assuming he had any.

Quick as a shark Villiars pivoted and went right back in, so fast Collum could barely follow, chaining attacks together in fluid sequence: hard upward left-to-right, then high right-to-left, ducking and spinning under the counterstrike into a low cut, a punch, a stamp to the ankle, the big blade always light in his hands. The Green Knight lumbered and doddered a beat behind, always seeming to be parrying and dodging the blow that had just happened instead of the one that was coming at him next.

"Come on!" Villiars shouted. "Fight like a shrub!"

The crowd chuckled. Villiars finished his next pass by stepping past the Green Knight, pivoting and booting him in his armored rump. The knights roared but it died a moment later when the Green Knight kicked back with unexpected speed and swept Villiars's leg, and he crashed down on his broad back.

He bounced up again and strode back in, striking hard, textbook moves but combined in unexpected ways, pushing the Green Knight back so far that people had to scramble up and drag their chairs out of the way. What could be going through the Green Knight's mind, inside that ancient corroded helmet? What green thoughts were twining through his green brain? Collum's own brain could only think: I am at Camelot, watching Sir Villiars battle a Green Knight.

His mind was already racing ahead to the divulging of the secret, the first crumb in the trail that would lead, somehow, to the crowning of a new king, the heir to Arthur, the next link in the golden chain—when a sudden change in the rhythm of the fight snapped him back to the present. Villiars chopped at the Green Knight overhand, but before the blow could land the knight parried, and for a frozen moment their blades were crossed in a bind, strength to strength. Then the Green Knight wound his blade past Villiars's, seeking a crack in his plate, and Villiars jerked his sword up, forcing the Green Knight's thrust off course.

The move left Villiars's legs exposed, and the Green Knight didn't miss his chance. Doubling his speed—he must've been shamming till now—he struck low and hard at the side of Villiars's knee. It bent sideways and Villiars staggered a little, but the Green Knight was already spinning and cutting hard at Villiars's upper arm, this time with shocking force. The sound was so loud even some of the watching knights startled, like someone had dropped a metal cook pot from a high rooftop. Underneath it you could hear the meaty snap of a thick bone.

"Ah!" Villiars barked.

Collum's stomach seized. Villiars swayed, looking like he was trying not to black out. The Green Knight tagged the knee again, savagely, two-handed, and Villiars toppled onto all fours, sagging on the side with the wounded arm like a broken cart. The Green Knight hammered down hard on the top of Villiars's head and he collapsed forward onto the ground stunned, his rear end in the air. It had all gone horribly wrong horribly fast. Half-swording—guiding the blade with his free hand—the Green Knight stabbed straight down, under the edge of Villiars's helmet, right through his mail coif and down through his neck at the nape.

Everyone was on their feet shouting at the top of their lungs. Villiars spasmed as masses of blood pulsed out from under him. Setting his foot on Villiars's shoulder like it was a log he'd just split, the Green Knight jerked the blade out, stepped back, and resumed parade rest, exactly as if nothing had happened.

Constantine froze with his long arms reached out for Villiars as if there were some way he could bring him back. Dinadan came sleepwalking, half tripping on a chair leg, and knelt beside Villiars's body. A dark pool spread out from under it and then stopped spreading. Bedivere and Palomides and even Collum were on their feet shouting outrage and abuse at the Green Knight.

A few people crossed themselves. A servant ran out of the room at a sprint. Tenderly Dinadan started to work Villiars's helm off, but then stopped because the neck wound was too terrible. He gave up and just knelt by the body, whispering something, tears streaming down his face. They all lifted Villiars together, Dinadan carefully supporting his flopping head, and laid him out on the Table: Villiars the Valiant, who had fought the Eleven Kings and beat Collum hollow not more than two hours ago, only to die on the floor of his own hall at the hands of some itinerant wood spirit for the sake of a secret he would never hear.

Sir Palomides caught Collum's eye and held it for a heartbeat, and a pang of shame shot through Collum so hot it scalded his insides. *This was my fault. It was my idea. It happened because of my arrogance. What did I expect? That a little brachet would come and lead them on a merry chase? The world has gone dark, and I, a common thief, an impostor, invited the darkness inside.*

The shame was more than he could stand. *God is a great optimist.* Before he knew what he was doing he was on one knee in front of Bedivere.

"My lord, I beg of you the favor of this trial!"

Bedivere didn't even look at him.

"Be silent, child."

"Sir Bedivere—"

"Can you not once in your life be silent?!" he shouted. But Collum couldn't be silent.

127

"I brought this challenge upon us! It is only right that I face it!"

"Get him out of here," Bedivere muttered to nobody in particular. Nobody moved.

"For pity's sake, haven't you caused enough trouble?" Nimue glared at him. "Did you not see what just happened? You do realize I was joking before, about putting you on the Table!"

He did realize. He'd lied his way into Camelot and opened the way for the Green Knight to enter, and now Villiars the Valiant was dead, so he would be the one to banish this monster or die trying. He was ready to beg. He needed it as badly as air.

"At the risk of being pedantic," Palomides said, "Villiars beat you, the Green Knight beat him—you see? The logic is self-evident."

"It doesn't matter!" Collum flushed. He stood up and walked up to the Green Knight. "I challenge you. I will fight you for your secret."

He said it fast, before anyone could interrupt him, before he could lose his nerve. The Green Knight inclined his head slightly.

"I accept."

Nimue turned away, shaking her head at his folly.

"Well, God protect you." Bedivere rubbed his forehead with his stump. Collum noticed for the first time that his hair was thin on top.

"Thank you, my lord."

Just like that it was settled. Servants were already going over the flagstones with a mop and rags, painting them with Villiars's blood in circles that grew wider and wider and paler and paler pink. No one spoke to Collum. Why should they? Why would they admire the vainglorious posturing of a young churl doomed by his own arrogance? This would be over quickly enough.

But Dinadan at least caught his eye.

"You want—?" He knocked his knuckles on his armored chest. Collum shook his head.

"I won't countenance suicide," Bedivere growled. "Put on some plate."

"I know what I'm doing!"

Bedivere shrugged and turned back to Sir Villiars.

It was a calculated risk. Without full armor Collum's defense would have to be perfect. A single solid hit could cripple or kill him. But against that he'd be faster and nimbler than the Green Knight, and he could see better. The Green Knight would tire first, if Green Knights got tired. And plate hadn't saved Sir Villiars.

Collum did accept a mail shirt, a pair of heavy leather gloves, and a steel cap. In what seemed like an eyeblink his sword was brought up from the gatehouse and then he was setting up facing the Green Knight with only twenty feet of swept stone floor between them. He fisted and unfisted his hands.

Now I've fucking done it, he thought. Collum bounced a few times on the balls of his feet. The cool weight of the mail on his shoulders anchored him reassuringly to the ground. He was terrified and unprotected, but at least, at least he felt some relief from the shame that was burning his insides like lye. He closed his eyes, took a breath, willed himself to sink into the familiarity of single combat.

It wouldn't come. It was like he'd never done this before in his life. He'd forgotten everything he ever knew. He opened his eyes and saluted the Green Knight with his sword. At least he hadn't had to borrow that.

Though he wasn't its first owner. His stepfather got it used from a dealer in Dunadd when Collum was fourteen, by which time it had probably already spent thirty or forty years hanging from the hip of some other knight, probably several others. But his stepfather had chosen well, more by luck than by design. It was a solid piece of work: the hilt didn't rattle or move when you twisted it, and the blade had a raised ridge running down it for added stiffness. When you knocked it with your knuckles it made a pleasing chime. The whole business balanced neatly on your finger at a point four inches up from the guard.

When the proud swordsmith had delivered it to its first owner, whoever that was, it would have been polished to a mirror shine, but time had turned it a hard-serving matte gray, and the edge had a dozen tiny notches in it and two deep ones, the record of heavy blows badly parried. It was plain except for one decoration: while the blade was still hot the smith had etched a circular groove into it, and inside that circle a tiny *S*-shaped groove, and when the metal cooled he'd hammered brass wire into the grooves to make a pretty inlay.

What the *S* stood for was anybody's guess. *Sharp. Swift. Sic transit gloria mundi. Salvate me.* More likely the maker's name, or the buyer's.

He opened in the Ox: sword head-high, guard next to his ear, blade parallel to the ground, point aimed at his opponent's throat. With all the excitement in him the weapon felt like a toy in his hands. It was coming back to him now. Marshal Aucassin spoke reassuringly in his mind: *Watch the body, not the blade. Interrupt the enemy's strikes before they gain power. Turn parries into counterattacks. Meet edge with flat, strong with weak, weak with strong.*

The Green Knight began circling as before. Collum followed suit, pacing out the circumference of the little world they now shared. His feet felt numb. For the second time in his life he was fighting for his life and the fear was sharp and feral, like an animal's stink. As they paced they moved closer and then farther apart, as if they were testing an invisible band that stretched between them.

Suddenly the Green Knight feinted high then cut at Collum's forward knee, and he jerked it back out of harm's way, farther than he needed to, and at the same time cut high (his opponent's blade being at that moment low). The Green Knight leaned back out of the way. It had begun.

He was wound so tight that he swung twice as hard as he needed to, but if the Green Knight noticed he didn't capitalize. *A paradox,* said Marshal Aucassin: *To win you must attack, but in attacking you make yourself vulnerable, so you must defend. Discuss.* They both feinted and then cut for real and the two blades clashed and caught in a bind.

When Aucassin talked about the bind it was with an almost sexual fervor. It was the moment in the fight when you felt your enemy most directly—you shoved at him and he shoved right back, forming an electric connection through which you were supposed to be able to sense his true character. As far as Collum could tell, the Green Knight had the character of cold stone. He tried to shove his blade to the side and at the same moment the knight gave way and Collum almost fell down, but he staggered clear and got set again.

He feinted, feinted again, but the knight didn't bite. He hadn't fallen for Villiars's feints either. How was he going to beat the Green Knight when a knight of the Table couldn't? *The logic is self-evident.* Maybe God would take an interest. Collum would prove his righteousness on his body.

They clashed and withdrew, clashed and withdrew. In a fight you were constantly trying to interrupt and confuse the other party, which made the rhythms broken and unmusical. He had to grip his blade hard to keep his hands from shaking. Collum threw a hard overhand cut that banged off the knight's shoulder, striking sparks and scaling rust off the old metal, spun away from the counter and punched the Green Knight hard with his pommel in his steel-bucket face. They closed and grappled, and Collum smelled old moss and rotten iron. He tried to throw him but the Green Knight was too strong. His grip was starting to crush him. The knight let go but stomped on his foot, trapping him, and delivered a cannon of a clout with the flat of his sword to the side of Collum's head.

His steel cap flew off. For a heartbeat it felt like his brain was knocked about five feet outside his body and he was controlling his limbs numbly from a distance like a marionette. Collum stumbled over Constantine's long legs and almost sprawled right into his lap. He drew the business out as long as he could, playing for time while he tried to get his bearings back. He kept waiting for the fear to lift but it got worse. This was the end. He was going to die now, bleed out his life on these famous stones. No one would even be surprised; it was an old story, youthful pride brought low. They would lay him out like they had Villiars, though with fewer tears.

With a crazy shout he ducked a high strike and threw himself bodily on the knight again, chest to chest, getting a faceful of those thorny twigs, groping frantically for a joint lock. Did he even have joints? The Green Knight got a hand on his face and pried him off and chopped at Collum as he staggered away, bruising a rib through the mail. It was like a nightmare. He was locked in a cabinet again at Dubh Hall, he was drowning with his head in a bucket—

But that brought something else back. Did they fight like dirty cowards in the forest? Let's see if he knew this one. The knight chopped again and Collum caught his blade in a bind, then with a gloved hand he grabbed both swords together where they crossed. He pushed down and around—the leverage was all his—twisting till the knight's wrists crossed awkwardly, then he *yanked*—

He scrambled back holding both swords together in one hand. It was a silly trick, a schoolyard prank, but it worked. The Green Knight was disarmed.

Collum raised both swords over his head, declaring victory, though his arms were almost too tired to lift them, then dropped them with an almighty clatter. Technically the duel wasn't over, the Green Knight could keep on fighting bare-handed if he wanted, but Collum desperately hoped he wouldn't. The Green Knight regarded him, silent and expressionless, as if such childish antics as these were incomprehensible to his vegetable mind. But then he bowed very slightly.

It wasn't a glorious victory. No one was going to write a poem about it. But he was still alive. They didn't shout his name to the rafters, but a couple of hands touched his shoulders as he took his seat again, breathing hard, his body starting to shake in earnest with the floods of useless energy still in it. Bedivere leaned over.

"All right," he said. "Well done, boy."

Collum didn't look at anybody, just stared straight ahead panting. Villiars died like a knight, and Collum had won like a cheating schoolboy, but it was over and he was still alive, and now the Green Knight would have to give up his secret.

Something touched his knee and he startled out of his chair, wildly going for his sword, but it was just Dinadan trying to hand him a cloth for his nose, which was bleeding.

Bedivere addressed the Green Knight.

"Go on. Let's hear it."

The Green Knight reached up with two hands and removed his helmet. Collum braced himself for whatever new horror was about to be revealed, but instead a fan-shaped spray of leafy branches sprang out. The knight had no head at all, he was just foliage.

Something small and furry scuffled out from the armor's neck hole and peered at them through the greenery. Then it scampered out and perched on the knight's corroded metal shoulder, sniffing the air. It had round white-tipped ears and a sinuous little body.

"What the hell is that?" Dinadan said. "A ferret?"

"Stoat," Constantine said.

"Weasel," said Palomides.

"That is a polecat," Bedivere said with an air of authority.

Whatever it was, it raised its head and spoke in the voice of the Green Knight.

"Would you know my secret now, for which you have paid so dearly?"

Bedivere said nothing, just folded his arms and waited.

"One more of your number still lives."

"You mean a knight of the Table?" Dinadan said. "Who is it?"

"I can lead you to him."

The knights all sat there, unsmiling, turning it over in their minds. Collum turned it over too. They'd wanted a new king, and they'd called out to the world, and the world had given them an answer. It wasn't the one they were looking for, but this was a different world now. The language it spoke in was strange and harsh, its meaning obscure. They were strangers in this world, the world after Arthur.

But it wasn't nothing. It wasn't silence.

"All right," Bedivere said. "Show us. We leave at dawn."

Ten

A New Sword

No one formally invited Collum to join them at the Round Table, but when lunch was finally served Bedivere indicated that an extra place should be laid there for him. He sat, occupying a chair that had belonged to one Sir Patrise, presumably now deceased.

Collum's hands were still trembling. His ear hurt, his head hurt, his ribs ached, and his thigh was on fire. His nose still pulsed and throbbed from when Villiars smashed it. He wondered if it was broken again.

They were bunched around one short arc of the table, with the long empty curves of the rest of it stretching off into the deepening shadows. They made a pitifully small crew: Collum, the four surviving knights of the Table, and Nimue. It felt like the hall, the castle, the whole world should have shrunk to fit its newly diminished population, but it stubbornly stayed as vast and cavernous as it had ever been. Though at some point, when nobody was paying attention, the back wall had turned from a forest back into a solid wall again.

A silent hollow-eyed jester wandered in, collected some knives off the table, and began juggling them. He wasn't much of a showman—he never smiled or even acknowledged the worthies he was performing for—but he was incredibly skillful. He threw the knives all the way up to the rafters, watched them fall, spinning slowly, then scooped them up again by their heavy handles just before they hit the floor. He started with three knives and then added a fourth. Collum was fascinated, but the only other person who watched was Constantine.

The wine went round, and this time Constantine didn't turn up his nose at it. There was a strange mood in the room, a kind of bleary, teary mixture of grief and resignation and also a touch of relief. The great Sir Villiars had joined the many, many dead, but in the same moment a way forward had appeared, an adventure, however dark and tenuous.

"It used to be simple." Constantine had changed into a flowing green tunic stitched with a royal garden's worth of golden flowers. "Look at how Uther became king. His father, Constantine the Third, no r-relation, was descended from the last Dux Britanniarum in Eboracum. When he was murdered by a Pict, his oldest son, Constans, naturally took the throne. Then Constans was murdered by his c-counselor Vortigern, so the next brother—he had the wonderfully Roman name Ambrosius—took over from him and burned down Vortigern's fortress.

"Vortigern's son poisoned Ambrosius. Uther, as the third son, killed Vortigern's son in a battle, and that was that. Uther was king."

"Those were the days," Dinadan said.

"A king has the blood of kings," Constantine said. "A king is chosen by God. How do we make a king now, without blood or God?"

"But didn't Arthur name a successor?" Collum said. "He must've known it would be a problem."

"Arthur thought of everything," Bedivere said, "but he didn't always tell us what he thought."

"The Grail Quest was rather supposed to take care of this," Constantine said. "But it d-didn't work out that way. And then we thought God would give us a sign."

"But what happened on the quest?" Collum said. "You won, didn't you?"

"A Pyrrhic victory," Constantine said. "That was when God left."

"I don't understand."

"Well, have you seen Him around lately?" Dinadan said.

"But why? What happened?"

"Ask Sir Galahad."

"I thought he was dead."

"Exactly."

"Haven't we paid enough?" Constantine said. "What more does God w-want?"

"He always wants more," Palomides said. "He's insatiable."

The talk moved on to how best to ready Camelot's defenses against an attack by King Rience. They speculated as to which of the major local landowners were still loyal, and which of them had outstanding debts to the Crown and could be squeezed for men and money. They argued over how far the standards of age and fitness for military service could be relaxed in order to drum up some semblance of a fighting force. Stores needed to be inventoried in case of a siege. Clerks were summoned and lists made. There was no more talk of going home.

Eventually, as dim watery patches of light from the thick glass windows slid slowly across the floor, lunch blended seamlessly into dinner. The sun set, leaving behind the long afterglow of an early summer evening. Some of the dishes were gold; others were lustrous red Roman ceramics of a kind he'd only ever seen in Dubh Hall's cabinet of wonders, and those had been cracked and held together by wire.

"You're really sure Arthur didn't have a secret heir hidden away?" With a little wine in him Collum was starting to feel almost at ease. "The way Uther hid him?"

"Impossible." Nimue was the youngest person in the room besides Collum and the next closest thing to an outsider here, but she didn't seem eager to make common cause.

"I would've known," Bedivere said.

"But hasn't Merlin said anything?"

The room went quiet.

"Now you've done it. You said the magic word." Dinadan's voice had an edge. "What about it, Nimue? What about Merlin?"

"You may not be aware that Nimue was Merlin's apprentice, until she killed him." Bedivere gestured for more wine.

"How did you think she got her job?" Dinadan said.

"'No mere woman can kill the great wizard Merlin,'" Nimue said, not visibly cowed. "Or such is the prophecy. But since you bring it up, Master Collum, I put Merlin under a hill, which is where he belongs."

She didn't bother to look at him when she spoke. Evidently she still considered him beyond the pale. He caught himself looking at her though. She was striking, her large bright eyes full of cool confidence, like a sea captain scanning the horizon for prizes. From time to time she unconsciously touched the pinned-up coils of her braids, as if she were puzzled about how they came to be there.

"Is there something you want to tell us about Merlin, Nimue?" Palomides asked.

"Not really, no."

"If Merlin were free," Dinadan said, "I bet Arthur would still be alive."

"If Merlin were such a fucking great wizard then he wouldn't be stuck under a hill, would he?"

Collum sipped his wine and decided he wasn't going to ask any more questions for a while. He was belatedly trying to bring his manners up to Camelot standards; the others wiped their lips with a napkin every time they drank, and they never seemed to have to scratch or burp. Back at Dubh Hall he was more accustomed to eating alone, if at all; he used to hide food around the house in case the kitchen turned him away.

"Maybe God doesn't want to talk about it," Palomides said, "but we should discuss who will be king."

"The quest will show us," Bedivere said curtly.

"We should discuss Mordred's son."

"Oh for Heaven's sake," Constantine said. "No one wants Sir Melehan on the throne!"

"I suspect Sir Melehan does," Palomides said. "And half the realm rose for his father. And being of Arthur's blood, however polluted by bastardy and incest, he has a claim, and therefore we will have to deal with him."

"He can't be more than ten years old."

"Even Rience would be better," Bedivere said.

"Does anybody support King Rience?" Collum asked, breaking his resolution almost immediately. "I mean, besides the Franks?"

"Rience is smart." Bedivere refilled his cup. "Arthur could do many things, but he couldn't lie, and Rience will say anything to anyone. He tells the Christians he'll throw out the fat decadent sinners of Camelot, and the pagans that he'll throw out the fat scoldy Christians."

"He's consistent on that one point anyway," Constantine said. "Quite h-hurtful really."

"He has men putting up broadsheets proving conclusively that he is descended from King David," Palomides said.

"We could write to the pope." Constantine stretched; with his long limbs he could never seem to get comfortable. "He always seems to h-have an opinion."

"What about you, Constantine?" Nimue said.

"What about me?"

"Maybe you should be king."

"Thank you, no." He gave a thin smile.

"You have royal blood," Nimue said. "Good royal name. You have as much a claim as anyone."

"You don't want to be High King of Britain?" Dinadan asked.

"I prefer my ambitions thwarted, thank you." Dropping even the thin smile, Constantine crossed one long leg over the other and changed the subject. "Could Sir Bors still be alive?"

"If we are talking about Bors," Palomides said, "we should talk about his cousin. We should talk about Lancelot."

Bedivere looked up sharply. Heavy royal cutlery clinked in the silence. Another magic word.

"Lancelot is Frankish." Nimue pulled thoughtfully at the end of her sharp nose. "But he's royalty."

"He made me duke of Provence during the siege," Palomides said. "I must go there one day."

"Lancelot is the last of the great ones," Constantine said gravely. "He's not like us, he's a hero."

"Lancelot is scum," Bedivere said. "Worse than scum."

"You can't betray the crown and then wear the crown," Dinadan said. "And anyway, no one knows where he is."

"He'd do well to stay there," Bedivere said.

Collum kept his own face carefully blank, but in that moment he felt absolutely certain that the path they were on would lead to Lancelot. Maybe he'd made mistakes, maybe he had things to atone for, but Collum knew that he would fight and die for a King Lancelot.

He also realized, later than he should have, that it was time for him to go. Time for bed—he wasn't making that mistake again. If the knights were going to argue about the future of Britain, they weren't going to want to do it in front of him. Better disappear quietly before they kicked him out. He rose and excused himself with as much gravitas as he could muster.

As he walked the length of the hall, exhausted and half drunk, he wondered if Camelot's hospitality was going to extend to a room for the night. He felt queasy with all that rich food in him. He would've happily slept right here on the floor of the hall—it was what he was used to—but as the alleged son of a nobleman he should probably pretend to have higher standards.

He paused in the darkness at the far end. He could still hear Dinadan's high clear voice.

"We should go back to the lake. The Lady could give someone the sword."

"I can never keep them straight," Constantine said, "between Excalibur and the s-sword from the stone."

"The sword from the lake was Excalibur," Nimue said patiently. "The sword from the stone broke. I suppose if we still had the pieces somewhere we could reforge it. Like a symbol."

"I am tired of symbols." Suddenly Palomides did sound very

tired. Weary unto death. "I am tired of putting my faith in things that break. I have had enough of it."

"So have we all."

Bedivere pushed back his chair and stood, much as he had just that morning, a thousand years ago, though he was less steady on his feet now. He'd consumed a truly heroic quantity of wine.

"Gentlemen. And lady." His voice, usually so flat and hollow, was resolute and full of emotion. And only a little slurred. "I put it to you that we are bound now. Even more than before. We are not Camelot's best, not nearly, we are not heroes"—his voice broke a little here—"but we are all Arthur has left, and together we shall see his kingdom whole again or die trying.

"Swear it with me. Swear it. We shall have a new sword, and a new stone."

Palomides was the first one to his feet.

"A new sword, and a new stone."

He raised a cup, and then the others raised theirs, all of them.

"A new sword. A new stone."

Collum swore it, too, in a whisper. He knew in his heart that having sworn, these people would never yield. Heroes or not, they would not let the great age pass away if they could help it. They would drag the sun back across the sky if that's what it took. And he would help, if they would let him.

Then he did slip out, into the nighttime stillness of the court-yard. The light and heat of the hall drifted off and away into the cool air. The laundry tubs had been emptied, and the geese were gone somewhere for the night. The smith had gathered up his tools and dragged his anvil in under the eaves. The gulf between the world now and the world he'd left behind that morning was so vast it gave him a moment of vertigo. It had still been the Age of

Arthur then, or he'd thought it was. Whose age was it now? It would be two hours' ride back to the inn in the dark, if he didn't get lost, but let it be known, he thought, even in the age of No One, that Collum of the Out Isles has supped in the Great Hall of Camelot. He fought a duel and won. It was easily the worst and the greatest day of his life.

"Not quite what you were hoping for. Was it."

Squinting into the darkness, Collum made out a small, skinny man with prominent eyes sitting on a wooden bench. It was the fool, the one who'd been juggling knives earlier.

"What wasn't?"

"What do you think? Camelot. The Table Round."

He whispered something else and shuddered in a way that made Collum wonder whether he was entirely sane.

"Well, I'd hoped the king would still be alive. My name's Collum. Of the Out Isles."

"Dagonet."

Ah. Now it made sense. Improbably enough, this man wasn't a jester at all, he was another surviving member of the Round Table, though the others hadn't considered him worth mentioning. Sir Dagonet had been King Arthur's fool until one day the king knighted him, even though he'd never held a sword in his life. In the stories, Sir Dagonet was the butt of every joke. Collum had imagined him a lot jollier.

"What they won't tell you," Sir Dagonet said, "is that we lost this game a long time ago."

"What do you mean?"

"Take it from an old carny, God conned us good. He took our money and took the prize, too. Oldest game there is."

Sir Dagonet still had one of the knives from the Great Hall and now he threw it spinning straight up into the darkness. Collum shied away but the Fool Knight picked it out of the air effortlessly.

"I'll think on your words, Sir Dagonet." Though he wasn't sure that he would. "Good night to you."

He made for the archway that led to the outer bailey.

"They won't tell you this either," Dagonet called after him, "but the Table needs you as much as you need them. Never let them pretend otherwise."

"Sir Collum?"

A servant had appeared out of the darkness, a chinless man, tiny and stooped. Collum wasn't a knight, and therefore not a sir, but he didn't correct him.

"If you would—?"

The little man gestured for him to follow. Collum expected to be shown to the gate, but instead the servant led him through a narrow doorway and up steep spiral stairs to a neatly kept solar with a low fire in the fireplace and a colossal barge-like four-poster bed.

"We'll bring your things up."

Collum did his best to keep his composure as he thanked the man and dismissed him the way he himself was used to being dismissed at Dubh Hall. As soon as he was alone he collapsed face down on the crisp bedcover, still in his clothes. All the strength flowed out of him. He had his own room and his own bed. Not a mattress on a cold crowded floor, not a haystack or a shared bed at an inn, his own bed in his room.

He felt the rich fabric of the coverlet under him. It was red and scratchy and stiff with embroidery. He could hardly believe they were leaving him alone with it. And he had his own candle. Beeswax, not smoky, runny tallow.

All his injuries throbbed together in time with his heartbeat. Tired as he was, Collum didn't know if he could fall asleep in a room with no one else in it. He wasn't even sure he wanted to. He might never be back here again. He didn't want to miss anything.

But he was out the moment he closed his eyes.

A PLUMP VALET WOKE him at dawn and led him to a wooden bath with a silk canopy over it that soon filled up with warm steam. He rinsed Collum in rose water, which stung his cuts and scrapes deliciously, then helped him into his armor, expertly buckling and tying and hooking and catching. Some sharp-eyed soul had replaced the fastening pin he'd lost in his duel in the meadow. Collum felt guilty when he caught himself enjoying it all—he was only here because Arthur and his best men were all dead—but wouldn't Arthur have wanted him to take joy in whatever he could? As if he knew what dead King Arthur would want after one night at Camelot.

A scrofulous-looking boy met him at dawn at the postern gate with his horse, who looked well groomed and fed and watered and happier than he'd ever been in his life. Sir Bedivere and Sir Dinadan were there, too, sitting stock-still on their mounts, their long shadows streaming across the wet grass.

They were in full harness except for gauntlets and helmets. Bare steel, no surcoats. Bedivere's breastplate had a sun etched in the center from which gilded rays emanated in all directions, so that his entire body was striped steel and gold. He bore a sun on his shield, too, half-eclipsed, on a silver field; the sun's face appeared distressed, as if at the pain of being partially obscured. At first glance Dinadan's armor seemed almost ostentatiously plain, but when you looked closer you saw it was subtly engraved with birds and beasts and portraits of various saints with their attributes. On his shield was a sheaf of arrows gripped in a disembodied fist.

The Green Knight was there, too, on his horse of twisted branches, looking even weirder in full morning sunlight, the polecat presumably curled up safely back inside his chest. A handful of squires and servants dressed in Camelot's azure and gold were fussing around a cartload of food and wine and bedding and bundled lances and what Collum took to be a folded-up pavilion.

"Coming?" Bedivere asked.

Collum did his best not to grin like an idiot.

"I'm coming."

"Collum, how do you feel about defending ladies?" Dinadan asked.

"Good."

"And the helpless?"

"Good."

"Loyal to your king? I mean if there was one?"

"Yes."

"Speak the truth? No treason or murder?"

"I—yes. And no. And no." In fact he might possibly have been a murderer, but it didn't seem like the moment to split hairs.

"You forgot the church," Bedivere said. "And bravery."

"Right," Dinadan said. "Are you going to serve the Lord? And be brave?"

"Yes and—"

Collum's right ear flashed with pain. It was the same ear the Green Knight had smashed the day before, and the pain was so intense he clutched at it and lost his balance and fell heavily off his horse onto the muddy grass in his freshly polished armor.

Someone had hit him. He lay there on his side, breathing and rubbing at his ear, waiting for the pain to go away. He seemed to find himself in this position a lot around the knights of Camelot. The monumentally heavy hooves of a destrier clumped past him.

"Arise, Sir Collum of the Out Isles!" Sir Palomides called back over his shoulder. "Adventure awaits!"

Eleven

THE TALE OF SIR PALOMIDES

The first time Palomides heard the word *Britain* it was in the *suq al-warraqin,* the paper-seller's market. Vast tides of words, both familiar and strange, written and spoken, ebbed and flowed and sloshed around the marketplace as if it were a great verbal ocean. But he'd never heard this one before.

"It's a Christian city," Hassan said with authority. Hassan sold copies of mathematical tracts from India that were so abstruse as to be indistinguishable from poetry. "Situated on the shore of the Western Ocean, the seventh clime, very cold and quite barbarous. Britain is ruled by seven kings, and if a stranger tries to enter it a magic idol puts them to sleep. When they wake up the Britons interrogate them as to their business there."

"And you know this how?"

Tahir passed a hand through his rich, lustrous hair. It was his shop they stood outside of, down a stubby little alley littered with fallen palm fronds and crammed with long uneven tables piled with books. Tahir trafficked in medical textbooks, mostly from

China, and he was also the handsomest man Palomides had ever seen, a fact of which he seemed completely oblivious.

"A book," Hassan said. "The writer was a prisoner of war in Constantinople."

"Constantinople is a long way from the Western Ocean. Which I think is more correctly named the Encircling Ocean." Ziyad had to squint up at them when he talked from under his wickedly hunched back. His shop dealt exclusively in lavishly inlaid pen boxes.

The three men liked to try to outdo one another in pedantry. It was a game they played.

"I've never heard of either of them," Palomides remarked. They ignored him.

"There is no such thing as the Encircling Ocean," Tahir said, "unless you mean the Green Sea, or as it's also known, the Sea of Darkness. Apparently its water appears black, but when you scoop it up with your hands, it runs clear."

"The text specifies the Western Ocean," Hassan said. "They can't all be the same one."

"How many oceans can there be?" Tahir asked.

"And seven kings sounds like quite a lot of kings for one city," Palomides said. "A highly unstable arrangement." Here in the paper-seller's quarter Palomides was a nobody, a dilettante, a slumming aristocrat from the royal precinct. Men like Ziyad and Tahir and Hassan were the princes here.

And they were right, he was a dilettante. He had no idea what any of them were talking about. But it all sounded very thrilling and romantic.

As far as the knights of the Round Table were concerned, Sir Palomides was a Saracen. In actual fact, when he arrived in Britain he'd never heard the word *Saracen* before, and it took him a while to figure out that they were using it to refer to him. But the British were so deeply convinced that "Saracen" was the correct name for people like Palomides—that is, for Muslims—that they further concluded, reasoning backward in their stolid British way, that he must come from a place called Sarras.

They had a lot of feverish fantasies about Sarras, which was supposed to be located somewhere near Egypt. In fact there was no such place. It didn't exist.

Palomides had long since given up explaining this. The British could wear you down that way. And the truth would've been harder to explain, because Palomides was from Baghdad, a city that in magnificence and sophistication far outshone even the fever dream of Sarras.

When Palomides was first ushered into the presence of the Round Table he did his best to look impressed, but while the Table was indeed large and undeniably Round, Palomides came from an entire city that was ruled out in a perfect Euclidean circle four miles in circumference. The city's founder, Caliph Abu Ja'far Abdallah ibn Muhammad al-Mansur, had paced it out himself on the empty sand and had it marked with cotton balls soaked in naphtha, so that at night they could be set alight and you could see the shape of the city-to-come burning in the cold darkness of the desert.

Ring-walled, four-gated Baghdad was a city of markets and squares, mosques and schools, baths and markets, bridges and canals, mansions and slums. Everything was built in stucco and brick, stone being a relative rarity in the fertile floodplains of the Tigris, which rubbed affectionately up against the city walls like a cat. Everybody came to Baghdad: Sunni and Shia, Arabs and

Persians, Africans and Bedouins, Greeks and Christians, Jews and Indians and Slavs, scientists and scholars and slaves and singers and shoemakers and swordsmen and silk weavers. In the precise center of the city was a second perfect circle, a much smaller one, and within it stood the Great Mosque and the homes of the caliph and his extended family, which included Palomides. Baghdad was a prince among cities, and Palomides was a prince of Baghdad.

The royal precinct was a lush enclave of fragrant wood and lavish tiles, scented with rose water and shadowed from the desert heat. The young Palomides grew up among its numberless villas and colonnades and belvederes. Its courtyards were planted with orange trees, their branches artfully interwoven and heavy with fruit and the doves and parrots that gathered there. At the very center of this circle-within-a-circle was the caliph's home, the Palace of the Golden Gate, surmounted by a great green dome, 150 feet high, that was itself topped by a golden horseman who carried a golden lance in his golden hand. The horseman had been magicked in such a way that it turned and pointed its lance in whatever direction the caliph's enemies would come from next.

Palomides used to stare up at the golden lancer, hoping to catch it at the moment when it spun to point at a new foe. Every once in a very great while, he did.

A large, well-made boy, bright and curious, Palomides was fed on lamb and fish tongues and sweet melons that arrived from far northern lands packed in snow to keep them fresh. His mind was fed by a brace of tutors versed in mathematics, music, poetry, law, economics, medicine, astronomy, and above all the Hadith and the Quran. He was an avid polo player—polo was one of the pillars of *furusiyya*, the martial art of mounted combat. He trained with a sword as well, practicing a thousand strokes a day until he could slice through twenty reams of paper with a single blow without cutting through the soft cotton cloth they rested on. Though it seemed like a waste of good paper to Palomides.

He was a prince, but he would never be a king. He was well insulated from the throne by three hearty older brothers, and as a result nobody paid him much attention. His brothers absorbed all the love and honors his parents had to bestow. Years later he would discover that in Britain it was customary for a fourth son to carry the image of a swift on his shield, because a swift was a bird that was believed to have no feet and spent its entire life on the wing, never landing, from birth to death.

Palomides knew perfectly well that swifts have feet, but he understood the symbolism. That was the rootless, landless life of a fourth son, heir to nothing, fated to wander the world in search of a place, even as places were handed free to his siblings.

Palomides enjoyed every possible luxury, but as he grew older he looked at the life of leisured irrelevance that stretched out ahead of him and found himself troubled. There was a nagging hollowness to it all, the endless round of dinners and hunting and polo, backgammon at the club and flirting in the gardens. Wasn't there something more—some way to make his mark on the world? He wanted to be a hero. But of what story?

Another ornament of Baghdad's royal precinct was its great library, the House of Wisdom. The caliph was obsessed with books, and his agents scoured the world for them, buying them at great expense, exhuming them from ancient sand-flooded tombs and temples, claiming them as spoils of war, extorting them from foreign potentates as gifts and favors. The caliph didn't let these books lie fallow, he brought in scribes to copy them, and scholars to study and translate them and debate the merits of their contents, and cooks and cleaners and servants to serve the scribes and scholars, who sometimes slept in the House of Wisdom when their labors were so all-consuming that they couldn't even leave them to go home to their families.

But Palomides didn't much care for the House of Wisdom. He found its hushed halls oppressive and its denizens insufferably pretentious. When he wanted intellectual talk he betook himself outside the great circular walls of Baghdad, to the saltier, less salubrious alleys of the suq al-warraqin. Three or four times a week Palomides balanced his way across the Tigris, over a bridge of colorful skiffs that were permanently moored together in a chain, which the current tugged into a gentle crescent, to visit them.

"The Sea of Darkness is a mystery, my friends," Ziyad was saying. "Nobody knows how big it is. Sailors hug the shore for fear of getting lost forever. Waves sweep across it big as castles. Massive sea creatures live in it, with black skin and white flesh, so big the British build houses from their bones."

"Who or what exactly *are* the British?" Palomides asked.

"That's what Hassan has been busily misinforming us about. In point of fact Britain isn't a city at all, it's an archipelago, twelve islands, all shrouded in the mist and rain that blow in from the Encircling Ocean." He held up a finger to hold off both Tahir and Hassan from correcting him. "The British are a primitive people. The seventh clime is excessively cold, and the cold corrupts their humors. Also birds grow on trees there, like fruit, and the British roast and eat them."

"That raises so many questions," Tahir said. "For example, are these bird-fruits plants or animals?"

"They possess characteristics of both," Ziyad said, not very il-luminatingly.

"And the British eat their bird-fruit in their bone-houses?" Hassan asked. "The ones they make out of the giant fish?"

"Correct."

As the men talked, Palomides began to hear a strange roaring in his ears, louder and louder. It was as if a great wind had come rushing in off the desert—because this was it. It was so obvious. This was the story, this was how he would make his mark. This was how the swift would take wing. He felt his life turning like the golden lancer spinning on top of the caliph's great green dome. Where would it stop?

"Gentlemen," he announced, "I will settle this argument for you."

The three other men looked at him without much interest.

"You will?" Tahir said. "Really?"

"How do you intend do that?" Hassan said.

"Very simply. I will go to Britain myself and find out."

It took him two years.

It was perverse, and impulsive, and foolish, as not one single member of his family failed to point out to him. But that was the beauty of it! It was a magnificent gesture, a pure act of will, spitting straight in the eye of fate! Every time he thought of it the same wild thrill went through him. No one would ever forget Palomides, prince of Baghdad, who one day on a whim turned on his heel and lit out for the edge of the world.

As exits went, it would never be beaten. And anyway he couldn't very well go back to the paper sellers now. The die was cast. He would not be a caliph in a golden cage, he would be a citizen of the world. Maybe he would bring back seeds from those bird-fruit-trees and plant them in the royal courtyards alongside the orange trees. He would throw a feast of roast tree-bird-fruits and invite all the paper sellers.

He went by camel at first, following the Silk Road west to Mo-sul, bobbing easily on the current of jade, paper, cardamom, frank-incense, myrrh, cinnamon, slaves, and, of course, silk. From there he passed to Sivas and Ankara and finally, after ten months, to Constantinople.

Palomides loved Constantinople. It was a true rival to his be-loved Baghdad, full of life and color and confusion, a babel of voices, dirt and smells and beautiful women and strange birds. But nobody there knew much more than he did about his ultimate des-tination. Europeans were fascinated with the east, they obsessed and raged and fantasized about it, but their fascination was not requited by the east except on a strictly commercial basis. Some Europeans were good, some were bad. All were tall, drunk, pro-miscuous, and incredibly smelly. What else did you need to know?

Also they were fiercely devoted to Christianity, an outmoded faith that had long since been superseded by Islam. The only new fact Palomides gleaned about Britain was that it was currently ruled by a king named Arthur.

He at least was intriguing, this Arthur. Apparently one reason the Britons were so obscure and mysterious was that they had long been too busy fighting one another to have much to do with the wider world beyond their misty archipelago. But under Arthur that had changed. The Britons had made peace and were becoming prosperous and mighty. This Arthur must cut quite a figure.

Sailing to Venice, Palomides was racked with both sea- and homesickness. But for those rumors of Arthur and the tales of his glorious court, he might have given up. Instead he let them pull him forward, westward, ever westward, into the setting sun. It was in Venice that he acquired his new name. He was tired of listening to people stumble through his Arabic name so he adopted a new one, easier for a European to pronounce: Palomides. It had belonged to a minor figure in the Trojan War, legendarily clever, credited by some with inventing dice, or numbers, or certain letters of the alphabet. The original Palomides met a bad end in the war, but never mind. This Palomides would write a better ending for himself.

Now there was a thought—he would write a book! Of course he would! It would be copied out in numberless editions and shelved in the House of Wisdom. Handsome Hassan would sell it at his shop, telling his customers, *I was there the day Prince Palomides departed for Britain. We all thought he was mad! But then . . .*

Palomides joined a convoy of merchants headed first for Milan, from there to Cologne, and from there north to the Frankish city of Bruges. There, by dint of a lot of royal charm, memorized phrases, hand gestures, and gold, he booked passage on a ship that would brave the Western Sea, or the Encircling Sea, or the Green Sea, or the Sea of Darkness, beyond which lay at last the land of Arthur.

No MAGIC IDOL PUT PALOMIDES to sleep. There would be times when he wondered if it had, and if what followed was one long tortuous idol-induced nightmare.

In the cold stone hall of Camelot he presented gifts to King Arthur, a tall, rangy man, handsome in a long-nosed kind of way, who thanked him graciously but not overly effusively. *He* might have been a magic idol for the way his pale eyes seemed to bore into Palomides's own, warmly but insistently, as if to divine intentions that even he, Palomides, might not be aware of.

Palomides was then drawn aside by a berobed individual with long, lank hair and a brusque manner who startled him by speaking rapid, fluent street Arabic with no trace of an accent. This Merlin, as he called himself, accepted Palomides's homage—which was not a word that Palomides would have used, but he let it pass—on Arthur's behalf and in return offered him the hospitality due a visiting diplomat from the great city of Sarras. An officious undersecretary was assigned to show Palomides to his room and acquaint him with the wonders of Camelot.

The wonders. Of course Palomides knew he was an emissary from a more advanced civilization, and it was important to be charitable to those less fortunately situated. But even so it was hard not to feel like, after all that, it was a bit of an anticlimax.

In Baghdad there was a palace with an artificial pond at its center, and in the center of the pond was a tree made of silver. The tree had eighteen branches, and each branch sprouted innumerable twigs and leaves, and on each twig sat a mechanical bird that could, by means of a concealed mechanism, be made to sing and flutter its wings.

By comparison, the great treasure of Camelot was a table in the shape of a circle. Likewise Palomides absolutely enjoyed his tour of Camelot's Rose Garden, which took (he was being generous) a quarter of an hour, but there were rose gardens back home that covered a hundred acres and were irrigated by waterwheels powered by captive ostriches. He was more saddened than awed at the sight of the two miserable lions in the Royal Menagerie, which his tour guide referred to as leopards. The caliph had a hundred lions, and a hundred leopards too. And while the shelves of Baghdad's House of Wisdom groaned under a million books, the royal library of Camelot consisted, optimistically, of about thirty-five, most of which were copies of the Christian Bible.

Also they were all on parchment. Britain had not yet discovered paper.

There was no sign of any bird-trees at all. He didn't have the heart to ask.

As soon as possible Palomides retired to his cold chamber, where he lay down in a swoon of homesickness. He should've stayed in Constantinople. He rose again and by means of astronomical readings and spherical trigonometry determined the direction of Mecca so that he could pray facing the proper way.

He'd come this far, so Palomides determined to make the best of it. He set about parsing the social cosmos of Camelot, making careful notes for his book. King Arthur was at the center, naturally. Working outward you came to Merlin, and Arthur's one-handed shadow Sir Bedivere, he of the melting, adoring eyes, which he turned jealously on anyone who got too close.

And of course there was the universally revered Lancelot, whose dominance in the realm of personal combat was so extreme as to be almost bizarre. He pondered Arthur's motives in keeping someone like that so close, a foreigner with the power to kill at will. If they were closer to home he would have taken Lancelot for one of the *fedayeen*, an assassin in deep cover.

The queen of the Britons was a tall, skinny thing with the kind of beauty that one admired more than desired. She struck Palomides as highly intelligent and dangerously bored, an unstable combination. The evidence suggested that she was also infertile, another dangerous quality in a queen, to herself most of all. People spoke freely around Palomides, on the assumption that he couldn't understand them, and there were those at court who wanted to replace her by whatever means necessary with someone, anyone, who could give the nation a legitimate heir.

As for Arthur himself, he was a curious combination of irresistible and inscrutable. In this sleepy country, with its fading trappings of Romanity, he was one of a handful of people who seemed fully awake. Arthur was ardently Christian—if his toast landed butter-side up he was on his knees thanking God before you could say "knife"—but he wasn't afflicted by that aggrieved obsession with converting others from which so many Christians suffered. As befitted the center of the royal cosmos, he had a charisma that was almost solar in its intensity—even Palomides didn't like to look at it directly, lest he be drawn in and disarmed by it like so many others.

His troops liked to call him Black Arthur. Though he was as pale as the rest of his race.

Also like the sun, King Arthur was a furnace of energy. Hassan had said Britain had seven kings, and he wasn't wrong; Arthur was seven kings in one. He was trying to keep his barbarian nation from sliding into complete savagery by main force, single-handedly. When he wasn't off fighting or adventuring or surveying coastal defenses or treating with the clergy, he was commissioning public buildings or reviewing foreign intelligence or vetting some new judicial appointee or entertaining some sycophantic delegation from somewhere or other. He never stopped. By custom nobody at court was allowed to sit down until the king did, and by the end of the day they were all drooping with exhaustion because Arthur never sat down.

What fuel kept that furnace burning so bright and so hot? All fires consume something. It seemed to Palomides that a fire that is not fed, yet still burns, must be consuming itself.

PALOMIDES LINGERED IN BRITAIN through the summer. The court moved from place to place, Camelot to Caerleon to Londinium to Canterbury (slightly better library) to Cair Ebrauc and back to Camelot, in a great circle, dragging behind it a dragon's tail of clerks and cooks and courtiers, knights and whores, priests and fools and barbers and lumbering, clinking carts. As the season waned, Palomides felt his sojourn here was drawing to a natural close. It was time to start the long journey home. He'd done what he set out to do. If Britain wasn't quite ravishing enough to fill a book, well, he'd just make some stuff up.

Just knowing he was leaving put Palomides in a good mood, so when a group of women of the court asked him to chaperone them on an outing into the countryside, he graciously accepted.

It wasn't the first time. The ladies of Camelot were fond of these excursions, and they always took along a couple of knights for protection against bears and bandits and whatever else they might run into. Palomides was a popular choice because it was widely believed that he understood no Latin, which meant they could gossip in front of him freely.

In fact Palomides's Latin was quite serviceable by this time, but he still didn't much care what the ladies said. He stood on the fringes of the gathering, stiff as a marble statue, while they spread out their skirts on the grass and sang and embroidered and told riddles. The women of King Arthur's court were odd creatures:

bold, wittering, thin of blood and pigment, they put him in mind of albino peacocks. They plucked their eyebrows and, perversely, whitened their already pale faces even further with a paste made of flour and rose water.

Though they were undeniably feminine, and even beguiling at times to a lonely traveler in their form-fitting tunics, the sleeves so tight they had to be sewn into them by their ladies-in-waiting. One of them had a pet squirrel that scampered around on a golden chain.

As they talked, Palomides gazed off into the middle distance. He liked to imagine himself walking the streets of Baghdad. In his mind he strolled out through Khorasan Gate, across the Tigris via the curving boat bridge, and into the paper-sellers' market. To the awe and acclamation of all he presented them with the book of his travels. *A Journey to the Edge of the World and Back.* Or *The Book of Routes and Realms.* Or more formal: *Concerning the Island of Britain, Its People, Climate, and Geography.* Or more playful: *The Pleasant Wanderings of a Curious Traveler* . . .

The women were talking about him.

"He has a noble profile, don't you think?"

"Oh, stop. Could you even imagine?"

"Well, why not? He's terribly handsome—he is! Look at those shoulders! And he's probably a prince or a duke or something. They wouldn't send just anybody."

Peals of laughter. Palomides didn't distinguish very carefully among the ladies of court, but he had noticed the woman who spoke last because she was a recent arrival and extremely pretty, for a Briton anyway, with mischievous pointy eyebrows and an edifice of blond ringlets piled on top of her head.

Adding to her winsomeness was the very slightest overbite. He'd forgotten her name.

"Don't be ridiculous." A redhead with a wen on her cheek. "They only like boys. Didn't you know?"

"Nonsense, he's always trying to look down our dresses." A tall, ghostly pale woman made skeptical eyebrows.

"Never!" The pretty overbitten one again. "I believe that our Sir P. has only the healthiest possible inclinations. And as for looking down a woman's dress, Sir P. is far too respectful. Not like our men."

Sir P. thought it best to feign incomprehension.

"Which of us do you think he prefers?"

"Oh, honestly."

"Palomino, tell us!" the redhead called. "Which one of us are you in love with?"

Hilarity of the picnickers.

"I'm sure he has a beautiful dusky fiancée waiting for him back in Sarras. Pining for him in Oriental splendor. Don't you, Sir P.?"

The pretty one looked up and favored him with a wink, tiny but perfect. All gallantry aside, he couldn't help seeing down her dress, and the view was compelling. He was about to hazard an answer when—

"Ho ho! What have we here?"

Three men came swaggering across the field toward them. They were sunburned and red from rough living and wore linen jacks and cheap-looking swords. They appeared to be of a rather lower order of Briton.

"God give you good day, my ladies! You've got nothing to fear from us." The man who spoke had a boxer's nose and blond hair plastered down on his scalp. "But I'm afraid it is my duty to inform you that this field you are so comfortably enjoying belongs to us."

Palomides thought he must be misunderstanding something, either the man's Latin or some point of British law.

"No," the woman with the overbite said, "it doesn't. This is the king's land, so go scamper off up your own arses, all three of you."

"That is as it may," the boxer said merrily. "We shall take it up with the good King Arthur next time we see him. In the meantime you must pay your rent. Must they not, George?"

George, a heavy, soft-looking man with mournful eyes, confirmed that they did.

"Nothing you gracious ladies can't afford, just a quick tumble and your jewelry." He stuck his thumbs in his belt. "Now. Who will be first to settle her debt?"

Palomides felt no fear of these men. If anything he felt relief. He was tired of being an observer, a tourist, looking around passively at the scenery. Before he left he wanted to show them what a prince of Baghdad could do—that a great story was unfolding before them, and that he was its hero. The marble statue came to life, and Sir Palomides strode across the picnic blanket, scattering silverware and stepping in a pot of jam.

"The debt in question is yours, and you will settle it in blood." In the heat of the moment the Latin language leapt with alacrity to his lips. "Or yield to me as the recreants you are."

The women stared helplessly from the suddenly Latin-speaking Sir Palomino to the would-be rapists and back again. It was hard to say which they found more shocking. The thieves stared at Palomides too. Then they burst out laughing.

"Who brought the chimney sweep?" the boxer said.

"They left this one in too long!" Even mournful George was delighted. "He's overdone!"

The boxer grinned, yellow teeth. Palomides supposed that he wasn't what their idea of a knight looked like. Maybe his skin was too dark. Maybe he wasn't dressed right—maybe it was his turban, fine though it was, laced with golden thread. And they did have him three to one. Palomides drew his sword, a straight double-edged blade that bore an inscription in gold: *There is no Sword but the Zulfiqar, and there is no Hero but Ali.* The only sound in the meadow was the chittering of the golden-chained squirrel.

Palomides took a sudden jerky half step toward the boxer, who startled and stumbled back. Palomides had left his right side undefended, and George took a big unbalanced swing. The watching women gasped—but of course he'd done it on purpose to draw George out. He spun away from the cut, all the way around, and whipped his sword halfway through George's neck.

The dying man dropped, and Palomides freed his sword and sprang at the boxer. To his credit the man didn't freeze, and he didn't run. He didn't lack for courage. But his swordplay was slow and sloppy, and his weapon was a toy next to Palomides's. The blade of a caliph's son was forged from Damascus steel, smelted in Syria from Indian iron, and it held an edge like no blade in Britain.

Palomides smiled as he fought. A ream of paper would've given more trouble. Bewildered by the unfamiliar loops and rhythms of his swordwork, the boxer thrust awkwardly, and Palomides simply lopped off the top half of his blade, then severed his forearm. Then he tripped him and stabbed him briskly through the heart.

By this time the third man was running. Palomides strode back across the blanket, avoiding the jam pot this time, and leapt into the saddle. This horse was no polo pony but he rode it like one, darting and turning, heading the man off every which way, running him all over the field till he finally sank down, gasping and weeping, bewildered, and surrendered. Palomides flipped a mental coin, shrugged, and spared him, on the condition that he swear on his mother's life to convert to Islam and make a pilgrimage to Mecca. Then he returned to the women.

Most of them were hiding behind trees and bushes. One had fainted. Two had been sick into their skirts. The squirrel had escaped up a tree; its little body would be found months later hanging from a branch, hopelessly tangled in its golden chain.

But the lady with the overbite and the blond curls hadn't hidden or fainted or been sick. Instead she rose to her feet and with a curious gesture detached one of the sleeves of her dress and gave it to Palomides.

"Best clean your sword," she said.

Isolde was her name, that was it—they called her Isolde the Beautiful, or Isolde the Blonde—and at that moment Palomides fell madly in love with her.

BOOK II

A GOD OF
SAND AND DUST

In th'olde dayes of the Kyng Arthour,
Of which that Britons speken greet honour,
All was this land fulfild of fayerye.
The elf-queene, with hir joly compaignye,
Daunced ful ofte in many a grene mede.
This was the olde opinion, as I rede.

— "The Wife of Bath's Tale," from
The Canterbury Tales by Geoffrey Chaucer

Twelve

THE NOVICE

The Green Knight led the way. After him came Bedivere, watching for any signs of trouble. Palomides guarded the rear. They put Collum in the middle, under the supervision of Sir Dinadan, so he couldn't cause any problems, but he wasn't going to dwell on that. He was Sir Collum now, knighted by no less a hand than that of Sir Palomides the Saracen. Even with Arthur dead, even with all that had happened, he had that to hold onto. He was Sir Collum, and he was on a quest with the knights of the Round Table.

Or three of them anyway. Constantine had stayed behind with Nimue to get the defenses in order and rally the nobility and try to pull some kind of army together out of mud and hay and spare pennies in the event that King Rience turned up at the gates. They left Dagonet behind, too, because he didn't want to come, and nobody wanted him to.

The Green Knight led them west, staying off the Roman roads and following crooked, thready old footpaths instead, winding through forests and slipping through gaps in hedges and hacking across fields. It was June, and nature wasn't in mourning for King

Arthur. Martins whipped in and out of the trees, and the roadsides were deep with drifts of white wildflowers, wild carrot and cow parsley and white campion. The south was a land of huge meadows, thousand-acre meadows, rippling oceans of tall feathery grasses frosted with seed.

In the woods their horses waded through lakes of ferns, and you could smell wild garlic in the air. In places the trees had been cut back from the road the length of a bowshot, as a defense against bandits, but mostly they pressed in close, and the tree branches met overhead forming a tunnel of leaves, the green light like the light inside the barrel of a breaking wave.

The Green Knight refused to say anything about their destination. Collum wondered if he would lead them all the way to the Other-world. He would follow the knights of the Table anywhere, but he rather hoped he wouldn't have to go there. Arthur himself had led an expedition to the Otherworld with three dozen picked knights to find the Cauldron of Annwn, which would produce all the food a brave man could eat. Only seven men came back, whispering hoarsely about the gates of Hell and a fortress made of glass. If that was the best King Arthur could do, Collum didn't much like their chances.

Dinadan wasn't overjoyed to be stuck with minding Sir Collum, but he liked to talk—he couldn't seem to leave a silence unfilled—so they talked about the quest. Did it come from God? If so why would God send something like the Green Knight as His messenger? Why would He kill Sir Villiars? What if it was a trap from Fairy, or the devil?

Dinadan wasn't overly concerned. "If it's a trap then we'll spring it and give whoever set it the beating they deserve. It's like Bedivere said, we're in a new world now. We must divine its nature. And we must show it that our own nature has not changed."

Dinadan asked Collum about his life on Mull, and instead of owning up to yesterday's lies, Collum compounded them by describing his upbringing there as the golden child of Lord Alasdair (Collum gave Alasdair a courtesy promotion from baronet to viscount), groomed in every way for greatness and given every possible advantage. *They won't let you lie like that when you're a knight*, the fairy-woman at the inn said, but now he was a knight and he couldn't stop. It felt like even a word of the truth would dispel this whole miraculous scene, it would vanish like a fairy castle at dawn, and he'd be left trudging on to Astolat, just another rootless sword for hire.

They spent a night in the remains of a magnificent Roman villa surrounded by acres of ruined gardens turned savage and unruly by time. Palomides explained how the Romans used to pump hot air under the floors of their houses, through a system of channels, so that they had warm tiles to walk on in winter. Nobody believed him.

On the afternoon of the second day Bedivere told the Green Knight they were making a detour, and he led them a short way east to where a convent stood by the side of a cracked Roman road, a proud building of honey-colored stone in the shape of a Greek cross, which he identified as Amesbury Abbey. Maybe they were going to hear Mass and make confession? Never a bad idea on a quest. Bedivere announced them through an iron grille.

"Say nothing," he whispered to Collum.

"Less than nothing," Dinadan said. "Don't even think anything."

They were ushered into a sparse high-ceilinged receiving room.

Collum hung back; he felt like they were besmirching the immaculate quiet of the place with their every move. Bedivere had a word
with a lay sister, then a more extensive hushed negotiation with a
severe-looking abbess, who though plainly dressed wore a conspicuous gold cross on a chain and a ring with an exquisite sapphire.
She shot disapproving glances at Sir Palomides. Finally two nuns
brought in a chair and then laboriously set up a heavy red-leather
screen around it.

There was the swish of soft-soled shoes from behind the screen.
Collum felt the atmosphere in the room change subtly. Palomides and Dinadan knelt. Collum followed suit, though he didn't
know why.

"Stop. One doesn't kneel to a nun."

The voice of the woman behind the screen was clipped and
slightly nasal. It spoke of generations of wealth and breeding.

"You will always be our queen," Palomides said. "Your Majesty."

"But I won't, Sir Palomides. That is precisely why I took the trouble
to become a nun. And it wasn't easy. You should see what they did to
my hair."

The knights obediently got to their feet. Collum could hardly
breathe. That was Queen Guinevere herself behind that screen,
barely three yards away. She must have taken refuge here after
Camlann.

"To what do I owe the honor of this visit?" Guinevere said. "I do
hope Sir Lancelot didn't send you."

"You really think we'd run that treacherous fornicator's errands?" Bedivere snapped. He alone hadn't knelt.

The words echoed in the stone room. Instead of replying, Guinevere let the silence stretch out, tacitly inviting Bedivere to think
on his words and perhaps regret them. That must be one of the

ways a queen learns to wield power, Collum thought. She would be dressed as a novice, but he could only imagine her on an imperial throne wearing a golden crown.

"Go on, Bedivere," she said finally, more softly. "Speak your piece."

"We seek a new king," Bedivere said curtly. "Did you and Arthur ever discuss the succession?"

"I can't help you with that."

"You didn't speak of it? Not once in twenty years of marriage?"

"Did he discuss it with you?" The fallen queen's courtly tones sharpened. "You may think me a dizzy fool, or worse, but I always believed that God would provide us with a new king. And I still do, though I'll admit He's not going about it quite how I expected. In the meantime I am doing my best to ready my soul for the kingdom to come."

"Many congratulations, Your Majesty," Palomides said, "but your old kingdom lies in ruins, and we are doing our earthly best to put it back together."

"And what is it you'd like from me, Sir Palomides? In the past year I have been falsely accused of treason, nearly executed, then abducted and finally widowed. What is it you're hoping I have? A divine communiqué? Secret baby? A coded letter, in Arthur's hand? When my opinion mattered most no one listened to me, and I feel disinclined to give it to you now. I will tend to my own virtue, since everyone else seems so concerned about it."

"You have many years left, God willing," Palomides' deep voice rang in the convent hall. "If you were to marry again—"

"Silence, you revolting blackamoor!" The abbess spoke with such vitriol she had to wipe her chin. "This interview is ended!"

But the woman behind the screen must have checked her with a gesture. She might be a novice, who had forsworn her earthly station, but some power was not so easily set aside.

"The past may be gone," Guinevere said, "but it is very far from forgotten. The people of Britain hold me responsible for my late husband's lamentable downfall and death, as you very well know. Any cause I support would only be tainted by association with the Whore of Camelot."

"No one would dare call you that."

"Pray do not patronize me, Sir Dinadan. Everybody calls me that and worse. Some of the sisters in here are quite inventive. I remain devoted to Arthur and all he stood for, but for now I must pursue my own interests in my own time.

"But think on this. Arthur and I each had a duty to the realm. Mine was to provide the king with an heir. Arthur's duty was not to fall. We both failed. I loved my husband with all my heart, but if you are seeking another king, do not seek another Arthur.

"Good day to you all, gentlemen."

There was a creak and rustle as the unseen woman rose.

"Wait."

Dinadan spoke in a low voice.

"Would you give us your blessing?" He kept his eyes on the floor. "Not as our queen, but as a sister of Saint Benedict?"

Nobody moved. Guinevere was silent again, this time for so long that Collum was sure she'd left. But finally the queen, or the queen that was, uttered a quiet prayer. Collum found himself closing his eyes and breathing deeply, as if to physically imbibe the grace she offered.

Then there was the retreating hiss of slippers on dry stone. The knights shuffled meekly out, and the abbess slammed the door behind them. Collum supposed that if he was going to go questing with the knights of Camelot he would have to get used to engaging in intimate chats with royalty.

"Her own interests," Dinadan muttered. "What the hell interests does she have left besides Lancelot and his holy cock?" He already seemed to have forgotten whatever solemn impulse had caused him to ask for the queen's blessing.

"Her cousins," Bedivere said. "The Eastbrooks must be weighing their options. Perhaps they intend to marry her to someone else, like Palomides said."

"It is what I would do," Palomides said. "I only hope it is not to Rience."

"She should've had fewer cousins," Dinadan said, "and more sons."

NEVER HURRYING, never dallying, the Green Knight led them deeper into the south and west.

Britain felt different now that Collum knew Arthur was gone. Small signs of disorder kept catching his eye: trampled mud, the charred smear left behind by a campfire, a column of circling birds over a field. Britain was like a vast ship that had broached in a storm and was beginning to break up. Helmless and dismasted, its ribs cracking, seams starting and spraying seawater. Midmorning the next day Bedivere abruptly summoned Dinadan to the front of the line. He pointed: far in the distance two tiny figures on horseback were descending the flank of a green hill, leading a riderless third horse behind them.

They all stopped and stood in their stirrups. Collum could barely make them out as separate figures, but Dinadan said:

"That's Scipio."

"What?" said Bedivere.

"That's Sir Scipio, on the back of that horse."

"Are you sure?" Palomides said. "Scipio only ever wore scale, not plate. Also I am fairly certain he is dead."

"Not the riders. He's a prisoner. They've got him tied up naked on the back of the second horse."

Collum didn't see how Dinadan could possibly recognize any-body at this distance.

"Should we rescue him?" Palomides said.

Dinadan looked at Bedivere, who considered the question for longer than Collum would've thought necessary. Sir Scipio was ev-idently not the object of their quest.

"Come on," he said finally. "Principle of the thing."

When the riders saw they were pursued they didn't try to escape. They picked a spot on the road, turned their horses, and waited. It was a double-wide cart track beaten through pastureland, with loose stands of beech trees on either side. Dinadan was right, there was a naked man flung over the second horse like saddlebags, tied hand and foot, his pale back and buttocks burned red by the sun. He must have been hideously uncomfortable.

"Ho there!" Dinadan called out when they were close enough. "Who are you and what the hell do you think you're doing with Sir Scipio?"

The two knights were a mismatched pair, one small with a neat pointy beard, the other tall with a long equine face. The tall one's shield bore two swimming fish, and his breastplate was etched with fish scales. If they were cowed by the sight of three knights of Camelot—or four, assuming they didn't know that Collum wasn't one; or five, depending on what on earth they thought the Green Knight was—they didn't show it.

"Well, well, well," the short one said. "I do believe we've found the last leg of the Round Table!"

"And a lame leg it is too." The fish knight chuckled.

"I asked you," Dinadan said, "who—"

"We're two honorable knights of Glamorgan. I'm Sir Germaine and this is the Knight of the Borders."

"Charmed," Palomides said. "Give us Scipio, and we might let you live."

"This man is a thief." The Knight of the Borders had a raspy voice, as if he'd suffered some kind of throat injury or ailment. "We caught him looting bodies after Camlann."

The tied man groaned something unintelligible.

"But you've saved us a trip," Sir Germaine said. "We were on our way to Camelot to collect a ransom, but you can have him on the spot for—what would you say, Borders?"

"Ten pounds."

"Ten it is. What say you, gentlemen?"

Bedivere snorted.

"Keep thyself."

He turned his horse away.

By tradition whichever knight currently stood highest in the unwritten martial pecking order would have had the honor of representing Camelot in the joust, but with so many of the leading lights of the table gone Collum wasn't sure there even was an order anymore. But there was no arguing or even any discussion about it: Sir Palomides fitted on his helm and accepted a lance from a retainer as one by one the others patted him on the shoulder and muttered a word or two of encouragement or advice. He ambled his horse into the road. His armor was in a fascinating Eastern style, a thick coat of double-riveted mail with heavy steel plates sewn into it, lighter and more flexible than your standard British knight's gear. The plates were gilded and inscribed with words in intricate, ornate Arabic script. His helmet was a turban sculpted in steel.

A hundred and twenty yards further down the road Sir Germaine waited alone, looking very small. The arms on his shield were three golden cups arranged above a single disembodied blackbird's wing. Somewhere a woodpecker knocked on a tree. Off to one side Sir Scipio still hung face down and exhausted over his horse's rear end, his hair hanging limp, apparently oblivious to the fact that his fate was being decided.

"Watch this," Dinadan said quietly.

Palomides didn't milk the moment. With no fuss he saluted his opponent and barked a curt foreign syllable to his horse. They were off, accelerating rapidly into a gallop.

Collum was only a fair-to-middling jouster himself. It was the mental challenge more than the physical one. You had to force yourself to relax because if you tensed up your lance would bob up and down as you rode and you'd never place the point properly. You couldn't let yourself shy away from your opponent even slightly, because the rules required you to present your body as a target. You had to keep your eyes on your adversary's shield, because if you let them stray even for a heartbeat to the approaching tip of his lance—and it attracted your gaze like a lodestone—it would look like it was coming straight in through your visor and the urge to flinch would become uncontrollable.

But the hardest part was simply that at the moment of impact you had to keep your eyes open, because when the enemy loomed up before you, looking like a mirror image of your own terrible armored self, and the lances hit with all the combined weight of horses and men and armor behind them, it was only with your eyes open that you could aim your point with the precision of a master.

And that was just tournament jousting, *à plaisance*, with blunt caps on the ends of the lances, and special jousting armor, and a fence between the horses to keep them from crashing head-on. Even then there were accidents; men broke limbs or lost eyes or even died. Out here in the wild—fighting *à outrance*, with weapons of war—the stakes were higher and the odds much worse.

None of that seemed to bother Palomides. He effortlessly absorbed the motion of his horse's strides, reins held lightly in his left hand, the tip of his lance as still as the center of the earth. A lance was too heavy to hold out straight for long so the knights kept them pointed up at an angle till they got close. Sir Germaine lowered his early, but Palomides waited till the absolute last moment, an instant before impact, before he let his point drop smoothly into place.

Sir Germaine's spear bent and scraped off Palomides's shield while in the same moment Palomides slipped his point neatly past the bearded knight's shield, where it found a mark just inside his left armpit. It stuck fast and wrenched Sir Germaine violently around and back before shattering into a cloud of spinning splinters.

Germaine flopped backward onto his horse's rump, then slid limply out of the saddle to the ground. That one blow had hammered all the fight out of him. Palomides rode through the spray of fragments, already decelerating. He tossed aside the stub of his lance and loosened his gauntlets and checked over his tack as if he hadn't just performed the most gorgeous physical feat Collum had ever witnessed. Some things at least were every bit as good as in the stories.

"Per Aristotle's *Physics*," Palomides said, "the application of violence produces unnatural motion."

An embarrassing scene followed in which Sir Germaine wanted to surrender rather than face Palomides on foot with swords, and the Knight of the Borders tried to convince him to keep fighting, whereupon Germaine suggested Borders fight Palomides himself, and Palomides calmly declared himself willing to fight anybody as soon as they decided who that was going to be.

When it was clear that they were done for the day, Borders went back to insisting that Scipio was rightfully their prisoner.

"We caught him looting!" he rasped indignantly. "After the battle!"

"You're lying," Bedivere said.

"We took him fair and square!"

"Two knights against one," Palomides said, "is neither fair nor square. It is at best triangular."

"If I might be allowed to speak."

It was Sir Scipio.

"Cut him loose, Collum," Bedivere said.

Germaine and Borders glared but didn't try to stop him as he sawed through Sir Scipio's ropes with his knife. He did his best to ease the poor man down onto the grass as gently as possible, where he lay limp and boneless. A startling amount of his bare skin was covered in whorled blue tattoos.

"They fell on me when I was sleeping." Sir Scipio didn't attempt to rise. His Latin was perfect. "Took me unawares."

"You were awake," Germaine said.

"No, I wasn't."

"Well, you should have been, it was halfway terce. And we saw you looting after the battle."

"I lent a gilt dagger to Sir Gumret le Petit, God rest him. His having died, I took it back."

"That is simply false!"

"Unless you're prepared to defend your claim more effectively than you have thus far," Bedivere said, "I suggest you get back on your horses and consider yourselves the most fortunate knights in Christendom that we don't kill you for the recreants you are."

"You know what?" In his weakened state it took Germaine three tries to swing himself up into the saddle. "You know what? Go fuck yourselves!" He was close to tears. "And fuck the Round Table! Where do you think you're even going? Still a-questin' after adventure? Grow up! You're pathetic, everybody thinks so!"

"We are not too pathetic," Palomides said, "to knock you off a horse."

"Arthur's dead! The Romans are gone! No one cares anymore!"

"God cares," Bedivere said.

"Does He? Really? You'd better hope He cares when the peasants come for your heads. Except something tells me He won't."

Sir Germaine made an obscene gesture and the two men rode away.

"'Knight of the Borders,'" Dinadan said. "Get a damn name."

"I fought him once," Bedivere said. "Mêlée at Canoel. About what you'd expect."

The woodpecker, who'd gone silent during the joust, went back to its knocking. Scipio was on his hands and knees throwing up on the grass, but all he managed was a few strings of bile. He spat. When he was done they gave him water and a piece of bread and an apple. Palomides chafed his ankles.

"We thought you were dead," he said.

"Wished I was." Scipio spat again. "How many of us are left?"

"Six. No, five." Dinadan corrected himself because of Villiars.

"That's all? What about Sagramore?"

Bedivere shook his head.

"Those pricks were right, we really are finished." Scipio struggled to his feet, unkinked his neck, and pressed both hands to his lower back. "Right. What's next?"

It appeared to have taken him all of about five heartbeats to process the fall of the Round Table and move on. His tattoos really were very striking, whorls and faces and crude runes. A few of the loops even crossed his face.

"There's one more of us alive," Dinadan said. "We don't know who, but we're on our way to get him."

Scipio nodded as if that were about what he expected. His clothes and armor were in a bundle on the back of the horse, and he carefully, patiently, unpicked the knot. His tattoos gave him the air of a wild man, but now that he was up and about his manner was more that of a fastidiously orderly person whom fate had thrown some disorderly turns.

"Did you really lend Sir Gumret that dagger?" Dinadan asked.

"Course not." Scipio stood wobbling on one foot to put on his undergarments. "I always wanted that thing."

THE NEXT DAY THEY SAW a burned village where a dead man was strung up in a charred tree. His head was in a sack and hung down at a dejected angle. There were no other bodies, and Palomides thought the inhabitants must have torched their own village to keep it out of someone else's hands. A goat chewed on the blackened remains of a thatch roof. A broadside was nailed to the corpse's chest, but weather had blotted the words. The warning was unreadable, the verdict lost. The ship was breaking up.

They made camp in a field. Their attendants were extraordinarily skilled at turning an ordinary meadow into comfortable accommodations—they combed through it for any stones larger than a baby's fist and used them to piece together a firepit. After dinner they erected a pavilion made of striped canvas rubbed with beeswax to keep out the wet. It wasn't Camelot, but it was a long way from the louse-infested haystacks Collum was used to.

Scipio was already gone again, off on some mysterious errand of his own. The knights ate boiled hare and drank sour red wine as the stars came alight overhead. Collum felt the warmth of the fire on his face and the cool darkness at his back. Crickets kept jumping into his lap. In this new age Britain felt vast and mysterious. It had become a foreign country, as strange and unknown as distant Cathay.

"How'd you know it was Sir Scipio on the horse, Dinadan?" Collum said. "He must've been a mile away."

"Mile and a quarter," Dinadan said.

"You can really see that far?"

"It's a gift."

"There is an initiation when one is raised to the Table," Palomides said. "Some people come out of it with a special talent. Dinadan can see farther than any man in Britain."

"Not everybody gets something," Dinadan said. "Bedivere didn't. Constantine didn't. There's no rhyme or reason to it. Gareth could do a standing jump of twenty feet. And when it rains, Palomides doesn't get wet."

"Lancelot," Palomides said, "never shits."

"What?" Dinadan said.

"Have you ever seen him shit?"

"When would—never mind."

"What happens at the initiation?" Collum said. "Or is that a secret?"

"It's not a secret," Dinadan said. "But once you've been through it, you never want to talk about it ever again."

"I have something to say." Bedivere was sitting well back from the fire. He wore a brass hunting horn round his neck, though Collum had never seen him blow it. He'd called for wine as soon as they made camp and had been drinking steadily ever since. "I think Arthur might still be alive."

From all around them came the slow creaking of the crickets. Collum wondered if he'd heard right.

"Alive as in—not dead?" Dinadan said.

"I mean that after the battle something happened." Whatever it was Bedivere obviously didn't want to talk about it, but he couldn't keep it to himself any longer either. "After the fight with Mordred Arthur was badly wounded but still alive. My brother Lucan and I helped him off the battlefield. We found a little chapel and laid him down there."

"Why the hell didn't you tell us this before?" Dinadan said.

"Because I didn't want to."

"But why—"

"This was given to me to witness. Not you." Bedivere took another drink. "And I don't know what it means. Probably nothing."

Some big animal startled close by and went crashing away through the bushes.

"Arthur gave me Excalibur and told me to get rid of it. Throw it back in the water. I don't know why, maybe he thought somebody might use it for ill. Maybe Merlin made a deal with the Lady. I'd never held it before, and I'll admit I cut the air with it a few times. Never felt anything like it.

"There was no lake anywhere near so I threw it in the ocean. A woman's hand rose up and caught it by the hilt."

The sword's in the sea, Collum thought. The fairy-lady. She knew.

"I sat with the king all that night with his head in my lap. I left his helmet on, I think it was the only thing holding his skull together. The chapel was abandoned, and there were wild roses climbing the walls. You could hear the sound of waves on the beach."

"Did he say anything?" Palomides asked.

"Just babble. He called out to Jesus and the Virgin and some of the old gods too. Taranis. Lug. Durelas—there was a shrine to her at Little Dunoak. He spoke of the Grail, and a pair of birds, and a ring of stones. He begged for forgiveness for something, I don't know what. He called for his old nurse.

"I kept waiting for him to die. Lucan died—I didn't even know he'd been wounded, but he was like that. Got it in the guts. Kept it to himself. His son will be king now in Dyfed.

"Then around dawn I heard a bell outside. A boat was waiting in the surf, a barge with a silk pavilion on it flapping in the wind, azure and gold. There were people in it—I recognized the Queen of Northgalis and the Queen of the Waste Lands. They told me to bring Arthur on board. I didn't want to move him, but I didn't know what else to do."

Bedivere waved his empty cup; an alert groom appeared out of the darkness to refill it.

"The wind was sharp and the waves almost knocked me over. They had a pallet spread out on the deck, white satin, and I put him on it. A woman spoke to him, I didn't know her. She touched his face. 'Ah, dear brother,' she said. 'Why have you tarried so long from me? Alas, this wound on your head has caught over-much cold.'

"Arthur's eyes were closed, but he said something then. 'I will into the vale of Avalon, to heal me of my grievous wound.'

"Then the barge started moving. No sails or oars, it just moved by itself, shoving through the breaking waves. I tried to climb in but some force pushed me back and I fell down into the water. I chased it but it was too far out, and I couldn't swim. I was still in armor."

There was no moon, and the firelight was an island in the starry black.

"Avalon," Palomides said. "What is that?"

"It's a fairy tale," Dinadan said. "A made-up place. Probably his nurse told him about it."

"Arthur thought it was real," Bedivere said. "He thought he was going there."

"Arthur had just had his head split open."

"Well, he was in a magical barge at the time so I didn't feel like I was in a position to argue with him. Now shut up, there's more."

The crickets chirped slower and slower as the air cooled.

"I sat there in the shallows till the barge was out of sight. Then it started pissing rain, lashing down, I could barely see the beach. I started walking—I'd lost my horse. I walked all day and night till I got to the church at Glastonbury. The priest there turned out to be the archbishop of Canterbury, he was hiding out from Mordred. I told him about Arthur.

"He told me that some ladies had come to him in the night and given him a body to bury and some money for candles. I asked him what ladies, but he didn't know them. He showed me the grave."

"And?" Dinadan said.

"On the gravestone it said *Here Lies Arthur, King That Was, King That Will Be.*"

A light drizzle had started, matching the rain in the story, making the embers hiss, but nobody moved. What was Bedivere saying? That everything was saved, or that it was all lost? The world was so much stranger than he ever knew.

"I don't understand." Dinadan sounded more irritated than awed. "Either he went to Avalon, which doesn't exist, and he didn't die, or he didn't go to Avalon and he died and he's buried at Glastonbury. But then if he didn't go and he did die then why does the stone say 'will be'? What's the 'will be' if he's already dead and buried?"

Collum didn't know whether to hope or not. Dinadan was right, it wasn't an answer, just another riddle from a maddeningly evasive world.

"Maybe they thought he would live," Collum said, "but he died on the way to Avalon and they had to turn back and bury him here."

"And they had already paid for the inscription?" Palomides said.

"Maybe the grave is empty," Bedivere said.

"But he told you it wasn't. He said they had a body. What, the archbishop of Canterbury is lying?" Dinadan's voice was getting higher and higher. "And when is 'will be'? How long do we have to wait?"

"I told you I didn't know what it meant," Bedivere said. "I don't understand it either. But I believe that we will see Arthur again. His story is not over. He'll come back when we need him, when Britain needs him, and we'll just have to muddle through till he gets here."

"But we need him now!" Dinadan shouted. "How could things get any worse? How could we possibly need him more than we need him now?"

There was another rustle in the bushes, and a snapping twig, and for a heartbeat Collum thought it must be King Arthur himself, making a surprise entrance. But it was just Sir Scipio back from his errand, his tattooed face like a mask in the firelight. He tossed a couple of heavy lumps into the circle and sat down.

The lumps were human heads. Collum recognized Sir Germaine by his neat beard.

"Peasants must've got 'em," Scipio said. "What did I miss?"

Thirteen

THE TALE OF SIR PALOMIDES, PART II

That moment in the meadow divided Palomides's life in two like a swordstroke. When word of his adventure got out he was the toast of Camelot, praised and feasted and embraced as never before, but his only thoughts were of Isolde. Publicly she honored him along with the rest, but he could find no way to meet her privately.

He learned everything he could about her. Isolde was a princess, it turned out, from the kingdom of Munster in Hibernia. Palomides had known women in Baghdad, plenty of them, but he understood now that he'd never been in love before. The way Isolde looked at him—her gaze had a terrible, irresistible warmth, both girlish and maternal in equal measures, that made him think, She alone knows me for who I truly am, and delights in me, and favors me above all others. He believed that even as he saw her bathe others in that same terrible, irresistible gaze.

But true love rarely comes without impediments. One impediment was that Isolde was married, to a certain King Mark of Cornwall. Another was that she was well known to be in love with King

Mark's dashing nephew, a knight of the Round Table whose name was Sir Tristram of Lyonesse.

But these barriers felt trivial to Palomides compared to the magnitude of his love. Surely it would sweep them away like a howling tempest. Surely a feeling this strong could not but be reciprocated. He realized that this was what he'd traveled the breadth of the world for. Not bird-trees, not Arthur, *this*, this barbarian angel waiting for him at the world's end like the fabled northern lights. This was where the story had been leading all along.

He forgot all about leaving Britain. Instead he threw himself into the social whirl of Camelot. He danced. He feasted. He falconed. Palomides quickly learned that it was no secret that he was besotted with Isolde, and furthermore that nobody was particularly surprised or shocked. People fell in love with Isolde the Beautiful all the time, and one of the social quirks of upper-class British life, it turned out, was that it was considered normal, even admirable, for a knight to have passionate feelings for a married woman. They called it "courtly love," and it represented a kind of aspiration of the heart toward an unattainable perfection. His love for Isolde only demonstrated the noble refinement of his sensibility.

Privately Palomides thought that that was all right for the likes of Lancelot, but he had every intention of attaining Isolde. Though admittedly it wasn't immediately clear how he was going to do it.

He experimented with becoming more British. He allowed King Arthur to knight him, then to raise him to the Round Table. (His arms: a golden swift on a field of green.) He began entering tournaments and quickly became a dominant force in the lists. He was a horseman like nobody had ever seen, and his elegant, unconventional bladework gave other knights fits. His armor was lighter and more mobile than the lumbering metal coffins his British opponents wore. He beat Sir Percival hand to hand and fought Sir Gawain to a standstill. The only knights against whom he could never quite notch a victory were the indefatigable Sir Lancelot and, maddeningly, his rival in love, Sir Tristram.

Isolde didn't appear to notice any of this. He still had the grisly trophy of her silk sleeve, stained a brittle brown with the blood of George and the boxer, but that was all he got from her. By now she'd left Camelot and was spending most of her time in Cornwall rejoicing in the drama of her love triangle.

Maybe it was his accent? Or the color of his skin? Should he ask Merlin to change it? But why would she care about that? Palomides's other new friends didn't seem to, particularly. They lamented his Muslim faith, but only because they were worried he'd go to Hell when he died. As for his skin, they insisted that it was only dark because his homeland was so close to the sun, and here in Britain it would naturally fade to a healthy, robust pallor.

Palomides went on adventures, and as he did he saw more of Britain, and it was a stranger and more complicated place than he'd first taken it for. Arthur and his knights were clearly in charge, and they spoke Latin and comported themselves like worthies of the Western Roman Empire, which as far as Palomides knew no longer existed. But there was an entirely different British people here, too, the Britons, who spoke an older language than Latin, and who mostly didn't own the land they broke their backs to plow. This was a divided country. The Romans had cloven it in two and it had yet to heal.

Britain was not quite the unbroken expanse of pallor he first took it for either. The Romans had stationed North African and Middle Eastern soldiers here, and their descendants were every possible shade a person could be. There was a knight of the Table named Sir Moriaen, who was the son of Sir Aglovale and a North African queen, and his skin was darker than Palomides's. There were other travelers here, too, Egyptians and Jews and Arabs and Berbers, diplomats and adventurers and transients and traders lugging carpets and silks and spices and pearls.

These men were friendly toward Palomides, and he knew he should have made common cause with them, but instead they made him uneasy. He felt like they were studying him for signs of disloyalty, whether to the old country or the new one he wasn't sure. Was he fitting in well enough? Or perhaps rather too well? Their faces and accents and the smells of their spices reminded Palomides of the home he'd left behind, which he longed for but could not return to, because his heart was pinned to Britain as if it were snagged on a thistle, and to leave would be to tear it apart.

But was it not ridiculous, this appalling fixation on a woman whom he barely knew? Who was half a savage? She wasn't even his type! It was so indecorous, so unbecoming of a man of his breeding and station. But love ground him under its heel, humiliating and degrading him. His daily prayers became spotty, and he took to drinking wine like the British, which made him surly and snappish. He quarreled with other knights and even killed one in an argument. It dawned on Palomides that he was not the hero of this story. Somewhere along the way he'd become a minor character in the big fat romance of Tristram and Isolde. He was the villain, at best. Or wait, no, the villain was King Mark! Palomides was the comic relief!

It was around this time that he began chasing the Questing Beast.

The Questing Beast was a true magical oddity, bizarre and unique. The front half of her body was a leopard and the back half was a lion. She had the cloven hooves of a deer and an eerie sound came from her belly like a faraway pack of hounds baying. Strangest of all was her head, which was that of an enormous banded serpent. Her name was Glatisant.

For years King Pellinore of the Isles was famous for hunting the Questing Beast, and he wore out horse after horse chasing her all over Britain, but when he died the post of Knight of the Questing Beast came open, and Palomides immediately stepped into the vacancy. He had the swift on his shield painted over and replaced with Glatisant's likeness.

He didn't really expect to catch the Questing Beast. She would have been a glorious trophy to bring home, a magnificent addition to the caliph's menagerie, but King Pellinore had always maintained that only he or one of his kin could catch her; against that Merlin had prophesied that only Sir Percival could catch the Questing Beast, though he never took much of an interest in her. Nobody thought that Palomides could catch her, not even Palomides.

But he needed something to take him away from Camelot, and when had Sir Palomides the Saracen ever shrunk from a lost cause? If he didn't stop brooding and sulking over La Beale Isolde he would go mad or kill himself. Hunting Glatisant soothed him like ice on a burn. He galloped after her along the stony coast of Cornwall, across the purple moors of Ebrauc, north as far as Pictland. Once she even led him into the Otherworld, where he glimpsed its infamous queen, the notorious Morgan le Fay, who was Arthur's half sister. She waved to him familiarly, as if she knew him, and called off her fairy hounds: *Stay*, she told them. *He is not ours. Not yet anyway.*

In her own bestial way Glatisant was as unattainable as Isolde, and he was as fiercely possessive of her as he would have been of his beloved. Palomides felt a kinship with the Questing Beast. He imagined that she, too, had a homeland elsewhere, teeming with vast herds of frolicking Questing Beasts, but something had brought her to Britain where she was a curiosity, just like him, alone in a strange land, and she would or could not leave. He never got close enough to touch her, but once in a while she would turn and look back at him, from the next hill on, looping her snake head over her leopard's-fur shoulder, and their eyes would meet.

But he saw nothing in her cold, reptilian stare: not love, not hate, not even recognition.

AFTER A YEAR HUNTING THE QUESTING Beast Palomides returned to Camelot, and his old passion for Isolde came roaring back as bad as ever. His love was a terrible parasite that devoured him from within. In his absence Lyonesse had sunk into the ocean and been drowned because of some dire divine curse, but unfortunately it didn't take Sir Tristram of Lyonesse with it.

One day, deep in despair, Palomides sought out Tristram alone in a forest and goaded him into a private duel. He half hoped Tristram would kill him and put him out of his misery, but Tristram wouldn't even give him that. He was too damned decent a chap, dash it all! Instead he battered Palomides into semiconsciousness, then dragged him to a nearby chapel in a daze to undergo the one disgrace he hadn't sunk to yet: he was baptized Christian.

Even after everything else that had happened, the depths to which he'd sunk, Palomides was still shocked when he came to himself. This was a new low. He was destined now for Jahannam, where he would be crucified forever on a burning pillar with the other apostates, his flesh peeling off his bones like the bark off a dead tree.

As for Sir Tristram, he expressed only mild disappointment. He'd been sure the holy water would turn Palomides's skin pale like his.

What did it mean? Was he actually a Christian now? Had he become a barbarian? In truth he didn't know what he believed anymore, or who he was. He was not unfamiliar with Jesus as a prophet of Islam, but he found the idea of God having a son hard to swallow. He'd always thought of Christianity as a crude faith, mystical and rather monstrous, with its incarnation and resurrection and its bizarre triple godhead. But had he not spent years now worshipping a goddess made flesh, in the form of Isolde? In the House of Wisdom there were old books that were written on parchment taken from even older books—the scribes had scraped off the old ink and written a new text over it. Palimpsests, they were called. Now Palomides was a palimpsest, a prince of Baghdad scraped clean and rewritten as a Christian knight. That was how he felt, scraped and scoured and raw.

At least now something would surely change. How could it not? The old Palomides was gone. Maybe Isolde would love the new one.

And something did change, though not in the way he'd hoped. Palomides expected more of the usual chaffing when he returned to Camelot—Kay had a running comic riff about the hypothetical offspring of Palomides and Isolde, whose skin would be checkered black and white like a chessboard. Old Palomides, always good for a laugh. He was funnier than Dagonet.

But the knights must somehow have perceived that it was not

the moment for it. The joke had gone far enough. When he came trudging into the hall a bright double ring of faces turned to him in welcome. They were worried about him. They sensed how lost he'd been of late. The king himself left his place at the table and embraced him, kissed his cheeks, and led him to his accustomed chair.

Palomides found himself blinking back tears. His own father the caliph wouldn't have embraced him the way this British king had. In Baghdad he was a fourth son, an inconvenient extra, the laughingstock of the paper-sellers' quarter. But these men had seen him at his absolute worst, humiliated, rejected, wallowing in sin, and here they were waiting for him. They didn't care what was written on him. They saw the parchment beneath the letters.

After that Palomides left off both his hunting and his wooing for a while. For the first time he began to take an interest in Camelot's scraggly, threadbare gardens, and he shared with the groundskeepers some of the advanced irrigation practices of the royal gardens in Baghdad. He gave a public demonstration of his astrolabe, which, granted, only Nimue attended, but she gave him her warmest attention. When a dome was wanted for a new chapel he showed the architect how to calculate its proportions by means of the novel mathematical discipline of *al-gebra*, fresh from the House of Wisdom.

He even went back to writing his book, *The Pleasant Wanderings of a Curious Traveler*. He who had felt so utterly worthless began to wonder if he might not have something to give after all.

But even as he embraced Camelot, it came apart in his arms.

Two years after the quest for the Holy Grail, Lancelot was surprised with Queen Guinevere in her chamber. The Table broke in half, and the two halves fought each other. Palomides didn't know which way to turn, but in the end he went to Benwick with Lancelot, who had always been kind to him. And if Lancelot was an adulterer—he denied it, but even if he was—well, Palomides was in love with a married woman, too, a woman who was in fact herself an adulteress. And God knew he would've given her a good adultering himself if he'd had half a chance.

But it was during the siege of Benwick that the news reached him: King Mark of Cornwall had finally run out of patience and killed Sir Tristram with a poisoned lance. Isolde the Beautiful had thrown herself on Tristram's body and died of sorrow. They were dead, their story was finally over, and Sir Palomides's long dream of love was over too.

When they told him the news Palomides cried like a child. Not for himself—he'd shed enough tears for himself—but for Isolde. Poor Isolde. What an ass he'd been. For all his passion he'd never even really come to know her, not even a little bit. All he'd cared about was himself. He'd never imagined what it might be like to be her, a woman married to a man she didn't love, shackled by love to a man not her husband, stalked and mooned over by a weird foreign knight. She had loved perhaps unwisely but with great power and constancy. What an unspeakable waste of life and love and beauty. He kept to his room, unable to face another human being.

Then one morning the castle woke to find Arthur and his host gone, leaving behind only smoldering fires and garbage pits and empty, flapping tents. Mordred had seized the throne of Britain, and Arthur and his host had taken ship back across the Channel to reclaim it. Gawain had drowned at the landing, trying to take the beach, though he'd already been half-dead from the beating Lancelot gave him in a duel. Lancelot rallied his men and followed after to help. Even then he still considered Arthur his liege lord.

But they arrived to find that the last battle had already been fought.

Corpses lay everywhere in drifts. Some had already started to bloat and inflate inside their armor. Broken standards and pole arms and the stiff, upturned legs of dead horses like turned-over tables stuck out from among the heaps of bodies. It was early spring and the smell was of shit and sun-spoiled blood.

What a truly comprehensive calamity. There was nobody left even to bury the bodies.

Plenty of people had turned out to loot them, though. They kept their distance from Palomides, but most of the intact weaponry was already gone, and the boots, and the belts. The knights' gilded spurs were a popular item. They'd started to pull off gauntlets and snip off fingers for the rings. A separate contingent was busy butchering and roasting the horseflesh.

Palomides didn't linger. Lancelot would be on the move soon, to sweep the surrounding area for any of Mordred's surviving forces. He would go with him.

But as he walked back to camp he wondered what he would do after that. He reviewed the accomplishments of his recent past: he'd discarded his homeland and his family on a whim in favor of a cold and primitive island; he'd wasted years pining for a married woman who died for love of someone else; he'd hunted a beast he was fated never to catch; betrayed the religion of his birth; sought a Grail he could never find; and finally been besieged by his own liege lord, who was then promptly killed by his incestuous bastard son.

It was almost enough to make him question the soundness of his judgment.

But Palomides the palimpsest didn't want to be scraped clean and rewritten again. He'd already been scraped too many times. Any more and he feared the parchment would tear beneath the pen.

He stopped at the edge of the woods, a straggling line of beech and sycamore, and stood there for a long time as the sun descended and the thin shadows of the bare trees shifted, and behind him the ravens pecked and screamed and fought over the flesh of his dead brothers.

After a while he lay down on his back on the cold spring grass. His adopted home lay in ruins, and how could he ever hope to find the strength to rebuild it, or find another one, or face his old home again? All he wanted, he thought, as he stared up at the deepening sky, was a cause that was not lost. Was that too much? But all causes were lost sooner or later. The ones he picked were just un- usually expeditious about it.

The problem with this clever insight was that it brought with it a terrible paralysis. He couldn't move, because there was no longer any reason to move. There was no golden lancer to point his way. *The Pleasant Wanderings of a Curious Traveler* would simply stop here, midsentence. Had fortune any greater fool than Sir Palo- mides the Saracen? Had anyone ever sought so zealously and found so little? When would he gain the wisdom to finally give up? He thought of the Baghdad he would never see again, of the silver birds on the silver tree, and the bobbing bridge of boats over the great brown Tigris. Ziyad's lovely pen boxes. Burning naphtha flares in the darkness. He thought of the sweet melons packed in snow that he ate as a child. Where had they come from? Not Brit- ain. Some even colder and more distant land.

Eventually he must have dozed off because something woke

him, something soft and feathery brushing his face. It was a tongue. A snake's tongue. He opened his eyes to find two huge yellow lidless eyes staring down at him.

It was Glatisant. She was close enough that he could smell her warm mineral breath. She didn't startle when he raised a hand and stroked her trembling side, where the tawny lion fur and the spotted leopard fur met and became one. He'd never touched her before. She was warm and very, very soft.

The Questing Beast gazed down at him for a moment more, her eyes lamps lit with some secret knowledge, as if to say: *not yet.*

Then she bounded away, her inner hounds barking and baying, and Sir Palomides watched her vanish into the trees. He lay there a minute longer. Then, slowly, stiffly, the weary traveler got to his feet and followed.

Fourteen

THE WELL OF INK

The next morning the knights reached the coast. They followed it south and west, past the scars of old Roman lead mines, into Cornwall.

Cornwall had always held itself proudly apart from the rest of Britain, and it felt like a different world. It was one of the Unconquered Lands that had never fallen to the Romans, or to anyone before King Uther. It was Igraine's land, and therefore Arthur's. (Also King Mark's. Palomides hated Cornwall, as he did not forbear to remark.) The constant wind bent the trees over like match flames. The coastline was humped up in huge salt-scoured hilly heads furred over with wiry scratchy, gorse that gave way to sudden dizzying drops and secret coves.

"We should've brought Sir Constantine," Collum said.

"Just as well we didn't," Bedivere said. "He's not much more Cornish than you are. His grandfather was a wealthy lord from Northgalis, who Uther installed to beat the Cornish into submission. You can imagine how much they love him."

The ocean here seemed to be made of different stuff than the dull gray water around Mull. Cornish seawater was a luminous turquoise liquid that rolled itself out on the strand in clear lustrous sheets, one after another. They camped on a beach made of round gray stones, each one circled by a white band like a painted egg, and Palomides stripped down and charged into the waves even though the water was cold beyond belief.

The rest of them followed, all except the Green Knight, and Dinadan, who never took off his clothes, even at night. He bathed in private. The others gave him a hard time about it but Dinadan, who would joke about just about anything else, didn't find it funny.

That night Collum lay awake listening to the sea. Each wave tossed a load of stripy pebbles onto the beach with a clatter then pulled them back down again, hissing like it was sucking its teeth. He felt the dark enchantments of night going to work on him again, the grasping coils of acedia embracing him. Why were they even bothering? A fool's errand to retrieve one more lost soul would change nothing. The great chain of succession had snapped, its golden links were scattered in the grass. The age of Arthur was over, there was no reviving it.

But the next morning he kept going.

As they rode they talked about Bedivere's story, about Arthur and Avalon. It should have inspired them but instead it just made them irritable and restless. Was he alive or not? Was he coming back or not? How long would it take for Avalon's magical surgeons to heal a fatal head wound? There was no way to know, and at the same time it was hard to think about anything else. Hope was all well and good but when you only had a little of it, a tiny fragment, it nagged at you like a splinter.

Collum proposed a naval expedition to Avalon, wherever it was. They could invade it, claim it for Britain, and liberate Arthur.

"He must heal first," Bedivere said. "Give him time."

"Why would he come back at all?" said Scipio. "When the party barge comes to take me to Avalon, believe me, that'll be a one-way trip."

Now that he was on his feet again Sir Scipio was a martinet, neatly shaven and crisply turned out. He could've been on military parade. It made a curious contrast with his barbaric tattoos. He also seemed to enjoy needling people.

"He'll come back because we need him," Bedivere said. "Britain needs him."

"Personally I tend to avoid places where I've had my head caved in."

"That's because you're not Arthur."

But before he could push it any further they reached the top of a headland, where two guards with spears stood in the road, their broad-brimmed kettle hats flashing in the seaside sun.

"Good morning!" The soldier hailed them with a big smile. "Got any wax?"

Bedivere stared at him stonily.

"You want to know if I have any wax?"

"We're collecting tariffs. Got any?"

Somewhere a cow was mooing repetitively.

"No wax. Any wool then? Cloth of any kind?" The other guard was shorter, with a broad chest and a big stubbly cleft chin. "What else? Tin, cheese, lard, hides—?"

"Move," Bedivere said.

"We're traveling on royal business," Dinadan said.

"Got you. We'll waive the tariffs then." The first soldier's cheery manner was undimmed. "You'd better take this at least."

He held up what looked like a coin-sized scrap of porcelain.

"What the hell is that?"

"It's a chit. You take it down to the house"—he pointed down the hill—"and they'll give you a pass."

Bedivere put his hand on his sword. The soldier still didn't move.

"You're in Cornwall now, friend. Camelot still owes us a duchess, and now that the king is dead I don't believe you have any business here at all, royal or otherwise. I'll let you pass, because you have an escort." Collum supposed he meant the Green Knight—but how could he see it? "But do yourself a favor and take this down to the house"—he held out the chit—"or you'll be eating shit from here all the way to Castle an Dinas."

"I'll go," Collum said. If shit was going to be eaten then he was going to be the one to eat it.

There wasn't much of a path down the hill. It was fenced into small pastures, and he had to clamber over one stone stile after another. He stepped in cow poo. One field had an old standing stone in the middle, an enigmatic obelisk with an unreadable word chiseled on it, which three cows were taking turns lustily scratching their rumps on.

There were stones like it all over Britain, even on Mull. Only a few fields over from Dubh Hall was a fine old stone circle, nine toothy slabs in a perfect ring in the middle of a muddy sheep meadow, plus a couple of odd extras off to one side. Not even the druids knew what they meant, before the Romans rounded the druids up and slaughtered them. They were that old. But even Collum, zealous Christian though he was, could feel that they meant something. They were a very different proposition from Christianity, which promised you everything, peace and happiness everlasting, but in the next world, a world no one living had ever seen, and only if you kept to His rules in this world, and His rules were a pain in the ass.

But the stones made no promises, so they couldn't break any. They didn't speak, and therefore they couldn't lie. They asked for nothing. They just were.

It was hard to say what God made of it all, the stones and the fairies and the pagan gods and all the rest of it. The more he saw of it the more the world seemed to Collum to be possessed of two incompatible, irreconcilable natures, the divine and the magical. It was a contested world, grasped at and fought over. No wonder it was such a mess. Collum sometimes wished God and the old gods would just have it out and settle things once and for all, one way or the other.

At the bottom of the hill Collum crossed a road to a large stone barn with a turf roof, gently swaybacked like the spine of a whale. An affable soldier relieved Collum of his chit and sent him inside.

The barn looked somehow larger on the inside, and instead of hay and stables it contained a vast sprawling garden, long beds planted with peas and runner beans and squash and pumpkins and artichokes. He searched in vain among poppies and marigolds and honeysuckle for someone to collect his travel pass from. There were even a couple of palm trees. (Were they the source of Dubh Hall's precious coco-nut?) Finally he stumbled on a tiny old man, magnificently dressed in green velvet embroidered with silver birds, sunning himself on the stone rim of a well.

Nearby was a little table covered with parchments weighted down by stones. When he saw Collum, he began busily turning the crank to bring up the bucket of the well. It came up full of a trembling glossy black liquid.

"Ink." The old man smiled, and his teeth were a glossy jet black, too, as if he'd been drinking the stuff. "Got your chit?"

With waning patience Collum explained that he'd given the chit to the soldier outside, that's how he got in here in the first place. The tiny old man seemed irritated by this and ordered him to go back and get it. A gust blew a few of the parchments off the table; the garden downwind was covered with them.

But somehow Collum must've gotten turned around because he couldn't find the door again—it was like the garden had grown even bigger while he'd talked to the old man—and when he finally did find it the guard wasn't there anymore. By now it felt like hours since he'd left the others atop the headland. They had a knight to find! And a king to crown! He still had cow poo on his boot. He spotted a small porcelain pot with rosemary growing in it and in a frenzy of frustration he stamped on it—it was tougher than it looked—until it smashed into little chit-size pieces. Feeling both clever and ashamed he took one and went to find the well-dressed old man.

But now Collum couldn't find him either! He ran out of patience and stormed out of the stone barn. He got it now; it was all a Cornish practical joke. He was being made a fool of. Well, he always had been the last one to get a joke. In a black mood, he struggled back up through the fields and over the stiles and through the standing-stone paddock till finally, finally, after what felt like weeks, he crested the green dome of the hill again.

But there was nobody there. They were all gone, knights and soldiers and horses alike.

Well, damn it all to hell and back.

They must've decided he wasn't worth the wait. Sir Collum closed his eyes and let himself savor just a drop of the miserable balm of self-pity. One wrong step and out he stumbled, out of the golden circle. How slippery were the slopes of Mount Olympus.

He blundered back down the hill, vaguely thinking that if he could somehow lay his hands on a horse he might still be able to catch them. Darkness was falling and a cold, briny Cornish drizzle closed in. He saw a lighted window in the distance, way up a hillside, and he clambered grimly toward it, up a gully with a stream running down it, icing his feet in the freezing water, trying not to turn an ankle on the stones rolling under his boots.

The few patrons inside went quiet when Collum walked into the tavern. Probably they didn't get a lot of northern knights staggering onto the premises dripping wet in full armor. Well, feast your eyes, ladies and gentlemen. A great feeling of heaviness descended on him.

There was something sharp digging into his palm: after all that he realized he was still gripping the useless porcelain chit in his fist, the counterfeit one he'd made in the garden.

He set it down on the dark oak tabletop in front of him. A barmaid passed by and swept up the chit and replaced it with a silver cup full of a trembling dark liquid.

It wasn't wine, it was ink. He looked up, and it was the strangest thing: the barmaid had short auburn hair. She looked just like that woman he'd met in the inn on the way to Camelot.

"Welcome to the Otherworld," she said.

THE INN'S ROOF SPLIT open overhead and its walls fell outward in all four directions like a box unfolding, revealing a vast blue sky striped like a trout with golden-pink sunset clouds. Collum threw his arms over his head.

"God's knees!" he shouted. "And toes and bollocks! What in God's Hell is this?"

"The Otherworld," the barmaid said pleasantly. "As I think I said. God's Hell is the next world over."

"Send me back! Now!"

"No."

"Please! I can't be here!"

The woman wasn't a barmaid anymore. She now wore a long emerald silk dress trimmed in gold, fit for a queen, and a gold circlet on her head.

Collum looked around wildly for an exit, but what was left of the tavern was now floating on water. He was on a peaceful river. The collapsed walls were floating away on its glassy surface, and the floor had become a raft. Now that he looked at it the whole place had been as thin and unconvincing as a stage set. The other customers were just painted silhouettes. It was never real at all. How could he not have noticed?

"Please!" He put his hands together imploringly. "It's not too late!"

"Oh, but it is. It has been for quite some time."

Collum turned around and kept turning, trying and failing to get his bearings. When had he stumbled, all unknowing, across the invisible border? Beyond the banks of the river, smooth plains stretched out in all directions. A distant tower loomed. The rust-colored light of a setting fairy sun was smeared out across more rivers, striping the land as far as the horizon.

He'd always pictured the Otherworld as something more in the way of a misty forest, or for that matter a glass castle. It was the flattest place he'd ever seen.

You're a knight of Britain, he thought, show some spine.

"I don't think we were ever properly introduced," he said. "I'm Sir Collum of the Out Isles."

"Sir Collum is it now? Well, congratulations. My name is Morgan. People call me le Fay."

He hung on to his composure, but inside him the world fell apart all over again. He'd gone through the ice and sunk deep in the cold, cold water, and now the sea monsters had arrived to devour him.

"I am honored to meet you," he said weakly. He sketched an unsteady bow. "My lady."

"I'm not your lady, I'm a queen. You may call me 'Your Majesty.'"

"Beg pardon," he said meekly. "Your Majesty. Why am I here?"

"As I understand it, you're looking for a knight of the Round Table."

"I—you mean the knight we're looking for is here? In the Otherworld?"

"Sadly, yes."

A swarm of bees came humming down out of the sky and circled the raft. I've fallen into the Otherworld, Collum thought, but I'm still on the quest. All is not lost, or not yet. I just have to keep going.

"Where is he?"

"Well, I'm not just going to tell you, you have to look for him. Isn't that how you knights play your game?"

"It's not a game!"

"People always say that, right up until they lose." Morgan le Fay sounded even less charmed by him than she had been at the inn. "As much as I revel in your wit and wisdom, Sir Collum, I'm wanted elsewhere. Just stay on the raft, if you know what's good for you."

The bees circled Morgan three times, and on the third circuit she vanished.

He wasn't sure if he was better off with or without her, but at least now he didn't have to make conversation. He could concentrate on finding the knight—Bors, Aglovale, Tor, whoever it turned out to be—and bringing him back home. If Morgan expected Collum to scamper around the Otherworld looking for him like a prize in a scavenger hunt, well, he wasn't too proud to do it.

A mild current took hold of the raft, swirling and spinning it downstream. Collum caught snatches of music in the far distance, discordant chromatic scribblings. What he had thought was a distant tower suddenly moved and scratched itself thoughtfully, and he realized it was actually an enormous man, fifty feet tall at least. A giant. He wasn't stomping around smashing things like giants were supposed to do. Collum wondered if it was true what Father Conall said, that the race of giants had been fathered long ago by angels who lay with human women. He didn't look especially angelic.

The river gathered strength and purpose, pushing him along at a steady clip. Good. The faster the better. Carefully he lowered himself onto the bench, the last remnant of the inn, staying well away from the edges. Deep rivers were the implacable enemy of armored knights.

A road ran along beside it, and soon Collum was overtaking a file of soldiers in dusty mail marching in two clanking, jingling columns. Their sandals slapped the ground loosely, and their long pikes pointed every which way. One soldier bore a battered battle standard with a weary eagle on top.

"Good evening!" Collum called.

"Is it?" The man at the head of the file looked round at him from under a studded silver helmet with a nose guard. He squinted—he had a twitchy eye. "Can't tell if it's morning or evening in this damned place. Servius Oppius, Optio, First Cohort, Twentieth Valeria Victrix legion."

"You're—are you soldiers of Rome?"

"Where else?"

Collum couldn't believe he was seeing them with his own eyes. These were the great ones, the vanished fathers, who'd brought the fire of civilization to Britain and then left it to gutter out again. But civilization hadn't saved them from the Otherworld. They must've wandered into it like him and been lost ever since.

"The Picts are on the move," the officer said. "They'll be over the Wall by now. We have to get word to Eboracum. We started out from Aesica this morning and we've been marching in circles ever since, years it feels like! Can you point me the way to Epiacum?"

"I'm sorry, I don't know where that is."

"Cocksucking Hades. They must think we're a lost legion by now."

For them it's still the old days, Collum thought. They must still think the empire will go on forever. Just like he'd thought Arthur's would, till a few days ago.

"That medal round your neck." The officer fixed his twitchy eye on it. "Where'd you get it?"

"What, this?" Collum put a hand on it protectively. "Why? What is it?"

"You can't wear that. Against regulations. Give it here."

"I don't think so."

The raft was moving faster than the soldiers could march. He was already leaving them behind.

"Look, just get word to the Dux!" The Roman had to shout to be heard across the widening gap. "First Cohort, Twentieth Valeria Victrix! Tell him we're not lost!"

Collum watched the soldiers till they disappeared. There was nothing he could do, and he had his own quest to finish. They would have to make their own way. See how they liked being abandoned for a change.

The sun still hovered at the horizon like it was nailed to the sky, a perfect semicircle, either half set or half risen. No wonder the Roman couldn't tell what time it was, it must be always in between here, neither day nor night. Collum knelt on the raft and prayed, though it was hard to believe God could hear him all the way from the Otherworld. His prayers were greeted with an even more resounding silence than usual.

A soft wind blew, feathering the surface of the water and bringing with it a flight of dead leaves. The river wound into a deep forest of oaks, black branches that were so low in places he had to duck.

A big knight on a black horse hove into view, trotting smartly along the bank on a narrow path, his shield showing a turning mill and two scarlet bands. Searching brown eyes set in pale crow's-feet peered out through his open visor. The knight rode with his bare sword in his hand, and his helmet had the stub of what must once have been a purple plume on it, ripped off near the base.

"Ho there!" he shouted heartily. "What news, Sir-on-the-Raft?"

"Ho there! My name is Sir Collum! I seek a knight of the Round Table!"

"You have found one, Sir Collum! But I mean what news of the Grail, sir? I am Sir Ganadal of the Cold Hills, and I have sought it these many months now."

Collum knew the name. From Bryneich, respectable knight. Couple of tournament wins, and he'd killed a griffin once. But Collum didn't think this could be the knight they were looking for. He'd disappeared years ago, on the Grail Quest.

"I have good news, Sir Ganadal!" Collum called. "The Grail has been found!"

Like the centurion, the knight seemed not to really hear him.

"I have seen strange things. Silver dragons that scored white lines across the sky. Steel cages with men inside, that moved of themselves. In Gorre I saw a man kill a damsel, swapped her head right off and threw it in a fountain. I slew him in turn, but then my sword froze to my palm, and now I cannot put it down! I sleep with it in my hand! Do you know the meaning?"

Collum shook his head.

"But listen to me, the Grail was found! The quest is done!"

"What?"

"They found the Grail! Bors and Galahad and Percival!"

"Where?!"

"Corbenic."

"Well, where the hell is that?!" Sir Ganadal said indignantly. He urged his mount to a trot to keep up with Collum.

"It's an island off Listenois. I think. But the quest is over!"

"But I've searched for years! Buried my squire by the roadside!" Sir Ganadal kept his eyes carefully on the path, which was narrow and ran perilously close to the river's edge. "Was it all for nothing?"

"I'm sure not, Sir Ganadal! It's all part of God's plan!"

He didn't know what else to say. He was overtaking him, too, like the Roman soldiers.

"Hast seen the knight of Three Scepters?" Sir Ganadal called. "Hold a little, I would speak with you!"

"I can't, I'm sorry! But who is the knight of Three Scepters?"

"Please, you must lead me out of this place! Help me find Camelot again!" Despair cracked Sir Ganadal's voice, and he let out a sob. "It's not a quest, it's a massacre! God is tearing us to pieces! Tell the king! God in Heaven, I never should have come!"

But the water was quickening, rustling and muttering and growing little standing waves, stealing Collum away faster and faster.

"I'm sorry! I wish you well! God will provide!"

"Wait, damn your eyes! Wait! Whoa!"

Ganadal's mount missed its footing on the path and stumbled. Its balance lost, it made a furious leap out over the water in a hopeless attempt to reach the far side, then splashed down thunderously into the river.

"Sir Ganadal! Ganadal!"

The horse slewed over on its side, legs working furiously, churning up foam, dumping Sir Ganadal into the water in his armor, heavy and ungainly as a statue. He made no sound as the black water swallowed him. The last Collum saw of him was his cursed sword, still stuck in his hand, till even that disappeared.

The current bore Collum around a bend, drawing a veil over whatever happened next. He sat down on the raft again and shivered and hugged his knees, blinking away tears.

"Damn it," he said. "God damn this place."

He was cold. His mouth felt gummy and dry, and the dark water looked inviting, but he didn't drink it. Where did your soul go if you died here? He hoped Ganadal would have some reward for his years of wandering. Something must've gone wrong on the Grail Quest. There must have been a price to pay, a high one, something that wasn't part of the stories the smith told him. But what?

Not that this current quest was going very well either. A deep clinging mist closed in, hiding the overripe, low-hanging sun and beading on his cold armor. He heard the baying of hounds, and the winding of a distant horn:

Rooooooooooo! Barooo barooooooooooooo!

He wondered if the others were here too, somewhere, or if he was the only one stupid enough to get trapped in the Otherworld. Maybe the Otherworld had stalked them like a lion and picked off the weakest of the herd. The river flowed through an orchard, trees with huge, grotesquely swollen buds the size of ducks, and into a fairy city.

The buildings were packed in tight and stretched to enormous heights, story after story, impossible steeples, crazily precarious, a city reflected in a convex mirror. The river was running along an aqueduct now, raised high above the streets. Gray ocean filled them, swirling around the bases of the towers, so far below it looked like it was moving in slow motion, and Collum could look down and see drowned squares and avenues and houses. He smelled the tang of ocean fog. Something told him he would have to find a way off this raft soon.

The distant sound of men's shouts and the unmistakable off-key clanking of steel on steel were so familiar in this strange place that Collum's head whipped around like a dog hearing its master's voice. There—on a terrace not a quarter mile away three knights were fighting, orange sun touching dull steel plates and bright blades.

Bedivere, Scipio, and Dinadan. No sign of Palomides.

They faced three fairy knights. They were the first fairies Collum had ever seen, assuming Morgan le Fay still counted as fully human, and they were stranger than he expected. Bedivere's opponent looked like a small, wiry woman, but in place of her hair a cloud of dense black smoke hung around her head. Scipio's had a frog's head, goat's legs, and a fluffy bunny tail. Dinadan's seemed to be made out of sheaves of wheat. All three wore deep-green armor. Their weapons were curious, oddly curved and too thin. The frogman's was red and translucent, as if it were made from cut ruby, and the wheat fairy's flickered in and out of visibility when struck.

Alarums and Excursions, Volume Seventy-Seven, Appendix Ex Ex Eye, in which odds are evened and quarter is given, but no halves or thirds.

It was Morgan le Fay's voice, calm and neutral. It seemed to come from everywhere at once, but she herself was nowhere to be seen. The words flirted with sense but didn't quite make it, and Collum ignored them, staring longingly at the mêlée. A fight, that's what he needed. Enough of this damned drifting.

There was something utterly honest about a person in a fight. You could lie with words, but swords, like angels, could only speak the truth. In the face of death you could only be who you were. Bedivere was a dancer. Big as he was, he was light on his feet, quick and deft. He fought not with a sword but with a massive war hammer with a spike on the back that looked too heavy to lift, let alone swing and twirl the way he was doing. Whereas Dinadan was water, a breaking wave, bending and curving, always moving and somehow never where his opponent's blade was. There was nothing funny about him now. His style was like nothing Collum had ever seen—no discrete moves or stances at all, it all flowed together. Now that he'd seen fairy weapons, Collum realized that Dinadan's must be one too.

Eventide finds spriggan-class entities Pharon, Odd Franklin, and Rainy Minster fully imbricated—

Scipio's fighting was just anger, pure ungovernable rage. Everything Collum had seen of him was neat and precise to the point of fussiness, but here was the tattooed wild man—he was getting an idea of why Bedivere wasn't sure whether to rescue him or not. His blade had an old-fashioned design, with no cross guard and an eagle pommel, and he barely even cut with it, just thrust and chopped and punched and grappled like a roughneck in a street fight. Collum watched him force his opponent, the frog-woman, back until he hopped over a railing into empty air, spreading a pair of gray-feathered kestrel wings. With total disregard for life and limb, Scipio leapt after him and bear-hugged him, and the two spiraled down together out of sight, still struggling, down into the drowned city.

"Courage, my friends!" Collum shouted.

Twilight interchange, cross-radial loss limits, pedin i phith in aníron, a nin ú-cheniog—

Enough. Collum backed up, eyeballed the distance from raft to bank, came to no clear conclusion, and ran and leapt anyway. He hung for an instant at full extension over the water, perfectly horizontal—then he smashed down into it, the tips of his middle fingers a foot short of the side.

Collum knew how to swim, but you couldn't swim in armor. He fell smoothly down through the cool water, windmilling his arms, through green glass into emerald and then deep nighttime forest-green darkness. The river was deeper than he thought. Now what? How incredibly stupid, to think of drowning in an aqueduct. Like Sir Ganadal. Or Sir Gawain, the Lion of Orkney, drowned in his armor in a foot of seawater.

Before he leapt he'd taken note of a stone staircase leading up the side of the aqueduct. No problem! He would simply walk to it across the bottom. But the current was unexpectedly strong, and the moment he raised one foot the force of it took him sideways, dragging him away downstream like a leaf in a high wind.

His lungs were starting to strain. It all seemed very unreal. This couldn't be how he died. Something struck his drifting feet and he instinctively grabbed on to it: an iron ring bolted to a square stone in the aqueduct floor. What if he pulled it out, like the giant plug of a giant bathtub? It seemed no crazier than anything else in this place. He set his feet on either side of the stone, straightened his back and heaved. Nothing.

Hm. There must be some fairy-logic trick to this. He twisted and jerked the ring and then pulled again. Was it wishful thinking or did the stone shift ever so slightly?

But it was too late, he needed air now, right now, his chest was filling up with stacks of hot, heavy rocks, one by one. He heaved on the ring again and something stirred inside him. Some weird strength struggled to break free, wanted to be unleashed, like a chick scratching at the inner surface of an egg. A mass of voices was rumbling somewhere, deep voices singing to him in a language he couldn't recognize. Daring him to answer. A strange glow lit the jade blackness around him, and suddenly he could see the ancient floor of the aqueduct littered with rubble and sunken detritus and shining fish hanging puzzled in midair all around him.

Which was all very well, but the fucking stone still wouldn't move! It was no good, his lungs were bursting, ripping out of his chest! He dropped the ring and leapt and scrabbled at the water, trying to thrash his way back to the surface but—

An enormous force tore him upward through the water and into the air. In another moment he was high over the aqueduct, in the cold air, coughing and vomiting river water and whatever he'd eaten for breakfast a hundred years ago. Floods of water drained out of his armor.

It was over. He had drowned, and God had fished his sodden soul out of the drink.

So that was how it all ended. Well short of a satisfying conclusion by any standards, but he'd tried his best. Tears of sadness and gratitude mingled with the canal water. He twisted around, trying to get a look at whatever angel had hold of him.

He stared into an enormous brown eye. It blinked. It wasn't an angel, it was the giant. He'd dragged Collum out of the water by the scruff of his neck like a drowning kitten. He wasn't misshapen the way Collum expected a giant to be; in fact he was on the handsome side, with a long nose and heavy-lidded eyes. His breath had a not unpleasant yeasty bread smell.

He hoped that after all that, the giant wasn't going to eat him. But he just placed Collum on the ground, where he rolled over on his back, still panting and coughing.

"Thank you." It came out as a croak. He tried again louder. "Thank you!"

But the giant was already striding away through the drowned city, running his hand along the edge of the aqueduct like it was a banister, with an aura of great dignity and loneliness, giving no sign of having heard.

Collum lay there in a sodden alleyway like a hank of washed-up seaweed. He'd come so close to dying. He could no longer hear the noise of the fight, or Morgan's voice in his head either, or anything but the faint sloshing of water through the streets of the empty fairy metropolis. He'd lost any sense of where the others were. Groaning, he got to one knee and felt for his sword.

Shit. He must've dropped it in the canal. The sword his step-father gave him, with its two notches and its little S for Something. No retrieving it now. He felt the joy of his miraculous delivery fading, and he sank back down. He was cold and wet and lost and spent. It hadn't been much of a sword, but at that moment it felt like he'd lost something precious and irreplaceable.

This is how it happened, he realized. This is how you became one of the Otherworld's lost souls, like the Romans and Sir Ganadal. Now he would wander for untold centuries, a cautionary tale, and if he ever finally blundered his way out again it would be a thousand years later and everyone he knew would be dead and gone, and the world transformed beyond recognition.

No. Not yet. He couldn't believe that was his fate. He forced himself to his feet and stumbled down the alley to where it opened onto a vast plaza, a quarter mile on a side at least. Across it on the far side was the strangest thing Collum had ever seen: a castle made entirely of glass. You could see right through it.

Fifteen

THE GLASS CASTLE

He wasn't sure if his luck had turned or if it had finally run out, but either way this was the end. Had to be. The castle loomed over the square, the cold glass heart of the Otherworld, lit from within by hearth fires and torches like will-o'-the-wisps frozen in ice. A dozen delicate branching towers rose toward the fairy sky like a forest of icicles. A thin skim of cold seawater washed through the plaza in the twilight. Collum slogged doggedly toward the open gate.

The mist had cleared enough to show that the sun still hadn't moved, but a flotilla of six or seven small, pale moons had swum into the sky to join it.

Even Arthur and his picked men hadn't been able to take the glass castle by force, but now the drawbridge was down and the glass portcullis was up, and Collum walked right in. The closest he came to mortal danger was when he nearly lost his footing—the glass floor was extremely slippery. Not very practical as a building material. Looking down at his feet was like standing in midair, or on a clear frozen lake. He thought of his mother, and where they found her.

Through a wall he could see ghostly figures moving in the depths of the castle, and he crossed a glass courtyard toward them. It was a Great Hall, just like Camelot's, and the other knights had somehow gotten there ahead of him—Bedivere, Dinadan, and Scipio, who had apparently survived his heroic plunge, plus Palomides, who had reappeared from whatever detour he'd taken. They were sitting at a long table crowded with glass goblets and pitchers and bowls and spoons and platters of pork and venison and fritters and jellies, laughing and talking uproariously like they were home at Camelot in the old days.

Across from them sat four fairy knights: the three he'd seen before and a fourth, presumably to make up the numbers, who appeared strangely blurred—their outlines and features were hard to make out, more so the longer you stared at them. Dark puffs and whorls floated up from the head of the fairy with smoke for hair. They sat silent and motionless, no expressions on their faces, the ones that had them—the wheat fairy had no eyes or mouth at all.

At least it was warm in the hall. There were fires in the fireplaces— you could see gray smoke going up the glass chimney; Collum wondered where people went to the bathroom. At the head of the table Morgan le Fay was laughing at some apparently hilarious story Scipio had just finished telling.

"Sir Collum!" she called. "You made it!"

"Collum!" the other knights chorused.

"You look terrible," Morgan said. "What happened, did you fall in?"

"I did." What else could he say? "Your Majesty."

More hilarity. He summoned a waterlogged smile. Even Bedivere was laughing, a sight almost as weird as a glass castle. They seemed to be under some kind of enchantment. Well, at least they were enjoying themselves. In a corner a fairy musician was silently plucking at an oak branch as if it were a musical instrument.

At the far end of the room a gilded throne stood on a dais with a stupendous tapestry behind it, a great silver thistle on a green background. The man on the throne had a broad red face, a salt-and-pepper beard, and a faraway stare. He wore armor that had been polished mirror bright and a golden crown that was slightly askew.

"Is that him?" Collum said quietly. "Is that—is that who we came for?"

Dinadan nodded, his mouth full.

"Sir Kay. The one man of the Round Table nobody missed."

Collum walked over. He looked older than Collum had imagined.

"Do I have the honor of addressing Sir Kay?"

The red-faced knight turned his head slowly, hesitantly, as if he were afraid of what he might see.

"Not I," he said quietly. "You are Kay."

"He's even less funny than he used to be," Dinadan said. "Kay, he's not you, he's Sir Collum."

"Of the Out Isles!" Benedict and Palomides said it together, then laughed hysterically.

"No," Sir Kay whispered. "It is you."

He closed his eyes.

"I accuse you."

There was a scabbed-over cut on his cheek. His skin was sallow under the alcoholic flush. This didn't feel like much of a prize, it felt like another dead end. And a poor trade for the life of Villiars the Valiant. By all accounts Kay was only ever on the Table because he was King Arthur's foster brother. Had they really come all this way for next to nothing? Maybe Kay knew something about Arthur, remembered something from their childhood together, a clue to the way forward . . .

But Collum didn't think so. There was nothing left behind those lost, empty eyes. Collum couldn't help feeling sad for him. In the stories Kay was a sour man, touchy and sarcastic, who never resigned himself to serving and honoring the boy he'd once lorded it over. He must've led a miserable life.

"The fairies found him wandering the woods after the battle. They're attracted to mad things." Morgan had come up behind him. "A word with you, Sir Collum, if you would."

She led him away from the table and the throne, toward the far end of the hall.

"It's just the two of us, I'm afraid. Your friends are drunk as lords. It's not the wine, it's the food—fairy food drives men off their heads. This will all be like a dream to them later."

"You'd think they would've known better. It's in all the stories, you never eat the food in the Otherworld."

"Well, that's what they get for not reading the stories." Morgan seemed to be trying out a more affable tone with him. "The fairies told me you'd fall in, by the way. They've seen everything for the next ten thousand years, or so they claim. I think that's why they don't seem to care about anything very much, for them it's all happened already. I sent Ysbaddaden to pull you out."

"Thank you for that. If the fairies can see the future, do they know when Arthur's coming back?"

"Oh, that." She rolled her eyes like it was a tiresome topic that he wouldn't shut up about. "Probably. But you'll never get it out of them."

Collum couldn't quite make out who he was dealing with. Was it possible that Morgan le Fay wasn't really as bad as people said? The stories about her couldn't all be true; certainly the number of knights who claimed to have been seduced or ravished by her was so large as to be physically impossible. And some of what she got up to was just mischief, like when she sent Arthur a magic drinking horn that only a faithful wife could drink from without spilling. It wound up at King Mark's court, where it caused a lot of embarrassment. But there were worse stories than that. Supposedly it was Morgan and the queen of Northgalis who boiled Elaine of Corbenic alive for five years, before Lancelot rescued her. And it was Morgan who stole Excalibur's magic scabbard, the one that kept Arthur's wounds from bleeding.

But why not kill Arthur outright? It couldn't be that hard for an enchantress. Why tease him like that? He wondered if her feelings about Arthur were more complicated than she let on. Collum felt like a yokel playing at diplomacy with a wily aristocrat, probably because he was one.

"Your Majesty," he said, "everybody knows you're no friend to the Table. If you wanted to get rid of Sir Kay, you didn't need us, you could've sent him back to Camelot with the Green Knight. I think you used him to bring us here."

"But why would I do that?" she asked innocently.

"I have no idea."

"Goodness, you're terrible at this. What if I'm trying to mend fences?"

"What fences? Between what and what?"

"Human and Fairy. This world and that. Myself and Camelot. Don't you think it's time?"

Morgan sat down on a glass bench and patted the spot next to her. Collum stayed standing.

"If you want to do us a favor, you could start by letting us go."
He could feel himself lurching from one clumsy sally to another.

"Of course I'm going to let you go. You think I'd keep those
foodbags here forever?"

"And what will it cost us?"

She sighed deeply.

"I wish Palomides had stayed sober, he's the clever one. And I do
admire those shoulders of his. All I want from you, Sir Collum, is
your attention for a quarter hour. That's it. I want you to shut up
and listen while I tell you a story." She patted the spot beside her
again. "Every Briton should know this one, it's the story of your
hero, the great King Arthur."

This time he sat. He was alert for treachery, but how bad could a
story be? He'd know, if he were the clever one.

"I'm sure you know the bare facts already. I grew up at Tintagel,
in Cornwall. I was the middle one of three girls. My father, Duke
Gorlois, was always away fighting Uther's wars for him, but the
rest of us were very close.

"Tintagel is just a folly, a toy castle balanced on top of a big rock
sticking out into the ocean. The weather comes straight in off the
water—rain, snow, sleet, hail—and Tintagel takes it all right on
the chin. Probably not so different from Mull." She pursed her lips
as she sank into the trance of remembering. "We spent most of our
time huddled together in our furs in front of a smoky fire telling
stories, three girls and their mum. That was Queen Igraine, of
course, though she wasn't a queen yet, just a duchess. We were our
own little world.

"And it was an old world. We never heard a word of Latin, and
Jesus was just a fairy tale. We were the Dumnoniae, and we lived
by the old ways. My mother always wore one glove inside-out to

keep the piskies from leading her astray, and when we got sick as babies they would pass us nine times widdershins through a great rock with a hole in it.

"When I was six my parents were summoned to Camelot to celebrate Uther's having killed some more Saxons. But they came back in a hurry, with Uther right behind them. Uther had fallen in love with my mother, and he was coming to get her."

Collum knew that part. The great king Uther, seized by a passion that no earthly power could stay. He was given the likeness of Duke Gorlois, by Merlin's magic, so that he might lie with his beloved.

"We had two castles, and Mother kept us at Tintagel while my father went to the other one, Tarabel. We knew we were safe—it may be a folly but no army can take Tintagel. There's nowhere to land a boat, and only one narrow staircase in from the land. We could have held it ourselves, just the four of us. We had grain for a year and all the fish we could stomach.

"But it was already too late. We didn't realize our father was dead till our mother came into the nursery to explain that she and Uther were married now. Yes, I'm telling *that* story, Collum. Stop squirming.

"We never got to mourn our father. How could we? We were too busy celebrating! We were moving to Camelot, and Mother would be queen of Britain! That whole business about how Uther was the enemy, that was all a misunderstanding. We silly children had got it all wrong. Uther loved us. But there would be no more talk of piskies, no more talk in British at all, we would learn good Roman Latin. Our little world, the world of furs and smoke, the old magic and the old gods, that was gone. Dead and burned. We were dressed in pretty gowns and our lands were made over to those bastards Mark and Cador, and the man who murdered our father became our father.

"And shiny clean Jesus Christ, that slick little Jew on a stick, became our one and only God. We'd had a wealth of gods in Cornwall, there was a god under every rock, in every tree and pool, but at Camelot we were beggars. And He was a piss-poor God at that, who never dared to show Himself. Never owned up to all the trouble He caused. The coward.

"And how He hates the other gods! He has to be the only one—He wants to eat them all and then sit there, a fat little God in the middle of an empty world. When I prayed it was to the old gods. I prayed that the piskies would come and get me and take me home.

"Morgause was older than me, and she never forgave our mother. Never let her touch her again. Little Elaine just cried and cried, but she was only two, and our mother took her off by herself for a week, and when she came back she was changed, like a fairy-child, only I suppose it was the other way round, they took a fairy-child and gave us a mere human. Elaine was part of the new world. She loved Camelot. And why shouldn't she? It was big and warm and Uther gave her a doll's house with real ivory furniture. She forgot our father completely and forever.

"I forgot him too. I tried not to. He went slowly, scrabbling with his fingernails all the way down, but in the end I lost him. He went to pieces in my mind and I couldn't put him back together. I used to scream at my mother to say his name, but she never would. She never said it again. I know she thought she was protecting us, and you have to hand it to her, she really committed to the role. Never broke character.

"And she did protect us. We lived. But I had to pretend that my whole life till then had been a lie, and that this new lie was the truth, and that I loved it. Do you know what happens when you make a child pretend to love? Oh, they'll do it—you can make children do anything—but it has a cost, and the cost is that everything else becomes pretend. Nothing you feel or know or say or do feels real anymore.

"Except for hate. That you can keep. Do you think it was worth it, Sir Collum, for the sake of the great King Arthur?"

Mercifully she didn't wait for him to answer.

"Honestly, he was a sweet little thing. He was only with us for a month before they sent him away." For a heartbeat there was a little softness in her voice. Even Morgan le Fay couldn't quite bring herself to hate the baby Arthur that was. "We went to see him once afterward, out in the country, the three of us together, Elaine and Morgause and me. It took us ages but we found him. Little Arthur. I don't even know why we went, he was just a little boy.

"Merlin said they sent him away for his safety, but the truth was that Uther didn't want Arthur around. He wanted a real heir, a legitimate one. And I think he reminded Igraine of what Uther did to her. She loved Arthur, I'm sure she did, but he brought it all back. It was just easier to let him go.

"As for us, Morgause and me, when Uther realized he couldn't turn us he ignored us. Or he tried to. Once at dinner Morgause stabbed him in the hand. He's lucky she didn't cut a tendon. And then he paid attention when Morgause became a woman and started filling out. His eyes followed her everywhere after that. The pig.

"But that was the great King Uther for you. People talk about him like he was a giant, the great warrior-king, with his high Roman diction and white hair flying and sword streaming with gore, but he was just a big baby, that's all, one of those babies who has to put everything in his mouth. He was as bad as Jesus. He ate Britain, he ate my father, and he would've eaten us, too, but he couldn't choke us down.

"So he got rid of us instead—don't worry, I'm almost done. Morgause was fifteen when Uther sent her to King Lot in Orkney. She was supposed to be a sop to the Picts, though a fat lot of good that did. Elaine went to Garlot. I made myself so unpleasant that Uther couldn't marry me off at all—yes, it is a point of pride—so he sent me to a convent on the coast of Durnovar instead.

"He had no idea what a gift he was giving me. I was fourteen and half a lunatic, starving myself, cutting myself, and if anybody tried to help me I cut them too. But I wasn't the first half lunatic that was left on the sisters' doorstep. They were kind to me, and they were willing to take a few cuts for it.

"They couldn't change my mind about Jesus, though. I never stopped hating Him, and I wasn't the only one. All kinds of interesting people wound up at the convent, and it didn't take me long to sniff out a coven. They met at night in the buttery, led by the gardener, a humble-looking woman who was a shockingly powerful witch. It was there that I completed my education as an enchantress. They showed me that there was still power in this world that didn't belong to God, and I gorged on it till I practically glowed.

"And they helped me understand, really understand, what had been done to my family. You can call it what you like, war, or politics, or *un amour fou*, but I call it what it is: Uther murdered my father and raped my mother. Yes, I am absolutely going to rub your nose in it, Collum. Use your brain, you've got one in there somewhere. What did Uther want with a woman like Igraine? There were plenty of noblewomen in Britain who were unmarried and fertile, who spoke his language and shared his religion. But that was exactly it, that was the kink for him. It wasn't enough to force himself on my mother, he wanted somebody whose entire family and land and tongue and gods he could take away. He wanted somebody he could erase and destroy completely. The atrocity wasn't the price of his love, it was the point of it.

"I decided I would never leave the abbey grounds again. Britain's soil burned my feet.

"But in the end the abbess sniffed out our little coven, too, and it turned out the nuns' patience did have a limit. They set a local lord's house knights on us. We held them off for a while—we'd buried a family of black mice in a bottle under the threshold—but that snake Merlin showed up and tore it all down around us with his druid magicks. By rights he should've been on our side, but that man would betray anyone and anything for a little more money and a little more power. He changed the gardener into a sweetbriar and then burned her to ash. The rest they hanged.

"Me they couldn't touch—rank hath its privileges—so they sent me back to Camelot. On the way there I slipped my bonds and ran into the woods and changed myself into a rock till they gave up searching.

"After that I lived like an animal, on roots and berries, until one day I pulled up a wild carrot and it started to sing to me. I thought I was finally going properly mad, all the way this time.

"But then I heard a pheasant in a tree take up the song, and I followed it. Then it was a stripy snail singing in a meadow, and a young bull in the next one over, and when I climbed over the stile into the meadow beyond that I was in the Otherworld.

"You see, my prayers came true in the end. The piskies had come back for me after all."

. . .

WHEN SHE WAS FINISHED, Morgan le Fay, queen of the fairies, last surviving child of Igraine, High Queen of Britain, stood up again and looked out through the wall of the Glass Castle at the flooded square, the light from the half-sun brushing the water with apricot.

"I don't suppose you enjoyed that very much." She blotted her eyes with the back of her hand and took a sip of her wine. She was putting her armor back on.

"I don't suppose I was supposed to."

Collum realized they were looking down on the city. While she told the story the castle had risen into the air, so slowly he hadn't even felt it, and now it hovered over the plaza like a low-flying cloud.

It was true, Collum hadn't enjoyed her story, but what he did feel would've been harder to put into words. Of course he knew it all already, or most of it, but in the past he'd always successfully managed to avoid thinking about it too closely. It was a truth to be hastened past with a certain squeamishness, a dark thread in the otherwise golden tapestry of Camelot. He'd certainly never heard it the way she told it, as an upside-down fairy tale with Morgan le Fay as the hero and High King Uther the monster. And Arthur as a footnote, the misbegotten by-product of a rape. A king who never should've been.

But there it was. And it was terrible, of course it was. A bad, bad business.

"I know what you're thinking," Morgan said. "Not literally, mind you, but I don't need magic for that, it's written all over your face. You're thinking, *How long do I have to stand here looking grave and concerned? How long do I have to wait before the nice chatty Morgan comes back? I liked her so much better!*"

"That's unfair."

"Oh, do tell me more about unfairness, Sir Collum."

"I know it's terrible what Uther did," he said stiffly. "Obviously. I'm sorry, I can't imagine what it must have been like."

"Of course you can, you lost both your parents. You just don't want to."

"I'm sorry," he said again. "I wish I could do something."

"Is that why you think you're here?" She laughed. More wit and wisdom from Sir Collum. *"Behold, a lady in distress. Surely I, a knight of Britain, can save her!* But it's too late for that, Collum. Arthur at least understood that. He knew where he came from, and he hated it. A lot of heroes hate themselves, it's why they work so hard to make everybody love them."

"He was a victim just as much as you. You said it yourself—"

"Don't." Morgan stuck a finger in his face, suddenly deadly serious. "Don't you defend him. Arthur never apologized. He never repudiated his father. He could've given us reparations. He could've given us back Tintagel."

"You did try to kill him."

"If I'd wanted him dead he would've been. I left killing him to Morgause, and she left it to Mordred.

"But you're asking the wrong questions, Sir Collum," Morgan went on. "You can't change the past, so ask me what I want now. Ask me what I deserve. Why do you think I brought you here? To watch you squirm? Honestly, it's not that entertaining."

"I don't know." Collum realized he actually did want to help her somehow. She had been wronged, grievously wronged, obviously she had been, and no amount of his royalist blustering was going to change that. He could feel an invisible trap closing on him, but he couldn't quite tell what it was or how to get out of it.

"Maybe we can help each other." Morgan took a step closer. "You're waiting for God to tell you what to do, like He always has. Of course you are! But God's not coming. No, He's not, Collum, not this time. Instead I'm coming."

She bored her deep-gray unblinking eyes into his. He smelled that same cold, winter, wood-smoke smell he had at the inn.

"What do you mean?"

"I mean that I'm the greatest enchantress of this age. I have a thousand fairy knights at my command and the blood of High Queen Igraine in my veins. You came here looking for someone to fill the throne of Britain, and keep it filled, and you've found her. I'm your sword, and I'm your stone."

For a heartbeat Collum was lost for words.

"That's impossible."

"It's the only thing possible." She held his gaze. "The Round Table and I are the only powers left with any chance of saving Britain."

"Is this a joke?"

"On the contrary, as far as I can tell I'm the only one who's taking it seriously."

"If the Table joined with you then Britain would already be lost! Did you really drag us all the way to the Otherworld for this?" Collum heard his voice go embarrassingly high. "Is this what you killed Sir Villiars for? Just to begin with Britain would never accept a queen!"

"You're forgetting Queen Boudicca."

"Boudicca burned Londinium, then lost to the Romans, then killed herself!"

"You also seem to be forgetting that Camelot is mine already, by blood." Collum could almost see the power coming off her in waves like heat-shimmer. It prickled at his skin and raised the hairs on his forearms. "Whether I like it or not I am Arthur's oldest and closest living relative. By your own laws I stand next in the succession, and if the Table doesn't like it then the flower of British chivalry shouldn't have reduced each other to a pile of steel and guts."

Morgan was terrifying, but the real trouble was that a tiny treasonous part of Collum wondered if she was right. Camelot was dying, and God seemed to be in no hurry to save it, and here was the daughter of High Queen Igraine herself ready to step into the breach with an army of her own. He allowed himself to picture it for a moment: the throne of Britain held not by divine fiat but by the ancient magic of the land, the magic of oak and blood and stone and rain. A fairy queen ruling from a fairy Camelot, its crystalline towers rising up behind an enchanted curtain wall . . .

But his heart rebelled. That's not what he was fighting for. That wasn't what brought him all the way to Camelot. That was the Old World, that was Mull and mud and bonfires and standing stones, everything God and Rome and Arthur lifted Britain out of.

"What Britain needs is a king," he said, "and God will choose him like He always has. Like He chose Arthur."

"Well, God had better hurry. The boundaries between the realms have been weakening ever since the Grail Quest, and the Otherworld is vaster than you know. This city is only a jumping-off point." She pointed; they were high enough now to see the Fairy Sea, stretching to the smudged gray horizon. "Out there are the islands of the Bramble King, and the Duke of Sparks, and beyond them the Palatinate of Never-Better, and then the Lands of Sleeping Arawn himself. When this world spills into yours Britain will drown in fairy!"

"Then we'll fight to the last man. We will never trust you. How can we? You betrayed Arthur! We swore to serve him, and God will protect us!"

"God is gone, Collum." She almost sounded sorry for him. "Didn't they tell you? He made you grovel and praise His name, then He took His magic cup and His crying whelp Jesus and ran back where He came from, back to Israel where He belongs. He's a desert god, a god of sand and dust. This cool green island is beyond His remit."

"He'll come back." His own words sounded thin and distant to him. In the Otherworld it was God who sounded like a fairy tale. "When we show ourselves worthy God will come back."

"Why can't you face it?" Morgan raised her voice for the first time. "Why can't you face what's right in front of you?! Arthur's dead, God's gone, Rome's gone, and good riddance! You moon over the lost glory of Rome, the glass beads and the shiny coins, but you never look at what they took from us! Our gods and our druids, our crops and our metals, generations of warriors—"

"I'm sorry for what happened to you. And to your family. I am truly, truly sorry."

Collum's voice was tight with emotions he couldn't even name. His eyes were full of tears. Her raw, naked suffering was right there in front of him, demanding with absolute righteousness to be honored—but when he was drowning in an ocean of loneliness and pain on Mull, it was the dream of Arthur and Camelot that kept him alive. And now he would keep them alive. He would harden his heart, he would drown his own conscience, not because he wanted to but because Britain needed him to.

"What Uther did was terrible, but Uther is gone, and he left us Arthur, the greatest king Britain ever had. I know you know this or you would have killed him yourself. I know you could have!"

"Don't you dare." Morgan's face was white. "I would not kill my kin, and don't you dare tax me with that!"

Collum blundered on, stalked by the fear that it was himself he was trying to convince.

"And what good would it do, putting you on the throne? Would it bring your father back? Do you think you can make Britain whole again? I would love to help you but poetic justice is a luxury we cannot afford. What Britain needs is Arthur back, or the next king in his line, and that is what it shall have!"

Morgan set her glass goblet down on the bench so hard that the stem snapped. Irritably she threw the rest of it aside and it smashed on the glass floor.

"I don't know why I bothered, I truly don't. I'm a sentimental fool, and you're a pathetic idiot. Do you think you're in any position to bargain with me? Do you think I need the Table? I brought you here as a courtesy. When I come back to Britain it will be with fire and blood and black magicks! You have one God, but we have a thousand, and when Taranis goes to war, and Toutatis, and Joan the Wad and Jack o' the Lantern, oh, believe me, your man is going to shit His holy breeches!"

She snapped her fingers. The heads of the four fairy knights whipped round in unison. It was the first time they'd moved all evening.

"He's got a medal round his neck," Morgan said. "You'll know the one. Take it."

"What do you want with my medal?"

"Go to hell, Sir Collum."

The fairy knights rose as one and advanced on him four abreast, swords drawn, a mismatched murderers' row.

Come on then, Collum thought. He was almost relieved. He'd

had enough talk. He was bad at talking, everything he said felt wrong, and this at least was something he understood. He was unarmed, and one against four, but when it came to the prospect of his own imminent death he was not confused. On that point at least he knew where he stood.

Collum stutter-stepped back, eyes darting everywhere, feigning panic, then abruptly changed direction and darted at the leftmost fairy, the frog-woman who trotted on delicate goat hooves. She was tall and armed with a black flambard with a wicked wavy blade, but she'd underestimated him—he looked too big to be as fast as he was. Collum caught her sword-hand and punched her in her big golden frog's eye, then her soft pale frog's throat.

She staggered back and fell down, her sword clattering and sliding across the glass floor.

"Camelot!" he shouted. "For Camelot! For Arthur!"

What is the first rule when fighting more than one opponent? Aucassin whispered, and Collum whispered back: *Never stop moving.* He spun away and trapped the smoke-haired fairy's wrist in the crook of his arm and shoved her elbow till it bent back the wrong way and the ligament popped satisfyingly. She screamed, and Collum pushed her away and dove for the first knight's wavy-bladed sword.

He was back in the training yard, teaching those well-born boys a well-deserved lesson. Did time ever really move on, or was he always fighting the same fight? The wheat fairy took a big cut at him, their thin blade slitting the air, but Collum deflected the blow upward and then stabbed down, pinning the fairy's foot to the floor and cracking the glass under it like a spiderweb.

He left the blade there and caught the wheat fairy's sword as they dropped it and flourished it at the last of them, the blurry fairy, who startled backward and stepped on the remains of Morgan's broken goblet. Their foot went out from under them and the glass floor knocked them cold.

The hall was silent. The knights of the Table were staring at him like an apparition. The fairy whose foot he'd stabbed keened quietly, tugging weakly at the blade with their wheat-fingers.

All Collum wanted now was to leave this place. They'd wasted enough time on lies and false errands. He was tired of fighting Morgan and fighting himself, and there was so much that needed doing, and God only knew how much time had passed in Britain while they were here in the Otherworld. Breathing hard, he walked over to the dining table and lifted one end as high as his head. The plates and knives and dishes and jugs all slid in a clanging clattering mess onto the floor.

"Oh, bravo," Morgan said coldly. She indicated Sir Kay with the back of her hand. "Take that with you when you go."

Even the contempt was gone from her voice now. She'd lost interest in him again, just like she had at the inn. Looking at her, alone with the fairies in her glass fortress, Collum couldn't help but see the child she was, the stolen child, her family in ruins around her, but he tore himself away—how very many thoughts we have that we can't bear to let ourselves think—and walked over to the gilded throne. He put an arm round Sir Kay's shoulders and set his own shoulder in the old knight's armpit.

"Come on, big fellow." Collum hauled him to his feet.

"I have something in my eye," muttered Sir Kay.

Bedivere got up to help, too, and Palomides, and Dinadan—they were coming back to themselves. Scipio rooted around in the heap of food on the floor and rescued a leg of lamb. Bedivere whispered encouragingly to Kay, who just shook his head. His vacant, rheumy eyes didn't track.

They had their prize, for what that was worth, but Collum had no idea how they were going to get him home. The castle was very high up now, floating like a soap bubble. In the windows the sky had gone dark, and white stars sparkled all around them, the stars of the Otherworld. And what was above them? Was Morgan going to make war on Heaven?

"One thing before you go, Collum," Morgan said. "Look in a mirror."

Seating herself on the golden throne in Kay's place, she indicated a mirror on the wall.

Unsurprisingly Collum's reflection was damp and exhausted. His eyes were bleary and shadowed, his face scratched and un-shaven, his nose a little swollen. But behind him a pair of wide phantasmal wings rose up—butterfly wings, iridescent and trans-lucent like stained glass. They moved by themselves, slowly clos-ing and then spreading again like they were warming themselves in the sun.

He looked over his shoulder but there was nothing there. He reached behind him to feel them, but the wings were only there in his reflection. And something else too: a crown floated above his head, a golden circlet sprouting oak leaves of silver.

He looked to the other knights, but they just stared back at him as if they'd never seen him before.

"What is this?"

"You are not who you think you are, and Britain is not what you think it is. I return you now to Camelot. Your disaster is already in progress."

A distant bell rang, the room disappeared, and the roar of shout-ing men rose up all around them.

Sixteen

THE BATTLE OF CAMELOT

The Great Hall of the Glass Castle ripped apart like an old carpet and revealed behind it, as if it had been there all along, a lumpy, sloping green field seething with more people than Collum had ever seen in one place at one time in his whole life.

Crowds of men were strewn across the grass in big, messy double handfuls, thousands of them, in loud reds and yellows and blues and greens. The bright hazy air was full of cries and clashes and dust and smoke. Prickly stands of spears and pikes and lances stuck upward at odd angles, with flags hanging off them drooping in the slack air: stripes and crosses and suns and stars and heraldic animals, foxes and leopards and birds and fish.

"God's blood," Dinadan said. "That cock-eating whoreson really did it."

"Who?" Scipio shaded his eyes. "Did what?"

"That shit-eating bastard Rience. He marched on Camelot."

How long had they been gone?

"He'll rot in hell for this," Bedivere said.

"I find the tricky thing with people like Rience," Palomides said, "is getting them there."

"He's got some of the Old North with him." Dinadan was scanning the lines with his keen eyes. "Elmet. Rheged. The eastern dominions, and some Orkney too. Anyone Arthur ever checked or demoted. He's picked up where Mordred left off."

"Bastards," Bedivere said.

"And it looks like they picked up a few along the way south. There's Lord Anvyl and the Earl of Catuvel. People do love to join a parade."

"They must have come for a siege, and Constantine rode out to take them before they could dig in," Palomides said. "It appears we are just in time."

The knights seemed to have recovered from the effects of their fairy feast. If anything they were refreshed and alert, as if they'd woken from a long sleep. They didn't even seem especially curious about how they got here, though Scipio was still clutching his leg of lamb. He took a last bite and tossed it aside.

"I hope he survives the battle," Collum said, "so we can hang him as a traitor."

"He'll do the same to us," Scipio said. "The losers are always the traitors."

Traitors to what, though? *Britain is not what you think it is.* He tried to scrub Morgan's words out of his mind, like graffiti off a wall. A pitched battle should help with that, though there didn't seem to be any actual fighting yet. All the clatter and shouting was the sound of the soldiers trying to arrange themselves in more or less orderly lines and rectangular formations, which were constantly being melted and distorted by the pressures of fear and confusion and contradictory orders and the skittishness of horses. The shapes rippled and stretched under a pale gray summer sky.

"Looks like Constantine found an army anyway," Collum said.

"Every lordling and baronet within a hundred miles must've chipped in a few men." Dinadan studied the banners. "Carmack, Blind Bainbridge, Oakbridge. The chough is King Cador—daddy's here. There's Lackland the Younger, Blackbow, Wylde and Wylder . . ."

That's right. It's not an atrocity. Camelot isn't what Morgan said. It's a shining light, a North Star for all to sail by. Now was their chance to prove her wrong.

He had often, very often, thought about battles and how amazingly well he would one day acquit himself in one. But now that he had an actual battle forming right in front of him—for Camelot!—the idea of involving himself in it, submerging himself in that swirling human maelstrom, was less appealing than he'd imagined. All else being equal he would've preferred to wait a little longer, and gone off somewhere and lain down and had a sleep first. Too much had happened, he needed the sorting angel of dreams to come down and sift it all into piles for him, make it into stories and tell him what it all meant and which bits he could safely forget.

Sir Kay seemed to feel the same way. He sat down on his rump in the tufty grass.

"Looks about even odds," Bedivere said.

"There's Constantine." Dinadan pointed. "With the mounted guard, and Nimue's with him."

"Is that bitch still around?" Scipio said. "Dame Fortune has a peculiar sense of humor."

"That bitch was right," Collum said. "She told us this would happen."

They set off across the field at a brisk pace, leaving the king's mad foster brother blinking at the daisies and butter-and-eggs like a child. Excitement was goosing Collum back into a state of brittle, exhausted alertness. Morgan could wait. Everything could wait. As they walked he reached back and touched the place on his shoulder where he saw the phantom wings in the mirror, but again he felt nothing.

Collum thought Bedivere's estimate of the odds was generous: there were a lot of people at the far end of the field, most of them in the sulfur-yellow of King Rience, and who knew how many more in the woods beyond. It was harder to guess Camelot's numbers because they had no uniforms—the troops had come dressed in the colors and badges of whatever lord had mustered them. As the knights mixed in with the rearmost ranks he caught a giddy carnival atmosphere, loose talk and nervous laughter and the fairground smell of crushed grass and horse piss. A peddler strolled by hawking protective talismans and magic salves to keep your weapons sharp.

"Not a bad spot, considering," Bedivere said. "Slight slope in our favor. And we've got the Brass and the woods on our flanks—they'd be damned lucky to get cavalry through those trees."

Collum nodded sagely, as if he had evaluated the tactical scenario too and come to that exact same conclusion.

With his height and his long hair Constantine was easy to spot, safely back from the lines between two squares of mounted knights, even apart from Camelot's blue-and-gold dragon standard. In full armor his height was more intimidating than gawky. He was talking a mile a minute, sometimes stopping to confer with Nimue beside him, sometimes leaning down from his horse and grabbing people so he could shout in their ears, then a herald would go sprinting away into the crush. He was red in the face and drenched in sweat, but Collum could see something in him that he hadn't spotted before, some steel showing through his foppish exterior. Whatever Constantine felt about being king, or said he felt, command suited him.

His face lit up when he saw his old comrades. They traded big clanking embraces.

"Is that Sir Scipio I see?" The heat of battle had temporarily banished Constantine's stutter. He wore no helmet, and his long blond hair was in a warlike braid that put Collum in mind of a Saxon warrior, not that he'd ever actually seen one.

"Back from the dead. Like Jesus."

"Wait—was Scipio the lost knight?" Nimue looked confused.

"No, that was Kay," Dinadan said. "And it was Morgan le Fay who had him, so you missed a real first-class adventure. Now tell us how we're going to destroy this treacherous toad."

Constantine laid out the battle plan, which was so simple even Collum could follow it: regular infantry front and center, companies of archers on both wings, and two groups of heavy cavalry waiting stolidly in the back. They would stand and fight the enemy till the enemy had had enough and went home.

"That's it?" Dinadan said. "No hidden reserves, feigned retreat, what-what? Arthur would at least have had a double envelopment."

"You think these men have drilled together?" Nimue said. "Or with anybody ever? We emptied the prisons. We'll be lucky if they're all facing the right way."

Constantine estimated that Rience had the advantage by about five hundred men, but as against that Camelot's men hadn't just marched three hundred miles from Rheged. The grade and firmness of the field was discussed, the ratios of cavalry to infantry to archers, wind conditions, the possible presence of disguised enchanters, on down through the humidity and its probable effect on the archers' bowstrings. Collum would stick to trying to kill the man opposite him. And facing the right way.

"Where do you want us?" Bedivere said.

"Palomides with the left cavalry. Bernivan's in charge there, don't let him run when things get hot. Bedivere and Dinadan on the right with Percy. Dinadan, pick a wing of archers. And, ah, Collum, let's have you in front with the infantry. God be with you all."

"God be with you." The knights turned and started pushing their way through the press in all directions. Scipio had already wandered off during the talk about bowstrings.

"Let the men know you're here!" Nimue called after them. "They'll want to know the Table's here!"

Collum—Sir Collum, he thought—headed in what he hoped was the general direction of the front line. He caught a last glimpse of Dinadan slapping backs and clapping shoulders as he made his way out toward the flank. Then he was alone in the crowd.

He wondered how long till the battle started. Only now did he feel the first cold itch of fear. If they lost, that was the end. He'd be hanged or worse, and Rience would sleep in Arthur's bed tonight.

As he waded deeper into the ranks he got a better look at who he was fighting with. There were a few proper soldiers, grimly composed and kitted out with jacks and brigandines, but only a few. The lines were generously stuffed with farmers, tradesmen, adolescents, and old men. Collum spotted a missing arm here, a limping gait there. They carried an extraordinary menagerie of weapons: rusty heirlooms, cheap sixpenny blades bought in a bundle and handed out this morning, fat falchions like meat cleavers, monster two-handers, all manner of hammers and clubs. One man nervously clutched a pitchfork, another a felling ax, another a knotty tree branch with a nail through it. A shirtless man was carrying some kind of exotic curved Turkish weapon that must have traveled a thousand miles to end up here, gripped awkwardly in a sweaty farmer's fist in a British hayfield.

A few had pole arms, too, named not for the long poles they were mounted on but for the polls—heads—that you split with them. Most farmers could lay their hands on a bill, which was good for trimming tree branches but doubled as an excellent anti-knight weapon. Its blade sliced through reins and its hooks and spikes would catch on armor and drag you out of the saddle to where the mob could finish you off.

You could hardly blame them. A lot more farmers would die today than knights. Officers on horseback shouted at the men to stay together like they were children in danger of straying into the woods. "With me! With me! With! Me!" Then the sergeants repeated it in British for the ones who didn't speak Latin.

Bottles circulated. He caught whiffs of vomit and voided bowels. He heard prayers, to Jesus Christ but also to Cocidius, and Belatucadros, and Mars Gradivus. As he got closer to the front ranks things got quieter. The lines got straighter. Collum's palms began to sweat, and he had a sudden urge to pee. The two very front lines were in good order, heavily armed men standing silent and stock-still, swordsmen reinforced by a few dismounted knights like himself, then behind them a line of spearmen and axmen ready to strike through the gaps, and every fifth man an archer. These were the big hard bastards. They faced the right way. No one wanted to make room for Collum, but when they saw he was a knight they grudgingly let him through.

And then there was nothing between him and the rebel army but two hundred yards of thin British daylight. All the chaos and tumult behind him died away to a faraway rumble.

Even Collum knew that if you had to fight a battle then it was better to receive the charge than to do the charging. You wanted to be the ones holding a line, not running at it trying to break it. As a result neither side wanted to go first. He wondered how long they'd been waiting here.

Birds chirped sweetly and insects clicked in the creeping bent-grass. There was the smell of hot steel in the sun. The oxeye daisies and meadowsweet and a hundred other flowers he couldn't name seemed touchingly unaware that they were about to be trampled by ten thousand human feet. An ancient beech tree stood alone in the middle of it all, holding itself aloof from the drama unfolding around it. The Otherworld seemed like a distant memory now. Morgan le Fay, the Romans, the giant, Sir Ganadal. There was nothing here but this place and this moment. Collum scanned the enemy lines for Rience—supposedly he was a half-giant, eight feet tall, with a cloak trimmed with the beards of all the kings he'd defeated. He ought to stick out. But Collum couldn't spot him.

Every once in a while one side or the other would start banging their swords and shields together and yelling taunts, but the officers held them back and eventually the noise would die out again. A knight rode out from the opposing line and shouted something inaudible and capered his horse skillfully in a circle. A few arrows fell just short of him. Collum's stomach growled. He said some prayers.

"Hey. Sir Prance-a-lot." It was the man on his right. "Get yer sword out."

"Eh?"

"Draw your fucken sword. When it starts we'll be packed in tight."

He was an older man with heavy gray eyebrows and a big gray mustache. He wore a pointy metal cap with a veil of riveted links hanging down to protect his chin and throat. Only then did Collum remember that he didn't have a fucken sword. He'd lost it in the Otherworld.

"Oh for Christ's sake." The man barked hoarsely over his shoulder: "Sword!"

Collum flushed red, but within a minute a sword arrived, passed hand over hand from back in the ranks. He thanked the man, checked the grip, knocked it against the bottom of his foot a couple of times, edge and flat. Bit short, bit stiff, bit heavy in the hilt, but if you hit somebody with it hard enough, they would die.

A flicker of movement on the right flank caught his eye. Down by the river a couple of arrows lofted over from the Camelot side, thin shafts floating in high, lazy arcs. Waste of good arrows.

Except when he followed them Collum saw that they could actually just about reach the front ranks of the enemy. The slight grade and a breath of wind were enough. There was a line of stakes hammered into the turf in front of the archers, angled to protect them from a cavalry charge, but a few had cheated forward a little past the line to get in range.

It was a good game. More and more archers were edging forward and letting loose, laughing and cheering, and one or two shafts turned into a light drizzle. They were rewarded with wails and shouts from the other side, pain and anger. The enemy infantry formation shifted under the arrows like a restless animal.

One lucky arrow must have caught a breeze because it drifted farther back, past the infantry, to the cavalry. These were knights in heavy armor. They weren't in much danger from a windborne arrow, but they had titles and reputations to defend, and they weren't going let a bunch of smug Camelot fat cats dribble arrows down on their heads. Another arrow came down, somebody shouted a curse, and all at once the cavalry square lost its collective temper and charged like a young bull.

The knights didn't care that there was infantry in front of them. Officers shouted at the foot soldiers to hold but they weren't the ones with a line of giant horse-borne hotheads right behind them. They ran for it. Then the lord commanding the center line saw the left moving, and he wasn't going to let them grab all the glory, and just like that it all passed the point of no return. The whole of Rience's army shifted forward like a muddy hillside losing its grip and becoming a landslide.

Collum watched it come. Camelot's archers were shooting in earnest now, straight and hard and flat, right arms dipping for arrows and nocking and drawing and loosing clothyard shafts. Collum saw a horse rear up in pain with an arrow sticking straight out of its chest. Archers weren't knights, they didn't give a shit about chivalry, and if they didn't snuff out that cavalry charge before it got to them they were dead men.

He squeezed his borrowed sword tight then forced himself to relax. The oncoming line looked like one long breaking wave bearing down on a beach. Nobody could stop this now. Not out of fear but from some even deeper animal instinct, he pissed himself.

Camelot's officers were shouting: "Hold now! Hold with me, hold! Hold!"

An arrow loosed from just behind Collum's right ear flashed out and away in a strangely foreshortened curve and vanished into the oncoming mass. On his left a long spearhead appeared. Another arrow flew, and one of the attackers lost his feet and went down and was trampled. One of Rience's men was coming straight at him: a big man with pink jowls, some kind of rash creeping up his neck, big sad eyes, and a yellow cross surcoat, jogging stolidly with the pack. He trampled down a bushy weed a hundred yards away.

The fear was mounting and mounting in Collum, but he was between them and Camelot and he could not move. In his whole life up to that point Collum had only ever seen two men die by violence, Sir Villiars and the nameless knight of Three Scepters, a Chevron Or, but now a dark flight of arrows hissed out from behind him and ten, twenty men took them face- and chest- and neck- and eye-first and staggered and were overrun. Yellow Cross kept coming, though.

A roar rose up around Collum like a sudden storm, and Collum roared, too, without even meaning to, the roar roared right through him. They were almost here, the fear got worse and worse until for a heartbeat it was infinite and unbearable, and then Yellow Cross was ten feet away and all the fear melted away completely the way the white cap of a volcano vanishes just before an eruption, and Yellow Cross was—

Collum was on the ground, flat on his face with his ears ringing and grit in his mouth and a boulder on top of him. It was pitch dark and the boulder was crushing him. He heaved; the boulder was a heavy struggling body. On his third try he got up onto his hands and knees, then he got a knee up and dragged up his sword, which two people were standing on. He was bashed from the side and almost went over again but forced himself grunting back into the light and onto his feet.

251

Shouting, struggling, surging men were jammed like cattle shoulder to shoulder and chest to chest. He couldn't have fallen over again if he wanted to. He had no idea which way he was facing. Maybe twenty yards away horses were rearing and plunging, their riders furiously smashing and lashing the heads of those around them. Twisting wildly, Collum slung an armored elbow into the head of the man opposite him, and as in a dream it became the snarling face of the man-at-arms who'd given him his sword. The man glared at him but then grimaced and threw his head back—a thin warrior behind him in an old-fashioned bascinet had somehow found enough room to jam a sword into his back.

Collum wrenched his arm free, lunged past the man-at-arms and shoved the point of his borrowed sword into the freckled hollow of the attacker's throat. The man jerked his chin down sharply as if he'd just seen something of which he seriously disapproved, then coughed blood out of his mouth and neck at the same time. The crowd spasmed and pushed Collum chest to chest with the dying man, who spluttered out more blood right in Collum's face. He could taste it, hot and salty along with the cold, bitter dirt he'd eaten. He tried to spit it out.

"Jesus," Collum whispered. "Holy precious baby Jesus."

He doubted precious baby Jesus could hear him. He couldn't hear himself. There was no semblance of a battle line. He looked for the gray-eyebrowed man-at-arms but he'd vanished, dead or dragged under. He started shoving his way toward the rampaging horsemen, Rience's men—the horses were in yellow barding. That's what must've happened: right as the two lines met Rience's cavalry must have shock-charged Camelot's undefended left flank.

Collum was wading against the tide; most people were fleeing the cavalry. He remembered to clank down his visor, but the world shrank to a slit and he had no idea what was anywhere so he opened it again. Something was scratching at his armor—he swung around to see a man with a blond mustache trying to get a short sword between the plates. Collum punched him and wrapped an arm around his narrow shoulders, hanging on to him like a rock in a maelstrom, and forced his sword into the man's side and through his kidney and jerked it out again.

"Camelot!" His voice broke. "Camelot!" The word had lost all meaning.

The two armies were crushed and fused together. Everywhere Collum looked he saw unthinkable things. A man out of armor was trying desperately to climb the lone tree, one foot dangling by a strip of skin. A sharp sword cut a smooth flat section off a man's skull, exposing a flash of pale gray-pink brain before it erupted in gore. An axman with a long red braid removed a horse's right foreleg at the knee with a big two-handed swing. The horse staggered down onto its face, screaming, and another rider hewed right down through the axman's collarbone into his chest.

"For—!" Collum's voice died. This cannot be how kings are made. You couldn't make order out of chaos. Something had gone terribly wrong. There must be some way he could explain it to everybody—

A horned knight on an armored horse came crashing through the press like a rolling boulder, clipping and crushing everything in his way. In a tournament he would have dismounted out of courtesy, Collum thought stupidly, even as the horseman smashed down at him with a long-handled war hammer and he parried clumsily and his arm went numb. He stabbed back up but the man kept hammering him, a god raining down thunderbolts, and Collum was crawlingly aware of how exposed he was from behind.

The horse bit at him and a hoof clanged off his chest. In a spasm of fear he pulled a knife from his belt left-handed and shoved it in to the hilt between the horse's ribs. It tore itself away, rearing and plunging madly.

The mob had thinned out around him a little, and he rolled his shoulders and reset himself. It was coming back to him what this was about. These men wanted Camelot and they couldn't have it. He wouldn't let them. He pushed forward in what he hoped was the direction of enemy lines, sweat streaming off him. He passed the lone beech, a relic of the sane world of moments earlier.

He was remembering that he knew this game. Strange faces goggled at him and shied away: a chinless beanpole in yellow, a devil with beard almost up to his eyes. A man in a kettle hat painted red thrust at him with a gilded sword, a neat twisting thrust that must have cost him years of practice. He was quick but not that quick: Collum caught the tip of his blade in his gauntleted fist. The man backed away but he didn't want to let go of that fancy blade, and while he was struggling with the decision Collum struck him hard with his own very unfancy sword, not penetrating his mail but definitely cracking the man's collarbone. Before Collum could finish him, a pop-eyed spearman's thrust skated up his breastplate, tearing apart Alasdair's marvelous velvet. Collum snapped the head off the spear with his sword and then surged swiftly forward— why was everyone else moving so slowly?—and amputated one of the man's hands at the wrist. A blunt blow on his shoulder spun Collum around: a huge bushy-bearded Orkney, mouth crammed with yellow teeth at all angles, swinging a heavy ax. A local hero, small-town Goliath, probably not unlike Collum himself.

But nobody was like Collum now. He felt rampant with power. This was a battle. He was fighting a battle! As the man reared back for another blow a gap in his armor winked open just above his kneecap and Collum darted his sword into it, feinted, then did the same on the other side, and when the man staggered Collum batted his ax aside and collapsed the side of his head.

All this *talk talk talk* about birth and blood and crowns and claims. Finally, here was something real! A sword in your head: *that* was a God damned claim. He would prove it upon their bodies. A circle was clearing around him. From the lofty height of battle rage he looked down on his everyday self and saw it for what it was, a miasma of doubt and inward-falling confusion, a queasy nightmare from which he had at last awoken. Almost casually he kicked a ratty axman in the groin, a Pictish mercenary maybe, who'd come all this way to get Collum's foot in his fruits and then his blade in his stomach. It came out skimmed with red and brown.

"Camelot!" he roared. "The Table!"

He smashed a shield with a candle-sigil so hard it knocked in the teeth of the man holding it. He risked a look back and saw that the wound inflicted by Rience's cavalry in their flank was clotting. Camelot's own cavalry had finally arrived to engage them, strength to strength—Palomides had found a dappled stallion somewhere— and a mob of men with billhooks was tearing a struggling rebel knight out of his saddle. The world was recovering its order, pulling itself together after its earlier disastrous collapse.

Now there was a ragged line of infantry on either side of Collum pushing back at the attackers, and a crowd of archers was shooting over their heads, volley on volley on volley.

"Camelot! The Table!"

He lowered his shoulder and charged and smashed deep into the yellow ranks, ran until the press of men slowed and stopped him. He wondered if he'd just made a fatal error, but then his holy bloodlust reasserted itself. A mistake? No, this was so much better! There were so many more enemies here! Somebody was already knocking on the small of his back with the point of a snapped-off lance, looking for a way in, and Collum gracefully spun past the sharp tip and got a glimpse of a furious dark-faced man with a riveted cap and a big gap between his two front teeth before his fist bashed the man thunderously in the face.

He jabbed a bug-eyed staring man in the thigh, made him drop his sword, then caught an ax blow on his armored forearm—that would bruise later—and slithered the point of his sword past a round buckler and into the man's rich, soft entrails. An arrow exploded into shards off his shoulder. The enemy front wavered, uncertain whether to flee or mob him.

Flee, he thought. Hie ye from this place.

"Camelot!"

Collum's own men caught up and enveloped him again, trying to turn the moment into the start of a proper rout. The front line overtook him and he chased it. See: they didn't need Morgan. They would build the Table again themselves, the old way, blow by blow, meadow by meadow, and not stop till all stood as it was before.

Bedivere brushed past Collum at a jog, brusque and businesslike. He snatched a black studded club away from a man, wresting it out of his grip one-handed with such authority that the soldier just turned and fled, slipping on the mud.

"Arthur! The Table!"

Ahead of Collum the rush met a wave of enemy reinforcements, fresh men who pressed back at them. Where the hell had they come from? The woods? For a heartbeat the whole battle paused in equilibrium, army to army, both sides screaming and pounding and shoving at each other. Far back in the enemy host Collum glimpsed an enormous roaring horseman who could only have been King Rience himself. He really was exceptionally large.

A dark cloud of arrows passed overhead going the other way and bit into the rabble behind Collum. The enemy flank was wrapping round them to the left, curling around the end of Camelot's line and making it unravel. Collum saw three of his fellows go down in a row, one-two-three, overpowered and stabbed and overrun. The world was crumbling again, back into chaos. *No.* Collum stepped on something that rolled and sat down on his ass. Immediately a man with a long, tall shield fell on top of him.

It was the most beautiful shield Collum had ever seen, a carved, gilded dragon curled around a green oak tree. What a terrible waste, he thought stupidly. It should be hanging on a wall somewhere, not out here getting scraped and ruined. He writhed out from under it, lost his sword, scrabbled for it again and stumbled to his feet, but a hard shove from behind immediately sent him reeling, and he had to snap his head around when an arrow came flashing straight at his eyes; it clattered off the side of his helm . . .

HUMP. The earth was a giant bass drum, and God beat on it once.

The shock froze the whole battlefield. Everything stopped. Fifty yards away, back in the enemy lines, a great dome of mud rose up and dark shapes flew gracefully away from it, pinwheeling bodies and fragments of bodies and weapons and armor. A heartbeat later a circular shock wave rippled the bloody mud under Collum's feet, and he heard the whine of metal fragments.

In the breath of silence that followed a man screamed brokenly. Both sides looked around wildly for whatever had done it and whether it was going to do it to them next. Collum looked, too, and for a moment his eye skipped over her, then slid back.

It wasn't God, it was Nimue. She was striding forward across the churned muck, tiny between the four house knights escorting her.

"Clear!" they shouted. "Clear a path! Clear!"

Her lips were moving but Collum was too far away to hear. She pointed and lightning struck, once and then again, leaving a searing pink broken vein of light across Collum's vision. The thunder almost knocked him down.

Like a startled school of fish the mass of Rience's army turned as one and ran. Nimue pressed her two small hands together and squeezed her eyes tight shut, and her whole body shuddered, and the mud of the churned meadow opened underneath a knot of horses and men and then closed over them.

Collum stared, not at the magic but at the woman working it. When she cast a spell Nimue's whole soul was there in her face, naked and exposed. She was so strong and so vulnerable at the same time, with a thin sweaty lock of brown hair that had got free pasted across her pale forehead, as she summoned power from beyond to break men's bodies.

Collum thought he had never seen anybody so beautiful.

Her right hand glowed, then pulsed so bright Collum had to turn away, though he caught the afterimage of a searing white beam, a crack into an otherworld of intolerable alchemical brightness. Where it lanced through the crowd men lit like torches. Later the scavengers and looters picking over the battlefield would find chunks of cracked glass where the beam had touched the ground. Some of Rience's men were withdrawing in good order but others downed weapons and sprinted.

Collum knew he should run after them, but all at once he found himself spent, a slack empty skin, a sponge with all the strength squeezed out of him. All that joy and power had drained back down to whatever sunless sea they came from. He was turning back into himself again.

The lone beech tree was split and smoldering. It was over. They'd won. Do you see, Morgan, from your glass castle? But how then could he feel so empty? A hollow armor defending a hollow fortress, and Arthur's empty bed. He bent over and put his hands on his knees and closed his eyes, and in the black he saw the city, the drowned fairy city, the tall towers and flooded streets. His forearm was throbbing, and low down on his right side was a wound he didn't remember getting. The stubs of broken arrows hung off his armor where they'd lodged in the gaps. A bit of his helmet had been bent in by a blow and was cutting into his temple, and the blood and sweat stung his eye.

Hoofbeats. He opened his eyes again in time to see Scipio race past him on horseback at a gallop, laughing and singing, sounding completely berserk. Dinadan was close behind, waving his thick sword. Together they were riding down the stragglers.

Seventeen

THE TALE OF SIR DINADAN

L ord Dugfall had a small, remote fastness called Greenstone House at the head of the Great Wold Valley in Ebrauc, a green vale of thinly scattered farms watered by the Gypsey Race. It was an ancient land, haunted by long barrows and gangs of old standing stones. It hadn't been much troubled by the arrival of the Romans or by their departure.

Lord Dugfall had two children, a girl and a boy, Orwen and Oriel. They were twins, though the two children didn't especially resemble each other. They were the same height, but Oriel was broad and heavyset while Orwen was on the slender side. Oriel had gorgeous curly blond hair that the ladies of the castle were always running their fingers through, to his endless irritation, while Orwen's hair was straight dishwater. Her features were neat and unremarkable, while Oriel had a bruiser's jowly face, with a nose that looked broken even before it was actually broken, which happened for the first but not last time when he was eleven.

He was a relentlessly physical little boy, always climbing things and falling off them and hitting them with other things to see which of them would break. He was especially devoted to a violent form of football that was played with several dozen boys from all over the area. Oriel captained one team, and the other was led by an exotic-looking child named William Colingham, who had dark eyes and long, loose black hair—the Dugfalls and the Colinghams were the two large landholding families in the Great Wold Valley. The ball was an inflated pig's bladder filled with dried peas, and the playing field was the whole town and the fields around it. The game generally left crops and fences and small outbuildings in ruins and only ended when the bladder popped or someone got seriously hurt.

Orwen was intensely curious about football, violent and unseemly though it was, and about all of Oriel's world, the boy's world of hunting and fighting, hitting and shouting, running fast and spitting in the dirt. It wasn't that she disliked girl-things, she was given dolls and she dutifully took care of them, clothed them and fed them and organized their social schedules and put them to bed. Her dolls did not go neglected. But it was more like a chore than play.

The boys staunchly resisted Orwen's efforts to insinuate herself into their football games, but those were the rules, weren't they? You stuck to your team. Girls with girls and boys with boys.

Though it wasn't just girls versus boys in the Great Wold Valley, the teams were also Dugfalls and Colinghams. The two families had been embroiled in a more or less constant feud for decades; it waxed and waned and heated and cooled in an endless round of lawsuits over property lines, accusations of poaching, mysterious fires, fouled wells, missing livestock, perceived slights, contested appointments to bailiff and mayor of this or that, displays of disrespect between drunken underlings, and so on. Orwen and Oriel were Dugfalls, and when they were nine the feud ran sufficiently hot that it was deemed prudent to get the children out of town for a while for their safety. They were sent to their cousins in the next valley over.

For extra security Orwen was disguised as a boy. She was dressed in stockings and a short tunic and her hair was summarily chopped off at chin length, leaving eight inches of dishwater locks on the lawn behind the house. Everybody stopped what they were doing to have a good laugh at the result, and someone proclaimed Deuteronomy in ringing tones: "The woman shall not wear that which pertaineth unto a man, neither shall a man put on a woman's garment: for all that do so are abomination unto the Lord thy God!"

Hilarious. They bundled her into a covered cart. It was six hours to Harwood in the freezing cold, and they stopped halfway so everybody could have a piss. Orwen got out and found a puddle and stamped on the glaze of ice on it so she could look at her reflection and see what everybody else found so funny.

But she didn't laugh at what she saw in the shivering water. She recognized that translucent apparition. The identification was immediate and electric. She'd never seen him before, but she realized she'd been looking for him for years. Look at that boy, she thought. Just look at him. I'd know him anywhere.

He felt real, realer than she did, as if she were the rippling insubstantial reflection and he the real thing. She knew at that moment that she didn't want to be insubstantial anymore, she wanted to be real. She wanted to be that boy. No, she already was him—that boy was who she'd always been. She was he.

But on arrival Orwen was packed off to a girls' school attached to the local convent. Meanwhile Oriel was taken into the cousins' household in training to become a knight.

Orwen knew who he was now, but at the convent school he dutifully tried to stuff the whole of himself back into the small girl-shaped space life had allotted him. He spun and weaved and painted and read. He improved his manners and his moral conduct. But the boy in the puddle called to him, like a mer-boy with his siren song. He stole a pair of sewing scissors and gave himself regular secret trims, at night, to keep his hair short, which perplexed the nuns to no end.

The other girls could smell his difference, even if they could or would not name it. Some were repelled, others attracted.

Orwen itched with boredom and restlessness. He regularly went over the wall to the big house to watch Oriel training with a sword. He liked to play along with a stick sword, and he always got in one or two good clouts before they chased him away. He would be *so* much better at it than they were, Orwen thought.

Or at least as good. Probably. Anyway they could at least give him a chance.

A creeping fear began slowly consuming Orwen, a fear that no one would ever see him. He would never be at home anywhere, because his body itself was a foreign country to him, and the person who other people saw was a stranger to him. How was it not obvious to them that he was a boy? Everybody else looked like who they were. Why not him?

Orwen studied the precedents. Whatever Deuteronomy said, a surprising number of female saints had dressed and lived as monks and male hermits. Saint Pelagia, the holy harlot of Antioch. Saint Thecla, who rode with Saint Paul himself, and not only dressed as a man but baptized herself by leaping into a pool full of angry seals. Saint Apollinaria of Egypt, and Saint Euphrosyne of Alexandria, and Saint Theodora, also of Alexandria, which apparently

263

was a hotbed of holy transvestism. Most awesome of all was Saint Marina the Monk, who lived in a monastery in Lebanon under the name Father Marinos until she was finally kicked out—not for being a woman but because she was accused of fathering a child. She only revealed her secret on her deathbed, after which everybody presumably felt suitably chastened.

The only person Orwen confided in was Oriel, and he needn't have bothered. He snuck into his brother's room one night and woke him up.

"I have a problem."

"Me, too," Orwen said. "My fool sister won't let me sleep."

"Do you ever wonder if you were really meant to be a girl?"

"That is the stupidest thing I—"

"Because I was supposed to be a boy, and something went wrong, the devil cursed me or something, and now I'm stuck in a girl's body."

"That means you're a girl. Having a girl's body *means* you're a girl."

"How do you know what bodies mean?" Orwen asked. "We're just going to throw them away anyway when we die, like orange peels, and then at the Last Judgment we'll be given our perfect bodies, so what does this body even mean?"

"It will mean something to you," Oriel said, "when I punch it in the face."

"Come on then, fight me!" Orwen put up his fists and danced around the room on the balls of his feet. He didn't know much about fistfighting. Yet.

"I don't hit girls. Look, what's so bad about being a girl anyway?"

"Do you want to be one?" Orwen asked.

"No."

"Why not?"

"Because I'm a boy!"

"So am I!"

Oriel pulled his blanket over his head. Orwen punched his blanketed head and went back to his bedroom but not back to bed.

He felt the walls of his world closing in. He wondered whether, if he tried very hard, he could go mad. Or grow a beard like Saint Uncumber. Maybe sorcery could help, but sorcerers were scarce in Ebrauc. The only one he'd even ever heard of was Merlin, the young King Arthur's wizard, and he was far away at Camelot. He wondered if the devil really had cursed him, and if he ought to try to summon him so they could have it out face-to-face.

But instinct told him he should leave Satan out of this, if possible, and the Almighty too. You didn't want to get caught up in that holy slugfest. They were the big guns, and this matter called for some delicacy.

But there were other beings for whom delicacy and nuance were a specialty. Who did not take sides in the titanic struggle between good and evil. Whose very nature was to slip and slide between worlds and across boundaries, and after all that was precisely what he was trying to do. What God wrought wrong, maybe Fairy could put right.

But how to ask them? The precautions for keeping fairies out were well known. You hung a pair of iron tongs on the wall over your bed. You drank milk from a cow that had eaten pearlwort. You made the sign of the cross with burning straw. But how did you invite fairies in? Did you do the opposite? You could put tongs *under* your bed. You could drink milk from a cow that *hadn't* had any pearlwort. Or probably not. It wasn't like you could ask it.

Maybe a gift would help. Orwen scavenged a little honey cake from the kitchen and put it on a dish on the windowsill. Then he fetched a handful of hay from the meadow behind the house. Instead of burning it he soaked it in well water and—screwing his courage to the sticking point—he held it up and solemnly made the sign of the cross backward.

Nothing. He threw the wet straw over his shoulder and flung himself down on his bed. It was late. He was tired. For tonight at least he was ready to sink into despair and its kissing cousin, sleep.

In dreams all was fluid. Nothing was fixed. Everything, even your body, was mist.

But some sixth sense caused Orwen to open his eyes again. He wasn't alone. That damp straw he threw behind him had settled on the head of a little old man, four feet tall, who now stood by his bed.

The old man brushed it off impatiently. If he was a fairy he was a bit bigger than Orwen had hoped. He'd imagined a tiny, unthreatening, dragonfly-winged fairy, a cute one that trailed glowing motes, who could sit on his shoulder or nestle in the palm of his hand like a baby bird.

This one wasn't cute. Kind of shabby actually; his green jacket was rubbed shiny in places with grease and dirt and wear, and he wore a green hat that looked like it had been sat on a few times. He watched Orwen, moonlight gleaming in his large black eyes—his pupils were hugely dilated. His face was serious and deeply seamed.

"Well?" he said. "What d'ye want?"

"I—"

Terror had him by the throat.

"What?" the fairy snapped. "Spit it out!"

"I want to be a boy. I mean I am a boy, but I don't look like one. I want you to turn me into—turn me into what I am."

The little man studied him. He seemed to be both there and not. It took Orwen a minute to figure out that he could only see him with his left eye; to the right he was invisible. In a flash—he moved unnaturally quickly—the fairy-man was right up close to him, loudly sniffing his shoulder, an animal sound.

He grunted.

"Yuh. Somethin' off there, arright."

He should have thought this through more. He really hadn't thought the summoning would work. But fairies were the in-betweeners, fence-jumpers, locksmiths at the gates between realms. Surely they could open the one between girl and boy.

At least he could see there was a problem. No one else had ever seen that before.

"Can you fix it? Fix me?"

"How?" He blinked his black eyes.

"Well, I don't know! You're the fairy! Change me! Make me right!"

The fairy pouted thoughtfully. Behind him a wooden picture frame was sprouting branches and leaves.

"Can't change who ye'are. Soul-cutting, 's a bloody business. Makes me sick, just thinkin' about it."

"Well don't cut my soul! Obviously!"

"Body swap then? Ye couldn't afford it."

The frame fell off the wall with a clatter. It was a nest of twigs and leaves now. Orwen wrung his hands and bounced on his toes. This was agony.

"So what'll it be?" the fairy said. "Ye'll be paying whatever happens, yeh might as well get somethin' out of it."

267

He blurted it out.

"If you can't change my body . . . I want to fight. Like a knight. Make me a knight!"

It was all he could think of.

Before Orwen even got out the final *t* of *knight* the little old man had lowered his head like a bull. He ran at Orwen and with unnerving strength threw him over his shoulder and jumped out the window.

As the fairy hurdled the sill he neatly grabbed the honey cake off the dish with his free hand and crammed it into his mouth.

By the time Orwen started screaming they were already across the field behind his house. But it was only a startled scream anyway and it stopped fairly quickly. He raised his head far enough to see the warm, candlelit convent disappear in the distance. It was a brisk autumn night and he was only in his nightdress, and the fairy's shoulder was narrow and sharp and dug into his stomach. He was carrying Orwen backward, and the turf blurred by like the earth spinning beneath him. His stride lengthened into long bounds.

He stopped at a little round lake called Cow Pond. Orwen had been there plenty of times, for picnics and such, and he'd never seen anything particularly eldritch or mystical about it.

The fairy dumped him down on its black, muddy edge.

"The name's John Punch." He stooped and picked up a pebble. "Take this."

Orwen took it and immediately dropped it because it weighed as much as a rock the size of his head. John Punch picked it up and gave it to him again, and this time, using both hands, he managed to hang on to it.

"Follow me."

The fairy waded straight into the dark, gnat-swarming water. He didn't seem to care about his clothes. Hesitantly Orwen stepped into the cold water up to his ankles, his knees. He'd hoped maybe it was magic water that would feel like nothing, or a nice warm bath, but no, just regular water, wet and freezing. The country silence was loud around him.

"Come on!" John Punch called. "Ye'll pay anyway! Whatever happens!"

The black lake water closed over his hat. A bit of duckweed spun where he'd disappeared, then slowed and stopped. He didn't come up again.

Orwen walked deeper, lugging the heavy pebble with aching fingers. Maybe I'll drown, he thought bitterly. He would drown his body, and good riddance. That'll show it. His shoulders shook violently as Cow Pond soaked through his nightgown. He stopped when the water was up to his neck.

A heedless spill of stars filled the sky overhead. He couldn't do this. But when he thought of going back to the village, and the convent school, he couldn't do that either. A night bird cried.

And at least John Punch could see who he was. No one else ever saw. Orwen took one more step, and there was no bottom under his foot.

He dropped straight down through the murky water, the weight of the pebble yanking him head down into the blackness. If he thought it was cold and dark before, now it was like being frozen in black ice. Five heartbeats. Ten—no, forget it!—but just then he felt, of all things, warm air on his hands, then his face, and the next moment he'd slipped down out of the water, like a calf being born, and slapped down on his back onto wet stone.

He was on the bottom of Cow Pond in an enormous round

bubble of air. The water hung low over his head, smooth and taut like a black silk tent. A tiny silver fish flipped and flopped on the stone step next to him, expiring in the air even as he, Orwen, came back to life. It was warm and wet like a greenhouse. A steep stone staircase led down to a little grassy field in the center.

The tiny field was dominated by a green beech tree. Its branches were full of birds, cheeping and chattering, and each bird glowed with a soft light like a miniature star.

John Punch was waiting for him along with another personage of similar age and size. In fact he looked exactly like John Punch, they could've been twins, too, except that he was dressed formally, in a magnificent green jacket with silver buttons, like a miniature lord.

"This is John Matchstick," John Punch said. "He'll teach ye how to fight."

John Matchstick bowed.

"He don't speak."

"What, not ever?"

"Ye might say his actions speak for themselves. Ye'll report to him every evenin' at vespers. He'll train ye all night, every night, till dawn, when ye'll go back home."

John Matchstick looked Orwen up and down critically. John Punch translated:

"Dress appropriately next time."

He turned to go. The star-birds twittered. Everything echoed strangely in the dome under Cow Pond.

"Wait!" Orwen called. "Won't the nuns notice I'm gone?"

"A fairy'll sleep in yuir bed, wearin' yuir likeness."

"You said before that I had to pay. What do I have to pay?"

"A boon."

"What 'boon'?"

"Part o' the price is that ye don' know the price."

Those sorts of boons were always something bad and tricky. But trickier than the trick that had been played on him at birth?

"I don't have a sword."

John Matchstick gallantly drew his own weapon, a beautiful shining length of narrow steel, and held it out to Orwen on his upward-facing palms.

Orwen took the sword, and whatever doubt he had evaporated like water thrown on a bonfire. This was good. This was better. He held it up to the light and power coursed and thrilled through him. A sword of his own. The star-birds cheeped and chattered. Starlings, he would've called them, if that weren't already something else.

"Can I start tonight?" he said.

The little lord looked at John Punch. John Punch interpreted:

"John Matchstick says ye can start tonight."

ORWEN STARTED THAT NIGHT, and he didn't stop. Every night at vespers he slipped out of bed and out the window into the country twilight, into clear nights, or hard freezes, or storms or rain or wet snow. At first he walked the two miles to Cow Pond, but as he got stronger he ran there without stopping and dived straight down into the water, headfirst, arriving all warmed up and ready to go. Sometimes in winter he had to break ice to get down there.

Every morning Orwen stole back home over the dew-soaked fields, with the dawn warming up in the east, and the distant bells ringing prime. As far as he knew no one ever saw him, though he had more than one close call with night owls and early risers. Certainly no one ever tried to stop him.

As soon as the door to his bedroom closed a fairy who looked just like him slipped into his bed, he knew, though he never once saw her. At dawn when he dropped back into bed, tired and sweaty, the fairy was always gone again, though sometimes he imagined he could smell her on his sheets—a savory smell, like thyme or oregano. She always remade the bed, always with the pillow at the wrong end.

Although his strength and power grew all the time, to the nuns it looked like Orwen had become gravely ill. He couldn't rouse himself in the morning, or even for lunch, and regularly slept on till early afternoon, when he awoke, his muscles aching, and demanded a huge meal. The nuns alternately beat and blessed him, and barbers and surgeons bled him. They whispered darkly about fairies stealing away his vitality. But the truth was precisely the opposite.

They were lonely, his silent sessions with John Matchstick under the sparkling, twittering beech tree under Cow Pond, but they were satisfying in a way that nothing else had ever satisfied Orwen. John Matchstick taught him a different style from what Oriel was learning back home in the practice yard. Orwen was neither as big nor as strong as the other boys, at least most of them, but John Matchstick was small too, and he taught Orwen to fight like he did, a fairy fighting style that made a virtue of his light, lithe frame. He couldn't beat the other boys on strength, but he could be quicker, and more flexible, and better balanced. He could use their power and weight against them. He learned to fight from his core and from his legs. John Matchstick taught him odd sinuous parries and thrusts, and acrobatic twirls and flips, and bewildering eye-bending feints to lead the big boys astray, lure them off balance and off-center.

At the end of his first year, to the day, John Matchstick presented Orwen with a gift: a sword. Not a hand-me-down, a sword of his very own. The blade was huge, wide and thick, and it took some getting used to. The metal was midnight blue and matte, not shiny, with silver filigree that showed only when the fighting got hot. The pommel was in the shape of a steel acorn.

He loved it. But every morning when he bid goodbye to the pond and returned to the world above, he had to leave it behind.

By the time he was fifteen Orwen had put on real muscle and become a serious menace with a variety of different weapons. The sword was his first option, but he practiced with mace and poleax and bow and unarmed too. Whenever Orwen wasn't training he felt like he was wasting time. He lived in an inverted universe where the world was a prison and the only freedom was in a bubble at the bottom of a pond.

But the thing was, Orwen was in a bubble in time, too, and sooner or later that bubble was going to pop. The adult world was closing in on him. He had muscle now, but he also had breasts. He'd wondered whether his body would really make good on its threat to develop and blossom, and it had. When people looked at him now they saw a woman. And my how they looked—strangers, his brother's friends, even his father's friends, even the village priest. His chest drew male eyeballs to it like a lodestone.

Shortly after he turned sixteen, Orwen's parents informed him that a match had been found for him. He would be married to William Colingham.

They'd met. William was the wild black-haired boy who captained the other side in the local football games. Orwen hadn't seen him since he was nine. Well, he'd been a little monster then, and he was probably a big monster now. Orwen wished him much joy on his wedding day, but he personally didn't plan to be there for it. He would run away, bind his chest, pack his crotch, and become a soldier of fortune. Or a pirate. Or a monk, like Saint Marina. Or a knight.

Except that, maddeningly, it wasn't that simple. The match between Orwen and William had been brokered only after long and exhausting negotiations by the sheriff, who'd been appointed by the Crown to keep the king's peace in the valley, and who was tired of arbitrating endless disputes between Colinghams and Dugfalls. (Thanks very much, King Arthur!) The purpose of the wedding was to put their long and mutually destructive feud to an end. It was not an exaggeration to say that lives depended on its successful completion.

Orwen couldn't even say it was unfair. It was just that without knowing it they were asking him to commit a kind of suicide, to destroy who he really was and replace that person with William Colingham's wife. The mother of William Colingham's children. It was so absurd it was almost funny. Almost but not. Orwen didn't know what to do. He couldn't stay, and he couldn't flee.

The night before the wedding, when Orwen should've been praying and washing and receiving ominously veiled erotic advice from his mother, he reported to John Matchstick for the last time. He trained as hard as he ever had. He didn't say anything about what was going on in the upper world—over the years Orwen had become almost as silent as John Matchstick was—but he was sure the fairy knew something was up. They always knew things like that.

When he couldn't wait any longer, when dawn was almost on him, Orwen stopped. He took a moment to look over his beautiful sword. He brought it to his lips and kissed its strange blue blade. Then he offered it to John Matchstick, as he always did.

But John Matchstick didn't take it. He shook his head. *No thanks.*

Orwen hesitated. The fairy made a shooing gesture at him. *Go on, take it.*

"I can't. You know I can't."

The fairy's expression didn't change.

"I'm getting married tomorrow, John Matchstick. This is the end, my training is over. I have to go and live a different life now."

John Matchstick cocked his head and narrowed his eyes skeptically. *Do you, though?*

"It's not what I want." Saying it out loud Orwen felt it more keenly than he ever had. His voice didn't break but tears spilled down his cheeks, mingling with the sweat from his exertions. "I loved all this, it was my favorite thing, and it always will be, but it's over now. I have a different destiny."

John Matchstick folded his arms.

"Take it, you pigheaded leprechaun!"

Dawn was coming. Orwen had to be off.

"Fine," Orwen said, less graciously than he would've liked. "All right. Thank you. It can be my dowry, I'll stick it in my hope chest." It wasn't the goodbye he'd wanted. He mastered himself and said, with proper feeling and respect: "Thank you, John Matchstick. These nights have been the happiest times of my life."

Orwen bowed and walked away, up the wet stairs, for the last time, as the star-birds winked out one by one.

HE DIDN'T RUN BACK to the convent that morning. He trailed slowly back over the wet fields like a sulky schoolboy, his sword stuck in his belt. He didn't care who saw him now. He was ready to collapse in his fairy-warm bed and sleep till it was time for his God damned wedding.

But he didn't make it that far. The moment Orwen stepped into the convent somebody grabbed him from behind and a strong arm wrapped around his throat. He writhed and scrabbled at it—John Matchstick had trained him to break holds like this, but for all his training Orwen had never been in a real fight before, and he panicked. He strained futilely at the arm and struggled to breath while his attacker's wine-scented breath rasped in his ear.

The man dragged Orwen back outside into the predawn hush. Orwen managed to wrench his throat around into the crook of the elbow and get a sip of air. Three more men were waiting there— they must have been hiding in the bushes.

"Good morrow to you, girly!" A man in a scarlet tunic cut so short it barely covered his privates stepped forward. Orwen knew him; he sold candles in town. He'd always thought the man had a kind face, lopsided but honest looking. But he didn't look so kind now.

"Where've you been so early this fine morning?" He stuck his thumbs in his belt.

"None of your fucking business, thanks."

"If you're marrying our cousin then your fucking is very much our business, Lady Whore-wen," the chandler said. His wit was rewarded with some droll chuckles. "You're fresh from some lucky fellow's bed, and we'd like to know whose."

So that's what this was. He'd thought he'd been so clever.

"If you're wondering if I'm 'intact,' you idiots," Orwen said, "you've got nothing to worry about."

"What we're worried about," said a skinny man with a huge brown beard, "is our brother marrying a Dugfall slut."

"Looks like your fellow gave you something to remember him by." The third man was bald and big as a knight out of armor. He pulled the sword from Orwen's belt and held it up, puzzled by its curious shape and alien metal. Now Orwen stopped laughing. He didn't care what they said about him, but they could take their filthy hands off his sword.

"I'll ask you again," the chandler said. "Who you sleeping with, girly?"

"Nobody," Orwen said. "You dumb shit. I don't have a lover."

"Well, you'll have four of 'em in a minute."

Baldy sauntered forward, loosening his hose. The other men cheered him on. Orwen took a wild kick at his crotch but he danced back out of reach, and the arm around Orwen's neck tightened so hard that his vision grayed out.

But Orwen hadn't expected the kick to connect, he'd just wanted them to keep on thinking he was helpless. He'd had a minute to calm down and it was all coming back to him. The men were still cheering when Orwen reached back and grabbed his captor's fruits and squeezed hard. The man yelled and his grip loosened enough for Orwen to jab him hard with an elbow in the solar plexus.

He scrambled to his feet, gulping air. The strangler turned out to be a squat, square-headed man with a greenish complexion. He was doubled over, groaning. Orwen kneed him in the face and felt his nose snap.

"Ooooh!" the burly bald man said with a huge grin. "We've got a fighter!"

Orwen grinned back. That was exactly what they had.

Though he'd never fought four full-grown human men before, at the same time. They weren't expecting his strength, and his skill—his first move was to hit Big Bald hard and sharp right in the pressure point in his armpit, cutting off all feeling to his arm—but the men were strong, too, and three of them had knives. Orwen had never been hit hard in the face before, and it hurt. He took cuts on both hands and another along the side of his neck that he was lucky to walk away from. Skinny Beard walloped him in one ear with a cupped hand, and he would never hear well out of that ear again.

But Orwen felt a perverse gratitude to these men. Thanks to these assholes he could finally let it out, all of it. He could finally show somebody who he really was. It cost him an eardrum, and a scar or two, but so be it. And when he finally got his hands on his sword, his beautiful fairy sword, the fight was over very quickly indeed.

ORWEN WAS HARNESSING A HORSE in the convent stable when Oriel found him. The sun was up, and the church bells were ringing prime. Somewhere tables were being laid, flowers arranged, a jeweled and overwhelmingly embroidered dress spread out for him on a blameless white coverlet.

Orwen had a strange warm floating feeling after the morning's excitement. His head, his hands, and his ribs were all in significant pain, and one ear was singing a single insistent high note, but the membrane that separated his fairy-life from his real life had finally been ruptured. The two had become one and combined into a new as yet unexplored third life, rich and strange, and he had no idea what would happen next except that now everything could really begin.

Not inappropriate sentiments for one's wedding day.

"I heard there was trouble," Oriel gasped. He'd been running. "By the convent. God's holy knees!" That last was when he got a look at Orwen's face.

Oriel wasn't a bad young man, Orwen reflected. He was obnoxious and arrogant and pretended to be dumber than he was, but he wasn't like those shitheads who'd come after him either, whom Orwen had left with a smashed nose, a missing finger, a missing earlobe, and assorted stab wounds. They wouldn't die, but they would never forget.

"Let me guess," Orwen said. "You heard I was attacked by robbers, and by sheer grit and manliness four Colingham men fought them off and saved their cousin William's bride-to-be."

"Something like that, yes. Why?"

Orwen took a deep breath.

"Only thing those men got robbed of was some serious fucking misconceptions."

"Well, are you all right? And what the hell are you doing now?"

"What the hell's it look like?" Orwen said. "I'm leaving the valley and I'm never coming back." He gently positioned the saddle and cinched it in place. The horse was a fine black palfrey, presumably belonging to one of the wedding guests. "Or not for a long time anyway."

"Is this about—" Oriel lost heart in the middle of the sentence but then manfully soldiered on. "Is this because you think you're a boy?"

"I don't think I'm a boy," Orwen said. "I know that I am a man."

Oriel's brow furrowed and his eyes got shifty, usually a sign of mental effort.

"There weren't any robbers. Were there?"

He sat down heavily on a hay bale. Orwen shook his head and yawned. He hadn't been to bed yet and wouldn't get there for a long time. He had some distance to put between himself and Greenstone House.

"So then what happened?"

"They jumped me and tried to rape me. We fought. I beat them up."

"But . . . how?!"

"The fairies have been teaching me how to fight under Cow Pond."

"See, this is why I can't take anything you say seriously. You know those assholes are going to start another war now?"

"No, they won't," Orwen said. "Because they would die before telling anyone I beat them. I'd best be off, brother of mine, before it's too late."

He swung up into the saddle. He wanted to keep the number of people who saw him galloping out of town on the morning of his wedding day to a minimum. Oriel rose wearily from his hay bale.

"Where are you going?"

"To seek my fortune."

"What fortune?"

"Well, I won't know till I've sought it, will I? Maybe I'll become a knight."

"A knight?!" He laughed, though not as meanly as he might have. "Sir Orwen?"

Oriel did have a point. He was going to need a new name. He supposed it didn't really matter what it was, knights had all kinds of weird names. He'd heard there was one called Sir Bleoberys.

It could be anything. Sir Ringading. Sir Falala.

"Dinadan."

"What?"

"I'll be Sir Dinadan."

"What the hell does that mean?"

"Nothing," Sir Dinadan said. "I just like it."

"Well I'm glad you're taking this seriously—listen!" He grabbed Dinadan's bridle. His face was a little desperate. "Listen. I know you don't care about this place, I know you don't want to come back, but if you don't marry William Colingham we'll never have peace! It'll be worse than before!"

"I've thought of that. Go look in my bed."

"What?"

"You don't need me to marry William, you just need someone who looks exactly like me to marry him. Take a look. She's in my bed. No one will ever know the difference."

"I don't—"

"Trust me when I say that she'll make a far better wife to him than I ever would have. Just tell him to keep a lot of honey cakes handy. Good luck to you, my brother. I'll see you again, I hope."

With that Sir Dinadan rode out of the Great Wold Valley forever.

He rode for hours, at first through woods and then out into yellow grasses that went on for miles, broken here and there by clumps of poplars. Not much cover, anybody who was looking for him could see him a mile away, but Dinadan would've seen them, too, and he didn't.

At noon he took a nap under an oak, then pressed on till he was past Harwood—somewhere along the way he must've passed the puddle where it all began. The sun was setting and the light was failing when he saw something glowing in a tree up ahead. It was a flock of those little birds, the star-birds, the ones from the tree under the pond, hopping and chirping away just like they always used to. The whole tree sparkled with them. Underneath it sat John Punch, taking his ease.

Dinadan wasn't completely sorry to see him again. John Punch was the first one who'd seen him for who he really was. He wouldn't forget that. The fairy toasted Dinadan with a little silver cup.

"Congratulations on completin' your education," he said. "Now there's just the wee matter o' yuir fee to settle."

"I hadn't forgotten."

"No more had we."

"Well?"

"We'll be requirin' ye to kill Merlin."

Dinadan laughed, louder and longer than he had in a long time.

"Merlin? The wizard?"

"Well, ye could kill Merlin the butler but he'd mostly likely've died of natural causes sooner or later. Merlin the wizard, though, I'm not so sure about him, which is why he will indeed require killin'. By you."

"Why?"

"He knows what he did. That's all ye need to know."

Dinadan shook his head, still chuckling. Was that all? Well, life was a rum business and no mistake.

"I'll see what I can do."

"Yes, ye surely will."

Dinadan rode on.

He had a destination now anyway. He was riding south, riding for Camelot and the Round Table. He'd pay his debt to the fairies, probably, by and by, though it seemed to him that the killing of King Arthur's personal wizard, the greatest sorcerer in all of Britain, would not be a simple thing. Not the sort of thing you'd want to go rushing headlong into.

He would bide his time, and in the meantime he would live as a man, just like Marina the Monk had in Lebanon. He would bind his breasts and stuff his crotch and bathe in private. He would pretend to shave his face and learn to piss standing up. He would have lovers, and a hundred brothers, and he would be happy, because at long last he'd done what he always dreamed of doing. He'd turned into what he already was.

Eighteen

A SILVER SHILLING

They'd won the day, but in his head Collum was still stuck back in the battle. Shadows kept turning into swords and spearpoints, lunging and stabbing at him. He was drinking hard to try to get them to turn back into shadows again. But they wouldn't go.

At least he wasn't drinking alone. The victory feast wasn't held at the Round Table but in a smaller, more private chamber in the stony quiet of the keep, the walls lined with shields and the horns of beasts, some of them utterly unidentifiable. The knights of the Table were there, plus every lord and lordling and king and kinglet who'd brought a few men to the battle. There were even two bishops, Caerleon and Londinium, and a papal legate.

And Collum. It wasn't a round table, but it was a very long one.

The hot glory of the fight had cooled and congealed inside Collum into something sticky and clammy that he couldn't get rid of. The room felt close and warm and smoky from candles and torches. Outside the night rang with the sound of crickets and the shouts of the drunken victors—the clumsy rabble of this morning were tonight's legendary heroes. Mingling with those sounds were the moans of wounded men suffering the dark mercies of the surgeons. In the distance an abandoned siege engine burned like a dying dragon.

Collum had killed six people today. Maybe more. You couldn't exactly call it an accident, or unforeseeable, since it was exactly what he'd been single-mindedly training to do ever since he was a child, but till now he'd never really understood what it meant. It suddenly felt like a terrible mistake. What a great and awful power God had given to men, the power to revoke His divine gift of life, to unlock one another's chests with the blunt key of a sword and roughly evict the ghost within. A pile of steel and guts, like Morgan said.

He touched a wound he'd gotten on his right side, just above his hip—a hard blow had ground his mail right into his flesh, giving it a scaly, macerated appearance. They'd dressed it with bandages soaked in wine, but it still hurt.

His stomach hurt, too, as if he'd eaten those men and now they were down there in his guts, groaning and aching, indigestible like roots or gristle: the ratty axman, the yellow-toothed giant, all the rest of them. After the battle he'd washed in the river, and then again back at the castle, but he still didn't feel clean. He waved at a servant and pointed to his empty cup. Drank. Pointed again. Keep 'em coming. Maybe if he drank enough he could puke them out.

Bedivere looked at him searchingly.

"All right?"

Collum gave him a sullen nod—*sure, why wouldn't I be?*—and looked away. Whatever this was, he wanted to be alone with it.

From the chatter going on around him Collum was coming to understand better what had actually happened today, which was

that they'd come very close to losing everything. The archers who'd
started the battle were unable to stop the cavalry charge they'd set
off, and it made a bloody mash of Camelot's right flank. Moments
later another mounted formation exploded out of the woods straight
into their unguarded left. Constantine and Scipio got into a sharp
exchange over why they'd thought it wasn't possible to get horses
through that wood, and how Rience's men had managed to do it
without anybody noticing.

After that unpromising start the weight of numbers would've
carried the day for Rience if Camelot's infantry hadn't been fresher,
and even then it was only Nimue's arrival on the field that turned
the tide irreversibly in Camelot's favor.

But everything came at a cost. Two lords had died, and a dozen
knights, along with hundreds of archers and infantry. As soon as it
was clear that Camelot was out of danger, Nimue collapsed and
had to be carried back to the castle on a litter. She lay now in a feverish half sleep, rousing only to swear blisteringly at any physi-
cian who tried to examine her. The only person whose medical
attentions she would accept was Palomides.

Still: it was a victory. Rience himself had escaped but not many
of his noble allies had. Some were cut down running, others were
found hiding in the woods or hunting desperately for a church to
take sanctuary in. A mob of armed peasants caught up with the
Earl of Aeron halfway to Londinium, dressed as a woman. They
butchered him right there in the road. A roving detachment led by
Sir Dinadan had stumbled on a segment of the enemy baggage
train bogged down in a muddy field. It yielded some richly gilded
weapons and Rience's own royal cache of wine, which the party
was currently enjoying.

"And did you see—*did you see*—Bedivere catch an arrow?" Dinadan mimed it, like he was catching an invisible fly. His face was red, and he looked a little stunned; he'd gotten a glancing mace blow to the head while trying to save a few of the luckless archers. "Like in the old days! And then"—he plunged a knife into the tabletop, startling an archbishop—"he stabs a man right in the eye with it!"

Everybody turned to Bedivere for confirmation, but Bedivere seemed more interested in whatever was at the bottom of his cup of wine.

"He turned the tide *single-handedly.*" Scipio waited for the laugh, but either people didn't get the joke or just didn't feel like laughing. Scipio was as neatly turned out as if he'd spent the day primping instead of laying about him in the press; Collum noticed for the first time that he wore a wedding ring. Dinadan was having some trouble getting his knife unstuck from the table.

They were all doing their best to feel celebratory. Constantine had changed into party clothes, complete with shoes with upturned toes so long they had to be fastened to his knees with fine golden chains. But he sat staring at his food without eating, bleary and worn out, sweating in his finery in the hot, smoky room.

"My friends." A flushed King Cole the Old lifted a silver cup, not his first. "To Camelot." Cole was an immensely distinguished royal figure who had only thrown in with King Arthur after having occupied and then lost the thrones of three different kingdoms in the Old North, where he was known as Coel Hen.

Collum was glad to have an excuse to drink more. The table was crowded with bowls and saucers and goblets and gold plates.

"And many happy returns!" shouted Lord Argente of the Straight Marches, a beat late. Argente was even older than King Cole and completely bald except for two white puffs coming out of his ears, which made him look like something was on fire in there. But when Camelot called he'd come straight from the Straight Marches, wherever they were, with a half dozen house knights.

"Now." King Cador of Cornwall clapped a heavy hand on his son's shoulder. "How goes the pursuit of the stragglers?"

Cador had the long, rookish face of a very tall man, though he still wasn't as tall as Constantine.

"Lord Lum is leading it." Constantine seemed to have shrunk by a few inches in his father's presence. "Rience's men n-need food and rest, and he will deny them both."

"Have they crossed the Thames?"

"D-don't think so."

Cador pouted thoughtfully.

"So they still hold the Salt Ford."

"Yes."

"And the Galafort?" Constantine shrugged. His father shook his head. "War's a game of castles, boy! Battles are nothing—"

"Don't lecture me, Father. Rience is retreating through land that he already burned and pillaged on the way in. He's left himself nothing to live on, and the locals hate him."

"They don't hate him," Cador said. "They fear him. Big difference." Cador gave Cole a knowing look. *They should leave this stuff to us real kings, eh?*

Collum had assumed Cador was at Camelot to advance his son's fortunes, even put him forward as High King, but he seemed more intent on undermining him. Constantine muttered something about Vegetius's *De re militari* and the dangers of pursuing a retreating enemy. The steel he'd shown on the battlefield was gone again.

"Everybody is waiting for us to overcommit," Palomides said, coming to his aid. "If we overextend ourselves west they will descend on Camelot en masse. Indeed, Rience's entire campaign may well have been nothing more than a feint to draw us out."

"Who is 'everyone' in this scenario?" asked the papal legate, a mild-mannered man in an ecclesiastical-looking red hat, which he wore even indoors.

"The Picts," Palomides said. "Saxons, Orkneys, Scotti. Take your pick."

"It's the Franks we should worry about."

"Lancelot would keep the Franks in l-line," Constantine said.

"Oh, like he kept his cock in line?" Dinadan snapped, with sudden bitterness. The churchmen scowled. "A king has to master a country. He couldn't even master himself. And I'll tell you something else, it wasn't Frankish gold in that baggage train, those coins were minted in Cameliard, which means the Eastbrooks. The queen's family."

No one knew what to say to that.

"There's six keels of Mordred's Saxons still running up and down the east coast," said King Cole. He shifted in his chair, trying to ease a gouty foot. "Who's going to pay them now?"

"There's always money in the monasteries," Scipio said, "if you shake them hard enough."

"You would plunder the church to pay heathens?" the archbishop of Caerleon said.

"Just sell some more indulgences, you old fraud! If God doesn't like it He shouldn't've left all those gold reliquaries lying around."

"Enough." Bedivere massaged his forehead as if he had a sudden headache. He must get tired of being the grown-up in the room, Collum thought. "We won today, but the next army of any size that turns up at Camelot will take it. We must act."

"Pray," the papal legate said.

"God's not listening," Constantine said.

"Another quest then," the archbishop of Caerleon quavered. "You could find the Holy Lance, no one's ever found that!"

"There are no adventures left in Britain," Bedivere said.

"What would we do with a Holy Lance anyway?" Scipio pointed at Bedivere's pheasant in sauce. "Are you going to finish that?"

"When we were in the Otherworld I spoke with Morgan le Fay," Collum said, trying heroically not to slur his words. "She told me she's coming back to Britain."

Even the servants stopped what they were doing and stared.

"Oh, that's good," Dinadan said. "What's she going to do when she gets here?"

"She says that as Igraine's daughter the throne is rightfully hers. She offered to join forces with the Table. I declined on your behalf."

"Well, that was prudent. How long till she gets here?"

"I don't know," Collum said. "But she seemed eager to get started."

"You must've had quite a long conversation."

"It definitely felt long."

"Would somebody please get me some wine?"

Collum hadn't noticed Nimue come in. She looked chalky and a little unsteady but not any less startlingly beautiful than she had on the battlefield. How strange that he hadn't noticed it before. Collum poured her some wine and then some more for himself.

"I'll summarize our options for the late arrivals, as I understand them," Bedivere said. "We can choose a lesser royal and try to raise him to the throne and make it stick. We can forcibly marry someone to Guinevere. We can wait for God to pull another king out of a hat. Or apparently we can bend the knee to Morgan le Fay."

The room was silent. Maybe they'd expected the list to be

longer. Was that all, after all that fighting and killing and dying? In a corner Sir Dagonet sat mechanically vanishing and producing a silver spoon.

"Or we can wait for Arthur come back. If anybody has any other suggestions, I'm eager to hear them."

"Constantine?" King Cador said pointedly. "Do you have anything to say?"

"I support Sir Lancelot."

"Very well," King Cador said. "I offer my services to Britain as high king."

"What is your position on the Pelagian heresy?" the papal legate asked politely. King Cole looked amused.

"We should consider Morgan le Fay's offer," Palomides said.

"Morgan le Fay is a pagan and a moral cesspool!" said the bishop of Londinium. "And a woman!"

"She has Igraine's blood. She has a claim. Perhaps it is time for the old Britain to have its say."

"Only the church can crown a king in this land," growled Caerleon. "Our hand will not be forced."

"It is easier to crown than to dethrone," Nimue said.

"I want to say something about Morgan le Fay," Bedivere said. "When we met her in the Otherworld, I recognized her. I'd seen her before.

"She was on the ship that came and took Arthur away. It was her who touched his head and called him 'brother.'"

Was it possible? Collum struggled to fit that idea in with what he'd seen of her. Was Avalon part of the Otherworld? Just offshore, in the Fairy Sea? Could she be keeping Arthur prisoner there, injured but alive? If she was then she'd kept very quiet about it.

"I cannot understand what any of you are talking about." Lord

Argente pulled anxiously at one of his ear-tufts. "Could we not ask the Grail King?"

"King Pellas left Britain along with the Grail," Palomides said gently.

"Well, could not Joseph of Arimathea be had?"

"Oh sure," Dinadan said. "He's only been dead for five hundred years!"

"Nonsense! He popped up on the Grail Quest every five minutes!"

"I think that was his ghost." Dinadan rubbed his face. "Though right now a ghost king doesn't sound that bad."

This is going nowhere, Collum thought. Mud and blood and murder, drunken bickering in a smoky room. There must be another way to make a king.

"We need the blood of the Pendragons," said Old King Cole.

"Oh, people always say that. But as soon as they've got it, well, there they go, spilling it everywhere."

Heads turned. It was a boy's voice, high and piping, from the far end of the room. He was leaning languidly against the doorframe, finely dressed in black velvet trimmed in silver. He couldn't have been more than ten or eleven, but he spoke with a man's confidence. Two exasperated-looking soldiers hovered behind him.

"Who the hell are you?" Bedivere said.

"God's bones." Nimue put her hand to her forehead as if to check if she was still feverish. "Here we go."

"I don't understand." King Cador looked around helplessly. "Who is that?"

King Cole pointed ominously, his face darkening: "That is scum begotten by scum!"

Bedivere rose, half drawing his sword, but something in the boy's face made him stop there.

"For those of you who don't know me," the boy said, with uncommon self-possession, "my name is Sir Melehan. My father was Sir Mordred, begotten by that notorious scum King Arthur. As his only living male descendant, I am here to take my rightful place on the throne of Camelot."

THE FEAST WASN'T SO MUCH adjourned as it was abandoned. Sir Melehan explained that he'd come with an army, two thousand men down from Orkney and Elmet and another five hundred from across the Channel. They were camped ten miles away, ready to descend on Camelot if he did not reappear, unharmed and newly crowned, within three days.

Lord Argente spat at his feet and Scipio called him a liar. Having accomplished that much, they sent Sir Melehan to the dungeons and went to bed.

Alone in his bedchamber, sweating vinous sweat in the summer heat, Collum lay fully dressed on his field of golden lions, each one framed, or maybe caged, inside its golden diamond. He ached and stung in half a dozen places. He tried to work out the last time he'd actually closed his eyes and slept. Before the battle. Before the Glass Castle, before his journey across the Otherworld, before the old man in the garden. It must've been on a stony beach in Cornwall, a thousand years ago. It felt like Britain was drifting apart, piece by piece, disintegrating into a shapeless, kingless archipelago. He'd thought Camelot would make him whole and new, it would fix what was broken, but Camelot was no better off than he was.

He wanted to close his eyes but he was afraid of what he might see. He felt desperate not to be alone, but there was no one at Camelot, or anywhere else for that matter, whom he could wake up at this hour. Eventually he got up and went to the window. Down in the courtyard someone was kneeling on the grass, all alone, under a fat setting summer moon that was very slightly flat on one side. It was Nimue.

He picked his way carefully downstairs in the torchlit darkness; the spiral staircases at Camelot were pitched so steeply that they slung knotted ropes down them from the top floor to hang on to so that people didn't break their necks. He'd gone past tiredness into some exalted spiritual state on the other side. The summer air felt like a calm sea he was drifting through like a jelly.

Nimue was digging a hole with a small shovel in the carefully tended lawn. She worked diligently, uncomplainingly, like a forest creature burrowing in the dark. A handful of glowing golden-green motes hung around her head: fireflies. She must've bewitched them. He could see the shape of her narrow shoulders through her dress as she worked.

He cleared his throat to avoid startling her.

"Good evening, my lady," he said. "Are you feeling any better?"

"Yes. Don't hover."

Suddenly he did feel awkward and looming. He took a step back.

"Is there something you need?" she said.

"No. I couldn't sleep."

"Well, I could, but I have work to do. And before you ask, I'm out of sleeping draughts."

The vulnerability he'd seen on the battlefield was gone as if it were never there.

"Maybe I could help you. With—this." Whatever this was. "I dug a hole or two back in the Out Isles."

Because I was a servant, he didn't add. He was a thief and a liar bandying words with King Arthur's beautiful sorcerer. He would've panicked completely if he weren't so tired. As it was he couldn't think of anything else to say. He was about to make his excuses and go when Nimue handed him one end of a skein of string.

"Hold."

She walked away from him backward, unspooling it as she went; Collum immediately dropped his end and had to run after it and pick it up again. When she'd paid out its full length, she marked the spot and started another hole there.

Collum followed, rewinding the skein.

"I'm not looking for an apprentice," she said.

"That's all right," Collum said. "I already have a job."

"Or a husband."

"I'll just hold the string then."

He waited while Nimue dug another hole.

"Could I ask you," he said, to break the silence, "what it feels like? Doing magic?"

"Feels like?" She frowned. "Why?"

"Because I've never done it."

"I don't know, what does it feel like killing people with a sword?"

Nimue's shovel hit a rock, and she stooped to root it out.

"Good at first. Fantastic actually." Collum fiddled with the string. He couldn't think of a good lie so he just told the truth. "I felt like a god today, like I could do anything and whatever I did was right. But now none of it seems right. People say battle is supposed to show you who you are, and I wanted it to show me. Very badly. But I know less about myself than I did this morning. Except I guess that I'm not a god."

That probably wasn't the answer she was looking for. Having pried the stone out, she flung it off into the darkness.

"Well, you must be good at it. You know Dinadan took bets when you were fighting the Green Knight? The odds on you were not short. How many people did you kill today?"

"Six, I think."

"I killed a hundred and seventy-three. Not that it's a competition."

"Maybe I took up the wrong trade. You're sure you don't need an apprentice?"

"I'm sure." She finished the hole and paused. "You feel each one as they go, like bubbles popping. It's part of the magic. Seven of them were ours. One was a woman. There must be a better way."

"I thought the same thing. But I can't figure out what it is."

She refilled the hole and patted the turf once with the back of the shovel, then they did the business with the string again. The green-gold light from the fireflies showed her delicate features in the dark. There was a smudge of dirt on her forehead where she'd wiped it with the back of her wrist.

"Arthur would've found some way to get Morgan and Rience fighting each other," she said. "Solve one problem with another. But I could never see the angles the way he did."

After two more strings and two more stones Nimue straightened up and planted her hands in the small of her back.

"Done." She stretched and groaned and crossed herself and said a brief prayer over the final hole. Her eyebrows were just a bit on the unruly side.

"Good. What did we do?"

"Strengthened the boundaries around Camelot, so that your friend Morgan can't see in. She may be a pagan cesspool or whatever that mitered whoreson called her but she's a very competent sorceress. And the barriers are getting thin."

"Morgan said that too," he said.

"What did you make of her?"

"Impressive."

"Most men think that. Would you want her on the throne?"

"She wasn't that impressive."

"But then who?"

The night was black and humid around them, with dark windblown clouds, smooth and rounded gray as river stones. He knew that she was indulging him, but he didn't care. He was enjoying himself too much.

"I would choose Lancelot," Collum said. "I know what people think of him, but at this point I'm not even sure it matters what he did or didn't do. People would follow him. I know he's a monk now but he has to see that Britain needs him. Why, who do you support?"

"God." She sat down on an old stone block that had been left there as a bench. "I'm still waiting for God. Because I'm a sorceress people think I must fly through the night to copulate with the devil in the form of a goat, but I didn't give up my faith when I took up magic. I practice sorcery, but I still pray to God."

"I suppose I did think that. I mean, not about the goat." He blushed furiously. It had never occurred to him that there were Christian wizards. "But you have to admit God's been pretty quiet lately." *A desert god. A god of sand and dust.*

"God doesn't come when you snap your fingers, He comes when you're ready for Him." Nimue snapped her delicate fingers, producing a strikingly loud *pop* in the quiet. "That's the difference between a spell and a prayer."

"We'd better get ready then."

"And quickly too." Nimue stood up, declining Collum's offer of an arm, and slapped the grass off her dress. "I didn't answer your question about magic before, Sir Collum, but I think maybe you answered it for me. It's like sword fighting, it feels good and bad. Right and wrong. I love God, and I know He loves me, but the only power I have in this world comes from the other side, and I don't know why that is."

They were close enough that he could smell the sweetly sour tang of her sweat. Someone in the next courtyard was singing "Fowls in the Frith" in a sonorous baritone. Collum was trying to think of an elegant but manly way to wrap up the conversation when she went on.

"I think you've been honest with me, Sir Collum, or as honest as you can be, so I should be honest too. You fought well for Camelot today but I don't trust you. You're keeping secrets."

At that moment all Collum wanted to do was tell her everything, good and bad, start to finish. It would almost be worth it just to have had this be a genuine conversation between two people in the middle of the night in a courtyard at Camelot.

But it wasn't quite. He wasn't quite brave enough.

"Everybody has secrets," he said.

"Of course they do. Bedivere certainly has them. And Dinadan, and Scipio—Scipio is made of secrets. But you want to be particular about which secrets you keep, right? Because they require a lot of care and feeding. In my experience it's almost never worth it."

"Well," he said sheepishly, "fortunately I'm not very good at keeping them."

"I suspected as much."

"I have a feeling you're the opposite."

"It's a mixed blessing." Nimue smiled, and Collum almost felt like himself, whoever that was, for the first time since the battle. She took something out of her bag and tossed it to him. "Here."

It was a silver shilling.

"I won it off Dinadan. I have a feeling you're going to need it more than me."

Nineteen

THE LION IN THE DESERT

ollum woke to a torrent of summer sun pouring in through his narrow windows. It took him a few moments to remember where he was and what was wrong with him: he was at Camelot, and he had a hangover. Another thing they didn't mention in the stories. He scraped himself out of his luxurious bed, head splitting, horribly thirsty, drank a bucket full of cold water from a well and was sick in the bushes. Then he went off in search of the only thing that would make him feel better, assuming Nimue didn't have a draught for hangovers.

Collum grew up training in a neglected courtyard behind Dubh Hall, thirty yards on a side, overgrown in the corners and muddy in the middle. The training yard at Camelot was ten times that size. Its carpet of grass was perfectly smooth. In the center was a worn old Roman mosaic, wide as a man was tall, depicting the severed head of Medusa gazing up at the sky open-mouthed, as if she'd just spotted a falling star.

Not one but four pells graced Camelot's training yard, each set in its own perfect circle of fine white sand. (The red devil-faces painted on them bore a family resemblance to the old pell-devil Collum had left behind.) There was a ring chalked out for wrestling and stuffed canvas clouts for archery, each one with a peg in the center for a bull's-eye. Lined up neatly along the base of a wall were heavy stones for lifting and throwing, arranged by size, from a modest cannonball to a boulder a foot and a half in diameter that looked like it had sat there unmoved for several centuries.

An airy high-beamed hall floored with smooth slate opened onto the yard with rank on rank of unstrung bows on its walls, each one resting horizontally on two nails to keep it from warping, and bins of arrows fletched in Camelot blue and gold. A small arsenal of wooden training weapons stood along the back wall: swords and pikes and bills and spears and axes and glaves. Collum chose a sword, measured it, knocked it against the stone floor a few times, put it back, tried another one, then went back to the first. He took a deep breath. The fragrance of all that lovingly worn, seasoned wood was already making his head feel better.

First he traced circles and squares in the air, at full extension. Then he cycled through all fourteen guards, five major and nine minor, then the eight cuts, a hundred of each, and the four thrusts, same. His wounds from the day before flared hot, and sweat stung them, but he didn't care. He couldn't believe he was getting to practice like this, with nobody making fun of him or threatening to beat him if he didn't clean their boots. The throb in his head grew fainter. The phantoms from the battle began to fade and crawl back to wherever they came from. For a while anyway.

After the swordwork he shot some arrows out in the yard. It was all so easy! No wonder the knights of the Table were so damn good at everything. He picked up one of the gargantuan throwing stones. The grass under it was yellow, and the underside was crawling with pill bugs, which made him drop it even faster than he otherwise would have.

By this time the toothy shadow of the castle wall was dividing the yard in half diagonally like a shield, and the bells were ringing for nones. He dragged an arm across his sweaty forehead. The wound on his hip had bled through his tunic, but he felt almost human again.

And look at him, nobody from nowhere, the whipping boy of Mull, standing here in the quiet green heart of Camelot. This world was worn out and cold, its future was uncertain at best, but it could still play host to wonders.

"Sir Collum. We need to talk."

Bedivere was standing in the open doorway of the hall, hands clasped behind his back, looking somber as usual. He must have been there for a while. Dinadan was sitting astride a wooden horse they used for practicing mounts and dismounts.

"It's a delicate topic," he said. "There are certain standards to which a knight of Camelot must be held."

"Oh." He'd rather hoped they were going to praise his diligence in the yard, or his valor on the battlefield. "What standards?"

"Your armor," Dinadan said. "It's cheap and ugly."

"And the fit is poor," said Bedivere.

Yesterday he'd felt like a lord in it, but as soon as they said it, Alasdair's old armor immediately became embarrassingly shabby, with its replacement plates and its red velvet, tacky even before it was ripped down the middle.

"Come with us," Bedivere said gravely.

Collum followed them into an older part of the castle, where the walls were Roman stone, and across a courtyard with a well in the center and down a half flight of steps that were worn slanted and slippery with age. Bedivere unlocked an iron-clad wooden door to reveal a long chamber half sunken below ground.

The air was dry as dust. All was still. Collum's breath caught.

All along the walls were rows of armors. It was a frozen army of silent steel. They stood two and three and four deep, gray and black and blue and silver, shiny and matte, spiked and scalloped and painted and damascened. Some were battle-scuffed, some looked like they'd never been worn. They were grouped by their country of origin, their size, their age, their style. It was a library of armors.

"God's knees," Collum whispered.

"The armory of Camelot," Dinadan said.

"Left here by our betters." Constantine had appeared from somewhere, with a solemn Palomides behind him. Suddenly it was quite a gathering.

Dinadan pointed out a few that had belonged to famous knights now gone: King Pellinore's armor, fire-gilded with crosses and grails and the Questing Beast; and the enormous armors of Sir Balin, Knight of the Two Swords, and his brother, Sir Balan, their chests so big they looked like cauldrons. They'd slain each other in a duel, neither one knowing who he was facing. The men inside were beyond repair, but their armors had been fixed up good as new. The helmets sprouted a wild profusion of horns and ruffs and crests. An old Roman legionary's armor—ragged, scarred scale, *lorica squamata*—stood at attention on a wooden rack.

"We've picked one out for you," Bedivere said.

"You have?" Collum had hardly dared to hope. His voice was husky. "Thank you. That's very generous of you."

They strolled down the aisle all together like generals inspecting the troops, past the rows of puffed-out metal chests. It seemed a little silly that all the knights had turned out for this, but why not. He would live and probably die in this armor. Outside, through the windows, he could see the little courtyard with its old well.

"Here it is," Dinadan said.

"You earned it."

They stopped. In among the steel soldiers a long wooden chest had been stood up on one end. Collum stared at it stupidly. It was made of plain unpainted boards cheaply knocked together.

Not a chest. A coffin.

Shit. His heart froze an instant before the iron hoop of the Saracen's massive arms closed around his chest. The breath went out of him. He opened his mouth to shout and someone forced an oily gag into it and cinched it sharply behind his head. A rough sack jerked down over his head and the sun went out.

For an instant Collum was too confused to react, and when he did kick and squirm it was too late. Deft hands were already binding his ankles tightly, then his wrists, and shoving him forward into the coffin. What did they think he'd done?! Someone banged in nails, sealing him inside. Whatever this was they must have planned it carefully because it was all over in a few heartbeats. The coffin was hefted up unto strong shoulders.

He couldn't speak and he could barely move, but he could hear them talking.

"You know he lied about his father?" Constantine said. "After all that he was nothing but a w-wool broker!"

"And that was not even his real father." Palomides. "He is a bastard. *Filius nullius.* Lying is surely one of life's least pleasurable sins."

They knew. Of course they did. But how?

"And he stole that armor," Bedivere said. "From his own liege lord."

"Thick as thieves with Morgan le Fay herself," Dinadan said. "And he's not from Mull either, whatever he says. Even Nimue can't figure out where he was born."

"And have you seen how he drools over her?" Sir Dagonet was here too.

There was a chorus of raucous laughter. Well, Collum didn't suppose Dagonet got too many laughs these days. He tried to shout through his gag but they ignored him, and he didn't even know what he would've said. I *am* from Mull! And my drooling was very discreet! The coffin was set down roughly on stone. He panted through his nose in the confined space. Were they going to bury him alive?! Jesus. Surely not. Beloved Jesus. He'd lied, he'd pretended, but he didn't deserve that. The coffin swayed slightly, as if it rested on some narrow fulcrum.

It came to him where he was. He was outside in the courtyard. They'd set him down on the edge of that old well. He kicked wildly with his bound feet.

"His table manners are worse than poor old Villiars's were." Constantine sighed. "I suppose he thought to take advantage of our depleted numbers."

"He won't be the last," Dagonet said.

"It's a shame," Dinadan said. "I was almost starting to like him."

Collum had been about to try shouting again but it died in his throat. What difference could it possibly make. He moaned and squeezed his eyes shut under the hood. Wood grated on stone, his weight shifted, and the world tipped head downward.

FOR A LONG MOMENT the horror was so pure he couldn't distinguish it from physical agony. Weightlessness told every cell in his body that it was about to die—

Something banged him on the head so hard that the darkness flashed solid white light, then shattered into dying red shards.

At first he thought the well must've been dry and he'd smashed his skull on the bottom, but cold water poured in on him, pressing on his clothes, penetrating them. The fall had clubbed the wind out of him, and he tried frantically to suck in a little air around the gag into his collapsed lungs. He doubled his bound body inside the sinking broken coffin, pushing with his knees against the wood, thrashing like a grub, a half-smashed larva, something degraded and injured and not human. He was a fetus trapped by the womb, a breech baby, unable to be born. It would not release him. It would drag him down and drown him.

He heaved with his back and felt the wood crack and start to separate. Three nails dragged hot lines across his face and then he was free and wriggling desperately upward like a worm. Apparently even this degraded, humiliated, rejected grub still wanted to live.

He humped himself up over a couple of boards from the coffin and shook the rough sack off his head. The darkness was total. Slowly and awkwardly, by kicking his bound legs together, he managed to get his chin over another board. One by one he collected as many as he could, like a horrible, exhausting children's game. But when he was done and had them all he could just about rest and catch his breath without going under.

He'd thought they abandoned him in Cornwall, and he was wrong then, but this time seemed pretty definitive. He'd flown too high, too close to the sun of Camelot, and his waxwork wings had melted and flowed and scalded his arms and he'd fallen to earth. Or even farther than that, he'd sunk deep underground. He closed his eyes and lay like that for a long time, a turtle on a log, shivering as the cold water leached the heat from his body.

When he finally opened them again he saw something: a tiny smudge of gray light in the blackness. He thought it was a figment but it didn't move when he moved his head. It looked like it was far away, but that was impossible. He kicked toward it. He expected to hit his head against the side of the well but he didn't, because there was no more well. The light was miles away, over the horizon. He was in the ocean, the well water had become salty, and the light was dawn.

Well, this time he'd definitely drowned. No giant was going to fish him out of this one. In a way it was a relief. He'd thought it would hurt more.

But even when you were dead it seemed that you had to drag yourself to the afterlife. He kicked some more. Gentle waves were now helpfully washing past him, urging him on toward the east. Below the rising sun he could make out a low, flat slip of land.

The moment he touched the smooth beach all the strength went out of him. He inched like a worm the rest of the way up onto it. By this time the whole world was washed with pearly morning light. His eyes closed again and he lay there with his head throbbing, his muscles aching, his cheek in the cool sand.

When he opened them again the sun was well up and someone was standing there gazing down at him. Not an angel. A man. He was well dressed. He looked like somebody important.

"Hrrurrr." Collum tried to make a sound like a greeting through his gag. He tried to sit up but failed. "Hrr."

"That's all right. Everything's all right now." The man smiled—he had golden-stubbly cheeks and a heroic cleft chin. He knelt and started working on the ropes. "You are welcome to Astolat."

So HE STILL wasn't dead. He'd just moved on to the next castle down the road, which was Astolat. Of course it was. It made perfect sense. That was always the plan if things didn't work out at Camelot, which they apparently hadn't, since the knights of the Round Table had thrown him bodily down a well.

It wasn't what Collum had dreamed of, but he mastered his disappointment sufficiently to admit that Astolat was nice enough, a long narrow stone keep stretched out along a low ridge, with barley fields rolling away on all sides like well-smoothed bedclothes. The man with the cleft chin who found him on the beach was in fact the lord of Astolat, who bore the fine old Roman name Numerius.

And more luck: Lord Numerius had need of a good strong knight. In a wood not far from Astolat was a fountain. By tradition it was considered sacred, and only the lord and his family were allowed in the grove where it stood. Numerius wanted a knight to guard it. Times being what they were, Collum was grateful to have a job. He swore his sword to the Lord of Astolat.

It was even an adventure of sorts: he would be known as the Knight of the Fountain now. He was given comfortable quarters and a fine new armor. All black, none of that tacky velvet. No one here seemed to mind about his accent or his table manners. They were ordinary men. That's what Bedivere said, and that's what he was. *Grails and spirits, marvels and quests. Time to let it all go.* Camelot and all that. And who was he trying to fool, he'd never even had it in the first place.

For days and then weeks he rode out each morning to defend the fountain. It was a pretty spot, and the beeches all around were crowded with songbirds. Once in a while a passing knight would challenge him, and he would fight them and see them off. Mostly they were just amateurs and upstarts, no one who gave him much trouble, and he served them accordingly. After a while the Knight of the Fountain began to acquire something of a reputation. He wasn't really on an adventure, it was more like he *was* the adventure. He was a part of the scenery now, here for other knights to come and test themselves against. Then they would ride on to other dramas, other chapters of their various epic stories, while he stayed behind. It wasn't such a bad berth, all things considered. And he was getting a lot better at jousting.

The sacred fountain was a stone statue in the shape of a woman, probably a pagan deity or an allegorical figure for some virtue or other, though her precise nature had been forgotten long ago. She held an upraised sword in a fierce martial salute. The sculptor had given her a winsome face and a knowing expression, her thin, straight hair skillfully rendered in marble. Collum liked to imagine her watching his battles and silently cheering him on.

It all seemed very easy—but why shouldn't it be? He'd tried working hard, and his reward was getting chucked down a well. He'd been going about life all wrong. He'd been trying too hard, aiming too high. He'd had some idea he was a hero, steering the fate of the world. He couldn't believe he'd been so arrogant. As if everything would all go to smash if Sir Collum didn't come galloping in to save it! *Here's a lady in distress. Surely I, as a knight of Britain, can save her!*

As if the future of mankind hung trembling on which overfed Narcissus sat the throne of Camelot. Kings rise and fall, but the world was wide, and from this distance the kings looked very small. Even Arthur looked small.

One day a knight appeared at the far end of the meadow, bearing a blue rooster on his shield. He saluted Collum.

There was something dreamlike about Collum's life at Astolat, and it was only at moments like this, when lance met shield and steel met steel, that he came fully awake. Both spears shattered at the first pass, and the two knights wheeled round at far ends of the field. Blue Rooster waved off another lance and drew his sword instead, and they got into it hand to hand.

But this challenger wasn't like the others. Blue Rooster was no upstart. His first blow tore the shield right off Collum's arm, almost spraining his elbow. He batted Collum's sword back and forth like it was a toy. Inside of ten minutes Collum was down and stunned. The knight tied him hand and foot, flung him over the back of his horse, and rode away with him as a prisoner. God's blood, Collum thought through the pounding in his head, this must be what Scipio felt like. At least he let me keep my armor on.

The knight of the Blue Rooster rode with him for three days, never saying a word, out of the green valley of the fountain and into an empty land, a desolate rocky country of red dirt bristling with stunted trees. He dumped Collum there and rode away.

How false and foolish life is, Collum thought. And how easily one life is changed for another.

. . .

COLLUM MIGHT HAVE DIED of thirst, but that night he heard an un-
earthly yowling from not far away. Creeping closer he saw a black
lion wrestling with an enormous banded serpent that was trying
to crush it. Collum drew his sword, waded in, and slew the snake.

After that the grateful lion followed him everywhere, padding
along beside him like a loyal hound. For weeks Collum and the
lion wandered the desert together, until a bandit chief and his company ambushed them and took Collum prisoner. He languished in
a cell until a servant girl took pity on him and slipped him a magic
ring that would turn him invisible. Once he'd escaped he discovered that the ring was cursed and wouldn't come off his finger, and
he spent six more months roaming the countryside invisibly, like
a ghost, stealing food when he had to, searching for a sorcerer or
holy man who could undo the spell.

The sorcerer who finally lifted the curse charged him with rescuing his daughter, who was being held captive by a giant. This
Collum did, and in the giant's castle he met a fairy knight with
whom he agreed to change places for a year. When the year was up
the fairy knight revealed himself to be none other than Blue
Rooster, the same knight who'd dragged Collum into the desert in
the first place. That whole affair was a case of mistaken identity!
Blue Rooster had confused him with another black knight who'd
slain his father. In fact the two of them hit it off, and they agreed to
travel together.

From then on Collum's whole life seemed to go like this, in loops
and cycles, round and round the mulberry bush, turning and turning back on itself, like a children's game. It was enough to make

him dizzy. He saved a damsel, and she turned out to be the same servant girl who'd rescued him from the bandits, the one with the cursed ring. Once he glimpsed the black lion from a far distance, but it didn't seem to know him. Sometimes tales would even reach him of the great Knight of the Fountain of Astolat and his legendary prowess, no doubt told by some knight he'd beaten to make his defeat seem less embarrassing.

He was caught in an eddy, spinning in place, but how to get out? One day at a tournament, a lord challenged Collum to a wager over who could cut down the thickest tree with a single blow. Collum won, and he used his winnings to book passage to the Frankish kingdoms, where he joined a free company, fighting for the highest bidder. He spent a winter laying siege to a castle in the Alps, huddled freezing among the towering snow-frosted engines. There wasn't much talk of Arthur over here on the Continent. No one had cared much for the British king, bastard spawn of the despised Uther and too Christian by half. When they finally raised the ladders Collum was first over the wall.

Life as a mercenary was never boring, but Collum still felt like he was growing older to no purpose, pursuing bootless errands, falling through life the way he'd fallen down that well, faster and faster, never touching the sides. The feeling came over him at odd moments, when he glimpsed moonlight through the trees, or heard a distant voice singing an old song. Like there was something he'd left undone. But what? What did he expect? Life was but a dream, till one and all awakened on Judgment Day.

One day he was riding through the Frankish countryside when he saw a peasant family straggling along the edge of the road. Among them was a girl, a daughter or a young bride maybe. Her face reminded him of someone—he stared at her, and the world around him vanished for a moment. His fellows laughed at him. He'd always had a weakness for a pretty face. He shook his head, tossed her a shilling, and rode on.

But that night he thought of the stone statue, the one in the fountain at Astolat, and just like that he was awake again. For years he'd been blown sideways like a ship in a gale, and now he saw that he must seize the helm, bring the ship around or be dashed upon a lee shore. This was the moment. It was almost too late. In the morning he passed command of his company to a lieutenant and rode away alone to Calais, where he took ship for Dover.

From Dover Collum set out for Astolat. His route took him through a mountainous region where he chanced upon a remote and lonely castle. The lord there explained that his land had once been green and fertile, but it was blighted by an evil monster. The beast's venomous breath spread like a mist over the land, shriveling and stunting everything that grew there. It made its home in a cave not far away.

He charged Collum with slaying it in return for a rich reward. Collum swore to do it, without a second thought.

It wasn't hard to find the cave, a raw crack in a hillside, blackened with scorch marks around its mouth and littered with discarded bones. As he strolled down into the cavern, deeper and deeper into the earth, Collum felt only a mild curiosity as to the nature of the monster he was hunting, as if his fate had been settled long ago, and his duty was merely to dance the steps. Before long he'd lost the light from the entrance and stumbled on by torchlight. He could feel the weight of packed rock above him.

The deep darkness made him think of his ordeal in the well, all that time ago. He'd never been so cold or so frightened. He touched the scar on his face where the coffin nails had scratched him, three faint straight lines. How had he gotten out? Had he even left the well at all? Was he in there even now, lying dreaming across his broken coffin, waiting to drown?

By the light of his torch Collum could see that he wasn't the first human being to come down this far. There were marks on the walls: whirling wheels and labyrinths, streaming rivers and fields of stars. In among the patterns were drawings in red ochre, birds and wolves and giant deer. A magnificent hermaphrodite sorcerer. This was the work of the Old Ones, who'd raised the standing stones. Long before the Romans came, before Jesus was born, before even the druids came, this land was theirs. What happened to them? Maybe they were called back to another place, like the Romans. Maybe their king was slain by his own treacherous incestuous bastard. It had been known to happen.

The cave opened up into a grotto awash with gold, lit by a hellish glow from pools of lava. The monster's hoard was heaped up in a messy nest, drifts of it in a sloppy circle six feet deep. There was more gold here than on the whole island of Mull. The whole of Britain maybe. But all Collum saw was a sword, lying carelessly in among the old coins. The scabbard was old leather, so dried and charred that it turned to dust when he picked it up, but the blade inside was clean and smooth, and its edge was still fine.

When he looked up again, the monster was there. It was a dragon.

There were no dragons in Britain anymore, hadn't been since ancient days, but he couldn't very well argue the point with this one. It only distantly resembled the heraldic beast of the Pendragon arms: this one was broader, flatheaded and wide-mouthed like a lizard. Uglier. Also it was very big. In all the stories he'd read about them nobody had ever managed to accurately convey just how enormous dragons were. It filled the cavern to the roof. It didn't seem possible that anything that big could be alive, but its eyes were alert and watching him.

Its broad mouth opened a crack and red light leaked out between its interlocking teeth, as if its belly were full of more lava. Collum stood up straight, spun the ancient sword once, and raised it over his head with both hands—the Roof Guard, for maximum intimidation. His nerves stretched taut. He was awake and alive like he hadn't been in years.

The dragon lunged, its dagger claws spraying gravel and gold coins at the walls. Collum ran.

He'd fought the Green Knight, he'd faced Morgan le Fay and survived the Battle of Camelot, but he couldn't fight that thing. Nobody could, it wasn't possible! He dropped his torch and pelted back up the way he came, bouncing off the walls in the dark, gagging on the acid air. He could feel the heat on his shoulders as the dragon surged after him. Any moment he expected to feel its claws in his back—but then something shot past him going the other way. It flew out of the darkness and right at the dragon's enormous face.

It was the lion, the black lion! His old friend from the desert! It must have been following him and caught up just in time. How he'd missed that brave, beautiful, foolish beast! The dragon seemed uncertain—what was it dealing with? Cautiously it batted at the big cat with a foot the size of a knight's shield. The lion held its ground and roared. Then the dragon opened its mouth wide and that red light grew brighter and brighter . . .

It was no good. No good. Collum ran again. The heat at his back was blistering; it felt like his mail must be melting into his skin. That poor poor beast, more loyal and faithful than any man, far more than he was. It shouldn't have come, and now it had died for him. He shed a tear as he ran, but he didn't stop running—he would not let its sacrifice be in vain!—and when he couldn't run anymore he staggered along gasping, passing the cosmic spirals and ochre beasts unseen in the dark. Sir Collum of the Out Isles, onetime aspirant to the Round Table, now hobbling away from battle in tears.

After an eternity of exhaustion and terror he saw the jagged crack of the cave mouth. But when he emerged blinking into the sunlight, he wasn't in the mountains anymore.

It was all different now. He was in a forest. The light was lush and green with the shadows of swaying branches. He looked around confused. Had he somehow succeeded, in spite of his cowardice? Had the land been reborn and grown fertile again? But no, this was a different place entirely. The cave must've forked in the darkness and he'd taken the wrong path back. He squeezed his way through dense scratchy bushes, crawled up a mossy bank, through more trees and finally out, panting and blinking, into a sunny clearing.

He knew this place. There were the green trees, teeming with singing birds. There was the fountain, with the marble maid he'd so foolishly fancied. He was back in Astolat. Turn, turn, turn. Sitting on the rim of the fountain, as if he'd been waiting there for Collum all these years, was Lord Numerius of Astolat himself, older but still hale, his cheeks still rough with blond stubble.

Collum dropped to one knee.

"My lord."

"Sir Collum. It's been some time."

"It has," Collum said. "I beg your forgiveness, my lord. I regret my absence."

"You swore an oath to me," Lord Numerius said. "I can only assume that all these years you have been trying your utmost to return to your duties."

"I am sorry, my lord. I have not."

It would have been an easy lie, but somehow Collum didn't have the stomach for it. He was worn out with running in circles, fleeing who he was. He couldn't run any longer.

"You have much to answer for, Knight of the Fountain. You broke your oath. You fled battle like a coward. You abandoned your only friend, the only creature loyal to you in this world."

On cue the black lion padded silently out of the trees. It was missing the tip of one ear, and an inch or two of tail, but it had survived. It settled on the grass like a sphinx, licking a singed paw with its pink tongue, eyeing him reproachfully.

"I did. I am sorry." He apologized to the lion. "I'm glad to see you alive, old friend."

"I took you for a knight, but you're a liar, a thief, and a coward. A bastard and a commoner."

Everything Lord Numerius said was true. He'd thought that it would destroy him—that the shame of it would blast him to nothing—but the strange thing was that hearing the truth spoken aloud, dragged into the daylight, was a relief. Nimue was right, keeping secrets cost too much.

"I own it, my lord."

"I take it you're ready to resume your service, Knight of the Fountain?"

Collum almost said yes, he was on the absolute point of saying it. He could finish out his days here, and he would be damned lucky to. He looked up at the face of the stone statue, still as beautiful as she always had been. Like an idiot he'd missed her. But now that he was here he realized it wasn't her that he'd missed at all; she reminded him of someone else, somewhere far away. So many times he'd let time and tide and fate have their way with him. He'd been going round and round for so long he didn't know who he was anymore.

But that wasn't true. He knew, if he wasn't too much of a coward to admit it. It was time for him to wake up and start his life again, this time for real, and be who he was meant to be.

"I'm grateful, my lord," he said, "but I can't stay here."

Numerius frowned.

"Who else would have you? Where else would you go?"

"You know where."

"But you don't belong there, you pathetic fool. They've made that very clear."

"They're wrong. Or maybe they were right before, I don't know. They can do what they like with me, but I know who I am, and where I belong."

Lord Numerius heaved a sigh and shook his head. The statue in the fountain was no longer smiling.

"It will cost you everything you have."

"I'll pay."

"Will you?" Lord Numerius said. "Then go ahead. Pay her."

Mutely the statue held out a smooth gray stone hand toward him, the one without the sword in it.

Collum hadn't thought the bill would come quite so soon. He had nothing to pay with—he should've pocketed some of the gold from the dragon's hoard—but when he put his hand in his pouch there was a silver shilling in it. It was the one Nimue gave him.

Somehow it was still here after all these years. He'd forgotten he ever had it. He didn't want to give it up, but he placed the coin in the statue's hand anyway. The stone maiden climbed nimbly down out of the fountain, holding up the edge of its stone gown. The water in the fountain was already draining away, sinking down out of view, leaving behind an empty shaft with slick dripping sides.

Collum walked over. It was a long way down, out of the sunlight, into the cold depths. It wasn't a fountain anymore. It was a well. He supposed it always had been.

"They threw you away," Numerius said. "Just like your stepfather did. Just like Lord Alasdair."

"They may do so again if they choose. I can't stop them."

Collum stepped up onto the edge of the well, balancing unsteadily. He couldn't see the water at all now, not a glint, it was that far down. Lord Numerius was right, he was a fool, but he thought again of that first day he walked into the Great Hall. He would not take one step backward. If he could do nothing else, Collum thought, he knew how to double down on a rash decision.

Cool air rose up from the depths.

"Collum," a voice asked. "Do you know what doomed King Arthur?"

More questions? He thought he was done with them.

"It was Mordred's treachery," Collum said.

"Mordred alone could never have brought down Arthur. If you would build Camelot again, you must first learn why it fell."

It was only after Collum had stepped over the edge that he realized it wasn't Lord Numerius who had spoken. It must've been the lion.

He fell feetfirst, windmilling his arms backward trying to keep himself from turning over. The earth was always so hungry to pull things down to it! Too late he wondered if he should've dived headfirst. A roaring wind kicked up and just when it felt like his stomach was going to climb up his throat he crashed into the freezing water.

The blow shocked his legs and compressed his spine and it was long, long seconds before he made his way back up. He treaded water in a daze. *What the hell have I just done?*

He began a methodical survey of his prison. He circled it, groping with fingers that were already shivering. He reached down underwater and then up, slapping the wall as high as he could. Twice he found fingerholds substantial enough that he could pull himself up, but to what end? He'd fallen too far to ever climb out.

So instead, like the Old Ones, he delved downward. He stripped to his smallclothes, duck-dived and ran his hands over the rough slime-slick stones underwater, over and over, deeper and deeper, poking with the tip of his ancient sword, till he thought he would pass out and drown. He never found the bottom of the well, but he did find what he was looking for. He almost wished he hadn't.

It was a round hole in the wall, a yard or so across. He would have to swim into it.

Collum would never know how long he waited in the darkness, getting colder and weaker, his fingers jammed into a crack between stones, his only support in a drowned world. It was hard to believe that somewhere above him the sun still rose and set and clouds heedlessly roamed the sky. Was this really the way back to the upper world? Could he even face that place again, after they'd flung him down here and forgotten him?

Well, it hadn't killed him. Yet. He offered a desultory prayer to God, then counted thirty deep breaths and went under.

Even then it took him three more tries before he could make

himself swim into the hole. The last time he just scrubbed out all thought from his head and kicked frantically, mechanically. It was a cramped, crumbling pipe lined with old Roman terra-cotta, with no room to stroke with his arms, so he kept kicking his way along into the black, pulling himself forward with his hands where he could.

The bubble of air in his lungs began to ache, like it had in the river in the Otherworld, but even worse now, like he'd been speared through the chest. He kicked and kicked, harder and harder. White lightning flashed in his vision, a storm coming on. Phantasmal flowers, blousy peonies and roses. Some part of him must still have been holding on to the dream of turning back because it wasn't till he realized that he couldn't, that it was too late and the passage was too narrow to turn around in, that he truly panicked.

He'd made a terrible mistake. He should've stayed in the well. He should've stayed at Astolat, on Mull, anywhere but here! He regretted everything. How could he have left behind the paradise of air to drown in the black like this? He thrashed like a burning spider. He groped inside himself for that strength he'd felt in the battle, in the Otherworld, any strength at all, but it was all gone. His need to take a breath and his terror of taking water into his lungs were both absolute, they were tearing him apart. A hurricane raged in his eyes, his head was vibrating, his chest was bursting, he coughed out all his air in one and then—*no*—*he MUST NOT*—

In an instant of agony beyond agony he saw with total clarity a woman's face, kind and beautiful and forgiving. It was his mother's.

His head broke the surface.

Collum fell forward onto smooth stone and took a long, croaking, spasming inward breath, the longest breath of his life, then choked as he vomited convulsively and inhaled the burning acid vomit and coughed it out again. He slipped back into the water and then scrabbled his way back out again in terror and lay there half in and half out, lungs heaving.

The air was cool on his wet back. He spat. Bit by bit it came to him where he was. He was in a pale stone church. Candles were lit, but there was dawn light rising in the windows too.

"Huzzah. It worked."

A voice that dull and depressed could only have belonged to one person: the Fool Knight of Camelot, Sir Dagonet. Collum raised his head. They were kneeling in a circle around him, all of them: Bedivere, Dinadan, Dagonet, Palomides, Constantine.

"Welcome back," Bedivere said. "Sir Collum of the Table Round."

Twenty

THE TWISTED STAFF

hey hauled him out of the water, which turned out to be a kind of ceremonial pool built into the floor, and stripped him and rubbed him with linen towels. Then they made a bridge with their swords and he balanced along it out of the chapel, wobbling, cold as hell, still coughing up water, still stark naked, his bits flapping in the wind in the soft morning light—a passing maid winked at him. They took him that way all the way from the church up to the castle, through the Rain Gate and across the bailey, Dinadan leading them in a Roman marching song:

Urbani, servate uxores, moechum calvum adducimus.
Aurum in gallia effutuisti, hic sumpsisti mutuum . . .

He felt like he'd been gone for years, but it was all still here—the grass, the geese, the linens, the gardens, the sleepy blacksmith fussing with his tools. Everything looked raw and new, as if the paint were still wet on it. They had not cast him out. Or they had, but only so he could claw his way back and even further in, all naked and undeserving, into the golden circle itself. It couldn't be, but here he was.

The sword bridge ended at the Great Hall, where they dressed him in white samite and plied him with food and wine. They would have bathed him, too, but Dinadan pronounced him wet enough already, what with his sojourn in the well, plus all the tears he was shedding. The chandelier was lit overhead, pale fire in the thin morning light, and he was given another knighting ceremony, a proper one this time, and another oath. Sir Bedivere buckled a set of gold spurs on him, deftly, one-handed.

When it was all finished a falcon came swooping in low through the open door of the hall and perched on the back of a chair, Arthur's chair, stamping its feet severely and staring around at everyone with an air of furious self-importance. It was Goose, Arthur's gyrfalcon. He hadn't been seen for months, not since the day the king took ship across the Channel to lay siege to Benwick, and he'd shed his bells and jesses somewhere, but now he was back.

They all agreed it was a good sign.

AFTERWARD COLLUM WENT UP to his chamber and slept like a dead man for seven hours, and in the afternoon they came and took him back to the armory.

On the way they passed servants and soldiers staggering under bundles of firewood and barrels of grain and wine and sugar and water. Camelot seethed with activity—its brush with a besieging army had awakened it like a fairy-tale kiss. Whitsunday had passed but nobody was going to Glamorgan this summer. Workmen clogged the stairways and courtyards, patching crumbling masonry and whitewashing walls and queuing for garderobes.

The knights walked Collum down the aisle of the armory again, like a bride being ushered to the side of her steel groom. Even after all the pomp and ceremony he was relieved when they showed him to an actual armor this time and not a wooden coffin.

Though at first he did have to hide a little disappointment. It was a plain armor, no fancy velvet or filigree or enamel or damascening. Not even any paint, just smooth bare steel. But the longer he looked at it the more it grew on him. It wasn't flashy, but the workmanship was of the very highest standard. The maker's mark was a running leopard, sigil of the oldest armoring family in Milan, home of the greatest armorers in the world. This was proper fighting harness, case-hardened, not just for show. There were no gaps or showy fluting that might catch a point or an edge. The gauntlets were delicately articulated—you could've threaded a needle wearing them—and the work around the shoulders and armpits, a perennial weak spot, was an intricate play of gardbrace and pauldron and vambrace. Collum found and tested every stud and spring and hinge, and they were all set precisely in place and snapped and clicked just as they should. It was perfect.

The helm had a steel crest running back to front like a fighting fish. Its visor was a full-face steel plate pierced with dozens of tiny crosses, large enough to see through but too small for any blade or missile to penetrate. It was fastened in place with a neat sprung stud, and when not needed it could be swung upward on tiny hinges.

He smiled. The helm gave him back a cryptic, intimidating stare. *Do you mean to be my next occupant?*

"Try it on," Bedivere said. "It should fit, our man does it by sight."

"There's a hauberk too," Constantine said. "Riveted rings. Mail of p-proof."

The door at the far end of the gallery banged open.

"They told me there's a new knight of the Round Table and he's not drunk yet," Scipio proclaimed, "but I didn't believe it!"

"I only thank God," Palomides bellowed, right behind him, "that Arthur did not live to see this shameful day!"

Two servants followed them rolling a rumbling, bumping iron-bound barrel of wine.

The knights sat down right there on stools and boxes and on the stairs and on the floor and started drinking. While Collum got out of his clothes and into his new armor, they made learned conversation about the quality of the wine and debated whether it really was from Bayonne or if the merchant had cheated them. They discussed court cases involving their cousins who were accused of poaching, and hunting prospects for the fall in the Wychwood, and memorable feats of archery performed by women, and the unpleasantness of crossing the Channel in March. There was nothing to hide and no appearances to keep up anymore. He was one of them now. Probably he wouldn't be if most of the Table weren't already dead, probably he never would've got through the door, but there they were, and here he was. He could breathe, really breathe, for the first time since he got to Camelot. Had it fixed him after all, like he'd hoped? It was a start.

Collum told the others what he remembered of his time in the well. It felt like years to him but up here only a day and a half had passed, and the details were already fading like a dream. But he still had the scars from the coffin nails, that much was real, and the sword he'd found was still stuck in his belt. There were letters engraved on it, neither Latin nor Ogham. Palomides studied the script for a long time, tracing it with a fingertip.

"I can read many alphabets," he said, "but that one I have never seen. We should take it to the House of Wisdom, though if we did the caliph might not give it back. I can tell you it is old, older than it should be—men have not known how to make steel for that long. So perhaps it is a fairy blade, though that is not any fairy script I know."

"Is it magic?" Collum would dearly have liked to wield a magic blade.

"Not that I can tell. Maybe Nimue could." He shaved a few hairs off his forearm with it. "Very fine edge, though."

It came out that the initiation was different for everyone, but they'd all made it through, even Dagonet; the sole exception was Sir Scipio. It came out now that Scipio wasn't actually a knight of the Round Table at all, which was why he hadn't been part of the circle when Collum came out of the well. He was a regular guest at Camelot, well known as a good fighter and a basically solid fellow, with a rough edge or two, but he was too erratic to ever quite make it onto the Table. They'd put him up for membership a few times, but he always found a way to sink his candidacy at the last minute by blaspheming or breaking something or offending somebody.

"We did actually put him through the initiation once," Dinadan said. "Down the well. We waited and waited, but he never came back up. Then a month later he turned up at the Rain Gate riding a donkey."

"It spat me out of a tin mine in Cornwall." Scipio was flushed with drink. "I left a shoe down there."

He didn't say it with his usual bravado, and Collum realized he was actually embarrassed. Some part of him must really have wanted to join the Table, but he couldn't quite let himself do it, he couldn't give himself that gift, like a stray cat who came to the door to be fed but was too wild to go in the house where it was warm and dry. Some deep defensive instinct, either of self-preservation or self-destruction, made him slink away instead, back out into the cold.

"You're probably wondering if you should be embarrassed about all those things we learned about you," Bedivere said.

"You definitely should," Dagonet said.

"Nobody cares," Dinadan said. "We all have plenty to be ashamed of."

"I coveted another man's wife," Palomides said.

"A lot," Dinadan added.

"But can you really let somebody in with my—background?"

"People have come in with a lot worse sins on their hands," Dinadan said. "If God can forgive, shouldn't we?"

"Big if," Dagonet said.

"It's not us who decides anyway, it's Camelot. But in my experience the question isn't so much about whether you're lying to us, it's whether you're lying to yourself."

To go with his armor they presented Collum with a new shield that had a golden sheep on it.

"The sheep's for—" Constantine began.

"I get it."

Collum held it up. Sooner hung for a sheep as for a lamb. The artist had given the sheep wings, and it was gazing up at a moon above it in the sky; like him it had ideas above its station. It was no northern sheep, this was a fat puffy southron breed, but a sheep was a sheep.

"Golden sheep, golden fleece," Scipio said, in his elegant Latin. He'd recovered his poise. "It's a classical allusion."

"I told you he would see the joke," Palomides said. "Constantine thought you'd be offended."

"Got any special gifts?" Dinadan asked. "Still shit and piss?"

"I'll let you know."

The afternoon wore on. He asked after Sir Melehan, and it turned out that after his dramatic entrance and subsequent confinement his army had utterly failed to materialize, at which point Melehan freely confessed that he'd been bluffing. He'd been on the run and sleeping rough since Camlann, and eventually he'd decided he'd be safer in the dungeon at Camelot, where they were fussier about summary executions than the roving mobs outside.

Palomides sang a couple of songs from Sarras, and Dinadan recited a long and impressively filthy poem for which he did the voices with great comic effect. A big-pawed ginger cat wound its way between the legs of the empty armors, and they tried to pet it but it wouldn't let them catch it. Scipio and Dinadan sparred and wrestled till Dinadan accidentally gave Scipio a bloody nose. Dagonet did some drunk juggling. Constantine invented a game where you threw a grape and saw how many armors you could get it to bounce off of, which brought out the knights' competitive streak. Collum did in fact have to piss, so he went outside and pissed down the old well. Served it right.

At some point a silence fell. The yellow squares of light from the windows had lengthened into deep orange bands. It would be time for dinner soon.

"So," Dinadan said. "What now?"

"Now we choose." For the last hour Bedivere had been sitting off by himself, mechanically downing cups of wine one after the other. Now he looked around at the other knights with his steady blue eyes and his granite features. His knees popped audibly as he stood. "No priests, no kings, no wizards. Just us."

He was right, Collum thought. It was time. If they waited for that costumed rabble from the other night to reach a consensus, they would wait forever.

"We need a sign from God," Constantine said.

"We cannot tell God what to do," Palomides said. "I have tried. He seems to have a problem with authority."

"Let's wait for Arthur." Scipio dabbed at his nose. "Path of least resistance."

"We've waited long enough," Bedivere said. "I will not watch everything he stood for burn while we wait for him to come back and do our duty for us. He wouldn't wait. We must choose ourselves."

"Who then?" Dinadan said.

"King Cador."

Bedivere said it without a single particle of enthusiasm, but with finality.

"What?" Constantine said.

"We must do something. If not him, then who? You?"

"You know who."

"I will die before I see Lancelot on the throne," Bedivere said evenly.

This was it, Collum thought. The other part of life. He'd been basking in his miraculous elevation, and now here came the inevitable disappointment, the compromise of everything. It called for a different kind of bravery than being thrown down a well.

"My father is a monster," Constantine said, his face going red, "and I will kill him before you can crown him."

"Bors then," Dinadan said.

"A Frank," Bedivere said. "We're going in circles. King Cador is strong enough to want the throne and weak enough that he can be led. And"—he spoke over Constantine—"if you don't like it, you can grow a pair and take the throne yourself."

"And become a monster like him?" Constantine stood up too. He towered over everybody else in the room.

"It is time to set aside personal feelings," Palomides said.

"I'll h-happily set them aside," Constantine said. "I'll leave Britain and enjoy a comfortable exile—"

"That's fine," Bedivere said. "We don't need you, we need someone who can do what has to be done."

"You've given up, h-haven't you? You don't believe anymore! You're not even going to try!"

"Say that again."

Bedivere took a step toward him. A line had been crossed. Searing pain lit up Collum's chest just below his collarbone.

"Ow!"

It was like someone had dropped a hot coal down the front of his armor. He jumped up clawing at his front, kicking over his cup of wine.

"God's blood!"

Something was burning him like metal fresh out of a forge, searing into his skin! It was the medal—the one he'd got from the knight, the one Morgan had found so intriguing. He tried to rip the thong off his neck but it wouldn't give, so he tore it over his head and threw it on the floor.

Everybody stared at him, then at the medal where it lay on the bare stone. It glowed like a firefly. A rich, sweet smell filled the room, smoke mixed with jasmine. The medal shone brighter, now pure white light, like a sunstruck crystal, then like a fallen star, till the whole room was full of a pitiless silver light so bright they had to cover their eyes and look away.

Then it faded, leaving behind only a hot green blob in Collum's vision. He touched his chest. Nothing. The heat hadn't burned him at all.

"What the hell was that?" Dinadan said.

Everybody was blinking and rubbing their eyes. Scipio crouched down and fearlessly picked up the medal.

"Is this yours, Collum?"

"I got it off a knight I fought."

"Know what that is?" Scipio showed everybody the symbol on it, the twisted stick. "It's the *vitis.*"

"The what-is?" Dinadan said.

"The vitis. A vinewood staff. Centurions used to carry them. Staff of office. Useful for beating people with too."

"So?" Dinadan said.

"Ah," Palomides said. "I see. Saint Longinus was a centurion, present at the Crucifixion. It was his spear that pierced Jesus's side. That spear became the Holy Lance."

Scipio tossed the medal to Bedivere. Spilled wine was pooling on the flagstones.

"So it's from God. God." Bedivere repeated it as if he'd never heard the name before. "The Holy Lance." He looked around the room. "This is it. Isn't it? Is this it?"

Nobody answered. But nobody said no either. The old knight's features recomposed themselves. He'd decided for himself.

"We will seek it." Bedivere's voice gathered conviction as it went. "The way is before us. We will find the Lance and win back Britain for God, and all will be as it used to be. As it was meant to be. It will be Arthur's Britain again."

There was silence in the room, and the knights were as still as the armors. Then Dinadan stood.

"Arthur's Britain. God has spoken." Cups were retrieved, from the floor and elsewhere, hastily filled, and held up.

"Arthur's Britain!"

Collum drank too. It was almost beyond belief, but here it was at long last. God had spoken. Or at any rate He'd winked broadly at them. He'd certainly drawn out the question as long as possible, milked it for all its drama, but He'd finally answered. It was incontrovertible. Like Nimue said, they must finally be ready.

"It can't be worse than the Grail Quest," Dinadan said.

"Don't even joke about it," said Constantine.

One by one the knights kneeled and prayed, all except for Dagonet, who never seemed to pray. Thank you, merciful God, Collum thought. Now the tears came. He'd been so desperate—he only realized now that he'd lost all hope. Thank you. God had provided. And what a banquet He had laid! Not only was he a knight of the Round Table, now the quest of all quests lay before him. The picture was complete.

In spite of itself Collum's mind played host to the men he'd killed in the battle—convened them as a jury of his peers. I am sorry, he thought, to the long-haired spearman and the yellow-toothed Orkney giant. But see now: it had to be this way. I had to kill you so that this could come to pass. It was all part of it. It was all worth it. And then to Lord Alasdair and his son Marcas: I was right all along, you jackasses, Camelot was always the way. And to Morgan too: say what you like about Him, but the Jew-on-a-stick was listening after all.

His mind stayed with Morgan, and her grief and her rage, which he couldn't seem to set aside—God knew he would've liked to but they wouldn't go. He'd been right but she was not wrong. God had returned to reclaim this cool green island, but when it was all over whoever was king must turn his hand to paying for the cost of it all. Reparations must be made. Whatever it took.

And then all would be well. There was a way forward now, and it was the way back, the old way: *grails, spirits, quests, angels.* The Old World was shattered but all the pieces had been saved, and it was only a matter of gathering them back up and sticking them back together. It was a second Grail Quest, this one for the future of Britain itself.

Not that the first Grail Quest was much of a success, from the way they talked about it, but whatever errors had been made, they could correct them this time. They would right this great storm-wracked ship. The tempest would blow in reverse, re-step the mast, reweave the rigging, mend the sails. The waves would sweep the hapless crewman back on deck.

"Christ!"

Bedivere dropped the medal. It was leaking drops of blood.

"That's the holy touch, all right," Dinadan said. "He does love a bit of blood."

Dark crimson pooled around the medal on the stone floor, mingling with the garnet puddles of wine.

"Everyone confess tonight." Bedivere wiped his hand on his tunic. "Sit a vigil if you can. We leave tomorrow at dawn."

More toasts were drunk, to God and Arthur and Saint Longinus. In his mind Collum drank to that nameless knight of Three Scepters, a Chevron Or, too, the first casualty of the quest for the Holy Lance. He must not have known what he had, and Collum had killed him and robbed him of it like a common highwayman. But maybe that was just God's plan to get it to Camelot. Maybe the mystery knight was burdened with sins of his own, and his death was just and necessary. Only God could wholly grasp the system of the world.

Bedivere began to sing:

Te Deum laudamus: te Dominum confitemur.
Te æternum Patrem omnis terra veneratur

They all took it up, Dinadan an octave up from the others, Bedivere an octave below, Palomides supplying some curious harmony in between. Still solemnly singing, the knights trooped out the door and up the half flight of stairs together, back out into the early evening air, so cool after the hot closeness of the hall.

Tibi omnes Angeli; tibi Caeli et universae Potestates

Collum could already feel yet another hangover starting but he didn't care. Onward, onward, onward to glory. It would be the Grail Quest all over again, and this time they would get it right. And Nimue would be happy; she loved God. This would be what she wanted. Collum couldn't wait to tell her.

But before they could spread the news a servant met them coming the other way with news of his own: even as the Round Table had gained one member, it had lost another. Sir Kay was dead. He'd hung himself in his chamber with his own sword belt.

Twenty-one

The Tale of Sir Dagonet
and Sir Constantine;
or, the Quest for the Holy Grail;
or, the Very Last Adventure

O f all those who set out on that grandest of errands it was Sir Dagonet the Fool, the very lowest of them, who was the first to suspect its real nature. He was its prophet, though nobody would've listened to him if he'd even bothered to say anything, which he hadn't—he was a lazy Cassandra. But if life had taught him anything it was that the worst disasters come dressed as miracles, and it followed that a miracle this glorious and beautiful could only mean disaster on the grandest possible scale. The end of the good years, the time of legends, the age of Arthur. The beginning of the end of everything.

Dagonet grew up in the flooded Fenlands, a vast network of meres, washes, bogs, and marshes fed by rivers on one side and the ocean on the other, half fresh and half salt. He first came to Camelot with a troupe of traveling minstrels. No one had ever seen anything like him. The master of ceremonies introduced Dagonet as the Boy Who Could Steal from the Angels.

He started his act by asking King Arthur for his chunky royal golden signet ring, which Arthur duly handed over. Dagonet made it disappear right out of the palm of his hand, and then when he tried to bring it back he pretended he couldn't find it. Over the course of the evening Dagonet kept discovering the ring in more and more unlikely places—in someone's nose, or a sealed bottle of wine, or the stomach of a fish that had been freshly baked in a pie—and then immediately losing it again. At the close of the show Dagonet and his assistant—a learned dwarf named Oswald, who had in fact taught Dagonet most of what he knew—pretended to get into a fight over some oranges they were juggling. Dagonet vanished each orange one by one, but Oswald managed to grab the last of them. He climbed up onto the Round Table and ran a gleeful victory lap while the knights cheered and scrambled to get their cups and plates out of the way. Then he sat down cross-legged in front of Arthur, peeled the orange, and took a big juicy bite. He yelped in surprise and spat out Arthur's ring.

It was a good act. Part of what made it funny was that Dagonet did the whole thing absolutely stone-faced, as serious as a merchant banker calling in a debt. The knights loved it and by popular acclaim Dagonet was immediately plucked out of the company and made Camelot's new fool.

But Dagonet's straight-man act wasn't as funny once the knights realized it wasn't an act. He was like that all the time.

Even as a little boy Dagonet had had an odd manner. He was nervous and distracted. He had a mania for cleanliness and hated anything associated with any bodily function, especially eating or drinking. It was harmless enough as far as it went, but as he grew older Dagonet began to be gripped by nameless fears and rages and black miseries. His mind sloshed around inside his skull, always off-kilter. Some days he felt vastly powerful, like an unacknowledged emperor; other times he felt revolting, a loathsome spider too degraded even to be stepped on. Often he wished to die, but he lacked the courage. Some dark god had left his heavy thumbprint on Dagonet.

He tried to contain these feelings but they overflowed into his body, making him hunch and shiver and argue with himself at odd moments. Sometimes he wondered if he wasn't mad at all, if he was the only sane one, because when other people looked at the world they seemed to see a paradise of ease and order and meaning. But when Dagonet looked he found only a wasteland of empty signs, transient and meaningless as the shapes in clouds. The worthless currency of a vanished empire.

His salvation arrived in the form of a company of minstrels who were so down on their luck that they were making a swing through the sodden, isolated fishing villages of the Fens. When Dagonet watched their juggler perform, it seemed to him that he'd stumbled on a trace of that mysterious hidden paradise. That same evening he chose three round stones from a streambed and began his study of the art.

Juggling soothed him, made him feel safe from the feelings that stalked him. He juggled till he couldn't lift his arms anymore; if anything he was afraid of what would happen when he stopped. It was silly, a party trick, a carnival act at best. But to Dagonet it was everything, it was the movement of the spheres writ small, a glimpse of the clean eternal order that lay beyond the filth and chaos of this fallen world. And it was he, the lowly Dagonet, none other, who made it visible.

DAGONET OFTEN WONDERED what Arthur thought he was doing by knighting him. It was an uncharacteristically awkward gesture, with a cruel edge to it, a whiff of mockery, which was strange because even Dagonet had to admit that Arthur was not a cruel man. But he did not do things by halves either. He had Dagonet swear the real oaths, got him a sword and a shield and armor and a horse and a squire. His arms were a silver cloud on a deep blue background. More shapes in more clouds. Any knight who forgot or refused to accord Dagonet full knightly honors received a hilarious public spanking.

Meanwhile Arthur got a new and much funnier fool, a man with a genuine lust for foolery. Not much of a juggler, but he could walk on his hands while farting actual musical notes.

Perhaps Arthur was poking fun at the knights of the Table, to teach them humility. Perhaps he saw—as no one else did, not even Dagonet himself—that Dagonet was fighting as hard as any knight ever had just to stay alive and sane. Perhaps, too, Arthur saw a bit of himself in Sir Dagonet. They'd both begun life at the lowest of stations, only to be raised on a divine whim to dizzying heights. Did Arthur, too, not feel a bit ridiculous at times? Something of a fraud? A bit of a fool, perhaps?

The sword in the stone had made a fool a king, and the king had made a fool a knight. But the Grail would make fools of them all.

It arrived on Whitsunday in the twenty-third year of Arthur's reign. Sir Dagonet watched from the back of the Great Hall while the king, as was his custom, declared that he would not eat till he had witnessed some miracle or marvel. Then the knights waited in the early summer cool, the vast chamber alive with their expectant rustlings and shushings, until an excited servant arrived and delivered a whispered message to the king. A block of solid marble had been spotted floating in the river Brass with a sword stuck straight upright in it.

The hall emptied out in a hurry as the knights raced one another down to the muddy riverbank. By the time Dagonet got there a few had already waded up to their thighs into the bronze-colored water to get a better look. The marble slab rode heavily in the water, hardly bobbing, a massive bloody red stone veined with blue and white like a raw steak, lapped at by the current. Dagonet found it troubling to the eyes—a wrong thing, that shouldn't be. A heavy thing that should sink but would not.

"Sword in a stone." Sir Dinadan tapped his upper lip in thought. "Reminds me of something, but I can't think what."

Funny, Dagonet thought. If he'd only shown some ambition in life he could've been a fool.

Arthur studied the miracle with his active, intelligent gaze, Nimue on one side and a visiting archbishop on the other, both leaning in to whisper advice in the king's ear.

"My lord!" Sir Villiars was one of those who'd waded out. "There's something written on it!"

"Is that right?"

Now the king strode out into the water, too, up to his waist, heedlessly ruining a cloth-of-silver cape. Overhead the sky was divided, half sunny blue, half cloudy gray.

"Arthur," Nimue called. "Don't touch the sword."

"Don't worry, I've done this before."

That got a ripple of laughter. Arthur squinted up at the blade.

"It says"—he read it out to the crowd—"'*Never shall man take me hence, but only he by whose side I ought to hang, and he shall be the best knight of the world.*' Lance!"

More laughter. Everybody looked around.

"Where's Lancelot?"

Like Dagonet he was hanging back at the rear of the crowd, modestly, a tall man with a wave in his brown hair and a dancer's narrow waist. Lancelot had a reliable sense of humor, but he wasn't in a laughing mood.

"I don't think so." The great du Lac spoke so softly he could barely be heard over the rippling of the river. "It's not for me."

Arthur frowned.

"If you're worried about the sin of pride, we've got the archbishop right here to absolve you on the spot. Now come."

"Forgive me, Your Highness." Lancelot folded his arms. "I would sooner this honor fell to another."

For Lancelot to decline a marvel was as rare a thing as the marvel itself. The man's lust for the miraculous was insatiable. A sword in a stone—Dagonet was surprised he hadn't already proposed marriage to it. Did the great Frank know something the king didn't?

"As you wish." Arthur surveyed the crowd on the riverbank. "But it must be meant for someone here."

Everybody found somewhere else to look than at the king. They'd all heard about the disaster of the Holy Lance. The divine punishment for overestimating one's worthiness was instant and severe. Dagonet found himself seized from behind by Kay and a couple of his cronies, who tried to force him into the water, but he dug in his heels and writhed so furiously that they had to give it up.

Finally Sir Gawain gave an audible huff of irritation and splashed into the river. *Christ's crutches, it's a holy adventure and the will of our liege lord, so let's fucking get it over with.*

"Good man," Arthur growled, clapping him on the shoulder.

Gawain was small for a knight but handsome and well formed. He and his four blond brothers—Morgause's boys, Gareth, Gaheris, Agravaine, and Mordred—were Picts, from Orkney in the far north. The Picts had resisted the Romans longer and more fiercely than anyone, and they never let you forget it. Arthur was the only southern king who'd ever made them bend the knee. They had a reputation as wild men with knotted hair who went naked but for blue tattoos and a sword belt.

But the Orkney brothers surprised everyone by being dignified and well mannered. They spoke good Latin, and their teeth weren't filed to points, and they didn't try to sacrifice anybody to their strange northern gods. They looked uncomfortable in their southern finery, but they wore it. Gawain in particular had an appealing air of disciplined intelligence and an amused, fatalistic worldview. Though he also had a dark temper when he drank, and he got into more scraps with other knights than the rest of the Table combined.

He waded out to the red stone with no fuss, like a farrier getting ready to shoe a badly behaved horse. For him this was also, Dagonet knew, about showing up Lancelot as a coward. Gawain was the eternal runner-up to Lancelot in the standings, and he'd made it clear that he considered Lancelot's Christian fussiness about God and sex and chivalry to be the worst kind of southron bullshit. He boosted himself nimbly right up onto the slab, river water streaming off him, set himself, and gripped the silver sword by the hilt.

It didn't move. Dagonet was disappointed. He realized he would've liked Gawain to get a win for a change.

Nothing daunted, the Orkney knight gave the sword a resounding kick with his boot, and it twanged in place. The archbishop put his hand over his eyes. Gawain turned and bowed to the crowd as if to say, *See, Lance? Nothing to it. You big baby.*

Lancelot was shaking his head.

"One day that sword will wound you, Gawain," he said. "Badly."

Gawain bugged his eyes out just a little. *I'm so scared.*

"Who's next?" Arthur said. "Percy?"

After Lancelot passed and Gawain failed, Dagonet assumed the prize would go to Percival, a rangy knight from darkest North-galis with a bowl haircut. Gawain gave up his place to make room, doing a jaunty backflip into the water, which earned him a smattering of applause. Gawain had bad blood with Percival, too, because Percival's father—King Pellinore—had killed Gawain's father, King Lot, in battle, after which Gawain and his brothers had killed Pellinore. It was one of many cracks running through the Round Table.

But Percival couldn't pull the sword out either, and he graciously made way for Bors and Gareth and the freshly converted Palomides, but none of them could budge it either. Arthur called for Lancelot again—enough's enough—but the *preux chevalier* had slipped away. Probably gone back to the hall to get an early start on the haddock in saffron sauce.

Gawain and Percival left, too, to dry off. A line of lesser knights formed, trailing from the reedy bank out into the water, strivers who mostly just wanted to be able to say they'd been there and they'd tried. Arthur stayed to cheer on each and every last soul, until the very last one had failed. The rest of the crowd drifted back toward the castle. The king had had his marvel, even if the mystery had gone unsolved. It was time to eat.

But the marvels weren't over. They were still at lunch when a strange boy dressed in white samite walked into the Great Hall trailed by a stooped, elderly monk whose hands shook with palsy. The boy looked about fourteen and was almost comically handsome, with high cheekbones and fine, almond-shaped eyes. He had the air of someone who was late for an important appointment. Without waiting for permission, and with the barest of nods to his king, he circled the Round Table till he came to the empty seat next to Lancelot.

That seat was always empty, not because Lancelot was unpopular but because the actual chair itself was either blessed or cursed, depending on how you looked at it. When the Round Table was first convened Merlin had explained that it was reserved for a knight who had not yet arrived.

With all the wine and loose talk in the Great Hall, it's not surprising that sooner or later somebody would test that idea. A certain Sir Grivous made a great show of lowering his bottom dramatically onto the empty seat. The moment he touched it every candle and torch in the hall went out, and Sir Grivous exploded in blue flames in the darkness, as if he'd had brandy poured over him and set alight. He died screaming and begging for God's mercy, which, true to form, God denied him. After that they named the chair the Siege Perilous, and they draped a blue silk over the seat for safety.

So when the boy in white whipped the silk off the chair like it was a damp towel, half the room leapt to their feet shouting. But he sat down before anyone could stop him. Nothing happened, except that golden letters appeared on the back of the chair that read:

SIR GALAHAD

"Right." The boy looked around at the staring faces, bemused by all the attention. "Now would any of you happen to have seen a sword in a stone around here somewhere?"

. . .

Just like that the whole center of gravity at Camelot changed. It felt like the hero of a great story had finally arrived, and everybody else, even Lancelot, even Arthur, was now a minor character in the grand triumph of Sir Galahad. The cargo had shifted, the balance altered. The ship began to list.

It was all the same to Dagonet. His position hadn't changed.

Everything that followed Galahad's arrival passed immediately into legend. How he claimed the sword from the marble block in the river, making a perfect leap from riverbank to stone and back again, without even getting his white boots muddy. (Dinadan remarked that he could just as easily have walked across.) How the sword fit perfectly in an empty serpent-skin scabbard that Galahad just happened to already have hanging from his belt. How Arthur convened a great tournament, and how Galahad did wondrously well in it.

How afterward a sunbeam seven times the strength of daylight pierced the Great Hall, and a mighty thunder shook it, whereupon the Holy Grail itself appeared. How it floated the length of the room, held by no visible hand, filling the air with good odors and giving each knight that which he most longed for to eat and drink. How in its presence all wounds healed without scars; two ladies in the hall were startled to find their virginities restored.

Even Dagonet felt it. His mind calmed. He felt a hope and ease he hadn't felt for years, maybe not since the womb, maybe not ever. But when his gaze happened to light on Galahad in the crowd, it was quite clear from the expression on the young knight's fine pleasant face that while everyone else in the hall was in transports of holy gladness, he felt nothing at all.

. . .

UNTIL THEN QUESTING had always been a relatively private matter, an amateur affair conducted decorously among friends and colleagues, in ones and twos and threes. But now every knight of the Table was mobilized in pursuit of a single object, the Holy Grail. It gave the whole business a jolly competitive spirit, like a steeplechase or a scavenger hunt, and devil take the hindmost.

The only off note was that King Arthur, of all people, wasn't going. He firmly declined to seek the Grail. It made no sense: Arthur was as piously Christian as any of them, and more than most, and he loved adventures and had personally called for this one, but now that it was here and the other knights were busily packing for the quest of a lifetime he sat on his hands, like a teetotaler turning his wine cup over to indicate that, no, thanks, he did not care to partake this fine evening. Bedivere's obvious and bitter disappointment was embarrassing to witness.

Arthur mentioned his age, and his obligations as a ruler. After all, he was a king before he was a knight. He said he wanted to make room for the younger generation to distinguish themselves. None of it quite rang true to Dagonet. Like Lancelot, Arthur was never one to pass up a marvel.

But there was another, more convincing theory making the rounds, though people uttered it only in lowered voices. It started out as nigh-treasonous scuttlebutt, but the more Dagonet thought about it the more it made sense. It was obvious to even an uninterested, deeply depressed observer like himself that at this point Arthur and Guinevere weren't going to have a child. Arthur's only heirs were his three unbearable half sisters and his one incestuous illegitimate son, hardly the stuff of which peaceful successions are made. The last time Britain faced a disaster of this kind was also the last time it had seen a miracle of this magnitude, namely the Sword in the Stone. The purpose of that marvel was to designate Arthur as the true heir to the crown.

It followed that with Britain once again in need of an heir, God had once again inaugurated a miraculous contest with deliciously high stakes. Whoever found the Grail, the theory went, would succeed Arthur as king of Britain. The real prize wasn't the Grail at all, it was the throne.

When it came to forming adventuring parties the knights of the Round Table could be as cliquish as schoolchildren, and there was a lot of gossip and shy, stuttering asking out and some catty talk and bruised feelings too. Dagonet wasn't expecting anybody to ask him until Sir Constantine did. Dagonet was without question the hundredth- and last-ranked knight on the Round Table.

But Constantine wasn't too far ahead of him. Despite his height and his ungodly long reach he wasn't taken very seriously as a fighter. Those praying-mantis arms didn't carry much muscle. He was probably best known for his affable good nature and for the frequency and resourcefulness with which he violated the royal sumptuary laws, which stated that it was illegal to dress better than the king. Everybody liked him, but they assumed he was only on the Table as a sop to King Cador. Constantine himself assumed that.

Dagonet told him he could take his pity and fuck off with it. But Sir Constantine gently but firmly, with only a hint of his ridiculous affected stutter, declined to fuck off. He would accept no other arrangement. Eventually Dagonet gave in. It was less trouble. He supposed Sir Constantine thought he was doing a good deed.

Sir Dagonet the Fool and Sir Constantine of Cornwall set out together from Camelot in search of the Holy Grail on the third day following its miraculous appearance. They were among the last to go, and Camelot was all but deserted. Dagonet just hoped they would fail quickly and without dying. For the first few days their conversation consisted mostly of Constantine commenting unflatteringly on the food and the accommodations, and Dagonet saying nothing, or shuddering involuntarily. It was on the fourth day that they came across Sir Turquine's castle.

It bore the sinister name of Blackfast, though it didn't look especially sinister, just a modest-sized country keep, low and blocky, round gray stone towers topped with square-toothed battlements. Out in front on a wide rolling lawn stood a spreading oak in all its summer splendor. An old copper basin, greenish and dented, hung from a low branch. Dagonet didn't get it, but Constantine knew what to do. He banged on the basin three times with the butt end of a lance.

The hollow clanging faded into the quiet of the June afternoon. Nothing happened. They sat down to wait. Metallic dragonflies, delicately wrought from blued steel, skimmed the warm, still moat.

A quarter of an hour later the portcullis rattled up and Sir Turquine rode out on a great liver-chestnut horse. A chronically angry man, he wore a square bucket helm bolted to his bull shoulders, and the sigil on his black shield was a burning tower. He carried a festive red-and-white candy-striped lance. Constantine listened patiently while over the course of another quarter hour Turquine recounted at length the ill-defined and largely imaginary grounds for his hatred of the Round Table.

On the first pass Constantine broke his spear against Sir Turquine's broad black breastplate, but Turquine kept his seat. On the second Turquine found the dead center of Constantine's shield with his point, and Constantine tumbled backward over his horse's rump and landed in a tangle of lanky limbs. He tried to rise but grabbed a knee and yelped. He was done for the day.

Sir Dagonet surrendered without a fight.

Twenty-two

THE TALE OF SIR DAGONET AND SIR CONSTANTINE, PART II

Sir Dagonet and Sir Constantine spent eight months in Sir Turquine's dungeon.

Their stay at Castle Blackfast was not enlivened by much in the way of incident, and afterward Dagonet found he barely remembered it. He passed the time by juggling, using a carefully curated collection of stones pried out of the wall and dug out of the floor, selected for their weight and roundness and smoothness. He was not much more miserable there than he was anywhere else. Constantine prayed and paced and did push-ups and climbed the bars and ran in place. The filth of it all was a trial for both of them—they were the two most fanatical bathers the valets of Camelot had ever seen. Constantine built a great city out of dirt and pebbles and fragments of brick and tile, which he named New Constantinople to avoid any confusion with the original. He thought of devastating bon mots directed at his father.

On two unforgettable occasions Constantine cherished the sight of a woman's ankles strolling by his narrow, heavily barred window.

He suggested that Dagonet use his sleight-of-hand skills to free them—surely the Boy Who Could Steal from the Angels could steal a key from Fat Fucking Felix, the jailer of Castle Blackfast. But he

350

couldn't, because F.F.F. of C.B. didn't carry any keys, because he hardly ever unlocked their cells. On his bad days Sir Turquine came down himself and shouted and wept while he beat them with thorny branches, and one night his men held them down while he for some reason branded their buttocks with the Turquine Tower.

The pain was excruciating; Dagonet would remember that part. He understood that God was punishing them for their arrogance at having attempted the quest for the Holy Grail. But in their defense He'd made it very hard to refuse.

Michaelmas, All Saints' Day, the feasts of Saints Martin, Catherine, Andrew, Nicholas, and all the rest flew by unobserved. Outside their narrow windows, which were positioned level with the ground, summer swelled the trees full of sap, then autumn came and the leaves flooded down in torrents. Finally the forest was embraced and conquered by frost. By March it seemed like their ordeal would never end, and that their lives before the dungeon were only a dream.

That was when Sir Galahad arrived, with a white shield with a red cross on it; later when Dagonet saw it close up he realized the cross was actually dried blood smeared on the white canvas with somebody's thumb (the thumb in question, and the blood, belonged to the Grail King, King Pellas, Galahad's grandfather). Galahad banged on the basin just like they had. Then he broke Sir Turquine's collarbone and set them free.

THUS BEGAN ONE of the strangest stories of the Grail Quest. It was Galahad who suggested that Dagonet and Constantine travel with him for a while. After nine months in the dungeon they were thin and weak and lice-ridden, in no shape to be adventuring on their own.

"Just . . . you'll have to keep up," he said, not unkindly.

They found out pretty quickly what he meant. That same afternoon they spotted two knights ahead of them on the road. One carried a silver shield with three diagonal red stripes, the other's was all little gold crosses on a purple background. Without a word both men challenged Galahad. The boy knight smote the first one so hard that not only he but his horse went down, struggled to rise, then lay still again in the dust of the road. He split the second man's helm open with his holy silver sword.

Then he got back on his horse and trotted on, leaving his vanquished opponents unconscious on the ground. Dagonet and Constantine tried to keep up.

"Dagonet," Constantine said quietly. "Do you know who those knights were?"

"Should I?"

"Well, you're the only man in Britain who wouldn't. You s-s-saw their shields: Argent, Three Bendlets Gules, and Purpure, a Semy of Crosses Or." Constantine was a fiend for heraldry. "The first was Lancelot and the second was Percival. Those were the two greatest knights in Britain, probably in the world, and Galahad beat them both hollow inside of five minutes."

"With Arthur and Galahad running around I don't know why people even bother having legitimate children anymore," Dagonet said. "Bastards are clearly the superior product."

"See?" Constantine said. "You can be funny. Don't worry, I'll n-never t-tell."

That night they found shelter in a castle. In front of it stood a cursed fountain that boiled ceaselessly. Engraved on the fountain's stone rim were these words:

THE KNIGHT WHO LIFTS THIS CURSE WILL DISPEL THE ENCHANTMENTS IN THE KINGDOM OF ADVENTURES AND PUT AN END TO ALL ADVENTURES FOREVER

Galahad—never one to read a warning—stuck his hand right in. The water stopped boiling.

"It's because I'm free from lust," he explained.

Lancelot loses again, Dagonet thought.

The lord of the castle had been declining for years with a wasting illness, and on their arrival he expressed his final wish, which was to die in Galahad's arms, which he promptly did. The young knight cradled the old man awkwardly, like a bachelor who'd just been handed a baby. In the morning when they left, the lord's daughter swooned for love of Galahad, and the moat teemed with miraculous fishes.

DAGONET AND CONSTANTINE understood that by riding with Galahad they had moved from the margins of the world to its very center. They had joined the Hero, the main character of the story of Britain, taking on the roles of two mismatched background players who were about to have an absolutely magnificent view of God's will being worked on earth.

"This has to be the most important thing that's ever happened to two unimportant people," Dagonet said. He'd spent so much time in Constantine's company that he hardly loathed him anymore, and found himself talking almost freely.

"I suppose we're here to accentuate Galahad's p-perfection by comparison. Throw it into high relief, as it were."

"Plus if he let us roam around unsupervised he'd just have to rescue us again in a couple of days."

"We are anti-Galahads," Constantine declared poetically, "the sh-shadows cast by his brightness!"

"If this is what God likes," Dagonet said, "why didn't He make us all that way?"

And now that He's finally got it right maybe he'll stop making people forever. And crumple up all the rough drafts and throw them in the fire.

For the whole year that followed, spring to spring, Dagonet and Constantine followed Galahad around Britain. It really did seem like he was bent on finishing every last adventure at breakneck speed, at the rate of two or even three a day, just like the words on the fountain said. He seemed neither daunted by the challenges nor elated by his triumphs; he went about his work the way a baker bakes bread, blithely doing his job.

It wasn't as if he had much choice, the adventures wouldn't leave him alone. They came at him from all sides, harassed him, in forests and in meadows, at chattering river fords and in dry wastelands, in bogs and fens and on bare, sere winter beaches. There was no refusing them. But Galahad won every time.

If this is the story of Britain, Dagonet thought, it's distinctly lacking in dramatic tension.

Improbably enough Dagonet, who hated almost everyone, found himself becoming fond of Galahad. He was as exalted by the world as Dagonet was despised and neglected by it, but for all that Dagonet suspected they were equally lonely. Galahad had slain giants and banished demons but never kicked a ball or kissed a girl. He seemed to have been put on earth to make a point, but it was God's point, not his. His own life wasn't about him, he was just a helpless onlooker. He was as much a prisoner of his own strange nature as Dagonet was.

Perhaps Galahad felt some distant, lofty affection for his mismatched companions, too, because one night as they were making camp he volunteered an incredible fact, apropos of nothing, which was that his father was none other than Sir Lancelot du Lac.

Dagonet didn't know what to say.

"Are you sure?"

"Yes."

It was well known that Galahad was illegitimate. He'd always deflected questions about his paternity, but the truth made a certain kind of sense. His mother was Elaine, the daughter of King Pellas, who was that selfsame maiden whom Lancelot had pulled damp and pink and naked from Morgan le Fay's magical cauldron of boiling water. Afterward matters must have taken their course.

But Dagonet had always assumed Lancelot was a virgin.

"Why didn't you say before?"

"I didn't want to embarrass him at court. You won't say anything, will you?"

"Of course not, but—" Constantine pursed his lips, then made up his mind and went on. "But you and he fought in the road, and you beat him. Your own father. And neither of you said a word to each other."

Galahad lay back and looked up at the first stars. He always slept on the ground, even when it snowed, with an air of comfort and contentment that Dagonet had never experienced even on the most sumptuous of featherbeds.

"It's a mystery." Galahad's clear brow was as close to troubled as Dagonet had ever seen it. "My father sinned, and from his sin came me. And then I bested him. But how could someone as strong as I am"—Galahad had no modesty, false or otherwise—"come from his father's lowest moment of weakness? By rights I ought to be a twisted homunculus. A warning against all those who would stray and sin. Instead I am a champion."

Lancelot should've had me, Dagonet thought. That would've taught him a lesson.

"But for Lancelot maybe this is worse. To be humbled by his own son. Do you think God sent me to punish my father?"

"God must've had more on His mind than that," Constantine said generously, if not entirely honestly. "You're a great gift to the world, and to your father. He must be proud of you."

"Perhaps he is." Galahad didn't sound very sure about that. "Maybe I'm a sign of God's forgiveness. So maybe I was supposed to let him win."

"Maybe he let you win." Dagonet shifted to try to get a hard root out of the small of his back. He rarely—never—went to the trouble of lying to spare someone's feelings, but he found himself doing it for Galahad without thinking. Lancelot would've sold his own mother for an extra point in the tilt.

"I don't think so," Galahad said. "I know he does well in tournaments but his form's a sieve, I could've beaten him six different ways. Better would've been not to fight at all. I don't think much good can come from sons fighting fathers, do you? Jesus never tried to overthrow His father, for all that He suffered."

"I would pay to see that fight," Dagonet said.

Dagonet thought of his own father, who'd been so ashamed to have him for a son—a short, skinny, half-mad minstrel boy—and how much his father would've loved a proper son like Galahad. Whereas Lancelot felt humiliated by his son. And Galahad struggled to feel even the rage of a son at his unloving father. Dagonet was amazed once again at how unfailingly the world taxed people with the very thing that would try them the most.

FROM TIME TO TIME they met other knights along the way and exchanged news, and generally the news was bad. They seemed to be the only ones who were making any progress toward the Grail at all. Some of the knights had given up or been sent home by scoldy angels and hermits. Others had died or gone mad, and accounts of the deaths were disturbing. Sir Brian de les Isles was discovered turned into a figure of ice, and his companions watched helplessly as he melted away to nothing. Sir Felot of Listenoise had gone down fighting something that somehow attacked him inside his armor, leaving great bulges and dents in the metal. It ate him alive. The quest for the Holy Grail, which had begun in such a spirit of adventure, with such high hopes and good fellowship, had become something very much rougher and darker.

There was grumbling about it, especially among the older knights, especially since raw skill at arms didn't seem to count as much as it used to. On the Grail Quest it was nakedly apparent that victory really did go to the pure of heart, no matter how disgraceful their swordsmanship, and whose bright idea was that? Questing's a hunt for glory, sir! The great game! The whole enterprise stank of the seminary. This one was for the kneelers, the cross-kissers. Any knight with red blood in his veins ought to quit while he still could.

Maybe that's why the great King Arthur was afraid, Dagonet thought. Too much red blood.

Sir Percival reappeared one morning, wading out of a driving wet snowstorm at dawn. He'd recovered from the beating Galahad gave him with no ill effects or even any particular ill will; ruefully he parted his shaggy blond hair and made them feel the permanent groove Galahad had put in his skull. From then on he and Galahad fought as a pair, side by side, and the pace quickened even further. Not long after that Constantine and Dagonet woke one morning to find that they'd been left behind.

The two champions had broken camp before dawn and left them sleeping. Percival had made them redundant, or even more redundant than they already were.

They'd always known it would happen, sooner or later. The truth was that it was a relief. Galahad set a punishing pace, and they didn't have his heroic constitution. Dagonet had been nursing a low-grade feverish cold for a week, and Constantine's knee had never fully recovered from the fight with Sir Turquine. They were ready to go home. They retired to a warm inn and sat drinking mulled wine in front of a roaring fire, basking in the heat.

Constantine ordered them a feast. He was giddy with his new-found freedom.

"We've been spared, Dagonet!" He knocked Dagonet's cup with his own. "I n-never thought we'd make it as far as we did. I thought we'd end up like Gournevain!"

They'd found Sir Gournevain's armor, shield, and skeletonized body swimming in a pit full of colorful banded snakes.

"Personally I'm disappointed in God," Dagonet said. "I thought He had higher standards." A dry cough wrenched at his narrow chest.

"But here's what I want to know: Why didn't you quit before this? Long ago? You don't care about any of this stuff!"

"Why didn't you?"

Constantine squeezed cold water from his long hair.

"It's a fair question—excuse me, have you got any more of those apple f-fritters?" The serving girl went to get them. "I suppose I could say I'm doing it for the glory of Cornwall, or my family, or God. But really I think I'm on this quest for Arthur. Which is ironic since he d-didn't seem to want us to do it at all.

"But you see, my whole life my father's been building me up with one hand and cutting me down with the other. He tells me I'm destined for the throne, then he t-turns around and humiliates me to show me I'll never be worthy of it. I suppose he sees me as his replacement—a reminder that he will age and die. And he could never accept that. As long as he kept me down, he would never die.

"And in fairness he hasn't. It's worked so f-far. Still I really ought to have overthrown him, like Galahad did with Lancelot. But instead I ran away to Camelot.

"I knew you and he aren't close, but Arthur's been a father to me in ways my real father never could. He must have seen I was desperate for a f-father of any kind—I don't suppose I hide it very well—and he was kind to me. It's doubly generous of him really because he never had a father of his own. He gave me what he never had, without a second th-thought.

"And I believe that whoever wins the Grail will succeed Arthur on the throne. And that would make him Arthur's son. Symbolically at least. Wouldn't that be something, to be Arthur's son?"

"So King Galahad then," Dagonet said.

"Maybe." Constantine scrutinized the ragged edge of his once-magnificent tunic. "But I can't quite see that, can you? Galahad doesn't seem worldly enough to me to s-sit a throne. I can't see him levying taxes and all the rest of it. I think this quest is m-more like coursing with hounds, and Galahad's the hare. He's not here to win, he's here for the rest of us to chase after, to set the pace."

The fritters arrived, though they were still too hot to eat.

"My other theory is that we're to bring the Grail back to C-camelot so that Arthur can drink from it, or Guinevere, or both, and then they'll be able to have a child. It will make them fertile. But that can't be why you're here. Can it."

It was true, Dagonet didn't care about that. But he did care about finding the Grail. Very much.

When it appeared that day at Camelot, drifting through the air the length of the Great Hall, its curved silvery sides smeared with the stretched funhouse reflections of gaping knights' faces, Dagonet felt something he hadn't since he was very small: he was happy. Dagonet had no physical wounds to heal, but he had spiritual ones, grievous and profound, and the Grail made them better. He looked around at the world and instead of a wasteland of empty signs he saw for the first time that paradise of order and meaning that other people saw.

How could he never have seen it before, when it was all around him and always had been? He was blind, but now he saw. Tears of joy flowed freely down his face. He supposed it was what people meant by grace.

Once the Grail was gone the clouds gathered again, and his thoughts dove back down into the depths where they habitually resided. But he remembered what it was like to feel at peace. He would do anything, anything, to feel that again.

He didn't say any of this to Constantine, and the prince of Cornwall had learned to accept Dagonet's nonanswers without offense.

"There's a problem with my theories, though." Constantine lowered his voice even though the hall was empty. "About the Grail."

"What do you mean?"

"Well, it's not going very well, is it? How many knights have died so far?"

"I don't know. Thirty maybe."

"Thirty-eight. And I'll bet you there's m-more we don't know about. A lot more."

It was a good bet. Galahad had told them he'd seen three other knights dead in Simeon's tomb alone—they'd suffocated down there, on the sulfurous smoke. And how many more such bolt-holes must there be all around Britain, where God had squirreled away more of those corpses he loved to make?

"I'm worried that at this rate there will be few survivors. Maybe none at all. It's as though God released the hare and set us coursing and now he's cutting us down as we chase it. The huntsman is hunting his own hounds. But why? This was supposed to be like the Sword in the Stone, but if you failed at that you didn't die, you just went off for a pint and watched everybody else fail too.

"This is different. If you want to know what I really think, I think there's not going to be any succession. God has turned on us. He set a trap for us, and the Grail is the bait. He's ending the adventures and smashing the Table and terminating Arthur's line."

"But why would he do that?"

"I don't know." Glumly Constantine kicked a scroll of bark into the fire. "Or it'll go the other way. God will give us the Grail, but the price will be too high. He'll keep killing and killing till only one knight survives, and King Galahad will wear a crown of bone and sit on a throne of blood.

"But I put it to you, Dagonet: Who would serve the God who did that? A God as bloodthirsty as any pagan death idol? Either way, it's the beginning of the end."

Outside the wind whispered hoarsely. Sleet and darkness were closing in. The beginning of the end, Dagonet thought. He didn't know whether to be terrified of the coming disaster or relieved that it was all going to be over soon.

Twenty-three

THE TALE OF SIR DAGONET AND
SIR CONSTANTINE, PART III

Someone woke them in the middle of the night. A woman.

She had a round face, plain but wonderfully open, and a gap between her two front teeth. Something about her looked familiar, but Dagonet couldn't place it. She'd crept into their room at the inn and shaken them awake.

"Come with me now," she said earnestly, "and I will show you the most lofty adventure a knight has ever seen."

"What, really?" Constantine still had his eyes closed.

"Can you show it to us in the morning?" Dagonet asked.

"The thing of it is, we were just on our way home." Now the prince of Cornwall sat up. Even in bed he looked dashing, in a silk nightshirt trimmed with ermine and matching sleeping cap. "Are you a-absolutely sure you have the right kn-knights?"

"Come now," the young woman said.

So the quest wasn't over after all. They weren't getting away that easily. They'd thought they were free but it still had them. It felt like a divine joke, except that in Dagonet's experience God wasn't that funny. The woman waited as they gathered up their things. Curiously she was almost completely bald—Dagonet hadn't noticed at first because she wore a hood, but her head was covered only by a fine blond fuzz.

They rode with her for two days. It was late February and the cautious new sun shone through dripping branches dipped in ice. Badgers and hedgehogs emerged wobbling from underground along with the very earliest of spring flowers, snowdrops and violets.

Only once did they spot another knight, and only from a great distance. They were crossing a stream burbling with meltwater.

"My goodness," Constantine said. "Look at that."

"What?"

He pointed. Dagonet's eyes were bad. He could barely make out a small, dark figure, very erect, fording the creek far upstream from them on a white horse.

"Azure, Three Scepters, a Chevron Or," Constantine said. "That's Sir Bleoberys, unless I'm very much mistaken. He's been out a long time."

"What, longer than us?"

"Much longer. He left before the Grail Quest even started. In all honesty I thought he was dead."

"What's he looking for?"

"Don't know. He was very mysterious about it. I don't think even Arthur knows."

Constantine waved to the knight, but if he saw them Sir Bleoberys, if it really was him, didn't wave back. The young woman with the gap teeth hurried them on.

When they reached the coast they found a ship waiting for them, a great big cog with a huge square-rigged sail, white with a bold scarlet cross. Galahad, Percival, and Sir Bors the Younger were already on board. The moment Dagonet and Constantine stepped onto the deck a wind came roaring over the stern and the great sail filled with a dramatic *whuff*. No one steered it, the tiller worked by itself.

They'd been returned to the story as mysteriously as they'd left it. It was like a game of snakes and ladders, they'd shot down a snake only to come upon a ladder that took them all the way right to the top, or almost. The ship cleared the bay and headed straight out into the steel swells of the open sea.

Dagonet spent much of the journey that followed alone, sitting up in the high prow of the cog. Whatever else he was, he was still a child of the Fens, and he'd always felt at home on the water. He allowed his mind to rove ahead and consider what would come next. Even a committed pessimist like himself could see that Constantine's theories must both have been wrong. They weren't being killed, unless God was herding them toward some really spectacular Old Testament–style ritual slaughter. Nor was it likely they would win the Grail either, but it was looking increasingly like somebody would. Much blood had been shed, barrels of it, but in the end perhaps the scales would balance after all. Galahad would claim the prize and bear it in triumph back to Camelot. Arthur and Guinevere would sip from it and then retreat for some marital fornication. They would install it in its own glorious chapel, lined with gold and lapis, a beacon for pilgrims and the envy of princes and potentates the world over.

Or maybe they would build a cathedral for the Grail in Londinium. The pope would declare a new feast day for it, when it would be paraded through the streets in a bejeweled palanquin, and everybody would be bathed in its healing glow as it passed, while two mummers—a jester and a man on stilts, playing himself and Constantine—followed after in comically hopeless pursuit.

Its mere presence would permeate the whole island with grace, the way incense perfumed a room, inaugurating a new age. Britain would become an enchanted isle, like Avalon.

The ship's passengers existed in a state of grace. They didn't have to eat or drink. No one was hot or cold or seasick, and Dagonet's cough cleared right up. No one even slept. There was a chamber belowdecks with a large and sumptuous bed in it, on which lay yet another holy sword, silver on one side, crimson on the other. It presented Galahad with a puzzle, because the blade was clearly meant for him, but he was already carrying the sword from the block of marble, which was also meant only for him, and how many magic swords was he supposed to carry? In the end he shrugged and swapped them, belted on the new sword, and laid the old one on the bed.

The young woman explained that she was Sir Percival's sister, which solved the mystery of her vague familiarity. Her name was Agnes, and she'd spent her entire life till now in a convent, until one day an angel had told her to cut off her long blond hair and put it in a box and go fetch Dagonet and Constantine and bring them here. She kept rubbing her fuzzy scalp—it didn't itch, she said, but it felt so funny she couldn't resist. Dagonet developed a formidable crush on her.

On the fifth morning a white seabird sloped across their path on tilted wings, and he knew they must be at the end. A towering spur of rich red-brown stone stood all alone in the ocean, a thousand feet tall, with a castle on its highest point, its foundations worked into the living rock. Great flocks of white birds circled the spire, drifting and changing shape, lit up in peachy orange by the descending sun.

The waters were too rough to risk the cog, so they unshipped a dinghy that hung from the stern. Galahad clambered down the side into it, then Percival, then Bors. Dagonet and Constantine waited their turn uncertainly until Agnes stepped in front of them.

"Sirs, you will accompany us no further. Yonder is Corbenic Castle. No man may set foot there who is not pure in body and spirit, with no sins upon his conscience."

They nodded like a pair of mismatched twins. The young woman forbore to enumerate their particular sins but Dagonet could've reeled them off without much effort. Despair—he'd barely ever felt anything else. Wrath, a constant companion. And of course there was Lust. Even here, on a holy ship of grace, he'd managed to conceive a desire for Sir Percival's sister. I do confess it, he thought, I did envision her in all her nakedness.

They'd both known this moment would come. What followed was the business of saints and heroes, not fools and gangly princes. Dagonet handed Agnes down into the bobbing dinghy, cherishing the feel of her fingertips on his. Bors used the point of his sheathed sword to fend them off from the ship's side while Percival unshipped the oars and Galahad studiously averted his eyes from the lady's bared ankles. Dagonet couldn't help noticing that Galahad had a new sword belt for his new even-more-holy magic sword, and that it was made from lengths of shining blond hair.

Well, add that to the list of my sins, he thought. Envy.

Now there was nothing to do but wait, while God rendered His final judgment and chose a king and made His peace with man. Dagonet and Constantine sat down on the smooth black wood of the deck.

"I do wonder where Lancelot is," Constantine said. "If he's not in there, then wherever he is he must be m-mightily pissed off."

A great shattered sunset blew up behind the castle, arcs of cloud flaring pink against the deepening blue. Later Sir Bors, who would be the only knight to return from Corbenic, would tell them that the landing party was met by King Pellas. A broken sword was brought in, and Galahad fitted together the parts and mended it— still another magic sword, but it turned out that Bors was allowed to wield this one. A great suffocating hot wind blew up that made the ocean steam.

Next a tiny bright spark appeared high in the deepening sky, an infant star, falling through the air till Dagonet could see that it was actually a man garbed as a bishop, with a miter and a crozier. He was escorted by four great rainbow-winged angels. They were descending from Heaven.

"He does know how to put on a show," Constantine said.

Every door in the castle slammed shut at once—you could hear them from across the water like a rattle of cannon fire. The man from Heaven was Joseph of Arimathea, who took Jesus's body down from the cross, and who first sent the Grail to Britain, and he held a Mass assisted by the angels. Thunder cracked and rolled. Distant trumpets rang out from every point of the compass. As Holy Communion was given a spectral child with a fiery face appeared.

Dagonet felt it again, the grace of the Grail. He was calm and content. It came so easily, as if it had always been there, if he had but thought to reach out and grasp it.

Sometime after midnight an angel appeared on top of one of Corbenic's towers, under a sky flecked with millions of icy stars. He stepped up onto the battlements, spread wide his tremendous many-colored wings, and let himself fall forward and glide in a long, easy spiral down to the deck of the cog, where he checked himself with a couple of big noisy flaps.

Dagonet felt the wind on his face. It smelled sweet. The rainbow wings marked the angel as one of the higher ranks, a virtue maybe, or a dominion.

Sir Dagonet, he said. *Sir Constantine. Your journey has ended. Praise the Lord. Rarely have any so humble been granted an adventure so great.*

From a distance he'd looked like a winged man, but up close they could see he was bigger than that, nine feet tall at least and perfectly muscled. His skin was white as marble, like an ancient statue come to life; even his lips and his hair were white, and his eyes were liquid gold with no pupils. His deep voice echoed as though they were in a cathedral. He was so handsome he filled Dagonet with intense confusing feelings—love, longing, desire, devotion. An oversize golden dagger was strapped to his massive hairless calf.

This ship will return you to Britain. From there you may go where you will.

"Thank you," they both said, and Constantine added: "We'll probably go back to Camelot."

"Will the Grail come with us?" Dagonet said.

No. The Grail has left Britain forever.

The wood of the cog creaked, and the sail flapped softly.

"It has?" Dagonet said. "But the quest succeeded. We found it— they found it—it's just there in the castle."

And now it is gone.

"Gone where?"

Far away, to a city in the east. God has left Britain as well. There will be no more marvels.

"But why?" Dagonet felt like he'd had a blow to the head, and another to his heart. "I don't understand."

Because you weren't worthy.

"But we found it," Constantine said. "Or they found it anyway. Doesn't that prove we're worthy?"

Three knights of Britain proved their worth. Three, out of how many?

"Yes, all right, the arithmetic isn't very impressive," Constantine said, a little peevishly, "but so many others died! And we all tried so hard! Was it all for nothing? And what about the heir—the new king?"

That was never the Grail's purpose.

With no miracles to work, Dagonet thought, Lancelot will run mad within the week.

"So it was just a test," he said. "To find out if we were good enough. As if He didn't already know."

Suddenly Dagonet felt no fear or awe of the angel at all. Annihilate me if you want, go ahead. Blast me with a divine bolt. Chop me up with your golden knife.

"Why let us hope?" he said. "Just tell me that! Why set us a task that was too hard? Does He love suffering that much, that He likes watching us play His games and lose?"

The angel didn't seem bothered. Around his head was a faint, shimmery halo like a paper-thin cloth-of-gold ribbon. It shifted constantly, spinning one way and then the other, words and numbers and stars and more obscure characters forming in it and then fading away.

"Where is Galahad?" Constantine said.

Galahad is dead.

The boy had barely even lived except to run God's errands the length and breadth of the island, and now he was gone. Dagonet supposed Heaven was probably pretty nice, but he would've liked to see Galahad enjoy himself a little on earth first.

"He did everything you asked," Constantine said quietly.

And he has gone to his reward.

So after all that fuss nothing was going to change. There would be no gilded cabinet, no enchanted island, no new king. God wasn't even going to kill them all before He left. Just some of them. And Dagonet would go back to how he was before too.

But no. He couldn't. Please not that.

He got down on his knees on the deck in front of the angel and clasped his hands together. Some part of him was looking down at himself with withering contempt. *You pathetic sniveling hypocrite.* But he did it anyway. He couldn't stop himself.

And maybe God would like it. He did have a taste for humiliation.

"I am sorry," he said. "I spoke intemperately before, out of grief for those who died. I must ask you a boon: when I saw the Grail at Camelot I felt calm. I felt . . . happy. I'd never felt that way before. I don't know why, it's something to do with my mind. Now I'm afraid I'll never have that feeling again. And I'm afraid of what I'll do without it."

He didn't dare look up. The angel seemed to consider his reply. Dagonet imagined the whirling prismatic thoughts inside that great marble skull.

Why? the angel said finally.

"Why?! Because I cannot feel joy! And I can't stand it anymore! I can't go back! I don't know what I'm going to do!"

Dagonet's chest seized up and he sobbed. He couldn't stop. He'd never felt so degraded and disgusting in his degraded disgusting life. Constantine put a hand on his shoulder but he shrugged it off angrily. Completely unhinged, he threw his arms around the angel's smooth, hard calves; its skin gave off an unsettling buzz of power when he touched it. He gripped the cool, silky stuff of the angel's robes in his fists.

"It would cost you nothing!" Constantine said.

The angel looked down at Dagonet impassively.

You are not wrong. You see this world as it truly is: a vale of tears, empty of meaning. But if you honor God in this world, you will have your reward in the next.

He addressed them both.

If you wonder why you were brought on this journey, it was because of Galahad. He prayed for you, and God heard his prayer.

The sweet wind from the angel's wings swept the deck and his smooth feet slipped from Dagonet's grasp. He flew away. Dagonet lay there on the cold deck for a long time.

They'd thought to bring home a new spiritual heart for Britain, but in their unseemly haste to grab at grace they'd fumbled away what little they had to begin with. The worst disasters come dressed as miracles. The despair came on hard then, like a great dark wave breaking over him, cold and strong, driving him down to the bottom, grinding his face into the grit and gravel. The vile black toxins of his thoughts sloshed in his head, soiling his brain. He was remembering who he was.

That's right. Him again.

His teeth were chattering. He went belowdecks. Constantine was there, his absurdly long body looking somehow even longer lying down, stretched full length on the bed, the one that had had the magic sword on it. He hadn't wanted to risk touching it so he'd rolled it up in a blanket and shoved it rather unceremoniously underneath the bed.

Dagonet lay down next to him. It would be a long voyage home, and what would happen when they got there? When Icarus flew too near the sun he lost his wings and fell and died. That's what happened to heroes who played heavenly games. But Death didn't bother with the ordinary folk, the extras. They had it tougher, they had to keep on living, crawling forward in the dark, with no moon or even any stars to light the way.

And there is no path back from whence we came. Can you lead us out of this darkness, King Arthur? Or are you lost in it too? How could a good man like him serve a God so cruel?

Dagonet was not a good man, and neither would he serve. Your promised land is no doubt wonderfully pleasant, but I think it is too far for me. His hands were sticky from the sea salt, a feeling he hated. But it was a very comfortable bed.

"I'm sorry the angel didn't g-give you what you asked for," Constantine said.

"Fuck him."

"That's right. Fuck that angel." He stretched, which made him even longer. "Nice a-ankles, though."

Constantine really had gone on about those ankles. Dagonet didn't say anything more for a while. He was forgetting again how to talk to other people.

"I did get something," he said finally.

"You did?" Constantine propped himself up on an elbow. "He gave you something?"

"He gave me nothing. I took something."

Dagonet slid it out from under his cloak and held it up: a golden dagger. He turned it this way and that, and it flashed as bright as if the sun shone on it.

"I stole it from the angels."

BOOK III

THE
BLIND GIANT

The land was all laid waste
by such deeds; and they said openly,
that Christ slept, and his saints.

—*The Anglo-Saxon Chronicle*,
Year 1137 CE

Twenty-four

THE INDIGO KNIGHT

Under the circumstances a little pomp would've been justifiable. A brass fanfare, some scattered *huzzahs!*, even just a ragged cheer from the sleepy guards at the gate. But the quest for the Holy Lance began in silence.

They met at the postern gate, seven knights and an enchantress, all sober and solemn, morning fog beading on hard leather and cold engraved steel. Everybody was coming this time: Bedivere, Palomides, Scipio, Dinadan, Constantine, Collum, Nimue, even Dagonet, who turned up punctually and in full armor. It was odd to see Dagonet the Fool in harness, blued steel with gilded rivets, closely fitted to his pipestem limbs, his arms a white cloud against a dark blue sky, almost black.

He looked tiny next to the big men of the party, broad-shouldered Bedivere and towering Constantine, whose armor was engraved and enameled and fire-gilded to within an inch of its life. Constantine's arms were ten black birds—Cornish choughs—and the surface of his armor was alive with even more of them, engraved, with gold accents, as if they'd taken flight from his shield and alighted on his person.

Scipio wore only light scale and carried an oval shield with three arrows and a golden boar on it. Collum felt suitably noble and heroic in his own new armor. Its plate was thicker than his old one but it fit better, and hung on him better, so that it felt lighter. They brought no squires or bearers; they would build their own firepits this time. The world was wrapped in mist, the sun and sky smothered and buried in it miles deep.

Nimue was dressed practically, in black boots and a gray dress with a skirt big enough that she could tuck it under her legs as she rode. No witch's robes for her. Collum hadn't seen her since the night before his ordeal.

"Thank you for the shilling," he said. "You were right, it did come in handy." He couldn't guess within a thousand miles what she thought of him. He wondered if she'd known everything already, that night in the courtyard.

"I hope you spent it wisely."

"I gave it to a lady made of stone, so she would let me jump down a well."

Her bold eyebrows arched.

"I hope it was worth it."

"If you trust me a little more now," he said gallantly, "then it was worth it."

Nimue didn't answer that but touched his arm and went forward to talk to Bedivere. God's holy bones, she was beautiful. He hoped he hadn't drooled too much.

After a short prayer they wound their way down through the castle grounds quietly, skirting the gardens and the tiltyard, the pond and the deer park. The air smelled like wet bark, and the mist was so thick that Collum couldn't even see the end of the castle gardens—the rows of squash and peas and cabbage and turnips led off into nothingness. They filed out through the Gate of Three Queens, crossed the Brass, and headed north along a dirt road that after a couple of miles joined up with the Fosse Way. But Bedivere didn't follow the old Roman road, instead he led them straight across it and through a gap in a hedge into the damp fields on the far side.

By midmorning the fog had burned away and they stopped in a ragged field, unmown and ungrazed, where a ring of old standing stones loitered. A man was waiting there with a cow, and Nimue led it into the circle and cut its throat and daubed each of their foreheads with the blood. Constantine made a face when she got to him, and Dagonet flinched, but nobody declined.

"For luck," she said. "Be glad it was just a cow, Scipio wanted to sacrifice Sir Melehan."

They kept off the main roads, sticking to the old paths, ragged ways that wound through fields, past old farmland and the edge of the Blackash Woods, the great oaks at maximum late-summer green. They circled the lonely encampment of a solitary charcoal burner, the ground around it blackened and smoking like the entrance to Hell.

Around noon the second day they crossed a river where it fanned out and flowed an inch deep over dark brown pebbles, chattering loudly but barely wetting the horses' hooves. A thready goat track through shoulder-high bracken took them into the cool, green, rolling uplands of Sorelois. From the peak of a hill they looked down on a flat, dark lake where a mass of men and horses milled around on the shore, forty or fifty of them, weapons glinting dully in the summer sun.

"Ours?" Collum asked.

Bedivere shook his head. "Look at the shields."

"And no helmets." Dinadan knocked on his own with his knuckles. "Those aren't Britons. That's a Saxon warband."

Collum had never seen Saxons before, not in the flesh. They didn't wear braids after all.

"What are they doing this far west?"

"Having a drink and a piss, it looks like," Bedivere said.

"They must be part of Mordred's gang," Dinadan said. "Their employer having died, they'll be collecting their salary from the populace in the form of rape and pillage."

"God's hair." Bedivere stared at them so intently that Collum wondered if he was actually considering taking them on.

Finally he shook his head.

"Not our fight," the old knight said. "We're hunting God, not Saxons."

THE NEXT DAY the wind became steady and relentless, bending the trees and whistling in the gaps in their armor and hissing through fields of wheat as women tied it into sheaves. The blue sky was full of foolish white swashes of cloud. They flushed a couple of meaty pheasants which took lumbering flight, clapping their wings together. The land was crawling with Saxons—Collum wasn't sure if they were the same ones or different, but they had to divert twice more to avoid them. So far their grand quest was worryingly aimless and furtive.

Palomides spotted the ruins of an old Roman gold mine.

"See where they ran aqueducts from higher ground." He pointed to a couple of decapitated columns barely visible above the shrubbery. "They brought in water at high pressure to blast away the topsoil and lay bare the ore."

It was hard to believe such things had ever been possible, or ever could be again.

They came to a grand estate set all by itself in the middle of the fields, surrounded by a high wall. They entered through an iron gate that got stuck in the dry grass—it must have been years since it was opened. Inside was a pleasure garden of tall trees, neatly trimmed bushes, and an immense tidily kept lawn. The walls kept out that ceaseless wind, though it still pushed at the tops of the trees.

Along one edge of the lawn stood seven knights, motionless, like chess pieces waiting to be put in play. The knights' armors and surcoats were all different colors, arranged like a rainbow from red to violet. Beside them a herald carried a standard bearing a silver key on a field of black.

Only now did Collum feel for the first time like they were really on a quest. Till then it had felt just a little like playacting, striking heroic poses as they wandered an empty world to no particular purpose. But now the game was afoot.

The Red Knight stepped forward. Bedivere dismounted and crossed the lawn to confer with him. Somewhere a yellowhammer called in the silence: *a-little-bit-of-bread-and-no-cheese.*

"It's a tournament," Bedivere said, when he returned. "Joust and then a mêlée."

"Terms?" Palomides said.

"The joust is three passes, mêlée is sword and shield only. Rights of way observed, no trampling, no blows from behind, no striking a helmetless knight."

"Should we ask permission before we fart?" Scipio said.

"No farting," Dinadan said.

"I must say, it's all very civilized!" Constantine had given in to boyish excitement. "I don't remember even Galahad getting anything like this, do you, Dagonet?"

"Galahad's dead," said Dagonet.

Bedivere informed the rainbow knights that their challenge was accepted, and immediately the place sprang to life. Grooms in black-and-white livery appeared leading horses. Servants set up a table and laid out food: cold pheasant and lamb and meatballs in aspic and dark rye bread and pyramids of apples, plus a barrel of red wine. Constantine sampled it.

"*Very* civilized."

Nimue kept to herself, nibbling nervously at some bread and butter.

"Any advice?" Collum asked. "On matters magical or supernatural?"

She popped the rest of the bread in her mouth and brushed the crumbs off her hands.

"We're past advice," she said with her mouth full. "At this point there aren't really any choices left at all. We're taking our cues directly from God now. How are you in the tilt?"

"Fair to middling."

She swallowed.

"Well, full marks for honesty."

"It's often considered a virtue."

"Might give you a tactical advantage. God does look kindly on virtue. Collum, you do realize you have to win this?" He saw for the first time how worried she was. Her lips were pale. Nimue liked to be in control, she wasn't cut out to be a spectator. "There's no choice about that either. This quest could end right here, today."

Collum nodded. He wasn't hearing "I believe in you" or "it's all going to be all right," but he'd already gathered that Nimue didn't care much for empty words. For a wild moment he thought of begging her for a favor to wear in battle, but either his courage failed him or common sense got the better of him.

"You could pray for us," he said.

"I'll pray for you."

But she didn't look any less nervous.

Bedivere trotted to the head of the lists, his broad armored shoulders striped steel and gold with beams from the sun on his chest. At the far end of the field, a hundred yards away, a knight rode out to face him, the yellow one; his horse wore yellow barding to match. The two standards hung limply in the still air, Camelot's at one end of the tilt and the silver key at the other. Everything was silent as a dream.

Bedivere saluted his opponent and barked a quiet *hya!* at his horse. He shot away down the field, a narrow green road with no turnings, the point of his great yew lance up at an angle, his horse accelerating smoothly into a gallop, the cheeks of its great shiny rump working, big hooves kicking up grass and beating bass thumps on the ground in the quiet. Collum's stomach tightened and the knights sent up a thin cheer.

Both lances dropped into line and a sharp *crack* announced the impact. Bedivere's point hit his opponent's shield, but the Yellow Knight shrugged it off while his own lance took Bedivere in the chest, bent and shattered, sending a spectacular fountain of spinning splinters as high as the treetops. Bedivere swayed backward perilously but kept his seat.

He would be judged the loser in that exchange. Tournament jousting was really just a game, which was one of the reasons

Collum always had trouble taking it seriously. The object was to break your lance against your opponent, the way the Yellow Knight had done, for which you were awarded points. Further points could be awarded for damaging the other knight's shield or armor, for knocking him off his horse, or for knocking down his horse completely. Likewise you could lose points for breaking your shaft too close to the tip, or touching the barrier with your horse's rump, or losing your helmet or your stirrups or your lance, or hitting your opponent below the waist. The judges would add up the totals and declare a winner.

Bedivere managed a tie in the third and final pass by breaking his lance against his opponent's helm, a difficult blow that earned him extra points. His duty done, he doffed his helm and his gauntlets and rubbed his face and ruefully accepted everybody's congratulations and mockery while attendants rushed out to clean up the broken wood and replace the divots.

Constantine was ungainly on a horse, and he looked like far too large a target, but his innings ended early when he took the Red Knight down and his horse with him. Palomides, as natural in the saddle as a centaur, the gilded plates of his armor flashing in the sun, unhorsed the Blue Knight spectacularly on his third pass. By contrast, Scipio was not only knocked down by the Green Knight, his foot caught in the stirrup and his horse dragged him half the length of the field. When he finally shook himself free, miraculously uninjured, he got to his feet and bowed to torrents of imaginary applause.

Collum knew he was in for his own measure of humiliation. In spite of all his practice as the Knight of the Fountain, he still was not a Camelot-caliber jouster. On his first pass, buoyed up by a wild last-minute surge of confidence, he aimed for his opponent's forehead like Bedivere had and missed by at least a foot, the shaft bouncing juddering off the man's shoulder. It was only by sheer good fortune that the Violet Knight missed his mark as well. From the far end, he heard the other knights laughing and somebody, Scipio probably, made a convincing sheep's *baaaaah*. On the second pass Collum panicked completely and his mind emptied, whereupon his training took over and he shattered his lance satisfyingly on the other man's shield. Point to Camelot. It seemed both wrong and undeniably true that he wanted to do well to find the Holy Lance and save Britain but equally as much he wanted to impress Nimue.

Nothing daunted, he attempted the same difficult helmet strike again on the third pass with exactly the same result, except that this time his opponent didn't miss but landed a solid hit on his own shield. That gave him an even outcome overall, like Bedivere, unless he'd scored it wrong. When he got his helm off, Dinadan clapped him on the shoulder.

"At least you didn't fart."

Dagonet was last in line but he refused to joust, so it was decided that Palomides would joust a second time, this time with the Indigo Knight as his opponent. The afternoon had become hot in the walled garden, but the sun was dropping, promising relief before too long. After the most perfunctory of salutes they both shook their reins and surged forward in perfect synchronicity toward each other, mirror images, a stone dropping toward its reflection in a pond.

Then the Saracen's lance was spinning end over end in the air. Indigo's point had taken him full in the chest and laid him out flat.

Collum wouldn't have believed it. Palomides jounced once or twice in the saddle like a rag doll, then slumped sideways to the ground, stunned. His riderless horse cantered on, looking relieved to get away while it still could.

The Indigo Knight finished up at Camelot's end, patted his horse's neck, and flipped the end of his broken lance casually to a servant. Scipio immediately strode up and challenged him to another pass, but he didn't respond, just rode off back to join the rest of the rainbow.

Scipio watched him go, hands on his hips.

"I am going to mêlée the shit out of that fellow," he said.

After the joust Camelot held a narrow lead of just one point, but the mêlée was more Collum's thing—nothing cute or clever, just proper scrapping. You want to touch the barrier with your rump? Go right ahead. The seven knights of Camelot lined up mounted along one edge of the field. Collum was second from the left, matched up against the knight in orange, who'd knocked Scipio out of the saddle. He was shorter and broader than the others, a bandy-armed brawler, and he wore an old-fashioned bucket helm with a sinister chevron-shaped eye-slit.

Collum bent forward and whispered a few words of encouragement to his horse. A mêlée was rough on horses, who didn't like having their ears bumped and sharp objects waved around their heads. He tried not to think about what hung in the balance. At the far end of the line Bedivere raised his sword.

"Camelot!"

And the knights answered from deep in their chests: "*Camelot!*"

They trotted forward across the cooling green, the sun behind them, long shadows racing out ahead. Collum drew his sword, the ancient blade he'd dragged up from the world in the well, and held it low and to his left, across his body, a guard that looked awkward but kept his options open and his intentions unclear. It also kept his sword clear of his horse's head; one's first victim in mounted fencing was often one's own mount. Discreetly he slipped his right foot out of its stirrup.

You had to work fast in a fight like this because blows from horseback landed twice as hard as they did on foot, and you wanted to make sure yours landed first. At the last moment Sir Orange surged forward just a step quicker than Collum expected, but the exhilaration of the fight was like a magic draught that slowed time down around him. He slid his sword sidewise under Orange's thrusting point, under the man's armpit, while with his free right foot he deftly kicked Orange's left foot out of its stirrup. Grunting with the effort, Collum grabbed him by the armored crotch with his free hand and heaved him bodily out of the saddle.

The Orange Knight hit the ground on his back with a mighty clatter. He tried to rise but Collum smashed him down with his sword, again and again, guiding his horse in a tight circle with his knees, raining strikes on his head and shoulders while Orange tried to protect himself with one hand and grope for his dropped sword with the other. With all the leverage and momentum and unfairness of a mounted man beating an unmounted one, Collum hoisted his blade over his head with both hands and brought it down on the man's trapezius. The Orange Knight burst apart.

It happened in a heartbeat: man and armor were gone, and in their place a dozen or so birds went fluttering up and away around Collum in a little flock. Doves maybe, all white except for one gray one. They flapped up into the sky, clear of the struggling, thrashing humans below them.

He didn't even have time to be surprised. That's got to be worth a point or two, was all he thought.

For the first time Collum heard the sounds of the fight all around him, the shouts and curses and the sound of metal sliding on metal like giant shears. You could see the occasional lively spark when two swords met. Dagonet and Constantine were down—and there went Scipio, too—but the other side was down to four men, too, then three as Dinadan disarmed the Yellow Knight. The defeated knight simply bowed to him, knelt on the grass, placed his palms together, and became a flock of doves, which circled the field once then settled in the lower branches of a tree to watch.

But there was a problem, and it was Sir Indigo. Bedivere was dueling him now, with a sword instead of his signature hammer—house rules—and it was obvious that Palomides's loss in the tilt was not a fluke. It was an incredible sight: Bedivere was broader and two or three inches taller, and his massive ironbound shield was like a wall between them, but the Indigo Knight was striking him at will while Bedivere blundered after him like a blindfolded child in a party game. Finally—and to all appearances he could've done it at any time—the knight pirouetted and struck him with an overhand blow, two-handed, the hardest cut in the swordsman's arsenal. It was enough to dent Bedivere's helm. He fell down backward.

For a long, uncomfortable moment the old knight lay without moving, till finally he stirred, dragged himself to his feet and trudged resignedly to the sidelines. The victor skipped back fresh and alert as ever, bouncing just a little on his toes.

Collum found the man's cockiness irritating. A purple popinjay.

He dismounted and slapped his horse on the rump, sending it to the sidelines. Then he spun his sword once and stepped into the Indigo Knight's line of vision. The quest wasn't going to end here.

Collum started with speed, forcing the pace, double-time, throwing out a volley of cuts and thrusts and feints, high to low, low to high, no letup. It was like he wasn't even there, and the Indigo Knight was serenely practicing perfect, clean forms all by himself. Their swords met in the bind and Collum felt for Indigo's strength and found it. It wasn't like the Green Knight's, cold granite, this was a living, surging, hungry strength, unshakably confident in its power to overcome and consume. What insatiable phantom haunted that armor?

But there had to be a way in. The knight took a hard cut at him, and Collum got his blade on it and steered it down into the dirt and stomped on the blade so it stuck there. Not for long, but long enough for him to swing his own sword around behind the Indigo Knight's head and lock it there with his other arm while he kicked the man hard behind the knee once, twice, and felt it bend. Something caught fire inside him, just as it had in the battle. He wasn't the frightened boy from Mull anymore, he'd left that boy in the well under Camelot. He imagined himself as he must look to the other side, huge and gleaming, his face a cryptic mass of crosses. That was him, he was the young blood of the Table, and he was going to win this thing for Arthur! Distantly he heard the others shouting his name.

He heard something else too. For the first time the Indigo Knight made an actual sound, a low and very unbirdlike growl as he strained against the sword lock, harder and harder, his strength was incredible, holding him was like trying to keep the sun from rising.

It was too much. He tore free and Collum staggered back, boots slipping on the uneven grass.

Now the knight abandoned his decorous reserve and just a little bit of that perfect form. He was the one pushing the tempo now, chaining his attacks together until he caught Collum with his sword at a weak angle and knocked it aside. What had happened to all that power from a moment ago? Where had it flown? Wheezing and blundering he tried to get back into it but he'd lost his rhythm, and Indigo stepped in hip-to-hip and wrapped his own sword behind Collum's head, gripping it with both hands, and did exactly what Collum failed to do to him: forced him to the ground as gently as if he were teaching a naughty puppy to submit.

Face down in the dirt, Collum's helmet showed only dark. He slapped the ground three times to show he yielded.

Safely on the sidelines he slipped his helm off and let his vision clear. His breathing slowed in the cool twilight. For once he didn't even reproach himself. It hadn't been a near thing. There was no world in which he could've beaten that knight. All that was left was to accept defeat and face the consequences. The shadows of the trees stretched across the green like taffy, their branches full of birds. Constantine licked his finger and rubbed at a scratch in one of his choughs. Collum watched with a sense of detached fatalism as the delicate tracery of Palomides's bladework shattered against the indigo champion's matchless form, and he was sent off to join the rest of the defeated. It was over.

By Collum's count they'd lost the tournament. Narrowly but inarguably. Would that be good enough? It didn't sound good enough for God, from what Collum knew about Him, but they had no more to give. Like Nimue said, there were no choices left. This must be what the end looked like.

The Indigo Knight stood alone, his armor melting into the indigo sky. Maybe he was an angel after all, put here by God to teach man humility. Well, job well done. He undid a catch at the nape of his neck with a delicate gesture, like a queen unclasping a necklace in the privacy of her chambers after a long and exceptionally wearying night at the ball.

Collum waited expectantly for the angel of judgment who would send them home. But it wasn't an angel, or a demon, or even a flock of birds. Collum had never seen that gaunt, handsome face before in his life, but he recognized it instantly. The knight who'd beaten them all hollow was Sir Lancelot du Lac.

Twenty-five

MIRACLES

It was like they'd seen the face of Medusa. The knights of the Round Table were stone statues in a sculpture garden.

Lancelot was a half generation younger than Bedivere, but you could see he'd spent most of those years outdoors, roaming Britain in search of adventure, getting beaten and battered by sun and rain and sleet and snow. There was a leanness to him, too, that spoke of extreme discipline—he'd so punished his body in the pursuit of perfection that it contained not one particle of surplus fat. The skin was stretched tight over his prominent cheekbones.

But he was still handsome, with wavy chestnut hair and narrow eyes that had reflected a dozen miracles. Those eyes had looked down on every knight in the kingdom as they sprawled on the ground in front of him in abject defeat. Every knight except Galahad. Whose father he was.

But Galahad was dead, like all the other great ones—Gawain, Gareth, Percival, Tristram, Lamorak, Lionel, Bors. The runaway landslide of fate had caught up with all of them, one after another, and buried them. But the great du Lac had outrun them all.

"Well met, old friends," he said.

There was a moment more of silence, then Constantine ran over and wrapped him in a big gawky embrace.

One by one the others followed. They didn't all hug him but they shook his hand and looked him in the eye and clapped him on the shoulder. Even Dinadan did. The only ones who hung back were Dagonet, who never shook hands with anybody, and Bedivere, who just folded his massive arms and watched.

And Collum, who didn't want to presume. But as soon as he could disengage himself Lancelot came straight over.

"We haven't met. I'm Lancelot."

"Collum. Of the Out Isles."

"A pleasure." They shook hands. "Well fought, Sir Collum."

"It was a great, great honor." His voice went inexplicably hoarse in the middle when he said it, but Lancelot pretended not to notice. He was probably used to it. He turned to Sir Bedivere.

"Don't touch me," Bedivere said.

Lancelot didn't look surprised. He didn't smile or try to ingratiate himself either.

"I know what you think of me," he said. "I know what you think I did. I'd probably feel the same way. But I swear to you that I never betrayed Arthur, and I would never have left him had I not been driven from his side. I swear it to you by our lord Jesus Christ."

"Swear it by whoever the hell you want." Bedivere was tall enough to look down at Lancelot. "I know what you are."

"You know nothing, Bedivere, but I'm not asking you to believe me, I ask only that you come inside and eat a meal. Have a drink. Sleep in a bed for a change. You're tired, and we were comrades once."

Bedivere just stared at him.

"Come on, Bedivere," Scipio said. "For God's sake."

"You go ahead."

"Bedivere," Palomides said. "We are not here by accident. God put us here."

"Maybe so." Bedivere kept his arms folded, as if he was concerned about what they might do if he didn't. "I don't presume to know what God does or doesn't do, but I know I'm not spending a night under the same roof as this traitorous sack of shit." Now he pushed a thick finger into Lancelot's chest. "And if I hear you speak Arthur's name again I'll kill you."

He walked away across the torn-up grass and back out through the gate into the darkening fields beyond. No one followed him. The doves watched silently from the trees.

THEY WERE AT HOXMEAD ABBEY, which was the monastery where Lancelot had elected to spend the rest of his life in holy seclusion. Hoxmead had a well-appointed guesthouse with a high-vaulted hall built of pale blond stone, and the knights dined there on mackerel in a fresh green herb sauce and drank the monastery's own ale. Lancelot sat with them but ate almost nothing, just leaves of lettuce from the garden, and drank only water. He appeared to be taking his vows more seriously than Guinevere had.

Both sides were hungry for news. Dinadan and Constantine did most of the talking, and when they got to the Battle of Camelot Lancelot made them go through it almost minute by minute, listening intently, eyes unfocused, quizzing each of them in turn, as though he were restaging it stroke for stroke in his mind.

When they were finished, he told them his story.

After the disaster of Camlann, Lancelot wanted to disappear.

He had never betrayed Arthur, never, not in his heart or anywhere else, but he hadn't saved him either, and the shame of that failure ran so deep that he didn't know how to face it. He couldn't look his own men in the eye. He went off by himself, hunting what was left of Mordred's army alone. Some part of him was praying that he would come across an enemy force large enough to kill him.

But Lancelot had always found defeat to be an elusive quarry, and it escaped him again. He triumphed over everyone he met. When he stumbled on this abbey he decided that if he couldn't arrange an honorable death for himself he could at least put an end to his old life and start a new one. He begged the monks to take him in as a novice. He'd been here ever since.

"Why didn't you tell us who you were?" Collum asked. He'd recovered the power of speech but his heart still raced every time those starry brown eyes fell on him.

"Couldn't. Last night I had a dream that you were coming, and when I woke up the armor was waiting for me in my cell. As soon as I put it on I couldn't speak. I guess God didn't want me to spoil the surprise." The great knight's manner was never anything but affable and unassuming, but it was somehow very clear that he was accustomed to being the center of everybody's attention, including God's. He honored you with his presence and in return you felt, ever so slightly, through no fault of your own, that you were taking up his valuable time.

"Lancelot." Palomides pushed his plate aside. "Did God tell you why we are here?"

"I'm guessing it has to do with the succession."

"We are looking for the Holy Lance," Palomides said. "If we find it then God will give us a new king."

"You know this?"

Palomides explained about the glowing medal.

"Will you come with us?" Constantine asked.

The great knight folded and unfolded a lettuce leaf with his huge callused hands. From the moment Lancelot had taken his helmet off Collum had done nothing but hope for exactly this, for Lancelot to come with them, as their companion or as their king. But after a thoughtful pause he shook his head.

"I belong here. And even if I didn't, Bedivere wouldn't have it, and it would tear everything apart all over again. I don't think your quest is over, even though you lost today. I think I would know. I've played my part, but God gave this task to you."

"And he led us to you," Palomides said. "And even if we did not need you, the Round Table is currently ninety-four knights short of a quorum. Camelot needs you. Britain needs you."

"Why else would God have put you in our path?" Dinadan said.

"To test you. To test me, maybe, to see if I would abandon my new vocation. I don't know, I've always been bad at those guessing games. Bedivere would say I was put here to tempt you from the right path, and maybe he's right. But the questing game is something I know a little bit about, and believe me when I say that you don't want me anywhere near it."

"Why not?" Collum asked.

"Is it because you slept with the queen?" Dinadan asked.

"No." If Lancelot had to master any emotions at Dinadan's remark, he did so with no obvious effort. "But I've got enough sins on my conscience without that one."

"Don't be dramatic. You can't be worse than Scipio."

"How many knights of the Round Table has Scipio killed? Thirteen came to arrest me when I was with the queen, and I killed twelve of them. And I killed Gareth and Gaheris while I was rescuing her."

"We were all there that day, it was a madhouse," Constantine said. "Were you supposed to let Guinevere burn?"

"Like I said, I'm no good at guessing games. Maybe there were only wrong answers that day, I don't know. But I know that what I did was wrong."

"Then redeem yourself," Dinadan said.

"What the hell do you think I'm doing here?"

A hugely fat tabby cat pounced up onto the table and stalked along it stiff-legged, sniffing at the cups of ale. Lancelot swept it onto his lap, where it suffered itself to be stroked by the great du Lac. Collum strongly suspected that the other knights still had no idea whether or not Lancelot had done what he was accused of. He was impossible to read. Maybe that was part of being the best knight in the world, keeping your intentions veiled, so no one could exploit them. Maybe he'd mastered and armored his exterior so completely that nothing, not even his own emotions, could get out. Or maybe it wasn't so much that he was unreadable as that somewhere in his long pursuit of invincibility he'd lost the ability to be read.

"Have you seen her?" he asked.

"She told us to fuck off," Palomides said.

Lancelot smiled at that, the lines piling up on his weathered face. "I'll bet she did."

Not long after that they went to bed.

They could've left the next morning, nothing was keeping them there, but one way or another they all found reasons to delay their departure. Palomides said he wanted to examine the cellarer's bee-breeding experiments. Dinadan was resting a strained calf muscle. Nimue wanted to consult the monastery's library, which included a rare copy of *Asteroskopita*, Zoroaster's five-volume treatise on astrology. Though it turned out that women weren't allowed in the reading room, and she gave the librarian a furious talking-to and went to camp with Bedivere in the fields.

Collum caught only a glimpse of Lancelot during the day, weeding the garden with the same intense concentration he must've brought to his knightly training. He wondered what the other novices thought of receiving instruction alongside King Arthur's fallen champion, who must've been three times their age. Collum certainly didn't know what to make of him. He didn't seem to have a message for them, or any desire to join them. If only there had been a little pride left over, a little lust for power, some envy maybe, they could've used it to tempt him out of seclusion, but whatever titanic contests Lancelot's soul had played host to, between greatness and weakness, love and loyalty, lust and purity, they'd apparently left him cool and devoid of any further earthly desires. Nothing left but incorruptible ashes.

Though that night he appeared for dinner in the guest house as before, with his cup of water and his lettuce leaves. He couldn't resist sniffing the air of Camelot that still clung to them one last time.

"I wonder if you've ever heard this story." They'd finished eating, and he dipped his already clean fingers in a finger bowl and wiped them on a cloth. "It was one of my very first outings after I joined the Table. I was in Roevent Forest near Lanvenic when I spotted a black hunting hound following a bloody trail."

"The good ones always started with dogs." Constantine hung on Lancelot's words even more obviously than Collum did.

"It led me to a great manor house where there was a dead knight on the floor. A lady came out, weeping and wailing, said she was his wife and he had to be avenged. It turned into one of those endless adventures with far too many twists and turns, but in the end it came down to Sir Meliot de Logres having a wound that could never heal till somebody brought back a bloody cloth from the Chapel Perilous."

Lancelot never once stuttered or hesitated when he spoke, he was always perfectly composed, but Collum noticed that his fingers were constantly at work, tapping or twiddling or twisting the bristly edges of his rough novice's tunic.

"Well, the name was spot on. It was guarded by thirty knights and an enchantress who said she was in love with both Gawain and me. Gawain had already been there, but he never got the holy cloth or whatever it was, he just slept with her and left again. He always complained about me getting all the miracles, but it wasn't that I was so much better, it was just that at the end of the day he liked sex more.

"But the point of the story is that I finally got back to Sir Meliot de Logres and touched his wounds with the cloth, and they healed. It was the first time I ever did a miracle.

"I shouldn't be talking this much, but I feel like I have to get it all out before I take my vows. Have you ever seen a wound heal by magic? You never forget it. The skin pulls together by itself, the two edges meet and become one, the scar fades. Even the little hairs grow back. It's not like healing so much as it is like time running in reverse. But what's truly wonderful is how it makes you feel."

Lancelot's eyes began to lose focus.

"In that moment you know, you know for a certainty, that God is with you. Of course He's everywhere all the time, but when you do a miracle you actually feel it. He's looking directly at you, working through you, holding your hands, like a father dancing with his child. You are loved, and you are in love, not just with Him but with yourself and with the whole world. At that moment I loved Sir Meliot as much as I ever loved my mother or father or Arthur or anyone. I laughed and cried and kissed him and babbled like an idiot. In that moment I knew in my heart that all that ever happened or would happen was good and right.

"It was like I'd been cold all my life and hadn't known it, because I'd never known anything else. And then in that moment I discovered warmth, and I knew what I'd been missing."

Lancelot blinked, returning to earth, but slowly, a drifting feather.

"I also understood why my life till then had been so strange. I was a very ordinary child—please, I'm done with tall tales and false modesty, just know that I was undistinguished in every possible way. My parents died when I was young, and my father's cousins were happy to inherit his castle but less happy to inherit his ten-year-old son, and the first chance they got they sent me to the Lady of the Lake.

"There was a quid pro quo with the fairies, something to do with a water mill that my guardians had an interest in. You probably thought 'du Lac' was a family name, but it's not. I actually grew up in a lake. I expect you all had rather lonely childhoods, too, to have grown up into the heroes you are now."

"Not me," Palomides said. "I grew up in a palace."

"Well, I lived under a lake for seven years. I came up four times a year on the quarter days, then right back down again. It's all like a fever dream to me now. It was the Lady who taught me how to fight—you must be fairy-trained, too, Dinadan, I can see it in your style, as I'm sure you can see it in mine."

Dinadan gave a very slight nod.

"And I can see your brow wrinkling, Collum, so before you ask, she wasn't the same Lady who gave Excalibur to Arthur. Lady of the Lake was her title, not her name. There must be lots of Ladies, of lots of Lakes. I never did learn her true name.

"The agreement expired when I was seventeen, but before she let me go the Lady said I owed her a boon, and the boon was that I would sleep with her." Lancelot kept his eyes on the candle flame. "But I wanted to stay a virgin and be a perfect knight. And it wasn't as tempting as you may be thinking, she had grasshopper legs. And she was practically a mother to me, for God's sake!

"The Lady flew into a rage and tried to kill me. But she'd trained me too well. Afterward I swam up to the surface, and her blood washed off me in the lake, and I came back to the land of men.

"It's an awful story—but then when I performed my miracle, and healed Sir Meliot, it all made perfect sense to me. Why my parents died, why the cousins sent me away, why the Lady trained me and then tried to seduce me. By His grace I saw that it had all happened to get me to that moment, so I would be there to follow that hound and find the dead knight and heal the wound. It was like a crystal, perfect in each part and in the whole. God had laid it all out and He was pleased and proud that I had carried out His will.

"While it's happening you think you're going to feel that way always, but you don't. The moment passes. You remember it but you can't feel it. The next day Sir Meliot was still healed but I no longer loved him, he was just a strange knight with an ill-trimmed beard who was stupid or unlucky enough to have run afoul of a cursed sword.

"The only difference was that now I knew what warmth was, and I had to feel it again. Whatever I did after that, all the training and adventures and tournaments, it was for that. It was all I wanted, and God help anybody who stood in my way. People thought I wanted to be a perfect knight, and I told myself that, too, but I see now that what I was really trying to do was to control God. I knew that if I was perfect then God could deny me nothing, not even if He wanted to. He would have to love me. I would force His hand.

"I wonder sometimes if it would've been better if I never did that first miracle." The cat leapt back into his lap, purring thunderously, but Lancelot didn't seem to notice. "Maybe man isn't meant to feel what I did. Like King Midas, God should never touch His children."

This wasn't the story Collum was expecting. He'd been looking for something more along the lines of an unswerving commitment to helping the weak and rescuing maidens and so on, but it did make sense of Lancelot's almost uncanny calm. After you'd known a happiness beyond what the human soul was ever meant to feel, what could possibly disconcert or distract you? And what else could have driven Lancelot that hard, to train the way he did? He must've been powerless to do otherwise. A man made of lesser steel would've collapsed, or gone mad, but God's love had pounded Lancelot like a red-hot sword on an anvil till he was sharp and unbreakable.

"For a long time, for years, it worked," Lancelot said. "Even after I slept with Elaine, God let me do miracles. God is terrible, and He is merciful, and the really hard thing is that you never know which you're going to get. Sometimes it actually made me angry, because I knew He shouldn't love me anymore. I was unworthy, and contaminated with sin, and I knew God knew, but He loved me anyway.

"Elaine was a miracle, too, of course, but she was also the beginning of the end of miracles, the miracle that undid all others, because she was the first crack in my perfection, and that crack let Galahad into the world. And Galahad ended it all.

"But it's wrong to put it that way, because God must've wanted that crack. The crack was part of the crystal."

A sudden deafening *pop* from the fire punctuated the sentence. Wind gusted outside, and the candles trembled. Dagonet had acquired an egg somewhere and was making it appear first in one hand and then the other without apparently traveling in between.

"There's a little coda to this story," Lancelot said, "which is that the night Mordred came for me in the queen's chamber, twelve knights came with him, and Sir Meliot de Logres was one of them. The same knight whose wound I healed, who I laughed with and loved and kissed, came hoping to catch me committing adultery so that Arthur would have me executed. Truly whatever God gives us we deserve, and more."

The cat lost patience and scrambled down from his lap. He took a chaste sip of water and sat back in his chair.

"Do you feel God's love here?" Collum asked. "In the monastery?"

"Not yet. But I will pray and honor God until He returns or until I die."

"Lancelot," Palomides said, "God's love is all well and good, but Britain needs a king."

"I know that." Lancelot balled a lettuce leaf up and tossed it into the fire. "And I know that you are going to find one."

"Help us then. Do God's will again."

"I'm doing it here."

"What if God called you to be a king?" Collum said.

"He won't."

"You're being disingenuous!" Dinadan was out of patience. "You're the son of a king, best knight in the world, last of the heroes of the Table! God led us right to you! What more do you want? I won't pretend my feelings about it are uncomplicated but who the hell else are we going to get?"

"I have—"

"Of course you've fucking sinned! Good God, you think that makes you special?! As if Arthur didn't sin? He screwed his own sister! We need a king, not a saint! The people will love it: Lancelot gave his life to God, and God said unto Lancelot, *Raise up this nation that your careless lust destroyed—!*"

"That's enough."

"But it's not enough." Constantine turned pale at his own daring, but he kept going. "It's not over, the miracles are coming back. Collum's medal proves it. What if the very love you seek is waiting for you on the throne of Britain, Lancelot? All you would have to—"

"Stop!"

Lancelot's voice echoed in the guesthouse hall, and a couple of brothers—night owls, staying up after sunset—turned to watch from the far end of the hall. He'd half risen, and he froze like that. It was the first time Collum had seen him lose his composure, other than that growl he gave in the mêlée. A crack in the crystal. But he got it back just as quickly.

"You came here looking for a king, but it's not me." He sat down again. "Even I want it to be, but it's not."

"Why not?" Dinadan said.

Lancelot took a deep breath and blinked his eyes hard.

"That night, the night it all happened, a boy brought me a message from the queen. It said that she required me to come to her chambers. It was late. Of course I questioned whether it was appropriate to see the queen at that hour, but I was flattered too. I wanted to go. I told myself that whatever a queen requires is by definition appropriate."

He paused, considering.

"That's not the whole truth. The truth is that I was in love with Queen Guinevere. After the Grail and the miracles, I never thought I would love again, but then there it was. God's love went out like the tide, and when it did it revealed my love for Guinevere like a precious treasure in the sand.

"So of course I went. But when I came to her door she looked at me like she'd never seen me before. She didn't know what I was doing there."

"You are saying—" Palomides narrowed his eyes.

"The message wasn't from her. I believe Mordred must have sent it, so that I would come to the queen's chamber and he could surprise me there and say we were lovers, and nobody could prove otherwise. He'd planned it all along, and I think it's fair to say his plan worked better than even he could possibly have imagined."

"So you weren't naked," Scipio said.

"Naked? I was calling on the queen of Britain." Lancelot gave a ghost of a smile. "I wore the best clothes I owned. I looked almost as good as Constantine. And no man could beat a dozen knights naked and unarmed, not even me. Well, maybe Galahad could have, but Galahad would never have been there in the first place.

"But I'm not trying to tell you I'm innocent. I would have committed adultery with Queen Guinevere that night, I have no doubt of that. But I did not, for the sole reason that she didn't want me.

"And there you have it, gentlemen, the great romance of Lancelot and Guinevere. I don't care if you forgive me, or Britain forgives me, I don't even care if God forgives me. I will not forgive myself."

He stood up awkwardly.

"Good night, and may God protect you all and bring you glory on your quest."

They left the abbey the next morning at sunrise, when the bees were still asleep in their hives. Nimue and Bedivere met them at the gate without a word, and they rode north. The monks of Hoxmead had already been awake for hours.

Twenty-six

THE WASTE LAND

King Arthur had had the high-beamed hall of Great Standing
cleared and vigorously swept. Then he'd filled it with orderly
rows of oak tables and chests and dressers and whatever other
furniture he could commandeer on short notice, and on each piece
of furniture stood a ziggurat of scrolls, each one bound with a ribbon. It was a city of parchment.

And not a messy British city of crooked alleys and roundhouses,
this was a proper Roman city, the kind where they actually planned
it in advance before they built it. Neat and square. Sleet patted
softly at the shutters in the quiet. Great Standing was the oldest of
the royal hunting lodges—the moldings still had Uther's grandfather's arms worked into them. Crossed hammers. Force of arms.

His name was Magnus, the grandfather. But whom did he marry?
Guinevere couldn't think of the wife's name.

And what was her device? Nails, probably.

"Currency reform." Arthur pointed to a heap of parchment rolls,
and she retrieved her attention from the moldings. He pointed to
another heap. "Great survey of Britain."

405

Guinevere curtsied politely to the rolls. It was cold in the hall, even though two fires roared in two monumental fireplaces, one at each end. Great Standing wasn't really a winter lodging. The king strolled down the rows and aisles, uneven boards creaking, pointing to one pile of parchment after another. He was like a little boy sometimes.

But all was not well with the royal boy. He hadn't shaved, and his stockings were filthy. Where was Bedivere when you needed him? He never would've let Arthur go around like that. And Arthur looked gaunt; he'd lost easily fifteen pounds in the last year, since the Grail appeared.

It couldn't go on. A crisis was coming, Guinevere suspected, a great change, and she was rarely wrong about these things. She had come to observe it.

"Naval construction. Judicial corruption. Expulsion of the Jews."

"You're not actually going to—?"

"Of course not. But people will keep bringing it up."

He had a pimple next to his long nose, and he toyed compulsively with that old coin, the only thing he still saved from his rustic childhood, as far as Guinevere knew. Arthur's mind was always clear, but the strain spoke through his body.

"This one's forest law, which badly needs reform." Good God, more scrolls. "Did you know Uther would blind a man just for poaching one of his pigs? Pictish rebels. Adulterine castles. The ribbons are color-coded too."

"You're just showing off now."

"Yes." Arthur picked up a roll and looked at her through it, end on. "I'm going to start putting all this into books. Scrolls are just impractical, the way you have to keep rolling and unrolling them.

In a book you can jump from place to place. And it saves on parchment, too, because you can use both sides."

"According to Palomides," the queen said, "it was Julius Caesar who invented books. He was tired of unrolling papyrus all day to read his military reports."

"And then he burned the library of Alexandria."

"Complicated man, Caesar."

Something struck Arthur, a thought or a memory, because with no warning he picked up a silver knife off a tray where it sat next to an uneaten cheese and threw it hard at a window. The knife hit handle-first and bounced off, leaving a white star on the pane. Irritated, Arthur took a poker from the fireside to finish the job, then strode out into the courtyard—an alert footman opened the doors just in time.

Freezing air blasted in.

"How long since the king slept?" Guinevere asked the footman.

"Not since Wednesday, Your Majesty."

Guinevere slung the heavy train of her gown over her arm and followed her husband out onto the grass, which was coated in an inch of gray slush. Even in February the King's Wood couldn't manage a proper freeze. The stuff was translucent, you could see right through it down to the dead grass and leaves underneath. Arthur stood looking out at the winter woods with his hands clasped behind him, indifferent to the flecks of freezing rain that settled on his black hair, still without a strand of gray.

"I always wanted to do that," he said.

"What? Break things like a spoiled child?"

"Make a scene. Act the fool. What's the point of being a king if you can't be a mad king once in your life?"

"And? How was it?"

"In truth it was less satisfying than one had hoped."

He was embarrassed. Dramatic gestures didn't come naturally to him; at times like this you could tell he didn't grow up a pampered prince.

"Well, don't be discouraged, it was just a first try." The queen hugged herself in the cold wet. "Though you know a poor family could've eaten for a month for the price of that window."

"I'm creating work for the glaziers. Promoting industry. Basic economics. Tell me the news?"

"Inside." The slush was soaking through her silk shoes.

The footman opened the doors for them again, and another was already waiting on all fours with a rag to mop up the slush they would track onto the floor. Guinevere went and stood by one of the fires to try to get warm.

It had been eight months since Galahad parked his saintly arse in the Siege Perilous, and in that time the quest for the Holy Grail had declined from a glorious miracle to a lingering curse, and Camelot had become a hive of gossip and a sinkhole of grief. Arthur had temporarily relocated here to Great Standing to escape it all, but he couldn't bring himself to make a clean break. He'd brought his clerks and his counselors and his parchment with him so he could continue conducting matters of state, and fresh misery arrived daily in the form of riders with the news from Camelot. Today Queen Guinevere had come to deliver the news herself.

For eight months she'd watched Arthur struggle to understand the disaster of the Grail Quest and give it a meaning. It was fascinating—viewed in a cold, detached way—to watch an intellect as powerful and remorseless as his throw itself full force at a terrible divine mystery. What the devil was He punishing us for this time?

Apart from the usual? Arthur's mind demanded answers from itself, and when answers were not forthcoming it put itself to the question, applying the hot irons and the pliers. Arthur abhorred cruelty in others but he could be quite cruel to himself.

In a crisis it was Arthur's habit to channel chaos into orderly patterns, and to that end he'd taken down the stuffed heads of wolves and bears and stags from one long wall and replaced them with ninety-nine slates, four rows of twenty and a fifth top row that was one short. On them a scribe recorded the comings and goings and risings and fallings of each knight of the Round Table on the great Grail Quest. The top two rows you had to reach with a ladder.

Each slate had a knight's name chalked on it and below that a series of symbols. A little slantwise dagger indicated combat, followed by the name of the antagonist, or a *G* for a giant, or an *F* if they'd met with a fiend or a demon. An *A* meant they'd encountered an angel or other divine being, and a cross (similar to the dagger, one had to be careful) to show they'd been shriven or attended Mass. There was a star for any marvel witnessed. And so on. When a knight was reported dead his slate was turned to face the wall and the date and place and cause of death, if known, were written on the back. It was Arthur's way of feeling like he was in control, but to Guinevere's eye the slates were an oppressive, looming presence, like tombstones. The reversed slates of dead knights were shuffled to the right-hand columns, which meant that the ranks of the dead were gradually marching their way relentlessly across the wall from right to left.

He dwells too much on the effect, Guinevere thought, *and not enough on the cause.*

It didn't help that Arthur had replaced his regular scribe with his teenage son, Mordred, when he came back from the quest. Mordred was one of the few things she and Arthur still fought about. He wouldn't have had to do much in order to irritate Guinevere, the mere fact of his existence was enough, but he went above and beyond. He was a changeful young man, by turns charming and cold, innocent and knowing, aggressive and vulnerable, with the spotty country manners you'd expect from someone who grew up in the northern backwater court of Lot and Morgause. (Although— Guinevere forbore to point out—his half brothers, Gawain and that lot, had somehow learned to act like gentlemen.) If he absolutely had to go and have a bastard, why couldn't he have had one like Galahad? Maybe he and Lancelot could arrange a swap.

He did write a neat hand though, she'd give him that. And his presence made Arthur happy in a way that nobody else's did, not even hers.

Guinevere waited to deliver her news while Mordred was summoned. He was the spit and image of Arthur, lean and tall, though Mordred tended to hunch in a way that was either good-naturedly self-effacing or falsely humble, depending on who you asked. He affected ragged clothing, to add to the air of the exiled prince. Like many teenagers he thought he possessed guile, whereas in fact he had none.

When he was ready with his chalk she delivered her news, which was that Lancelot was back from the quest.

"What?" Arthur asked. "When?"

"Don't know. A maid went in to clean and found him in his room praying. He may have been back for days. He won't talk to anyone. Or eat anything."

"And he didn't find it?"

"Definitely not."

She said all this evenly, to make it clear that she wasn't avoiding the topic, because it wasn't a topic and there was nothing to avoid. There was always a particle of tension in the air when Lancelot came up, because sometimes he would pretend to woo her, in strictly platonic fashion, and she would gently spurn him, in the same fashion. It was a game, a courtly ritual. Lots of the knights played it with some married lady or other. It was nothing, the sort of breath of wind that adds a little texture to the placid surface of a marriage. And after all it wasn't as though she'd gone and had a child with her half sibling.

In one night. And then a thousand nights with me, and nothing.

Guinevere went on—a litany of deaths and defeats—and Mordred's chalk squeaked and clacked in the quiet. When he was done Arthur gave him a manly approving nod—*Well done, son!*—as if he'd just slain a dragon. Pretty much anything Mordred did elicited this nod from Arthur, which meant they were at best meaningless and at worst actively unnerving to the boy. Arthur was a great king but as a father he appeared to have no natural instincts whatsoever.

I can't be the first person to observe, she thought, how often those best placed to take care of a child have the least idea what it needs.

"Did Lancelot say anything else?" Mordred asked, because why leave well enough alone?

"Not to my knowledge. I expect he'll go back out again. I think he's quite ashamed that he didn't make it further."

A lot of the Grail survivors felt that way. They skulked around the castle avoiding one another's eyes and serving out endless penances, starving and beating themselves for their failures. Some woke up in the night shouting battle cries. Some of them couldn't sleep in their beds at all, they slept on the floor or camped out in the courtyards at night.

"Thank you, Mordred," Guinevere said. "You may go."

That was another thing: Arthur would never, ever dismiss Mordred. He seemed to think his son was so fragile the slightest brush of his fingers would destroy him, which meant that Guinevere always had to be the one to say *Bye-bye, off you go!* Which made her even more the evil stepmother.

"Shall we walk?" Guinevere said. It wouldn't be long now, the crisis, but he would need her help. Keep him moving, keep him talking, that was the thing. She knew Arthur extremely well.

Once she was properly cloaked and shod it was good to be outside. Arthur gulped the fresh air like a swimmer surfacing. Sheets of white mist hung motionless in the still air. The silver birches on the edge of the lawn stood bowed down with slush as if in shame, like Lancelot.

"So what are you going to do?"

"I don't know," he said. "Yet. I flatter myself that I'm a man of action, but at present I can think of no actions to perform."

"If the Saxons did what God has done, killed fifty-eight knights of the Round Table, you would cross the North Sea and burn Saxony to the ground."

"Well, I'm not going to make war on God and burn Heaven, if that's what you're suggesting. You're being deliberately provocative." His breath was white in the air like smoke. A dragon's breath. A Pendragon's. "You see how this will end, don't you?"

"I could make an educated guess. Galahad will achieve the Grail, and maybe a few others. Maybe Percival. But that's all. And I think God will consider the whole business a failure."

"I agree. This is not God making peace. He is washing His hands of us. And where does that leave us?"

"Out with the bathwater, I suppose."

Numerous tender little pawprints crossed the gray slushfields around them. Mice. Or shrews. Or voles. Arthur would know.

"Maybe it's a cleansing," he said, "like the Flood. Or God felt we were getting too familiar. Camelot is the Tower of Babel, and He is showing us our place the same way He did then, with confusion and ruin."

"You need a distraction. This is a hunting lodge, let's go hunting."

"Nothing's in season."

"There's always foxes," the queen said. "Or do the shepherds a favor, hunt some wolves."

"Good God, woman, a king can't hunt wolves! And I can't go hunting while knights are dying." Arthur blew into his cupped hands. "Maybe I should join the quest. Maybe God is waiting for me to come personally."

"God will kill you if you go."

"Perhaps a sacrifice is necessary. The king must die, so the land may live."

"That would be very pagan of Him. But I don't think this is about you, Arthur. If you won't hunt then we'll go hawking."

But an elderly cadger informed them that the falcons were moulting and could not be flown, and any lesser bird was of course unsuitable for a king. So off they set again into the sunless morning. A heavy mass of wet snow slumped off an angle in the roof and landed with a thump a yard behind them.

At Camelot Arthur had spent much of his time walking like this, through the empty halls and colonnades of his deserted castle, like the lonely leopard in Camelot's bestiary who paced ceaselessly, never doubting that she would one day find the door that led out of this damp grim enclosure and back to the hot savannas of her youth. Arthur had probably covered as many miles as the Grail knights, all told, a spiral quest wound in on itself, going nowhere.

Off in the mist a crow cawed loudly.

"You're not sulking, are you?"

"I'm thinking," Arthur said.

"They can look similar to the untrained eye. Common mistake. Trap for young players."

"You know people are saying I planned it all?" he said. "That God and I are in on it together? Most of the knights are childless, so when they die their properties revert to the Crown. It's all a great big royal land grab."

"Is it?"

"Well, it's an ill wind."

"They must have a high opinion of your relationship with God if they think you're running a scam together."

"The king of the Franks thinks the Grail is a holy weapon that I'll use to conquer the world," Arthur said. "He's sent out a party of his own to try to find it first."

"Good luck to him," Guinevere said. "They say Sir Harry le Fise Lake has left the Table to start a free company. It's called the Ugly Mugs—that's a Grail joke."

Arthur managed to laugh at that. A good sign. She remembered after the wedding when her father presented them with the Round Table. Arthur's elaborate gratitude, then his expression slowly turning to tragic dismay as an endless parade of servants carried it into the Great Hall, piece after piece after piece. It was their first real joke together.

The sun seemed to be beaming down cold, not heat. She slipped on some ice and nearly went down. There was a slow leak in her boot.

"I'm going inside," Guinevere said. "And when I'm warm again I'm going to the archery butts. Meet me there, if you dare."

To GUINEVERE'S CRITICAL EYE Great Standing wasn't very well situated. They'd built it in a bosky hollow for some reason, dark and damp. But to get to the butts you crossed a bridge over a lovely little brook, and then beyond the brook you burst out into some glorious flat open hayfields, snow with hummocks of dead frosty grass showing through, declining gently toward a bank of low hills in the distance.

Servants were sweeping off the earth mounds where the targets were mounted. You could barely see them in the mist. A dog barked far away. A sprinkling of little birds were left that hadn't flown south, robins and redwings, hopping from branch to branch.

A frozen land. And it felt frozen in time. Nothing would happen here till either the Grail was found or the last knight fell trying.

But of course that wasn't true. It only felt like that here, within the enchanted penumbra of Camelot. All over Britain people kept on being born and dying, Grail or no. They were spinning and hunting and spreading manure and planting new vines and waiting for spring. If anything people were taking advantage of the Table's unhealthy preoccupation with the Grail. A self-proclaimed bandit king had set himself up in the Forest Sauvage. There were debauched monks in Astolat. Half of Gore was delinquent in its taxes.

The realm was being neglected. Camelot needed to catch up. It was time for this to be over. Past time.

She knew what people said, that the Grail was meant to be a cure for her infertility, but she didn't believe it. She knew a poisoned chalice when she saw it. She could feel it out there somewhere, crouched in some remote grove or chapel like a silver spider in its web, a hidden thing that drew knights to it, and retreated from them as they came. One by one they burned up as they approached it, as stars did falling to earth, a whole flock of Icaruses—Icari?— descending in a cloud of feathers. And one Daedalus to mourn them all.

She supposed she should show the Grail more respect, and God for that matter, but Guinevere's approach to religion had always been pragmatic, as it was to all things. As a princess she'd expected to marry for politics, not true love. Likewise as a Christian she didn't feel the need to be virtue incarnate. She wanted to achieve goodness, not perfection. After all if God had nothing to forgive her for then how would he maintain his hard-earned reputation for mercy?

Perhaps that was why she had no child.

Arthur was different. Guinevere's marriage to Arthur was a political marriage, but it had come with unlooked-for blessings: Arthur was handsome, and kind, and faithful, and he didn't (often) drink to excess. He'd also turned out to be one of the few people Guinevere had met in her life who was as intelligent as she was and could keep up with her in conversation. But there was another surprise waiting in her marriage, which was this absurd craze for divine adventuring, this obsessive pursuit of the miraculous. Arthur wasn't a pragmatist like her, he had a hunger for perfection. If there was a third party in their marriage it wasn't Lancelot, it was God.

She supposed it must have to do with his absent father, or fathers. Arthur's real father, Uther, had tossed him aside, and his foster father Ector hadn't been much better. No more had his heavenly father, God. Not a lot of cuddles at bedtime. All boys need a father's love, and they'll do anything to get it, and Arthur had tried being good, and it hadn't worked, so that left only greatness. Perfection. If only, if only Arthur had had a father there to say, it's all right, this is good enough. You can stop now, I will love you whatever happens, whatever you do, whoever you are. But there was no one there to say it. God would never say stop. And so Arthur never would.

(No wonder Arthur fell all over himself to baby Mordred, who wasn't even particularly good, let alone great. Because he was starved for love Arthur thought Mordred should be glutted with it, stuffed like a goose, but there's such a thing as overcorrection. Trap for young players.)

And now Arthur's passionate wooing of God had gone south, God in His wisdom had set the bar too high, and what to do? A more reasonable man would take it on the chin, hang up the questing gear with a rueful chuckle, chalk it up to the sad fallible nature of humanity, which could never by its very fallen nature achieve the lofty ideals of etc., etc. But she knew that for Arthur it must be like being run through the heart. He couldn't take it on the chin, he lived to prove to God and himself that he was who the sword said he was, he was God's chosen king. That his goodness could pay for his monstrous father's crimes, even undo them. And God was telling him no. No one else knew what it cost him, because Arthur had the kind of strength that kept you moving and talking and smiling even when you had your death wound, till you fell down a corpse. But his wife knew.

Arthur would never be good enough for Him. And when Arthur finally realized that then something would have to give. But what? And what exactly would it give?

To her irritation Arthur didn't join her at the archery range till the bells were ringing nones and the sun had sunk low in the sky. The whole world was drained of color. She'd already shot a dozen arrows, with indifferent results, and she didn't feel like shooting anymore. Oceans of shadow washed across the snowfield from the western woods, as if the trees had been drawn there and the ink had run across the page. She was chilled to the bone all over again.

When Arthur did finally turn up he suggested they play rovers, like children did, so they wandered around the field calling out targets: a bush, a tuft of grass, a stump. Whoever got closer won that round and got to pick the next target. Once they flushed a hare and both shot at it and missed. It wouldn't have mattered, the arrows were blunts anyway.

"I'm sorry I took so long," Arthur said, "but King Erec came to beg an audience in person. He told me the most extraordinary story, about some knights causing trouble in Destregales—it was Lavaine, Hellaine le Blank, and Bellangere le Beuse."

"What sort of trouble?"

"Apparently there was an old giant named Umfrey who lived in the hills north of Carnant. He was a gentle enough soul, didn't eat people, just took a sheep every week or two. He slept most of the time. King Erec said he slept on his belly like a little boy. Well, Sir Lavaine got it into his head that this Umfrey was a monster, an enemy of God, and therefore he was their next adventure on their glorious path to the Grail. So they searched him out and chopped him up with axes while he slept."

"Not very knightly."

"It was a damned atrocity. Umfrey woke up halfway through and broke Hellaine's leg before he died."

"Serves him right. The fool."

Hellaine was an ignorant man who grabbed the maids' bums. Guinevere aimed an arrow at a young oak by itself in the middle of the field, picturing Sir Hellaine. She held the bow at full draw for a count of ten, just to show she could, then shot and hit it. Arthur applauded, then missed with his own shot. Point to Queen Guinevere, who leads ten to seven. A spot on the inside of her forearm was starting to burn where the leather guard didn't quite cover it.

"What did they do with the body?"

"Nothing. They left it lying there and rode away. Wolves and bears came from miles around. You can imagine the stench. The sky was black with birds."

"At least the shepherds were happy."

"But that's just it, they weren't! They were furious! Apparently they worshipped Umfrey, to them he was the god of those hills, and if he took a sheep every week or so they considered it a necessary sacrifice to keep the rivers flowing and crops growing. When they found out what happened they set up on the road back to town with bills and bows and axes and ambushed the knights in a mob. Killed all three of them."

"What did Erec do with them?"

"Well, the knights had killed four already. Erec hanged the ringleader and put the rest in the stocks, but that was all. He's worried they'll revolt.

"But that's not even the point. The point is that they didn't care, Guinevere. I thought that at least, at least, people would be proud if we found the Grail. I thought they would want to see us claim it for Britain. But they don't care! And why should they? Imagine what we must look like to them: a bunch of wealthy Christian killers, walking around in a fortune's worth of steel armor, trampling their gardens and yelling about our God in a language most of them don't even understand. Look at us go, chasing divine marvels, while they break their bodies to plough our land! Of course they don't care!

"And does God even care? I trusted Him for so long, Guinevere. So long. But now He's asked too much, we'll never bring home the Grail, and even if we did I wonder if it would be enough. I don't think it would. His discipline has always been harsh, but I thought His harshness was love, it was how badly He wanted to us to be good. But it's become something else.

"Maybe he's simply inhuman, like a storm, or a fire."

Arthur stared up at the nothingness of the sky, shaking his head.

"I don't know what it all means, and I suppose I never will, but I won't beg anymore. I can't. He was my father's God, Uther's God, but He is not mine. We'll find our own way. Or maybe we'll go to war with Him, like you said."

Now we reach the matter of it.

"But if God isn't your God," Guinevere said quietly, "then who is? Jupiter? Sol Invictus? Umfrey the Giant?"

"Of course not! Of course not! I don't know! I don't know what I'm saying!"

Arthur threw down his bow and then, still unsatisfied, he swept off his hat and threw it in a half-frozen puddle, where its ermine lining began soaking through. His hair was a mess. He was still handsome, though, with his long body in a black-and-blue surcoat and stockings. Black Arthur. He always dressed as if he expected a funeral might break out at any moment. Guinevere unstrung her bow with practiced ease and leaned it against a tree, the same little oak that she'd bull's-eyed earlier. She went to her husband and took him in her arms and held him, pressed her smooth cheek against his cold scratchy one.

"I had a grail," she said in his ear. "It was a child, our child. A prince or a princess of Camelot. We have sought that grail these twenty years, you and I, and never found it. And now I fear it's too late for us. God hid it too well.

"So just know this: God may abandon us, Arthur, but I will never abandon you. Never. If I must choose between Arthur and God, I choose King Arthur."

What a thing it was to be married to a king, to be the only other person who knew his secret, though it lay right out in the open, every day, for all to see, which was that he was just a man and nothing more. Guinevere's marriage to Arthur had come with many surprises, but the biggest surprise of all was that they loved each other, as much as any man and wife, as much as any lovers in any story. She loved him more than he loved himself. And was that not the point of a marriage, to love a person more than they can love themselves?

"Now tell me," she said. "If God truly is leaving, what will happen to Britain?"

Guinevere let him go but kept hold of his hand. Both of their noses were running in the cold. Her feet were numb.

"I don't know," Arthur said. "I suppose it will become a waste land. Empty of grace. But then how will we survive?"

The light was failing, and the world was as still as a painting. These days when you never saw the sun, it hardly felt like a day had passed at all.

"I suppose," she said, "we'll have to find some way to live in a waste land."

Arthur rescued his hat from the puddle, but it was too wet to put it back on so he just stood there gazing down at it in his hands.

"Either that," he said, "or we'll find some way to bring it back to life."

Twenty-seven

The Barrow

Collum was fast asleep when somebody stepped on his hand.

The foot was wearing a smooth-soled sandal, and it stepped lightly and cautiously, a hunter's step. He almost didn't wake up, but then his knuckle ground painfully against a pebble.

"Ow!"

He tried to yank his hand back but it was trapped under the sandal. He opened his eyes. A caped man carrying a spear towered over him, looking like a marble colossus in the moonlight.

For a long, uncomprehending moment they stared at each other while Collum tried to blunder his way out of the maze of sleep. Then the stranger gave a little shriek and jumped back, pointing his spear at Collum.

"*Eálá!*" he shouted. "*Eálá!*"

Collum was shouting too: "Arms! Arms!"

The spearman scrambled backward till he fell down into a bush. Collum lunged after him, and the sharp end of a woody branch scraped burning along the side of his neck. The man's face was all gray beard and big wide eyes and gap teeth—he was much older than Collum. He dropped the spear and the two of them wrestled each other and the bush at the same time.

The stranger wasn't alone. The woods all around were full of men, mixed in confusingly with the trees, and knights sleeping on the ground were stirring like slumbering corpses when the last trumpet sounded. Collum's adversary was panting and straining to free a thick, blocky knife from a leather sheath, but Collum bit his cheek, the wiry beard rough on his lips, and the man gave up on the knife and clawed at Collum's eyes instead while Collum tried to shove a knee into his crotch.

A thunderbolt struck him in the side.

"Ahhhhhh!"

The thunderbolt kept going, digging into him, prying his ribs apart, and Collum rolled out of the bush, desperate to get away from it. It was a spear—another spearman, broad-shouldered and moonfaced, was advancing on him, jabbing as he came.

Somewhere Bedivere was bellowing: "Get them all! No one gets away!"

And Dinadan's higher voice: "Camelot! Camelot!"

The attackers were shouting, too, in a language Collum didn't recognize. It felt like there was a hot coal lodged between his ribs, and he put his hand to his side to feel his death wound and only then remembered that he'd gone to sleep in his mail shirt, so it was probably just a bad bruise or a broken rib.

And these men must be Saxons. That was it. They'd been asleep in a forest and a band of Saxons had stumbled on them. The big round-faced spearman harried him backward. Collum could've parried and countered a thousand ways if he had a sword, but instead he just dodged and grabbed weakly at the shaft while its owner snatched it back, like they were playing a game.

Then the Saxon quit the game. He dropped the spear and arched his back and tried desperately to scratch an itch halfway down his spine. The tattooed face of Sir Scipio appeared behind him, having stabbed him in the back. Scipio tried to pull his blade out, and when that turned out to be harder than expected he picked up the dying man's spear instead and went looking for more prey.

A man with a thick, heavy knife emerged from a bush like a wood-spirit and went stalking after Scipio: it was the first Saxon, the graybeard who'd stepped on his hand. Gritting his teeth against the pain in his ribs, Collum charged him, and the two of them went down together for a second time. They wrestled, but fully awake Collum was stronger by a good margin, and he twisted the Saxon's knife out of his grip.

The Saxon broke away and ran but Collum tripped him and he fell back down, and Collum pounced on his back and sawed his throat open with his own knife. He was getting better at that, he noted dispassionately. Killing. Quicker and more efficient in the act, and quicker at shoving down the horror and guilt, too, down somewhere where he couldn't feel it.

A thrown ax brushed the back of his head like a feather. Luck. Or divine providence.

The night forest was washed in moonlight and alive with soft sounds, not the roaring and banging of a proper battle but rustling leaves, hoarse breathing, men groaning and grunting and straining. But it was getting easier to tell friend from foe, and the friends were winning. Most of the knights had got swords in their hands now and were routing the Saxons, who didn't seem to be at all properly armed for this encounter. They were doing their best to melt back into the forest the way they came, but the knights wouldn't let them go—Collum saw one pelt off into the darkness only to be staggered by an arrow between his shoulders, traceable back to Dinadan, who'd climbed on top of a boulder and was already nocking another one.

Collum still hadn't found his sword but he had the Saxon's knife. The man Dinadan shot was crawling away, painfully, the point of the arrow stirring and shredding his delicate lungs with every movement. He had thick red hair and Collum dug his fingers into it, pulled the man's head back, and chopped out his throat too.

Then it was over. Hardly a proper battle at all. Scipio was already going from body to body collecting and comparing those chunky knives, which all Saxons seemed to carry, so he could take the best one. The blades had a curious broken-backed shape. Scipio plucked the one Collum was holding out of his hands, held it up in the moonlight, then handed it back.

Collum stabbed it into a tree and left it there. Those men didn't belong here. Once he and the knights found the Lance, the next thing they would do was hunt down the Saxons and clear them out. They knew they didn't belong here, they must know it. But then why cross the sea to come here, and die here, hunting for a meal in our woods? What the hell was wrong with Saxonia, or wherever they came from?

Constantine was on his knees praying. Dinadan was seated on his boulder, feeling cautiously under a cuisse, trying to figure out how bad a cut on his thigh was. When Collum offered to look Dinadan snapped at him to leave him alone.

"Not the rudest awakening I've ever had," Scipio said, "but close to it." Ever the spit-and-polish man, he was already packing up his kit.

"I couldn't sleep anyway." Constantine got to his feet. "I will never leave Camelot without a pavilion again. Come to that, I might not leave Camelot at all."

"We were lucky," Nimue said. "That was a hunting party. Not a sword or shield among them. They weren't looking for us."

"We will not get lucky twice," Palomides said. "They will be hunting us now."

"Let them hunt," Bedivere said. "We'll keep going."

"Bedivere," Palomides said reasonably, "we can fight Saxons, and we can find the Lance, but we cannot do both at the same time."

Bedivere didn't answer. Dagonet hung and dropped from a branch. He'd climbed a tree when the fighting started.

THAT WAS ALL THE sleep they'd get that night. They waded through a soft moonlit sea of knee-deep ferns in a half-dreaming state. In the deep woods, massive boulders and interlocked branches mingled with gulleys and gaping pits pulled up by the roots of fallen trees, so that sometimes it was hard to tell up from down. Collum spared an envious thought for Lancelot, having a cozy night's sleep in his monastic cell.

Twice they startled families of placidly feeding deer. The Saxons might've had a good night if they hadn't had such a bad one.

"I miss hunting," Constantine said. "For game and not for exalted holy weaponry."

"Three motes for the uncoupling," Bedivere said softly. "*Hoo sto ho sto, mon ami, ho sto.*"

After an hour, the trees thinned to the point where they could ride. Collum was dozing in the saddle when Bedivere and Nimue overtook him on either side.

"We need to speak with you," Bedivere said. "That first night at Camelot you asked us if Arthur could've hidden a child away somewhere, the way Uther did with him."

"You said you would've known."

"I did say that. But now I'm wondering if it's you."

"What?"

"The child, the one Arthur hid away. Is it you?"

"Of course it's not me!" Collum said it so loudly that Bedivere shushed him.

"I'm sure you've been called worse." Nimue seemed to find the whole idea amusing.

"I think I would know!"

"Arthur didn't know," Bedivere said.

"Don't waste your time," Collum said. "We have little enough as it is."

"Why are you trying to wriggle out of this?" Nimue said.

"I'm not! Because I'm not in it!"

"Just think about it. The minute Arthur's dead a big strapping boy from the middle of nowhere turns up. Handsome, good with a sword, peddling a story so flimsy even Dagonet could poke a hole in it. Miserable childhood in pagan obscurity, never knew his parents—in the old days they would've called you Le Bel Inconnu."

"I never met my father, but I know who he wasn't." Collum felt irrationally irritated at both of them. "I've spent my whole life living down being the dead fisherman's bastard. Now I'm supposed to be a prince in disguise? Do I look like King Arthur?"

"Not really," Bedivere admitted.

"But then why is Morgan le Fay always sniffing around you?" Nimue said.

"She's perverse. She's practically a fairy."

"Arthur had a touch of that too," she said. "I guess it ran in the family."

"Well, I'm not perverse."

"I'll take your word for it." She smirked.

Handsome, though, he thought. He would take that. The path split to either side of an enormous fallen beech tree, then met itself again.

"Besides," Collum said, "Arthur would never have sent his own son away, after Uther did it to him. Would he?"

"Maybe not," Nimue said. A night bird whistled and trilled. "But fathers cast a long shadow. Some sons outrun it, but others get caught, and then they act out their father's sins over and over, like mummers in a play, even when they have the best of intentions."

"If anybody could outrun a shadow," Collum said loyally, "it was Arthur." What kind of shadow am I trying to outrun? he thought. What kind of shadow did a dead fisherman cast?

Up ahead Constantine slowed and stopped.

"More Saxons?" Dinadan said.

Constantine sniffed fastidiously.

"Bit of an odd smell."

At first Collum thought it was a rotting animal, but it had a smoky whiff to it.

"Fire, and something else," Palomides said. "Sulfur."

"Brimstone," Scipio said.

"Sulfur and brimstone, they are the same thing. Though in fact the element itself is odorless; the smell arises only from its combustion in air."

They rode on, slower now. The smell bit at Collum's nostrils and made him cough. Constantine had produced a scented cloth from somewhere and held it over his mouth and nose. A large moon was sinking behind the trees, almost harsh in its brightness.

"I might know where we are," Nimue said. "But I hope I don't."

"If you did," Dinadan said, "where would we be?"

"The last time I smelled anything this bad it was at Merlin's Hill. The one where I buried him."

"How the hell would we end up there?"

Nimue shook her head.

"God must have brought us here. Or maybe it was Merlin, if he can reach this far. I wouldn't have thought so."

"Probably he's just lonely," Scipio said.

"Perhaps he could help us," Constantine said.

"Merlin only helps Merlin," Nimue said.

"That is not a problem," Palomides said, "if our interests align."

"I'll do the talking. If it comes to that."

But the smell got stronger as they went and the trees around them got drier and browner and more stunted. Now they could make it out through the dimness: a low hill all by itself in a clearing. The forest surrounded it but the mound itself was bare except for traces of grass and the sharp stumps of shrubs, burned out and snapped off. It looked like the charcoal-burners' land, or like a monstrous anthill.

The horses stopped, and when they tried to make them keep going they trembled and rolled their eyes. This was as close as they wanted to be. Leaving them there Collum walked out into the clearing and squatted and placed his palm on the ground. It was warm, feverish, as if the earth itself had contracted an infection. Was the great wizard Merlin really under there somewhere?

Scipio surveyed the scene with hands on hips.

"Mounds," he said. "Gods, I do hate them."

Ignoring Nimue's protests he went trotting up it. He looked down at them from the top: *Now what?* Then he turned away and urinated down the other side.

Nimue raised her voice.

"Merlin, I know you can hear me. What do you want?"

The night was quiet. Collum didn't even hear any insects. They must not like the smell either.

"This could be providence, Nimue," Constantine said. "The hand of God. First Lancelot, now Merlin. Put your quarrel aside and let him help us."

"He's right," Dinadan said. "You've humbled him, Nimue. You've made your point. Maybe it's time to let him redeem himself. He was the making of Arthur, maybe it's time for him to make someone else."

The knights looked at her expectantly. Collum couldn't have said he disagreed with them. How bad could he be?

"We make the kings around here," she said. "Us and God. If we must parley with him, give him no information. The less he knows about us and what's going on in Britain, the less he can hurt us."

"What, did you have a lovers' tiff?" Scipio called down.

"Fuck you. Merlin, I know you're—"

Nimue.

Everyone startled but her. The voice was deep and resonant and quite loud. It came from all around them, the earth itself vibrating like a drumhead, shifting the dust under their feet.

"What do you want, Merlin?"

My old friend. It's good to see you.

"What do you want?"

Really? Is that all? Aren't we friends? Or colleagues at least? You are my peer, Nimue, you have proven that. Let us show each other some professional courtesy.

"Is that what you showed me, Merlin?"

Well, I'm sorry you feel that way. Bedivere is still my friend, aren't you, Bedivere? We go back even further. We were there the day Arthur pulled the sword from the stone.

"I have no quarrel with you, Merlin," Bedivere said quietly.

Of course not. We only ever did what was best for the king, we two.

You know I can feel you all above me, through the earth? I can't see you, but I've been here so long that the ground above me has become like a second skin. There's Palomides, of course, and Constantine. Dinadan. Scipio. And you've brought the fool too. How droll. Collum imagined the wizard in the darkness, pale and thin, fingering the low cavern roof above him—he could almost feel fingertips pressing against his boots through the earth. It made the soles of his feet crawl. *Or could it be* Sir *Dagonet now? Well, well. Will wonders never cease?*

"I thought they already had," Dagonet said.

I do miss the upper world and its many surprises. It's very quiet down here. Very still. I've been down here a long time now.

"Not long enough," Nimue said.

Many, many surprises. You, for instance.

The ancient wizard's invisible attention had turned to Collum, and the hair stood up on his arms.

"Sir Collum of the Out Isles," he said.

So you are. Well, welcome, Sir Collum. You are a curious company indeed. What noble cause brings you all here tonight?

"You tell us," Nimue said. "You dragged us here."

Interestingly, I did not. I suspect greater forces than myself are at work.

"Our cause does not concern you."

Of course it concerns me, Nimue. Of course it does. Britain has been my life's work, and I have had a very, very long life. Everything that happens on this blessed isle concerns me. Every footfall, every raindrop, every heartbeat. You live only for yourself, Nimue, but I have only ever lived for Britain.

So tell me. Something has happened, something grave.

"Arthur is dead," Bedivere said. Nimue looked daggers at him. "There was a battle, and he and Mordred killed each other."

The earth shifted under their feet, as if a huge sleeping form were stirring restlessly under a thin blanket. Nimue took out a small flask and began shaking drops of a clear liquid from it onto the dust in a circle around them.

That is a tragedy, Merlin said finally. *What a terrible thing. Though it wouldn't have taken a prophet to see it coming. It would merely have taken a competent magician, but well, there it is, isn't it? The fall of Camelot began with Merlin's fall. Were you there?*

"Yes."

What happened to the sword?

"I threw it in the sea."

I see. Good enough. Good, good, good.

"Please don't insult us by pretending you care about anything besides yourself, Merlin," Nimue said.

I pretend nothing. If it is God who brought you here, then I doubt it was for my sake. He knows you need my help.

Merlin spoke calmly and slowly, drawing out every word with a slight purr.

"If you have something to offer us then get to the point," Nimue said.

If you want to know everything I can offer you, well, we'll be here all night! Grim Bedivere, I could fashion you a new hand. I could alter your nature, to better suit the practices of God and man. Or you, Dinadan. I could give you what you desire more than anything in the world. What even the fairies couldn't give you. Nimue, I suspect, cannot. Can she? No, I thought not. She lacks my skill with bodies.

But I could do it, if you let me out. I could do it tonight. No? Your famous wit has flown?

Dinadan's face was blank. If he had a clever comeback he kept it to himself.

"No one's impressed with your boasting, Merlin," Nimue said. "If you can help, do it. If not, we'll be on our way."

But you won't, though. Your bluff is sadly transparent. So go on, ask. Ask me. Why wouldn't I help you? I gave everything for Camelot, I did nothing but serve, and you see how this treacherous whore thanked me.

"Watch your mouth," Collum said.

Oh dear. Sauce from the fisherman's bastard. Tell me, what are you questing for? I hope it isn't some last holy toenail that God left behind on His way out the door.

But it is, isn't it? Oh, dear. Oh, how disappointing.

Well, I don't expect you'll find it. A quest is hero's work, hero's business, and that's just not quite you lot, is it? You're the other ones, the sidekicks, the spear carriers. The stage is empty now but for the stagehands, and who will play the story?

But the heroes could come again. It was I who hid away Uther's child. When the moment came it was I, Merlin, who revealed him, by the miracle of the Sword in the Stone. God worked through me to set a new king on the throne. Me, and no other.

I could do it again. But not while I'm down here.

"End this, Nimue," Constantine whispered. "You've made your point. We n-need him."

"He's lying."

Collum wanted to leap to Nimue's defense, but even after what Merlin called her he wondered if Constantine could be right. It was a calculated risk. Merlin wasn't going to be pleasant to have around, but they could find out what he knew, and then if it went wrong, well, Nimue beat him once. Surely she could do it again.

"You said you kn-knew everything he knew," Constantine said. "You said—"

"I said I was a better magician! He's a monster, and if you let him out now then nothing will stop him!"

"Why would we want to s-stop him? He put Arthur on the throne!"

"Because it served his purposes to do so. By the end Arthur was the only thing keeping him in check. Who do you trust, Constantine, me or him? And don't say *it's whom.*"

Constantine didn't answer, just sniffed his handkerchief.

Do you remember that hill at Tam's Head, Nimue? Merlin's voice was gentler now. The thunder had faded to distant waves. *Streaks of meadowsweet down its sides and that one great hornbeam right on top, with a knot in that looked like Sir Lionel's face. We used to gather mistletoe there together on the equinox. Do you remember?*

It's dark down here, but I can see it in my mind. I wish you'd buried me there instead.

"I'm glad I didn't. This hill is a wasteland. You poison everything you touch."

I have been down here a long time, long enough to grow bitter,

I know that, and nothing grows from bitterness. I have spoken harshly. I should not have.

"What about a gesture of good faith then?" Collum said.

Nimue narrowed her eyes at him, but he pressed on. She was right, he knew who he trusted.

"The lands between here and the north are crawling with Saxons and rebels and God knows what else, and Britain is running out of time. Your magic brought us here. Is there a spell that can send us to the north, as far as the Ouse? And take us over or under or past the land in between?"

And what would I get?

"Nimue will give you the key to the cave," Bedivere said. "So you can work God's will, whatever it may be."

Moonlight brushed the burned, blasted surface of the hill with silver. A jet of steam hissed from a fissure upslope, as if from the pressure of Merlin's thoughts. The wizard was silent for a long time; then he spoke crisply and rapidly.

Find a smooth round stone from a river. Are you listening, Nimue? Find one with three bands around it. Strike it three times with a brass hammer. If it breaks then find another one.

He must have instructed her with this same voice, master to apprentice.

When you find a stone that will not break, write ξύπνιος on one side and κοιμισμένος on the other with the blood of an animal that has no hooves. Make a fire with birch sticks and bake the stone in the embers. When you rake it out it should cut easily with a silver knife. You'll find the word you need inside.

Bedivere looked to Nimue, who nodded.

"All right," Bedivere said.

He turned and walked away, back toward the horses at the edge of the clearing. Collum and Nimue followed.

What are you doing?

"We're going to find God's holy toenail," Collum said.

"Careful who you call a whore next time," Nimue said.

One by one the rest of the knights followed. Steam jetted from cracks all over the hollow hill, and the last of the ditherers, Constantine and Scipio, broke into a startled trot to get clear of them. Dawn wasn't far off, but stars still ruled the night sky.

You lied.

"What did you think confession was for?" Dinadan said.

"You're right about us, Merlin," Bedivere called out. "We're not the heroes, we're the odd ones out. The losers. But did you ever think that might be why we've lived so long? Losing makes you tough."

Nimue, I'll leave Britain forever, if that's what you want. I'll tell you my true name. Just open the hill and let me out.

"If you and God are such good friends, let Him do it."

You fools. I could give you a king. I could give you everything you wanted.

"And by the way, there is no key," Nimue said, "because there is no lock, because there is no door. I'm never going to let you out."

Single file they picked their way through the dry dead trees back into the forest, where the horses waited. In the darkness Nimue found Collum's hand and gave it a quick squeeze.

It will not hold me. I have grown strong under the earth, Nimue, stronger than you know. Did you forget who I am? Did you forget I am a devil's son? I WAS BORN UNDERGROUND! HELL IS WHERE I COME FROM!

The thunder was back, loud enough to hurt their ears. Something beat three times on the ground from below, and it seemed like the earth was about to give way, but it held. When Collum looked back for the last time every crack and fissure on the hill was glowing red, a spidery network of bright lines lighting up the circle of wasted trees around it. Hot veins ran as far as the edge of the clearing, and trees burned where they touched.

LET ME OUT, DAMN YOU!

A dab of bright molten rock appeared at the mound's summit.

LET ME OUT!

Twenty-eight

THE TALE OF NIMUE

At first Nimue didn't pay any special attention when the king's great sorcerer Merlin came stumping through Rutupiae. She had enough on her mind. She was a fifteen-year-old laundress in the household of Lord Castic and well on her way to worse.

Rutupiae was an old Roman fortress town on the coast of Cantium, one of the famous Saxon Shore forts, with ruined temples and a crumbling amphitheater and massive seawalls stained with the rust of old Roman iron. It was said to be the spot where the invading Romans had first landed in Britain, and Castic claimed descent, on no grounds whatsoever, from the Count of the Saxon Shore himself.

The laundry was belowground, a dank, dimly lit place that smelled of lye and urine, which they used shocking amounts of as a stain remover. Silks and samites and velvets and furs came through it in incredible profusion, heaps and hampers and bundles of them with the most astounding assortment of stains and messes. Fortunately Nimue was exceptionally resourceful at finding new recipes for soap when ingredients were scarce, as they usually were. A laundress had to be a bit of an alchemist too.

But alchemy wasn't going to keep her from starving. Count Castic was prosperous enough, but he paid his laundry girls practically nothing, and Nimue also had the care of her little sister, Mary, eight years younger, ever since their parents were carried off in a wave of typhoid. Mary was a good girl who tended a wooden sheep named Moo that lived in a house made of butter.

After two years on the job, Nimue came to the conclusion that it was impossible, she and Mary simply could not live on what she was paid. The castle steward had apparently been waiting for her to reach this conclusion, because that was when he made it clear that laundresses were expected to supplement their wages by having sex with the castle's highborn guests for money. It was an arrangement of long standing.

Nimue didn't want to be a prostitute, but that left the question of how to not be one and not starve. So she prayed. And God, in His own inscrutable fashion, answered.

Merlin arrived on foot, unannounced and alone, as if he'd just moments ago been deposited at the gates by some capricious zephyr. She would've expected a wizened, bent-backed sorcerer, but he was, or appeared to be, a vigorous, thick-bodied man in the prime of middle age with an easy smile and a searching gaze that put you at ease even as it made you wonder what exactly he was searching you for. He wore a druid's dun robes, with long sleeves that he was always hitching up, though she would learn much later that the outfit was pure theater, as were the tattoos. They were only there to impress the Court—Merlin's idea of a British lord's idea of what a scary old wizard should look like.

Unlike the rattling amulets round his neck, which were entirely real. When he arrived, his hands were coated with bright yellow powder to the wrists, as if he'd just plunged them into a barrel full of buttercups. The first thing he did was ask for a basin to wash in.

Merlin gave no explanation for his presence at Rutupiae, or any indication as to how long he'd be staying, but then Merlin wasn't in the explaining business. Rumor had it he was the oldest man in Britain, the last of the druids—the word came from *dru-wits*, which in British meant "oak-knowers." They were the adepts of sacred groves, god-whisperers, dealers in silver sickles and mistletoe and moonlight and acorns and blood sacrifice, and even the Romans were scared of them. That was why when they conquered Britain they slaughtered the druids en masse.

The druids wrote nothing down, they had always passed their knowledge from one to the next by spoken word only, so when they died all that they knew vanished. The lore and culture and memory of Old Britain went out like a candle.

Except for Merlin. It was simply not in his nature to be slaughtered. He slipped through their net. Or no, he didn't slip through it, he became part of it.

Merlin knew how to make himself first unthreatening, and then useful, and finally indispensable to the Romans. There was no problem he couldn't or wouldn't apply himself to. You want a stone wall that stretches all the way across the north, eighty miles, from Segedunum to Maia? Not a problem. Merlin would bring the stones flocking through the air from all points of the compass and burrowing their way up from unknown depths like fish rising to the bait, to take their assigned places.

Great works like these required sacrifice, sometimes even human sacrifice, but slaves flowed freely into the empire from all over the world. The Romans were rich in nothing if not human blood.

So Merlin survived and even thrived in Roman Britain, on through the decades and then the centuries. In the fourth century, Rome turned Christian and paganism was banned, but by then Merlin was as much a permanent monument as Hadrian's Wall and about as easy to move. Go ahead, baptize him! Water off a duck's back. Even when the Romans left Britain, he wasn't much bothered. Power was Merlin's real medium, even more than magic, and power, like heat, was never destroyed, only redistributed. Somebody somewhere always had it. You just had to figure out who it was and how to get close to them.

His arrival at Rutupiae set off a flurry of cooking and sweeping and beating of carpets and airing of linen and bringing up of fine wines from the cellars. Two days after he appeared a series of crates began arriving by ship, from which he extracted the gleaming components of a large and complex mechanism, each piece packed in straw and wrapped in silk. Merlin commandeered Lord Cantic's great hall to assemble it.

Nimue, who had an inquisitive nature, would peer in from time to time. The machine was taller than a man, a confabulation of interlocking tracks and hoops and toothy gears and clockworks and transparent spheres of different sizes, from tiny peas all the way up to whopping melons, filled with colorful marbled liquids. Merlin called it an armillary sphere, and he explained to anyone who would listen that it was a representation, in steel, gold, glass, porcelain, and finely engraved brass, of the universal mechanism of the cosmos. It mirrored God's creation. In many ways, he added dryly, it represented a considerable improvement.

But unlike God's creation it didn't move. It looked like it should, but it didn't. When his work was complete everybody expected Merlin to leave, but he didn't move either. He stayed on at

Rutupiae for days, then weeks, as if he were waiting for something. To make matters worse, he started to hold grand parties in the Great Hall, every night, with dancing and reveling around his great enigmatic machine. People came from all over Cantium to attend.

For Nimue this meant a bounty of overnight guests' clothes stained with every possible edible and potable substance plus the full range of bodily fluids and the occasional insect infestation. But that was the least of her problems. She was having dizzy spells from hunger. More than once Nimue stared ravenously at a smear of (hopefully) jam on some baron's stocking and even took a furtive lick.

Catching sight of her reflection in a basin of gray water one night she saw that she was getting a blurry, haggard look. Her hair looked thin and sick. Pretty soon even prostitution wouldn't be an option, she thought bleakly. Her market value was declining.

If she went into debtor's prison she'd have no home and no job when she came out. And who would take care of Mary? They had her in a trap. The iron vise of circumstance was closing on her, tighter and tighter, just because it could, until sooner or later the unstoppable world would make her do something unspeakable. If not for herself then for Mary, with her fairy braids and her little pie face and her Moo.

But not yet, she thought. You sons of bitches. You'll have to squeeze me tighter than this. With thready hunger-logic she decided she would slip upstairs and steal some food from the party. Nothing simpler. She made her way alone up the stone steps to the kitchen and through it to the Great Hall.

It was a waking dream. The air was full of the clinking of silver, the thunder of footsteps, the massed roar of chatter and aristocratic laughter. The light was mellow, elegant candlelight, not the guttering rushlight of belowstairs. Nimue stared at all these pretty people, whose clothes she knew so intimately, who didn't smell like lye and piss, who owned themselves. And the food. There was mounds of it, cheeses and pasties and tarts and puddings—

Someone grabbed her from behind. It was the steward. She would've cried out but the collar of her dress bit into her neck and choked her. He was dragging her backward out of the room.

A voice louder than any voice she'd ever heard before shouted: "STOP!"

The musicians scraped to a halt; the flautist was a moment late. A stocky man in a brown robe was striding across the room directly toward her. It was that man, the king's wizard. Morton. Marvin.

"Take your hands off her, churl," he said, almost absent-mindedly backhanding the steward across the face. He pursed his lips and took a closer look at Nimue: "Hm."

No one else was looking at her, because behind the wizard his glittering machine was moving at last. Its innards whirred and ticked. The spheres trundled along on spindly arms like aging courtiers taking to the dance floor.

The partygoers whispered and shuffled away with nervous faces. Nimue prayed silently to God and to the Virgin Mary, the great forgiving mother, that it wouldn't hurt when Marvin fed her to his gleaming machine. She prayed for little Mary, too, her Mary, that after Nimue was dead she would enter a convent and be safely wedded to God.

Little stars embedded in the brass housing of the great apparatus blinked on in constellations: a swan, a ship, a serpent, Hercules. The crowd gasped, delighted now, and there was scattered applause. It was all part of the show! Even in her weakened and terrified state

Nimue had to agree that it was beautiful. If it were to consume her, that wouldn't be the worst possible fate.

Forgetting herself, Nimue approached the machine and held out her hand to it. With a deep *woof* the golden sun at the heart of its works ignited. The crowd gasped. *Ooooooh.* A rich solar warmth flowed over her. It was almost like it recognized her. Her fear evaporated: it wasn't going to eat her, it was a little cosmos that had been waiting for its god, and its god was Nimue, a laundress who'd just come within an ace of selling her maidenhead for half a shilling.

Merlin—that was it—folded his arms and sighed. He looked no happier than before. Somewhere inside the apparatus tiny bells chimed: the music of the spheres.

"Well," he growled. "I guess it's you."

A silvery comet sputtered to life, shedding bright white sparks as it went.

THAT VERY SAME NIGHT Nimue agreed to become Merlin's new apprentice, until such time as he deemed her a master of the art of sorcery and competent to practice on her own. She was the one. The machine had spoken.

It was no kind of job for a good Christian girl, but how could she refuse it? It was deeply confusing to her, even hurtful, that the only way she could survive in God's world was by practicing pagan magic, but it couldn't be worse than starvation or prostitution, could it? Or maybe this was a test, maybe she was supposed to starve herself to death and be a martyr. Well, she could always come back to that.

Merlin didn't much care about her Christianity one way or the other, to him it was just an odd personal choice, like an eccentric hairstyle or a vegetarian diet. Fine with him. Just keep it to yourself, I don't want to hear about it. Her first job was to break down the machine, rewrap its components in silk, and pack them gently back into their crates. To slumber, Nimue supposed, till he needed a replacement apprentice. How many had Merlin run through over the centuries? Where were they all now?

Never mind. What mattered now was that she could eat. The steel vise of hunger and fear released her from its grip, and she could pay her debts.

But her apprenticeship came at a price: she would be taking care of Merlin now, he was to be her sole concern, and he would tolerate no distractions. So she had to say goodbye to Mary and Moo. They would be packed off to a distant cousin's farm near the ruins of Calleva. They would be well provided for, but Nimue would be permitted to visit her precious sister-child, her pride and joy, only once a year on a date of Merlin's choosing.

It was a bitter pill. Even long afterward the taste of it was still sharp in Nimue's mouth. Even though Mary was married now, not to God but to a fat farmer in Garlot, and had forgotten all about Moo. Nimue hadn't forgotten.

She had a lot of other things to remember, though. Some of what Merlin taught Nimue were spells, which drew on the invisible forces of the world, or the hidden powers within oneself. She had such powers, that was the lesson of Merlin's whirling armillary sphere.

But much of what Merlin did was of a very different and more transactional nature. The landscape of Britain, though it appeared empty, was alive with spirits. He showed her how to see them and how to call to them: nymphs and genii, naiads and dryads and demi-deities, spirits of hill and tree and bog and river and great stone and calm hidden pool. Some were the embodiments of natural boundaries, like beaches and streams, or the days when the seasons changed, or the hidden seams and folds within the earth. They were the geniuses of Britain's many places.

With the coming of God to Britain, many of them had either departed for the Otherworld or gone to sleep, like frogs hibernating in freezing mud, till the long winter of Christianity passed. But others, the proud hardy survivors, could still be roused and spoken with. It was part of Nimue's job to keep on good terms with them, to acknowledge and propitiate them, against the hour when they might be useful.

It was hard work—and it seemed not impossible that she was blaspheming, and consigning her immortal soul to damnation—but she did it. Day to day it was a bit like feeding a lot of farm animals: some of the spirits were beautiful, some grotesque, some genial, some abrasive and petty, some listless and depressed at the dark turn the world had taken. She wasn't permitted to speak to the real powers, mind you. The great antlered war god Belatucadros, the shining one, spoke only to Merlin. Likewise the God of the Gate, and Lugh, lord of light, and the triple Mother, and the thunder god, Taranis, who carried a lightning bolt in one hand and a wheel, the great wheel of the cosmos, in the other.

It was the smaller fry, the little local gods, that fell to Nimue. She would talk to them and find out what they wanted: a freshly killed squirrel, or a wooden doll in the shape of a child, or a copper bracelet, or three of her hairs, or a secret. Over the years she'd been asked for her blood, and her urine, and a kiss. And like children they would always want to know what the others had got.

Nimue didn't worship them. Her devotion to God never wavered; if anything it made her fonder of God that in His mercy he allowed this curious rabble to live on in His domain. But she grew fond of her charges, too, or some of them at least, and she liked to think that they liked her, too, or at least tolerated her. Nimue didn't grovel and abase herself before them the way some sorcerers did. She didn't flatter or wheedle. Sometimes she bargained, but she'd learned never to beg. She gave them respect and demanded it back, and they gave it. Most of them. Sooner or later.

As for Merlin, he was more opaque to her than the strangest nymph or spirit. He never threatened or mistreated her, or even paid her much attention at all, but for reasons she would have had trouble articulating she never once, in the three years she spent as his apprentice, felt entirely safe.

ONE MORNING MERLIN summoned her to his library.

She found him sitting in a massive shabby armchair reading a tiny book no bigger than the palm of his hand. Its pages were crinkled and wavy, as if it had spent some time underwater. He squinted at them through a clear, round reading stone held between thumb and forefinger.

The library took up the top two floors of Merlin's Tower, and it dwarfed Camelot's royal library. Its curved walls were lined not only with thousands of books but with animal skeletons, obscure weapons, unidentifiable medical devices, a vivarium for a poisonous moth, glass jars, oddly shaped leather cases, and exotic astronomical instruments. Teetering ladders on casters ran up to the upper shelves.

The tower migrated around Britain according to an irregular

schedule; today it was in a chilly meadow in Ystrad Tywi. Merlin turned a tiny page of his tiny book, blinked, turned another.

She waited. He ignored her. He seemed to relish these tiny assertions of power.

Finally he closed the book and looked up.

"Why do you suppose King Arthur has no heir?"

"I couldn't say, master. Perhaps the queen—"

"Guinevere's not the problem, she's fertile as a dungheap. You could grow mushrooms on her."

"I would as soon allow the king of Britain's bedchamber to remain a private—"

"As would I! Believe me. But we cannot. It is a cruel paradox of monarchy that the king's private life is the foundation of Britain's public well-being." Merlin stood up and began to pace the perimeter of the room. "We know very well that he is not an invert, and that his, ah, apparatus can function, witness his performance with his half sister Morgause. So why with her, and not with Guinevere?"

"I don't know." She hated herself for blushing. Merlin's vague allusions to sexual matters were another way he had of making her feel awkward and vulnerable.

"Come, come, don't play the schoolgirl with me! Unless I miss my guess, Arthur suffers from a classic fear of intimacy." He stopped pacing and clasped his hands behind his back. "To open himself to another, as one does in the act of love, would be to risk revealing the terrible secret at the core of his being."

"But what secret could Arthur possibly have?"

"My dear Nimue, when it comes to guessing the terrible secrets concealed in a man's soul, one's choices are sadly limited. There are three or four at most to pick from. Arthur's is that he believes that he is worthless. Discarded by his parents, raised in obscurity, condemned, as far as he knew, to life as squire to an ill-natured jackanapes. Those were his formative years, and once formed a man cannot be re-formed—no, not even by a sword in a stone. The world tells him he's a king, but he feels he is a fraud, and he's terrified the world will find out."

The wizard picked up a flask of orange powder from a shelf, held it up to the light, flicked it.

"Our red mercury has become denatured. Please send to Hispania for more."

"Of course, master."

"And then there is the sad business of Arthur's conception, for which I bear some of the blame." Merlin hung his head in mock penitence. "The rape of pagan Cornwall by Christian Britain. In Arthur's mind every blow he strikes for Camelot must reprise the primal sin that made him. To draw his sword, literal or metaphorical, is to repeat what Daddy did to Mummy. No wonder the poor man can't get it up!"

The old wizard paused by a window, sixteen squares of wavy glass.

"My own father raped my mother. He was a devil, she a priestess. Hardly the stuff of which great romance is made, but still, one can get past it. One must. Do you know that Uther cried out for him, on his deathbed? 'Arthur! My Arthur!' Bit late for that!"

"Speak more plainly, master, I'm afraid I do not follow." Nimue kept her expression calm and apparently fascinated, as always, but her mind was full of warning trumpets and bells and cries of alarm. This was careless talk, and Merlin adored the sound of his own voice, but he was never, ever careless.

"I rather thought you were quicker than that. If I must be absolutely clear then: Arthur is a flawed vessel, cracked in the firing. It's a wonder he's made it this far. His weakness puts all of Britain at risk. Guinevere must be bred like a heifer, and swiftly, or Britain will come apart."

"But how—"

"Let us not dwell on details, but much as I did with Duke Gorlois, I will give a man the seeming of Arthur. If the matter is neatly handled no one need be the wiser."

"You cannot be serious."

"Don't look so shocked!" His tone was cheerful and avuncular, but his eyes weren't cheerful. Merlin was watching her very closely now. "I may do the job myself if it comes to that. And then if the king should meet with some accident, the child would require a wise regent"—he modestly indicated himself—"to—"

"What you're saying is treason." Her lips were numb, as if they'd been brushed with poison.

"We will start afresh," he said, exactly as if he hadn't heard her. "It is the old druidical way and still the truest: a blood sacrifice. The king must die so the land may live."

She'd learned many things in her apprenticeship with Merlin, and one was that he was inhumanly intelligent, but another was that she herself was very far from stupid, and a sixth sense had always told her that she must never, ever let Merlin know that. He must always think she was a step slower than she really was.

"Ordinary men live but a brief span, even kings come and go, but I have lived for centuries and needs must take the long view. My loyalty is to Britain before all else, before even the king. As your loyalty is to me, Nimue."

Abruptly he stepped toward her, pulled her against him, and kissed her on the mouth.

Her very first kiss, as it happened. It was deeply unpleasant. His lips were hard. He smelled of nothing—he lacked a man's smell the way cursed spirits lacked a shadow. She jerked her head back.

"Stop."

He pulled her to him again. She turned her head and pushed against his chest but his grip was shockingly strong.

"No! Stop!"

What a fool she'd been. She thought the great wizard had rescued her from the trap, but she was still in it. She'd been in it all along. He was part of it. Nothing had changed.

"I've wanted you for so long—"

"I said no!"

His fingers were as tough as old roots.

"Don't be difficult, Nimue," Merlin said in a gentle singsong, as if to soothe an agitated horse. "If you don't desire this form, you need not have me as I am." Even as he spoke he became Sir Lancelot, then a Pictish savage, naked and hugely endowed.

"I can be any man for you."

A Saracen. A winged angel who towered over her.

"Or any woman, if you prefer."

He was Queen Guinevere. He was a mirror image of Nimue herself. She kept her eyes on his; the eyes were always the same. Those he couldn't change.

"Or is it—?" Merlin became a smiling Arthur. "You're so valiant in his defense. But I believe you'll find I'm very much more of a man than he is—"

With a flick of his wrist Arthur-Merlin threw a handful of fine yellow powder in her face. It stung her eyes and she reeled back, scrubbing at them with her hands. He must've palmed the stuff, the old carny.

"You Christian girls." She couldn't see but Nimue could hear the smile in his voice. "I don't like it this way, but you leave me no choice."

Backing away, feeling blindly with one hand, Nimue sank down on a couch. The dust was pollen. She spat. You'd think pollen would be sweet like nectar but the taste was bitter.

"The flower is *Archaeamphora longicervia*, and it's been extinct for one hundred million years, so you can imagine how hard it is to get ahold of." He was so calm. He must have done this many times. So this was what happened to his apprentices. "But you're worth it, my darling. It's in your eyes and your nose and your mouth now, and from there it will enter your bloodstream, and from there your brain. It will render you pliant and cheerful.

"Don't fight it. Resistance will only increase the damage."

Through streaming eyes she saw Merlin's satin slippers arrive on the thick rug in front of her.

"I think that's long enough. Look up at me." She did. "Yes. Dear, dear"—with an affectionate chuckle—"your face is a very vivid saffron. Like a beautiful dandelion. Let's clean you up, then we'll have that kiss. Oh, we will have—"

Nimue grabbed those ratty amulets round his neck in a bunch and with her other hand whipped a knife out from under her robe and sliced through the thongs. She'd practiced the motion. The blade was slivered glass, not metal, or he might've sensed it. Could've gone for his throat but the glass would probably have shattered against his leathery skin. It did not do to forget that Merlin was not wholly human—he left behind scales when he bathed—and if the legends were true then no woman could kill Merlin. Only a man. And where Merlin was concerned legends had a tiresome tendency to be true.

But she'd got those amulets off him, and now he was vulnerable. Nimue spoke a word. She had it from a *marid*, a very senior category of djinn, for a small fortune. She didn't know what it meant but she knew if you said it wrong it could break your jaw. She said it right.

The word exploded.

The results exceeded her expectations. Money well spent. Merlin shot backward like he was fired out of a cannon, smashing through the bookshelves behind him in a cloud of splinters and loose pages and right out through the wall of the tower in a spray of stones, and on out into the quiet countryside.

She wondered how long it had been since somebody got the drop on Merlin. She'd known all about his special pollen. She'd come across it in his notes and arranged an immunity months ago.

Cool sunlight flooded into the library through a cloud of stone dust. A few fallen books of magic flopped around on the carpet like fish out of water or jetted in circles as sparks sprayed from their cracked bindings. Nimue stepped up to the hole in the wall, waving away the dust and blinking at the light. A pair of startled ponies were running in circles. The only questions now were what could she do to him, and how far away she could run once she'd done it. Would it be too much to ask to find him sprawled unconscious in a neatly Merlin-shaped impact crater?

But here he was, already striding spryly back toward her across the grass, a fixed smile on his face. If a woman could've killed Merlin he would've been strewn in pieces across the innocent green countryside. As he walked he raised his fist and a gray stone the size of his head ripped itself out of the grass and flew to him, smacked into his palm. He wound up and threw it at her like a catapult.

She bolted for the stairs as the stone shattered against the back wall. She had to move; she couldn't fight Merlin here in his sanctum. Behind her he made the five-story leap and popped back inside through the hole in the wall. Immediately a carpet rose up at him as if caught in a high wind and wrapped itself around him. She'd woven a few strands of her own hair into it to secure its obedience. She pelted downstairs and out the door. She'd never been safe here, never ever, not for a moment.

The morning sunlight dimmed. The oak and ash trees around the tower were bending, leaning down, surprisingly quick, like an anemone closing around its prey. She tried to dodge, but their cool woody arms snagged her clothes and clutched at her wrists and ankles.

"Ah well." Merlin's voice was already close beside her. "There's so much I never got to show you, Nimue."

"Drink hot piss in hell!"

She writhed and strained against the branches, but you weren't going to beat a druid in his own grove. So Nimue whispered a rhyme in Old Thracian, held her breath, and became smoke, a once-a-year spell. She slipped sideways on a light breeze through the massed branches. She knew this breeze—twice a year she left a silver pin on the roof for it. Chuckling softly to itself, it carried Nimue across a meadow and up a hill before she became flesh again, on all fours on the grass, gasping.

Merlin was still coming. He would never stop. Clouds were gathering over the field with unnatural speed.

"That's right, my dear, Taranis is on his way. I don't believe you've met yet."

He was calling in favors from the powers of the world. Well, she was owed a few favors too. She'd been hoarding them for years. Her friends were small and lowly, but there were a lot of them. It would've been nice if God helped out, too, but something told her He was going to sit this one out. Maybe she'd been supposed to starve to death after all. Or maybe He just trusted her that she could handle this one.

"Tumbo, you know me!" she whispered into the dirt. "Give me strength!"

She hadn't come here by accident. Tumbo was the spirit of the hilltop, a shy one whom she'd treated with many times, his soft rumbling voice issuing from a crack in a great boulder embedded in the hillside. He liked to play rhyming games.

"I don't forget," came the soft voice. "At least not yet."

Merlin aimed a slap at her—she'd always figured him for a slapper, and here it was. But Tumbo lent her his strength, the strength of a hill, its power and its mineral hardness, and with hands hard and heavy as rock Nimue stopped Merlin's slap and slapped him right back, knocking him sideways.

It shocked him. He scrambled away and she strode after him, back on the offensive. She was going to show him that he couldn't touch her. For his part Merlin was furiously whispering streams of spells and invocations, and as he did his body bulged and distorted crudely, adding big muscles and thick ligaments and overbuilt bones.

"No one." His new body's voice was deep and hollow; his newly thick tongue made him lisp. "No one strikth me and livth." He grinned, big yellow tusks.

They traded blows, punching and kicking, heavy with anger and magic strength but clumsy. She was strong as a seam of granite, but neither of them was skilled at using their fists. It felt good to punch Merlin in the face, God knew, but she wasn't going to beat him like this. She had to get away soon. She had all the strength Tumbo had to give, but Merlin was still getting stronger.

But now the whole landscape around them was coming alive. The spirits of Britain had a limited interest in the doings of men, but a fight between Merlin and his Jesus-loving apprentice would be drawing some attention. They'd be taking sides and gossiping up a storm. Merlin ripped a tree out of the ground and hefted it like a club.

"Awel, take me!" she cried out to the wind. "By the debt you owe me, take me away!"

With a rush and a roar the easterly wind of Awel dragged Nimue somersaulting into the air, like a large ungainly leaf, and she was racing over the land. This was all a joke to Awel—winds found everything funny—so it wasn't a gentle ride or a gentle landing. She chucked Nimue down carelessly on the bank of the river Slip a mile away. She sat up dizzy. Even from here she could see Merlin following at a run, the size of a young giant now, twenty feet tall, kicking down trees as he ran. One hand glowed red, and the air warped around it; the other was so cold it shed trails of mist.

Sometimes looking at raw feral magic like this made her feel like she was going mad. Merciful God, why do You allow such things?

"Let me go, Merlin! I'm not yours!"

"All you are is mine!" giant-Merlin boomed back. "That is all you are! You were nothing when I found you!"

"Aid me, beloved Slip! I call in my debt!"

The Slip had the face of a little girl, sketched in light ripples on its surface, but she was far older than Nimue. Now she answered the call and heaved herself out of her channel and rushed violently over the land. The torrent snatched Merlin's feet out from under him, bowling him over and sweeping him backward, smashing him into rocks.

Nimue became a common swift, crescent-winged and swallow-tailed; she'd thought about becoming a merlin as a *fuck you*, but a swift was faster.

She had to admit that when she'd thought this through ahead of time she'd rather hoped that Merlin would be down by this point, and that she would be beyond his reach. More trees grabbed for her as she went up but she slipped and fluttered between their twiggy fingers and bounded into the sky. She had to get free of him, free of this man and his grasping hands and his stifling tower. She beat up toward the clouds. She knew he'd be following, as a hawk maybe, an eagle, something big; she doubted he knew what she did, which was that no raptor could beat a swift in level flight.

She urged herself higher and higher, calling out to other birds, crows and choughs and ravens and rooks. *Mob him!* she twittered. *Mob him!*

But no one answered her. A quick glance over her shoulder told her why. He wasn't a hawk. Merlin had become a dragon, big as a blue whale but coal black, with poisonous golden stripes, snorting smoke, ripping his way up into the sky on billowing black wings.

She was grudgingly impressed: a dragon was not a natural form, and she had not thought it was within even Merlin's abilities. But was it fast? Let's find out. Her own featherlight wings took her higher and higher—

That was when she realized her real mistake.

Clouds. Stupid. *Stupid.* The dragon wasn't the trap. She'd flown right into the trap.

The clouds had been thickening all afternoon, and they were swollen with power now, crackling with it. Nimue couldn't see it but she felt the great starry outline of Taranis above her, hefting the wheel of the world jauntily in one hand, a thunderbolt in the other. She'd been so close, she was almost free, but the trap had closed on her in the end. Nimue could feel the lightning building. She only wished she'd had time to tell someone what Merlin was planning to do. Or at least tell Merlin himself that she was glad to die because she would rather be dead than be touched by him ever again. *Mary—!*

Everything went quiet. All color vanished. The green earth far below turned suddenly gray. The sky was black. The sun was gone.

What just happened? The air was blowing with what looked like black snow.

Was she dead? If so, this didn't look like Heaven. Nimue clung to the thin notion that she couldn't be dead because she was still flying, and, logically, if the lightning had hit her then her human body would've been restored to her in death. A technicality at best.

You are not dead, a voice said. *You are in the realm of dreams.*

It was another swift, a black one, flying along beside her. So not dead, not yet. But how? She doubted she'd dozed off on the wing.

I am Durelas, the liminal god, the other swift said. *I keep watch over the doorways and boundaries of the world. Death and life, waking and sleeping, beginnings and endings.*

She had heard of such.

"The Romans called you Janus, the god with two faces."

The Romans cherished many misconceptions.

"So this is where dreams happen?"

Any attempt at explanation would be tedious and imprecise. You have come a long way. This realm lies beyond even the Otherworld, for even the fairies dream.

But you cannot stay here long. It is incorrect to be in this realm bodily, and in a waking state.

"Thank you, Durelas. I am grateful, you saved my life. I think. But why? Why bring me here?"

You have been gracious to some of my children. Fritu, and the spirit of the Whin Sill. Certain minor interstitial colors of the rainbow. They petitioned me on your behalf.

She remembered Fritu, a saucy, foul-mouthed spirit who looked like a tiny person made out of sticks. He embodied the place where a forest met a meadow. He'd asked Nimue for a small pearl. Thank you, little Fritu! She must get him another one, if she lived long enough. She had no idea what the Whin Sill was but they could have whatever they wanted too. Within reason.

"I thought the Great Gods were all on Merlin's side."

You are loyal to the Christian God, Nimue, which I cannot approve of, but at least you are loyal to someone. Merlin asks us for our loyalty while he sells his own to the highest bidder. Better he had died with the others on Ynys Môn.

Tell your Jesus that He owes us a debt.

"I will. And my Jesus will tell you that no one but a Christian would've been so kind to your children."

Instead of answering, the liminal god made a strange noise, a grunt of surprise or discomfort. Not a very divine noise. The black swift banked away sharply.

"What is it?"

Merlin has followed you here. Fly, little bird. Do not tarry.

But it was too late for that, there was nowhere for the little bird to fly. Nimue looked back to see a flash of the impossibly huge, horrible jaws of the Merlin dragon before they snapped shut on her. Then not just the sky but everything went black.

And still she didn't die. She was in Merlin's mouth, a thought as revolting as it was terrifying. She fluttered her wings desperately, but his great dry, black dragon's tongue had her tiny bird-body pressed to the roof of his mouth. He had not swallowed her yet.

She heard his voice in her mind.

I cannot let you go, Merlin said, or he thought, it was hard to tell the difference when you were literally inside his head, breathing his burned breath. She thought back at him.

Then kill me. You can screw a dead bird.

I must have you. You can't conceive of how much I want you.

Swallow me. I'll stick in your throat and choke you.

It is strange, at times our partnership was torture to me. And here Merlin's thought-voice turned plaintive. *There are times when I have wanted to marry you, Nimue.*

You are dreaming, Merlin. You could never love anybody.

It was one of the hazards of communicating by thought that one always said more than one meant to. She wondered how long he would keep her here before he killed her.

You cannot refuse me, Merlin said. *You would not, if you understood who I am. The druids chose me from among tens of thousands, and of those they chose, half died in the trials. The rest of us trained for twenty years before we were initiated. We were the lords of Britain. Armies followed us. Forests bowed to us. We spoke with gods. We passed judgment on kings.*

And then the Romans came and harried us west across Britain with dogs. They bayed us like animals on the beach at Ynys Môn.

With his mind Merlin made Nimue see it, the flat gray strand littered with sea wrack, bonfires burning behind it in the scrubby headlands. An army of druids, men and women both, howling and dancing on the sand at dusk, spinning torches, chewing acorns to bring on a trance state.

The Roman cavalry swam their horses over from the mainland, across the narrow, green strait, and then the infantry splashed ashore through freezing shallows from flat-bottomed boats. They were terrified but their officers lashed them on. Such was the druids' faith that they wore no armor. They called on their gods to destroy the invaders.

But their gods did not respond. Perhaps the Romans had bought them with gallons of slave blood. When the soldiers saw they were powerless it became a massacre. Ordinary soldiers, common men from the east, put the greatest minds in Britain to the sword.

But not you, Nimue thought.

Not me.

Goodness, only get him talking to a dead bird and it all comes out.

Because I had seen it all coming. I, Merlin the Prophet, saw the future, and it was not ours, so I did what the other druids would not. I groveled and humiliated myself and prostituted myself so that at least one druid could live, and our knowledge would live on within me. If I hadn't, then all of it, the treasure of centuries, would've been lost.

Nimue said nothing. There was nothing she could add that would make the inferno of his shame hotter. It was his soul that had been lost, and like so many who'd lost their souls, he had to insist the bargain was worth it and show contempt for those who still had theirs.

I have carried it for centuries in the fragile vessel of my mind. And why? To give it to you. A nobody, a pretty Christian whore who betrayed me. Damn me for a fool.

I *betrayed* you, *Merlin?*

She sensed the dragon landing, settling on its great haunches somewhere in the dark countryside of dreamland.

I will grieve for you, Nimue. Your death will hurt me, but letting you live would be careless, and I have lived too long for that. Time will dull the pain. I will mourn for a decade, or two, or three, but no more. You will not go to Heaven, Nimue. Your God will never find you here in dreams.

But I might visit you from time to time.

But still he didn't devour her. An idea had come to her, a guess as to what might really be happening here. Mary, pray for me, wherever you are. Give me strength and luck. You too, Moo.

I have prepared something special for your grave. I have called down a falling star, Nimue. Merlin showed her that, too, in her thoughts: a bright blue sky with a new light in it, a second sun, harsher and whiter than the old yellow one. *A meteor is its correct name, a great hot stone plucked from the Sphere of Stars. When it's all over there will be a hill here to remember you by.*

"You shouldn't have followed me, Merlin," Nimue said.

I didn't have to. The gods brought me to you.

She could hear the amusement in his voice. Still so calm.

"You never listen," Nimue said. "You talk and talk but you never listen, Merlin. I told you you were dreaming. You've lived too long. The hounds of Hell are baying for you."

The god of boundaries had told her she couldn't stay long, and he was right. She'd returned to the world.

But Merlin had not.

Perched on his snout, like a plover on an alligator, the little bird whispered the words in the ear of a sleeping dragon.

"Taranis didn't strike me with his thunderbolt. He struck you, and he knocked you senseless. Your sleeping mind is in the world of dreams, but your body is still here, where it cannot save itself."

In your extremity your wits have deserted you.

"I must away, Merlin, but before I go I will tell you a secret: Arthur frightens you not because he's weak, but because he's strong. Stronger than you.

"And another secret: Jesus will always win. Because unlike you He's not a shit."

His dragon-body was stirring, trying to wake up, but it was no good. Sleep held him fast. She must be gone, and soon. The falling star was not a dream, it was close now, she could see the flickering phosphorus glare of it pressing through from behind the clouds. She took flight.

When he spoke again, Nimue sensed that Merlin had grasped the change in his fortunes, but he could do nothing to reverse it.

No one will believe you when you tell them what I did, Nimue. That is your curse.

There was no panic in his thoughts. Give him that. He was an old pro.

I remember the day I found you, in the hall at Rutupiae. If it were anyone else Nimue would have taken his tone for fondness. *Your hair was loose. Your gown was filthy and you smelled of piss, but you were so beautiful I thought the gods must have sent you.*

The falling star wouldn't kill him but it would bury him deep. She flew all the way back to Merlin's Tower, now Nimue's Tower, where she alighted on the roof to watch it. She became human again.

No one ever made the comet sparkle before.

When it hit, the flash lit up the whole sky. It was so bright she had to turn away, and even then she had a sunburn for days.

Twenty-nine

The Wild Hunt

They stopped in a meadow flooded with wildflowers, pignut and yellow rattle and red clover. Nimue built a fire of birch wood to work Merlin's spell. When she raked the stone out of the embers it cut easily and there, inside, like a swirl of cinnamon in a loaf of sweet bread, was the promised word.

"Should've known that," Nimue muttered when she saw it. Collum tried to look but she pushed him away. "No peeking."

She threw the two halves of the rock into the woods.

"Wake the others. We're going."

While they broke camp, Nimue took a rabbit out of a bag and as its feet desperately paddled the air she cut its throat and called out the word from the stone—it was something long and sibilant that Collum somehow forgot as soon as he'd heard it. She shook the hot blood out on the grass and tossed the rabbit's little body unceremoniously into the trees where she'd thrown the stone.

Collum grimaced.

"Merlin didn't mention that part."

"Did you think magic was free?" Nimue squatted and wiped her hands on the grass. "But by all means, you can walk all the way to Bryneich."

Even as she spoke two beech trees reached out and touched their branches together, as if they were holding hands. The joined branches formed an arch, and under the arch was somewhere else, a rolling grassland with a thin seam of blue sea in the distance. One by one the knights stopped what they were doing to stare at it. It made Collum a little dizzy, as if he were standing on a high cliff and might fall down into it somehow.

"I'm sorry to have to say it," Constantine said, "but this is as far as I go."

"What?" Bedivere didn't even look round. "What do you mean?"

"I mean that I've been giving it a great deal of th-thought, and what I think is that we've found our king already. It's Lancelot."

"You must be joking." Now Bedivere stopped staring at the archway and turned around.

"I regret to say that I am not."

His cheeks were flushed. Constantine obviously disliked making speeches, but he wasn't backing down from this one.

"He's a traitor to the Crown," Bedivere said. "But even if he weren't I thought he said no."

"I don't accept his refusal."

"Constantine," Collum said, "I really don't think Lancelot wants to be king."

"The choice is not his to make. I don't think Arthur wanted it either. But you know, I find that it's the people who actually want to be king who are the problem."

"How are you going to change his mind?"

"I'm not. Guinevere will do it for me. From here I'll go to Amesbury and put my case to her. If she is willing to forgive him, I will bring her to H-Hoxmead. I believe that her blessing will be enough to convince Lancelot. Then we'll all return to Camelot together."

"You actually believe him," Bedivere said, shaking his head in disgust. "You believe that lying shit."

"What about the spear?" Nimue said.

"Well, the thing of it is—" The tall knight rubbed the back of his head uncomfortably. "No one ever came right out and told us to find the Holy Lance, did they? I mean to say, it's not as though we got a sword in a stone or a Holy Grail. And the stone at least had some instructions on it. We got a glowing button with a stick on it, that's all. It's not much to go on, is it?

"And even if it were, it's not as though any of us found the Grail the first time round. Dagonet and I came close, but then we had Galahad, and there aren't any Galahads anymore. I'm afraid Merlin might have been right on that particular score—this is heroes' work. Not really our department."

"Maybe he's right." Scipio unconsciously traced a tattooed line on his face. "Even if we do find the damn spear, Queen Morgan and King Saxon will probably be making royal monster-babies in Arthur's bed by then."

"Maybe the lance is Lancelot," Palomides said thoughtfully. "Wordplay—you see?"

Collum fingered the medal around his neck. It did feel very ordinary and mundane. Hardly a fitting conduit for the voice of God. And he wanted it to be true, he wanted Lancelot to be the answer. But finding Lancelot hadn't felt like the end of the quest.

"All right." Bedivere started kicking apart the birch fire. "Well, do what you want, Constantine, and good luck to you."

"I know what a king is." Constantine drew himself up, and Collum remembered how steely he'd looked that day at the battle, shouting orders in the press. "I grew up with one for a father, and frankly I don't much care for him. But I like Lancelot. When he sits on the throne, he'll feel God's love again, just like before. He'll have God, and we'll have a king. Dagonet, you'll come, won't you?"

But Dagonet shook his head.

"Not this time."

He said it almost inaudibly. A breeze made the magic arch sway, and the edges of the smooth green land shifted with it.

Bedivere stared up at the crossed branches. Then he walked back over to Constantine and for a heartbeat Collum was sure he was going to hit him, and the thought obviously occurred to Constantine, too, because he shied away, but instead Bedivere put his hands on the tall knight's shoulders.

"Go on." He patted Constantine's cheek. "Go. God will sort it out one way or the other. We'll see you at Camelot."

He turned away and led his horse through the arch.

"Thank you, Bedivere!" Constantine called after him. "I do hope you find it. And if God says it's me, please inform Him that I abdicate!"

THEY SPENT THE AFTERNOON crossing the high heather moorland of Bryneich, picking their way around soggy peat hags, two hundred miles or so from where they'd woken up that morning. They spent that night in an empty stone barn, by a crackling fire of thorny branches. The sunset looked red and sere and wintry. The barn was missing half its roof, and overhead the stars made silver skeletons of men and beasts and gods, who gazed down on them indifferently.

Then they pushed on, to the north, through an empty gate in Hadrian's Wall and into the land of the Picts.

The weather changed. The great door of autumn blew open with a bang and through it came cold wind and sudden squalls splashing them with cold rain. Red and yellow leaves went streaming through the air and across fields and down lanes like lost pages from a broken book, plastering themselves on rocks and grass.

It was true what Palomides said: he didn't get wet. No rain touched him. It parted like the Red Sea wherever he walked.

Collum knew this world, the world of the north. The land shed most of its trees and took on that familiar bald, threadbare lumpiness, as if the soil were a rug that was worn too thin to conceal the stony substrate underneath it. Valleys opened on valleys, vast bowls and hollows, huge stepped green promontories striped with skinny white streams. The weather was colder, the cold of the north but also of advancing autumn—the year was rushing past them, as if every night while they slept a week or two slipped away, like they were dreamers in a fairy cave.

But they were getting closer. When they first set out the Holy Lance had seemed ghostly and abstract, but now it loomed larger and larger in Collum's mind, more and more real, crowding out everything else. According to Palomides, the North Pole of the earth was a great black lodestone, thirty-three miles in circumference, standing all alone in the middle of a freezing sea. The spear felt like that, a lodestone at the end of the world, drawing them to itself.

Collum hoped it drew them fast, because everywhere around them were small signs of a great disintegration: burned fields, a dead horse, a stone bridge with a sodden, bloated body trapped against a pier by the current. Ragged, rainswept lines of displaced people straggled along the sides of the roads. Lone houses were boarded up and shut tight, and towns grew rings of hastily constructed walls and barriers. They entered a church once to find it empty, the bell stolen, the priest absconded, stained glass broken, and rain gusting in onto the altar.

The few people who would speak to them had no news, just confused rumors. That Camelot had been sacked and burned. That Arthur had never existed at all, he was just story spread by Christian propagandists. That there was a cult of Arthur that roved from town to town dressed in white, singing and preaching and beating themselves and urging people to do the same to speed the return of the king, who would arrive flanked by Galahad and Percival. There were rumors, too, of a rival cult that raped and pillaged and burned in an attempt to ruin Britain so comprehensively that Arthur would have no choice, he would be forced to come home and stop them.

"Wait'll he hears what he missed," Dagonet said. Since Constantine left the quest he'd become even quieter and more sullen.

One night they camped by a stream that was clear as glass, with a bed of rainbow-colored stones. The rain eased off for once. Sometime after midnight Collum rolled over onto his stomach and out of sleep. Something had woken him up, but he'd already forgotten what it was.

Then it came again: *Baroooooooo-doo-doo-doo-doo-doo-doo-oooo!*

A hunting horn, and not far away. Bedivere sat up, blinking and searching the darkness around him for his hammer. A few glowing embers had survived the rain, and the sky had cleared, revealing a host of stars.

"The *forlonge*," Bedivere said. "The stag has outdistanced the hounds."

"Who the hell's hunting all the way up here?" Dinadan asked irritably. "And in the middle of the night?"

"Shh!" Nimue held up a hand for silence. Now they could hear the baying and yelping of the pack.

A single hound shot through the camp at full tilt, pelting right through the campfire, kicking up a spray of sparks. Collum saw it only for a moment. It was a strange sort of dog, with bone-white fur and blood-red ears.

Nimue stared after it.

"Shit," she said under her breath.

"What in God's name was that?" Collum said.

More dogs bayed, all around them now.

"It looked like a fairy hound. The Cŵn Annwn, Arawn's pack. But they hunt the Otherworld, not here."

"I hate dogs," Dagonet contributed.

Now a tiny old woman galloped past them on a black goat. She was naked, her skin smeared with red ochre. She shouted something at them in a language Collum didn't recognize, then disappeared again into the night.

"It's the Wild Hunt," Bedivere said.

"Can't be," said Nimue, but without much conviction.

The horn sounded again, closer, and three more of the spectral hounds tore through the camp, whipping between the bewildered knights in a flurry of long legs, followed at a trot by something that looked like a horse but with black-and-white stripes like a tiger.

"What do we do?" Dinadan had one boot on. "Do we fight?"

"Don't touch them," Nimue said quickly. "Don't engage. We shouldn't've looked at it, but too late now."

The boundaries are getting weak, Collum thought. Fairyland is spilling into our world, just like Morgan said.

A bizarre procession emerged from the woods, hounds and beasts and fairies, male and female and otherwise, clothed and naked, hooting and shouting and leaping. They rode cows and pigs and ostriches and a giant bounding hare as big as a bear. One or two came walking upside down on their hands. A few of the fairy hunters rode piggyback on cursed men and women, naked and weeping. The hunters lashed them on with whips. Where is King Arthur? Collum thought. He would turn them back. Rebuild the boundaries. What more did he need than this? Would it help if he flagellated himself?

BAROOOOOOO-DOO-DOO!!!

Now the horn blower himself burst into the clearing, a brown-bearded satyr astride a giant black rooster with a livid red flapping comb.

BAROOOOOOO-DOO-DOO-DOO-DOO-DOOOOOOOO!!!! TROU-ROU-ROU-ROOOOOOO!!!!!

It was so loud Collum had to cover his ears.

"All right! We hear you!"

Right behind the satyr came a centaur—except not quite. Her lower parts weren't a horse's body, they were those of a mighty deer. From the waist up she was Morgan le Fay herself.

"Hello, Britain!" Her face glowed with triumph. "I'm back!"

A proud pair of antlers sprouted from her hair like an imperial headdress.

"Gods, can you believe it's Samhain already? Taranis spins his great wheel faster and faster. And I'm so pleased to see all of *you*— even you, Collum! Even though we had a fight! But look at you blushing. Does all this embarrass you?"

Morgan was magnificently naked from the waist up. The cold didn't seem to touch her.

"Oh, and your witch is here too! Love your work, Nimue."

"Thanks," Nimue said dryly.

"The Merlin bit especially. Couldn't stand that man."

"You're too old a soul to mistake me for a fellow traveler, Morgan."

"Oh, but we could be, Nimue! Perhaps you mistake yourself. But tell me: Whither the knights of the Round Table on this fine autumn night?"

"We're—"

"Not you, Collum, I need a grown-up."

"It's none of your business where we're going," Bedivere said.

Above them a fairy rowed a boat vigorously through the air. The Green Knight saluted them from his gnarled horse of roots and flint.

"I was going to pretend I didn't know," Morgan said, "just to spare your feelings, but you've forced my hand, damn your steely blue eyes, Bedivere. What do you want with Longinus's spear?"

"We hope to secure God's blessing for a king."

"You would hope that. Well, you'll probably find it, knowing you."

"Does that worry you?" Nimue said.

"Should it?"

"If God sees fit to put someone on the throne of Britain, it won't be you."

"I should hope not! But you know, Nimue, I find that if there's one thing you can count on in this world, it's your God doing fuck-all, especially when you need Him most. I mean, look at me! The Wild Hunt is running free in the north, and what does God do about that?"

"You think this is the Britain people want?" Dinadan said. "Freaks and fairies?"

Morgan raised an eyebrow at him.

"People want the old ways back, the British ways, and that is what I will give them. The world is finally broken enough that we can put it back together the way it should be."

"And what about God's ways?" Bedivere said.

"I'll never understand it." Morgan shook her head. "A man with your, shall we say, proclivities, fighting for a God who would send you to Hell just for being what He made you. There are other ways to live, man! I put it to you, to all of you: What can you say about a God who judges your worth by how infrequently you touch yourself?" She drew a finger suggestively along one elegant antler. "What can you say about a government that falls apart just because the queen got a poke on the side? You will find my Britain a wilder place but a much freer, much stronger one."

"What have you done with Arthur?" Bedivere asked.

"What?"

For the first time Morgan dropped her smile.

"I know you have him. What have you done with him?"

"I saved him." She drew herself up. "From your God."

"When is he coming back?"

"I wouldn't dwell on that, Bedivere. In my experience people don't come back. And if they do they're not the same."

BAROOOOOOOO-DOO-DOO-DOO-DOO-DOO-DOOOOOOOO!!!!

The satyr on the rooster waved Morgan on impatiently, then plunged ahead into the darkness of the birchwood.

"Look, I can't stay or I'm going to lose the pack," Morgan said. "Who's coming with me?"

Nobody answered.

"My friends, a visit from the Wild Hunt is not a social call." In her half-deer form Morgan towered over all of them. "The rules are as old as the standing stones, and quite clear, but it's been some time so allow me to remind you that the Wild Hunt doesn't hunt animals. Our quarry is souls. Now that you've seen us, one of you must join us.

"Any volunteers? No?"

Overhead a fairy in a diaphanous gown drifted by, dangling from a swarm of wasps by a fistful of gossamer leashes.

"You'll have to kill us all." Bedivere drew his sword.

"Nonsense."

"She's right," Nimue said. "The Wild Hunt is Old Magic. There's no denying it."

"There. You see?"

Collum took a deep breath and—

"Not you, Collum!" Morgan laughed musically. "Good God! Get back in line. And no, my sweet, sweet Dinadan, you have other debts to pay. You won't get off that easily."

Palomides stepped forward. He looked in no way afraid.

"I sense fate's hand in this," he said. "And it is a principle of mine never to turn down an invitation to travel."

Collum wasn't sure what to do. He had a wild urge to throw his arms around Palomides and try to drag him back, but something told him this fight was already lost. Morgan smiled at him, then whistled loudly.

"Your chariot awaits."

With a burbling, baying sound the strangest animal Collum had ever seen came trotting out of the woods. It had the powerful haunches of a lion but its legs ended in deer's hooves. Its front parts had leopard spots, and its head and neck were those of a snake, brilliant black banded with hot pink.

Palomides put out a hand and patted her neck admiringly, as if he'd been made a gift of the finest destrier in the land. Glatisant dipped her great reptile head, and he leapt lightly astride her with the air of a much younger man.

The beast shook herself and tasted the air with her forked tongue. Palomides turned to the knights.

"My friends, I am not from Sarras." Palomides smiled, a little sadly. "There is no such place. My real name is Uthman, and I am a prince of Baghdad. I will see you again before the end."

He clucked at the beast and they set off at a rapid prancing trot, his seat perfect as ever. Collum had the strange feeling that it was only then, just as he was leaving, that he was seeing Palomides for the first time.

"This fight was destined ever since this island was made," Morgan said, when he was gone. "It has always been coming. The reckoning is very near now, friends, very near."

She reared up on her hind legs, pawed the air with her hooves, and bounded off into the velvet night.

A reckoning. That sounded good to Collum. It was long past time that God and Fairy had it out and settled things once and for all. Probably that's why God had let Morgan in—probably He'd wanted the barriers to weaken, so He could lure her back to Britain for a final showdown. Then all would be set right, all would be answered for, all would be healed. No more messes like this one. No one is mightier than God. When He turns up.

With a crackling, crushing sound like a boulder rolling through underbrush the giant Ysbaddaden strode past, his head cresting along above the treetops. Collum suppressed the urge to give him a friendly wave. Then quiet descended on the clearing. The cold brook chattered in the chilly darkness. Collum kicked a few stray embers back into the firepit.

Bedivere squatted down and began feeding it twigs.

"I'm getting too old for this shit."

"There is no age," Dinadan said, "for which that shit was appropriate."

"I was so sure he was from Sarras," Collum said.

"It doesn't exist," Nimue said.

"You knew?"

"I know everything."

Scipio was to all appearances already fast asleep. Collum was on his way to the stream for a drink of water when one final creature appeared in the moonlight.

It was a white tiger as big as a horse, moving silently on paws the size of dinner plates. Its rider sat tall and straight and wore a nun's habit of plain undyed wool. The oval of her face, framed by a white wimple, was coolly beautiful. Collum was too exhausted to even react. Go on, he thought. Catch up with the rest. You don't scare me. God will sort you out, too, no fear.

The nun didn't favor them with a glance, but her tiger gave them a big whiskery grin, its face as ribald and hilarious as hers was solemn. Then both lady and tiger disappeared again into the trees.

Dinadan watched them go.

"There are times when I think will never understand anything ever again," he said.

"We'll get him back," Collum said. "She can't keep him."

"Oh, I know that. But I meant the nun on the tiger."

"The nun? What about her?"

He hadn't thought she was weirder than any of the rest of them.

"I forget that you've never seen her face. That wasn't just a nun, Collum. That was Her Royal Majesty Queen Guinevere."

COLLUM HAD ALWAYS supposed that if they kept riding north then sooner or later they'd have to reach the sea, and the next morning they finally did.

The coastline reminded Collum powerfully of Mull: the crumbling cliffs, blackened by salt and sea, and cracked boulders in shapes so bizarre they made one concerned about the God who made them. What divine brain would have conceived these tortured extrusions, upraised fists of stone, collapsed cathedrals, crazed chessboards? Once when he was about ten he stumbled on a remote cove where the outline of an ancient burning tree was imprinted on a basalt cliff. What kind of God, with presumably infinite options available to Him, would choose to make that?

With Morgan now at large in Britain the quest felt even more urgent, if that were possible, but the going was slower than ever. Wet snow closed in, and they cut inland in search of shelter, stumbling over mud half-frozen in ridges and potholes with white crusts that crunched underfoot. Heavy flakes draped themselves on the grass and soaked into every scrap of cloth they touched. When they left Camelot they hadn't expected the weather to turn so quickly, and all they had were light wool cloaks. They hunched over their horses, hungry for their warmth.

"I should've gone with Palomides." Dinadan's teeth were chattering. "I could be riding a giant fuzzy bunny right now."

There was general relief when they spotted an old stone manor through veils of gray snow, standing all on its own. But Collum wasn't relieved.

"I know this place," he said.

It didn't just look like Mull, this was Mull. The old stone manor was Dubh Hall.

"This is where I'm from."

"Collum," Bedivere said, "I freely grant that you're the expert, but I have it on good authority that Mull is an island."

"I'm telling you, I grew up in that house."

There was the great oak tree with the swing hanging from it. There was the well down which Marcas had once thrown a wooden spoon to see if he could retrieve it with the bucket (he couldn't) and then blamed it on Collum.

"If you say so," Dinadan said. "Shall we?"

Of all possible trials, God, you brought me this? *This?* Already he felt the mood of the place invading him; he was breathing in that old familiar feeling, acedia, like bad night air. He'd come all this way to make sure he would never have to feel like that ever again, but here he was, back where he started. He looked at Bedivere, but Bedivere just looked back at him, unyielding. No help there. Damn your steely blue eyes.

"All right," Collum said. "In we go."

The windows were dark but a thin trickle of smoke rose from one of the chimneys. Caps of snow stood on the two white marble urns on either side of the great door; Alasdair had had them shipped to Mull from Durnovaria along with a third one that got dropped and cracked somewhere en route and now stood in a corner of the yard where Collum used to practice, upside down so it wouldn't fill with rainwater. It was pathetic how well he remembered this dismal worthless place.

It was no servant who answered the bell but Lord Alasdair himself, wrapped in a heavy brown cloak. He was more stooped than

Collum remembered, and there was gray in his beard now, but he had that same long jester's grin.

His eyebrows lifted when he saw Collum.

"So," he said slowly. "The prodigal returns."

"Greetings, Lord Alasdair." Collum kept his voice cold, even colder than the wet snow that kept falling steadily. "Allow me to present to you the Lady Nimue of Camelot and four knights of the Round Table: Sir Bedivere, Sir Dinadan, Sir Dagonet, and Sir Scipio."

Sir Scipio was a fudge, since he wasn't officially part of the Table, but in the moment Collum found himself not giving a shit about fine distinctions. Alasdair observed them over Collum's shoulder. His breath showed white in the blue twilight.

"Well, well, well." He smiled wider, like an old crocodile. "Welcome, gentle knights, to Dubh Hall. I'm honored. And welcome back to you, Collum, of course."

"Sir Collum now," Bedivere said.

"We've come a very long way, on the most urgent of errands." Collum refused to speak with any familiarity or even any inflection at all. As far as he was concerned Alasdair was a stranger. "Will you permit us to rest here a short while and warm ourselves at your fire?"

"By all means. Come on in." With a scrape and a hollow iron clank Lord Alasdair unlatched the big door from the inside and ushered them inside. "Collum will show you to the hall."

Collum wondered what happened to the cosmically old butler, Duncan, whose features were practically erased by smallpox scars. But he couldn't honestly have said he cared very much. What the hell were they doing here? He touched the old sheela stone in the chimney as he passed, for luck. Maybe it would work this time.

The fire in the hall had gone out, and it was almost as cold inside the house as it was outside. Collum set about starting a new one, heaping up a pile of wood shavings in the cavernous stone fireplace. He'd done it a thousand times—and had himself regularly been beaten for letting the fire die—but now his fingers felt numb and clumsy, and after a frankly embarrassing number of failed attempts Dinadan gently relieved him of the flint and steel and told him to go sit down.

He took a seat at the old dining table. He wondered if they'd had to put up with shit like this on the Grail Quest.

"He seems nice enough." Scipio rummaged idly in a dark wood cabinet against one wall. "I thought you said he was an asshole."

"He is an asshole."

Nimue was watching him with concern. He tried to sit up a little straighter. All fine. Nothing to worry about.

"Maybe he turned over a new leaf," Dinadan said.

"He did not turn over a new leaf. He's just on best behavior to suck up to you."

Am I meant to take revenge on Lord Alasdair? he thought. Or even worse, forgive him? The sun was setting so early that they had to light candles. A couple of boughs of holly were nailed up pathetically in the rafters. It was Samhain yesterday, but Taranis's wheel had already spun them around to Christmastime. Alasdair returned with a platter of cold pork, some softening carrots, pickled turnips, stale brown bread, and a pitcher of red wine. He apologized for the humble fare and explained that the house was completely empty except for him: the men had all run off when they heard about Mordred's rebellion, then the women had run off, too, either after their men or back to their families and no one came back.

"What about Duncan?" Collum said.

"Dead. Finally. And do you remember that beautiful Roman bowl that went missing? The blue glass? He had it under his bed, the old crook!"

"You blamed me for that. You had me beaten and then banned me from the house for a week."

"Oh, I know, Collum."

"I had to forage in the woods for food. I was nine."

"If I didn't always do right by you, Collum, I am sorry."

It wasn't much of an apology. He said it like he'd accidentally stepped on Collum's toe. Collum said nothing, only poured himself some of Alasdair's sour wine, which he'd never been allowed when he lived here. It wasn't very good but he wanted to drink the whole cellar dry. Why was this so hard? He realized he couldn't stay in the room any longer, so he stood up abruptly and walked out like a sleepwalker. He wanted to go and hide in the old smithy like he used to. Instead he made himself useful and went to the shed behind the house to fetch some firewood.

He was coming back, his arms full of sticks and crumbling peat logs, when he met Nimue coming the other way. She examined him with a frown.

"Are you all right? I can't tell."

"I'm all right."

Though he knew he didn't look or sound all right. He tried to will himself back into a normal state of mind.

"Listen to me, Collum." The half-light of the winter afternoon made everything soft and unreal. Her pale face looked luminous, and her breath puffed white. She'd come out without a cloak. "I see you. I understand what's happening. You don't feel your own strength right now, but I do. That man in there treated you like you were weak, like you were nothing, but he was wrong."

It was true, that was what Alasdair did. That was exactly it. But how did she know? And then for a change Collum understood something.

"It happened to you, too. Didn't it. That's what Merlin did to you."

She nodded slowly.

"Yes. That's what he did."

"I didn't understand before."

"I didn't tell you."

"But you showed him. Didn't you. You showed him how strong you were."

"I did." Nimue leaned forward and pressed her warm lips against his. Collum's heart burst silently in his chest. "Now you show that son of a dog inside."

She held his gaze for a moment longer, then turned and went back in. The wood suddenly felt very much lighter in his arms.

The others made stilted conversation while Collum built up the fire. As the heat spread out from it, rooting out chill and damp as it went, he could feel the house relaxing around them—the beams, the floorboards, the tapestries. A good Christian forgave, Collum knew that. That was the test. Should he forgive Alasdair? He didn't want to. The light had sunk in the windows, and snowflakes pawed at the shutters. What with the wine and the intoxicating presence of so much nobility under his roof, Alasdair became positively chatty.

"A lot has changed since you've been gone, Collum. You couldn't know this, but Marcas is dead." He touched a tear from one eye with the tip of his finger. "A pack of Scotti came through looking for coin. You would've run 'em off, but Marcas never could fight like you."

"I'm sorry, Lord Alasdair," Collum said automatically. He did feel a little sorry for Marcas. A shit who'd had a shit for a father. One of Nimue's hopeless mummers. Collum tried to think what exactly he wanted from Alasdair. He wanted him to beg and grovel for forgiveness. He wanted to humiliate him the way he'd humiliated Collum.

Steady on. He remembered the feeling of Nimue's lips on his.

"You're not the one who should be sorry, Collum." Alasdair dropped his eyes and picked at a sticky spot on the table. "You were given into my care, and I didn't look after you the way I should have. But now look at you. A knight of the Table, traveling with the high lords and ladies of Britain. You were always greater than we knew."

He reached out a hand, speckled like the hand of the knight of the Chevron Or.

"Can you forgive an old sinner? At Christmastime?"

Everyone was watching. This was the moment to be moved by the angels of mercy and compassion. But something else moved Collum instead.

"No."

He slipped his knife from his belt and stabbed it down through the back of Alasdair's bare hand, pinning it to the table.

"Not even if you were Alasdair. I don't know what you are, but you're not him."

Everybody was shouting at Collum but Alasdair just looked down at his wounded hand, with no apparent discomfort at all.

"Ah well," he said. "It would've been funny if you forgave him, but trust a knight of Camelot to ruin the joke."

His eyes went wide and turned bright yellow. He stuck out a

tongue as long and red and forked as a decorative ribbon. The table burst into flames.

"He's a fiend!" Bedivere shouted.

Dagonet fell off his chair. Dinadan threw the rest of the wine in the Alasdair-fiend's face, followed by the pitcher, while the other knights scrambled back fumbling frantically for their swords. Only Collum didn't react. He kept sitting at the burning table, shaking with emotion. He didn't know if he'd passed or failed the test but at least he'd told the truth.

The fiend tugged the knife out of its hand and snapped the blade off easily. Belatedly Collum stood up and drew his sword. The devil was still transforming, its face stretching out in all directions, widening and darkening and distorting. A pair of jet-black horns grew out of its forehead, and two more sprouted from its cheekbones, and two more from its chin, so that its face was ringed with spikes. It stood up and grabbed the front of its own tunic and ripped it open to reveal a big broad belly with a huge second face on it, wide eyes and no nose and a toothy red-lipped mouth.

Scipio lunged forward stabbing, but the fiend just grabbed his battle-scraped old sword by the blade with one horny hand, jerked it out of his grip, and fed it into its giant belly-mouth. The mouth chewed it up noisily and belched.

"Damn," said Scipio.

"Collum!" Nimue shouted. "How do we get out?"

Right. Collum unfroze and led them at a run through the house to a back door—but where it used to be there was only a blank wall. The windows were gone too.

The house had become a prison. As he supposed it always had been. They could hear the fiend crashing through the house after them, shoving aside heavy furniture and splintering doorframes. It was still growing, already it was half again taller than Alasdair had been, and its crooked goat's legs were sprouting a pelt of black hair. Its two faces muttered to one another. Collum led Nimue and the knights at speed through a pantry and the kitchen and up a narrow back staircase to a dim landing where a skinny iron ladder was bolted to the wall. The ladder led up to a trapdoor—still there, God be thanked—that opened onto the roof.

Dubh Hall wasn't technically a castle so it couldn't legally have battlements, but Alasdair had always had pretentions to greatness, and he'd added a low stone parapet running around the flat roof to give it a martial look. There used to be a vine in back that was strong enough to climb down. The vine was gone, but there was a better way now: a gleaming white ladder that led up toward the low clouds.

"Dagonet, find out what's up there," Bedivere said. The Fool Knight set off up it, nimble as a monkey. "Can swords hurt this thing, Nimue?"

"I don't know! It's a devil, I don't do that kind of magic!"

"Come find out." The smiling fiend's shoulders were too broad to fit through the trapdoor so it broke the stone roof around it. God's blood, it was strong. The tips of its horns glowed red in the darkness.

"Where's Scipio?" Collum said.

The fiend belched.

"It's a road!" Dagonet's voice came down through the snowy air. "There's a road at the top! It's made of metal!"

"Good enough," Bedivere said. "Nimue, get up the ladder."

She didn't argue. This must be it, Collum thought. The final leg. We're almost there.

"Dinadan, go," Bedivere said.

"I—"

"You want Dagonet to win the fucking Lance? Go! Collum, you next."

"You go," Collum said.

"Get up the ladder."

"This is my stand to make. This test was meant for me, Bedivere, you know it was."

Someone had to hold off the fiend while the rest climbed. It was probably suicide but Collum felt strangely at ease, invincible enough to take on a whole pack of fiends. It wasn't that he'd finally faced Lord Alasdair—he hadn't faced him at all—but he'd faced something in himself. He had no more blame for himself. He forgave himself for not forgiving.

"Come on, you idiots!" Nimue called down. "Somebody!"

The fiend had acquired a massive blade from somewhere, black iron and thick as a roof beam, the tip glowing red to match its horns. It raised one leg and farted a jet of fire.

"Go, Collum!" Bedivere said. "I'll catch up!"

"We'll fight him together."

"Don't be stupid." Collum hadn't taken his eyes off the fiend, so he didn't see it coming when Bedivere picked him up by his belt one-handed and threw him bodily at the ladder. "Go. Bring it home."

He started climbing then immediately stopped and clung there in an agony of uncertainty. The old knight stepped forward, sword held high—the Ox. He stabbed, feinted high, and cut low at the devil's knees. It caught the strike deftly with its own massive blade, which it wielded as lightly as a dagger.

Collum climbed higher. Snow made the rungs slippery, and the narrow ladder swayed. Dinadan was far above him. He could still hear the off-pitch clanks and clonks of Bedivere's sword and the demon's. He blocked out everything and kept moving.

"For Arthur!" Bedivere shouted.

Collum recited the Lord's Prayer as he climbed, his fingers numb. Maybe the words would hurt a fiend. He stopped again. Maybe he should go back down and yell the Lord's Prayer at it.

"Come, Collum." Dinadan had reached the top and was looking down at him. "This is Bedivere's honor, not ours. Come."

The fiend had grown a long black lashing tail that it snapped like a whip, and between that and its red-hot blade it had Bedivere backed up against the parapet. Collum didn't think he could keep watching.

But then the fiend paused, as if it had heard something. It reached over its shoulder and pulled off something that was stuck there: a hatchet. Scipio had emerged from the trapdoor. The fiend hadn't eaten him after all, though most of the hair was singed off one side of his head.

"*Deus voluit*, you old bugbear." The fiend had eaten his sword, but Scipio had picked up a heavy iron poker from the fireplace, and he had a felling ax in the other hand. "Go, Bedivere!"

"Climb," Bedivere said. "I'll hold him off."

Scipio charged. The poker had a barb on one end and he used it to hook the fiend's blade to one side, at the same time chopping the ax into its hip, where it stuck as if the devil's flesh were hardwood. He rolled under its backswing and came up by Bedivere.

"I felt that," the fiend remarked.

"That's what your mother said. Go." The tattooed knight's voice had a note of command in it that made even Bedivere pay attention. "Go! Up the ladder!"

"No."

"Can't you see it?" There was desperation in his voice too. "You damn fool! Don't you understand? It's him! It's that pusillanimous little shit Collum! It has to be, he's the heir! So go, get him to the end!"

He actually thinks it's true, Collum thought. God's head. He's going to die because he thinks I'm King Arthur's son. How horrifically stupid. Without warning Scipio rapped Bedivere on the knuckles with his poker, Bedivere dropped his sword and Scipio snatched it up.

"Go on. Please." He was almost begging. "My cause was lost long ago, but it's not too late for yours. You can still win. So let me die like a man."

Collum wanted to shout, it's not true! I'm not him! But did he know that for sure? Of course he fucking knew it! He climbed higher up the ladder, furious at himself, willing himself not to think anything more. The voices from below were more and more distant. Damn me for a coward.

"You're not a martyr, Scipio!" Bedivere said.

"I am an officer in the greatest army that ever was." That ring of authority again. "I am a Prefect, First Cohort, Twentieth Valeria Victrix legion, and I've lived too long. So go now or I'll kill you myself."

At the top of the ladder was a road, and it was made of smooth steel, just like Dagonet said. It was so cold it might've been ice, and it was slippery as ice, too, so when Collum got to the top he had to sprawl on his stomach and be dragged up onto it. When he was safely there he crawled back to the edge and looked down.

Bedivere was climbing, one-handed, his face impassive. He'd

made his decision and wasn't looking back. Below him Scipio charged at the fiend, meeting the massive glowing sword high and stopping it, then again when the fiend cut low, its horns still burning red in the darkness. It grunted as the tip of Scipio's sword split its belly-face's obscenely fat lip. *Turn your parries into counterattacks.* Scipio advanced, putting another step between the fiend and the ladder.

"*Roma invicta!*" he shouted. "*Dominus nobiscum!*"

When he was sure Bedivere had reached the top, Scipio gave the ladder a shove and it toppled over. It seemed to fall slowly, as if through water, but then it smashed down hard onto the parapet, overbalanced, and tumbled down into darkness. Scipio bounced on his toes, alive with the flow of the fight. His voice came floating up from far below, even as snow drifted down all around him.

"*Pro deo et imperio! Dominus nobiscum! Roma invicta!*"

Thirty

THE SPEAR

The steel road was a strange thing, like walking along the flat of a giant never-ending sword, or like the sword bridge the knights made for him after the ordeal in the well. It hung in midair, supported by nothing more than divine grace. The metal was so slippery that all five of them had accidentally sat down hard on it before they'd gone half a mile. Eventually they accepted that the only way to make real progress was with an undignified and not very knightly knees-bent shuffle.

They'd left the horses behind at Dubh Hall, but Collum didn't think they would've liked the steel road anyway. They all agreed that they'd go back for Sir Scipio once the Lance was found, just in case he'd somehow beaten the fiend and survived, but nobody sounded particularly confident about it. With him and Palomides and Constantine gone there suddenly seemed to be very few of them left.

But of course the Holy Lance came at a price. The Grail had cost many more.

They walked for hours, deeper and deeper into the night. The knights stuffed rags in the chinks in their armor against the cold. The wind shoved at them and whistled through their helmets and snatched their words away even as they spoke them. Sometimes they could barely see ten feet in any direction, but Collum could sense the presence of great indistinct cliffs and masses of rock all around them. Once through a rip in the mist he glimpsed a sheer, steep slope with jumbled stunted trees, startlingly close. He tried to puzzle out what had just happened. Had he passed the test? The devil's temptation had been to forgive, which should've been the good thing, the compassionate thing, which seemed exactly backward. And if he'd passed, by not forgiving, then why did Scipio have to die? He gave up. It was too tangled a web.

After a while, Collum had no idea how long, they took a break and sat down. It felt wrong to waste time resting, but there were no barriers at the edges of the road, and if they got too tired somebody would wander right off it. Collum prayed for a while, then he lay down on his back and closed his eyes and felt the snow patting his cheeks, thinking, it's almost over. It had to be. They would find the spear and the world would go back to how it should be. Maybe Arthur himself would even come back, God would bring him back. Surely He could do that, if only they proved themselves.

Then Dinadan was nudging him with his foot. He'd fallen asleep in the cold, just like his mother in the blizzard. He got up slowly and painfully. His muscles had hardened into wood while he slept.

At first Collum thought the sun must finally be rising because the mist and snow ahead of them were getting brighter. But it wasn't the rosy-orange glow of sunrise. The steel road ended at a chapel, an almost ostentatiously humble building, just four walls of undressed fieldstone, a peaked roof, and a square Manx-cat stump of a steeple. Inside it there was something so bright that the little chapel could barely contain it. Light shot out of its windows in all directions, in great white spikes that pierced the night.

Collum felt someone take his hand—it was Bedivere. Nimue took the other. Collum found himself smiling at her, and she smiled back, painfully lovely. It was a funny thing to do, but for the last half mile they all walked together along the steel road in a line holding hands like schoolchildren, even Dagonet, who never touched anyone. The wind whirled the snow into great towering, spinning spirals around them. They were high enough that low-flying clouds drifted by, looking like steam in the pure white light coming from the church.

The chapel was set on a little plateau at the very top of a mountain, a sharp peak sliced off flat. Stepping from the steel road to solid ground felt like arriving on the beach after a long, unsteady ocean voyage. The relief came on so strong it was like being drunk. It had cost them so much, but it would all be worth it. They were going to put it all right now. The age of Arthur would come again. Morgan could bring on her reckoning, whatever it was, if she absolutely must. With the Holy Lance in hand they could stand against anyone.

The only fear Collum had left was that they wouldn't live up to whatever final test lay before them. He prayed that one of them would have the strength to lift the Lance, or pull it from a stone, or whatever needed doing with it. It flashed through his mind—which God could see into, Collum knew, you couldn't keep anything from God—that maybe Scipio was right, he might even really be Arthur's son.

But he didn't feel any Arthur inside him. Nothing in there but the mud of Mull. It would have to be enough. A memory came to him, of that day in the meadow when he'd fought the knight of the Three Scepters, and he thought he'd won, and what happened after.

The door of the church was plain wood, as ordinary a door as there ever was, but the light leaking out around its edges was so white it was almost blue. Bedivere didn't even break stride, just stiff-armed it open and walked straight in.

They threw their arms over their eyes—but as bright as it was the light no longer hurt to look at. You didn't even have to squint. It was like a sweet liquid that they waded through. The air in the chapel was warm and smelled like roses, and Collum shivered as the glorious ache of feeling returning to his fingers and toes and cheeks. The building was spare and elegant inside. The floor was made of intricate many-colored marble tiles set in patterns that re-peated and repeated to infinity. Now he understood that he'd been wrong to worry about the Holy Lance, or anything else. Whatever would happen would happen. No more questions; in this place there were only answers. This must have been something like the grace Lancelot spoke of: Collum felt weightless, enveloped in God's will, drowned in it like a bee in honey.

There would be no more fighting or struggling or hoping, only what He willed, and whatever He willed would be right. It always had been, if only he'd been able to feel it like he did now. Like a child dancing with his father.

At the far end of the chapel was an altar draped in white samite, and behind it stood a perilously thin, straight-backed old man in a mail vest that looked too big for him—it had evidently been made for a younger man, and he'd shrunk and grown old inside it. He had deep olive skin and his hair was scant, and what there was of it was short and curly and white.

Behind him a dozen slender candles floated unsupported in the air, each one as long as a man was tall. Faint, high ringing tones were audible, chiming and harmonizing. On the altar lay a long spear. Collum realized—not with self-reproach but with compassion for his old, fallible, cynical self—that until then a part of him had still been expecting some cruel trick, some divine bait and switch. But there was no trick.

The door closed behind them with a hollow boom.

"My friends. Please approach." The old man's voice was hoarse. "My apologies. It has been many years since I have spoken aloud."

Together the five of them walked the length of the chapel—but no, they were only four now. Nimue wasn't there. Collum looked around but she was nowhere in the chapel.

Wherever she is, that is where she belongs, he thought. We're in God's hands now. The four knights kneeled together in front of the altar. The spear was of a curious design, a long wooden shaft worn smooth and topped by two feet of slender black iron, slightly bent, ending in a small triangular point. From that iron point a droplet of blood trembled and then fell. The marble tiles below it were stained a rusty red.

"Do you know what this is?"

"The Holy Lance," Bedivere said.

"The spear with which I stabbed our beloved savior Jesus Christ in His side, as He hung helpless from the Cross."

"You're Saint Longinus," Collum said.

"My name was once Lucius, but yes, they call me Longinus now." The old man had a gentle manner.

"We are grateful to you," Collum said. "For waiting here for us. For welcoming us in."

It was a silly thing to say but the man was so gracious and good that Collum had to thank him for something. He thought of God's mercy, that had forgiven even Lucius-Longinus his terrible sin and raised him up to sainthood. If Lord Alasdair were here now Collum would've forgiven him in a heartbeat—that hopeless man, so gnawed from within by shame and greed that he would do anything to anyone to escape the pain. How unhappy he must have been.

"It is I who am grateful," Saint Longinus said. "You have come far and paid dearly to be here. Of late God and Britain have been estranged, but now you have come to study what I was born to teach: how broken things can be made whole, through the grace and goodness of Jesus Christ."

When he said the name a distant bell rang, and a warm wind caused the floating candles to flicker. The old saint smiled, showing white teeth.

"This spear is the last holy treasure in Britain." He touched it with one brown hand. "It was mine once, and now I will give it to you, and it will show you wonderful things. It will show you the one you seek, the rightful king of Britain."

Collum's eyes overflowed with tears. It was the sum of all his longings, all his life. Longinus took up the spear and held it balanced on his palms, gazing at it fondly as if to say goodbye.

"Will it bring Arthur back?" Bedivere asked.

A red drop fell from the spear tip onto the white samite table-cloth.

"All that should be, will be," the saint said. "Now begins the final age, a holy age, and it will last—"

The saint paused. He glanced up at the ceiling.

"It will—"

There was an odd creaking sound, as if the chapel were being shaken by a strong wind. Fine dust sifted down from the rafters.

They all looked up. A crack had opened in the masonry high up on one wall, where the timbers of the ceiling met the stone.

"I don't understand," the saint said softly. His hand wandered along the shaft of the spear, an old soldier's half-remembered reflex.

The crack in the ceiling yawned opened impossibly wide, a gust of snow blew in, and with a tearing, popping sound the roof cracked open to the night sky. Rafters splintered and Collum covered his head as a torrent of dust and slate shingles showered down. When he could look up again half the roof was gone and two huge hands like pale beasts were groping and pulling at what was left of it, tearing and crumbling it away piece by piece.

Cold and starlight rushed in. There, lit up from below with holy radiance, was the great face of the giant Ysbaddaden.

"No," Collum whispered. "No, not now."

He drew his sword. Whatever this trial was they would endure it like all the others. The saint was shouting at the giant. With an almighty bang the heavy wooden door of the church blew inward off its iron hinges so hard that it cartwheeled half the length of the room. Morgan le Fay stood in the doorway. She'd shed her deer half and become human again, garbed for war in magnificent gleaming green steel.

"Begone!" Longinus shook the spear at her. "You may not enter here!"

But Morgan did enter. She stepped into the chapel. There was a blue flash in the air around her.

"Morgan!" Collum shouted. "Please! Not now!"

"I know, I know," she said. "Don't girls just spoil everything?"

"Morgan." He was begging, but he didn't care. "You must let us have this. You must let it happen!"

"I will not. I will not let God choose the ruler of Britain. The chain of succession must be broken, now and forever. It is the chain that binds us, and we will be free of it. God's business in this land is done."

"You would defy Our Lord?" Longinus sounded more incredulous than angry.

"Your lord? That little carpenter pulled off the prank of a lifetime when he died, and you're still falling for it! He must be laughing his ass off, wherever he is. I've come for what is mine by birth."

"If the throne is rightfully yours then God will bestow it on you," Dinadan said.

"Don't patronize me, Dinadan."

"We earned this," Bedivere said.

"But my dear Bedivere, I earned it first."

Collum and Dinadan drew their swords and Bedivere unslung his hammer from across his back. Even Dagonet took a stand: the Fool Knight had produced from somewhere a short sword that seemed to be made of gold, except that its point and edges looked sharp and hard as steel, and it shone with its own light. Where the hell had Dagonet gotten a magic blade?

But Morgan looked past them at Longinus. She seemed to consider him the real threat. Ysbaddaden gazed thoughtfully down into the little church like it was a toy box full of dolls.

"You're a long way from Cappadocia, Lucius. Time to go home."

"This is God's house," the saint said, "and God's house is my home."

"You Christians have an answer for everything, don't you?" Morgan sighed. "The pageant is wearing very thin, my friends. The thousand gods have come back to Britain at last."

"God will not suffer you to trespass here any longer!"

Behind him the candle flames roared and flared into torches.

"Won't He though?" Morgan said. "Let's find out. "

She clapped and the knights' weapons fell out of their hands and hit the stone floor with a *bang*. Collum tried to pick his up but he couldn't; it was fixed to the tiles. The curse didn't appear to affect Dagonet's golden knife any, but with a wave Morgan threw him bodily sideways into the wall of the church . He stuck there.

Bedivere kept walking toward Morgan anyway, empty-handed.

"In Arthur's name," he said grimly. "Kill me if you must, but you cannot have the spear."

Bedivere reached for her arm, but Morgan threw a fistful of dust in his face, and his eyes closed and he fell backward; Collum reached him just in time to stop his head from cracking on the hard floor. He and Dinadan started for her, and Morgan opened her mouth as if to speak.

Then she stopped. In a flash her face and hair and her whole body had turned white. She'd grown a thick coat of frost.

"Leave this place."

Nimue came floating down through the torn-off roof. Morgan was still on her feet but doubled over, rubbing frantically at her frozen face.

"You can still leave unharmed." Nimue settled gently to the tiled floor.

"They wouldn't even let you in the church!" Morgan managed through numb lips.

"But it's not about me. I have treated with your gods, and for that I was kept from entering, just as Lancelot was barred from Corbenic. But I will tell you something about your gods: They are easy to love, because they are like us. They drink and fight and fornicate. My God may be harder to love, but that's because He is not like man. He is greater."

"Don't lecture me, Lady Laundry," Morgan spat. "I was educated in a nunnery. They taught me that the world is a dead place, that my body is sin, and the only life that matters is the next one. But they lied. The world is alive, and there is no other life. You know this, Nimue, I know you do."

As she said it she flicked the last of the melted frost from her face at Nimue and the drops became a torrent of green water. Nimue parted it easily with an outstretched palm—but even as she did Morgan's magic was stripping stone tiles from the floor and stacking them around her with a clacking sound. In a heartbeat Nimue was entombed like an anchorite in a marble box.

"You learned your magic from a man," Morgan said, "and he taught you much. But no man knows how to fight like a witch."

The stone box stood for one long moment, then it exploded in flying shards.

"You underestimate me." Nimue raised one hand with something shining and golden in her fist, starfire, blue light streaming out between her fingers.

"I suspect we underestimate each other," Morgan said. "We will have many more delightful arguments over the course of my long reign, but for now—"

Nimue jerked her shoulder irritably. The light in her fist flared and went out. Fairy knights became visible behind her, gripping her arms. Stepping forward Morgan produced a delicate green leaf from somewhere and brushed it across Nimue's lips. She opened her mouth but no words came out.

The fairy knights dragged her away.

The little church was filling with fairies now, crowding in through the door in every imaginable form—beast-fairies and fairy-beasts, tree-fairies, stone-fairies, a fairy made of iron, another of mist, another of parchment. Their armor was green and encrusted with strange, asymmetrical protrusions. Everywhere they stepped green plants burst up under their feet, grass and moss and shrubs, cracking the marble and popping tiles out of their places.

There were magical creatures among them, too, griffins and wyverns and others Collum didn't know the names of. Over it all the horn of the Wild Hunt sounded, and it was answered by more horns from all around the church, some higher and some lower, roaring and whistling in a thunderous cacophony. All his life Collum had known the fairies were here, hiding at the edges of things, but now they had stepped forward into the center. The great powers of the world had ceased their endless circling and were finally meeting face-to-face.

It would be a brief encounter, unless Collum was vastly underestimating Saint Longinus and his spear. He and Dinadan abandoned their cursed swords and retreated back behind the altar to join him, dragging Bedivere's sleeping body with them. The old saint kicked over the altar to make a barricade. With a practiced air he spun his spear and held it ready, waist height, two-handed.

"If you want my Lance, come and get it," he called out. "But I'll remind you that I stabbed Jesus Christ Himself with it. I won't think twice about stabbing you."

He pounded the floor once with the butt end and a shock wave flashed out, stirring dust and staggering the whole fairy host, shoving back the closest ones against their fellows behind them. At the same moment five stars kindled in the sky and then fell. When they struck they shook the earth, leaving vertical vapor trails hanging above them.

They were angels: two male and three female, two pure white, two black as ebony, and one that was all the colors of the rainbow.

They crouched with the shock of the impact, then straightened up, ten feet tall, with limbs thick as tree trunks. The rainbow angel hit the ground and rebounded into the air, wings spread wide, whipping out a fiery sword. She flew at Ysbaddaden's face like an angry wasp and slashed him across the eyes. The giant's scream sounded like the roar of a monster deep underground, echoing from a cavern. One arm pressed against his face, he fell backward over the edge of the plateau and down the mountain into darkness.

Then the angels sang all together, in unison, their voices as glorious as trumpets:

The spear is not a prize to be won! It is God's alone to bestow!

If Morgan felt in any way cowed she didn't show it.

"Hear this all of you." Her voice echoed in the ruined chapel. "The forces of Fairy, the true spirits of this land, deny you sovereignty here. You are invaders, and you are not wanted. You will leave, tonight, forever."

The heavy shape of a dragon came stooping down out of the sky and struck the rainbow angel with a resonant thump. It bore her to the ground, demolishing a wall along the way, and spat fire in her face, lighting up the night. Heedless of their fellow's fate, the remaining angels turned their calm, monumental faces to the front line of the fairy horde. They were unarmored, but they glowed like moons and dark stars. They drew their weapons—two swords, a hammer, and a staff—and golden light played on the walls.

The horn sounded again and the fairies swarmed them, crowding in out of the darkness, pouring in through the doors and gaps in the walls and gliding down from above. This wasn't a battle for mortals, but Collum was damned if he was going to stand there while they fought over the soul of Britain. He stepped up behind a fairy with a fish's head and got an arm round his thick neck, squeezing and squeezing till he dropped his fat-bladed sword.

You shall not have it, the angels sang together, their musical voices audible above the clamor. They changed from unison to harmony. *You shall not have it! Shall not! Shall not have it!* Above their heads, turning wheels and rings of letters and other symbols shifted and glinted.

"You shall not have it!" Collum shouted.

Morgan was in the air now, shouting and gesturing, and lightning struck an angel, once and then again, scratching a bright line across Collum's vision. The angel shook and spasmed, his wings smoking, but he didn't fall.

Collum moved around the fringes of the scrum, chopping and stabbing with his short, heavy sword. He cracked the blade off a boar-headed fairy's poleax, and the fairy knight charged him, and he hacked a wedge out of their thick neck. They fell clutching the wound, pale ichor gushing between their fingers. The first wave of fairy infantry was thinning out, but now the heavier fighters came forward. Five more angels shot down to earth, even bigger and brighter than the first five. These were of even higher rank, seraphim and cherubim. One of them wore a golden armor, and another was too charged with power and glory for human form, its body a grotesque mass of wings and faces and musclebound arms.

You shall not have it! It is God's to bestow!

Fire and magic and holy power lit up the snowy night in flashes. The ground dropped and rose under Collum's feet like a ship in a storm, and he wondered if Creation could withstand it all or if the whole world was about to break apart around them. He glimpsed Dinadan fighting manically against the Green Knight himself in his rusty mail and plate, holding his own better than Collum had. Behind the big fairies came beings even larger, with horns and antlers and triple faces with glowing eyes. One came swinging chains, another a burning branch, another a hammer in one hand and a chisel in the other. The god of the chains—a young woman dressed in furs, completely bald—lashed out with one, wrapped it around an angel's leg, and pulled him down. Smiling, she drew a sword six feet long from a sheath on her back.

A fairy knight came pushing through the press with long strides swinging a gigantic black sword. Silver sparks chased themselves across its blade. Here's my fight, Collum thought eagerly, but then he froze: that was no fairy, it was Sir Palomides. Reaching the front he sliced a great circle in the air and slashed at an angel, who blocked the blade with the flat of her own golden sword and grabbed for his throat. Collum's stomach clenched, but Palomides was wreathed round with fairy sorcery, deep and thick, and he brought up his shield in time, stepped in close, and chopped at one of those wide wings. Chalk-white feathers sprayed.

Space cleared around them. Collum didn't even know what he wanted to happen. The angel fought like a swan, beating Palomides with her wings, the wind scattering fallen bodies in all directions. Her oversize sword was wrought in an outlandish shape, strange curves and complex geometrical edges. She parried a cut, stepped close to Palomides, caught the edge of his shield with one hand and ripped it off his arm. She beat him to the ground with it.

The angel raised her foot to stamp on his head—but then she cried out, a sound like a tormented choir, and collapsed backward onto the ground, her leg bent awkwardly under her. Standing behind her, breathing hard, was Sir Dagonet. He held his golden knife in both hands, its blade running with what looked molten silver. He'd cut the tendons at the back of the angel's knee.

"There," he said. "See how you like it."

The angel's lip curled. Pushing herself back up to one knee, she grabbed him by his skinny leg and beat his whole body hard against the ground, once, twice, three times, like wet laundry on a rock. When she was done he lay without moving. The angel picked up the golden knife and buried it in his chest, right through him and down into the stone underneath.

She struggled to her feet, favoring one leg but already healing, ready to face off against Palomides again. But Collum kept staring at the Fool Knight's small body. For all the rage he'd felt in life, for all the indignities he'd suffered, Dagonet had probably only ever struck that one single blow in anger. That angel had never felt an instant of the wretchedness he'd lived with. She looked entirely different to Collum now. Grotesque. Angels weren't so different from the fairies, at the end of the day they were all of them monsters. They would do well to leave us humans alone. A cold rage took him. They would—

Peace.

A sun bloomed overhead.

Someone was descending from the sky. Not an angel this time but a young woman or a being with the appearance of one. Rays of light reached out from her in all directions, a rich, warm solar light different from the sidereal glare of the chapel.

Peace. A ragged section of wall collapsed. *One and all.*

She ceased her descent thirty feet above the battlefield. The fighting had paused. Everyone was watching her. They couldn't do anything else. Calmly, without hurrying, she extended a hand toward Longinus, and the spear tugged from his hands and floated up, up, up till it hung in the air by her side.

She put a hand on it as if it were an old friend, then smiled down at the broken chapel below her and all who were in it, wise and sorrowful and calm. Watching her, Collum forgot all about Dagonet and the angel. He forgot everything. He just wanted someone to set everything right. Was it too late for that?

Peace. We are all of us magic. We are all of us holy. I have come—

A great fist loomed out of the darkness and struck her full force. The sunlight was snuffed out, and the spear went spinning off into the snow.

Behind the fist, out of the shadows, came the shape of the blinded giant, Ysbaddaden, crawling, groping like a man who'd dropped a key in the dark. He found the spear where it fell, took it in both hands and bent it, grimacing, like a child with a twig. The air filled with sounds like a great sheet of metal warping and buckling, and a host of divine instruments playing climbing chromatic scales from all points of the compass. Morgan le Fay cried out something, an oath or an incantation or a warning. Longinus howled.

The Holy Lance broke in half.

The whole battlefield went white and silent, every crack, every crevice filled with radiance, annihilating all shadow. The flash clubbed Collum to his knees. The earth convulsed as though its spine had broken, and then a hot shock wave threw him hard against a wall.

His ears rang and his head throbbed. Blue afterimages pulsed in his vision. His eyes were still open but he couldn't move, his body felt numb and clumsy and drained of all strength. He couldn't think.

Then, slowly and uncertainly, his mind began reassembling it-self. Thoughts came again. Not that it mattered. He couldn't re-member at first exactly what happened, only that all urgency was gone now. Whatever it was had taken its course. There was peace.

But no, that wasn't it. Not peace. Something else. Despair. The peace of lost hope. Something had been carelessly mislaid, that could never be found again. But what? For a long time Collum just lay there with his face pressed to cold grit and stone. Then he tried to move and found that his limbs stirred, and it all came back to him.

When he could focus his eyes again it was on a scene of cold, blackened stillness. He smelled burned wood and flesh and metal. Dawn was coming on, and the ruins of the church stood out in un-even shapes against the lightening sky. Behind them loomed the rib cage of the dead giant, open to the heavens, like the skeleton of a wrecked ship on a beach.

The snow had slowed. Collum struggled to his hands and knees, coughed and spat. His chest felt hollow and sore, like he'd breathed in smoke. One of the black angels sat cross-legged on the ground nearby, her great head bowed. Her glorious wings were scorched, most of the feathers gone. She raised her head as he approached.

It is finished.

Her voice was still beautiful. It contained neither joy nor sorrow. She fixed him with her strange blank-looking golden eyes.

The spear is broken and cannot be mended.

Stiffly, shedding a few more feathers, she got to her feet. The other angels, scattered across the battlefield, rose with her at the same time. One held an extra knife—she was taking the one Dag-onet stole back up to Heaven. The rainbow angel was nowhere to be seen. Could angels die? Collum wasn't afraid or awed anymore. They were fellow veterans, that was all. Fellow losers.

"What will happen now?" he asked.

Nothing will happen, now or ever again. All the rest is empty time.

"But who was it meant for?" Collum called again, hoarsely. "Who would've won the spear?"

Your question has no meaning. That was for the spear to show, and now it never will. We cannot know what would have happened.

Without flapping her wings, as if she were lifted by an invisible thread, the angel rose silently straight up into the sky. The others went with her. They dwindled to points and disappeared.

Collum blew into his numb fingers. What now? He found himself struggling to care very much. Britain might still have a king, but not like Arthur, not like it would've been. The dead land would not live again. Instead one man would grab a gold hat from another and put it on his head, that was all. The old dream was gone, and the paths forward were winding and indistinct, lost in thickets of darkness and confusion.

Empty time, like the angel said. There would be no new age, not now or ever. The sun had moved, the shadows had shifted, and they would not move back.

Wind whistled through gaps in the ruined masonry. He needed to find the others. Dinadan sat propped against a wall, staring into space but apparently intact, with the remnants of what had been the Green Knight all around him, rusty plates and scattered branches. Collum wondered if the polecat had survived and scampered off somewhere. Nimue stood scanning the wreckage and chafing her stiff limbs, a thin, small figure, upright and whole. Thank God. Thank God, or Morgan, or Dame Fortune, whoever deserved the credit. Nimue was not lost. She still mattered. He picked his way through the wreckage toward her.

"All right?" he called, and immediately started coughing.

"I will be."

She could speak again. Together they went to Dinadan and hauled him to his feet.

"I guess Morgan won," he said.

"Morgan didn't have to win," Nimue said. "All she had to do was not lose."

It had cost her though, not losing. The bodies of dead fairies were all around them. Even as Collum watched they changed and became clumps of wildflowers, mixed in with discarded weapons and armor. Tidier than humans. Together Collum, Nimue, and Dinadan walked the length of the chapel to the broken altar. Collum found the samite cloth that had covered it, once white but now stained and trodden into the dirt. He shook it out and laid it over Dagonet's body.

He didn't even feel angry. The door to the golden world was closed forever, Morgan had slammed it shut in their faces, but he didn't see how she could've done anything else. How could any of them? They had acted according to their natures. They were all just parts in the blind mechanical engine of the world. Even God was, in the end. And then at the end of time, when the engine ran down, it would all mean something, or nothing, and they would all find out, or they wouldn't. Nothing he could do would change anything.

They found Bedivere in what was left of the nave, bending over Saint Longinus. Collum thought he might've gone up to Heaven with the angels, but the old man was sitting on a fallen stone sobbing into his hands. He'd stood guard over the lance for all those years, centuries, faithful and dauntless, and now it was all for nothing.

Bedivere had found a cloak somewhere and draped it over him.

"There you are, old soldier." He patted the saint's shoulder softly. "There you are. You can stand down now."

Thirty-one

THE TALE OF SIR SCIPIO

W here we going, chief?"

It was one of the soldiers who spoke. Scipio didn't really distinguish between them too closely, they were just *limitanei*, border troops, not regular army.

"Silence in the ranks," Scipio said.

"You go where the centurion tells you." Servius, his optio, rode at the rear.

"Maybe we're going to Rome," someone said.

That got some wry chuckles. Some of these men would certainly die for Rome. But none of them, just as certainly, would ever see it.

Scipio didn't turn around at any point during this exchange, mostly because he didn't feel like looking at his men, because his men looked like shit. Scipio was a spit-and-polish man, everything in good order, but their mail was streaked and stained with rust. Most of them didn't bother wearing helmets anymore, and the two that still did were each missing one cheek guard, which made them look ridiculous. But the smith died last winter and hadn't been replaced, and regulation army gear was hard to come by in these parlous times, in this parlous place, at the very northern edge of the very northernmost province of the Roman Empire.

Scipio looked good though, in immaculate bronze scale adorned with white leather strips and a sparkling silver-gilt helmet. He maintained his kit at his own expense and frequently with his own labor.

The company was eighteen men in all, two eight-man squads plus the two officers, Scipio and Servius, all straggling in a double file along the edge of a wide tufty field. The men walked, the officers rode. Scipio kept scanning the ridgelines. You had to keep your eyes on the edges of things, this far north of the Wall: skylines, tree lines, stone walls, the soft shadowy margins of forest.

Servius came forward to join him.

"Where, in fact, are we going?" he said more quietly. Servius had a fat face and a weird permanent squint on one side, some kind of palsy, which made him look like a fool. But Servius was a shrewd number two and nobody's fool.

"We're looking for trouble," Scipio said. "And if we can't find trouble, we'll go to Dogtown."

Scipio was a prefect and the commander of Fort Aesica, the ninth fort on the Wall, if you were counting east to west. He was much too senior an officer to be leading a raiding party but he needed some dead Picts, and if you had to kill Picts, you went where the Picts were. That was the job. And these days, in this army, if a job needed doing Scipio generally had to see to it himself.

Also he enjoyed it. Scipio had been sent to Britain to get things in order. He'd done it before in Numidia, and again in Germania. This was no different, really. They sent him wherever the borders were getting ragged. Scipio was a pure creature of empire, the quintessence of the Roman military machine. He ate barbarians, with pepper and fish sauce, and shat law and order.

They tramped along through silent meadows with their solitary oaks and alders, skirted bogs, negotiated bluffs and escarpments, tiny figures in the vast green expanse of Caledonia. They stopped at a ford in a river for lunch, but the midges were too much so they ate on the move instead. Five nights ago a Pictish warband had climbed over the wall between Aesica and Vercovicium and gone marauding from farm to farm, raping and plundering as they went, till the local garrison there chased them back north. That's not how things were supposed to work, and apparently the Picts needed reminding of that.

Around midafternoon, as they were traversing the side of a lovely hill covered in heather just starting to bloom, one of the soldiers took an arrow in the chest.

It was either a lucky shot or a very good one. Pictish arrowheads were sharp but they were made of flint and wouldn't penetrate even rusty Roman armor. But the bowman had slipped his shaft in just above the collar of the man's mail shirt at a high angle. Only the arrow's crude gray goose fletching was left exposed, like a decorative pin on his collar.

No one even noticed what had happened till the man sagged down onto his side, then rolled over on his back, groaning and stretching like a sleeper who couldn't get comfortable, and died. The other soldiers swore and edged away from him, as if arrows in chests might be contagious.

"'Ware arrows!" Scipio shouted belatedly.

"Arrows! Arrows!" Servius craned his head around to see where the attack came from. The top of the hill, pretty obviously, though they couldn't see anybody up there.

"Well?" Scipio said. "Go on! Up the fucking hill! Run! Up the hill, and I'll kill the last man to the top with my own hands!"

The men turned and started struggling uphill through the gorse, their boots slipping and sliding everywhere. What they needed were hobnailed boots, but they didn't have them, for the simple reason that you couldn't get nails anymore on this godsforsaken fuckwater island, because iron was too expensive.

Scipio urged his horse upslope after his men—she was a good hill-climber—and swung out in a wide arc to the left. He thought the Picts might run for it, because tactical retreat was article number one in the Pictish military playbook, but they chose to make a stand. Good. He would circle behind them. They sent down a few more arrows plus a flight of javelins, probably already regretting whatever rash impulse had caused them to take a potshot at a passing Roman patrol. Servius barked an order and the men dropped to their knees behind their round shields, each one bearing the gray wheel of Aesica. An arrow stuck in one shield with a hollow knock, and a javelin clanked off the metal boss of another. Then Servius got them up and running again.

These Picts were teenagers, most of them, probably grew up together in the same village, talking shit about what they'd do to the Romans one day if they ever got the chance, and now here it was. One of them even wore a looted Roman helmet. A light rain began, slicking Scipio's face. Cresting the hill, he became weightless for a heartbeat. Off to his right he heard the crash and the yells behind him as his men came over the top and bulled into the Pictish line, such as it was, shattered it like a hammer tapping glass. The yells were all Pictish; Scipio drilled his men to charge in silence, not screaming like a lot of barbarians. Silence was scarier.

The Picts were brave enough, he'd give them that. It was discipline they lacked. The Romans came on in three lines, swords and spears, while Servius and another man hung back, throwing heavy metal darts overhand. Servius was lethal with those things, and between him and Scipio and the swords and the spears, the Picts didn't know where to look.

When it was all over Scipio stood apart from his men, feeling his racing pulse settling, the high fading, as the soldiers stripped a silver pin off one of the Picts and reclaimed the looted helmet—it had both its cheek guards, for a wonder—and collected the thrown javelins from downslope. You couldn't waste anything nowadays.

But he felt good. He wouldn't even kill the last man up the hill, whoever that was. They left the corpses for the wolves, though not without first arranging one of the bodies face down on another one's crotch, so it looked like he was sucking his buddy's dick.

Now can we go home? they asked.

Now, Scipio said, we go to Dogtown.

DOGTOWN WAS A Pictish village. Scipio didn't know its real name, or why his men called it that. It was close enough to the Wall that over the centuries the Picts there had been more or less domesticated, and Scipio and his men swaggered through town, still jittery from the fight. They broke some pottery, spanked a few old people across the face with the flats of their swords, waved a burning brand around, just reminding people who's boss. Their little gang was down to sixteen now: the archer had picked off another man on his way up the hill. Mars, he'd been good. They'd buried the two men on the hillside, though Scipio couldn't even give them proper burials now, just chucked them into the raw bare ground.

Why? Because they had no coffins. *Because they had no fucking nails.*

They drank some of the brutally strong Pictish ale, which was brewed with heather, and ate some food, if you could call it that. These people wouldn't know what a fig was if it bit them on the ass. Didn't even have apples. Didn't even have fish sauce! In the damp depths of one of the dark longhouses, a couple of pale, yellow-haired Pictish women serviced them.

They left behind a few thin, clipped silver *siliquae*, three emperors out of date, bearing the words VIRTUS ROMANORUM.

Afterward Scipio went off for a ride by himself. He missed his wife. His kids would barely know him, he'd been gone so long.

A crowd of little Pictish kiddies was standing chattering around his horse, and Scipio shooed them away. They'd drawn white chalk circles on the ground around the poor thing, and on its haunches—some weird Pictish game. The rain was thickening, and his wool cloak gave off a musty smell, the pungent ghost of whatever sheep it was shorn from. He rode out of the village through the clouds of mist that flowed endlessly across the road.

Britannia was a weird place, no question. Growing up in a Mediterranean clime, Scipio never imagined in a thousand years that he would come here. Britannia was so cold and distant and insular and northerly as to be almost mythological, a miserably damp demi-realm confabulated out of gray stone and wet leaves and coarse grass. A different sun hung over Britain, a worn, debased tin version of the great golden coin that stared unblinking down at Rome.

Some people couldn't take it. The officer Scipio replaced out here, he sure couldn't. The day he arrived Scipio sat down with him for a debriefing, and the man—if you could call him that, he was one of those pussy milkwater Christians—started mumbling about the Picts and their scary guerrilla tactics and their singing and their creepy burial mounds, and finally Scipio just had to say stop. For fuck's sake. Stop. Mars Cocidius, are you listening to yourself? Get the fuck out of here. Go home. Go on. Go home and suck some Jesus dick, you're an embarrassment to the Imperial Army.

Scipio could take it. That was his job. This land cried out for Roman roads to bind it, for baths to wash its filthy people clean. It begged to be ruled into grids and planted so that its golden wheat could feed the appetite of empire. The tin moldering in its earth demanded to be freed and turned into strong Roman bronze. Spit and polish. Law and order.

The only trouble was that in a way that guy had been right, because the Picts were different. Scipio had been here two and a half years already, with the simple instructions to secure the border and spread Romanity, but for the first time in his career he hadn't been able to carry out his orders. Two and a half years since he'd seen Rome. Did his kids even remember him? Lucia might, but Linus would be only four. But the job wasn't done, wasn't even close to done.

It was hard to say exactly what it was about the Picts. They were just more Britons, after all, and the gods knew that Rome knew how to beat Britons. They did it all day long. South of the Severn-Humber line the Britons were forbidden to own swords. They spoke Latin and lived in sprawling country villas, the rich ones anyway. They'd forgotten they weren't Romans.

But Rome couldn't seem to beat these particular Britons. The Picts were spooky bastards, relics of the old times. They couldn't read or write, and they were useless as slaves, but if you tried to cross the Wall in force they would harry and ambush the piss out of you and then melt right back into the land. Caledonia ate Roman armies and shat more Picts. Eventually Rome just walled the whole place off.

Privately Scipio had a certain amount of respect for the Picts. He understood something most Romans didn't, which is that they had no idea who the Picts really were. They called them Picts because some chronicler who'd probably never even been to Britannia heard they tattooed *pict*ures on their skin, but they had their own name in their own language. A lot of them didn't even have tattoos. They left standing stones scattered around with runes and spirals carved in them, and nobody knew what they meant. Once he'd found a little carved ivory elephant in a house in Dogtown that must have come all the way from Africa.

Through a thin line of trees, smack in the middle of an otherwise empty field, Scipio spotted a mound.

He'd heard about these things—that cross-licker he'd replaced had whined about them. He left his horse cropping the grass and waded through the wet meadow toward it. The mound was maybe twenty yards high and fifty across. Roughly round, roughly symmetrical, though not quite either.

He took a running start and jogged right up it to the top. Easy-peasy. King of the castle. He stood there looking around, hands on hips, in the fog and the rain. If this thing was supposed to be a fort it was a pretty pathetic one. Though he guessed the Picts probably said that about the Wall. Rome didn't have enough men to man the whole thing, not nearly, so if the Picts wanted to go south they just found a spot with nobody on it and brought a ladder. Or they went to sea and sailed around it. Well done, Hadrian. Regular Oracle of fucking Delphi, you are.

Maybe the mound was a tomb. Maybe there was treasure here. He should come back with a few men and dig it up.

But there was something about this place, it felt not so much eerie as wild. Un-Roman. This, right here, this was the Caledonia they'd never been able to conquer. This big lump, this was the hard knot that Rome couldn't digest. It was the great heart of Britannia; he could almost feel it beating under his feet. He thought of drawing his sword and stabbing it. Take that. He would murder Britannia once and for all.

Scipio trotted down the far side of the mound but—the *fuck?!*— he missed his footing and fell the last ten feet with a high-pitched yelp. He scrambled to his feet, slapping wet grass off his backside.

There was a doorway cut into the side of the mound, and warm bronze firelight flickered inside it. There was a whole little room in there! Inside sat a woman at a table, tall and slim and pale. Her hair was red gold. She wore a rope of fine Pictish silver around her neck.

Scipio goggled at her. *This* was what they'd been missing. Caledonia had been holding out on them. He wiped cold dirt off his hands. This woman must be some kind of Pictish queen or high priestess or some such. Capture her and those sneaky Picts would bow down quick.

She was doing something at the table, it looked like metalwork. The table was strewn with tools. She turned to look at him, so quickly he almost startled.

"Who are you?" she asked, in pure Roman Latin.

Her small, pale face had swirly indigo lines on it—finally some of those famous tattoos he'd heard so much about. And her eyes were strange, they had no white and no pupil, they were a uniform indigo all across, the same color as the tattoos. But the way she looked at him, she didn't seem blind.

"Scipio Hostus," he said. "Prefect, First Cohort, Twentieth Valeria Victrix legion, is who I am. You live out here all by yourself? Where's your husband?"

"Where's your wife?"

The question took him aback.

". . . Rome?"

She tilted her head, amused.

"A prefect of Rome, nervous as a little boy. Well, come in, oh victorious one. You have work to do."

He could never explain it to himself later, but when she said that Scipio walked right into the smoky dimness of the mound and picked up a twig broom from the hearth. He'd planned on taking the woman hostage, then dragging her bound and kicking back to Aesica. But he lost track of those plans as soon as he was inside. Instead he started sweeping her floor.

It was hilarious, even to him. *If the boys could see me now!* he chuckled to himself as he swept out a corner. *Or Galla. Look, it's your fearsome husband, the Animal of Aesica, sweeping up after a Pictish queen!* They would laugh about it together. He smiled and shook his head at the thought.

After he was done Scipio chopped wood for his new mistress. He carried water from a well. He cut the grass. He drew her a bath. She never thanked him, in fact she barely took any notice of him except to give him orders and once to rap his knuckles, painfully, when he spilled water. He worked so hard for so long that finally he just lay down on the packed dirt floor and fell asleep.

He woke up outside on the grass. There were pink drifts of cloud in the morning sky. The dawn chorus was in full cry. What the hell was that? A dream? Did they slip something in his beer?

His horse was gone. It took him two hours to walk all the way back to Dogtown. When he finally got back to the Wall they said he'd been gone for three weeks. Everybody thought he was dead.

SCIPIO GOT RIGHT back to work. Whoever Madam Mound was she was right about one thing: he had work to do. And it wasn't getting any easier.

It wasn't just the Picts, there were threatening rumbles from the Scotti and the Attacotti and the Saxons and Angles across the North Sea. It was almost like the barbarians were communicating with one another somehow, if that weren't completely impossible. Meanwhile dark rumors ran up and down the Wall about what was happening on the Continent: the Visigoths shaking down the Senate for a fortune in gold and silver; the Rhine frozen over and Vandals pushing into Gaul in force. In the southlands usurping would-be emperors kept arising, and each one stripped more troops from the Wall to support his claim.

And the soldiers Scipio did have were barely even Roman. When it was first built, Fort Aesica had been garrisoned with Gauls from Belgica. Over the years they'd married and interbred with the local Britons, and then some Iberians showed up and interbred with them, and now a few centuries down the line Aesica was its own weird mongrel tribe, speaking a mongrel Latin-Belgic-Iberian-British dialect and worshipping a mongrel pantheon of Roman and barbarian gods. Sometimes he looked at his men on one side and the Picts on the other and all he saw was barbarians fighting other barbarians.

He set his men to refurbishing his local stretch of Wall, which after 250 years was nearly as old and weathered as those Pictish stones. They rebuilt the collapsed sections and cleared brush from the defensive ditches and reopened the milecastles. Scipio paid a long overdue visit to the advance fort seven miles north of the Wall that was supposed to be keeping an eye out for trouble. He found it in a sad state, with much undue fraternizing with the locals. Scipio sacked the commander and replaced him with Servius.

Every day and every night Scipio wrote urgent letters in black ink on wafer-thin slices of white birchwood. He wrote to the Dux

Britanniarum in Eboracum, and the Comes Britanniarum, and the Count of the Saxon Shore. He wrote to Londinium and Camulo-dunum and Rome itself, to any number of governors and quarter-masters and treasury officials, demanding and haranguing and pleading for food and arms and armor, and more men, and more money to pay his men. He barely slept.

It was hard to tell, because the outside world was silent, but it seemed the great imperial apparatus was not functioning as it should. It was starting to feel like Rome itself was the myth, and Britannia the reality. The only letters he got were from his wife, silver-haired, almond-eyed Galla, who spared him the news of the wider world and just told him about their little world. She wrote him about the mosaic he'd left half done in the atrium. The tiny colored cubes still lay all around the room in heaps—blues and greens, ceramic blacks and whites and reds and browns, and mar-ble for the in-between colors, the pinks and peaches and oranges. There were even a few silver and gold ones, the precious metals pounded thin and sealed under glass. The kids liked to trade them back and forth, she said, and build roads and cities with them.

She was too clever to tell him what he already knew, which was that it wasn't the mosaic, and it wasn't the empire, it was his family that needed completing.

In a desperate attempt to make payroll he raised the tolls for the traders who passed north and south through the wall. In a show of benevolence he picked a local chief at random and declared him governor of all Caledonia. In a show of confidence he had the camp's granaries expanded, to accommodate future bumper har-vests. In a show of strength he took a couple of centuries and marched on Dogtown—he'd make Servius the mayor there, see how they liked that.

But Dogtown was deserted, with human skulls set up on posts in a circle around it. He put it to the torch. Then Servius disappeared into thin air along with an entire squad of limitanei. He searched everywhere for the woman in the mound, the queen or witch or witch-queen or whatever she was, but in vain.

One morning in November, with the temperature dropping and the weather closing in, Scipio woke up to a letter from the governor, the Dux Britanniarum himself. Finally! It was the first official communication of any kind that he'd gotten in months.

It was orders. He and his officers were to return to Rome immediately, to assist in the campaign against the Visigoths. There would be no more coin coming, no more food or equipment. The limitanei could do whatever they liked. From now on Britain would look to its own defense, and good luck to it. The First Cohort, XX Valeria Victrix, was disbanded.

He stared at the little slip of wood for a long time. Then he threw it into the fire.

Those fools. Those piss-guzzling idiots. Scipio got dressed. He put on his armor and belted on his sword, threw his great officer's cape round his shoulders and donned his helmet with its white ruff a foot tall, and walked down the camp's muddy main street.

How dare they. How dare they give up. Had they forgotten that Rome had stood for a thousand years? Did they think this was the toughest scrape it had been in? Rome did not give ground. Rome would thrive and grow forever.

In something like a fugue state Scipio walked out through the East Gate and began stumping north. He knew what he was looking for. He walked for an hour, forded the North Tyne, two hours more to the advance fort where he commandeered a horse. From there he galloped even deeper into Caledonia, across roadless hills and moorlands, always north, into open country, humped and billowy meadows flocked with clumps of dark trees. A Pictish archer could've picked him off at any moment, a warband could have ridden him down, but somehow he knew they wouldn't. In his own way he'd let Britannia get to him after all. Well, he wouldn't stop until he'd gotten to it too.

That night he blundered into three Picts sitting around a fire, hunters. He threw himself on them out of the darkness with just a knife in his hand, stabbed one man in the guts, folded him over where he was, then beat another's sword strike up and over his head and bulled into him. Their momentum took them over the edge of a gulley, down a slide of wet leaves and into a rushing stream below, where he cut the man's throat, hot blood in the cold water.

The third Pict was covered in eczema or something that made his skin blotchy, and when he saw Scipio rise from the stream he ran, but Scipio threw a rock and hit him in the back of the head. Knocked him down for long enough that he could run up and stab him in the back. *Dominus nobiscum. Roma invicta.* He wasn't even frightened. Death would not touch Scipio Hostus, not today, not till his work was done. It was not permitted. It was contrary to regulations. That night he drank from cold pools thick with floating leaves and slept rough and shivering on the ground.

When he found the mound again he wept with relief.

Was it the same one? It looked the same, but this one had no door. He walked all the way round it three times but it was smooth and featureless. The heart of Britannia was closed to him.

Despair cut his knees out from under him and he fell to the grass. A cold drizzle began, sweeping in slack white lines across the flat, misty country. He stayed there he didn't know how long, head bowed, water running off his nose. *Let me in.* He almost prayed to it. *Please. Let me in. Please. I need you. I've been looking for you for so long.* He knelt for hours, till his knees ached, clenching his jaw to keep it from chattering.

When he looked up again the woman was there.

He was suddenly aware of how filthy he was. He was wet through and covered in dirt and blood and snot. He'd lost his helmet and he had leaves in his hair. She was as beautiful and composed as ever, with beads of mist in her red-gold hair like seed pearls and those strange eyes and that heavy silver rope around her neck. He was the one who looked like a damn barbarian. He dragged a forearm across his face and stared up at her with angry, bloodshot shame-eyes.

"Poor baby." She sounded amused. "Well, come on then."

He huddled by her fire, shuddering and rocking as he warmed up. When he had some strength back, he gathered himself and got to his feet, but before he could speak she slapped him across the face so hard he tasted blood. He raised a disbelieving hand to his face and she slapped him again, then knocked him down with her small, sharp fist.

Satisfied, she turned and strode out the door. She was gone for hours, but for all that time Scipio didn't move. He understood that he wasn't allowed to, and that she would know if he did, and punish him further.

When she returned she pointed to the broom, and he got up and swept the floor. Then he washed her dishes and built up the fire and brought her wine. Just like last time he did whatever she told him, though it didn't seem as funny now. He served her day after day, he lost track of how long. He worked the bellows as she forged and shaped things. If he was slow to obey her she hit him, sometimes with her hand, sometimes with a stick. Sometimes she had guests, strange ones, fairies and animals, emperors and corpses and stones and trees, and he waited on them, too, in the most servile manner possible, and ate the scraps they dropped on the floor.

All he could think was that if he served her well enough perhaps she would come with him like he wanted, back to Rome. He would parade her through the streets to remind everyone that there is nothing Rome cannot take, nothing it cannot control. Why not? How could she not want what Rome had to offer? Writing and money and glass and fish sauce? Rome was the whole world. How could she not want to be part of it?

AND THEN ONE DAY he came to himself as if from a deep sleep. He remembered who he was. She was absorbed in her metalwork. Smoothly he snatched a sharp tool from her table and stabbed her in the back, aiming for a kidney.

The blade broke against her pale skin. She laughed.

"What are you?!" He threw the broken blade into the fire. "Witch? Fairy? God?"

"There is no word for what I am." She kept working, twisting wire with her nimble fingers. "I was here long before you Romans came. Before the Picts, before even the fairies. I was here when the lush plains of Doggerland stretched all the way across the North Sea. And I will be here when the seas run dry."

"You will come with me now." He swallowed. "Now. To Rome." Scipio grabbed her wrist and pulled with all his strength, but she barely seemed to notice.

"Ten thousand horses couldn't move me from this place," she said, "because I am this place."

"Then one man will do it. I will drag you through the streets of Rome."

"Oh, you don't want to go there." Now she rose, picked up a stick of firewood and smacked him across the face with it. She broke it over his head and he fell down with stars dancing across his vision. "Rome is burning. Even as we speak Visigoths are sacking the Eternal City and putting whole families to the sword."

Lies. Sick lies. Whole families . . . how dare she. She reached into the fire and took out the broken knife—the heat didn't touch her—and did something to make it whole again. Then she crouched over him and began to draw searing lines of pain on his body and on his face with the hot blade. He couldn't move.

"For all the days you've stood on your wall, you still don't understand what it means. The wall is death. An empire that builds its walls in stone has stopped growing. And an empire that is not growing is dying."

She spoke over his screams.

"One day you will see that it is a mistake to love an empire, or a throne, or a crown, because those things cannot love. They can only die."

She took his chin in her hand and turned his burning face one way, then the other. Satisfied with her work, she beat him with the stick till he passed out.

He woke up outside on the grass. He sat up, rubbing his mouth and slapping the leaves out of his hair. It was November when he went into the mound, but now it was warm out. Could he really have slept the whole year round, from winter to summer?

He set off south for the Wall at a jog. He felt strangely light. Whatever else the woman from the mound had done to him, she'd broken the spell Britannia put on him. He was done. He could go now. He'd lingered too long on this enchanted isle, he saw that clearly now. He was a good soldier, and if Rome needed him to go home then home he would go. Back to Aesica, and from there to Eboracum, Londinium, and Dubris, where he would take ship for Rome. Where his wife and his children were waiting. He could still make up for lost time. It wasn't too late.

It wasn't till he reached the Wall that he understood what had happened. The great double doors of the East Gate stood open, and someone would get a good lashing for that. But no, they weren't open, the doors were gone. The roofs of Aesica's long barracks were sagging, and it looked like one of the granaries—so recently expanded—had fallen in. Grass swamped the base of the walls like drifted snow, and the well was overgrown with lilac and honeysuckle. The Wall curved away into the distance in both directions, broken and uneven, like the spine of a dragon long dead and turned to stone.

He'd been gone for a hundred years. Rome had fallen, and everyone he'd ever loved was dead.

LATER SCIPIO WOULD make his way south, and he would find a new ruler to serve, new laws to enforce, and new order to spread. He could never quite bring himself to join the Round Table, because once you've seen an empire fall you can never look at another one quite the same way again. All you can see is ruin. But his old Roman manners and military bearing marked him out as a man of importance, one of the right sort, and his bravery was famed all over Britain, for truly it was said of Sir Scipio that he fought as if he cared not whether he lived or died.

BOOK IV

THE
SAXON SHORE

Yet some men say in many parts of England that
King Arthur is not dead, but had by the will of
our Lord Jesu into another place; and men say that
he shall come again, and he shall win the holy cross.
I will not say it shall be so, but rather I will say:
here in this world he changed his life.

—*Le Morte d'Arthur*, Thomas Malory

Thirty-two

GALAHAD

It took them a week just to get down out of the mountains. The steel road was gone, and they had to pick their way through a steep, pathless, broken country of plunging cliffs, high wind-swept plateaux, and valleys choked with tumbled, ankle-breaking boulders. They would've died without Nimue, who made magical fires out of sodden bracken and diplomatically encouraged chilling squalls of rain and sleet to move on when it got too wet. Once or twice she ensorcelled a trembling deer to approach and stand still and be slaughtered.

She regarded her handiwork with glum satisfaction.

"At least I still have magic," Nimue said. "Though I'll be really disappointed if the great lesson of my life turns out to be that Morgan was right."

"I never cared about any of it," Bedivere said. "All I ever cared about was getting Arthur back."

When you were inside them adventures happened slowly, but the aftermath of a failed adventure was even slower. On the journey out they'd walked in a dream, pulled on by the quest, driven by their divine purpose, but now they just trudged. It was not a path to glory, or to anywhere really, it was just a lot of cold gray mountains in northern Pictland.

They didn't talk much, though there were plenty of things they urgently needed to talk about. Collum wondered if Morgan would keep pressing her claim now that the spear was broken. He wondered whether Constantine had managed to pry Lancelot out of his monastery after all. It was time to pick a new side and make more plans. It wasn't over, the millstone of history would keep turning till it had ground them all to fine dust that would blow away in the wind.

God's teeth, he thought a lot of crap when he was tired. They'd been walking for too long.

At a dour Pictish settlement built up against the ruins of the Antonine Wall they bought four horses for five times what they were worth and rode south, through Strathclyde and the Royaume Sauvage. They crossed the southern Wall at Banna. After another week Collum began to notice familiar landmarks. They'd picked up the same path he'd followed on his first trip south from Mull.

"Great," Dinadan said. "You can give us a tour of the finer coastal haystacks."

They passed churches, and ruined Roman temples, and pagan shrines, and stone circles, but they didn't stop. Let the gods play whatever games they wanted, or no games at all. Their playthings were tired out.

One morning they crossed a matted brown meadow. A crooked ash tree stood there. From a branch hung a weather-beaten old shield. Bedivere stopped.

"Look at that."

The meadow looked very different than it had in summer. The

long grass was bent and brown and dead, the ash tree bare but for its velvety black winter buds. But Collum knew that shield because he was the one who'd hung it there. Most of the white paint had worn and peeled away.

"Azure, three Scepters, a Chevron Or," Bedivere said. "That was Sir Bleoberys of the Wilderness."

"It was?" Collum thought he was past surprise at this point.

"Old Blueberries himself. I never thought to discover his end."

Collum nudged his horse forward, close enough that he could reach up and touch the weathered old leather that covered the shield. Could it be true? Was that the mystery of the uncouth knight? He'd come south looking for Sir Bleoberys, and he'd killed him instead.

Scipio was right, Dame Fortune did have a peculiar sense of humor.

"I wonder what happened," Dinadan said.

"I can tell you some of it," Collum said. "Because I was there."

It was his last secret. Nobody looked especially shocked when he told them, but only because nothing shocked them anymore.

"I'm impressed," Dinadan said. "Bleoberys was a hard man to beat. Beautiful form."

"I don't think I saw him on his best day," Collum said.

"Bleoberys wouldn't have acted like that, though. He wouldn't've said those things." Bedivere dismounted and squatted over the grave that Collum had dug with such effort. You could still see it: the ground was sunken, the grass a different color. "He had a soft heart—sentimental, in the Frankish way. Used to cry at old songs. But you never met a more courtly knight."

"It could've been an impostor," Dinadan said. "Someone fighting with his arms, in his harness. You never saw his face?"

"No."

"Maybe the news of Arthur's death drove him mad," Nimue said.

"Mad or not, he was carrying the medal of Saint Longinus." Collum still had the thing, for all the good it did them, and now he fished it out from under his breastplate. "So in a way he died for a purpose. Though it didn't matter much in the end."

"No, it didn't." Dinadan rubbed his chin. "But it's strange, you meeting him like that. Must've meant something."

But no one knew what. Maybe not everything meant something; certainly the available evidence strongly supported that conclusion. They rode on, and at sunset they stopped at the Two Moons, the very same inn where Collum passed a sleepless night before he came to Camelot.

He half expected to see Morgan le Fay tending bar, but there was only the innkeep with his thinning red hair. Collum would've welcomed a quiet dinner, lamb stewed with onions and a cup of sour wine to go with it, but the moment they walked in every eye was on the three road-spattered knights of the Table and their lady companion.

A lanky young man with big front teeth popped up from a bench.

"Is it Sir Bedivere?"

He had an easy smile. The stare Bedivere leveled back at him would have frozen most men where they stood, but he was either dauntless or oblivious because he kept right on talking. He looked about Collum's age, though Collum felt centuries older.

"We've orders to take you up to the castle, my lord. Soon's you get here."

"Whose orders?"

"The king's, my lord."

He had a companion with him, shorter and broader but equally young and smiley, with a head of brown ringlets. Both wore red-and-white livery, not the azure and gold of Camelot.

"Well then," Bedivere said wearily. "If the king wishes it, let it be done."

It was a still, cold night, but high overhead a wind was sweeping gray clouds briskly past. This was a surprise, but Collum wasn't sure yet what kind of surprise.

"We've been looking for you," Curly Hair said. "Everybody has. For months now."

"We didn't realize we had an appointment," Nimue said. "But since you mentioned him, who exactly is the king of Britain these days?"

"Who's the king?" The two men looked at each other, unsure if they were supposed to laugh. "Of Britain?"

"We've been gone a while."

"You mean—what's his name?" Curly Hair said. "It's Galahad. King Galahad."

"God's balls," Dinadan said. "Really?"

The lanky one gave him a sharp look.

"The king frowns on swearing, my lord. He's very devout."

"I've heard that about him."

"Very strict about the fast days too. He is a great champion of our lord—he's been converting pagans by the hundreds. Marches them into the Thames to be baptized en masse."

"All due respect to the king, of course," Collum said, "but we thought Galahad was dead."

"So he was, my lord, but he's come back. God returned him to us. It's a miracle."

"A miracle!" his companion said. "Praise God!"

"But he'll tell you himself. He's asked to see you personally."

Collum thought it over as they walked. Was it really possible? But why shouldn't it be? Why shouldn't Galahad be back from the dead and seated on the throne of Britain? It wouldn't be the most unlikely development of the past year. Or the worst. He might be a bit of a holy joe but by all accounts Galahad was the greatest knight who ever lived, the most virtuous, the most puissant. God had taken Galahad, and now in their hour of need He'd returned him.

But of course: this was always how the quest was supposed to end. It seemed obvious in retrospect. Whatever the angel said, this must be what would've happened if they'd claimed the spear. They'd tried their utmost, and they'd seen the blood of their fellows shed, and now God in his mercy had forgiven them their failure. God knew it was as hard won as any victory.

The others all knew Galahad, but Collum had only heard the stories of an aloof, inscrutable, indefatigable boy wearing white armor. *Magic boy*, Palomides would've said. And now he'd been to Heaven and back.

Collum's eyes had been dry ever since the Battle of the Spear, even since Sir Scipio died, but the sight of Camelot in the moonlight, cradled tenderly in the crook of the glistening river Brass, was enough to make them prickle with tears. It looked as perfect as a toy castle, gleaming with a few tiny yellow lights—a torch was lit in the very highest chamber of the Godsfall. He'd been so hopeful and so foolish the first time he'd seen it. Now he just wanted to get there and fall into bed in his tidy solar.

At the Gate of Three Queens their escorts whistled for a groom, who took their horses. The guards requested their swords and

Bedivere's hammer. Bedivere looked at them with cold contempt, but the request was repeated, and in the end they handed them over.

They were then escorted by a heavyset steward not to the Great Hall, or to the throne room, or to their own rooms, but to a private chamber Collum had never seen before. It was large and almost totally without adornment, just a row of torches on stands against the wall and a long, striped runner down the middle of the stone floor—red and white, Galahad's colors—leading to a throne. Though really it was just a large wooden chair, finely made but bare of any ornament. Collum wondered if King Galahad would still want the Round Table, or if that was too fancy too. A fire burned contentedly in the fireplace.

"In his humility," their escort explained, "the king eschews any trappings of luxury or excess."

"Good-o," Dinadan said. "Speaking of chewing, I'm starved. We never got our dinner at the Two Moons."

The man bowed and disappeared and came back with wine and a tray of fruit and cheese and bread. Shortly afterward the king himself entered, unannounced, through a rear door. He was dressed plainly apart from his crown and the red cloak of office in the Roman style—he hadn't eschewed those. He was accompanied by a moody, glowering boy in black and silver. It took Collum a moment to recognize Sir Melehan, Mordred's son, who'd made such a dramatic entrance at the feast after the battle of Camelot. Will wonders never cease.

But the king was even more of a surprise.

"No," Bedivere said.

"You're kidding me," Dinadan said.

"My friends," said Lancelot. "You are welcome at Camelot."

Collum could almost have laughed. Almost. Fate certainly had an artistic touch where Lancelot was concerned, and once again it had produced him out of nowhere, like one of poor Dagonet's sleight-of-hand tricks.

"I don't think I understand," Bedivere said coldly.

"I know how you feel." Lancelot smiled his familiar weathered smile. "Believe me."

"I don't believe a word you say."

"Well, I can't make you. Even a king can't make a man believe something. Or stop believing it either. Some useful royal wisdom I've acquired." He took his place on the throne. "But I'm sure the rest of you would be interested to know why I'm wearing Arthur's crown and using my dead son's name."

"Those were two of the questions that have crossed my mind, yes," Nimue said.

"But first, you all know Sir Melehan, yes? Mordred's son?"

The last time they'd met Melehan the boy had been full of sardonic wit, but now he looked subdued and sulky.

"I'm glad to see you all, for any number of reasons," Lancelot said, "but one of them is that you're the only people in Britain I can talk to about everything that's happened. Everybody else is either too terrified of me or too reverent or both."

Lancelot did look exceedingly royal. The power sat lightly on him—he handled it as easily as he did a blade. Melehan fidgeted and his face was flushed, as if his collar were too tight.

"First things first, I really am Galahad. I've been him all along. Lancelot was just a nickname, a family joke that stuck. I was baptized Galahad, but nobody ever called me that. I don't know how Elaine even found out about it when she named our son.

"I never thought about it, but it came up again when they

crowned me—yes, I'll get to that too. The archbishop insisted on using my baptismal name, and so that became my regnal name. I never liked 'Lancelot' anyway, *ancelot* is an old-fashioned Frankish word for servant, so *l'ancelot*—you see what I mean. It wasn't an affectionate nickname.

"And yes, obviously, it helped me with the people. Of course it did. Right away there were rumors everywhere that I really was the other Galahad, the perfect knight, back from the dead to succeed Arthur on the throne. I corrected whoever would listen, but like I said: when people want to believe something even the king can't stop them. It's just too good a story.

"Though they must wonder what I got up to in Heaven that I came back looking twenty-five years older.

"I'm telling the story backward, I know, but you can guess the rest of it. Constantine came back to Hoxmead. He'd been to Amesbury to look for Guinevere, but she was gone by the time he got there. At first I said no, but he was persistent, and by then we could see that things were going from bad to worse. The monastery was taking in refugees and fending off raiders and warbands day and night. I felt selfish hiding away and trying to pray my way into Heaven while Britain was dying. What did my own salvation matter compared to that? And then when you were so long coming back from the quest . . . I had to do something. I couldn't stay there."

"Where is Constantine?" Collum asked.

"Cornwall. Trying to persuade them that they have a High King again. But come eat. We've got a lot to catch up on."

"Sounds like it!" Nimue said.

They waited while Lancelot cut some cheese and a slice of apple; nobody could eat before the king did. It was the first time Collum had seen him eat anything other than lettuce. After that Dinadan tucked in, and Collum poured himself some wine. Why not. They were home, and Galahad was really Lancelot, but they could've done a lot worse. They could've had Morgan or Rience or half a dozen other pretenders. So here's to King Lancelot. And here's to good Sir Constantine—they should've listened to him. If they had they could've turned back after the Rainbow Tournament. Scipio and Dagonet would still be alive, and Palomides wouldn't be in thrall to Morgan le Fay.

He felt a little drunk.

"And what brings you here, Sir Melehan?" Dinadan asked politely.

"I was already here, if you remember. In a cell. Lancelot let me out."

"He has formally renounced his claim to the throne and endorsed mine," Lancelot said. "In return for which I made him king of Orkney."

"That was generous," Nimue said.

"Yes," Melehan said, "Lancelot has pointed that out. Many times."

"Orkney needed a king, and Melehan is Morgause's last surviving descendant," Lancelot said. "It simplified things. Mercy felt like the wisest course."

"It almost makes up for his killing all four of my uncles."

And Collum had no doubt that, as Melehan once observed, the blood of the Pendragons comes in handy. He wondered if Melehan looked like his royal grandfather.

"What happened to King Rience?"

"Dead. As soon as the Franks found out there was already a Frank on the throne they cut off his coin. What was the point? We caught him at Wallsend trying to take ship for Saxony. He demanded a trial by combat, which I granted him."

No need to ask how that turned out.

"And what about Londinium?" Nimue asked.

Apparently Londinium loved King Galahad. They welcomed him rapturously as the last hero of the Age of Arthur. People love a redemption story. And that was that. Welcome to the Age of Galahad.

"But I'm talking too much. Tell me your news."

Dinadan told Lancelot the story of their quest and how it had ended. When he was done Lancelot sat down on his throne again, rubbing his chin, and quizzed them sharply on the condition of Morgan's army after the Battle of the Spear. It was late and Collum was tired, and his attention drifted, slipped its mooring and washed out to sea. The quest was over, they were back home safe, and it was all for nothing, but everything had worked out anyway, more or less. In the end they'd made no contribution whatsoever. They could've stayed home for all the difference it made.

Though who knows, maybe things would've gone differently if they hadn't. *We cannot know what would have happened.* He wondered if even God knew, or whether the realm of Might-Have-Been was hidden from His mighty prying eyes. Collum stared into the fire, letting it blur into points and smears of light, letting the others talk.

"Collum?"

Lancelot was focused on him with his characteristic intensity, and Collum snapped awake like he'd been caught dozing in church.

"Yes?"

"In the Chapel of the Spear, did God speak to you personally? Or was it just Saint Longinus?"

"Just Longinus." That was a good memory, right up until Ysbaddaden ripped the roof off. "God never spoke. There were angels there during the battle, though, and they spoke. Or sang. And at the end a woman appeared, floating down out of the sky in a sort of golden glow. She wore a robe. I imagine she was a saint too. Being in the chapel made me think of what you said at the monastery, when you talked about doing miracles."

Lancelot nodded, breathing deeply, like a great wave of emotion was passing through him, almost too big to contain.

"I wish I'd been there," he said. "I would've stopped Morgan. I would never have let them break the spear."

"I don't think even you could have stopped it," Nimue said. "Not even the angels could."

"I could have."

His voice was different now—this was the other Lancelot speaking, not King Galahad, the real one, who'd been raised by the Lady of the Lake and then killed her. Or maybe King Galahad was the real Lancelot now. Who was to say? Lancelot picked up a poker and resettled the logs in the fire. Collum fancied himself a good judge of when someone was going to hit him—most people will shift their shoulders, reset their feet—but Lancelot was utterly relaxed and at rest right up until the moment he swung the hot poker at Collum's head.

It was Bedivere who saved him. He'd never once dropped his guard since they walked in the door. He caught the blow on his thick forearm—he'd have a bruise there and a burn on top of the bruise. Collum ducked a second swing that just nicked his shoulder.

"Shit!" Nimue began a spell but Lancelot dumped the cheese off a round silver tray and whipped it sidearm at her like a discus. It caught her square on the bridge of the nose, and she went down on her knees, her hands over her face.

"What are you doing?!" Dinadan shouted.

"I knew it," Bedivere said. "I always knew it."

Lancelot was standing on the runner, and Bedivere snatched it up and yanked on it hard, hoping to jerk him off his feet, but he leapt off just in time. God dammit, Collum thought, why couldn't they rest for a little? Why did everything good have to turn to shit so fast? He tried the door but it was barred from the outside.

Lancelot flourished the poker at them.

"Why did you come back? You could've run to Orkney, Hibernia, anywhere but here."

"This is our home," Bedivere said.

"It was," Lancelot said. "Best prepare yourself for Hell, Bedivere."

"I've made peace with who I am. Can you say the same?"

With a snarl Sir Melehan leapt onto Lancelot's back with a stubby knife in his hand. Lancelot barely looked at him as he caught the boy's wrist with one hand and wrapped a steely arm around his neck. He squeezed and twisted. There was a muffled pop like a root snapping underground. He let the boy drop to the floor.

"There," Lancelot said. "Didn't spill a drop."

The last of the Pendragons, Collum thought numbly. King Melehan of Orkney. God rest him, the poor child deserved better. With his eyes he ransacked the room for anything he could use as a weapon. Dinadan was wrapping a tablecloth round his shield arm as a makeshift buckler.

"What do you think really happened to Arthur?" Lancelot said. "Was it the wheel of fate that brought him down? Or me, or Guinevere, or Mordred? Sins of the father? Nonsense. I loved Arthur but he was a damned fool and a worse Christian."

"Least he wasn't a fucking liar," Nimue managed from the floor. "And a child killer."

"If you thought about it for even a minute, even a minute, you would see I have no other choice!" Lancelot actually sounded exasperated to the point of tears. "Arthur's Britain was broken, a land not even God could love. Galahad's Britain will be whole. And better than whole, it will be pure. Please, it's all so painfully obvious, when you just bother to think it through! I'll roll it all back, finish what the Romans started. Convert the pagans, demolish the temples, pull down the standing stones. Do the thing properly. If Arthur had had the grit to do it then we wouldn't be here! But he was always too weak.

"And when I'm done God will come back. That is the adventure."

It was like he could barely see them. In his mind it had all already happened. Compared with the glory that was coming they were a minor detail.

"Put a sword in my hand, coward," Collum said.

"I think not." Lancelot wagged the poker at him. "Take it as a compliment if you like."

Bedivere advanced with murder in his eyes. Dinadan picked up one of the wrought-iron torch stands and hefted it, doing his best to hold it like a pole arm though it was much too long and heavy. Nimue had both hands over her nose and was trying to sit up. Outside, somewhere far away, Collum heard a woman shouting, but he couldn't make out the words.

Dinadan circled to Lancelot's right so Collum went left, collecting a short broom from the hearth, which he would do what with exactly? Dinadan was trying to wiggle the torch out of the torch stand, but it was stuck. Lancelot fell back behind his throne as they came on.

"Don't forget that I've only ever lost one fight in my life," Lancelot said, "and that was to the other Galahad."

"Your victories were God's doing, Lancelot," Bedivere said. "Daddy's not here to help you now."

"God has turned His back while I do what must be done, but when it's over He'll return. Nimue, I'll spare your life in exchange for one favor: let Merlin out."

"Bugger yourself." Her voice was muffled by her cupped hands. Something large flickered by the windows, an owl maybe.

"Help me and you walk free. You once boasted of your faith in God, show it now."

She showed him her middle finger. Dinadan finally got the torch loose and threw it whirling at Lancelot's face. Collum and Bedivere charged.

In an instant Lancelot became a many-armed god of war. His speed was not inhuman but it was the absolute limit of what a human could achieve. With no sign of effort, not the slightest wasted movement, he dropped his poker, snatched the torch in flight by the handle and whipped it one-handed behind his back and straight into Collum's face. Catching the falling poker on the point of his toe, at its midpoint, like a juggler, he kicked it back up into Bedivere's forehead hard enough to snap his head back. Dagonet couldn't have done it any neater.

He high-kicked Dinadan in the chin and plucked the rebounding poker out of the air. Dinadan staggered and fell down sideways. Lancelot stepped over him and was closing on Nimue when the fire crawled out of the fireplace like a giant spider and embraced him.

"Go!" Nimue shouted, to the knights or the fire or both, one hand still on her nose. Whatever spirit lived in a hearth fire, she'd somehow coaxed it into joining the fray. Lancelot scrambled back, slapping at his smoking clothes. The fire followed him, expanding, growling with pleasure at being released from its fireplace. Moving slowly, half stunned, Bedivere seized another of the heavy torch stands and slammed it butt-first against the door as a battering ram. The noise was loud enough to wake the whole castle. Collum added his weight to Bedivere's and when they rammed it again something broke and the door shuddered open.

"Fire!" Collum shouted. "Fire! Save the king!"

Bedivere went back in and came out half dragging Dinadan and Nimue, one under each arm.

"I'm fine!" Nimue said, struggling out of his grip, though she sounded like she had a heavy cold.

They stumbled down the nearest hallway, then reversed course when they saw guards advancing three abreast and charged down another one. The castle was coming alive. They could hear Lancelot shouting behind them. The fire wouldn't confuse them for long. Bedivere led them down a punishingly steep spiral staircase, then back up it when they met soldiers coming the other way. They climbed till they burst out onto a high parapet.

The night was wild but clear, with a cool wind scouring the walkway and a generous slice of yellow moon overhead.

"Nimue!" Collum said. "Can you fly us out of here?"

"I don't think so." She had a thick, dark purple line of bruise across the bridge of her nose and two developing black eyes. Dinadan was still working his jaw with one hand.

"Why not?!"

"Because it's not that simple! It's the wrong wind!"

Bedivere picked up a loose building stone and heaved it back down the stairs the way they'd come. He was rewarded with a distant cry of dismay. He picked up another one.

"How long will that fire-thing hold Lancelot?" Collum said.

"As long as it feels like it. So not long."

"Soldiers." Dinadan pointed. There were men-at-arms at the far end of the wall with bows and spears, standing watch, the wind tearing at their torches in the darkness. They hadn't seen them yet. "Nimue, get us out of here! Somehow!"

"Let me think!" Biting her lip, Nimue leaned over the parapet and studied the drop to the grass far below with furious concentration.

They were trapped, Collum thought. And they didn't even have swords. It was looking very much like the end. But really hadn't that been true for a while now? He'd done everything possible to keep from admitting it, but this fight was already well and truly over. The king was dead, the Table shattered, the spear broken. They were like sleepy children who begged for the story to keep going, but there was no more story.

Bedivere threw another stone down the stairs, but this one came flying right back up. Lancelot sprang up after it.

"Ho there! Traitors here!" He was calling over their heads to the guards at the far end. "Secure the parapet!" And more quietly. "Nimue, my offer stands. Give me Merlin and you go free."

"And the others?"

Lancelot shook his head. He'd doffed his crown and armed himself with his sword. Arondight, Collum thought, that was Lancelot's sword's name—a fairy word, he never knew what it meant. It had belonged to a Gaulish king who'd raised it in anger at a dryad, whereupon lightning struck it and killed him.

"And where would I go?" Nimue's tone was acid. "To Cornwall? Like Constantine?"

"That's fair. Constantine is dead."

"He believed in you!"

"He believed in Lancelot. Not King Galahad."

They took their stand, three knights and a wizard, but it was no fight. The only man alive who could've beaten these odds was Lancelot, and he was on the other side. They would see Constantine soon enough.

"Hold," Lancelot called to the men-at-arms. "I'll take them."

Time slowed down and thickened. It took on an almost unbearable intensity—the whole rest of Collum's life that he would never live, all its richness and meaning, were being compressed and forced into these few heartbeats he had left. He felt everything: the smell of the night wind, the tingling sixth sense that told him Nimue was nearby, the complicated shapes in the stars above, a stand of reeds in the distance on the bank of the river Brass. There was the wall with the heavy dark ivy spilling down it that he'd seen on his first day here. He felt not just the roughness of the stone parapet but the satisfaction of the mason who'd cut the stones, his callused hands, the good meal he'd enjoyed when the day was done, his grateful sleep that night.

Such was the magic of death. Everything he must do, he must do now or never at all. Everything he must say.

"Arthur!" he shouted. "King Arthur!"

"Arthur's dead," Lancelot said wearily—*God give me patience.*

But he wasn't dead. In that moment Collum knew it. Bedivere was right, he was not gone, only sleeping, sleeping on the faraway Isle of Avalon. Collum would shout loud enough to reach all the way there and wake him up.

"Arthur!"

"Collum."

"King Arthur! Arthur!"

"Collum!" Nimue grabbed his arm urgently.

Lancelot twitched Arondight, batting something away, a thin stick that clattered on the stones. An arrow. He was staring over Collum's shoulder.

Something big had appeared in the night sky, over the towers and peaks of Camelot, coming on fast. It was a boat, scudding out of the darkness, heeled way over against the wind, its sails taut and full. Its keel clipped a rooftop, spilling slate shingles, and kept going. Its lone pilot was silhouetted against the moon. She was steering with her knees and had a bow in her hands.

Collum thought panic had unhinged him, but the others saw it too.

"Shoot her!" Lancelot shouted to the guards. He took advantage of the distraction and made a lightning thrust for Bedivere's side, but the old knight sidestepped, barely—the blade slit his tunic— and Collum snapped out of it in time to snatch up the arrow and try to poke Lancelot's eye out with it.

"Get in!" a woman yelled. "For God's sake, get in!"

It was the same woman's voice he'd heard shouting before, in the king's chamber. He knew it but couldn't place it.

"Get in!" the voice shouted. "I'm not stopping!"

With a solid crunch the boat ran aground on the walkway, crushing a section of parapet ten yards away. Its hull scraped forward across the stone, wood groaning, the wind straining at the sails trying to pull it free again. Collum threw his arrow-sword in Lancelot's face and broke for the ship.

"Come on!" Nimue was already vaulting nimbly in, Dinadan right behind her. Collum felt Lancelot's fingers just graze his elbow. He kept running. The ship scraped free of the parapet and surged forward just as Collum leapt. For an instant he was in empty air, a hundred feet up, then he landed with both feet on the transom and balanced there wide-eyed, windmilling his arms backward, till Dinadan caught his hand and yanked him in.

Looking back Collum saw Bedivere facing Lancelot empty-handed and had a sickening memory of watching from the steel road as Scipio faced the fiend. Silhouetted against the stars the big knight stepped in past a thrust with unexpected speed, hooked a foot behind Lancelot's leg and pushed him stumbling back with a hand on his chest. The boat wheeled around, its sails luffing madly, and as it came in for a second pass Bedivere took one running step and hurled himself over the broken battlements. For a frozen moment he hung spread-eagled in midair—

The ship lurched as he caught the stern with his strong right hand. Collum, Dinadan, and Nimue all frantically grabbed at his wrist and the shoulders of his tunic. Collum took one look down and squeezed his eyes shut. After an eternity of panicky struggling they finally dragged Bedivere up into the boat, and all four of them collapsed in a heap in the narrow bottom, panting.

The woman at the helm surveyed her passengers coolly. Arrows rattled against the hull, and one glanced off the mast.

"Ready about." She shoved the tiller hard to port, the boom swung over, and the sail filled on the other side. The ship curved sharply away over the treetops.

"And away we go," said Queen Guinevere.

Thirty-three

THE QUEEN

I t wasn't a big boat, maybe twenty-five feet long, curved up at prow and stern, with a single mast. The fishing boat that took Collum to the mainland from Mull was bigger. This one looked like it was built for lake sailing, or at best hugging the coast. It definitely wasn't built to fly or be shot at with arrows, but somebody had ensorcelled it into the air by main force.

Collum managed to climb out of the bottom and onto a seat. He was panting like a fish fresh from the net, dizzy with the fact that he was still alive, still alive and looking up at the sail and at the stars in a magnificent mess above them. He laughed, a little hysterically.

Guinevere hauled on a line and the ship nosed up even higher into the sky. Wind gusted and tore at the rigging, snapping and rattling it. They'd doubled back, and the roofs and towers and courts of Camelot were pouring past below them. A few more arrows rapped and scratched at the hull, but they were too high up for any real danger. The queen hiked out fearlessly on the windward side, a tall, thin woman in her early forties, all long arms and legs. Collum took an unsteady knee more or less in front of her and bowed his head.

"Your Majesty." He remembered too late that she'd told them not to call her that, but they were the only words that felt appropriate. "My name is Sir Collum of the Out Isles. Thank you, we owe you our lives."

"You are welcome, Sir Collum."

She sounded like she was presiding over a glittering drawing room and not sailing a boat two hundred feet above the countryside.

"But if I may ask," he said, "how did you come to be here to rescue us?"

"Possibly by an error of judgment. But all in good time. We have a long voyage ahead of us."

She went back to trimming the sail and studying the stars, and Collum made his way unsteadily back to his place. Gripping the wooden seat with white knuckles, he summoned his courage and looked over the side.

The fabric of Britain was laid out under them like a counterpane— the stuff of the world looked so much softer and smoother from here. Woods were dark coarse wool, fields a lighter velvet with its nap brushed different ways. A road wound through them like a seam, and there was a darkened village for a button. Camelot had already dwindled to a twinkling jewel in the distance. The Brass was a squiggle of dull silver in the moonlight, with whiskery tributaries branching off it.

Oddly the moon looked no nearer from here than it had from the ground. A mystery. He would have to ask Palomides about it, if he ever saw him again.

"In the matter of addressing me, I'm neither a queen nor a nun now." Guinevere tied off the mainsheet and shook out her fingers, which were tired from gripping the rope. She had a lot of unruly light-brown hair, barely restrained in a knot at the back of her head. She wore no jewelry, and she'd exchanged her habit for a practical brown dress and a woolen mantle. "My tenure at the convent was only ever a matter of a convenience. I needed somewhere safe and quiet to hide. It did cross my mind that I might find God there, or that God might find me, but somehow we managed to miss each other as usual. Ships in the night. As it were.

"Mostly I was there because I knew that sooner or later Lancelot would make a move for the throne, and when he did he would send someone to kill me, if he didn't come himself."

"He said you didn't sleep together," Bedivere said.

"Lancelot is a damned liar, but that much happens to be true. I'm going to tell you the rest of it too." From the way the queen announced it this was evidently a decision she'd been thinking over for some time. "Not because I have anything to confess, or because any of you have a right to know. Any of you. I did not save all your lives so that I could submit to an interrogation. But we will have a great deal to discuss when we get where we're going, and it will all go much quicker without a lot of tiresome mutual suspicion.

"And perhaps you do have some right to know. I know you all loved Arthur, too, in your different ways, just as I did. We are all that he has left. And he loved you too. He found it easy to love other people. He even loved Mordred, and that took some doing.

"But of course everybody loved Arthur too. They all wanted a piece, so I suppose it's no wonder he was torn to pieces in the end. I often think that if Arthur had loved himself a little more, and the rest of us a little less, this whole disaster might have been averted. He would've stuck to the business of governing Britain and fighting off Saxons, and this would be the mightiest nation in the world.

"But he had to be good, on top of all the rest of it. I can remember the very first day that he sat at the Round Table and called for a marvel, and it appeared—it was a bird that spoke. A wagtail. Do you remember, Bedivere? Everyone was in transports of wonder, and I suppose I was, too, but some part of me also thought, well, that's it then. I'm just a woman, how the hell do I compete with a talking bird?"

The air around them felt still but they must have been traveling at enormous speed, faster than any horse or ship, because up ahead Collum could already make out what he took to be the estuary of the Avon River, and beyond that the Severn Sea. They were four days' ride from Camelot. He could feel the warmth of Nimue's shoulder pressing against his. He thought of kissing her by the woodshed at Dubh Hall. Her warm lips against his in the cold. Now that he was alive for at least a brief time longer he wanted to do it again.

"But I shouldn't pretend I was better than anybody else," Guinevere said. "I had no children, and with the Round Table Arthur had a hundred of them, so I had a great deal more free time than I knew what to do with. I dressed impeccably. I greeted emissaries, or more often their wives. I prayed, I advised, I chose among shades and patterns. And occasionally I flirted.

"Lancelot was a skillful flirt, because he did everything skillfully. He was handsome enough, and I, like every other woman at court, found that the idea of seducing the greatest of knights, the *preux chevalier*, that most exalted and forbidden of men, was fantasy enough to beguile the occasional hour or two. I am ashamed to say it now but in my innocence I even imagined that Lancelot and I . . . shared something." The words came with difficulty. "I was in love with a king, you see, and Lancelot was in love with God. Neither of us could have all of our beloved. Some part of us was alone with our love and always would be."

Aerial sailing was in some ways better than the regular kind. It was certainly drier, and so far, knock wood, Collum had managed not to be sick. For a while they kept pace with a large aquiline bird that coolly ignored them. They were starting to feel their wounds: Nimue's nose had swelled up dramatically, and Dinadan was feeling his chin, and Bedivere his forehead and his arm. Collum had gotten off easily, and he spent his time thinking about poor Constantine, and poor Sir Melehan too. And Dagonet, and Scipio. Their little band had gotten away once again, they always managed to scrape through, but every time they did it cost somebody everything they had.

"But all that—as you knights like to say—is as it may. Please understand that when Lancelot arrived at my door that night, I was not at all pleased to see him. Not at all. There is such a thing as taking the joke too far. I need not explain to any of you that the first principle of courtly love is that it remain unconsummated.

"Lancelot wasn't even meant to be at Camelot, he'd gone hunting with Arthur in the Old Weald. He must have come back early."

"You didn't send for him," Dinadan said.

"No." Guinevere adjusted the jib, which didn't need further trimming. Wide, pale moonstruck beaches slipped by below them. "I had no idea what he was doing banging on my door. I told him to leave immediately. Immediately. I did not mince my words. There was no misunderstanding."

"He said that too," Collum said.

"Really. Did he tell you that he forced his way into my chamber? That I bit and scratched and tried to scream? But there are few men in the world physically stronger than our King Galahad. He held me down and bound and gagged me. Even then I didn't understand; I thought he was there to rape me.

"But there was no lust in his eyes. Understand this, too: he cared nothing for me. He didn't even desire me. Once I was immobilized Lancelot did nothing further, just took off his clothes and then sat down to wait. He was waiting for Mordred. Lancelot knew he was coming."

"He said someone told Mordred he would be there," Dinadan said.

"He would know, he did it himself. He made sure we were caught. And Mordred was punctual. It wasn't long before he was outside with his righteous dozen, crying treason and lechery and shouting all kind of filth. Like me they had not yet grasped the nature of their roles in the drama. Only Lancelot knew that."

She took a breath, lifted her chin, and continued.

"Colgrevance got busy trying to shoulder down my door. Lancelot let it open just wide enough for him to stumble through, then slammed it shut again and locked it. Colgrevance was brave, he must've known he was going to die, but he didn't beg or try to run. He'd fought the Saxons by Arthur's side when he was barely twenty, and won, but he lost in my chamber, ten feet from me, with his own sword in the hollow of his throat. Lancelot stripped him for his armor.

"Lancelot talked as he put it on, quite matter-of-factly. He explained how Arthur was a false king, in thrall to the devil and half a dozen barbarian gods, and it was his duty as a Christian to bring him down and return Britain to God. He'd sent Mordred an anonymous note saying that he would be in my chamber tonight, and he guessed correctly—and it wasn't entirely obvious—that Mordred would come and catch us. He'd thought everything through, and gambled, and won.

"I suppose a better woman might have felt some compassion for Lancelot. He was certainly as miserable a man as I've ever seen. There are plenty of people who think Lancelot is full of himself but that is exactly wrong. He isn't full of anything, he's empty. He's a bottomless sinkhole, endlessly falling into himself. Not his countless victories, not even the throne of Britain will fill the void inside him. He will take everything, throw everything into it, until there is nothing left.

"The only thing that would fill it is God. No lover, not even Palomides, ever longed as pathetically and desperately as Lancelot longs for God. I doubt whether even He wants to be loved as Lancelot loves Him. I sometimes wonder whether God wasn't a little afraid of Lancelot."

"I have to know," Dinadan said. "How the hell did he fight his way out? Even he said it was impossible."

"I think I mentioned that Lancelot is a damn liar. His genius is the committing of violence, and it works in his favor that violence itself does not excite or arouse him. If anything it makes him calmer. I doubt his pulse quickened even a little when a dozen knights pushed into my bedchamber.

"To my eyes it was bedlam, but to his I think it was its own kind of order. I saw him throw a knife backhand right through Sir Gromore Somir Joure's open visor from twenty feet away, without even looking in his direction. He shattered Agravaine's sword with his own, caught one of the flying shards with his free hand and stuck it up through Sir Lovel's chin and into his brain. Sir Curselaine he killed with a candlestick. He picked up Petipase of Winchelsea in all his armor and threw him out a window.

"He got them all except for Mordred, whom he let go on purpose. He needed one alive to be the messenger.

"I knew even then the story that would be told. Lancelot knew too; he is far from stupid. People love stories, I love them, but stories are like gods, they care little for the human beings in their care. They don't care if they're true or not. From that night on people would tell the story of Lancelot and Guinevere, and their fateful passion, and the king they betrayed, and the nation they wrenched apart, and they would weep over it but they would love it.

"But it's not true. I loved Arthur. You know that I loved him." She was talking to Bedivere alone now. "Because you loved him as I did."

Her cheeks shone with tears. Bedivere's didn't, but he sat still and let her dig her sharp nails into his one great hand.

"I loved him," he said. "As you did."

"Our love was not simple, but it was real. That's what no one understands. Our story was not a romance, it was a marriage."

"Why does it matter what the stories say?" Nimue asked.

"Because it is galling!" Guinevere snapped. "That's why!"

She let go of Bedivere's hand and wiped away her tears. The boat was well out over the ocean now, and the water was like beaten silver, the land behind them a thin stripe the color of ash.

"Of course it was a miracle that Arthur could love at all." Guinevere had recovered her composure. "Lancelot couldn't, or not so you'd know it, and Arthur's childhood wasn't so different from his. But love lived on in Arthur, underground, all that time. I don't know how.

"Though of course it was love that undid him in the end, too. His love for Mordred. That was his fatal flaw, the one that God could not forgive. Do you really believe that, having run him through with a spear, Arthur could not have escaped from his son? When Arthur gave Mordred his death blow, he knew it was his own, too, because killing his own son was not something he could survive.

"It was always going to happen. He was dead the moment he lay with Morgause. He was dead the moment Uther lay with Igraine and conceived him. The moment the first Roman bireme touched the sand at Rutupiae."

The sky behind them was lightening, but ahead there was only roughened sea and winking whitecaps under a dark sky.

"Where are we going?" Collum asked.

"We're going to Avalon."

"The island?"

"It's real?" Bedivere's eyes were fixed on Guinevere.

"Avalon the island. It's real."

"Is Arthur there?"

"Arthur is very gravely hurt. I don't want to mislead you. But you will see him there."

Thirty-four

THE KING'S DREAM

The wind slackened, and Guinevere let the boat, which was
named the *Errant*, drift gently down out of the sky, foot by
foot, in great spirals. Below them was a milky ocean of mist,
and they sank down into it, and for a long time everything was
white clinging fog, and they seemed not to be moving at all. Collum couldn't have said if they were still in the human world anymore or if they'd passed into the Otherworld or some even more
mysterious place.

Then without warning the hull slapped down onto a gentle swell-
ing green sea. The boat settled into it and with palpable relief became an ordinary sailboat again, gently patted and rocked by the
waves, parting the fog ahead of it, the sail filled by a whispery gossamer breeze that was barely there.

Time was hard to reckon. Everybody was tired. Bedivere and
Dinadan closed their eyes, and Nimue rested her head on Collum's
shoulder. Only Guinevere showed no sign of fatigue; Collum supposed it was not in the nature of a queen to look tired. He couldn't
see how she could tell where they were going, but after what might

have been five minutes or five hours she snapped her fingers at him and indicated that he could be of service to her at the bow. Even as he was clambering unsteadily forward she swung the boat round into the wind and with the sails flapping they bumped gently into a dock.

Knots were not Collum's forte, and ultimately Nimue had to do the actual tying-up. They all climbed out unsteadily onto a long, skinny jetty, which they followed to a wide white beach lapped at by a pale turquoise bay.

"Welcome to Avalon," Guinevere said.

Stepping out onto that fabled shore Collum trod carefully, as if it might dissolve or give way under his crude, heavy human footsteps, but it was real enough. It smelled real—the usual seaside odors, brine and rotting sea wrack, mixed with something sweet. There were tide marks sketched on the sand in black seaweed. The land further in was hidden by more drifting fog, as if it had been wrapped in it for safekeeping.

"I always imagined it . . . I don't know," Dinadan said. "Sunnier."

"You must not have been to a lot of enchanted islands," Guinevere said.

Avalon was warm anyway, and an atmosphere of deep tranquility lay over the place. The disaster of the Holy Lance and King Galahad and all the rest of it felt no less real, but they were very far away. Guinevere led them up the beach and over low dunes crested with coarse sea scrub. Bit by bit the sand gave way to deep green grass, which gave way to an orchard, long straight rows of apple trees. Their twisted, crooked branches were bowed down with clumps of heavy ripe fruit, like cows that needed milking.

"May I?" Nimue asked.

"I don't see why not," Guinevere said.

Collum realized he was ravenous. The salt air made the apples taste even sweeter. He slipped on a mashed windfall, and suddenly everybody was laughing, at him but also at the absurdity of the whole thing. Here they were on Avalon, the Fortunate Isle. A fairy tale. They were safe. No one could touch them, not here, not for a little while anyway.

But Bedivere didn't laugh, or eat.

"Where is he?"

"This way." Guinevere wasn't going to keep him waiting.

With her long legs she was a fast walker. She led them deeper into the orchard, along the aisles occasionally ducking between them. They tossed their apple cores carelessly onto the grass. Soon they saw a glimpse of sunlight up ahead: beyond the orchard, framed by an archway of trees, stood a tall green hill with a grand silk pavilion pitched on top.

Its taut silk walls were gaily striped in azure and gold, and at its peak was a golden sun in an azure sky. It had the jolly air of a circus or a tournament, as if there should've been crowds milling around it and music playing, but standing there all by itself there was something dreamlike about it. No one spoke as they climbed the slope. He'd come a thousand miles for this, crossed worlds for this, but Collum found his steps slowing all by themselves. He was unaccountably nervous. It felt like when he'd walked into the Great Hall of Camelot for the first time: an audience with the High King. He wasn't ready. *An it please you, my lord.* The door of the pavilion was a gauzy white curtain. The ladies went in first, followed by Bedivere and then Dinadan and, finally, Collum.

Inside lay King Arthur.

He was asleep on his back on a soft white bed, a white sheet pulled up to his chest. He wore only a long white nightshirt; they'd taken off his armor. His face was pale, his cheeks a little sunken. He was very thin. His head wound was carefully bound with gauze that had been soaked in honey. The blue silk of the tent turned the light inside a pale blue, as if all this were happening deep underwater.

There he is, Collum kept thinking. It's him. It's King Arthur. His eyes were riveted to Arthur's face. He was a handsome man, though few men were truly handsome when they slept. Someone had shaved his face. His lips were dry and cracked, and his skin had a waxy sheen. Sweat stood out on his forehead, as if just staying alive were hard work.

Everyone went to their knees and bowed their heads. Choking sobs rose up and burst out of Collum, he didn't even know where they came from. He hadn't wept like that for years, not since that first night when his stepfather sent him to Dubh Hall. There lay Arthur, the pillar of the world, who'd carried an entire age on his shoulders. It had taken all his strength, and in the end it left him none to defend himself with, and when they cut him down it all came crashing down in pieces on top of him. He'd saved so many, but there was no one left to save him.

In a way Collum had been looking for this man his whole life, and he'd always imagined that when he finally found him he would go to his knees and beg. He would beg Arthur to make him a knight, to let him sit at his table, to give him lands and honors and a home, to give him all the love that his own lost father never could. He wanted to beg Arthur to wake up, and come back, come back across the sea and mend what was broken, to whisper the secret that only he knew, that would bring the dead world back to life.

But now that he was here Collum couldn't do it. He didn't have the heart for it. All he wanted now was for Arthur to do what he never did in life, which was to rest and care for himself and get better. To mend himself and bring himself back to life. You can pass on the burden, he thought. You don't have to carry it anymore. You can give it to us.

Long minutes went by in silence. Then Arthur gave a soft snort—there was no other word for it—and shifted restlessly under the sheet. It broke the spell. As though they were waking from a trance, they rose to their feet with stiff knees, wiping their eyes and their noses, and shuffled back out blinking into the misty daylight. Where to now? Collum thought. Now that we've seen the fallen pillar of the world?

Morgan le Fay was waiting for them, arms folded, unsmiling. Sir Palomides stood beside her dressed in magnificent deep blue robes embroidered with red thread and wearing a matching turban.

"Oh," Nimue said. "Well. Are we going to have a fight now?"

"Do you want one?" Morgan said.

"There will be no fighting," Palomides said.

"We came here for Arthur," Bedivere said. "That's all. We're here for our king."

"You didn't come here, Guinevere brought you here," Morgan said. "And she did it so you could see for yourselves that Arthur is never coming home."

MORGAN LE FAY evidently considered herself to be their host on Avalon, though the party wasn't an especially lively one. She led them to a little jewel-box castle overlooking the sea, where she tended to their injuries in a brisk, professional manner and gave them lunch at a long table on the roof. Fairies brought them cold pork and mutton with sharp grainy mustard, apples and figs and nuts; one of the fairies seemed to be half cloud. They were tired after their escape from Camelot and their all-night voyage through the sky, but Collum had lost his appetite and only picked at his food.

Overhead was a trellis overgrown with grapevines that were, like the apple trees, heavy with fruit. Fat bees wandered among them, drunk and happy.

"Sir Palomides," Dinadan said. "Has Morgan harmed you?"

"Thank you, Dinadan, I am well."

Of everyone at the table he did look the most at ease. There was nothing wrong with his appetite; he was tucking into his lunch.

"Are you a prisoner here?"

"In truth," he said, "I do not know."

"You're not a fool, Palomides," Bedivere said curtly, "so don't talk like one."

"Perhaps I am a fool. Morgan tells me that I am free to leave whenever I choose, but so far I have not chosen to. Why that is, it is difficult for me to say, except that Avalon offers one a new perspective on things."

Bedivere snorted in disgust and turned back to Morgan.

"Wake him up, witch. Heal him and wake him up. Britain needs him."

"I didn't put him to sleep, Bedivere." Morgan said mildly. "Mordred did that when he broke his skull. We're lucky Palomides was here to translate al-Razi on the treatment of skull fractures; that and my enchantments are the only thing keeping him alive."

"You're waiting for him to die, so you can press your claim again."

"If I had more than a scrap of an army left, I wouldn't be waiting. But as things stand my campaign for the throne is on hiatus."

"Is she lying?" Bedivere transferred his cold stare back to Palomides.

"I believe she is not."

"Nimue? Is it true what she says about Arthur?"

"I would have to examine the king more closely."

Guinevere watched all parties attentively, giving away nothing, waiting for others to show their hands. Her relationship with Morgan was hard to tease out; there was no obvious enmity, but there was no clear alliance there either. Every once in a while the sun pushed through the drifting mists that muffled the island, and it felt like waking up from a dream and then, when the fog closed back in, rolling over and going back to sleep.

"What is Avalon, Morgan?" Collum asked. "Where are we?"

"It's an in-between place." Morgan seemed happy to talk about something else. "All fairy places are in-between but Avalon is even more so than most—it's somehow in between the world and the Otherworld. It took me years to find it—how Saint Brendan got here I'll never know. I suppose it's a sort of inside-out Garden of Eden: all apple trees, and nothing forbidden. Though you do get a little tired of apples after a while."

"That's always the trouble with islands," Dinadan said. "The food."

"I thought apples were Roman," Collum said.

"Where do you think they got them from?" Morgan said. "The Romans steal everything and then take all the credit."

From their vantage point on the roof of the castle you could get a sense of the shape of it: Avalon wasn't round, as Collum first thought, but long and thin and curved, pulled by time and tide and current into a gracefully elongated S outlined in white sand against the green sea, like a silk scarf that had been snatched away by the wind.

"Let us talk about the future," Guinevere said.

"I'm not interested in the future," Bedivere said. "I want the past back."

"There's no way back."

"There was," Dinadan said, "before your giant broke it."

"You may think me mad and evil," Morgan said, "but please don't imagine that I'm stupid. What did you think was going to happen, any of you, if Ysbaddaden hadn't done what he did? God would've given that spear to Lancelot and we would've ended up right where we are, only worse because he'd be armed with a holy relic. I told you before, people don't come back. Except for Jesus, and look how He turned out."

"Cease your arguing," Guinevere said. "Let us look at the things we share. None of us can tolerate Lancelot on the throne. We can still work together and find a way to bring him down."

"It won't be easy," Morgan said. "I believe Merlin may have joined with him."

"What?" Nimue's eyes went wide with shock. "That's impossible!"

"I cannot see inside Camelot, thanks to you," Morgan said, "but it's what my sources tell me. Lancelot took a hundred men to his barrow with picks and shovels and dug him out like a fox. He had a hedge witch summon a demon to break the final stone. Most of the men died, and what happened to the witch was worse, but I believe that Merlin is now free."

"Can't you kill him?" Collum asked. "With magic?"

"That is a very dark art," Nimue said. "Too dark even for Morgan, I suspect. And only a man can kill Merlin."

The sun broke through again, dappling the table with warm light through the hanging grapes.

"Morgan," Bedivere said, with an honest attempt at mastering himself, "you were there on that barge. I saw you. You heard what Arthur said. He will heal, and he will return."

"If that's really his destiny, do you think a lowly creature like me could stand in his way?" Morgan said. "What you heard was a dying man's fancy, nothing more. And don't forget that I was the one who came for him, Bedivere. God would've let him die, but I didn't."

"If you can't wake him up then all you've done is keep him out of Heaven."

"Oh, is that what you think, you stupid lunk?! God couldn't wait to get His fingers on Arthur! If He had His way Arthur would be burning in Hell right now with a red-hot pitchfork up his backside, like all the other incestuous fornicators! I hated the man, but he is all that I have left of a family and by all the gods God can't have him. I won't give Him the satisfaction."

Bedivere shoved back his chair and walked away.

Collum wasn't sure who to believe, but he knew that if Arthur had the strength to rise from his bed and go back to Britain and conquer it all over again, nothing would stop him. He would be doing it.

"I did think I could heal him," Morgan said quietly, mostly to herself. Palomides put a hand lightly on her arm. "I thought I could do it.

"If Arthur doesn't get better," Collum said, "what will happen to him?"

"Not much changes on Avalon. Things happen very slowly. He could stay like this for years. Centuries even. He would be like King Bran. But I don't think he would want that, do you?"

"I don't know what Arthur would want."

"Well, Bedivere does," Morgan said. "And that's what makes him so angry."

. . .

AFTER LUNCH COLLUM realized he barely knew what to do with himself. They'd been dragging themselves down Roman roads for so long, fighting for their lives, chasing the Holy Lance, racing the runaway disintegration of the world. But everything happened slowly on Avalon, Morgan had said, it was ruled by a great pause, and little time was passing back in Britain. It was like the land of the Lotus Eaters.

So he walked down to the sea for a swim. Palomides and Dinadan went with him. As they walked, Palomides pointed out the Questing Beast watching them, poorly concealed among the apple trees.

"The tables are turned," Palomides said. "She stalks me constantly now. Won't let me alone. I am beginning to understand how Isolde felt."

The first beach they went to was calm, and Collum wanted waves, so they crossed to the other side of the island—it wasn't even half a mile wide—which was besieged by ranks of big, heavy rollers. He and Palomides stripped down, and for a change Dinadan joined them. Collum had never seen Dinadan naked before.

Palomides looked at his face and then laughed so hard he had to sit down.

"I didn't know." Collum wondered if he would ever stop being amazed at the things that escaped his notice.

"There's nothing to know." Dinadan wasn't joking now. He was letting Collum in on something, on purpose, but he was still wary. "You can stare at my tits all you want, Collum, but I'm as much of a man as you are."

"Right you are."

He was happy to leave it at that. Well, now he knew what Merlin was getting at before. The wonders, they still had not quite ceased.

He let the first few waves smash right into him, then he picked one and dived under it and swam out past the break. Floating on his back, staring up at the gray sky, he slowly pedaled his legs while the swells lifted him up and dropped him down. The Fairy Sea felt pleasantly odd: not quite blood warm but close, and full of tiny bubbles like beer. A scattering of rain blew through, rinsing his face with fresh water.

He duck-dived and swam down to touch the bottom, which was where he made another discovery: he didn't need to come back up. He seemed to be able to hold his breath indefinitely. He thought it must be some magic of the Fairy Sea, but he made Dinadan and Palomides try and they both came up puffing and blowing.

"Look at that," Dinadan said, treading water. "It must be a gift from the well."

"Do not tell Bedivere," Palomides said. "He is in a bad enough mood as it is."

That evening they drank wine in the hall at Avalon Castle while a smoky applewood fire snapped and spat in the grate. Collum asked Palomides about the moon and received a lecture on basic cosmology. Palomides also taught everybody to play *gwyddbwyll*, which was a little like chess; you played it on a wooden board with pieces made of gold and iron. Collum wasn't bad at it, but he wasn't good enough to beat Palomides. Dinadan was.

Nimue retired early, pleading exhaustion, and Bedivere kept to his room. Outside a great wind came up, hurrying the mists through the ranks of apple trees.

Collum sat up alone listening to the gale slamming shutters in distant parts of the castle. He pictured the lonely tent on the hilltop where Arthur lay, its silk flapping, its ropes and pegs straining against the wind in the darkness. He hoped there was someone there with him, to keep him company through the storm. He hoped they'd spread a blanket over him against the chill. He wasn't tired. He decided to make sure.

Outside the wind was like a dense black liquid flowing over him. He leaned into it as he tramped stubbornly through the trees toward the hill where Arthur's tent stood. He would sit a vigil by the king's side. That was the right thing. He could do no less for Arthur. Nothing was far away on Avalon, and it wasn't long before he spotted the tent up ahead on its hilltop, lit up from within like a lantern, the silk walls glowing blue and gold. The last light in the darkness.

But there was something odd about the light. It wasn't candlelight or lamplight, it moved and flashed and pulsed in weird rhythms. Someone or something was in there with Arthur. Collum broke into a trot, up the slope of cold grass. The king was helpless, there was no one there to defend him. If some old enemy had found him, Merlin even—

But it wasn't Merlin. The tent was warm and full of white sweet-smelling smoke. A gout of white flame flared above Arthur's motionless body in the shape of a complex sigil and then vanished again, so bright Collum had to look away. A woman was kneeling on the floor by Arthur's bed, naked to the waist and slick with sweat, a half-dozen books spread out around her on the tent floor along with bowls full of liquids and powders, plus one with a dead bird in it. She was singing in a shaky voice, her arms were spread wide and her whole body was shuddering. Another flame-sigil half-formed over the sleeping king then collapsed and flickered out before it could properly take shape—a salamander trying and failing to be born. The next one faded even more quickly.

"God's bloody bones," Collum whispered. For a heartbeat he froze there in the doorway, afraid to interrupt the spellcasting—but then the woman's arms dropped and she slumped forward, bonelessly, her bare back heaving.

He went to one knee.

"I'm here, Nimue."

He put his hands on her shaking shoulders. She was panting almost too hard to speak.

"I couldn't do it."

"Do what?!"

"I thought I could heal him. Your hands are cold." Her skin was burning under his fingers.

"Just tell me you're all right."

"I thought Morgan was wrong but it's too bad. His skull's shattered. I can't fix it."

"You did everything you could, I know you did."

He hoped she hadn't done too much. Nimue shivered convulsively in spite of the heat, and her teeth were chattering. Collum shrugged out of his cloak and wrapped her in it. She was as starkly pale and beautiful as she had been that day on the battlefield. He gathered her up in his arms—she was worrisomely light, as if she'd given up some vital part of herself to the magic, but maybe that was just all she weighed. Her hands were stained bright blue from something she'd used in the spellcasting.

Arthur hadn't moved through all this. Collum wondered if any part of him felt Nimue trying to reach him, and knew they were trying to rescue him. The smoke was dissipating, and the tent was dark again except for a single candle.

"I called Brighid." She swallowed. "And Belenus. Probably shouldn't have. It didn't matter."

"Let's get you back to the castle. We're not losing you too."

She closed her eyes and rested her head on his shoulder.

"I might be sick. I'm just warning you."

A savage wind tore at his back as he made his way down the hill through the trees. The darkness seemed deeper than ordinary darkness, like they'd been dropped into a sack of velvet. He could smell the sweet smoke in her hair.

"Should I get Morgan?"

"No Morgan," she whispered. "Just tired."

"You've done all you can. More than any of us. Time for somebody to take care of you for a change."

She didn't stir in his arms, and he was terrified that she might die before he could get her inside and warm. He kept whispering encouraging words to her, willing her to stay awake with him. When he laid her on her bed in her chamber and lit a candle there was some color in her cheeks again. He covered her with a blanket, averting his eyes as best he could.

"Always so gallant," Nimue said with a weak smile, still shivering.

"Merely defending your modesty, my lady."

"At least I'm not copulating with a goat."

He could feel himself turning red for the second time that day. Eternally the country bumpkin. He busied himself with lighting a fire. There was wood already stacked in the fireplace.

"I wish you'd told me," he said. "I would've gone with you." The shavings started smoldering on the third try—he was doing better than at Dubh Hall anyway. He blew on them carefully.

"It wouldn't have made a difference. And you would've tried to stop me. I offered the gods my life for his."

Now he looked round at her. Nimue's straight brown hair was down. He'd seen her in battle, he'd seen her angry and frightened and desperate, but he'd never once seen her with her hair down before. She was so lovely he couldn't look away.

"I'm glad they didn't take it," he said. The fire was spreading through the kindling. It would catch on its own now. "And you know Arthur wouldn't have wanted to come back like that."

"And I would've said it's not about what he wants."

"Except you would've been dead." Collum stood up. "I'll get you some wine."

"I don't want wine."

Nimue propped herself up on her elbows, letting the blanket slip down again.

"Well," he said. "I'm all out of sleeping draughts."

It was a joke, but neither of them laughed. Somehow Collum returned her steady gaze even though his heart was fluttering wildly around the room like a trapped seagull. She smiled, and he was intensely conscious of being alone with her in a bedchamber, in a castle, on a magic island lost somewhere in the vast Fairy Sea. By all possible standards of decorum and chivalry he shouldn't have been here, it wasn't proper at all, but decorum and chivalry seemed to have gotten lost in the Fairy Sea too.

"I should go," he said. "But I don't want to."

"Then don't."

SOMETIME LATER THEY WERE LYING side by side in her bed.

The gale had blown itself out, and the sky had cleared enough that they could see a half-moon in the sky. Pale, heavy banks of fog lay on the sea like snowdrifts in the moonlight. The only light came from the low fire.

"You've got scars," she said. "More than I thought."

It was true, life at Mull had left its marks on him. Long welts on his back. Burn marks on his chest.

"I thought you'd have more tattoos," he said.

He touched the slight bump on Nimue's freckled nose where Lancelot broke it.

"Morgan fixed it," she said. "I asked her to leave the bump, to remind me."

"Remind you of what?"

"To duck, I guess."

"Well, I like it."

She propped herself up on one elbow.

"You won't get to do miracles anymore, you know," she said. "Now that you're not a virgin knight. Not the first-class miracles anyway."

"I would settle for a second-class miracle. Anyway, who says I was a virgin before?"

"You were the most virginal knight I have ever seen. And I knew Galahad."

"Were you? A virgin?"

She answered that with a snort.

"If you were looking for a convent girl you should've knocked on Guinevere's door. Or Morgan's. Though I suspect her bed is already occupied."

Collum hadn't thought of that. In the moment it was hard to pay attention to anything other than the smoothness of Nimue's warm ribbed side against his under the thin sheet. Collum had never been this close to a naked woman before. Most of what he knew about female anatomy came from the sheela stone in the chimney at Dubh Hall. He wasn't much used to being touched either, except by other men who were trying to kill him. It was good, but the intensity of it was almost too much to bear, and he started shaking.

It was embarrassing but he couldn't stop it, and the more he tried the worse it got. There were things he remembered from Dubh Hall, things he never thought about, that didn't leave scars.

"Shh." Nimue put a hand on his chest; it was still blue from the spellcasting. "It's all right."

"I know it's all right!"

"There's no shame. It's their shame, not yours. When I first saw you—*shh*—don't say anything, I'm trying to calm you down." She put her arms around him and squeezed; she was surprisingly strong. "When I first saw you at Camelot I thought you were handsome, but you looked so innocent that I figured you had to be either an idiot or a con man. Then when you volunteered to fight the Green Knight I ruled out con man."

"I was a c-con man though," Collum managed to say. "I lied."

"You only thought you were lying." She smiled in the darkness and put her forehead against his. "That's what I've figured out about you, Collum. You were so sure you were a false knight. Everybody always told you you were. You told yourself that. But you were wrong, you were a true knight all along. You just didn't know it yet."

Collum started to relax. The shudders came slower. It was a sin what they'd done together, of course it was, but at the moment he did not find himself much troubled by regret. Maybe it wasn't good but surely it wasn't evil. Maybe it was some third thing entirely. At any rate as sins went he much preferred it to acedia.

"You used to think I was King Arthur's son."

"I still wonder about it. It's too bad Arthur can't tell us. What are we going to do, Collum?"

"You mean—besides this?"

"God's gone, the spear is broken, the Table's down to four knights, and that's counting Palomides, who doesn't seem to know what side he's on anymore. Lancelot holds Camelot and now he's got fucking Merlin on his side! All we have is Arthur, and we probably don't even have him, and without him we're lost. I'm starting to wonder if we shouldn't just stay here and let Britain fend for itself."

Collum didn't think she meant it, but he couldn't deny that at this moment he was very glad to be far, far away from Britain and its many troubles. He would never give up, he knew that, but he couldn't say he was looking forward much to throwing himself back into the glorious struggle. They'd be outlaws in Lancelot's Britain, hiding in the woods, or in smoky caves in the winter, washing in freezing streams, standing watches by night, always listening for footsteps. There would be no more battles, or not for a long time. Instead they would have to sneak into towns in disguise, by night, like criminals, to drum up allies, treat with skeptical lords, stir up resentment against the Crown.

And most of the people who hated Lancelot would hate them too. There would be so much arguing, so much politics, so much talk, talk, talk, and he would be so terrible at it. It made him tired just thinking about it. And then even if they won, what kind of new Britain would they build? What would it look like?

"Have you talked to Guinevere?" he asked. "Maybe her family could help. Maybe she could rally Cameliard."

"Maybe." She took his large hand in her small ones, rubbed his thick fingers with her thumbs. "But it was her family that drove her here. Did you know they tried to marry her to Rience? And then Lancelot? Finally she went to Morgan and offered herself as a more politically palatable choice for queen."

"She could hardly be less politically palatable than Morgan."

"It's moot anyway, because Morgan lost her army at the Battle of the Spear. And Merlin will be busy turning every bush spirit and river sprite in Britain against me . . . I'm not giving up, Collum, but I don't know how we're going to win. I never thought God would let us lose. I never would've believed it. Maybe He really does like Lancelot better. Maybe we're the villains after all."

It was the closest he'd ever seen her to despair.

"God must think we're strong enough to take it. Though a wise woman told me once that God is a great optimist when it comes to how much people can endure." He kissed her. "We should get some sleep, it'll be dawn soon."

"Sayest thou so? But hold, gentle knight." Nimue took his hand and showed him where to put it. "Thy quest is not yet at an end."

THE NEXT MORNING BEDIVERE announced that he was going to visit Arthur again. He wanted Nimue to examine the king herself. Nimue explained that she already had; Bedivere didn't accept it. Guinevere said they weren't going without her, and Morgan insisted on chaperoning the three of them, so in the end they all went.

The mist was thick even around Arthur's pavilion on the hilltop. Heavy drops gathered and broke and ran down the waxed silk. It was warm and humid inside. Bedivere took a stool next to Arthur's bed and held the king's hand. Morgan and Guinevere stood watchfully by while Nimue paced a circuit around the inside of the tent, observing the patient carefully from different angles through a shard of crystal that she kept in a velvet case.

The lord of Camelot took his slow shallow breaths. His hair was lank and overgrown under the white bandage. No one had trimmed the king's nails, and they'd grown long.

"Well?" Bedivere said.

Nimue just shook her head.

Bedivere didn't argue this time. He didn't say anything. He looked like a boar cornered by hunting hounds. They were all still waiting for something, though Collum didn't know what anymore.

"Do you think he dreams?" Bedivere asked of nobody in particular.

"He might." Nimue wrapped the crystal in a cloth and put it away.

"The night after Camlann he spoke about a god of dreams. Her name was Durelas. There was a shrine to her near Little Dunoak."

"One of the Great Gods," Nimue said. "Not of dreams exactly, but close enough. I met her once."

Bedivere didn't seem to have heard her. He kept gazing into Arthur's sleeping face.

"I think I understand," Morgan said. "You want to see what he's dreaming. I can ask her, but the gods don't owe you any favors that I can think of."

"Durelas will remember Arthur." Bedivere's voice was husky. "I'm sure of it."

"Even if she's willing, she'll only do it once."

The old knight nodded. He didn't trust Morgan, but what trick could she play on him now?

"All right," Morgan said. "You must—"

"Show me too." Guinevere took her place on the other side of the bed.

The preparations wound up taking some hours and included the messy slaughter of two lambs outside the tent as well as much lighting of candles and drawing of chalk glyphs and singing in languages Collum didn't recognize. The ritual wasn't ready till midafternoon, but everyone waited, even though most of them had nothing to do except stand and watch. There was nowhere else to go.

Finally Morgan told Bedivere and Guinevere to take Arthur's hands. Then she told everyone to close their eyes and get ready because the goddess was coming.

As soon as his eyes shut Collum had an overwhelming urge to open them again because there was a presence in the room. The pressure dropped abruptly, the way it does right before a storm, and he felt something like a million needles pricking his skin, softly at first but then harder and harder, until it was all he could do not to cry out. There was the same sweet smoke as he'd smelled last night. Morgan spoke, odd sounds that barely sounded like words, and a voice answered, not loudly but somehow with such force that something metal in the room rattled.

Then the presence was gone, and Collum almost lost his balance because instead of darkness he was looking at a winter landscape. It was a wide, flat frozen marsh, mazed with crusted gray ice and hummocks and brown tufts, spread out under a white sky. It was hard to tell what was solid ground and what was water. He could feel cold air and smell snow coming on. He heard the calls of distant crows. The strangest part was that his eyes were still closed.

King Arthur sat astride a dappled gray courser scanning the horizon, dressed for the hunt in drab greens and browns, with dagged hems and a sharp bycocket hat. His black cloak, sumptuously lined with ermine, was thrown back boldly from his shoulders.

This was not the broken sunset king who lay in the pavilion on Avalon, this was Arthur in his prime, lean and strong, color high, back straight, breath puffing out proud and white. This was the Arthur that Arthur dreamed of, good King Arthur in all his power, with his best days still ahead of him.

Somehow Collum had fallen into his dream, or been pulled into it, or was simply put there by the divine whim of the goddess. Bedivere and Guinevere were there too. Collum felt like an intruder, this was too private a thing for him to witness, but he couldn't think how to banish himself. He tried to wake up but nothing happened. Arthur turned and looked back at the three of them with startlingly pale gray eyes. Collum had never seen them open before.

"Well met!" he called. "My good queen, and my good friend!"

The king didn't seem at all perplexed at their sudden appearance in the middle of his dream-hunt, though he did give Collum a curious look.

"My king," Bedivere said, "this is Sir Collum of the Out Isles, and lately of the Round Table. I wonder if you know him?"

Did he? How could he? Then it came to him: of course. This was why the goddess had put him here. Of course it was. All along he'd dismissed it as nonsense, a stupid fantasy, that he was some kind of long-lost bastard prince, but the goddess had recognized him. She'd seen him for who he was. His back straightened. Scipio was right after all, it was him all along, Arthur's long-lost son, banished or misplaced or maybe completely unknown but now at last restored to him. Surely his father would know him! His lost fisherman father suddenly felt like an absurdly thin fabrication, and his real father stood before him revealed at last.

He'd always denied it to himself but that was only because of how violently he longed for it to be true. Arthur's gaze seemed to pass all the way through Collum like sunlight through glass, meeting no resistance, registering every facet and flaw and bubble. He could almost feel it warming him from within.

But the king just shook his head and smiled.

"I know you not, Sir Collum. But you are welcome here."

Collum knelt and bowed his head.

"Thank you, Your Highness. It's a very great honor."

He kept staring at the ground. Bowing your head had the advantage that nobody could see the look on your face. It was the greatest triumph of his life to be greeted by King Arthur himself, but nonetheless in the same moment a little flame of hope went out inside him. He wasn't a prince. He was just a lowborn bastard after all, like he always thought, and with far more luck than he deserved.

When he looked up again the king was back to restlessly searching the edge of the meadow. He looked eager to be off, an arrow nocked and drawn.

"Arthur," Guinevere said. "My love. Stay with us a while. We miss you."

"And I you, my dear, but I mustn't linger. The game's afoot—there, do you see it? Look at that!"

He pointed. Just visible across the marsh, at the edge of a sere and leafless winter wood, were the pale hindquarters and stiff antlers of a great white stag.

"Shall we ride with you then?" Bedivere said. "And join the hunt?"

"I wish you could." Arthur smiled sadly. "But that beast is the king's alone to hunt, and no other's, and you still have other prizes left to seek. You all do—you too, Sir Collum."

Collum couldn't suppress a slight smile. He remembered my name. The white stag had turned to watch them. It looked restless, too, impatient to be hunted.

"In truth I don't like to leave." For the first time Arthur seemed troubled. "It has all cost so much, and come to so little. There's so much unfinished. But I cannot stay here. I thought I could, but I was mistaken. The world is sea-changed now, and I fear I belong to the Old World.

"But this world has marvels in it too. Never doubt it." Now he looked straight at Collum. "They are of a different kind now. No one will hand them to you. You can't pull them out of a stone, the way I did, but they're still there. It's not too late.

"Goodbye, my love." He leaned down from his horse and kissed Guinevere, awkwardly but with great sincerity, then straightened up again. "Farewell, my good Bedivere. No king could have a better friend than I have had in you. Now a recheat, if you please!"

Bedivere lifted a brass horn to his lips, smiling through tears. This wasn't the Bedivere of the waking world either, his face gouged by time and his voice flattened by grief. It was dream-Bedivere, hale and young, the boon companion of Arthur's glorious prime.

TRUT TRUT TRO-RO-ROW TRO-RO-ROW!

At the sound, a pack of dream-hounds appeared, flowing past them across the frozen fen in a bounding, barking mass. An answering horn sounded somewhere off in the woods. The great white stag bolted.

"We had it all wrong!" Arthur called. "We were whole all along! Don't you see? We'd only forgotten! We were always whole!"

His gray courser took off like a shot across the icy fields, and the dwindling sound of his voice came floating back to them on the thin winter air.

So how, so how! Sa say cy avaunt!

He disappeared into the frozen woods.

The day was still. Collum blinked—

He was back in the azure tent on Avalon. He was on the ground, looking up at the striped ceiling with the golden sun at the center, and Nimue was standing over him, her mouth quirked to one side as if she were trying to decide whether he needed medical attention. The air felt warm and steamy after the winter dream.

"You fainted."

"I guess I must have." He sat up, rubbing his head. "I'm all right. I'll tell you later."

Bedivere placed his hand on the king's cheek and kissed him on the forehead.

"Goodbye, my king," he said. "I shall love you all the days of my life."

Guinevere kissed Arthur as well, but she said nothing. She and Bedivere each took one corner of the thick linen sheet and drew it up over Arthur's face. Then, together, side by side, they walked stiffly out of the pavilion.

Only then did Collum understand that the king was dead.

He stayed behind for a minute, looking at Arthur's still features showing faintly through the white sheet, as though he'd been buried in drifted snow. For an instant he was back again in the Great Hall on that first day at Camelot, sick with grief, washed overboard. It had happened all over again: the king was dead, then he lived again, and now he'd died a second time.

But it was different this time. Collum felt no less empty and bereft, but his eyes were dry. Maybe it was just that having sought him all his life he'd finally gotten to see Arthur, and say a kind of farewell, but somehow something had eased inside him, the silver key had turned, and he could finally let go and start to mourn. Arthur was right, it was time.

Collum knew Arthur could've stayed like that for years, forever, and he would've waited for him, wasted his whole life that way, but now he was moving on, and his story could move on too. Maybe terrible things would happen in the future, maybe it was empty, a waste land. But there could be seeds buried there, too, deep down below the dry dust, where hidden springs still flowed. It was deep winter, but there was still hope for renewal. The grail could be found. A new king could rise. The land could live again.

Collum stepped blinking out of the pavilion into the sunlight. The weather, oblivious as ever to human tragedy, had finally cleared up. Bedivere was on his knees on the grass, but he wasn't praying. He was staring with wonder at his hands. He had two of them. He moved his ten fingers and made two fists. The right one was old and spotted and callused, but the left was as pink and clean and new as if it were fresh from a hot bath.

Thirty-five

THE LADY OF THE LAKE

Nimue or Morgan could have dug a grave with magic but instinctively they all knew that wasn't what was needed. It had to be hard work, the way grieving was hard. They wanted sweat and blisters and aching muscles.

After some debate they carried the king's body out to one of the thin, loose ends of the island, one of the tips of the S. They picked a spot that was high enough that it wouldn't be washed away in a storm but close enough to the sea that you could still see it when the mist cleared. There were a couple of trees to shade it. They chopped at the matted webs of roots under the grass and then on down into the soft sandy soil. Even in his grief Bedivere obviously relished the feeling of wielding a shovel with two hands for the first time in his life.

Collum remembered burying Sir Bleoberys under his tree. It was easier digging with a shovel and not a sword.

As they worked, the others talked about the Arthur they remembered, which over time led to Dinadan doing his impression of Arthur yielding in a tournament, once again amazed that his mediocre swordsmanship had somehow been bested, and it was so dead-on that even Bedivere laughed. Even Guinevere.

"I used to wonder how Arthur became Arthur," Bedivere said. "Coming from where he did. I mean, how the hell did he manage it? And I suppose he was trying to please God and atone for his father, and all the rest of it, but I wonder too if he didn't just make himself up. It was painfully obvious how much Britain needed a King Arthur, and once he saw that he had to become him. He couldn't give us anything less. It just wasn't in his nature."

No one said it but they could all feel the wound of Arthur's death, which had been open and festering for so long, being drained and cleaned and properly dressed at last.

"He went back in his dreams," Guinevere said. "In his dreams at least the prophecy came true."

They placed a rough gray standing stone at Arthur's head, and Morgan inscribed it using an enchanted knife that cut the stone as easily as if it were cutting soap:

HIC IACET ARTHURUS
REX QUONDAM
†

Bedivere blew a mournful call on his hunting horn. Then they walked back to the castle with the sun going down over the wide, flat glittering sea. They weren't so deep in the Otherworld that the sun didn't set.

THAT NIGHT NIMUE took a bath in a copper tub; Collum sat on a stool nearby and enjoyed the steam.

"I'm sorry you're not his son," she said. "After all that."

She looked if possible even more beautiful with her dark hair wet and smoothed back and her face glowing pink from the heat.

"I never really believed it. Or maybe I did a little, but not for long."

"Somewhere you had a father, Collum. Maybe he was a king, maybe he was a fisherman, I don't know, but whoever he was he missed his son. And he wished he knew you. And he would've been proud of you if he did."

Reluctantly Collum looked at himself in a mirror, a disk of polished silver in an ivory frame, searching for the traces of his father's features in his own face. It was like trying to read the secret scraped-off underwriting of a palimpsest.

"I'm just sorry Arthur's not coming back," he said.

"Honestly I don't know what to believe in anymore." Nimue looked if not exactly hopeless—she was temperamentally incapable of true hopelessness—then getting ever more thoroughly resigned to disappointment. "Maybe I don't have to know. I can be a good person without God, or fairy either. I guess I'll just believe in myself for a while."

"Well, I believe in you."

"It's a start."

"Did you really used to work in a laundry?"

"Yes. And so you know, whatever happens I will never wash your shirts. Not ever."

She was dabbing her face with tartar oil to keep her skin smooth. In the mirror Collum saw the wings again, over his shoulder, deep iridescent-blue butterfly wings, just like he had in the Glass Castle. It was an unpleasant, uncanny feeling, like he'd spotted a large spider clinging to his back, and he couldn't reach it to brush it off. He forced himself to hold still and study them in the cloudy metal, like seeing himself through sheets of driving rain. He had to keep wiping the steam away.

He showed Nimue, and she studied them, too, tilting the mirror different ways, while Collum waited for the inevitable grim diagnosis.

"What do you think?" he said, when he couldn't wait any longer.

"You definitely need a haircut."

"I meant about the wings! What does it mean? Am I a fairy?!"

"As much as I relish the idea of having a secret fairy lover, no, I don't think so. Or it's not exactly that. But there's something more to you that we haven't seen yet, and it's past time that we found it."

They went to bed not long after that, together, but they didn't do anything, just slept. For tonight sleeping was enough.

In the morning nothing obvious had changed—the apples still hung heavily on the trees, the green sea still rolled up onto the sand, the mists still wrapped everything in quiet—but the mood had subtly altered. It was time to go, and everybody knew it. Lancelot would be tightening his grip on Britain, and Collum wasn't looking forward to it but somebody had to fight back.

Morgan didn't try to stop them—Collum doubted she was especially sorry to see them go—but as a concession she did offer them a bigger boat this time, a two-masted caravel half again as long as the *Errant*.

"Guinevere couldn't have handled this one alone," she explained.

"Also I stole the last one," Guinevere added. "Or did you think it was Morgan's idea to come save you?"

The extra space would come in handy because Palomides was coming this time.

"I am still a knight of the Round Table," he said, "and I fear that you will screw things up without me."

"Are you sure?" Bedivere rumbled.

"I am sure you will screw things up."

"I mean are you sure you're still one of us?"

"I said the vows, just as you did, Bedivere. They are forever. I used to wonder why God or fate had brought me to Britain, if it was only to lose Isolde and then Arthur. But I know now that that is precisely why I came—precisely because Arthur was going to die. I came to see Britain through its difficult rebirth."

"Guard yourselves," Morgan said. "Change is coming. Dark times are on their way."

"They're pretty dark already," Dinadan said. "Some change would do Britain good."

"Maybe," Morgan said. "But be careful what you wish for."

They walked out to the end of the pier. Morgan whistled and the caravel came gliding out of the mist like a faithful hound. Curiously its hull was made entirely out of bronze; it didn't look like it should float, but it did. Palomides kissed Morgan soundly on the lips, in front of everyone, and climbed in. Guinevere and Dinadan sorted out the rigging and raised the sails. Collum tried not to get in their way. A fairy wind blew up and swept them out into the bay and then up into the sky.

Only once they were well away and aloft did the five of them start to discuss in practical terms what was coming next.

"We can start in Dyfed." Steadying himself on a stay—with his left hand!—Bedivere looked more alert and engaged than Collum had ever seen him before. Atlas hadn't shrugged off his burden, but the great globe of the world had become a little lighter somehow, and he'd straightened his spine and unbowed his head. "A lot of the west will be for Lancelot, but my nephew will support us, and there'll be a few other holdouts, mostly the same Camelot-hating malcontents who used to piss off my father. It's a start. Guinevere, what about Cameliard?"

Somewhere along the way Bedivere and the queen had gone from adversaries to something else, if not friends then fellow travelers.

"I've alienated most of my family, but I will try. I'll speak to my father."

"We need to find out where Cornwall stands," Dinadan said. "The old ways are strong there. And I don't know that King Cador loved his son much but I doubt he appreciated Lancelot's killing him."

"Someone will have to go there in person," Nimue said. "Who here offended him the least?"

Good God, what a long road they still had ahead, Collum thought as they talked. It was going to be a long, long game. But just then they broke out of the fog into sunlight and the shimmering ocean spread out underneath them in fathomless woad blue, and for a heartbeat it was impossible not to feel hopeful. A flag bearing Avalon's arms—an apple tree, one half of it green, the other half in flames—stood out straight from the top of the mainmast. Look at me, he thought. The wool broker's stepson, flying to Britain's rescue in a magic boat with Queen Guinevere herself, and Sir Bedivere, and Palomides, and Dinadan, and a beautiful witch with whom I am almost certainly falling in love. He ran a hand through his hair, stiff with salt, and thought about how long ago it was that he'd paid a hatchet to cross the Firth of Lorn in a fishing boat, wearing Alasdair's stolen armor.

"Collum."

Guinevere had been watching him from across the bronze ship's narrow deck.

"Collum, I'll admit that I felt some relief when I learned that Arthur was not in fact your father. I'm certainly not your mother, and one royal bastard was quite enough for my liking. But it caused me to give some thought to the question of who your father really was."

"My stepfather always said he was a fisherman."

"Maybe he was, but I have another theory. How old are you, Collum?"

"Eighteen. I think." It was a little confusing after the year he'd had, which had stretched and compressed and generally abused the even flow of time. He'd never known his exact birthday anyway, only that it was in the spring. "Maybe we'd better sit down for this."

Collum crossed to her side of the boat and sat. Guinevere folded her hands in her lap.

"There's a story—well, it's not much of one, court gossip mostly, and Morgan will know parts of it that I don't—but it more or less fits the facts. It goes something like this. A fairy came to see Morgan once, in the Otherworld. She was pregnant. The father was a human. A knight of the Round Table, in fact.

"Such romances do happen, though I must say I consider it more than a little perverse. She was a flower-fairy, presumably one of the more human-looking ones. Human enough, at any rate. The knight had fallen in love with her, and they had, as it were, dallied together.

"It was not a romance for the ages, not to her anyway, but the fairy girl became pregnant. It's customary in such cases, apparently, for the fairy to give birth and then go her merry way and let the child be raised by its human parent. This fairy didn't wish to stay with the knight, but she was reluctant to give the baby up either. To give you up. She must have had a tender heart, for a fairy."

Collum kept his eyes fixed on the faraway horizon, trying to hold back a mighty wave of confused emotions.

"What happened to her?"

"Morgan let her stay with her till the baby was born—yes, in the Otherworld, right there in the Glass Castle. But Morgan wouldn't have a son of Camelot raised in the Otherworld, and the fairy girl had no wish to remain with your father, so Morgan packed her off to the most obscure location she could find, namely Mull, to live as a human and raise her child. This she did.

"Eventually she did fall in love, I believe with the man you know as your stepfather. She had a tender heart indeed. And he loved her as well, though there is some question of whether she induced him to through magical means. The fairies don't consider it cheating."

Guinevere spoke with her usual precise formal cadences, exactly as if she were informing him that it might rain, or that she'd decided to have him executed tomorrow.

"Your father was a tenderhearted man too—Sir Bleoberys was his name, did I mention? A Frank. He remained in love with the fairy girl and never forgot her. In fact when she'd been gone a few years he left Camelot and went searching for her, and for his son.

"Of course she died, as you know. Fairies can live almost indefinitely, but they can die too. Morgan feels some responsibility. A flower-fairy was never going to flourish that far north. I suppose that's why Morgan looked in on you. To this day I don't know what happened to your father. He could still be out there searching for you."

"He's not," Collum said quietly.

"No? Ah well."

"He found me, and I killed him."

"Oh!"

There was some satisfaction at least in having gotten a reaction out of the queen.

He'd no sooner acquired a father than he'd murdered him. I am a father killer, he thought, as surely as Mordred was. Collum felt like he was floating up and out of his body. The memory of that day in that meadow came back to him in vivid colors and played itself out again in fast motion while he tried to claw back every last detail of his father. The knight in old-fashioned armor, under a crooked ash, his head in his hands. The desultory chat, then three passes with a lance—Collum had had to borrow one. His own bumptious excitement at his glorious chance, come at last. Then the duel with swords, and the ugly finish. Poor Old Blueberries, picked at last.

But now he did what he'd never bothered to do before, or known how to do, which was to think of it from the other point of view. Sir Bleoberys's. His father's. The heat, the weariness, the knowledge that he could always give up and go back to Camelot if he chose, and at the same time the equal certainty that he could not, not without his beloved, and not without his son. He couldn't let them go. And she already long dead by then. And Arthur dead too.

He must have arrived at the meadow, a perfectly ordinary meadow like any other, and somehow realized he couldn't go on. He'd sat down, throbbing with despair, and waited for the sun to melt him into nothing. And when it didn't, he must've looked up and seen, emerging from the forest, an apparition: a young knight, looking much as he must have once, years ago. And much like his son must now, or just about. They would've been of an age. And knowing that here was the dark angel come to see him out of this long life at last.

You never met a more courtly knight, Bedivere said, and Collum was sure it was true, even though his death was bitter and uncouth. They could both be true: his father was both a courtly knight and an uncouth one, a good man and a bad one, hero and villain. That was the truth. And wasn't it a good thing to know the truth of one's own father, whose sins he carried, even when it was too late to save him?

Nimue put a hand on his arm. He realized the whole boat had been listening.

"And to think he had finally found what he sought, and never knew it," Palomides said. "A blessed end, and a cursed one too."

But he'd loved his son. He'd never given up searching. It was love that brought him to that fatal meadow. And it was he who brought me the medal, for all the good it did, Collum thought. He tried to remember if their blades had ever met in the bind, if he'd ever felt his father's strength pushing directly against his.

"Thank you," he said to Guinevere. "Thank you for telling me."

"Half a fairy and a half a Frank," Dinadan said. "An intriguing inheritance. You could change your arms now, though I'll admit I've gotten used to the sheep. Maybe it could be carrying a few scepters."

"Problematic," Palomides said. "He is still *filius nullius*, if you take my meaning."

"No problem at all," Dinadan said, "you just add a baton sinister or a wavy bordure or some such. Happens more than you'd—"

The ship lurched. It felt like they'd clipped underwater rocks, except that they were a thousand feet in the air. Everybody looked at Guinevere.

"That wasn't me."

She peered over the side, trying to see the hull. Collum could feel in his stomach that the ship was starting to descend.

"Did we hit a bird?" Dinadan said. "Or an angel?"

"That was no angel," said Bedivere.

Guinevere gave Palomides the helm as she and Dinadan struggled with the sails, trying to find a new tack, but the ship kept losing altitude. Its bronze plates creaked and groaned. Something was very wrong.

"Nimue!" Guinevere shouted.

"I'm trying!"

At least they had land in sight: a stony gray coastline was visible in the distance, beyond a field of gray waves, looking plausibly enough like Cornwall. But it would be a tough swim, and there were ships in the water, three at least, between them and the shore, and they flew the red and white.

The deck tilted, and Palomides only just caught himself by hanging on to the tiller.

"What, did we run out of magic?" Dinadan said.

"Too much of it." Nimue's voice was tense. "This is Merlin's work. He's trying to force us down."

"He's doing pretty well at it," Bedivere said.

Nimue called out names to the empty sky—local winds, presumably—but she evidently got no answer because they began to drop so fast that Collum's gorge rose and he clung desperately to a railing. He was almost relieved when the hull smashed down onto the waves, so hard that the masts shook and a couple of stays snapped. So much seawater came over the side that Collum thought they would be swamped, and he wished ardently that the hull was made of something more buoyant than bronze, but somehow they stayed afloat. Masses of foaming green water poured off the deck, which stayed tilted at a worrisome angle.

Guinevere fought to get the ship moving, cursing very unregally, her hair half loose and flying in the wind, barking orders, trying to make some headway. They could see the other ships, not far off now, two cogs and a longship; one of the cogs was already coming about to intercept, its great sail rippling.

"They must've known we were coming," Collum said.

"I guess there are less conspicuous modes of travel than a flying caravel," Dinadan said. "Can we get back in the air?"

Guinevere shook her head definitively.

"We'll cut east along the coast," Bedivere said. "Make for Tintagel."

"Merlin will have the winds and the currents on his side," Nimue said. "We'll never make headway against them. We'll have to fight."

The longship was crowded with soldiers rowing for all they were worth right at them.

"I might be able to summon a whale," she said wearily. Nimue couldn't be relishing the thought of more spellcasting after the other night. "It would do for one ship, maybe two."

"Save your strength," Guinevere said.

The long game wasn't looking so long after all. He would die fighting with a sword in his hand, that much he knew. Unless one of the archers on those cogs got him first. Or unless—

Better hung for a sheep than for a lamb. Collum took Nimue's hand.

"I'm thinking of something."

"If you're going to fly away on your fairy wings, take me with you."

"Not that."

He kissed her, then made his way forward as fast as he could, stumbling over mounds of coiled rope, before she could ask any questions. He had that same feeling he'd had in the Chapel of the Spear: there were no more choices left. No more questions, only what must be done. The difference now was that it wasn't God's will he was doing, it was his own. I killed my own father to be here, he thought. Who else wants to get in my way?

Reaching the bow he took a few deep breaths, the way he had deep in the well of Camelot. Bedivere called his name, but he didn't turn around. If he tried to explain they would stop him, and if he waited any longer he wouldn't have the courage. Hastily he took off his boots and stepped up onto the gunwale. He looked down at the prow cutting through the water, throwing off clean, white spray on either side. By what means, he wondered stupidly, does dark water so suddenly become white?

The longship was closing. Another minute and they'd be in range of the archers.

He expected it but the water was still a shock. This wasn't the warm bubbly ocean of Avalon, this was the deep, freezing, unforgiving Atlantic that ate sailors by the thousands. But death waited for him in the world of light up above too. And he'd felt colder in the well. Now to find out exactly what my little gift is worth, he thought.

He kicked and swam and struggled downward, forcing himself deeper and deeper. Pressure pushed in at his ears, and salt stung his eyes, but he kept them open. Was there something down there, a light shining in the black?

But he couldn't reach it, it was so much farther than he could go, fathoms and fathoms farther. Cursing himself he turned for the surface and the sun. He bobbed up and then kicked down again but came up even quicker this time. He was already exhausted.

The bronze ship was coming around hard, chased by a swarm of arrows. Bedivere threw him a rope. He clutched it weakly and let himself be hauled, dripping and shivering and scraped, back up onto the deck.

"What in God's name are you playing at, Collum?" Guinevere snapped.

"No time. Explain later." They probably thought he was trying to swim away. Somehow he'd thought that when it came to it he'd be strong enough. He wasn't but he had to be. He fought free of the helping hands and staggered to the bow again. He caught a quick glimpse of Nimue working her war magic—a swell rose up out of nowhere and broke over the longship, spilling shouting men into the water. It gave him the last bit of courage he was missing. If he couldn't do this for himself he would do it for her. There was a wooden locker by the foremast where they kept the anchor. He hauled it out and with shaking hands undid the pin and detached it from the chain.

Grunting and shaking with the effort he heaved the anchor up onto the gunwale, then over the side. It jerked him unceremoniously down after it.

This time there was no coming back. Like a runaway horse the anchor dragged him straight down, tearing deeper and deeper into the lightless underworld of darkness and pressure and consuming cold. Day became twilight and then night and then a darkness deeper than night. There is a point, he knew, where any free diver turns around, where his instincts tell him that past this point only the dead go. The anchor sped him past that line and down, down, down, fathom on fathom, into the black.

For a time Collum lost all sense of motion, it was as if he hung suspended, frozen in black ice—then the anchor touched bottom. He hung from it upside down, his legs kicking overhead. Carefully he pulled his feet down and placed them gingerly on the sand. It was like he'd finally reached the moon after all. He looked up but couldn't even see the surface.

But there was another light, and it was down here with him. It was coming closer, across the sandy bottom, through a towering grove of seaweed. It was a woman, not sylphlike but full-figured, her white samite gown billowing around her as if in a high wind. The light came not from her but from what she carried in her left hand: a bright shining sword.

Collum went to one knee on the uneven ocean floor. *We shall not go this day to our meat until we have heard or seen of a great marvel.*

"I am the Lady of the Lake," she said.

"I'm honored to meet you. My name is Sir Collum of the Out Isles."

If she was honored to meet him she didn't mention it.

"At least Arthur had the good sense to stay in the boat."

The Lady's face was round and pleasant and looked like it was capable of joy and merriment, but it wasn't joyful or merry today.

"Lady, I beseech you, Britain has great need of that sword you carry."

"This is Excalibur, the Sword of Light," she said. "Or Caledfwlch, or Caliburnus, or Claidheamh Soluis. They are all one. But why should I care for Britain and what it needs?"

"You are a creature of Britain, for all that you dwell below the surface." It wasn't much of an answer but it was what came to him. "And you gave it to Arthur."

"Under false pretenses." Her long loose hair washed this way and that. "Merlin told me that Arthur would use Excalibur to expel the interloper Jesus from our shores. Gods forgive me, I believed him. But Arthur was just another Christian king. He did nothing for us. What lies do you have for me, Sir Collum?"

"Arthur was a good king," Collum said. "Christian or not, he was a good king and a good man. And before he died he returned what was yours."

"His lackey threw it in the ocean." The Lady examined the blade in her hand. The way she held it made Collum think she knew how to use it. "Perhaps he forgot precisely what I am the Lady of. The salt water does not agree with me. Tell me then, what kind of a king are you? You have the old blood in you, fairy blood, but sadly polluted."

"I am no king, my lady. I'm no one at all. I only want to strike a blow for Britain."

"A blow for Britain. Really. Is that all?" Her narrow eyebrows arched. A half dozen brownish cod flitted between them silently, each one a foot long. Collum startled, but she didn't blink. "The world is not now as it once was, Sir No One. The gods no longer make heroes."

"And yet I have a hero's work to do." Collum kept his eyes on hers. "How shall I do it?"

"The hard way," the Lady in the Lake replied.

She raised Excalibur in both hands, its blade flaring white in the darkness, reversed it and thrust it straight down into a rough stone outcrop jutting from the sea floor. She buried it so deep that only six inches of bright steel showed above the rock.

"It's all a farce." There was bitterness in her voice. "I can't stop you. So go on. Take it if you can."

A stray current lifted a whirl of floating silt around her. When it settled again she was gone. Collum was alone at the bottom of the sea with a sword in a stone.

Of course Excalibur wasn't the sword in the stone, they were two different swords, but somehow this one was both at once. There wasn't much time, the battle was already joined on the surface, but he took a moment to examine it.

Its grip was some exotic crimson leather, and its pommel was a silver thistle. On its cross guard was written SIC TRANSIT on one side and GLORIA MUNDI on the other. What he could see of the blade itself was so densely etched with writing in such a magnificently florid script that he couldn't read it at all. Its edge was so fine that it seemed to disappear when he looked at it.

As for the stone it was stuck in, it was pitted and misshapen and encrusted with barnacles and anemones. For a crazy moment Collum wondered if he could just pick the whole thing up, like one of the throwing stones in the yard at Camelot, and take it with him, sword and all. But it was far too big, and it looked like it was rooted in the bedrock of the earth. There had been writing on the stone in the churchyard: WHOSO PULLETH OUT THIS SWORD OF THIS STONE AND ANVIL and so on and so forth. But there were no words on this one. No instructions this time. No anvil either.

Collum set his hand to the hilt and pulled. It didn't move. He'd heard the stories about Arthur drawing the sword out of the stone, and they'd always said it came out effortlessly. But Collum wasn't Arthur. He wasn't even Arthur's bastard offspring. He braced his foot on the stone and pulled harder. The sword felt fixed in the rock as if it were part of it.

He climbed up on top of the stone—it was a little undignified, but there was no one there to see him except those brown cod. He thought about all the people who'd had to die just so he could be there. Valiant Sir Villiars, and Sir Ganadal, drowned in the river of the Otherworld, and all those men in the battle—six by his hand, and how many by Nimue's? More than a hundred. Sir Kay by his own hand. Sir Scipio by a demon, and Sir Dagonet by an angel.

And poor Sir Constantine, killed by Lancelot. And poor Sir Melehan too.

And his fairy-mother, and Sir Bleoberys, his father. And King Arthur.

And after all that Collum was still here. He doubted they would've picked him as their champion if they'd all sat down and had a vote, but he was who they got. Alone in the darkness, under the vast weight of the ocean, he set himself and pulled till his fingers hurt, with a lot of embarrassing grunting. The sword didn't move. Take it if you can? Well, he couldn't!

God damn it to hell. Maybe he really wasn't the one. He ought to go back up and fetch the others and give them a try.

But of course he wasn't the one, he thought, there were no ones anymore. The gods no longer make heroes. Wasn't that what Arthur meant? *You can't just pull it out of a stone the way I did.* But he wasn't going back up to the ship without it either. He would starve to death down here if he had to, his bony fingers locked around the hilt. For the first time Collum felt himself getting short of breath. Maybe this little gift of his wasn't going to last forever, and there was no friendly giant waiting to fish him out this time. Gawain had gotten some fairy strength from his fairy blood; if Collum had any this would be a good time for it to show up. What had the lady said? The hard way? It wasn't hard, it was damn impossible.

But he'd never done anything the easy way. He wouldn't have known how. Everything he had he'd either fought for or stolen, starting with the wooden sword he took from that wide-eyed, jug-eared boy back at Dubh Hall, that had felt like the lightning bolt of Jupiter himself in his hand. If he waited for God to choose him, or fairy, or anybody, he'd be waiting forever. He would have to choose himself.

I cannot draw it, but I must take it. *A paradox: discuss.* He heard Arthur's voice—*It's not too late*—and felt the hot ray of his all-seeing gaze go through him like a sunbeam through glass. *The crack in the crystal.* It was a new age, and he would have to write the story himself now or all the worst people would do it for him. His heart was a great hammer ruthlessly punishing an anvil. *May I start my training now?* I'm sorry I killed you, father, but maybe it won't be for nothing. He squatted down and hefted the anchor up over his head like a giant's mattock. Maybe you could even forgive me, wherever you are, as I forgive you for trying to stab me in the groin. I shall not repeat your sin. *Thy quest is not yet at an end.* Light bloomed around him in the depths, a fairy light that came from within him, and with his ancestors roaring inside him in a chorus Collum smashed the anchor down on the rough rock with all the strength he had or ever would have.

A spark flared in the deep. The stone split wide open with a crack that sent a shock wave flashing out across the ocean floor all around him in a circle. When the dust and sand had settled, the bright treasure lay exposed at last.

Collum lifted Excalibur from the rubble. A new sword, in a new stone. It shone like a torch. All around him the cod gazed at it in awe. Leaving the anchor behind, he crouched and jumped and with the last of his air shot up from the bottom of the sea, trailing bubbles, all the way to the surface, out of the darkness and into the light.

Thirty-six

THE NIGHT OFFICE

Camelot had never looked more magnificent.

It was a grand sunny afternoon in late May, two years after the calamitous end of the quest for the Holy Grail, and a crowd had gathered at the tilting yard for a tournament in honor of the Feast of the Ascension. Dozens of striped and spotted lances waved and pointed up at all angles. Ladies in samite and silk milled around and talked and laughed with delight at what a day it was and how beautiful everybody looked, and knights traded greetings and gossip and boasts, their surcoats alive with beasts and fruits and stars and crosses. Heralds competed to see how loudly they could announce new arrivals and sharply criticized one another's grasp of social protocol and the nuances of heraldry.

Snatches and skirls of music surfaced from the chatter, lute and pipe, and then were immediately drowned again. Little dogs went whipping and yapping wildly around people's feet in circles, chased by little children. Horses were shitting with a majestic lack of self-consciousness.

The tournament had already been going on for hours, but there was still no actual tilting yet. The knights had arrived in a parade at dawn, each one led by a lady on a silver chain. Since the adventures had ended, tournaments had compensated by growing and evolving into a wildly elaborate theater, with complicated and largely nonsensical storylines. This one involved a knight dressed as Oberon, King of the Fairies, and another one dressed as Hercules, and still others dressed as the devil and Thunar and an elephant and the pope and the emperor of Nubia. Somewhere in there a dwarf would symbolically abduct the Queen of May, played with undeniable flair by Isolde the Blonde.

And if it all didn't summon up quite the same sense of triumph as say, vanquishing a giant might have, or banishing a demon—if there was a certain hollowness to it, a great clatter of arms to no real purpose—well, the world was not what it was in those days. Change was inevitable, the river flowed, *panta rhei* and so on, as Heraclitus said, or at any rate as Merlin said he said. The time before the Grail already seemed like a lost world.

And after all, King Arthur thought, there was something to be said for not having to deal with giants and demons.

Change might have been inevitable, but time passed damned slowly in the royal box. He watched the marshal walking up and down by himself, nervously buffing his brass horn on his ceremonial jacket, and his mind drifted back to his very first tournament, the one in Londinium so long ago, a quarter of a century now, when he'd tried to make off with a sword set decoratively in an anvil on top of a stone and instead found himself being crowned High King of Britain.

"Remember, Bedivere?" he said. "All I wanted was to get drunk and see Sir Mador de la Porte knock Kay off his horse, and suddenly everybody was shouting that I should be drowned in holy water because I was a fiend in disguise trying to usurp the throne."

"I was shouting that," Bedivere said. "It was my first tournament, and you ruined it."

"At least you were there." Lancelot lounged languidly on a richly embroidered, wildly overstuffed armchair. "I was stuck under a millpond in Benwick. No flampets on offer there, I can tell you."

Lancelot had declined to compete in the present tournament, claiming an injury, though everybody knew the real reason, which was that if entered he would almost certainly have won everything.

"And I was sulking at home," Guinevere said, "because my father took my brothers but not me. They're still mad at you, by the way. Amador thinks he could've pulled the sword out first if he'd had half a chance."

"He had every chance," Arthur said mildly. "Security was shockingly lax. He should've shown a little initiative."

At last the jousting began, and many fine feats of arms were accomplished. Sir Gawain, Sir Dodinas le Savage, Sir Dinadan, and Sir Bruenor le Noire (universally known as La Cote Male Taile because he showed up on his first day at court in a torn surcoat— one of Sir Kay's jibes that stuck) were all awarded golden keys. Sir Uwaine les Avoutres and Sir Ozanna le Cure Hardy won ornamented belts.

The only unhappy note came when Sir Galleron of Galway broke a lance against Sir Kay de Stranges (not to be confused with the Sir Kay the Seneschal, he of the droll jibes). It was an able performance, especially considering that Galleron was still dressed up as Oberon, but when his lance burst a spinning scrap of ashwood caught him straight in the eye.

Even from the royal box you could see the pale wood projecting out of his visor as he finished his pass. Then he fainted and fell off his horse. The crowd watched him carried off in silence.

"He's going to lose that eye," Guinevere said quietly. "If he's lucky."

Arthur felt his mood darkening. That a man should lose an eye, and for what? A game, played for nothing. A footman handed round glasses of a pale golden wine from Gallaecia, chilled to a wonderful aching cold with ice saved in sawdust from the previous winter.

Though there was precious little ice to save, since the winter had been laughably mild. After the Grail Quest, after he'd turned away from God, Arthur had been sure that plagues and curses would rain down and make Britain a waste land, a sea of sand like the one he'd seen with Bedivere on the adventure of the Maimed King. Dead trees and white sky. Dust and ashes. But instead the last two years had been almost perversely fertile. The castle gardens ran riot with peas and beans and cabbages and onions and more, exotic plants that had never grown in Britain before: cumin and ginger, nutmeg and cinnamon. What, the king wondered, was God playing at?

Arthur supposed he could have asked one of his many bishops, but on the Feast of the Ascension they would be busy blessing beans and extinguishing the paschal candle, and they had no real interest in mending Arthur's breach with God anyway. To the contrary, without God always sticking his oar in, upstaging them with His showy marvels, the priests of Britain had finally taken their rightful place as the center of attention. God's absence was the best thing that ever happened to them!

"We should decide what to do about Sir Selises." Bedivere had noticed Arthur's faltering mood and was valiantly attempting to make conversation. "A night in the dungeon, maybe, to think on his wrongdoing."

"Stiff fine." Guinevere wore a ravishing dress of marbled yellow silk, embroidered with white roses and trimmed with silver thread.

"Spell in the stocks," Lancelot said. "Make him an example."

"I'm inclined to clemency," Arthur said stiffly. "The poor man was desperate."

"They won't let you off that easily," Guinevere said. "The crowd is out for blood."

Earlier that day it was found that Sir Selises of the Dolorous Tower had bolted the seat of his armor to his saddle to make himself harder to dislodge, a shameful thing but sadly not unusual these days. With no adventures to attempt, nothing holy or sacred to pursue, the knights of the Round Table would go to any lengths to win a tournament. How else was one to gain glory?

"Someone ought to look into Sir Floriant's lances too," Lancelot said. "To my eye they look an inch or two too long."

Arthur's own eye caught on something in among the milling crowd: a knight in blood-red armor standing there motionless, staring up at him. There was something uncanny about him—he was going to point him out to Bedivere, but when he looked again the Red Knight was gone.

After the joust came the mêlée, where Sir Scipio and Sir Palomides were judged the winners and received gold chains from the Duchess of Lyonesse in the guise of the goddess Juno. Then they fought each other, and Palomides won another gold chain, this one presented to him by the Queen of May herself, Isolde the Beautiful, safely recovered from her abduction.

He immediately knelt and offered it right back to her. She declined with a tight smile. Palomides flung the chain down on the grass and walked away in a distracted state.

"He's making quite an ass of himself," Guinevere said. "I fear the poor man may one day do himself harm."

"Suicide is forbidden to the Saracen," Lancelot said, "as it is to us."

"Lots of people do forbidden things," Bedivere said.

With the shadows lengthening and the contest over, knights and spectators alike drifted off through the cooling air to clean up and rest up and dress up for the feast, which would run late into the night. An exhausting prospect, the *après-tournoi*—the noise, the drink, the same old stories. He might have to feign an injury like Lancelot. Whence this sudden bout of melancholy? Arthur felt sometimes like his life was consuming itself like a lit fuse, dissolving into smoke and sparks as it went. Acedia, the priests called it, and it ill became a king. But how to banish it?

He was about to join Guinevere in visiting the wounded Sir Galleron when Bedivere begged a private word.

"My king," he said. "Are you entirely well?"

"Don't I look well?" Arthur said.

"Not really, no."

"Well, I feel fine. Don't fuss at me, Bedivere."

"You seem weary. I diagnose an excess of the black bile."

"Maybe a feast will help."

"That seems unlikely."

They descended the stairs from the royal box together. Arthur was aware that his impatience was just proving Bedivere's point, but Bedivere always did see things in him that he couldn't see in himself, both good and bad. And in turn Arthur saw the love in Bedivere, though he couldn't return it, not in kind. It was their Gordian knot, and they could neither solve it nor cleave it in two.

"When was the last time you went hunting?" Bedivere asked.

"Hunting? It's been a good while." Months. Years maybe.

"Why don't—?"

"Affairs of state. Pressing affairs. You know that."

"Delegate them."

"To—?"

"To me." Bedivere stopped, and with a strong hand on Arthur's shoulder he made him stop too. "I beg it as a boon, Arthur."

He hadn't heard that phrase in a long time.

"I can't," Arthur said.

"Why not?"

The king was rarely at a loss for words, they were among his most faithful servants, but now they wouldn't come when called. Maybe it was the black bile. A ragged line of groundsmen progressed slowly across the churned-up grass of the tiltyard, bending and picking up soiled papers and ash splinters. Hungry birds swooped in behind them to glean whatever they missed.

It had indeed been a long time since Arthur hunted, and even longer since he'd fewtered a lance, or done anything else with one. He'd been a knight once, as well as a king. *Dux bellorum.* Black Arthur. The river flowed. *Panta rhei.*

"I will admit," he said, "that of late I do feel a little lost."

"But that's exactly what you aren't, Arthur." Bedivere kept hold of his shoulder. "That's exactly the problem. You know exactly where you are. You need to get out into the forest like we used to, in the old days, and get properly lost."

FEASTS WERE NOT a trivial matter at Camelot. In lush years like these the cook thought nothing of laying on thirty courses, beef

and venison and partridge and eel, duck and pig and veal and ba-
con, peacock and heron, ten kinds of fish, lark pasties, civet of hare,
aspics and puddings and sausages, all in ever more elaborate preparations. He was fiendishly inventive. Tonight the pièce de résistance
was a trio of uncannily lifelike swans, their graceful heads propped
up on hidden wire and their beaks and claws painted with gold
leaf. They'd been plucked and roasted whole and then had their
feathers carefully reinserted, one by one. Their eyes were replaced
with flashing rubies. They swam in a marvelous pond of dry water, with reeds around the edges, fashioned entirely of sugar and
pastry.

Lancelot was telling a long and rather humiliating story about
something that happened to him on the Grail Quest—he seemed
to have an endless fund of them, all involving mysterious knights
unhorsing him and hermits scolding him and magic chapels that
wouldn't let him in. The younger knights hung on his every word.
Arthur had had to bring on a lot of them to make up for the losses
on the Grail Quest.

"I wouldn't've minded a few hermits," Gawain said. "I didn't see
shit on the quest."

"Maybe you were too busy killing eighteen knights," Lancelot
said.

"Nonsense," Gawain said, unruffled. "One of 'em slipped in the
tub. Death by misadventure. Happens more often than you'd think."

Lancelot smiled and turned away to talk to Sir Petipase on his
other side. Gawain could best him at that game anyway. Trap for
young players, Guinevere would say.

The feast swung into high gear. The knights seemed to have
taken the wrong lesson from the Grail Quest, which was that if
nobody could meet God's high standards, not even Lancelot, why

even try? Though admittedly it was hard to see the flaw in the logic. Everything seemed so insubstantial since then, himself most of all, like he would blow away in a stiff breeze if it weren't for this heavy gold hat on his head. And without God's blessing was it even his? Was he still a king? How did you make a king without God? He wondered if he could even pull the sword from the stone now, if he had it to do over again. He was just a middle-aged man, lugging the tattered standard of a fallen empire. Our strength is not now as it was in those days.

And yet Britain needed a king. Someone to show them the path. The inedible head of a roast swan stared at him accusingly with its one ruby eye—somebody had filched the other—from where it lay on its pool of dry water. Dust and ashes.

A roar of laughter and applause greeted Sir Kay, in full drag, leading in the unfortunate Sir Selises on one of those damned silver chains. And he had Sir Floriant with him, too, they'd done him for his oversized lances. It had been decided that as punishment the two men would be made to paddle each other in the Great Hall.

Kay began a speech. Arthur turned the old coin in his fingers, worn so smooth that the bear on it was just a shadow in a silver mist. He tapped it on the arm of his chair. Enough. He stood up, maybe a little too abruptly. There were whispers. *His Highness has perhaps overmuch partaken.*

"My friends, there will be no paddling tonight." Groans of disappointment, and a few approving *Huzzahs.* "I choose to exercise my royal prerogative and pardon Sir Selises of the Dolorous Tower. I pardon Sir Floriant as well."

The begowned Sir Kay gave him a furious look, exactly the same one he'd given Arthur a thousand years ago at Little Dunoak when he'd beaten him at skittles.

"Let no man hold them in contempt. They wished only to be better than they were, and who among us has not wished that? Come, my friends. Come here and be forgiven."

Arthur put his arms around the two prisoners. Selises, a big man with a lumpen, ogrish look about him, burst into a noisy flood of tears on his shoulder.

Fortunately the crowd's attention was already moving on. There was to be a spectacle, the story of Moses, with a burning bush that really burned and a mechanical sea that would actually part. After that the dessert course would rain down from on high: marzipan manna, dropped from the rafters. More miracles, more empty marvels. It was late, and distant bells were ringing for nocturns, the night office.

A footman approached Arthur and whispered in his ear.

Sir Galleron of Galway was dead of his wound. The splinter had penetrated the brain. There was nothing the surgeons could do.

Arthur thanked the man and dismissed him, but his heart was racing like a greyhound. Galleron's death was a tragedy, but it was dawning on him that it was part of some even larger disaster. At Camelot, the heart of the heart of the world, something was wrong. All this merriment was a mere distraction, the hectic flush of a dying land. God had cursed Britain after all, he'd made it a waste land, only he'd kept it a secret. The land had died and been replaced by an empty husk of itself, indistinguishable from the original, as uncannily lifelike as a roasted swan with all its feathers, except that nothing meant anything, and everything was only what it was and nothing more.

No one else knew. None but the king could see it. And how will we survive in a waste land? That was Guinevere's question, right as usual. Where is the Moses who will lead us out of it?

King Arthur motioned to Gawain and Lancelot to attend him.

"My friends, we must away from this place. Tomorrow, at dawn, we're going hunting."

NOT EVERYONE WAS BEST pleased to be up prowling the woods and sniffing fewmets at the break of dawn. Gawain in particular was hungover, and the huntsman's horn was very loud, but Arthur didn't let them off. The king would have his hunt. He'd left Bedivere with a pile of parchment and a long line of petitioners and the king's undying gratitude.

By midafternoon a great hart had been found and chased and exhausted and bayed. Master Huntsman Edward insisted that Arthur should make the kill, which he duly did, though it took him three arrows to find the heart. Guinevere would've got it in one. But in the end everyone was satisfied that the thing had been done properly.

But Arthur wasn't ready to go home yet. He couldn't. Not back to the counterfeit Camelot of dress-up knights and ruby-eyed swans. He'd come to get lost, and lost he would get. So while the huntsmen were breaking up the carcass, and the dogs were enjoying their reward of the neck and guts of the beast served up on the hide, he pushed deeper into the woods on foot.

Gawain and Lancelot trailed after him in silence. He felt either very wise or very foolish, but he kept going. *We shall not go this day to our meat.*

They were in a forest that was known simply as the Old Weald because, contrary to their time-honored modus operandi, the Romans had never seen fit to cut it down. As a result it contained some of the most wondrously ancient old trees in the kingdom, real monsters, bulging and misshapen and big around as towers, some of them resting their lower branches on the forest floor with weariness.

For all its wildness, the Old Weald was a good forest for walking in. The canopy was so thick that hardly anything grew under the trees, and the forest floor was like a darkened ballroom carpeted with leaves. They walked for a good hour or so, and then another, until he'd begun to wonder whether he would become the first British monarch to be usurped by a bear. Here was Moses, leading his people around and around the desert in circles, while years pass and the Promised Land eludes him—

He stopped in a clearing. There it was. That uncanny feeling from so long ago.

"This is it," he said quietly.

"What?" Lancelot had been showing some understandable signs of impatience. "What is what?"

"For once I agree with Lance," Gawain said. "This is not what I grudgingly signed on for."

"Fair friends," Arthur said, "I believe we have come upon an adventure."

"Not possible," said Lancelot.

"Not a new adventure, an old one."

"There's no such thing. You can't have the same adventure twice."

"Maybe it never ended," Gawain said. "Maybe he never finished it the first time."

Arthur knew where he was going now. The forest floor sloped gently upward, and he followed it to the outskirts of a sizable village, on the edge of rolling open land. A small stone castle stood at its center, mounted on the earthworks of what was once a hill fort. The castle's design was unusual in that it had four gates, one at each compass point. It was ringed by a placid moat, its glassy surface almost obscured by floating leaves.

The former waste land had become lush and green again. The castle's gates were open now, no Burning Brothers guarded them. The old wood of the drawbridges had grown decorously mossy with age. When they'd first seen it the castle looked almost abandoned, but now smoke puffed up from chimneys, and sentries walked the battlements, and a flag flew from the top of a tower, a complicated golden knot on a green field.

"Not sure I see the adventure here," Gawain said, "unless we're a-questin' for some poorly thought-out military architecture."

A one-armed guard had to consult with his captain before he admitted them, which he did with a bare minimum of politeness. At least he wasn't made of blue fire. The castle's interior hadn't changed much, not a cross in sight. The wooden beams were hung with bronze shields and carved and painted with sinuous spiraling sigils, just as before. Were they birds? Flowing flowers?

But more than the look Arthur remembered the smell of the place. It was like entering another country. It smelled like Sir Ector's hall, Little Dunoak: fennel and mint and wild marjoram, herbs not brought by the Romans. It was the smell of the Old World, the one the Romans couldn't root out. Pagan Britain. Ector's Britain. Twenty years ago he'd sniffed at it with distaste. It had reminded him too much of his childhood, when he was an unhappy boy of murky origin and uncertain status, heir to nothing but Sir Kay's muddy boots in need of cleaning. King Arthur was not much given to nostalgia.

But he was older now, and perhaps more curious. Now there were no more fiends to face, maybe it was time he faced a few of the demons of his childhood. And after all this was the world of

Igraine, too, his poor lost mother. His father had assaulted her, tried to wipe her away completely, but here was her world, very much still with us, with its old gods and old stones. It was all he would ever have of her.

Old King Bran was gone—Arthur had seen to that—but his children were flourishing. Ystradel and Elidir were well into their thirties now. She looked much the same, with her dark braids and ivory cameo face, but the many luxuries of kingship had filled out and softened Elidir's frame, and his facial hair was if anything even more magnificent than before. Their necks and wrists were heavy with gold and silver. They weren't waiting for him this time. They were eating dinner with their families and seemed to have no idea he was coming. They made King Arthur and his knights sit like lowly petitioners in a receiving room for an hour while they finished, and only the full weight of his royal authority kept Gawain from making trouble.

"Three Mothers have mercy," Ystradel said, when she finally appeared. "If it isn't the man they call King Arthur."

She had no smile for him this time.

"What are you doing here?" Elidir said bluntly.

"I apologize for calling on you unannounced," Arthur said. "We were lost in the forest and came upon your castle. I think some magic must have brought us here, as it did the first time."

"Well, it's not our magic," Ystradel said. "We have all the kings we need."

"And no more fathers for you to kill," Elidir said.

"Hang on," said Gawain, "this is finally getting good. You killed their father?"

Arthur thought everybody had heard the story.

"Their father found the Holy Lance and picked it up," he explained, "and God punished him for it. He was suffering and unable to die, and this kingdom had become a Waste Land. They were waiting for a promised knight to come and heal him."

"Probably it was supposed to be Lancelot," Gawain said.

"It wasn't me. I couldn't heal him, but I thought the poor man had suffered enough, so I released him. By which I mean I killed him. I cut his throat with Excalibur. I was young, or younger anyway, and I was proud, and stupid. I fancied myself a knight, and I badly wanted the adventure to succeed, and I couldn't think of another way.

"And I suppose in a sense I did succeed. The land was reborn."

"Your God took your side," Elidir said. "Unsurprisingly. But there was nothing wrong with our land in the first place, or our father, before He turned up."

It came to Arthur what he had to do now. Maybe this was why the adventure hadn't ended. Slowly, and a little creakily, he went down on one knee and bowed his head before King Elidir and Princess Ystradel. There were some gasps and whispers—the knights had never seen King Arthur kneel to anyone. Well, feast your eyes. A marvel, forsooth. Cutlery clinked at the dinner table at the far end of the hall as wide-eyed children turned to watch.

"I am sorry," Arthur said. "I acted heedlessly and arrogantly. I was too proud and stupid to admit the truth, which was that I did not know what to do. Can you forgive me?"

He kept his eyes on the floor. He was thoroughly out of practice in abasing himself, but he'd seen it done often enough over the years, God knew.

"When you came to us before, our father was under a curse," Ystradel said, "but I think perhaps you're the cursed king now. Perhaps it's your own land that is suffering."

"You could always cut off his head." Gawain tapped the small pale scar on his neck where the Green Knight had nicked him on his own famous adventure. "Fair trade. Quid quo pro."

Lancelot put his hand on his sword, but Arthur didn't move. The heavy weight on his heart had not lifted, but he felt it shift a little.

"At least for once in his life he asked the right question," Ystradel said. "What do you think, Elidir? Should we show them?"

Her brother took a deep, resigned breath and puffed it out his nose.

"Come on then. Gods give me patience."

Without ceremony Ystradel led them through the hall and out across a courtyard teeming with more children, playing some incomprehensible game on squares they'd scratched in the ground. Arthur smiled at them. The children ignored him. They continued on out of the castle, trotting down the stepped earthwork ramparts and out through the west gate.

"I still wonder that we're here," Lancelot said. "My son, Galahad, put an end to all adventures in Britain."

"Maybe this is a false adventure then," Ystradel said, favoring him with a smile. "It's so hard to tell the difference sometimes."

The sun was touching the tree line as they followed the two children of King Bran along a narrow path through tall scratchy blackberries and then out into an overgrown sheep meadow.

"Look," Ystradel said. "The children found it the other day. I told them to keep their grubby paws off it."

It was a stone circle, no different from dozens Arthur had seen across Britain, hundreds probably. When he was a child there had been two stone circles within an hour's walk of Little Dunoak, and Ector would always lead an outing to one or another of them on the quarter days. On Lughnasadh they used to offer up the first fruits of the harvest. Samhain was the masks and the turnip lanterns, which he found utterly terrifying. He could remember the names of the other two quarter days—Imbolc, Beltaine—but not what happened on them. How had he forgotten so much? He used to remember everything.

But in the center of this circle stood something unexpected.

"Merciful God."

Arthur wasn't even sure who said it. He sank to his knees for the second time that day.

"What the hell is that doing here?" Gawain said.

"Beautiful, isn't it?" Ystradel said.

"Yes," Arthur whispered.

"What is it?"

She really didn't know.

"No one truly knows its nature, princess," Arthur said, "but our name for it is the Holy Grail."

The party was silent for a long time. It was the Grail, the same Grail they'd scoured Britain for, humbled themselves for, ruined themselves for. Arthur had never chased it himself but he'd longed for it just like all the others had, and he'd feared and despised it, too, and now there it sat, twenty yards away, like an exotic bird, a cup on a stone table. The setting sun threaded its red beams between the ancient standing stones and stained the Grail's liquid, mirrored surface.

Like the red wine Christ drank from it at the Last Supper. It was quite a large cup, but then Jesus would no doubt have needed a stiff drink. Unless it was the cup that caught the blood that flowed from His side on the cross, after Saint Longinus stuck Him, as the other story had it. Or they might've been the same cup, though hopefully someone washed it in between.

"It's full of something," Gawain said.

"Elixir," Lancelot said softly.

"It's water," Elidir said. "There's been rain lately."

"Rain?" Lancelot said. "The Holy Grail was rained on?"

"Hope it doesn't rust." Gawain chuckled. At least he was getting to see something this time around.

"How can this be?" Lancelot looked a little green. "It's obscene!"

"Is it?" Arthur said.

"Or it's a symbol. Paganism bowing down to Christianity."

"It could just as easily be the other way round," Gawain pointed out. "Christianity submitting to paganism. Or sacrificed to it."

"They should not be near it." Lancelot pointed at their hosts. His voice actually cracked. "They shouldn't look at it."

"And yet." Ystradel obviously found Lancelot hilarious.

"I begged to see it. I crawled—you have no idea what I did!"

"And now look," she said. "There it is."

Arthur couldn't deny that he felt some of the same anger that Lancelot did. God made his knights chase it all over Britain. He killed them in forests and fens, He cut them down on roads and beaches, they froze and starved and drowned and worse. God took the strength of my Table for it, and judged us unworthy of it, and now He's left it out in a field like a birdbath.

But the Grail wasn't acting the way it had at Camelot. It wasn't up to its old theatrics, there were no sweet smells or thunderclaps or sevenfold sunbeams. It just sat there at rest on the rough stone, which was not so much a table as an obelisk that had fallen over. This wasn't like God, not at all.

But did the Grail even belong to God? Whom did the Grail

serve? It had never occurred to Arthur to wonder before, but what if the Grail ultimately answered to some even higher authority? Or if it were its own authority? It had challenged men, demanded they be better than they were. Maybe now it was challenging God. After all, there were both God and Fairy in this world. Might there not be something greater than either of them, that engendered them both?

Or maybe God had sent the Grail like the rainbow after the Flood. Sorry about all the mess. Won't let it happen again.

As if in answer to his thoughts two birds did flutter down to the rim of the Grail, a pair of tiny goldcrests. They sipped daintily from it, then threw modesty to the four winds and splashed their dusty feathers in the rainwater delightedly.

Lancelot started toward it with a strangled noise.

"No." Arthur used his tone of command. "Let it be, Lance. Whatever this is, it is the strangest of marvels, and I had not thought to see its like again in Britain."

"Nor I," said Gawain.

The folding star was up, and somewhere a shepherd was singing to his flock, urging them homeward. There was something deeply comforting about being near the Grail but not feeling like you had to actually go and get it. It's all right, he was fine where he was. Divine perfection is over there, and I, imperfect and fallible being that I am, am over here.

"It reminds me of a story," Ystradel said. "Unlike you, we pagans have no story about how the world began. It was all so long ago that even the gods have forgotten. But we do have a story about the Milky Way.

"Once in Britain there was a battle where a great hero was killed. The hero had a lover, and when he was buried she was so grief-stricken that she threw herself into the grave after him and died of sorrow and was buried with him. The king who'd won the battle was a jealous and vengeful man, and he'd had a passion for this woman. He had her body dug up and buried in a separate grave, so that she and the hero wouldn't be together even in death.

"But over time a tree grew on her grave, and another tree grew out of the hero's grave, and their branches grew toward each other till eventually they touched, and the two trees were joined. The king got even angrier, and he ordered the trees chopped down, but the next year they grew up and touched again exactly the same way as before. He chopped them down again. This happened several more times."

Bats wobbled past overhead. Why did they bumble along crookedly like that, Arthur thought. Why don't they fly straight like birds?

"Finally the king had had enough, and he ordered both bodies dug up, and he put each body on a ship. The ships sailed in opposite directions, to opposite ends of the earth, and there the two lovers were buried again, one on one side of the world, the other on the other, so that they could never touch ever again.

"But even then they found a way. No tree could reach that far, so instead a great arch of stars formed, reaching from one grave all the way across the sky to the other one on the far side of the world, connecting the two lovers. And that's the Milky Way."

They all dutifully looked up at the pale starry swash that was slowly appearing, sloshed carelessly across the sky.

"It's a lovely story," Arthur said politely. The Greek myths said it was a spray of Hera's breast milk from when she was nursing Hercules, but this explanation seemed just as good.

"The king doesn't come off very well," Gawain said.

"True."

"And the lovers are still dead. I thought they were going to come back to life, or meet in Heaven, something like that. I'd call it a mixed outcome at best."

"But it's not just a story about lovers, or kings," Ystradel said. "It's about something that was broken trying to become whole. You asked for my forgiveness, King Arthur, but I have no interest in forgiving you. In my eyes you are a collaborator in a great crime, the principal architects of which fled this island long ago. But I'm not the keeper of your conscience, the gods know I have better things to do. You're asking the wrong person. You should try to forgive yourself."

"Really?" Gawain frowned. "For what?"

But Arthur thought he understood what. He flattered himself that he'd always been quick off the mark, but he'd been very slow off this one. He'd spent an awful lot of time dwelling on the past, old hurts, old sins, but it was all in vain. There was no undoing them, no matter how much good he did, how many quests his knights completed, how fervently he prayed to anyone or no one. He could never stop Uther and Merlin, never defeat the Romans, or wind back time till they unbuilt their cities, buried the stones, and climbed back into their ships to be blown home backward over the sea. No more than he could go coursing after God and bring Him back like a pheasant, limp in his jaws.

The past was a cursed wound. No perfect knight would ever come to heal it as if it never happened. The best you could hope for was forgiveness. And even that was cold comfort.

It was the future that required attention. Understanding was filling Arthur as if from a miraculous spring—in that moment he saw it all, the whole world, past and future, as no one else could. Britain was a wounded land, cloven in two, British and Roman, pagan and Christian, Stone and Grail, north and south, old and new. It was born in blood and grief and greed, divided eternally against itself, its different natures so mixed it could never extricate itself from itself. No miracle would erase that wound either. But Britain didn't need a miracle, or a perfect knight, or even God. It would heal all on its own, slowly, the hard way. It would always be a scarred land, a complicated land, but complicated was not the same as broken. It would never be pure or perfect, but it might still one day be whole.

How do you live in a waste land? Is there really any such thing? You look for the buried seeds and deep springs. You watch the animals, the lizards and the foxes, and see how they do it. You wait.

And when the land was whole, perhaps the king would be whole too. Perhaps he always was.

But where would Camelot stand in that new complicated Britain? Arthur had always seen through illusions, that was his great gift, and now he found that he could see through the last illusion, and that was Camelot itself. Camelot was great and glorious, and it seemed like it would go on forever, but that was only because it couldn't change. Britain was changing, though, a new age was beginning, and one day the ground would shift under Camelot, and when it did Camelot would not shift with it. It would not stand. When that day came it would break and fall to ruin.

And new houses would be built from those old stones.

Somehow at this melancholy thought Arthur felt a great strength rising in him. Maybe not the strength of old, but strength enough. How late all this had come to him, but not too late. Not too late.

He was only forty-three. The Romans considered dawn the start of a new day, but the British had always counted the new day from sunset.

"My friends." Arthur looked around, at the prince and the princess and his two best knights. "We have found what we were seeking. There is yet something sacred left in Britain, and I would learn its nature. Will you come with me?"

He stepped into the circle of stones. The Holy Grail was only ten yards away.

"I'm not drinking that," Gawain said, "if that's what you have in mind. Not after those birds went in it."

From behind Arthur came the harsh unmistakable note of a blade leaving its scabbard. He turned to see Lancelot with Arondight in his hands. The great knight's eyes were strangely fixed and flat.

I am a sentimental fool, Arthur thought. I have left him behind. I have crossed where he cannot follow.

"You forget yourself, old friend," he said gently. "Put up your sword."

All around Arthur swords were being drawn, but he left Excalibur where it was. Truth be told it probably wouldn't make a difference, Lancelot could probably take them all single-handed.

"That is a false Grail," Lancelot said. "Sent by the Antichrist. And you are a false king." It was as though something inhuman had him, a holy fever, and Lancelot, strongest of men, was as weak as a child in its grip. "If you do this then Britain will be lost forever. We will never feel God's love again."

"Maybe so," Arthur said softly. "But we can't go back, Lance. Even God can't go back, only onward. That is the adventure."

The best knight in the world sheathed his sword and strode right up to Arthur. He put his hand on Excalibur where it hung at Arthur's side, ripped it from its scabbard, and stalked with it into the meadow, into the ring, right up to the stone table where the Grail rested. He raised it over his head with both hands and brought it down to cleave the cup in two.

But the Grail vanished before the blade could touch it, and the stone with it, and Excalibur buried itself in the earth to the hilt. Lancelot left it there and took off running as if the devil were at his heels. He ran all the way home, back to Camelot, all the way to the door of Queen Guinevere's chamber.

Thirty-seven

LANCELOT

Collum had always been a strong swimmer. He did grow up on an island after all.

Or he had been a strong swimmer at some point in his life, but on reflection it had been a while since he'd done any serious ocean swimming, and he'd forgotten how exhausting it could be. By the time he finally crawled up onto the flat Cornish beach, with Excalibur stuck in his belt, he was chilled to the marrow, and there was very little strength left in his legs or feeling in his fingers. It reminded him of washing ashore on the coast of Astolat, a lifetime ago, down in the dreamy well-world below Camelot.

At least he came armed this time. He knew what he was here to do. A thin gray rain was falling, darkening the sand and roughening and stippling the water of the bay. The longship was pulled up on the beach, and he hid behind it.

His first worry was that someone would've gotten killed in the shipboard fighting, but they were all there. Bedivere, Palomides and Nimue were on their knees, hands tied behind their backs, staring down at the ground in front of them. Nimue was gagged.

Two soldiers stood over each of them. Dinadan was bound, too, and for a lark they'd put him in women's clothes. They hadn't dared tie Guinevere up, but she was closely guarded like the others.

Lancelot was addressing his troops, two very straight lines of soldiers, well drilled, swords and spears, armor wet but bright, red-and-white surcoats hanging limp from the rain. The king himself—or was he an emperor now?—stood with his back to the sea, resplendent in a spotless scarlet twill doublet and an imperial purple cloak embroidered with golden eagles. Collum couldn't hear what he was saying, but he was obviously on good form: his men looked suitably stirred, and an occasional aside elicited some low laughter. Lancelot had added some Roman touches to Camelot's uniforms: helmets with cheek pieces, leather belts of office, a draco standard—a gold dragon's head with a silk body streaming out behind, borne by an officer with a lion-skin cape.

A stocky man in dun-colored robes, almost certainly Merlin, was keeping a close eye on Nimue. Lancelot stopped talking and drew Arondight, a narrow sword with an unusually long grip, the blade silver on one side and black on the other. Shit! Was he going to execute the prisoners? Hastily Collum stepped out from behind the longship, sooner than he'd planned, and drew Excalibur.

The great sword glowed in the gray afternoon light, looking less bright than it had in the darkness of the deep ocean, but still bright enough. It felt pleasantly light in his hand.

This was the end. *Change was coming,* Morgan said. See, I've got it right here.

A soldier's head turned, and he nudged his neighbor, then more troops started turning and stepping out of line to look. Lancelot looked, too, annoyed, and just for an instant Collum thought he saw those adamantine eyes widen.

But then Lancelot smiled easily, as if he were glad to see him.

"Well, well," he said. "Look what the tide washed in. They told me you'd drowned."

Collum didn't answer. Let Lancelot make the banter.

"It might've been a better choice, all things considered. What's that you've got there?"

"They know what it is."

Collum sheathed Excalibur again as he walked up the beach; the famous sheath hadn't been in the stone, but miraculously he'd found it at his waist when he broke the surface. He was conscious of looking like a drowned rat, and of wearing only a thin cotton undershirt and his stockings, sopping wet—he'd shed the rest of his clothes during the swim. He allowed his eyes to flick to Nimue's for just a moment. The light in them gave him as much strength as Excalibur did.

"I understand you've been enjoying the hospitality of your good friend Morgan le Fay."

"She sends her regards," Collum said, "and urges me to grant you a speedy and merciful death."

"Very considerate."

"I'm not going to, though."

He supposed he could do a little banter too, if it came to that. The arrival of Excalibur had had a satisfying effect on Lancelot's soldiers. No one surrendered, or knelt, or spontaneously came over to Collum's side, but a low buzz of talk was audible over the soft sloshing of the waves, and the lines lost a little of their ruler straightness.

"Be not afraid!" Merlin stepped forward. Collum would've thought that six years underground would've left him wasted and pale, but the old wizard looked fighting fit. Well rested. He doubted that killing Collum with magic was too dark an art for him to practice.

"Be not afraid! It may appear to you as if this man"—Merlin pointed—"carries the legendary blade of the great King Arthur. But I assure you, he does not. Nothing of the kind. He is a false knight, and the weapon he bears is just as false, as I will demonstrate. Your Highness, if you would do me the honor of holding up your own sword."

Lancelot was quick to catch on. With every appearance of confidence he raised Arondight, the lightning-struck blade. The wizard tilted his head and whispered something, then made a big sudden gesture with both arms, as if gathering in light from the air and hurling it into Lancelot's sword.

It lit up. It was a colder light than Excalibur's, more deep-sea fish than sun, but just as bright.

"You see? Nothing but a cheap trick from the treacherous witch Nimue"—Merlin pointed, in case there were any confusion—"who betrayed me, her own master, who taught her everything she knows. These men and women are traitors all."

Collum did his best not to react. Just wait it out.

"They have schemed and plotted to kill your king and usurp the throne of Britain." The wizard shook his head, incredulous at their collective folly. "You will find among them Guinevere, once your queen, twenty years Arthur's wife, who contrived through dark arts to murder his children in the womb. Who tried to seduce Sir Lancelot, thereby precipitating the great king's downfall.

"And these others are the dregs and sweepings of the Round Table, losers even before they lost. I give you Collum of Mull, a bastard and a thief." Merlin made an ironical flourish in Collum's direction. "Palomides, a heathen Saracen. Bedivere, a notorious sodomite. And Sir Dinadan." Here he paused with special relish. "Who is a woman."

Loud laughter. He was pulling them back, the troops were regaining their morale. Even Collum would've had to admit that he and his friends didn't make a very intimidating band at this moment, even if most of them hadn't been bound hand and foot.

"If I'm a woman, Merlin," Dinadan said quietly, "then you have nothing to fear from me."

"Quite right. And given your appearance, I can personally guarantee that your virtue is safe from any man here."

That got another round of laughter. Collum addressed himself only to Lancelot.

"You have nothing to fear from me either, if I am what he says I am. But you know what I hold, you saw it in Arthur's hand a thousand times. Merlin might fool your men with his glamours, but not you." He drew Excalibur again and laid it flat across his forearm. "Excalibur is the sword of the king of Britain. If that's you, come and take it."

"Why would I wager my life against a thief's?" Lancelot held up his hands, miming confusion, but his eyes never left the sword. *Watch the body, not the blade.*

"We're both thieves here, but I didn't think you were a coward."

"A king does not fight, Your Highness," Merlin said in a low voice. "A king commands."

"I'll make it easy on you." Collum sheathed Excalibur and held out sword and scabbard together in his fist. "You don't even have to fight me. All you have to do is draw it. Go on."

He honestly couldn't tell if it was a stroke of genius or if he'd just thrown it all away. Could Lancelot pull Excalibur from its sheath? Probably. But he wasn't sure, and it would be a rather public blow to his legitimacy if he tried and failed. The great knight's lips were parted in thought, and his hand strayed to the golden crossbow brooch at his shoulder that held closed his purple cloak.

Collum waited. There was no sound on the beach but the soft hiss of rain and the slow slap of the waves. A little fish thrown up by the tide was panting out the last of its life on the sand.

"No?"

Collum shoved Excalibur back into his belt. Lancelot undid the brooch, and an alert attendant caught his cloak before it could touch the ground.

"Come on then," Lancelot said wearily, like an indulgent father letting his son have a piggyback ride. "God save your soul, Sir Collum."

"God damn yours to hell."

Lancelot clucked his tongue sadly. Another day, another pretender to the throne who needs killing. He rolled his shoulders and undid the buttons on his doublet halfway. Neither one of them had on a scrap of armor. Whoever death came for today, it would come quickly.

A slow chant rose up among the soldiers, the king's name. They were young men, some even younger than Collum, brought on after Camlann, less susceptible to the romance of the Old Guard, Bedivere and Palomides and Dinadan, or even of Excalibur, which they would never have seen before. Merlin shook his head disapprovingly at the whole business, though Collum had the strong impression that it was because he thought a duel unbecoming of the king, not because he had any actual concern for Lancelot's welfare.

Collum walked over to the prisoners and, staring down the guards, gently relieved Nimue of her gag. What were they going to do? He was already a dead man.

"I would offer you some plate," Dinadan said. "But as you see . . ."

He was showing a black eye, and Nimue had a split lip. Bedivere had a nasty cut all the way across his chest.

"We would give you the benefit of our long experience and point out Lancelot's weak points," Palomides said, "except that unfortunately he does not have any."

"If you see an opening, take it," Bedivere said. "You won't get another."

"You did beat the Green Knight," Dinadan said. "Though admittedly he was made of plants."

"And a polecat." Collum tried to play it off lightly, but his hands were shaking. Death was very near. Bedivere was looking only at Arthur's sword. Collum held it out, and the pale light played over Bedivere's craggy features.

"You really saw the Lady? She gave it to you?"

"I saw her. And yes and no. I'll tell you all about it after."

"Listen to me." Bedivere raised his eyes from where he knelt to meet Collum's. "You can do this. You don't know it yet, but you can. I'm glad it's you, Collum."

"Bend down." Nimue was still on her knees too. "Further."

He squatted down in front of her and she kissed him. Her split lip tasted of blood. He felt the tip of her warm tongue.

"There's a green ribbon in my hair," she said. "Take it and tie it around your wrist."

"What does it do?" Her dark hair was tangled and sticky with salt, but he managed to get the ribbon out.

"What do you think it does? It's your lady's favor, fool."

"I love you."

"Good." Her face was white. "Now go kill the king of Britain. I believe in you."

Collum kissed her again and walked away. Palomides called after him.

"Teach him some table manners, magic boy!"

Collum paced down the beach, windmilling his arms, trying to warm up his chilled muscles, trying not to limp. The world had shrunk to this thin, scrappy stretch of sand. This is the last thing I'll see, he kept thinking. These rocks. That sky. He bounced on his toes and bent back one wrist, then the other. The clouds were so low they scraped the tops of the headlands at either end.

It occurred to him that he hadn't even taken a practice cut with Excalibur, and he drew it again. He remembered what Bedivere said about it, when Arthur gave it to him after Camlann, and it was true: its balance was so perfect it felt almost weightless. Its blade bore not one notch or ding, not like the old one he lost in the Otherworld. He saw now that the writing on it was illuminated with birds and beasts and trees and flowers and ships and stars in such detail, the lines so immensely fine, that it was as though the smith had worked all of Britain into the metal. According to the legends Excalibur was forged by fairies on Avalon, in dragon fire. Though that sounded a little too legendary to be true.

"Whenever you're ready."

Lancelot was watching him impatiently. Collum did his best to chuckle, as if the prospect of one or both of their imminent deaths was of no special concern to him—*nay, 'twas even an occasion for merriment.* The soldiers spread out in a loose semicircle around them. Lancelot flourished his sword with his left hand, then his right. That was all the warm-up he needed.

"I am the stone, Lancelot. If you would be king of Britain, then take this sword from me." Collum had thought up that line while he was swimming. Nothing if not prepared.

"My name's Galahad, you pathetic peasant, and I'm already king. And I'm not fighting you with that on your hip."

Collum stared stupidly for moment, then he realized he was wearing Excalibur's scabbard. He supposed he could insist on keeping it on—Arthur always had—but if Lancelot refused to fight he would lose the only chance he had. He unbelted it and in what he hoped was a heroic display of insouciance tossed it aside.

The soldiers had fallen silent. *A straight arm is the essence of manhood*, Marshal Aucassin whispered, all the way from Mull, or wherever he was in the wide cold world. Collum still didn't know what it meant. *Long the journey to the kill.* It had certainly been long enough. Collum's palms were slippery, and he dried them on his thighs as best he could, but his thighs were just as damp as the rest of him. It seemed not unlikely that he would die quite soon. Excalibur was great, but Lancelot was the greatest there was. The black lion of the desert padded through his thoughts. *I lost an eye for you*, she said. *Are you going to tell me it was for nothing?*

Lancelot assumed an easy, relaxed guard, a curious one Collum had never seen before, a fairy variant of the Back Guard maybe, but with the blade pointed the other way . . . Collum shook out his arms, slung his jaw from side to side and let his sword drop into the Fool's Guard: sword in front, angled down. A defensive guard, deceptively unthreatening, the better to tempt your opponent into an unwary attack.

They circled widdershins, scraping a circle in the sand with their footsteps, and then simultaneously reversed and went sunwise.

Collum had fought Lancelot once before, when he was the Indigo Knight, but that was in armor, and he hadn't known who he was facing till it was all over. And he'd still lost. Lancelot swayed Arondight side to side like a swimming snake, silver and black, drawing Collum's gaze hypnotically—no, wrong, *watch the body*—

In the space between heartbeats Lancelot somehow flashed across the circle and gave Collum an open-hand slap that made his eyes water. By the time he'd recovered Lancelot had already skipped back to his position.

The soldiers hooted. First touch to the king.

"I'm glad we're doing this," Lancelot said, exactly as if they were enjoying a long-postponed meal together. "Before I make Excalibur mine I want to see what it looks like from the other side. And you know, as king I don't expect I'll get to fight too many more duels, which is a shame because in truth I don't think anybody's ever seen what I can really do with a sword. No one's ever seen me try as hard as I can. I've never had to. Shall I try now?"

"Suit yourself," Collum muttered.

Fear and energy surged through him in massive waves, more than he knew what to do with, while Lancelot looked as comfortable as a cat in a sunbeam. Start, Collum told himself. Do something. *Draw your fucken sword.* Lancelot did something: he executed a balletic spinning kick at Collum's chin, almost lazily, both feet leaving the ground, which Collum just barely jerked back from in time. Trying to take advantage he sprang forward thrusting at Lancelot's hands, but the king diverted the strike, neatly and with contempt, and cut at Collum's bare midriff.

Collum lost his balance but turned it into a form, sort of, spun and slashed—but no, he couldn't slash because he had to parry an incoming high cut. He trapped Lancelot's blade in a bind and tried to wind past it, stabbing at his chest and grabbing for Arondight's long grip, but Lancelot melted away from the attack. *Meet strong with weak.* Guess he'd heard that one too.

They separated, Collum giving ground, already breathing hard, Lancelot strolling after him—was he humming? Some Gascon fucking folk song? This man had beaten every knight alive, and most of the dead ones too. *The logic is self-evident.* Collum feinted but Lancelot saw right through it, and now his blade whipped and flowed, his strokes almost too fast and liquid to read—he was like a man made of quicksilver. Excalibur was a wonder, light and strong and sharp as split glass, but Lancelot gave him no space to work wonders with it. Arondight's point flashed at Collum's groin. Collum hammered it down in a panic and Lancelot struck him smartly in the stomach with the guard. Their swords clashed and locked again and Arondight slid up over his shoulder and he had to twist away before it sliced open the side of his neck.

Minutes ago he'd been shivering, now he was sweating. He tried to tune out the roaring and cheering of the onlookers. A pebble bounced off his temple, thrown by an overeager minion. Lancelot held up a hand. No need. I've got this. *I shall prove my righteousness upon his body.*

Will you though? He kicked a spray of sand in Lancelot's face and stepped into an intricate form he'd worked up on his own, in the courtyard of Dubh Hall, though he'd never tried it on anyone besides a pinewood pell. Excalibur whistled in the air and rang and chimed when it collided with Lancelot's sword, striking rainbow sparks. Mine is the power, Collum thought. Mine. Nimue chose me. *I broke the stone and took the sword. Not you.* But Lancelot refused to give ground, and for a solid minute they snapped strikes at each other in wild flurry, triple-time, toe-to-toe. He knocked

Arondight aside, took a hand off his own sword and threw his arm around Lancelot's waist. Lancelot grabbed for Excalibur and they wrestled for it, staggering in a circle like a pair of idiots while Collum tried to throw him, but the man was solid muscle and seemed to weigh a ton.

He broke away, but Lancelot followed again—his sword kept coming at Collum from unexpected angles, it was never quite where he thought it would be, first the silver side and then the black. Pain stung his shoulder, and a moment later his thigh, then his cheek. It was like Arondight had become a swarm of stinging steel bees. Its guard cuffed his chin and he tasted blood.

He spat. Lancelot regarded him with professional calm. Everything right on schedule, we'll be done by nones. Collum studied the tip of Lancelot's sword, but it was steady as a stone. There was cold water around his ankles—God's bones, had he already backed up into the sea? This is what my father must've felt like, he thought, when he was fighting me. Collum knew how that story ended.

Enough pretty fencing. Lancelot liked to fight clean so Collum went dirty, filthy, bumping and bashing in irregular rhythms, trying to break up that smooth composure. He smacked Arondight off-center and pushed in close, past it, too close for fine blade-work, threw a knee at Lancelot's groin—blocked—and an elbow at his throat—connected but not hard enough. How stupid it was that anything of consequence should be decided like this, let alone the fate of Britain! An army of great sages should spend a lifetime of study on it, but instead you got two idiots brawling on a wet beach. He grabbed the front of Lancelot's pretty crimson doublet and tried to throw him again. His mind flashed back to the Green Knight. What did Bedivere say? *I won't countenance suicide.*

But Collum knew how that story ended too. He wondered if Lancelot had learned any schoolboy tricks under that pond. He caught Arondight in a bind again, the two guards grinding against each other, and grabbed both blades with his free hand where they met. Shouting he pushed them over and down till Lancelot's wrists crossed then he *jerked* upward—

But unlike the Green Knight, Lancelot didn't do his part of the dance. He didn't let go of his sword; instead he flipped forward over the crossed blades like an acrobat, wrenching Arondight out of Collum's grip as he went. He landed lightly on his toes, acknowledging applause from the crowd.

"Good lord, Collum!" He was laughing. "I haven't seen that disarm since I was a teenager! Full marks for cleverness, but I don't think it was worth it, do you?"

Worth it? Lancelot was looking at Collum's hand. The little finger of his right hand was gone, sheared off at the base and spurting blood, and the top half of his ring finger was dangling from a scrap of skin.

That couldn't be right. I'm afraid there must be some mistake. He looked away and looked back. Still there, just as bad as he thought. There was no pain yet, just an icy cold sensation, freezing numbness, but the temperature was rising. That cold was turning to hot, hot, hot.

Shitting Jesus, what the hell was he going to do now? His mind, seeing its chance, wisely fled from his body for a moment, leaving him standing there numb and confused. He twisted off the dangling knuckle and tossed it aside into the shallow waves. The feeling of his own rubbery severed finger in his hand made him dizzy with pain and revulsion, and his vision grayed out. For a moment he had no idea where he was except that his hand was burning and blood was dripping into the sea. His stomach seized, and he doubled over and threw up into the shallow water.

Collum leaned on Excalibur like a crutch, breathing hard. His hand was screaming, but over the top of the pain and the nausea came, even worse, a wave of sadness, sadness that it had come to this. He couldn't look at them, but he knew all his friends, the last of Arthur's faithful, were watching their last hope die. *I'm glad it's you*, said Bedivere, King Arthur's first companion. Still glad? That light he'd seen in Nimue's eyes would be good and faded now. They'd put everything they loved and wanted on the shoulders of a jumped-up country knight who never belonged on the Table, let alone in a fight with the greatest swordsman in the world. Not even with the greatest sword ever forged in his hand. They deserved so much better than this.

And it was Guinevere all along, of course it was. Obviously. But it was much too late for that. What did Bedivere say—losing makes you tough? Perhaps. But as a long-term strategy it had its drawbacks.

Lancelot had taken a decorous pause, displaying maximum chivalry toward an injured opponent, but the time had come. Even Collum was waiting for it. *Have you fucked your mother yet?* The crowd roared. He was waiting for his knees to give way, and his part in the drama to end, and the hard work of living in this world to fall to others.

Lancelot skipped forward, drew an invisible circle in the air and thrust at his heart.

The plough hit the stone. A spark flared underground. Just as it had that very first day when Sir Villiars had tried to throw him out of the Great Hall. *Fuck off back to those Isles you mentioned.* Collum looked in himself for the despair, the obedient submission to fate, but he couldn't quite find them. He found only the rock that the plough couldn't break.

He slapped the blow off-center with his bare hand, the hurt one, just hard enough to send it sliding past under his arm, then he snarled and charged, bulling into Lancelot, shoving him back up onto the beach, punching that flat hard stomach with the hilt of his sword. Lancelot grabbed him by the throat but Collum dropped Excalibur and got hold of Lancelot's belt and the front of his doublet and this time he got him off the ground, lifted him bodily and threw him down hard on the packed sand and heard the wind go out of him.

Collum tried to stomp on his Adam's apple but Lancelot caught his foot and twisted it and he went down, too, his hand flaring white-hot when the wound touched the ground.

But he was past caring. Pain was no longer relevant. Even hope was irrelevant. They were down in the mud, both of them, and the mud was where Collum came from. He gouged and thumbed and tore like a dirty coward, just like the boys had taught him. He groped for a fistful of sand with what was left of his right hand and ground it into Lancelot's handsome face. He was remembering who he was: not a highborn knight, not a *preux chevalier*, he was exactly what Lancelot said he was, a hedge-born bastard. Liar and a thief. Collum had always hated that boy, the boy he'd been, hated him for his misery and shame and weakness and his manners and his peat-bog accent.

But that boy was him. And he couldn't have been as weak as all that if he got through everything he did and still kept going. Could he. So give me what you've got, Sir Prance-a-Lot. Are you sad that God doesn't love you? He doesn't love me either.

"Are you trying yet?" Collum picked up his sword and scrambled to his feet. "Are you? Come on! Get up!"

Lancelot still had all his fingers, but somewhere along the way he'd lost that affable smile. His fine clothes were wet and sandy. With a growl that Collum recognized he kicked up to his feet—but Collum didn't wait a decorous interval, he was already on him. Lancelot parried the strike, but Collum was flowing into a kick to the ribs and a thrust that he meant to be blocked so his blade could whip around into a low cut that missed but forced Lancelot back a pace.

He was coming to understand Excalibur better, what it liked and didn't like. Bedivere always said that Arthur was a great king but no great swordsman, and Collum was no king but he knew what to do with a sword, and he fancied that Excalibur was rather enjoying being put through its paces for a change. Collum felt like he was coming to understand Arthur better too. Before he was king Arthur was like him, a boy nobody loved or wanted. Bastard-born, mother- and fatherless, raised in the back of beyond under a pall of humiliation. The world had tried to teach him to hate himself, but he'd seen through the lie and understood who he was. They carried scars, both of them, but scars were tougher than skin.

Collum felt Arthur very near, as near as when he was in his dream. They fought side by side, and maybe he was no swordsman, but Arthur was a peerless strategist. Collum broke out his grand cuts, huge arcs and lines that sheared through Lancelot's forms, breaking them up and turning them back on him, the geometry of it hanging pure and bright in the air all around him, pretty as one of poor Dagonet's juggling patterns. He heard his fairy blood singing in him now, and Excalibur sang with it. He moved faster and faster until even the raindrops around him slowed in flight.

But always Lancelot kept pace with him. Collum hoped Lancelot was trying after all that because he was never going to fight any better than this.

Strategy then. Lancelot would never fall for a feint, but if he could offer him something he wanted badly enough . . . Collum stepped in close, as if he meant to catch Arondight in another bind, but Excalibur's grip was slick with blood and between that and his missing fingers he fumbled it. Lancelot's attention flicked to the prize. It was right there, unsheathed, naked and ready. He snatched Excalibur out of Collum's faltering grip, and for an instant he held it, and his face lit up with ecstasy, the greatest knight in the world with the greatest sword ever made.

Collum's left hook broke his nose.

It had been some time, but Collum hadn't forgotten the stance: hands up, elbows down, chin down, knees bent, feet unsquare. A bare-knuckled scrap. *Now I shall fistfight a knight of the Round Table.* Lancelot was holding two named blades, and Collum had only one and a half hands to punch with, but he was inside the great du Lac's reach and hitting hard, two hard jabs to the solar plexus and a brutal uppercut that rattled that great square jaw. *That's for Constantine.*

Collum grabbed his arms to keep him from doing anything clever with those swords and flattened Lancelot's handsome nose even further with his forehead, then he kicked his legs out and the great knight went down, and Collum crashed down onto his chest with both knees and all his weight. He snatched Excalibur back and hammered that famous face with its fine silver thistle pommel, one, two, three, four, *five* times.

He paused. Lancelot spat a tooth and struggled to rise. Collum bashed him twice more, then reversed the sword and put its point to the hollow of Lancelot's throat—

"Collum."

The voice came from far away, very far. But it was very firm. It was a woman's. So not God, probably.

"Don't kill him, Collum."

"What?" A sword in the dead king's bloody throat, that was a claim. But his breath started to slow.

"Do not kill him."

The voice was Guinevere's.

He was waking from his dream of wrath. He was still straddling Lancelot's prone body, but the desire to kill was draining away, fading like a fiend at dawn when a church bell rings. As it went the pain came back, quite bad now. He looked down and for a moment saw L'ancelot, the lonely child, under the point of his sword. He clamped his maimed right hand in his armpit and squeezed, which didn't help as much as he'd hoped, and struggled to his feet.

There were a hundred staring faces in a semicircle around him, mouths open. The fallen king lay at his feet.

"Untie them." He pointed at his friends. His voice was a croak. "Do it. Now."

For a heartbeat no one moved, then one soldier, a small man with a week's worth of stubble, tossed down his spear and went to the prisoners. The dam broke, and more soldiers hurried to obey. Nimue came and knelt by Lancelot and felt his neck. Suddenly exhausted, Collum turned and walked a few steps away, blinking up at the sunless sky. He was still alive. It was raining with a little more conviction now. The whole world was still here, the lapping waves, the tiny shells, just as he'd left it. He would see a few more things.

Bedivere gripped his right wrist firmly.

"Told you you could do it." Grinning, he wrapped a rag tightly around Collum's hand, linen torn from his own bloody shirt. "I've got more fingers than you do now."

Nimue buckled the magic scabbard around Collum's waist to staunch the bleeding, which it did, though it couldn't staunch the pain. He put his good hand on her shoulder, and then his bones liquefied and he had to put almost his whole weight on her. Bedivere caught him by his other arm.

The fight was won, but there were still a lot of soldiers on the beach, quite a lot, and their king was very much beaten but they were still wearing Galahad's red and white. Very soon someone was going to have to tell them what to do. Stretched out unconscious on the sand, without his sword or his cape or his crown, Lancelot no longer looked like much of a king, but if not him, then who?

The fate of Britain was here on this beach, waiting to be seized. The wheel of fate was spinning like a top. That was when Merlin stepped forward. He had, of all things, a smile on his face.

"Well fought, young man. Bravely fought."

He said it pleasantly and with pure confidence. This, even more than magic, was his element, the decanting of power from one human vessel to another. He must've seen a score of kings rise and fall, in stranger ways than this. Probably he'd worked everything out two minutes into the fight. The air around Merlin's hands shimmered ominously, and the sand shifted and rippled around him in a perfect circle.

"These moments are delicate ones, the birth of a king, and an expert midwife—"

A slim dark shape emerged from the front of his robe. At first Collum thought it was part of the magic, but the smile left Merlin's face. The dark shape was the tip of Arondight. Dinadan had thrust it into Merlin's back and out through his chest.

With a sharp tug he ripped the blade back out again and the wound pumped a spray of blood, Tyrian purple, then another. The old wizard stood still with more blood in his teeth, pondering, as if the taste were unfamiliar. The shimmer around his hands faded. He fell forward on his face.

Life had clung to that body for so long, so tenaciously, that even with a sword through his heart Merlin died slowly. He rolled onto one side and looked up at Dinadan. Half his face was coated in sand.

"But . . ."

"But what?" Dinadan stabbed the long, thin sword point down into the sand, where it stuck. He nodded to someone else, someone Collum couldn't quite see. "You're welcome."

He turned to the soldiers.

"Now if it wouldn't be too much trouble I'd like my fucking clothes, please."

But Lancelot's soldiers were starting to argue with each other. Fingers were being pointed. Worryingly one or two had even gone to one knee in front of Collum. If there was one thing Collum had learned about himself in his short life it was that he was a knight, not a king. He hadn't come all this way to put a crown on his head. But how did you make a king without God?

Maybe you didn't. He pointed with Excalibur.

"The queen!" he shouted. "Guinevere the Good, God save her!"

He stumbled over to her, hoping he didn't look too alarming, and offered the blade to her on the palms of his hands.

"Your Majesty. Please."

Guinevere knew what to do. She might even have been waiting for it.

"Thank you, Sir Collum." She took the bright sword and flourished it over her head, her sleeve slipping down her long pale arm.

"The queen!" Collum shouted. "The Queen of Britain! By God's heart, I will kill any man here who does not swear it on that sword!"

A few soldiers shouted raggedly: *The Queen!* Nimue and the knights joined in. Guinevere raised the sword again, and again, and each time more soldiers joined in till they were all shouting it together. Bedivere went to one knee on the beach before her and bowed his head.

He was the first.

Thirty-eight

THREE WITCHES

I t was a sunny day at Sir Ector's castle, in the heart of the Weald, a proper baking-hot summer Sunday. Kay had fallen out of a tree that morning and been taken away in a state of howling despair, though Art was pretty sure he hadn't suffered any really serious injury. Art also knew that after Kay was coddled back to a state of relative sanity, he would be scolded for ripping his good Sunday clothes, and to get out of it he would say that Art pushed him out of the tree, and Art would be beaten.

He knew it for a certainty. It was coming, and then it would have happened. Time was always stealing away bits of your future and replacing them with memories, and then the memories faded. Like trading real gold for fairy gold, and who thought that was a fair trade? But God must, or He wouldn't have made time that way.

He had an hour maybe before his beating, during which he would be pleasantly unsupervised. For a while he threw stones in the stagnant brown moat, choked with masses of duckweed. He imagined being a fish under there, forcing his way through the soupy sun-warm water. Did they know that the world they lived

650

in was a circle? Or did they believe they swam on and on forever, in an eternal green darkness, world without end?

He peered into the dry well that they threw garbage down sometimes. Even his hair was hot. He balanced across a weir and stopped at the edge of the forest.

The Weald exerted a powerful fascination over both Art and Kay because it was forbidden, and unlike many grown-up prohibitions that seemed arbitrary, this one actually had some sound reasoning behind it. There were boars and bears and wolves and giants and bandits in there, any of which could and would kill you. Fairies too. Art had seen them once from far away, a fairy-man in shabby clothes and a fairy-woman in a fabulous swirling green gown, dancing together in a meadow.

They were small, not much taller than he was, and wherever they brushed against the ragged robin it bloomed a perfect pink, even though it was February and the rest of the field was frozen and dead. It would be about half an hour now till they came looking for him.

Here was a dilemma, though, because there was an excellent stick about twenty feet into the shadow of the wood, just lying there on the ground. When it came to sticks Art had the subtle eye of a true aficionado, and this was a stick of the absolute first water: straight and smooth and altogether swordlike. Aspen, he'd wager.

Stepping into the edge of the shadow made his heart hammer. He believed the fairies couldn't cross out of the shadow into the sunlight, though he wasn't quite sure why he believed that. He set himself, made a mad dash into the gloom, grabbed the stick, and sprinted back out into the sunlight again.

Made it!

"Is that him?" A girl's voice.

"That's him."

"God's nails!"

"God's bottom!"

This was followed by hysterical giggling.

There were three of them. One was a teenager, almost a woman really, one a bit younger than that, and one just a year or two older than Art. They'd appeared out of nowhere. The bigger two were staring at him and laughing and covering their mouths. The small one just stared. They wore dazzling dresses like princesses. At first he thought they were fairies.

"Where did you come from?"

"Nowhere!" The big one laughed like it was a joke.

"Camelot," the youngest one said flatly.

"Don't say!" the middle one cut in immediately.

"Who are you?"

"Witches!" The middle one bugged her eyes and waggled her fingers.

"Told you it would work," said the big one. "I could kill him. Should I kill him?"

"Can we go now?" the little one asked.

"We just got here!" The middle one. "You *are* Arthur?"

"Yes. Are you really witches?"

"Yes. I'm Morgan, this is Morgause—"

"Don't tell him!" Morgause hissed.

"It doesn't matter!"

"He looks like Elaine, don't you think?"

"No, he doesn't!" Elaine sounded more insulted than Art thought was strictly necessary. "He has Daddy's hair."

"Don't call him Daddy!" Morgause snapped. "I should kill him now."

Elaine sulked off to investigate the weir. Arthur ignored the threat to his life. People said they were going to kill him fairly often, but they never did.

"I found a sword." Art held up the stick. They didn't seem to appreciate its unusual fineness, so he demonstrated it by attacking a privet bush. "Yah! Yah! In the thickest of the press he smote him! Doubled his strokes, and dealt him such a buffet as did bear him to earth, horse and man!"

Trying for a big finish he accidentally hit himself in the face with the stick.

"He served them all in the same manner," he finished quietly.

By this time Morgause had wandered off to look at the turtles with Elaine. Morgan was the only one who actually seemed interested in him.

"Do you know who you are, Art?" she asked.

"Course."

"I don't think you doo-oooo!" she sang. She was obviously enjoying toying with him, but without the others for an audience she could risk showing some kindness, and she rubbed at a smudge on his face that the stick left behind.

"There you go."

Art was unused to gentleness, and it made him cry a little.

"Are you really witches?" He sniffled.

"Morgause is. She won't teach me yet."

"Morgan, let's go!" Elaine called from over by the weir.

"Morgan!" Morgause tried to sound commanding. "You've seen him, now come on! And don't tell him anything!"

"Can I come with you?" Art asked.

She shook her head, but not unkindly.

"Mummy used to call you Little Bear. Do you remember? Little Bear." Morgan crouched down to be on his level and whispered in his ear. "They'll tell you Arthur is a Roman name, Artorius, but it's not, it's a good British one, and it means *bear.*"

She pressed something into his sweaty palm, an old coin.

"It was Mummy's. So you remember. I love you, little brother. I hate you, but I love you too."

Art looked at her for a long, solemn moment while he took that in. No one ever gave him anything, and the feeling was so intense that he just said "Bye!" and ran away.

He would have to go the long way back to the castle, down to the causeway, because the other princesses were still on the weir, throwing pebbles at the turtles to make them move, and they weren't as nice, and he didn't want to go past them. But then he stopped, because he had the idea of giving Morgan his stick. He was an open-hearted boy, whose first impulse was always to be generous, even if it meant giving more than he had to give.

But when he turned round to tell her it was already too late. The girls were gone.

Thirty-nine

ANGLE-LAND

They were back in their flying caravel. They were sailing home to Camelot.

They'd buried Merlin on a high headland near the beach where he fell. When they dug Arthur's grave they'd used shovels, but for Merlin they didn't bother. No grieving required. Nimue dug his grave with magic, and she dug it deep, twenty feet down, even though it meant chopping straight down into granite bedrock. She was fairly certain that Merlin couldn't rise from the dead, but just in case she wanted something good and solid on top of him.

Before they tipped his body in, she took a green stone out of her pouch, pried open her old master's stiffening jaws, and forced it into his mouth, though she had to crack a few of his old yellow teeth to do it.

"Serpentine," she said. "A cursed stone. Can't be too careful about these things."

They left the grave unmarked. Anybody who comes looking for Merlin's grave, Nimue said, is somebody who shouldn't find it.

They'd all spent a good while fishing around in the shallows looking for Collum's severed fingers, which reminded him of nothing so much as looking for the fastening pin off his armor, in the bushes so long ago, after he fought Sir Bleoberys. He'd never found the pin, and they never found his pinky either, but by lucky chance Bedivere spotted the missing inch of Collum's ring finger, the top knuckle and the nail, washed up on the sand.

It looked sadly waterlogged and bloodless, a gray sea slug, but Nimue dried it off and tied it up with some salt in a twist of parchment that had some curious pictograms on it. She gave him willow bark to chew for the pain.

"I can't stick it back on," she said, "but maybe Morgan can. Merlin could have done it."

"Merlin would've taken the whole arm," Collum said.

His middle finger felt naked without its neighbors. He wanted to be healed, but at the same time the idea made him vaguely uneasy, as if getting his fingers back would mean taking back the price he'd paid for victory, which would mean fighting Lancelot all over again. So go ahead, he thought, take it. There's your druid's sacrifice, a finger and a half to the gods, plus a pint of bastard's blood. Not much to pay for the throne of Britain.

"You won't need your fingers so much anyway," Dinadan said, "now you've got Nimue."

Astoundingly, and very fetchingly, Nimue blushed.

The soldiers had given Dinadan back his clothes and his weapons, and Guinevere had offered him Arondight, too—spoils of war—but he declined. Dinadan preferred his curious fairy sword, which he dared to hope was still waiting for him in a guardroom at Camelot. Collum had worried about Dinadan at first. He'd paid a price the rest of them hadn't: his secret was out now, the one he'd guarded so carefully all these years. Merlin and Lancelot were defeated, but there was no taking back what people knew.

But Dinadan didn't seem overly bothered.

"I almost feel like I owe those sons of bitches," he said. "I'd kept the secret too long, and I knew it, but I didn't know how to let it out."

"It wasn't even much of a secret," Collum said. "You're the same man you always were."

"I wasn't lying. I suppose it was the secret that was the lie. Other people can worry about it if they feel they absolutely must, and I'm sure a lot of them will, but as far as I'm concerned it's the best thing King Galahad ever did. The highlight of his brief reign."

He produced from somewhere a silver goblet containing what he said was fairy nectar. It made the rounds—it was magic, apparently, and never ran out. The taste was sweet and tart; Palomides said he thought it was tamarind. They toasted one another, and Arthur, and Britain, and the boat, and anything else they could think of to raise a glass to. Whatever it was, fairy nectar was strong stuff.

It helped with the pain, too, a lot more than the willow bark did. And after all, Collum was half a fairy. That seemed like grounds for drinking more of it.

Only Guinevere declined the cup. She was keeping herself to herself, sitting forward of the others, gazing ahead and presumably into the future. (Palomides had taken the tiller; he was the best navigator and unlike Guinevere he seemed to actually enjoy it.) They had no crown to give her yet, her hair was restrained only by a silk cloth, but her back had an unmistakably royal straightness to it, and she held Excalibur resting across both thighs, its blade naked and alight.

Personally Collum couldn't imagine anyone looking more royal, but he knew not everybody would see it. It was one thing to hand Excalibur to Arthur's widow on a beach in front of a crowd of impressionable young men and proclaim her queen of Britain, but it was going to be quite another to persuade an entire empire of fractious kingdoms to bend the knee and pay taxes to a woman. It could be like the Eleven Kings all over again. They'd be lucky if there were only eleven this time. Bedivere had already attached himself to Guinevere's side, her body man, as he had been Arthur's.

They'd talked about waiting, perhaps proceeding overland and letting word of Lancelot's defeat spread out over the land, house to house, village to village. But the idea of a fait accompli won out: Guinevere would descend on Camelot in a flying bronze boat, with Excalibur in her hand and a battered, bound Lancelot in the hold. That would be her claim.

"Do you think you'll keep Arthur's old laws?" Nimue said. "Or are you going to write your own?"

"I wonder if even Arthur would've kept things the same." Guinevere traced the fine tangled figures on Excalibur with her fingertip. "He said it in the dream, the world is sea-changed. And seeing Lancelot on the throne certainly made the Camelot of old look a good deal less appealing. It's a new age, and I suppose even I am forced to concede that we no longer live in a province of the Roman Empire. It's apparent that Britain is . . . a more complicated land than I understood it to be. So I suppose I will have to be a more complicated queen."

Collum had no idea what that meant, but at this lofty, lightheaded moment anything seemed possible. Guinevere would know what to do. Arthur wouldn't have died otherwise. He would never have left them if he didn't know everything was going to be all right. Maybe she could give Morgan back her lands. Bring back the piskies, and the quarter days. That would make for a more complicated Britain. It would certainly go down well on Mull. He hoped it was what Arthur would've wanted. But what Arthur wanted was for them to find their own way.

"We could have British spoken at court," he said. Victory was making Collum feel generous.

"And will you be our ambassador to the Otherworld, fairy-child?" Guinevere permitted herself a smile. "Let's walk before we run."

Before they did anything they would have to clear the Saxons out of the midlands and run them back across the North Sea. The wheel of fate hadn't stopped turning. It hadn't stopped for Arthur, and it wasn't going to stop for them.

"Do you think," Palomides said from the stern, "that you will still want a Round Table?"

"What else would we have?"

"Almost anything. It is a uniquely impractical shape. Even an oval would have been better. Or an ellipse, or a trapezoid."

"I don't believe that all of those are real shapes," Dinadan said.

"Or four tables." Nimue found a piece of charcoal and sketched on the deck to show them. "Still a circle, but you break it into four arcs and turn them around to face each other. That way people won't always be shouting at each other to be heard."

"It would spoil the metaphor," Collum said.

"To hell with the metaphor."

Some sort of sea eagle was pacing them, white tail and yellow beak, eyeing them as if they might be a rival, or some new kind of fat and tempting prey. Collum wondered if it was the same bird they'd seen on the way out. He wondered if Goose was still in residence at Camelot. They were up and out of the mists of Cornwall now, and the wind and the air were cold but the sun was hot. He pressed his leg against Nimue's leg next to him, and she pressed back. He still had her green ribbon around his wrist. Great slumbering hills rolled by beneath them, with winding rivers slopping this way and that.

Only very occasionally could you spot the work of man: a thread of road or wall, a tiny huddled village, a field studded with haystacks. Seen from up here, Britain didn't look that complicated.

"There it is." Palomides pointed.

From far away Camelot looked exactly the same as when Collum first saw it. There was the Godsfall, there was the tiltyard, and the Bakehouse Tower. There was Merlin's Tower, thought it was really time they started calling it Nimue's Tower. You could see the field where they'd fought the Battle of Camelot, the grass lush and green from feasting on the dead. There was the menagerie. Collum was going to ask Guinevere to grant the leopard a royal pardon, so that she could spend her final years growing fat on royal deer in the Forest of Arden.

It was all beginning. The Age of Guinevere. And how long will this one last? Every age is a dream, but somehow it's still always a surprise when we wake up at the end.

"Sir Palomides," Guinevere called, "shall we descend?"

Suddenly the sea eagle angled across their path and landed boldly on the deck. With a flapping sound and a few stray downy underfeathers it became Morgan le Fay in a rich gray cloak.

"Not just yet," she said.

Morgan wobbled for a moment, finding her balance on her human legs again. It was funny how she kept turning up, you'd think she would've been dying to get rid of them. Maybe she was lonely. Long ago, before Uther and Arthur, she'd loved having a family. Now they were the closest thing she had to one.

"Oh dear," Guinevere said dryly. "I hope you're not having another evil scheme, Morgan."

"She is not," Palomides said. "At least I do not think so."

"There's something I have to show you," Morgan said.

Collum was feeling a little tired of being shown things. He'd seen plenty for now, thanks. But Palomides had the helm, and Camelot was already dropping away behind them.

"If possible I would like to be home for dinner," Dinadan said.

"Many things are possible," Morgan said.

Dinadan snorted.

"Hey Palomino, how long are you going to keep on playing sidekick to the Oracle of Avalon?"

Everybody else looked more or less bedraggled after the events of the day, but Palomides had somehow remained dashing in his spotless blue robes and turban.

"Well?" Morgan asked. "I think we'd all like to know."

"When I left home I told everybody I was an explorer," Palomides said thoughtfully, "and they all thought I was joking. Even I thought I might be joking. But I have been many things since then, and I have come around to the opinion that I was right the first time. I have more exploring to do, and Morgan makes an excellent traveling companion. And it was ever my way to love incautiously."

"At least I'm not married," Morgan said.

"And I have a book to write, too, and I am not coming back to Camelot till I finish it."

"A book?" Dinadan said. "That is a sadly degrading activity for a knight. What kind of book?"

"One where I am the hero." Palomides squinted up at the sail. "It has taken some time, but I am finally ready to write it. It will be about my travels in the obscure and savage backwaters of the seventh clime. I think it will do very well in the paper-sellers' quarter in Baghdad."

Palomides laid on sail and took them up higher where the winds were stronger. Morgan would say nothing about their destination, so to pass the time Bedivere quizzed them on the finer points of two-handed swordplay. They discussed whether Arondight was a cursed sword now, and if not then who should wield it. They gazed down at the miles and miles of trackless forest below them and speculated as to how many bandits and giants and bears and rogue enchantresses they were flying over.

Morgan took a long look at Collum's stumpy ring finger, which was still raw and oozing, and at the gray scrap of finger they'd salvaged from the surf, but in the end she shook her head sadly.

"I'm sorry. It's too late."

"We'll bury it with full honors," Nimue said. But Collum just chucked it over the side.

"The bears can fight over it."

By late afternoon they'd passed the furnace of humanity that was Londinium and were overflying the Fenlands, Dagonet's homeland, a lacework of glassy black waterways. It was cold in the caravel. Bronze was an impressive thing to make a ship out of, and no doubt advantageous in battle, but it didn't keep you warm. Beyond the Fens lay the Wash and then the North Sea. Even as high as they were the wind had the smell of salt. Maybe they were going to invade Saxony. See how they like it for a change.

But when they reached the coast they saw that the shoreline had grown a strange dark crust of some kind. Palomides banked the boat and spiraled lower. The sands were furred with beached vessels, and crowded with human figures, hundreds of them. Thousands maybe.

"God's holy bones," Bedivere said. "Who are they?"

"Saxons," Morgan said matter-of-factly. "Some of them anyway. And some Jutes, and Angles, and probably others whose names I don't know. They all look more or less the same from here."

They stared down at all the milling yellow-haired heads. Pale faces looked back up at them, too, and pointed and shouted, but they were too far away to make out the words. Collum wouldn't have understood them anyway.

"It can't be," Dinadan said. "There's too many of them."

The boat didn't linger over the beach but sailed further out to sea, close-hauled, the water deepening and darkening underneath them. There were more invaders out there, more boats, the ocean was littered with them to the horizon, bobbing like wood chips in the immense expanse, not just longships but cruder vessels too. Some had ragged sails, some struggled unsteadily through the swells pushed by thin oars that flashed wet in the sun. Some of them were hardly more than rafts, crowded with passengers and cargo to the point of swamping. You couldn't believe they'd made it a hundred yards, let alone all the way across the North Sea. Probably some of them hadn't.

For God's sake, Collum thought. Just when we've won. Can't we ever, ever, ever have a little peace?

"I wouldn't have thought Saxony held so many," Guinevere said under her breath.

"This can't be real," Bedivere said.

"Go home," Dinadan said. "What are you doing? Go home!"

"We'll stop them," Collum said. "They've always invaded and we've always stopped them. There has to be a way."

"Not this time," Morgan said. "Because they're not invading."

"Well, what the hell do you call it?!"

"Emigrating," Morgan said. "Fleeing. They can't stay in Saxony. The sea there is rising and flooding their lands, and the land that isn't getting flooded is being taken away from them by the Huns, which you'd better hope don't make it as far as Britain, because you'll like them even less than the Saxons. These people aren't invaders, they're refugees. They have nowhere else to go."

Wind was whipping spume off the tops of the swells like smoke.

"It looks cold down there," Collum said.

King Arthur had always stopped them, and King Uther before him, and King Constantine before him, but they'd never faced this. This wasn't half a dozen keels of Saxons, it was thousands of them. And they weren't warriors, or most of them weren't, he could see that even from here. The boats were groaning with women and children, sunburned and rain-whipped and salt-sick, whole families who were only just getting their first sight of Britain after days of seasickness and freezing spray in their faces and the terror of drowning. How could you fight them? They weren't fighters. It wasn't an army, it was a people.

"The damn Saxons," Bedivere said. "After all that." He spat over the side.

"Imagine how Britain must look to them right now," Nimue said. "They must look at it and see paradise."

"They've got some delightful surprises coming," Dinadan said.

"This is it. This is the change the fairies were talking about."

Guinevere was clutching Excalibur by the hilt like it was a mast in a hurricane. "I thought it was us, I thought we were the change. I thought I was the change! But it was them all along."

"What in God's name are we going to do?" Collum said. She was the queen, she was supposed to know, but Guinevere didn't answer. He thanked the stars that he wasn't king.

"I can tell you something of what will come to pass," Morgan said. "Or as much as the fairies have told me anyway. Nothing will stop the Saxons, you can be sure of that, they'll keep coming and coming and never stop. Some people will fight them and others will flee to the west to get away from them. The Saxons will rename those fleeing Britons *Wēalas* and later *Welsh*, which means *foreigner* in their language. They'll become foreigners in their own country.

"But then others will welcome the Saxons. Yes, you can make that face, Guinevere, but it's true. There are people in Britain who would rather be ruled by the Saxons than by Camelot, and if that surprises you then think about how your lot sucked up to the Romans when they got here. They'll trade with the Saxons, live with them, marry them, have children with them. They'll learn the Saxons' strange language and forget their own. A time will come, not so long from now, when few people in Britain will speak British at all, or Gaelic, or Latin, and the land all the way from Dover to the Solway Firth will be known as Angle-land, and then finally England. And they'll forget they haven't always been here, and they'll make King Arthur their national hero."

Morgan was obviously relishing their bitterness—*see how you like it*—but she was equally clearly feeling plenty of it herself. This wasn't the future she'd dreamed of either. She'd wanted the old times back.

"It could be worse," Palomides said. "Remind me to tell you about the Mongols sometime."

"Well, I'm not learning Saxon," Dinadan said. "Or Angle-ish, if that's even a language."

"I already know Saxon," Palomides said. *"Þes hāl!"*

"I only just finished learning Latin!" Collum said wearily.

"No, you haven't," Nimue said. "I wonder what language their gods speak. I'll have to ask them."

"We're not going to give them Camelot," Bedivere said grimly. "We still have that. We have to get ready. God's blood, what a disaster. What would Arthur have thought?"

"Oh, Arthur. You remember what he was like." Guinevere smiled sadly at him. "He would've thought of some clever way that it was all all right. That Britain with the Saxons was still Britain, it was just a different Britain, no better or worse than the old one. Or something. He would've quoted Heraclitus or someone of that ilk. *Panta rhei.* Change is the only certainty."

"He would have, at that." Bedivere looked down at his hands. The left one was getting rougher and less pink, so that by now they were almost the same color. "He was absolutely insufferable that way."

"You do realize that we arrived exactly like this?" Morgan said. "It was only a thousand years ago, give or take. I don't know what we were fleeing, or what we were looking for, but it can't have been much different. The Old Ones must've been absolutely appalled. They would've watched us arrive over the sea—Morimaru is the old name for it, the Sea of the Dead—and shaken their hoary heads and said *Now fucking what?* We stood up all those standing stones for nothing!

"And now they're gone and forgotten, and the Old Ones are us.

Even the fairies were strangers here once. We're all of us refugees from somewhere, we just don't like to admit it."

"I suppose we'll have to be brave," Collum said. "Though I'm getting pretty damn tired of being brave."

"You could always whine like a lot of giant babies." Nimue held out her hand and he took it with his good one.

Time to go back to whatever we were before this, he thought, like Bedivere said. Ordinary men. Were we ever anything else? Looking down at the ocean, carpeted with Saxons and all the rest of them, he could feel the old specter of acedia beckoning him with its seductive coils, waiting to welcome him back into its melancholy embrace. It was tempting.

But he pushed it away. He didn't want that. What he wanted was to live in a timeless castle, a world wrought of old gold, where everything was noble and glorious and nothing ever changed. He wanted the battle to be over, he wanted to win and have won and be done with fighting forever and ever.

But of course it wasn't over. Why would the future be simpler than the past? Stories never really ended, they just rolled one into the next. The past was never wholly lost, and the future was never quite found. We wander forever in a pathless forest, dropping with weariness, as home draws us back, and the grail draws us on, and we never arrive, and the quest never ends.

Till the Last Day, and maybe not even then. Who knows what stories they tell in Heaven.

"What are you going to do with Excalibur?" Collum asked. "Your Majesty?"

"I could throw it back in the sea for you," Bedivere said. "It would make quite a splash from here."

"Yes, the Lady had some thoughts about that," Collum said.

"We could make a ploughshare out of it," Dinadan said. "It would make one hell of a spectacular ploughshare."

"Or we could stick it back in a stone," Palomides said. "Or an anvil and then a stone."

"I don't think so."

The queen had been silent for a while, but now she lifted her chin and spoke with royal conviction.

"Not this time. Not even when I'm dead. In fact I want you to swear it to me, all of you. If we must have Saxons then we're going to have Excalibur too. The gods and fairies are welcome to sit and watch our earthly pageant if they find it so vastly entertaining, but they've washed their hands of Britain just like the Romans did, and their sword belongs to us now—us, the mortal ones, who have to live and die in this cold and decidedly imperfect world they made.

"And if the Lady of the Lake wants it back she can damn well come and get it herself. Now take us home, Sir Palomides."

"Very well, Your Majesty." He spun the wheel jauntily. "Ready about!"

They all ducked as the boom swung across and filled again on the other side. The ship moved faster on its new tack, running before the wind now, overtaking the sluggish waves that inched along below them, its shadow lost somewhere far out to sea behind it. They sailed west back toward Camelot, straight into the tangerine sunset, over the ocean like a great rippling meadow bright with millions and millions of sparks, while a broad bank of purple cloud hung just above the dissolving horizon, lit up from behind, as though it were holding back a mighty torrent of molten gold.

Forty

A Bright World

M any years later, after everything that Morgan said was going to happen had happened, and a lot more besides, Sir Dinadan would reach the marvelously advanced age of seventy. Camelot was by then the capital of a small kingdom, still holding out against the Saxons, under the reign of good King Bedivere, who was Guinevere's son by her second marriage to the erstwhile king of Glamorgan. He was named after his mother's most loyal protector.

Dinadan had married, too, and been widowed, but he was still hale and strong, and he was overcome by a sudden desire to travel, much as his old friend Sir Palomides had been, long ago in Baghdad. So he put on his old armor and left Camelot and took ship for the east.

He rode through many distant lands. He crossed the Ostrogothic Kingdom, and the Byzantine Empire, and that of the Sassanids, and the Turkic Khaganate, and even more lands beyond that. It was a pilgrimage to nowhere, a quest for nothing, driven only by a compulsion to keep moving and never stop, and the thrill of never knowing what would come to him next. His beautiful armor was regarded everywhere with wonder and admiration, for in those parts no one had seen its like before.

Dinadan rode until finally he came to a land where the names *Arthur* and *Camelot* had no meaning at all and produced only puzzled looks, and there he rested from his travels. He didn't know it, but by then he was the very last knight of the Round Table still alive. All the others were gone. And when at last his time came, too, he lay down on a hot dry hill in the shade of an ancient silvery-leafed olive tree, alone except for his horse, and a single tiny perching bird that almost seemed to glow from within, as if it had swallowed a star, though it could just as easily have been a trick of the light. He looked up at the empty clouds, and as he died he wondered, not for the first time but for the very last, why it should be that we are made for a bright world, but live in a dark one.

HISTORICAL NOTE

The very first appearance of King Arthur anywhere in literature is probably a passing mention in *Y Gododdin*, a Welsh poem that may (the dat-
ing is hazy) have been written as early as the late sixth century. *Y
Gododdin* is a collection of elegies for fallen warriors, and it describes
one of them as follows (the excellent translation is by Gillian Clarke):

> *Blazing ahead of the finest army,*
> *he gave horses from his winter herd.*
> *He fed ravens on the fortress wall*
> *though he was no Arthur.*

The poet didn't have to say which Arthur he was talking about. Everybody already knew.

Since then Arthur's story has been told and retold for 1,400 years, and
it's never been told quite the same way twice. Every age and every teller
leaves their traces on the story, and as it passes from one hand to the next
it evolves and changes and flows like water. By the time Geoffrey of Mon-
mouth wrote *Historia Regum Britanniae* in the twelfth century, already
half a millennium or so after *Y Gododdin*, Arthur had been promoted
from mighty warrior to king. Geoffrey was the first to supply King Arthur with a royal wizard named Merlin and also a traitorous nephew—
not yet son—named Mordred. A couple of decades later the Norman
poet Wace added the Round Table; the French poet Chrétien de Troyes

added the Holy Grail and the adulterous love affair of Guinevere and Lancelot; and so on. Arthur didn't spring to life fully formed, he was deposited in layers, slowly, over centuries, like the geological strata of a landscape. It's one of the things that makes him so rich and compelling. It also makes him, from a historical point of view, a complete mess.

If there was an actual historical Arthur (a debate I have no business being anywhere near), the consensus seems to be that he would have lived in Britain in the late fifth and early sixth centuries, after the departure of the Romans and before the Anglo-Saxons completed their takeover. He would have been a Romanized Briton, meaning an indigenous Celt who'd retained some of the ways of the Roman colonizers. He would have won fame as a general, fighting off the encroaching Saxons.

But the Arthur of our collective popular imagination comes primarily from versions of the story written a thousand years after that, in the high medieval period, by authors who weren't much interested in historical rigor. A historically accurate sixth-century Briton wouldn't have fought in plate armor, because there wasn't any in Britain at that time. He wouldn't have lived in England, because England didn't exist yet— England is named after the Angles, one of those Germanic tribes Arthur was fighting so hard to keep out. Likewise he wouldn't have competed in tournaments or lived in a castle, and if he did it definitely wouldn't have been Camelot, which was also made up by Chrétien de Troyes in the twelfth century. He couldn't have known Sir Palomides, because Palomides is a Muslim, and Muhammad wasn't born till around the year 570. This Arthur—the Arthur of Malory and Tennyson, of T. H. White's *The Once and Future King* and the musical *Camelot*—is a loose mash-up of a thousand-odd years of British history.

There are amazing writers—Mary Stewart, Bernard Cornwell, Nicola Griffith—who have stripped away that high medieval gloss and taken Arthur back to his sixth-century roots, with proper period armor and weaponry and culture and geopolitics. Then there's the other kind of writers, who want to have it all, the Dark Ages king and the pretty high medieval trappings, Camelot and all the rest of it, who pick and choose what they like from history and sweep the messy bits under the rug. I'm that other kind of writer, and *The Bright Sword* is that kind of book. It's full of a lot of authentic historical detail but also a lot of anachronisms and contradictions.

I stick to the facts wherever possible. Sixth-century Britain really was a chaotic place where all sorts of tribes and kingdoms and peoples and cultures were jostling and grinding against one another in an unmappable scramble. It was a postcolonial place, still reeling from the aftershocks of occupation and littered with literal and metaphorical Roman ruins. But in other ways I've tinkered with or ignored the historical record. Not only have I kept Sir Palomides, I've given him a backstory that starts in Baghdad, even though Baghdad wasn't founded till 762, more than two centuries after the historical Arthur would've died. The knights, or most of them, fight in high medieval armor with high medieval weapons. The place names are a salad of Roman and Brythonic and even Anglo-Saxon; the archbishop of Canterbury should really be the archbishop of Durovernum, or of Cair Ceint, but it doesn't have the same ring. I've also included a reference to blueberries, which—I know, I know—are a New World berry that would've been unknown in Europe in Arthur's time. This is a tribute to my late father, who thought it was funny to pronounce the name Bleoberys that way. Don't @ me.

It's messy, but the messiness is, I would argue, an authentic part of the Arthurian tradition. It's always been there—I don't imagine Malory or Tennyson sweated much over their world-building either. *The Bright Sword* is a dream of medieval Britain, where disparate elements from different periods mingle and fuse in ways they never did in the real world, and that dreaminess, that woven texture, has always been characteristic of Arthur's world. His ability to pick up bright shiny bits and pieces along the way as he goes cantering through history is one of the secrets of his eternal youth. He's always transforming, but somehow we always recognize him for who he is. Nations come and go, and centuries, and traditions, and kings, and writers, but King Arthur always returns.